More praise for
THE HELLFIRE CLUB

"*The Hellfire Club* scares you bad, and that's good."
—New York *Daily News*

"A complex literary puzzle brimming with old-fashioned clues and red herrings."
—*San Francisco Chronicle*

"Intricately layered, fiendishly complex."
—*The Miami Herald*

"*The Hellfire Club* is one hell of a novel. Peter Straub has done a brilliant job in creating two unforgettable characters: a terrific dame and a hair-raising monster. Wow, did I lose sleep over this one!"

—SUSAN ISAACS

"Peter Straub is a national treasure."
—LAWRENCE BLOCK

ALSO BY PETER STRAUB

Novels
In the Night Room
lost boy lost girl
Black House (with Stephen King)
Mr. X
The Hellfire Club
The Throat
Mrs. God
Mystery
Koko
The Talisman (with Stephen King)
Floating Dragon
Shadowland
Ghost Story
If You Could See Me Now
Julia
Under Venus
Marriages

Poetry
Open Air
Leeson Park & Belsize Square

Collections
Wild Animals
Houses Without Doors
Magic Terror
Peter Straub's Ghosts (editor)
Conjunctions 39: The New Wave Fabulists (editor)

THE
HELLFIRE
CLUB

Peter Straub

BALLANTINE BOOKS • NEW YORK

FOR
Benjamin and Emma

The Hellfire Club is a work of fiction. Names, characters, places, and incidents are the products of the author's imagination or are used fictitiously. Any resemblance to actual events, locales, or persons, living or dead, is entirely coincidental.

A Ballantine Book
Published by The Random House Publishing Group
Copyright © 1996 by Seafront Corporation
Excerpt from *In the Night Room* by Peter Straub copyright © 2004 by Seafront Corporation

www.ballantinebooks.com

ISBN 0-345-47727-8

Manufactured in the United States of America

First Mass Market International Edition: March 1997
First Mass Market Domestic Edition: August 1997
First Mass Market Canadian Edition: July 2004
First Mass Market Special Edition: October 2004

OPM 9 8 7 6 5 4 3 2 1

Hallucinations are also facts.

LOUIS ALTHUSSER, *The Future Lasts Forever*

CONTENTS

SHORELANDS, JULY 1938

AN UNCERTAIN AGNES Brotherhood brought her mop, bucket, and carpet sweeper to the door of Gingerbread at nine-thirty in the morning, by which hour its only resident, the poet Katherine Mannheim, should have been dispatching a breakfast of dry toast and strong tea in the ground-floor kitchen. Agnes selected a key from the thick bunch looped to her waist, pushed it into the door, and the unlocked door swung open by itself. More uncertain than ever, Agnes bit her tongue and braved the interior.

She put her hands on her hips and bawled out the poet's name. No response came from anywhere in the cottage. Agnes went into the kitchen and was dismayed to find on the floor an enormous coffee stain which had dried during the night to a tough brown skin. She attacked the stain with mop and bucket. When she had worked her way upstairs, she aired out the unused bedrooms and changed the linen on the poet's rumpled but unoccupied bed.

On her way to Rapunzel and its two terrible occupants, one a penniless ferret, the other a pitted bull toad with wandering hands, Agnes ignored a Shorelands commandment and left Gingerbread's door unlocked.

An hour after lunch, the novelist Mr. Austryn Fain carried a chilled bottle of Shorelands' best Puligny Montrachet to the same door, knocked, tried the knob, slipped in, and peered into every room before taking the bottle back home to Pepper Pot. There he swigged half of the wine and hid the remainder in his closet to protect it from his more successful fellow novelist Mr. Merrick Favor, Pepper Pot's other inhabitant.

After dinner the following night, the Shorelands hostess, Georgina Weatherall, led a deputation of anxious guests across the lawn from Main House and up the path to Gingerbread. Georgina trained her flashlight on the keyhole and declared the door unlocked. Directly behind her, Mr. Fain wondered how she could tell this from a merely visual inspection. Georgina banged the door open, stamped into Gingerbread, and threw on all the lights.

The search party found some of Miss Mannheim's clothes in her closet, her toothbrush and other intimate things in the bathroom on the landing, a photograph of two small girls, pens, nibs, and ink bottle on the bedroom table, a few books stacked beside the bed Agnes had made up the previous morning. Over the coverlet lay a slate-gray silk robe, ripped about the arms. Georgina lifted the robe with two fingers, pursed her mouth, and let it drift back down onto the bed. "I am sorry to say," she announced, not at all sorry, "that Miss Mannheim appears to have jumped the wall."

No manuscript complete or incomplete was ever found, nor were any notes. Agnes Brotherhood never spoke of her misgivings until the early 1990s, when a murderer and a kidnapped woman were escorted into her invalid's room on the second floor of Main House.

BOOK I

BEFORE DAWN

IN A TIME JUST BEFORE THIS TIME, A LOST BOY NAMED PIPPIN LITTLE AWOKE TO DEEP NIGHT.

1

AT THREE O'CLOCK in the morning, a woman named Nora Chancel, soon to be lost, woke up from the usual nightmares with the usual shudder and began for the thousandth time to check her perimeter. Darkness; an unknown room in which she dimly made out two objects which could have been chairs, a long table mounted with a mirror, invisible pictures in frames, a spindly, inexplicable machine out of Rube Goldberg, and a low couch covered in striped fabric. Not only was none of this familiar, all of it was wrong. Wherever she was, she was *not safe.*

Nora propped herself up on an elbow and groped for an illicit handgun on permanent loan from a neurosurgeon named Harwich, who had rotated back to a world neither one of them could actually remember. She missed Dan Harwich, but of that one did not think. (Good old Dan Harwich had once said, *A bullet in the brain is better than a bullet in the belly.*) Nora's fingers slid across the sheet and rifled beneath pillow after pillow until bumping against the mattress seam at the other end of the bed. She rolled over and sat up, having just heard the sound of distant music.

Music?

Her own dark shape stared back from the mirror, and the present returned in a series of almost instantaneous recognitions. At home with her chairs, pictures, striped couch, and her husband's unused NordicTrack, Nora Chancel had again murdered the demons of the past by scrambling out of sleep in her bedroom on Crooked Mile Road in Westerholm, Connecticut, a fine little community, according to itself a completely *dandy* community, thank you, except for one particular present demon who had murdered a number of women. Someday, she hoped someday soon, this would end. Her husband had spent hours

3

reassuring her that it would end. As soon as the FBI and the Westerholm police did their job, life would go back to normal, whatever that was. The demon would turn out to be an ordinary-looking man who sold bug zappers at the hardware store, who trimmed hedges and skimmed pools on Mount Avenue, who came to your house on Christmas morning and waved away a tip after fixing your gas burner. He lived with his mother and worked on his car in his spare time. At block parties, he was swell behind the grill. As far as Nora was concerned, half a dozen oversized policemen were welcome to take turns jumping up and down on his ribs until he drowned in his own blood. A woman with a wide, necessarily secret knowledge of demons, she had no illusions about how they should be treated.

The music downstairs sounded like a string quartet.

Davey was up, trying to fix things by making endless notes on a yellow pad. He would not or could not take the single action which would fix those things that could be fixed: he refused to confront his father. Or maybe he was lying down on the family room sofa, listening to Beethoven and drinking kümmel, his favorite author's favorite drink. Kümmel smelled like caraway seeds, and Hugo Driver must have reeked of caraway, a fact unmentioned in the biographies.

Davey often reeked of caraway on the nights when he climbed late into bed. Last night, it had been two when he made it upstairs; the night before, three-thirty. Nora knew the hours because both nights the familiar nightmares had sent her galloping out of sleep in search of an automatic pistol she had dropped into a latrine one blazing June day twenty-three years before.

The pistol lay rusting at the bottom of what was by now probably a Vietnamese field. Dan Harwich had divorced and remarried, events for which Nora considered herself partially responsible, without ever having stirred from Springfield, Massachusetts. He might as well have been rusting beneath a field, too. You couldn't fall in love that way twice; you couldn't do anything the same way twice, except in dreams. Dreams never gave up. Like tigers, they simply lay in wait until fresh meat came along.

2

DAVEY HAD KNOWN Natalie Weil, too. Half of Westerholm had known Natalie Weil. Two years ago, when she had sold them the three-bedroom raised ranch with downstairs "family room" on Crooked Mile Road, Natalie Weil had been a small, athletic-looking blonde perhaps ten years younger than Nora, a woman with a wide white smile, nice crinkles at the corners of her eyes, and a former husband named Norm. She smoked too much and drew spirals in the air with her hands when she talked. During the time when Nora and Davey were living in the guest wing of the Poplars on Mount Avenue with Alden and Daisy, the older Chancels, Natalie Weil had intuited the emotional atmosphere within the big house and invited her grateful charges for dinner at her own raised ranch house on Redcoat Road. There Nora and Davey had eaten chili and guacamole, drunk Mexican beer, and half-attended to wrestling matches on cable while Natalie anatomized, to their delight, the town where Nora's new husband had grown up. "See, you're from Mount Avenue, Davey, you see this town the way it was about fifty years ago, when everybody dressed for dinner and everybody stayed married forever and nobody knew any Jews. Forget it! These days they're all divorced or getting divorced, they move in and out of town when their company tells them to, they don't think about anything except money—oh my God, there's Ric Flair, one day I am going to humiliate myself and write him a really lurid fan letter. And we have three synagogues, all booming. Ric sweetie, could you be true to me?"

After selling them the house on Crooked Mile Road—a house paid for by Alden and Daisy Chancel—Natalie took them for lunch at the General Sherman Inn, advised them to fill the family room with babies as soon as possible, and disappeared from their lives. From time to time, Nora had seen her spiraling one hand in the air as she steered two new prospects up the Post Road in her boatlike red Lincoln. Six months ago, she had come across Natalie dumping frozen pizzas into a shopping cart already piled with six-packs of Mexican beer and Diet Coke, and for ten minutes they caught up with each other. Natalie had said yes, she was seeing someone, but, no, it wouldn't amount to anything, the guy was a prune. She would call Nora, you bet, it would be great to get away from the Prune.

Two nights before, Natalie Weil had disappeared from a blood-soaked bedroom. Her body had not been left behind, like those of the other four women, but Natalie was almost certainly as dead as they. Like Natalie, they were divorced businesswomen of one kind or another, and they lived alone. Sophie Brewer was an independent broker, Annabelle Austin a literary agent, Taylor Humphrey the owner of a driver-service company, Sally Michael-man the owner-operator of a lighting-supplies company. All these women were in their mid- to late forties. The younger Chancels had installed a security system soon after they moved into their new house, and after the first two deaths, on nights Davey came home late Nora punched in the code that turned it on before she went to bed. She kept all the doors locked when she was in the house. After Taylor Humphrey's murder, she began hitting the buttons as soon as it got dark.

Nora had heard about Sally Michaelman from an immaculate twenty-something two places in front of her at a checkout counter in Waldbaum's, the supermarket where she had last come across Natalie Weil. Nora first noticed the young woman because she had put on drop-dead makeup and a loose but perfectly fitted linen outfit to visit a supermarket at ten in the morning. She might have been drifting past fluted columns in an advertisement for a per-fume named something like Arsenic. In the baggy shorts and old blue shirt she had changed into after her morning run, Nora leaned over her cart to see what the twenty-something had put on the belt: thirty cans of gourmet cat food and two bottles of Swedish water, now joined by a third.

"Her cleaning woman called my cleaning woman," she was saying to the woman behind her, also an armored twenty-something. "Can you believe this crap? It's that woman from Michaelman's, and I was in there last *week*, looking for a, you know—"

"That thing in your entry, that thing just inside the door."

"For something like *you* have. Her cleaning woman couldn't get in, and with all the, you know—"

She took in Nora, glared, and swooped into her cart to drop a bag of plums on the moving belt. "We might as well be living in the South *Bronx*."

Nora remembered that woman from Michaelman's; she didn't know her name, but the woman had persuaded her to go ahead and buy the halogen lamp she wanted for the family room. She had been down-to-earth and handsome and comradely, the kind of person Nora instinctively thought of as a fellow traveler. Her first impulse was to defend this terrific woman to the two self-centered idiots in front of her, but what had they done besides call her that woman from Michaelman's? Her second impulse, almost simultaneous with the first, was to panic about whether or not she had locked the back door on her way to the car.

Then Nora had seen the bloody corpse of the terrific woman from the lamp store. This figure instantly mutated into that of a boy soldier on a gurney, his belly blown open and his life slipping out through his astonished eyes. Her knees turned to water, and she dropped her head, breathing hard until the twenty-somethings had moved away from the register.

The dying young man and others like him inhabited her better nightmares. The worse ones were much worse.

3

NORA DISMISSED THE nightmare, decidedly of the worse variety, and got out of bed. Because she wanted to look more in control of herself than Davey was likely to be, she rubbed her hands over her forehead and wiped her palms on her nightgown. Out in the hallway, the music no longer sounded like a string quartet. It had a wilder, more chaotic edge; Davey had put on one of the Mahler symphonies he had taught her to enjoy.

Nobody who did not enjoy classical music could stay married to Davey Chancel, who fled into music when troubled. Nora, the pride of the Curlews, had decided to marry Davey during his second proposal, six months after they met, one year after Springfield and her never-to-be-thought-of reunion with Dan Harwich.

Nora padded past a case filled with Chancel House books and reached the stairs to the front door. Beside it, the red light glowed reassuringly above the keypad of the security system. Nora went quietly down the stairs and checked that the door was still locked. When she started down the second set of stairs to the family room, the music came into focus. Indistinct voices sounded. She had been hearing a soundtrack. Davey, who never watched anything except the news, had turned on the television. She went down the last of the stairs, her sympathy hardening into anger. Again, Alden had again publicly humiliated his son.

She opened the family room door and leaned in. Startled but in no obvious distress, wide-eyed Davey stared at her, wearing a lightweight robe of Thai silk over his pajamas and holding a pencil upright over an open notebook. The surprise in his face echoed her own. "Oh, honey," he said, "did I wake you up?"

"Are you all right?" Nora padded into the room and glanced at the screen. A ragged old man waved a staff in front of a cave. *Pippin! Remember to be brave! You must be brave!*

Davey aimed the remote control at the set, and the soundtrack disappeared. "I didn't think you'd hear, I'm sorry." As neat as a cat in the even light of the halogen lamp, he placed the remote on top of the notebook and looked at her with what seemed like real remorse. "Today we ran into a problem, some nuisance Dad asked me to handle, and I thought I should watch this thing."

"It wasn't the TV. I woke up."

He tilted his head. "Like last night?" The question may not have been perfectly sympathetic.

"This business about Natalie—you know . . ." Nora cut herself off with a wave of a hand. "All the hags in Westerholm have trouble sleeping these days." She turned back to the television. A bedraggled boy of eight or nine shouldered a sack through a dripping swamp. Twisted, monstrous trees led into gleaming haze.

"And most of them have no more to worry about than you do."

Last night Davey had listed the reasons why Nora should not worry: she did not live alone or run a business; she did not open the door to strangers. If anyone suspicious turned up, she could push the panic button above the keypad. And, though this remained tactfully unstated, wasn't she overreacting, letting the old problems get to her all over again?

"I wondered where you were," she said.

"Well, now you know." He tapped his pencil against the notebook and managed to smile. Faced with a choice, he chose kindness. "You could watch this with me."

She sat beside him on the sofa. Davey patted her knee and focused on the movie.

"What is this?"

"*Night Journey.* You were making so much noise I got out of bed, and when I looked at the paper, I saw it was on. I have to see the thing anyhow, so I might as well do it now."

"You have to take notes on *Night Journey*?"

"We're having some trouble with the Driver estate." He pointed the remote at the screen and raised the volume. Distant in the hazy swamp, wolves howled. More peeved than she wished to be, Nora watched the boy make his way beneath the monstrous trees. "It'll be okay," Davey said. For an instant he took her hand. She squeezed it and tucked up her legs and rested her head on his shoulder. Davey twitched, signaling that she was not to lean on him.

Nora slid away and propped her head on the back of the sofa. "What kind of trouble?"

"Shh." He leaned forward and picked up the pencil.

So she was not to speak. So she was a distraction. For some reason Davey had to get out of bed in the middle of the night to take notes on the film version of *Night Journey*, Hugo Driver's wildly successful first novel and the cornerstone of Chancel House, founded by Lincoln Chancel, Davey's grandfather and Hugo Driver's friend. Davey, who took enormous pride in the association, had read *Night Journey* at least once a year since he was fifteen years old. Anyone less charitable than Nora might have said that he was obsessed with the book.

4

MANY WERE OBSESSED with Hugo Driver's first novel. One of Davey's occupations at Chancel House was answering the requests for photographs, assistance with term papers and theses, and other mail concerning the writer that flowed into the offices. These missives came from high school students, stock-brokers, truck drivers, social workers, secretaries, hairdressers, short-order cooks, ambulance drivers, people who signed their letters with the names of characters in the novel, also famous crazies and sociopaths. Leonard Gimmell, who had murdered the fourteen children in his second-grade class during an outing to the Smoky Mountains, wrote once a week from a state prison in Tennessee, and Teddy Brunhoven, who had appeared in front of a recording studio on West Fifty-fifth Street and assassinated the lead singer of a prominent rock and roll band, communicated almost daily from a cell in upper New York State. Both men continued to justify their crimes with complex, laborious refer-ences to the novel. Davey enjoyed responding to Hugo Driver's fan mail much more than the other duties, matters like crossword puzzles and paper plates, wished on him by his father.

Twice Nora had begun *Night Journey*, but she never made it past the chapter in which the boy hero succumbed to an illness and awakened to a landscape meant to represent death. Bored by fan-tasy novels, she could smell the approach of trolls and talking trees.

Davey also revered *Twilight Journey* and *Journey into Light*, the less successful sequels, but had opposed the decision to sell the film rights to *Night Journey*. On the movie's release a year ago, he had refused to see it. Any movie of the novel would be a failure, a betrayal. You could make good movies of second-rate books; movies based on great books left an embarrassing stink. Whether

10

or not this rule was generally true, it had applied to *Night Journey*. Despite forty million dollars' worth of special effects and a cast of famous actors, the movie had been greeted by hostile reviews and empty theaters. It disappeared after two weeks, leaving behind the stink Davey had predicted.

5

FORBIDDEN TO SPEAK, Nora slumped back and watched the disaster unfurl. All that money had bought unconvincing trees, tattered clothes, and a great deal of fog. The boy came through the last of the trees and found himself on a desolate plain. Here and there, plaster boulders floated up out of silver mist. Distant wolves howled.

Bent over his notebook, Davey frowned like an earnest student taking notes in a class he didn't like. Seriousness and concentration increased the accidental likeness between them. At forty, he still had the large, clear eyes and almost translucent skin that had both attracted and repelled her when they had first met. Her first coherent thought about him, after she had adjusted to the unexpected resemblance between them, had been that his version of her face was *too* pretty. Any man who looked like that had to be impossibly vain. A lifetime of being indulged, petted, and admired would have made him selfish and shallow. Added to these insurmountable failings was his age. Men about ten years younger than herself were still blind, ambitious babies with everything to learn. Most damning of all, an envelope of ease and carelessness surrounded Davey Chancel. Her father, a foundry worker and lifelong union man, had known that such people were the enemy, and nothing she had seen or experienced had taught her otherwise.

Eventually Nora had learned that only the last of her first impressions had been correct. It was true that he had been born into a wealthy family, but Davey was too insecure to be vain. He had been mercilessly criticized, not coddled, all his life.

Oddly vulnerable, he was thoughtful; his ambitions had to do with pleasing others and publishing good books. He had one quality that might have been considered a flaw, even a serious flaw, but Nora had decided that this was a *trait* rather than a serious problem. He was imaginative, and imagination, everyone agreed, was an exceedingly Good Thing. And he needed her. It had been seductive, being needed.

"It's like they set out to trash the book. Every single thing is wrong." He gave her an exasperated glance. "Whenever they come to a big moment, they squash it flat. Pay attention, you'll see what I mean."

Nora watched the boy trudge through the fog.

"The pace is all wrong, so is the *tone*. This should seem almost *exalted.* Everything should be filled with a kind of *radiance.* Instead of experiencing profound emotions, the kid looks like he's going out for a sandwich. I bet it's five minutes before we see Lord Night."

Nora had no idea who Lord Night was and in fact thought that Davey had said Lord Knight.

"He's going to plod along forever, and in the meantime, the Stones of Toon look totally fake." He made another note. "You saw Gentle Friend, didn't you? When you first came in?"

Nora supposed that the old man in rags must have been Gentle Friend. "I think so."

"That proves my point. *Driver's* Gentle Friend is a heroic aristocrat who has renounced the world, and this one's a dirty hermit. When he tells Pippin to be brave, you don't have the feeling that he knows any more about bravery than anyone else. But in the book . . . well, you know."

"Sure." Without ever telling an actual lie, Nora had allowed Davey to imagine that on her second attempt she had read the novel and seen that it was a masterpiece.

"Gentle Friend is passing on the central message of his life—that bravery has to be re-created daily. Because he knows it, Pippin can know it, too. In this travesty, the scene is pure cardboard. Okay, here comes Lord Night, completely wrong, of course."

A big, brindled animal that could have been either a dog or a wolf leaped onto the boulder in front of the boy. In pairs, dogs or wolves appeared on the other boulders. The boy looked up at the animals with an absence of expression which might have been intended to represent determination.

"Duh, and who, I wonder, might you be? See, you don't have any idea that *this* is why Pippin had to really *get it* about bravery. He has to prove himself to Lord Night, and he's scared out of his wits. Would that mutt scare you?"

"Probably," Nora said.

"Lord Night is scary, his teeth are like razors, he's magic. He's the reason for all the emotion that should have been, but *wasn't*, present at the start of this scene. We know we're supposed to meet this dangerous creature, and who shows up instead? Rin Tin Tin."

To Nora, the animal staring down from the rock looked exactly like a wolf. It had been fed before the scene, but just in case, its trainer had been standing immediately off camera with a tranquilizer gun. The wolf was the best thing in the movie. Utterly real, it was a lot more impressive than what it was supposed to be impersonating. The boy had so little expression on his face because he was too scared to act. He was a sensible boy.

Then Nora saw that Davey was right; the movie wolf was only a dog. She had turned him into the Wolf of Westerholm, the unknown man who had stolen away the corpse of funny, desperate, appealing Natalie Weil and murdered four other women. And the boy playing Pippin Little wasn't scared or sensible, he was just a lousy actor. Looking at him, she had seen her own fear.

"Of course they screw up the dialogue," Davey said. "Lord Night doesn't say, 'How are you called, child?' He *knows* his name. What he *says* is 'Pippin Little, do you travel with us tonight?' "

Some renegade part of Nora had overlooked the savagery of the unknown man to remark on his reality. The unknown man strolled here and there on Westerholm's pretty, tree-lined streets, delivering reminders. He was like war.

The animal in the movie opened his long mouth and said, "Will you come with us tonight, Pippin Little?"

Davey slapped his forehead. "I suppose they think that's an improvement."

Nora supposed that when she caught herself finding valuable moral lessons in murder it was time to get out. Year after year, Westerholm proved that Natalie Weil had been charitable about its pretensions. Leo Morris, their lawyer by virtue of being Alden and Daisy's lawyer, had chartered the *QE2*, all of it, for his daughter's sweet-sixteen party. One of their neighbors had installed a bathtub made of gold in the bathroom off the master bedroom and regularly invited his guests to step in and check it out.

For at least a year, an idea had been growing within Nora, retreating in the face of all the objections to be made against it, also in the face of Davey's certain rejection, and now this idea returned as a conviction. They had no business living here. They should sell the house and leave Westerholm. Alden and Daisy would bluster and rant, but Davey made enough money to buy an apartment in New York.

Yes, Nora said to herself, it is time to wake up. It was simple, it was true, it was overwhelming. The move would be difficult, a risk, a test, but if she could retain this sense of necessity, in the end their lives would improve.

She glanced over at Davey, almost fearful that he had heard her thoughts. Davey was giving her a look of shocked disbelief. "Isn't that incredible?"

"What's incredible?"

He stared. "You have to read the book again. They cut all of Paddy's tale and went straight to the Field of Steam. Which means that the first whole set of questions and answers is out, and so are the rats. It's crazy."

"Imagine it without the rats."

"It's like *The Wizard of Oz* without the flying monkeys. It's like *The Lord of the Rings* without Sauron."

"Like *Huckleberry Finn* without Pap."

"Exactly," Davey said. "You can't change these things, you can't do it."

We'll see about that, Nora said to herself.

6

SOMETIME LATER SHE came groggily awake with her head in Davey's lap. A wide-shouldered man with crinkly eyes and a heroic beard was carrying the boy through an enormous wooden door. The soundtrack, all shining violins and hallooing trombones, applauded. This stage of events was coming to an end. Nora remembered a sense of resolve, but could not remember what she had resolved to do. With the memory of her own determination came the return of renewed strength. She had resolved to act. *Time to wake up.* She and Davey would turn their backs on Westerholm and move the forty crucial miles into New York City. It was time to be a nurse again.

Or if not that, she immediately thought, something else. Nora's last experiences of nursing were a radioactive substance too hot to touch. Until the final month, the radioactivity had expressed itself privately, in nightmares, stomach problems, sudden explosions of temper, depressions. The gleeful demons had put in occasional appearances. Neither Nora nor Davey had connected this stream of disorder to her work at Norwalk Hospital until her last month, when Nora herself had become radioactive. An improperly considered but nonetheless necessary action had for a time brought her into the orbit of the police. Of course she had not committed a crime. She had behaved morally, not immorally, but recklessly. After she had agreed, naturally to the regret of all, to "take a sabbatical," she had signed half a dozen papers and left the hospital too unhappy to pick up her final paycheck.

Nora's reckless but moral action had at first resembled kidnapping. The year-old son of a prominent man had been brought in with a broken leg and bruising around the chest. A fall downstairs, the mother said. She had not seen it, but her husband had. Sure did, said the husband, a sleek item in a Wall Street suit. His

15

skin had an oily shine, and his smile was amazingly white. Took my eye off the kid for a second, and when I looked back, bam, almost had a heart attack. Half an hour after the child was admitted, both parents left. Three hours later, stuffed bunny under his pin-striped arm, back came smiling Dad. Into the private room he went, came out fifteen minutes later, even oilier, smiling hard. Nora checked on the child and found him all but unconscious.

When she reported what she had seen, she was told that the father could not be responsible for any injuries to the child. The father was a wizard, a financial genius, too noble to beat his own child. The next day Mom and Dad came in at eight. Dad left after half an hour, Mom went home at noon. At six, just as Nora was leaving, Dad returned alone. When Nora checked in on the child the next day, she learned that he had suffered a mysterious "failure" the previous evening but was now recovering. Once again she reported her suspicions to her superiors, once again she was rebuked. By this time, two or three other nurses silently agreed with her. The parents had been in again at eight, and these nurses had observed that the wizard seemed to be merely *acting* the role of a worried parent.

When the father returned that evening, Nora, after an hour railing in vain at administrators, planted herself in the child's room until Dad asked to be left alone with his baby, at which point she left long enough to make three telephone calls—one to an acquaintance who ran the Jack and Jill Nursery School on the South Post Road in Westerholm, another to the chief of pediatrics, the third to Leo Morris, her lawyer. She said, *I am saving this child's life.* Then she reported back to the room. The irritated wizard said that he was going to file a complaint and bustled out. Nora wrapped up the child and walked out of the hospital. She drove to the Jack and Jill Nursery, delivered the child into her friend's care, and returned to face the storm she had created. Four months after the turmoil had subsided, the wizard's wife issued a statement to the press saying that she was seeking a divorce on the grounds that her husband regularly beat both herself and their son.

"At least they got one thing right," Davey said. "The Green Knight really *does* look like a grown-up Pippin. But you can't tell that *Pippin* realizes it."

On the screen, electronic manipulation was transforming the bearded man's face, stripping away years by smoothing wrinkles, shortening his hair, drawing in the planes of his cheeks, leaving the beard as only a penumbra around a face almost identical to the boy's.

"You need the words. *His own salvation lay within himself. Pippin had come to the great truth behind his journey through vast darkness. Life and death stirred beneath his own hands, and his hands commanded them.*" Davey recited the words unemotionally but without hesitation.

"Oh, of course," Nora said. "Absolutely."

For less than a second, the boy's face shone out from within the shadow of the man's, and then the wild hair, frothing beard, and hard planes of the forehead and cheekbones locked back into place. The man carried the boy down a grassy slope. Sunlight gilded his hair and the tops of his arms. On the hill behind the man and the boy stood a huge door in a dark frame, like a mirage. Before them in the fold of a valley at the bottom of the hillside, oaks the size of matches half-hid a white farmhouse.

She turned her head to Davey and found him looking not at the screen but down at her with a suggestion of concern in his eyes.

"Kind of pretty," she said.

"So it's completely wrong." His eyes darkened. "That's not Mountain Glade. Does it look like there's a secret in that place? Mountain Glade isn't pretty, but it contains the great secret."

"Oh, sure."

"It's the whole point," Davey said. His eyes had moved backward into his head.

"I better go back to bed." Nora pushed herself upright without any assistance from Davey. "Isn't it almost over, anyhow?"

"If it *is* over," he said.

Onscreen, the bearded man faded toward transparency. When she stood up and took an undecided step away from the sofa, he vanished altogether. The boy sprinted toward the farmhouse, and then the cast list obliterated his image.

Nora took another step toward the door, and Davey gave her a quick, unreadable glance. "I'll be there in a little while," he said.

Nora climbed the stairs, again reflexively checking that the front door was locked and the security system armed. She slid back into bed, felt the night sweat soak through her nightgown, and realized that she had to convince Davey that her desire to leave Westerholm had nothing to do with Natalie Weil or the human wolf.

Half an hour later, he entered the bedroom and felt his way along the wall until he found the bathroom. Without really being aware that she had fallen asleep, Nora opened her eyes from a dream in which Dan Harwich had been looking at her with colossal, undimmed tenderness. She rolled over and pushed her head deep into the pillow. For a long time Davey brushed his teeth while the water ran. He washed his face and yanked a towel off the rack. He spoke a few reproachful words she could not make out. Like his mother, when alone or unobserved he often conducted one-sided conversations with some person not present, a habit which Nora thought could not technically be described as talking to yourself. The bathroom light clicked off, and the door opened. Davey groped toward the bed, found the bottom of the mattress in the dark, and felt his way up his side to pull back the duvet. He got in and stretched out along his edge of the bed, as far from her as he could get without falling off. She asked if he was all right.

"Don't forget about lunch tomorrow," he answered.

Once during her period of radioactivity, Nora had forgotten that they were due at the Poplars for a meal. Usually, Davey's reminders of this distant error struck her as unnecessarily provocative. Tonight, however, his remark suggested a way to put her resolution into effect.

"I won't," Nora said.

She could help them by drawing nearer to Daisy Chancel; she could soften the blow before it fell.

7

A FEW MINUTES after they had wandered out onto the Poplars' terrace early the next afternoon, Nora left Davey and Alden holding Bloody Marys as they looked out at the sun-dazzled Sound. The announcement that she was going upstairs to see Daisy had met only a token resistance, although Davey had seemed disgruntled to be left alone with his father so soon after their arrival. Davey's father had seemed pleased and even gratified by Nora's words. Alden Chancel had grown into a handsome, unruffled old age by getting everything he had ever wanted, and while he had certainly wanted his son to get married, he had never imagined that Davey would marry someone like Nora Curlew.

Nora quickly traversed the downstairs living room, came out into the marbled entrance, and turned to mount the wide staircase. On the landing she paused in front of the huge mirror. Instead of changing into her usual jeans and top after her morning run, Nora had dressed in white trousers and a loose, dark blue silk blouse. In the mirror these clothes looked nearly as appropriate for lunch on the Poplars' terrace as they had at home.

She pushed at her hair without significantly rearranging it and started up the remaining steps to the second floor. A door closed, and the Italian girl, Maria, the short gray-haired woman who decades ago had replaced the famous Helen Day, called the Cup Bearer, at other times referred to more mysteriously as O'Dotto, came out of Daisy's studio carrying an empty tray. The Cup Bearer, whom Davey had loved, had made legendary desserts, seven-layer cake and floating island; Maria was serviceable, not legendary, and in Nora's experience prepared excellent French and Italian meals.

Maria smiled at her and gave the tray a short, emphatic slap against the air, as if to say, *So! Here we are!*

"Hello, Maria, how's Mrs. Chancel today?"

"Very fine, Mrs. Nora."

"How are you?"

"Exactly the same."

"Would she mind company?"

Maria shook her head, still smiling. Nora knocked twice, then pushed open the door.

Seated at the far end of a long, cream-colored couch facing a glass coffee table and a brick fireplace, Daisy raised her head from the paperback in her hands and gave Nora a bright look of welcome. The white oak desk at her shoulder, placed at the top of the couch like the crossbar of a capital T, was bare except for an electric typewriter and a jar of yellow pencils; the glass table held a tall vase crowded with fleshy-looking, white Casablanca lilies, a pack of low-tar cigarettes, a gold lighter, a stone ashtray brimming with butts, books in stacks, and a tumbler filled with ice and pale red liquid. Mint green in their own shadows, white aluminum blinds were canted against the sun.

"Nora, oh goody, what a treat, come in and join me, where's your drink?"

"I must have left it on the terrace." Nora stepped into Daisy's atmosphere of flowers and cigarette smoke.

"Oh no, mustn't do that, let's have the Italian girl fetch it." She slid a postcard into the book.

"No, no, I don't—"

Daisy had already leaned forward and taken a little bell off the table. It uttered an absurdly soft, tinkling ring. "Maria," she said in a conversational voice.

As if summoned out of the air, Maria opened the door and stepped inside. "Mrs. Chancel?"

"Will you be a sweetie and bring up Nora's drink? It's on the terrace."

Maria nodded and left, closing the door behind her.   •

Daisy patted the creamy couch and set the paperback, *Journey into Light*, Hugo Driver's second posthumous book, on the glass table.

"I'm not interrupting anything?"

In the mid-fifties, newly married, forty pounds lighter, Daisy Chancel had published two novels, not with Chancel House, and ever since she had supposedly been writing another.

Nora had nearly, but not quite, ceased to believe in this book, of which she had never seen any evidence on her infrequent visits to the studio. Davey had long ago refused to talk about it, and Alden referred to it only euphemistically. Daisy's manner at evening meals, rigid and vague, suggested that instead of working she had been drinking martinis supplied by the Italian girl. Yet once there must have been a book, and that Daisy maintained the pretense of work meant that it was still important to her.

"Not at all," Daisy said. "I thought I'd read Driver again. Such an inspiring writer, you know. He always inspires *me*, anyhow. I don't know why people never took to *Journey into Light*." She gave Nora a mystical smile and leaned forward to tap the book approvingly with her thick fingers. Her hand drifted sideways to capture the tumbler and carry it to her mouth. She took a good swallow, then another. "You're not one of those people who think *Journey into Light* is a terrible falling off, are you?" Daisy set down the drink and snatched up the cigarettes and lighter.

"I never thought of it that way."

Daisy lit a cigarette, inhaled, and as she expelled smoke waved it away. "No, of course not." She tossed the pack onto the table. "You couldn't, not with Davey around. I remember when *he* read it for the first time."

Someone knocked at the door. "Your potion. Come in, Maria."

The maid brought in the Bloody Mary, and when she proffered it to Nora her eyes sparkled. She was pleased to see Daisy enjoying herself.

"When will things be ready?"

"Half an hour. I make fresh mayonnaise for the lobster salad."

"Make lots, Davey likes your mayonnaise."

"Mr. Chancel, too."

"Mr. Chancel likes everything," Daisy said, "unless it interferes with sleep or business." She hesitated for a moment. "Could you bring us fresh drinks in about fifteen minutes? Nora's looks so *watery*. And have Jeffrey open the wine just before we come down."

Nora waited for Maria to leave the room, then turned to find Daisy half-smiling, half-scrutinizing her through a murk of cigarette smoke. "Speaking of Hugo Driver, is there some kind of trouble with his estate?"

Daisy raised her eyebrows.

"Davey got up in the middle of the night to watch the movie of *Night Journey*. He said that Alden wanted him to take care of some kind of problem."

"A problem?"

"Maybe he said it was a nuisance."

At these words Daisy lowered her eyebrows, lodged the cigarette in her mouth, and picked up her glass. She nodded slowly several times before withdrawing the cigarette, blowing out smoke, and taking another mouthful of the drink. She licked her lips. "I always enjoy your visits to my little cell."

"Did you ever meet Hugo Driver?"

"Oh no, he was dead before Alden and I were married. Alden

met him two or three times, I believe, when he came here for visits. In fact, Hugo Driver slept in this room."

"Is that why you use it?" Nora glanced around the long, narrow room, trying to imagine it as it had been in the thirties.

"Could be." Daisy shrugged.

"But is your own work like Driver's—is that the kind of thing you've been working on?"

"I hardly know anymore," Daisy said.

"I guess I'm a little curious."

"I guess I am, too!"

"Has anybody ever read what you've been writing?"

Daisy sat up straight and glanced at the bookshelves next to the fireplace, giving Nora a view of soft, flat white hair and the outline of a bulging cheek. Then she turned to look at her in a way unreadable but not at all vague. "A long time ago, my agent read a couple of chapters. But over the years, we . . . *drifted* . . . away from each other. And it's changed a lot since then. Several times. You'd have to say it changed completely, several times."

"Your agent wasn't very helpful."

Daisy's cheeks widened in a brief, cheerless smile. "I forgave him when he died. It was the least both of us could do." She finished off her drink, dragged on the cigarette, and blew out a thin shaft of smoke that bounced like a traveling cloud off the vase.

"And since then?"

Daisy tilted her head. "Are you asking to read my manuscript, Nora? Excuse me. I should say, are you offering to read it?"

"I just thought . . ." Nora did her best to look placating. Her mother-in-law continued to examine her out of eyes that seemed to have become half their normal size. "I just wondered if . . . if a reader might be helpful to you. I'm hardly a critic."

"I hardly want a *critic*." Daisy leaned forward over her stomach and stubbed out the cigarette. "It might be interesting. Fresh pair of eyes and all that. I'll think about it."

A rap sounded at the door, and Maria came in with two tall drinks on a tray. She removed Daisy's empty glass and placed Nora's second beside her nearly untouched first. "I give you extra jar mayonnaise to take home, Mrs. Nora."

Nora thanked her.

"Are the boys doing all right down there, Maria?"

"Doing beautiful."

"No shouts? No threats?" Nora had rarely seen this side of Daisy.

Maria smiled and shook her head.

"Are they talking about anything interesting?"

Maria's smile went rigid.

"Oh, I see. Well, if they ask, which they won't, you can tell them that *everything* we're talking about is interesting."

It struck Nora that the closest relationship Daisy had was with Maria.

Daisy surprised her again by winking at her. "Isn't that right, dear?" This bright, lively Daisy had appeared immediately after Nora had suggested looking at her manuscript.

Nora said yes, it was interesting, and Maria beamed at her before leaving.

"What do you think they're talking about downstairs?"

"Want to make a publisher's heart go *trip trap, trip trap,* like the baby goat walking over the bridge? Show him a nice, juicy crime, what he would call a 'true crime.' " Daisy smiled another mirthless smile and took a swallow of the fresh drink. "Don't you love that term? I think I'll commit a true crime. Right after I commit a nonfiction novel. *Trip trap, trip trap, trip trap.*" She opened her mouth, rolled up her eyes, and patted her heart in mock ecstasy. "I know, I'll commit a true crime by writing a nonfiction novel about Hugo Driver!" Daisy giggled. "Maybe that's what I've been doing all these years! Maybe Alden will give me a million dollars and I'll go away to Tahiti!"

"Maybe I'll come with you," Nora said. It would be fun going to Tahiti with this Daisy Chancel.

Daisy wagged a fat forefinger. "No, you won't. No, you won't. You can't go away and leave Davey all alone."

"I suppose not," Nora said.

"No, no, no," Daisy said. "Nope."

"Of course not," Nora said. "Are you really writing a nonfiction novel?"

The older woman was nearly gloating, as if she knew secrets so outlandish that she could hint eternally without ever divulging them. Nora took in her shining, slightly filmy eyes and understood that Daisy was going to let her read her manuscript.

8

"SURE, EVERY WOMAN in Westerholm is frightened," Alden said. "They're supposed to be."

"What do you mean, supposed to be?" Nora asked.

"You think I'm defending murder."

"No, I just want to know what you meant."

He surveyed the table. "When Nora looks at me, she sees the devil."

"A *nonfiction* devil," said Daisy.

"Dad, I don't think I understand, either."

"Alden wants people to think he's the nonfiction . . . true crime . . . devil." Daisy had reached the stage of speaking with exaggerated care.

"The devil does, too," Nora said, irritated.

"Exactly," Alden said. "Wherever this fellow goes, he's hot stuff. He gets his weekly copy of the *Westerholm News*, and he's on the front page."

He helped himself to another portion of lobster salad and signaled Jeffrey, generally referred to as "the Italian girl's nephew," to pour more wine. Jeffrey took the bottle from the ice bucket, wiped it on a white towel, and went to the end of the table to refill Daisy's glass. He moved up the table, and Nora put her hand over the top of her glass. Jeffrey gave her a comic scowl before he went to the head of the table.

Nora had never known what to make of Jeffrey. Tall, of an age somewhere between forty-five and fifty-five, his speech without accent, his fair brown hair thinning evenly across his crown, Jeffrey was an unlikely relative of Maria. Nora gathered that she had produced him some ten years before when Alden had begun to talk about hiring someone to answer phones, open doors, run errands. Jeffrey had clever eyes and a graceful, guarded manner that did not preclude playfulness. Some days he looked like a thug. Nora watched him offer the wine to Davey, turn away to twist the bottle into the ice, and return to his post at the edge of the terrace. In a close-fitting dark suit and black shirt, Jeffrey was having one of his thug days. Daisy reminded her of her private theory about Jeffrey by saying, "You're usually more . . . original . . . than *that*," and tapping her fork on the table in rhythm with her words.

Jeffrey had been hired to cover for Daisy.

"I'm not finished, my dear."

"Then please, please enlighten us."

Alden smiled universally at the table. His perfect teeth gleamed, his white hair shone, a flush darkened the smoothly tanned broad face. In a blazer and snowy shirt, the top button opened over a paisley ascot, with bright, expressionless eyes and deep indentations like divots around his mouth, Alden looked just like the kind of person who hired someone like Jeffrey. Nora realized how much she disliked him.

"Think of how many copies the *Westerholm News* is selling. People who never looked at it in their lives are buying it now. And this isn't true just of our rinky-dink little paper. The tabloids in New York jump up and salute every time another lady is slaughtered in her bed. And do you think the security system business in Fairfield County is having the usual August lull? What about the handgun business? Not to mention fencing, yard lights, and locksmiths? How about television reporters, the photographers from *People*?"

"Don't forget publishers," Nora said.

"Absolutely. What's your best guess on how many books are being written about Westerholm at this minute? Four? Five? Think of the paper that will go into those books. The ink, the foil for the covers. Think of the computer disks, the laptops, the notebooks, the fax machines. The *fax paper*. The *pencils*."

"It's an industry," Davey said. "Okay."

"A darn bloody industry, if you ask me," said Daisy. Nora silently applauded.

"So was World War Two," said Alden. "And so was Vietnam, Nora, if you'll forgive me."

Nora didn't think she would.

"Ah, if looks could kill—but did or did not unit commanders have a certain amount of shells they were supposed to fire on a daily basis—not officially, I mean, but pretty specific anyhow? Didn't we use up a tremendous amount of uniforms and vehicles over there, didn't we build bases and sell beer and buy tons of food? Wasn't somebody manufacturing body bags? Nora, I know I'm flirting with danger, but I love it when your eyes flash."

He was flirting with her, not danger. She looked across the table at her husband and found him gazing at the napkin in his lap.

"Gee, I love it when your eyes flash, too, Alden," she said. "It makes you look so young."

"Actually, Nora, you're the oldest person at this table."

For both her husband's sake and Daisy's, Nora forced herself to relax.

"You were tempered in ways the rest of us were not, and that's why you're so beautiful! I've admired beautiful women all my life, beautiful women are the saviors of mankind. Just being able to see your face must have pulled a lot of guys through over there."

She opened her mouth, closed it, and looked back at Alden. "Aren't you sweet."

"You must have had a great effect on the young men that passed through your hands."

"I think your viewpoint cheapens everything," Nora said. "Sorry. It's disgusting."

"If I could snap my fingers and make it so that you'd never gone to Vietnam, would you let me do it?"

"That would make me as young as you are, Alden."

"Benefits come in all shapes and sizes." He distributed a smile around the table. "Is there anything else I can clear up for you?"

For a moment nobody spoke. Then Daisy said, "Time for me to return to my cell. I'm feeling a little tired. Wonderful to see you, Davey. Nora, I'll be in touch."

Alden glanced at Nora before pushing back his chair and getting up. Davey stood up a second later.

Daisy grasped the top of her chair and turned toward the door. "Jeffrey, please thank Maria. *Lovely* lobster salad."

Jeffrey's courtly smile made him look more than ever like a dapper second-story man disguised as a valet. He drifted sideways and opened the door for Daisy.

9

ALDEN AND DAVEY took their chairs again. "Your mother'll be right as rain after her nap," Alden said. "Whatever goes on in her studio is her business, but I have the feeling she's been working harder than usual lately."

Davey nodded slowly, as if trying to decide if he agreed with his father.

Alden fixed Nora with a glance and took a sip of wine. "Planning something with Daisy?"

"Why do you ask?"

Davey flicked his hair out of his eyes and looked from Nora to his father and back again.

"Call it an impression."

"I'd like to spend more time with her. Go shopping, have lunch someday, things like that." Alden's gaze made her feel as though she were lying to a superior.

"Terrific," Alden said, and Davey relaxed back into his chair. "I mean it. Nice thought, my two girls having fun together."

"Mom's been working hard?"

"Well, if you ask me, something's going on up there." He looked at Nora in an almost conspiratorial fashion. "Was that your impression, Nora?"

"I didn't see her working, if that's what you mean."

"Ah, Daisy's like Jane Austen; she hides all the evidence. When she was writing her first two books, I never even saw her at the typewriter. To tell you the truth, sometimes this voice in my head would whisper, *What if she's just making it all up?* Then one day a box came from one of my competitors, and she whisked it away into her studio and came back out and handed me a book! Year after that, the same thing happened all over

27

again. So I just let her do her thing. Hell, Davey, you know. You grew up in this crazy system."

Davey nodded and looked across the table as if he, too, wondered whether Nora possessed secret information.

"All my life, I've dealt with writers, and they're great—some writers anyhow—but I never understood what they do or how they do it. Hell, I don't think even they know how they do it. Writers are like babies. They scream and cry and bug the hell out of you, and then they produce this great big crap and you tell them how great it is." He laughed, delighted with himself.

"Does that go for Hugo Driver, too? Was he one of the screaming babies?"

Davey said, "Nora—"

"Sure he was. The difference with Driver was, everybody thought his dumps smelled better than the other brats'." Alden no longer seemed so delighted with his metaphor.

"Daisy said you met him a couple of times. What was he like?"

"How should I know? I was a kid."

"But you must have had some impression. He was your father's most important author. He even stayed in this house."

"Well, at least now I know what you and Daisy were talking about up there."

She ignored this remark. "In fact, Driver was responsible for—"

"Driver wrote a book. Thousands of people write books every year. His happened to be successful. If it hadn't been Driver, it would have been someone else." He struggled for an air of neutral authority. "You have a lot to learn about publishing. I say that respectfully, Nora."

"Really."

Davey was combing his hair off his forehead with his fingers. "What you say is true, but—"

His father froze him with a look.

"But it was a classic collaboration," Davey continued. "The synergy was unbelievable."

"I'm too old for synergy," Alden said.

"You never told me what you thought of him personally."

"Personally I thought he was an acquaintance of my father's."

"That's all?"

Alden shook his head. "He was this unimpressive little guy in a loud tweed jacket. He thought he looked like the Prince of Wales, but actually he looked like a pickpocket."

Davey seemed too shocked to speak, and Alden went on. "Hey, I always thought the Prince of Wales looked like a pick-pocket, too. Driver was a very talented writer. What I thought of him when I was a little boy doesn't matter. What kind of guy he was doesn't matter either."

"Hugo Driver was a great writer." Davey uttered this sentence to his plate.

"No argument here."

"He was."

Alden smiled meaninglessly, inserted another section of lobster into his mouth, and followed it with a swallow of wine. Davey vibrated with suppressed resentment. Alden said, "You know my rule: a great publisher never reads his own books. Gets in the way of your judgment. While we're on this subject, do we have anything for our friend Leland Dart?"

This was the most exalted of their lawyers, the partner of Leo Morris in the firm of Dart, Morris.

Davey said he was working on it.

"To be truthful, I wonder if our friend Leland might be playing both ends against the middle."

"Does this have something to do with the Driver estate?" Nora asked.

"Please, Nora," Davey said. "Don't."

"Don't what? Did I just become invisible?"

"You know what's interesting about Leland Dart?" Alden asked, clearly feeling the obligation to rescue the conversation. "Apart from his utter magnificence, and all that? His relationship with his son. I don't get it. Do you get it? I mean Dick—I sort of understood what happened with the older one, Petey, but Dick just baffles me. Does that guy actually do anything?"

Davey was laughing now. "I don't think he does, no. We met him a month or two ago, remember, Nora? At Gilhoolie's, right after it opened."

Nora did remember, and the memory of the appalling person named Dick Dart could now amuse her, too. Dart had been two years behind Davey at the Academy. She had been introduced to him at the bar of a restaurant which had replaced a mediocre pizza parlor in the Waldbaum's shopping center.

Men and women in their twenties and thirties had crowded the long bar separating the door from the dining room, and the menus in plastic cases on the red-checked tables advertised drinks like Mudslides and Long Island Iced Teas. As she and Davey had passed through the crowd, a tall, rather fey-looking man had turned to Davey, dropped a hand on his arm, and addressed him with an odd mixture of arrogance and diffidence. He wore a nice, slightly rumpled suit, his tie had been yanked down, and his fair hair drooped over his forehead. He appeared to have consumed more than a sufficient number of Mudslides. He had said something like *I suppose you're going to pretend that you don't remember our old nighttime journeys anymore.*

During Davey's denial, the man had tilted back his head and peered from one Chancel to the other in a way that suggested they made an amusing spectacle. Nora had endured ironic compliments to her "valiant" face and "lovely" hair. After telling Davey that he should come around by himself some night to talk about the wild rides they'd enjoyed together, Dart had released them, but not before adding that he *adored* Nora's scent. Nora had not been wearing a scent. Once they reached their table, Nora had said that she'd make Davey sleep in the garage if he ever had anything to do with that languid jerk. Give me a break, Davey had said, Dart's trying to get in your pants. He gets it all from old Peter O'Toole movies. More like old George Sanders movies, Nora answered, wondering if anyone ever got laid by pretending to despise the person he wanted to seduce.

Midway through the tasteless meal, Nora had looked up at the bar and seen Dart wink at her. She had asked Davey what his old pal did for a living, and Davey had offered the surprising information that Dick was an attorney in his father's firm.

Now Davey said to his father what he had explained to Nora at Gilhoolie's, that Dick Dart lived off the crumbs that fell from the tables of Dart, Morris's wealthier clients; he took elderly widows to lunch in slow-moving French restaurants and assured them that Leland Dart was preserving their estates from the depredations of a socialist federal government.

"Why does he stay on?"

"He probably likes the lunches," Davey said. "And I suppose he expects to inherit the firm."

"Don't put any money on it," Alden said. Nora felt a chill wind so clearly that it might have blown in off the Sound. "Old Leland is too smart for that. He's been the back-room boy in Republican politics in this state since the days of Ernest Forrest Ernest, and he's not going to let that kid anywhere near the rudder of Dart, Morris. You watch. When Leland steps down, he'll tell Dick he needs more seasoning and pull in a distinguished old fraud just like himself."

"Why do you want Davey to know that?" asked Nora.

"So he'll understand our esteemed legal firm," Alden said.

"Maybe Leland's wife will have her own ideas about what happens to Dick," Nora said.

Alden grinned luxuriantly. "Leland's wife, well. I wonder what that lady makes of her son going around romancing the same women her husband seduced forty years ago. Leland took them to bed to get their legal business, and Dick sweet-talks them to keep it. Do you suppose our boy Dick climbs into bed with them, the same way his daddy used to do? It'd be a strange boy who did that, wouldn't you think?"

Davey stared out at the Sound without speaking.

"I suppose you think the women are grateful," said Nora.

"Maybe the first time," Alden said. "I don't imagine Dick gives them much to be grateful for."

"We'll never know," Davey said, smiling strangely toward the Sound.

Alden checked the empty places as if for leftover bits of lobster. "Are we all finished?"

Davey nodded, and Alden glanced up at Jeffrey, who drifted sideways and opened the door. Nora thanked him as she walked past, but Jeffrey pretended not to hear. A few minutes later, Nora sat in Davey's little red Audi, holding a Mason jar of homemade mayonnaise as he drove from Mount Avenue into Westerholm's newer, less elegant interior.

10

"ARE YOU UPSET?" she asked. Davey had traveled the entire mile and a half of Churchill Lane without speaking.

It was a question she asked often during their marriage, and the answers she received, while not evasive, were never straightforward. As with many men, Davey's feelings frequently came without labels.

"I don't know," he said, which was better than a denial.

"Were you surprised by what your father said?"

He looked at her warily for about a quarter of a second. "If I was surprised by anybody, it was you."

"Why?"

"My father gets a kick out of exaggerating his point of view. That doesn't mean he should be attacked."

"You think I attacked him?"

"Didn't you say he was disgusting? That he cheapened everything?"

"I was criticizing his ideas, not him. Besides, he enjoyed it. Alden gets a kick out of verbal brawls."

"The man is about to be seventy-five. I think he deserves more respect, especially from someone who doesn't know the first thing about the publishing business. Not to mention the fact that he's my father."

The light at the Post Road turned green, and Davey pulled away from the oaks beside the stone bridge at the end of Churchill Lane. Either because no traffic came toward them or because he had forgotten to do it, he did not signal the turn that would take them down the Post Road and home. Then she realized that he had not signaled a turn because he did not intend to take the Post Road.

"Where are you going?"

"I want to see something," he said. Evidently he did not intend to tell her what it was.

"This might come as a surprise to you, but I thought your father was attacking me."

"Nothing he said was personal. You're the one who was personal."

Nora silently cataloged the ways in which she had felt attacked by Alden Chancel and selected the safest. "He loves talking about my age. Alden always thought I was too old for you."

"He never said anything about your age."

"He said I was the oldest person at the table."

"For God's sake, Nora, he was being playful. And right then, he was giving you a compliment, if you didn't notice. In fact, he complimented you about a hundred times."

"He was flirting with me, and I hate it. He uses it as a way to put people down."

"That's crazy. People in his generation all give out these heavy-handed compliments. They think it's like offering a woman a bouquet of flowers."

"I know," Nora said, "but that's what's crazy."

Davey shook his head. Nora leaned back in the seat and watched the splendid houses go by. Alden had been right about one thing: in front of every estate stood a metal plaque bearing the name of a security company. Many promised an ARMED RESPONSE.

He gave her a brief, flat glare. "One more thing. I shouldn't have to say this to you, but apparently I do."

She waited.

"What my mother does up in her studio is her business. It doesn't have anything to do with you, Nora." Another angry glare. "Just in case you didn't get what Dad was telling you. Pretty damn tactfully, too, I thought."

More dismayed than she wished to appear, Nora inhaled and slowly released her breath as she worked out a response. "First of all, Davey, I wasn't interfering with her. She was happy to see me, and I enjoyed being with her." In Davey's answering glance she saw that he wanted to believe this. "In fact, it was like being with a completely different person than who she was at lunch. She was having a good time. She was funny."

"Okay, that's nice. But I really don't want you to wind up making her feel worse than she already does."

For a moment, Nora looked at him without speaking. "You don't think she does any work up there, do you? Neither does your father. Both of you think she's been faking it for years, and you go along because you want to protect her, or something like that."

"Or something like that." Some of his earlier bitterness put an edge on his voice. "Ever hear the expression 'Don't rock the boat'?" He glanced over at her with an unhappy mockery in his eyes. "You believe she goes up there to work? Is that what you're saying?"

"I think she's writing *something*, yes."

He groaned. "I'm sure that's nice for both of you."

"Wouldn't you like your mother and me to be, maybe not friends, but more like friends than we are now?"

"She never had friends." Davey thought for a second. "I suppose she was friends, as close to it as she could get, with the Cup Bearer. Then she quit, and that was that. I was devastated. I didn't think she'd ever leave. I probably thought Helen Day was my real mother. The other one certainly didn't spend much time with me."

"I wish you could have seen the way she was with me. Sort of . . . lighthearted."

"Sort of drunk," Davey said. "Surprise, surprise." He sighed, so sadly that Nora wanted to put her arms around him. "For which, of course, she has a very good reason."

Alden, Nora thought, but Davey would never blame the great publisher for his mother's condition. She tilted her head and quizzed him with her eyes.

"The other one. The one before me, the one who died. It's obvious."

"Oh, yes." Nora nodded, suddenly seeing Davey, as she had a hundred times, seated in the living room under a lamp from Michaelman's with *Night Journey* in his hands, staring into pages he read and reread because, no less than the killers Leonard Gimmel and Teddy Brunhoven, in them he found the code to his own life.

"You think about that a lot, don't you?"

"I don't know. Maybe." He checked to see if she was criticizing him. "Kind of—thinking about it without thinking about it, I guess."

She nodded but did not speak. For a moment Davey seemed

on the verge of saying more. Then his mouth closed, his eyes changed, and the moment was over.

The Audi pulled up at a stop sign before a cluster of trees overgrown with vines that all but obscured the street sign. Then across the street a gray Mercedes sedan rolled toward the intersection, and as Davey flicked on the turn signal before pressing the accelerator and cranking the wheel to the left, the name of the street chimed in her head. He had taken them to Redcoat Road, and what he wanted to see was the house in which the wolf had taken Natalie Weil's life and caused her body to disappear.

11

BESIDE NATALIE'S DRIVE was a metal post supporting a bright blue plaque bearing the name of a local security firm more expensive than the one the Chancels had chosen. Natalie had taken account of the similarities between herself and the first victims and spent a lot of money for state-of-the-art protection.

Davey left the car and walked up along the grassy verge of Redcoat Road toward the driveway. Nora got out and followed him. She regretted the Bloody Mary and the single glass of wine she'd taken at lunch. The August light stung her eyes. Davey stood facing Natalie's house from the end of the driveway, his trousers almost brushing the security system plaque.

Set far back from the road, the house looked out over a front yard darkened by the shadows of oaks and maples standing between grassy humps and granite boulders. Yellow crime scene tape looped through the trees and sealed the front door. A black-and-white Westerholm police car and an anonymous-looking blue sedan were parked near the garage doors.

"Is there some reason you wanted to come here?" she asked.

"Yes." He glanced down at her, then looked back toward the house. Twenty years ago it had been painted the peculiar depthless red-brown of information booths in national parks. Their own house was the same shade of brown, though its paint had not yet begun to flake. In design also Natalie's house replicated theirs, with its blunt facade and row of windows marching beneath the roof.

A white face above a dark uniform leaned toward a window in the bedroom over the garage.

"That cop's in the room where she was killed," Davey said. He started walking up the driveway.

The face retreated from the window. Davey came to the point where the yellow tape wound around a maple beside the drive, and continued in a straight line toward the house and garage. He put out his hand and leaned against the maple.

"Why are you doing this?"

"I'm trying to help you." The policeman came up to the living room window and stared out at them. He put his hands on his hips and then swung away from the window.

"Maybe this is crazy, but do you think that you wanted to come here because of what you were talking about in the car?"

He gave her an uncertain look.

"About the other one. The other Davey."

"Don't," he said.

Again the Chancel tendency to protect Chancel secrets. The policeman opened the front door and began moving toward them through the shadows on Natalie Weil's lawn.

12

NORA WAS CERTAIN that Davey's fascination with *Night Journey*, a novel about a child rescued from death by a figure called the Green Knight, was rooted in his childhood. Once there had been another David Chancel, the first son of Alden and Daisy. Suddenly the infant Davey had died in his crib. He had not been ill, weak, or at risk in any way. He had simply, terribly, died. Lincoln

Chancel had saved them by suggesting, perhaps even demanding, an adoption. Lincoln's insistence on a grandson was a crucial element of the legend Davey had passed on to Nora. An adoptable baby had been found in New Hampshire; Alden and Daisy traveled there, won the child for their own, named him after the first infant, and raised him in the dead boy's place.

Davey had worn the dead Davey's baby clothes, slept in his crib, drooled on his bib, mouthed his rattle, taken formula from his bottle. When he grew old enough, he played with the toys set aside for the ghost baby. As if Lincoln Chancel had foreseen that he would not live to see the child turn four, he had purchased blocks, balls, stuffed bunnies and cats, rocking horses, electric trains, baseball gloves, bicycles in graduated sizes, dozens of board games, and much else besides; on the appropriate birthdays these gifts had been removed from boxes marked DAVEY and ceremoniously presented. Eventually Davey had understood that they were gifts from a dead grandfather to a dead grandson.

Ever since the night drunken Davey had careered around the living room while declaiming this history, Nora had begun to see him in a way only at first surprising or unsettling. He had always imagined himself under the pitiless scrutiny of a shadow self—imagined that the rightful David Chancel called to him for recognition or rescue.

13

THE DETECTIVE SKIRTED a dolphin-colored boulder and came forward, regarding Nora with a combination of official reserve and private concern. She could not imagine how she could have mistaken his blue suit and ornate red necktie for a police uniform. He had a heavy, square head, a disillusioned face, and a thick brown mustache that curved past the ends of his mouth. When he came close enough for her to notice the gray in the Tartar mustache, she could also see that his dark brown eyes were at once serious, annoyed, solicitous, and far down, at bottom, utterly detached, in a way that Nora assumed was reserved for policemen. Some portion of this man reminded her of Dan Harwich, which led her to expect a measure of sympathetic understanding. Physically he was not much like Harwich, being blocky and wide, heavy in the shoulders and gut, a Clydesdale instead of a greyhound.

"Are you okay?" he asked, which corresponded to her unconscious expectations, and when she nodded, he turned to Davey, saying, "Sir, if you're just being curious, I'd appreciate your getting this lady and yourself away from here," which did not.

"I wanted to see Natalie's house again," Davey said. "My name is Davey Chancel, and this is my wife, Nora."

Nora waited for the detective to say, *I thought you were brother and sister,* as some did. Instead he said, "You're related to the family on Mount Avenue? What's that place? The Poplars?"

"I'm their son," Davey said.

The man stepped closer and held out a large hand, which Davey took. "Holly Fenn. Chief of Detectives. You knew Mrs. Weil?"

"She sold us our house."

"And you've been here before?"

"Natalie had us over a couple of times," Nora said, for the sake of including herself in the conversation with Holly Fenn. He was a hod carrier, a peat stomper, as Irish as Matt Curlew. One look at this guy, you knew he was real. He leveled his complicated gaze at her. She cleared her throat.

"Five times," Davey said. "Maybe six. Have you found her body yet?"

Davey's *trait,* that which had caused Nora second and third thoughts about the man she had intended to marry, was that he stretched the truth. Davey did not lie in the ordinary sense, for advantage, but as she had eventually seen, for an aesthetic end, to improve reality.

Davey was still nodding, as if he had gone over their visits and added them up. When Nora added them up for herself, they came out to three. Once for drinks, a week after they started looking at houses; the second time for dinner; the third time when they had dropped in to pick up the keys to the house on Crooked Mile Road.

"Which is it?" Fenn asked. "A couple of times, or six?"

"Six," Davey said. "Don't you remember, Nora?"

Nora wondered if Davey had visited Natalie Weil by himself, and then dismissed the thought. "Oh, sure," she said.

"When was the last time you were here, Mr. Chancel?"

"About two weeks ago. We had Mexican food and watched wrestling on TV—right, Nora?"

"Um." To avoid looking at the detective, she turned her head toward the house and found that she had not been mistaken after all. The uniformed policeman she had seen earlier stood in the bedroom window, looking out.

"You were friends of Mrs. Weil's."

"You could say that."

"She doesn't seem to have had a lot of friends."

"I think she liked being alone."

"Not enough she didn't. No offense." Fenn shoved his hands in his pockets and reared back, as if he needed distance to see them clearly. "Mrs. Weil kept good records as far as her job went, made entries of all her appointments and that, but we're not having much luck with her personal life. Maybe you two can help us out."

"Sure, anything," Davey said.

"How?" Nora asked.

"What's in the jar?"

Nora looked down at the jar she had forgotten she carried. "Oh!" She laughed. "Mayonnaise. A present."

Davey gave her an annoyed look.

"Can I smell it?"

Mystified, Nora unscrewed the top and held up the jar. Fenn bent forward, took his hands from his pockets, placed them around the jar, and sniffed. "Yeah, the real thing. Hard to make, mayonnaise. Always wants to separate. Who's it for?"

"Us," she said.

His hands left the jar. "I wonder if you folks ever met any other friends of Mrs. Weil's here."

He was still looking at Nora, and she shook her head. After a second in which she was tempted to smell the mayonnaise herself, she screwed the top back onto the jar.

"No, never," Davey said.

"Know of any boyfriends? Anyone she went out with?"

"We don't know anything about that," Davey said.

"Mrs. Chancel? Sometimes women will tell a female friend things they won't say to her husband."

"She used to talk about her ex-husband sometimes. Norm. But he didn't sound like the kind of guy—"

"Mr. Weil was with his new wife in their Malibu beach house when your friend was killed. These days he's a movie producer. We don't think he had anything to do with this thing."

A movie producer in a Malibu beach house was nothing like the man Natalie had described. Nor was Holly Fenn's manner anything like what Nora thought of as normal police procedure.

"I guess you don't have any ideas about what might have happened to your friend." He was still looking at Nora.

"Nora doesn't think she's dead," Davey said, pulling another ornament out of the air.

Nora glanced at Davey, who did not look back. "Well. I don't know, obviously. Someone got into the house, right?" she said.

"That's for sure. She probably knew the guy." He turned toward the house. "This security system is pretty new. Notice it the last time you were here?"

"No," Davey said.

Nora looked down at the jar in her hands. What was inside it resembled some nauseating bodily fluid.

"Hard to miss that sign."

"You'd think so," Davey said.

"The system was installed a little more than two months ago."

Nora looked up from the jar to find his eyes on hers. She jerked her gaze back to the house and heard herself saying, "Was it really just two weeks ago we were here, Davey?"

"Maybe a little more."

Fenn looked away, and Nora hoped that he would let them go. He must have known that they had not been telling him the truth. "Do you think you could come inside? This isn't something we normally do, but this time I'll take all the help I can get."

"No problem," Davey said.

The detective stepped back and extended an arm in the direction of the front door. "Just duck under the tape." Davey bent forward. Fenn smiled at Nora, and his eyes crinkled. He looked like a courteous frontier sheriff dressed up in a modern suit—like Wyatt Earp. He even sounded like Wyatt Earp.

"Where are you from, Chief Fenn?" she asked.

"I'm a Bridgeport boy," he said. "Call me Holly, everybody

else does. You don't have to go in there, you know. It's pretty bloody."

Nora tried to look as hard-bitten as she could while holding a quart jar filled with mayonnaise. "I was a nurse in Vietnam. I've probably seen more blood than you have."

"And you rescue children in peril," he said.

"That's more or less what I was doing in Vietnam," she said, blushing.

He smiled again and held up the tape as Davey frowned at them from beside a bank of overgrown hydrangeas.

14

ONE OF THOSE men who expand when observed close-up, Holly Fenn filled nearly the entire space of the stairwell. His shoulders, his arms, even his head seemed twice the normal size. Energy strained the fabric of his suit jacket, curled the dark brown hair at the back of his head. The air inside Natalie's house smelled of dust, dead flowers, unwashed dishes, the breath and bodies of many men, the reek of cigarettes dumped into wastebaskets. Davey uttered a soft sound of disgust.

"These places stink pretty good," Fenn said.

A poster of a whitewashed harbor village hung on the wall matching the one covered by their Chancel House bookshelves. In the living room, three men turned toward them. The uniformed policeman for whom Nora had mistaken Holly Fenn came into the hall. The other two wore identical gray suits, white button-down shirts, and dark ties. They had narrow, disdainful faces and stood side by side, like chessmen. Nora caught the faint, corrupt odor of old blood.

Davey came up the last step. Abnormally vivid in the dim light, his dark eyes and dark, definite brows made his face look white and unformed.

Fenn introduced them to Officer Michael LeDonne, and Mr.

Hashim and Mr. Shull, who were with the FBI. Hashim and Shull actually resembled each other very little, Mr. Hashim being younger, heavier, in body more like one of Natalie's wrestlers than Mr. Shull, who was taller and fairer than his partner. Their posture and expressions created the effect of a resemblance, along with their shared air of otherworldly authority.

"Mr. and Mrs. Chancel were friends of the deceased, and I asked them if they'd be willing to do a walk through here, see if maybe they notice anything helpful."

"A walk through," said Mr. Shull.

Mr. Hashim said, "A walk through," and bent over to examine his highly polished black wing tips. "Cool."

"I'm glad we're all in agreement. Mike, maybe you could hold that jar for Mrs. Chancel."

Officer LeDonne took the jar and held it close to his face.

"These people were here recently?" asked Mr. Shull, also staring at the jar.

"Recently enough," said Fenn. "Take a good look around, folks, but make sure not to touch anything."

"Make like you're in a museum," said Mr. Shull.

"Do that," said Mr. Hashim.

Nora stepped past them into the living room. Mr. Shull and Mr. Hashim made her feel like touching everything in sight. Cigarette ash streaked the tan carpet, and a hole had been burned in the wheat-colored sofa. Magazines and a stack of newspapers covered the coffee table. Two Dean Koontz paperbacks had been lined up on the brick ledge above the fireplace. On the walls hung the iron weathervanes and bits of driftwood Natalie had not so much collected as gathered. The FBI men followed Nora with blank eyes. She glared at Mr. Shull. He blinked. Without altering her expression, Nora turned around and took in the room. It seemed at once charged with the presence of Natalie Weil and utterly empty of her. Mr. Shull and Mr. Hashim had been right: they were standing in a museum.

"Natalie make any phone calls that night?" Davey asked.

Fenn said, "Nope."

It occurred to Nora as she tagged along into the kitchen that she did not, she most emphatically did not, wish to see this house, thanks anyhow. Yet here she was, in Natalie's kitchen. Davey mooned along in front of the cabinets, shook his head at the sink, and paused before the photographs pinned to a cork-board next to the refrigerator. For Natalie's sake, Nora forced herself to look at what was around her and recognized almost instantly that no matter what she did or did not want, a change had occurred. In the living room, a blindfold of habit and dis-comfort had been anchored over her eyes.

Now, blindfold off, traces of Natalie Weil's decisions and preferences showed wherever she looked. Wooden counters had been scarred where Natalie had sliced the sourdough bread she liked toasted for breakfast; jammed into the garbage bin along with crumpled cigarette packets were plastic wrappers from Waldbaum's. Half-empty jam jars crowded the toaster. Smudgy glasses smelling faintly of beer stood beside the sink, piled with plates to which clung dried jam, flecks of toast, and granules of ground beef. A bag of rotting grapes lay on the counter beside three upright bottles of wine. Whatever Norman Weil and his new wife were drinking on the deck of their beach house in Malibu probably wasn't Firehouse Golden Mountain Jug Red, $9.99 a liter.

Blue recycling bins beside the back door held wine and Corona empties and a dead bottle of Stolichnaya Cristall. Tied up with twine in another blue bin were stacks of the New York and Westerholm newspapers along with bundles of *Time*, *Newsweek*, *Fangoria*, and *Wrestlemania*.

"I wish my men looked at crime scenes the way you do."

Startled, Nora straightened up to see Holly Fenn leaning against the open door to the hallway.

"Notice anything?"

"She ate toast and jam for breakfast. She was a little sloppy. She lived cheap, and she had kind of down-home tastes. You wouldn't know that by looking at her."

"Anything else?"

Nora thought back over what she had seen. "She was inter-ested in horror movies, and that kind of surprises me, but I couldn't really say why."

Fenn gave her a twitch of a smile. "Wait till you see the bed-room." Nora waited for him to say something about murder vic-tims and horror movies, but he did not. "What else?"

"She drank cheap wine, but every now and then she splurged on expensive vodka. All we ever saw her drink was beer."

Fenn nodded. "Keep on looking."

She walked to the refrigerator and saw the half-dozen magnets she remembered from two years before. A leering Dracula
and a Frankenstein's monster with outstretched arms clung to
the freezer cabinet; a half-peeled banana, a hippie in granny
glasses and bell bottoms dragging on a joint half his size, an
elongated spoon heaped with white powder, and a miniature
Hulk Hogan decorated the larger door beneath.

Holly Fenn was twinkling at her from the doorway. "These
have been here for years," she said.

"Real different," said Fenn. "Your husband says you don't
think Mrs. Weil is dead."

"I hope she isn't." Nora moved impatiently to the corkboard
bristling with photographs. She could still feel the blood
heating her face and wished that the detective would leave her
alone.

"Ever think Natalie was involved in drugs?"

"Oh, sure," Nora said, facing him. "Davey and I used to come
over and snort coke all the time. After that we'd smoke some
joints while cheering on our favorite *wrestlers*. We knew we
could get away with it because the Westerholm police can't
even catch the kids who bash in our mailboxes."

He was backing away before she realized that she had taken
a couple of steps toward him.

Fenn held up his hands, palms out. They looked like catcher's
mitts. "You having trouble with your mailbox?"

She whirled away from him and posted herself in front of the
photographs. Natalie Weil's face, sometimes alone, sometimes
not, grinned out at her. She had experimented with her hair, letting it grow to her shoulders, cropping it, streaking it, bleaching
it to a brighter blond. A longer-haired Natalie smiled out from a
deck chair, leaned against the rail of a cruise ship, at the center
of a group of grinning, white-haired former teachers and sales-
clerks in shorts and T-shirts.

Some drug addict, Nora thought. She moved on to a series of
photographs of Natalie in a peach-colored bathing suit lined up,
some of them separated by wide gaps, at the bottom of the cork-
board. They had been taken in the master bedroom, and Natalie
was perched on the bed with her hands behind her back. Uncomfortably aware of Holly Fenn looming in the doorway, she saw
what Natalie was wearing. The bathing suit was one of those
undergarments which women never bought for themselves and

could be worn only in a bedroom. Nora did not even know what they were called. Natalie's clutched her breasts, squeezed her waist, and flared at her hips. A profusion of straps and buttons made her look like a lecher's Christmas present. Nora looked more closely at the glint of a bracelet behind Natalie's back and saw the unmistakable steel curve of handcuffs.

She suppressed her dismay and stepped toward Fenn. "Probably this looks wildly degenerate to you," he said.

"What does it look like to you?"

"Harmless fun and games." He moved aside, and she walked out into the hall.

"Harmless?"

Nora turned toward the bedroom, thinking that maybe the Chancels had a point after all, and secrets should stay secret. Murder stripped you bare, exposed you to pitiless judgment. What you thought you shared with one other person was . . . She stopped walking.

"Think of something?"

She turned around. "A man took those pictures."

"Kind of a waste if her sister took them."

"But there aren't any pictures of him."

"That's right."

"Do you think there ever were?"

"You mean, do I think that at some point he was on the bed and she was holding the camera? I think something like that probably happened, sure. I took your picture, now you take mine. What happened to the pictures of the man?"

"Oh," she said, remembering the wide gaps on that section of the board.

"Ah. I love these little moments of enlightenment."

This little moment of enlightenment made her feel sick to her stomach.

"I'm kind of curious to hear what you know about her boyfriends."

"I wish I did know something."

"Guess you didn't notice the pictures, last time you were here."

"I didn't go into the kitchen."

"How about the time before that?"

"I don't remember if I went into the kitchen. If I did, I certainly didn't see those pictures."

"Now comes the time when I have to ask about this," Fenn said. "Did you and your husband ever join in your friend's games? If you say yes, I won't tell Slim and Slam in there. Got any pictures at home with Mrs. Weil in them?"

"No. Of course not."

"Your husband's a good-looking guy. Little younger than you, isn't he?"

"Actually," she said, "we were born on the same day. Just in different decades."

He grinned. "You probably know where the bedroom is."

15

THROUGH THE OPEN door Nora saw a rising arc of brown spots sprayed across an ivory wall. Beneath the spray, the visible corner of the bed looked as if rust-colored paint had been poured over the sheets.

Fenn spoke behind her. "You don't have to go in there if you don't feel like it. But you might want to reconsider the idea that she isn't dead."

"Maybe it isn't her blood," she said, and fumed at Davey for having made her say such a thing.

"Oh?"

She made herself walk into the room. Dried blood lay across the bed, and stripes and splashes of blood blotted the carpet beside it. The sheets and pillows had been slashed. Stiff flaps of cotton folded back over clumps of rigid foam that looked like the entrails of small animals. It all looked sordid and sad. The sadness was not a surprise, but the sense of wretchedness gripped her heart.

Slumped in the far corner beside Officer LeDonne, Davey glanced up at her and shook his head.

She turned to Fenn, who raised his eyebrows. "Did you find a camera? Did Natalie have a camera?"

"We didn't find one, but Slim and Slam say all the pictures in there were taken with the same camera. One of those little Ph.D. jobs."

"Ph.D.?"

"Push here, dummy. An auto-focus. Like a little Olympus or a Canon. With a zoom feature."

In other words, Natalie's camera was exactly like theirs, not to mention most of the other cameras in Westerholm. The bedroom felt airless, hot, despairing. A lunatic who liked to dress women up like sex toys had finally taken his fantasies to their logical conclusion and used Natalie Weil's bed as an operating table. Nora wondered if he had been seeing all five women at the same time.

She was glad she wasn't a cop. There was too much to think about, and half of what you had to think about made no sense. But the worst part of standing here was standing *here*.

She had to say something. What came out of her mouth was "Were there pictures in the other houses? Like the ones in the kitchen?" She barely heard the detective's negative answer; she had barely heard her own question. Somehow she had walked across several yards of unspattered tan carpet to stand in front of four long bookshelves. Two feet away, Davey gave her the look of an animal in a cage. Nora fled into the safety of book titles, but she found no safety. In the living room Fenn had said something about Natalie's affection for horror novels, and here was the proof, in alphabetical order by author's name. These books had titles like *The Rats* and *Vampire Junction* and *The Silver Skull*. Here were *They Thirst, Hell House, The Books of Blood,* and *The Brains of Rats*. Natalie had owned more Dean Koontz novels than Nora had known existed, she had every Stephen King novel from *Carrie* to *Dolores Claiborne*, all of Anne Rice and Clive Barker and Whitley Strieber.

Nora moved along the shelves as if in a trance. Here was a Natalie Weil who entertained herself with stories of vampires, dismemberment, monsters with tentacles and bad breath, cannibalism, psychotic killers, degrading random death. This person wanted fear, but creepy, safe fear. She had been like a roller coaster aficionado for whom tame county fair roller coasters were as good as the ones that spun you upside down and dropped you so fast your eyes turned red. It was all just a ride.

At the end of the bottom shelf her eyes met the names Marletta Teatime and Clyde Morning above a sullen-looking crow, the familiar logo of Blackbird Books, Chancel House's small, soon-to-be-discontinued horror line. Alden had expected steady, automatic profits from these writers, but they had failed him. Gaudy with severed heads and mutilated dolls, the covers of their books came back from the distributors within days of publication. Davey had argued to keep the line, which managed to make a small amount of money every season, in part because Teatime and Morning never got more than two thousand dollars per book. (Davey sometimes frivolously suggested that they were actually the same person.) Alden dismissed Davey's argument that he had condemned the books by refusing to promote or publicize them; the beauty of horror was that it sold itself. Davey said that his father treated the books like orphaned children, and Alden said damn right, like orphaned children, they had to pull their own weight.

"Mrs. Chancel?" said Holly Fenn.

Another title shouted at her from the bottom shelf. *Night Journey* protruded at a hasty, awkward angle from between two Stephen King encyclopedias as if Natalie had crammed it in anywhere before running to the door.

"Mr. Chancel?"

She looked at the *D*'s, but Natalie had owned no other Driver novels.

"Sorry I wasn't more helpful." Davey's voice sounded as if it came from the bottom of a well.

"No harm in trying." Fenn stepped out of the doorway.

Davey shot Nora another anguished glance and moved toward the door. Nora followed, and LeDonne came along behind. The four of them moved in single file toward the living room, where Slim and Slam faced forward, automatically shedding any signs of individuality. Davey said, "Excuse me, I have to go back."

Fenn flattened his bulk against the wall to let Davey get by. Nora and the two policemen watched him go down the corridor and swerve into the bedroom. LeDonne quizzed Fenn with a look, and Fenn shook his head. After a couple of seconds, Davey emerged, more distressed than ever.

"Forget something?" Fenn asked.

"I thought I saw something—couldn't even tell you what it was. But—" He spread his hands, shaking his head.

"That happens," Fenn said. "If it comes back to you, don't be shy about giving me a call."

When they turned to go down the stairs, the two FBI men split apart and looked away.

16

"WHAT DID YOU think you saw?"

"Nothing."

"You went back in the bedroom. You had something on your mind. What was it?"

"Nothing." He looked sideways at her, so shaken he was white. "It was a dumb idea. I should have just gone home."

"Why didn't you?"

"I wanted to see that house." He paused. "And I wanted you to see it."

"Why?"

He waited a second before answering. "I thought if you looked at it, you might stop having nightmares."

"Pretty strange idea," Nora said.

"Okay, it was a rotten idea." His voice grew louder. "It was the worst idea in the history of the world. In fact, every single idea I've ever had in my life was really terrible. Are we in agreement now? Good. Then we can forget about it."

"Davey."

"*What?*"

"Do you remember when I asked if you were upset?"

"No." He hesitated, then sighed again, and his glance suggested the arrival of a confession. "Why would I be upset?"

Nora gathered herself. "You must have been surprised by what your father said about Hugo Driver."

He looked at her as if trying to recall Alden's words. "He said he was a great writer."

"You said he was a great writer." After a second of silence she said, "What I mean is his attitude."

"Yeah," Davey said. "You're right. That was a surprise. He sort of jolted me, I guess."

For Nora the next few seconds filled with a hopeful tension.

"I've got something on my mind, I guess I was worked up. . . . I don't want to fight, Nora."

"So you're not mad at me anymore."

"I wasn't mad at you. I just feel confused."

Two hours with his parents had turned him back into Pippin Little. If he needed a Green Knight, she volunteered on the spot. She had asked for a job, and here one was sitting next to her. She could help Davey become his successful adult self. She would help him get the position he deserved at Chancel House. Her other plans, befriending Daisy and moving to New York, were merely elements of this larger, truer occupation. *Start,* she commanded herself. *Now.*

"Davey," she said, "what would you like to be doing at Chancel House?"

Again, he seemed to force himself to think. "Editorial work."

"Then that's what you should be doing."

"Well, yeah, but you know, Dad . . ." He gave her a resigned look.

"You're not like that disgusting guy who takes old ladies to lunch, you're not Dick Dart. What job do you want most?"

He bit the lining of his cheek before deciding to declare what she already suspected. "I'd like to edit Blackbird Books. I think I could build Blackbird into something good, but Dad is canceling the line."

"Not if you make him keep it."

"How do I do that?"

"I don't know, exactly. But for sure you have to come at him with a plan." She thought for a moment. "Get all the figures on the Blackbird Books. Give him projections, give him graphs. Have lists of writers you want to sign up. Print up a presentation. Tell him you'll do it on top of your other work."

He turned his head to gape at her.

"I'll help. We'll put something together that he won't be able to refuse."

He looked away, looked back, and filled his lungs with air. "Well, okay. Let's give it a try."

"Blackbird Books, here we come," she said, and remembered seeing the row of titles by Clyde Morning and Marletta Teatime in Natalie's bedroom. Unlike Natalie's other books, these had not been filed alphabetically, but separated, at the end of the bottom shelf.

"You know, it might work," Davey said.

Nora wondered if putting the books together meant they were significantly better or worse than other horror novels. Maybe what was crucial about them was that they were published by Blackbird—Chancel House.

"I was thinking once that we could do a series of classics, books in the public domain."

"Good idea," Nora said. Looking back, she thought that the Blackbird Books on Natalie's shelf seemed uniformly new and unmarked, as if they had been bought at the same time and never read.

"If we can put together a serious presentation, he'll have to pay attention."

"Davey . . ." A sense of hope and expectancy filled Nora, and the question escaped her before she could call it back. "Do you ever think of moving out of Westerholm?"

He lifted his chin. "To tell you the truth, I think about getting out of this hole just about every day. But look, I know how much living here means to you."

Her laughter amazed him.

BOOK II

PADDY'S TAIL

THE FIRST THING PIPPIN SAW WAS THE TIP OF A LITTLE TAIL, NO
WIDER THAN FOUR HORSEHAIRS BOUND TOGETHER, BUT IN
SEARCH OF THE REST OF THE ANIMAL, HE FOLLOWED THE TAIL
AROUND ROCKS, THROUGH TALL WEEDS, IN GREAT CIRCLES, UP
AND DOWN GREAT LOOPS ON THE GRASS, AND WHEN AT LAST HE
REACHED THE END OF THE LONG, LONG TAIL, HE FOUND
ATTACHED TO IT A TINY MOUSE. THE MOUSE APPEARED TO
BE DEAD.

17

ALTHOUGH DAVEY SEEMED moody and distracted, the following five days were nearly as happy as any Nora could remember. One other period—several weeks in Vietnam, in memory the happiest of her life—had come at a time when she had been too busy to think of anything but work. Looking back, she had said to herself, *So that was happiness.*

Her first month in the Evacuation Hospital had jolted her so thoroughly that by its end she was no longer certain what she would need to get her through. Pot, okay. Alcohol, you bet. Emotional calluses, even better. At the rate of twenty to thirty surgical cases a day, she had learned about debridement and irrigation—clearing away dead skin and cleaning the wound against infection—worms in the chest cavity, amputations, crispy critters, and pseudomonas. She particularly hated pseudomonas, a bacterial infection that coated burn patients with green slime. During that month, she had junked most of what she had been taught in nursing school and learned to assist at high-speed operations, clamping blood vessels and cutting where the neurosurgeon told her to cut. At night her boots left bloody trails across the floor. She was in a flesh factory, not a hospital. The old, idealistic Nora Curlew was being unceremoniously peeled away like a layer of outgrown clothes, and what she saw of the new was a spiritless automaton.

Then a temporary miracle occurred. As many patients died during or after operations, the wounded continued to scream from their cots, and Nora was always exhausted, but not *as* exhausted, and the patients separated into individuals. To these people she did rapid, precise, necessary things that often permitted them to live. At times, she cradled the head of a dying young man and felt that particles of her own being passed into him, easing and steadying.

She had won a focused concentration out of the chaos around her, and every operation became a drama in which she and the surgeon performed necessary, inventive actions which banished or at least contained disorder. Some of these actions were elegant; sometimes the entire drama took on a rigorous, shattering elegance. She learned the differences between the surgeons, some of them fullbacks, some concert pianists, and she treasured the compliments they gave her. At nights, too alert with exhaustion to sleep, she smoked Montagnard grass with the others and played whatever they were playing that day—cards, volleyball, or insults.

At the end of her fifth week in Vietnam, a neurosurgeon named Chris Cross had been reassigned and a new surgeon, Daniel Harwich, had rotated in. Cross, a cheerful blond mesomorph with thousands of awful jokes and a bottomless appetite for beer, had been a fullback surgeon, but a great fullback. He worked athletically, with flashes of astounding grace, and Nora had decided that, all in all, she would probably never see a better surgeon. Their entire unit mourned his going, and when his replacement turned out to be a stringy, lint-haired geek with Coke-bottle glasses and no visible traces of humor, they circled their wagons around Captain Cross's memory and politely froze out the intruder. A tough little nurse named Rita Glow said she'd work with the clown, what the hell, it was all slice 'n' dice anyhow, and while Nora continued her education in the miraculous under the unit's other two surgeons, one a bang-smash fullback, one a pianist who had learned some bang-smash tendencies from Chris Cross, she noticed that not only did geeky Dan Harwich put in his twelve-hour days with the rest of them but he got through more patients with fewer complaints and less drama.

One day Rita Glow said she had to see this guy work, he was righteous, he was a fucking *tap dancer* in there, and the next morning she swapped assignments to put Nora across the table from Harwich. Between them was a paralyzed young soldier whose back looked like raw meat. Harwich told her she was going to have to help him while he cut shell fragments from the boy's vertebrae. He was both a fullback and a pianist, and his hands were astonishingly fast and sure. After three hours, he closed the boy's back with the quickest, neatest stitches she had ever seen, looked over at Nora, and said, "Now that I'm warmed up, let's do something hard, okay?"

Within three weeks she was sleeping with Harwich, and within four she was in love. Then the skies opened. Tortured, mangled bodies packed the OR, and they worked seventy-eight hours straight through. She and Harwich crawled into bed covered with the blood of other people, made love, slept for a second, and got up and did the whole thing all over again. They were shelled in the middle of operations and in the middle of the night, sometimes the same thing, and as the clarity of the earlier period shredded, details of individual soldiers burned themselves into her mind. No longer quite sane, she thrust the terror and panic into a locked inner closet.

After three months she was raped by two dumbbell grunts who caught her as she came outside on a break. One of them hit her in the side of the head, pushed her down, and fell on her. The other kneeled on her arms. At first she thought they had mistaken her for a Vietcong, but almost instantly she realized that what they had mistaken her for was a living woman. The rape was a flurry of thumps and blows and enormous, reeking hands over her mouth; it was having the breath mashed out of her while grunting animals dug at her privates. While it went on, Nora was punched through the bottom of the world. This was entirely literal. The column of the world went from bottom to top, and now she had been smashed through the bottom of the column along with the rest of the shit. Demons leaned chattering out of the darkness.

The second grunt rolled off, the first grunt let go of her arms, and they sprinted away. She heard their footsteps and realized that now she was on the other side, with the gibbering demons; then she gathered the demons into her psychic hands and stuffed them into an inner container just large enough to hold them.

Nora did not tell Harwich what had happened until hours later, when she looked down at the blood soaking through her clothes, thought it was hers, and fainted. A grim Harwich accepted her refusal to report the incident but followed her out of the OR on a break to pass from his hands to hers a dead officer's handgun. This she kept as close as possible until her last morning in Vietnam, when she dropped it into the nurses' latrine. Even after Dan Harwich left Vietnam, vowing that he would write (he did) and that they had a future together (they didn't), she used her awareness of the gun beneath her pillow to fend off nightmares of the incident until she could almost think that she had forgotten it. And for years after Vietnam it was as if she really

had forgotten all about it—until she had reached a kind of provisional, static happiness in Westerholm, Connecticut. In Westerholm, the ordinary, terrible nightmares of dead and dying
soldiers had begun to be supplanted by the other, worse nightmares—about being pushed through the hole at the bottom of the
world.

Long after, Nora sometimes looked back at that exalted period
before the war slammed down on her and thought: *Happiness
comes when you are looking elsewhere, it is a by-product, of no
importance in itself.*

18

EVERY NIGHT THAT week, Nora and Davey delved into Blackbird
Books, playing with figures and trying to work out a presentation
that would convince Alden. Davey remained moody and remote
but seemed grateful for Nora's help. To see what Blackbird Books
were like, Nora read *The Waiting Grave* by Marletta Teatime and
Blood Bond by Clyde Morning. Davey sounded out agents; he and
Nora drew up lists of writers who might sign up with a revitalized
Blackbird Books. They learned that Blackbird's greatest appeal
was its connection to Chancel House, but that Chancel House had
done even less with the line than Davey had imagined.

In 1977, its first year, Blackbird had published twelve paperback originals by writers then unknown. By 1979, half of the ten
original writers had left in search of more promotion, higher
advances, and better editing. In those days an assistant editor
named Merle Marvell had handled the line. Marvell's secretary,
shared with two other assistant editors, copyedited Blackbird
novels for fifteen dollars a book. (Alden would not waste money
on a professional copy editor.) Blackbird stubbornly refused to lay
golden eggs, and by 1981 all of its original writers had moved on,
leaving behind only Teatime and Morning, who had produced
their first books. No longer an assistant editor, Merle Marvell

bought one first novel that won an important prize and another that made the best-seller list and thereafter had no more time for Blackbird. Since then, Blackbird's two stalwarts sent in their manuscripts and took their money. Neither had an agent. Instead of addresses, they had post office boxes—Teatime's in Norwalk, Connecticut, Morning's in midtown Manhattan. Their telephone numbers had never been divulged. They never demanded higher advances, lunches, or ad budgets. Clyde Morning had won the British Fantasy Award in 1983, and Marletta Teatime had been nominated for a World Fantasy Award in 1985. They went on producing a book a year until 1989, when each of them stopped writing.

"Chancel House has been publishing these people for more than ten years, and you don't even know their telephone numbers?"

"That's not the weird part," Davey said. They were devouring a sausage and mushroom pizza delivered by a gnome in a space helmet who on closer inspection had become a sixteen-year-old girl wearing a motorcycle helmet. Room had been made on the table for a bottle of Robert Mondavi Private Reserve Cabernet Sauvignon and two glasses by shoving papers, printouts, and sheets torn from legal pads into piles. "The weird part is what I found on a shelf in the conference room today."

Like the old Davey, he raised his eyebrows and smiled, teasing her. Nora thought he looked wonderful. She liked the way he ate pizza, with a knife and fork. Nora picked up a slice and chomped, pulling away long strings of mozzarella, but Davey addressed a pizza as though it were filet mignon. "Okay," she said, "what did you find on this shelf?"

"Remember I told you that every new manuscript gets written down in a kind of a ledger? Now all this is on a computer. Whatever happens to the submission gets entered beside the title— rejected and returned, or accepted, with the date. I was wondering if we might have rejected books by Morning or Teatime, so I went back to '89, the first year we used computers, and there was Clyde Morning. He submitted a book called *Spectre* in June '89, and the manuscript never left the house. It wasn't rejected, but it was never accepted, either. He didn't even have an editor, so no one was actually responsible for the manuscript."

"What happened to it?"

"Precisely. I went down to the production department. Of

course nobody could remember. Most of the scripts they work on are kept for a year or two after publication, why I don't know, and then get returned to the editor, who sends them back to the author. I looked at all of them, but I couldn't find *Spectre*. A production assistant finally reminded me that they sometimes squirrel things away on the shelves in the conference room. It's like the dead letter office." Davey was grinning.

"And you went to the conference room"—he was nodding his head and grinning even more wildly—"and you . . . you found the book?"

"Right there! And not only that . . ."

She looked at him in astonishment. "You read it?"

"I skimmed it, anyhow. It's kind of sloppy, but I think it's publishable. I have to see if it's still available—I suppose I have to find out if Morning is still *alive*—but it could be the leadoff in our new line."

She liked the *our*. "So we're almost ready."

"I want to go in on Monday." He did not have to be more specific. "He's still in a pretty good mood on Monday afternoons." This was Friday evening. "I got a call back from an agent this morning, sounding me out about a couple of writers I'm sure we could get without breaking the bank."

"You devil," she said. "You've been sitting on this ever since you came home."

"Just waiting for the right moment." He finished the last of his pizza. "Do you want to play around with the presentation some more, or is there something else we could do?"

"Like celebrate?"

"If you're in the mood," Davey said.

"I definitely feel a mood coming on," Nora said.

"Well, then." He looked at her almost uncertainly.

"Come on, big boy," she said. "We'll take care of the dishes later."

Twenty minutes later, Davey lay with his hands folded on his stomach, staring up at the ceiling. "Sweetie," she said, "I didn't say it hurt, I just said it was uncomfortable. I felt dry, but I'm sure that's just temporary. I have an appointment with my doctor next week to talk about hormone replacement. Look at it this way—we probably don't have to worry about getting pregnant anymore."

"I have condoms. You have your . . . thing. Of course we don't have to worry about that."

"Davey, I'm forty-nine. My body is changing. There has to be this period of adjustment."

"Period of adjustment."

"That's all. My doctor says everything will be fine as long as I eat right and exercise, and probably I'll have to start taking estrogen. It happens to every woman, and now it's my turn."

He turned his head to her. "Were you dry last time?"

"No." She tried not to sigh. "I wasn't."

"So why are you this time?"

"Because this is the time it happened."

"But you're not an old woman." He rolled over and half-buried his face in the pillow. "I know what's wrong. I got too excited or something, and now you're turned off."

"Davey, I'm starting to go through menopause. Of course I'm not turned off. I love you. We've always had wonderful sex."

"You can't have wonderful sex with someone who wakes up moaning and groaning almost every night."

"It isn't . . ." This was not going to be a fruitful remark. Neither would it be fruitful to remark that you couldn't have sex with a man who would not come to your bed, or who left your bed to worry about work or Hugo Driver or whatever it was Davey worried about late at night.

"Well, a lot of nights, anyhow," he said, taking up her unspoken comment. "Maybe you need therapy or something. You're too young for menopause. When my mother went through it, she had a lot of white hair, she was over fifty, and she turned into a total bitch. She was impossible, she was like in a rage for at least a year."

"People have different reactions. It's nothing to be afraid of."

"People in menopause don't have periods. You had one a little while ago."

"I had a period that lasted more than two weeks. Then I didn't have one for about six weeks."

"I don't have to hear all the gory details."

"The gory details are my department, right. But everything's going to be all right. This is *temporary.*"

"God, I hope so."

What did Davey hope was temporary? Menopause? Aging? She moved across the sheet and put an arm over his shoulder. He turned his face away. Nora kissed the back of his head and slid her other arm beneath him. When he did not attempt to shrug her off or push her away, she pulled him into her. He resisted only a second or two before turning his head to her and slipping his arms around her. His cheek felt wet against hers. "Oh, honey," she said, and moved her head back to see the tears leaking from his eyes. Davey wiped his face, then held her close.

"This is no good."

"It'll get better."

"I don't know what to *do*."

"Try talking about it," Nora said, swallowing the words *for a change*.

"I sort of think I have to."

"Good."

Now he had a grudging, almost furtive look. "You know how I've been kind of worried lately? It's because of this thing that happened about ten years before I met you." He looked up at the ceiling, and she braced herself, with a familiar despair, for a story which would owe as much to Hugo Driver as to Davey's real history. "I was having a rough time because Amy Randolph finally broke up with me."

Nora had heard all about Amy Randolph, a beautiful and destructive poet-photographer-screenwriter-painter whom Davey had met in college. He had lost his virginity to her, and she had lost hers to her father. (Unless this was another colorful embellishment.) After graduation they had traveled through North Africa. Amy had flirted with every attractive man she met and threw tyrannical fits when the men responded. Finally the two of them had been deported from Algeria and shared an apartment in the Village. Amy went in and out of hospitals, twice for suicide attempts. She photographed corpses and drug addicts. She had no interest in sex. Davey once said to Nora that Amy was so brilliant he hadn't been able to leave her for fear of missing her conversation. In the end, she had deprived him of her conversation by moving in with an older woman, a Romanian émigrée who edited an intellectual journal. He had never explained to Nora how he had felt about losing Amy, or spoken of what he had done between the breakup and their own meeting.

"Well," Nora said, "whatever this is, it couldn't have been much stranger than life with Amy."

"That's what you think," Davey said.

19

"IT WAS ABOUT a month after Amy left. You know, I think I was actually kind of happy for her. Some people acted like they thought I should be disturbed by what she did, but I didn't know why. Amy never liked sex anyhow, so it was more like getting worked up about who she *wasn't* doing it with than who she was, and that's ridiculous. Anyhow, after about a month, I repainted my apartment and put new posters on the walls, and then I got a really good stereo system and a lot of new records. Whenever I found anything that reminded me of her, I threw it out. A couple of times when she called up, I hung up on her. Because it was all over, right?"

"You were pretty angry," Nora said.

Davey shook his head. "I don't remember being angry. I just didn't see the point of talking to her."

"Okay." Nora reached over the side of the bed and picked her bra and blouse off the floor. She tossed the bra into the clothing bin and put on the blouse.

"I wasn't angry with Amy," he said. "Everybody kept telling me that I had to be, but I wasn't. You can't get angry at crazy people."

Nora gave up and nodded.

"Anyhow, I was in a funny mood. After my apartment was all redone, I reread Hugo Driver—all three books—after I came home from work. Then I read *Night Journey* all over again. I felt like Pippin."

In other words, Nora thought, he felt as though Amy had killed him.

"I couldn't stand being in the apartment by myself, but I hardly had any friends because Amy, you know, made that difficult. I didn't want to spend time with my parents because they hated

63

Amy, and they *loved* telling me how lucky I was. I went through this weird period. Sometimes I'd spend the whole night staring at the tube. I'd listen to one piece of music over and over, all weekend."

"I guess you got into drugs," Nora said.

"Well, yeah. Amy always hated drugs, so now that I was free . . . you know? A guy in the mailroom named Bang Bang sold stuff, which Dad didn't know about. So one day I saw this guy coming out of the mailroom on a break, and I looked at him, and he looked at me, and I followed him outside. I got some coke and some pot, and I pretty much did those for about a year. At work I stayed pretty straight, but when I got back to my apartment, boy, I poured myself a glass of Bombay gin on the rocks, did two big, fat lines, rolled a joint, and had a little party until I went to bed. Or didn't. I was thirty, thirty-one. I didn't need a lot of sleep. Just take a shower, shave, drop in some Murine, couple lines, fresh clothes, off to work."

"And one day you met this Girl Scout," Nora said.

"You sure you want to hear about this?"

"Why don't you just say, 'Nora, once when I was fooling around with drugs I had this messed-up girlfriend, and we got crazy together'?"

"Because it's not that simple. You have to understand where I was mentally in order to understand what happened. Otherwise it won't make any sense."

It occurred to Nora that whatever he had to say, strictly factual or not, would be instructive. Maybe Davey had been a weekend punk!

"This isn't just about a girl, is it?"

"Actually it's about Natalie Weil." He pushed himself upright and pulled the sheets above his navel. "Look, Nora, I didn't tell you the truth the other day. This is the real reason I wanted to get into Natalie's house."

She tucked up her legs, leaned forward, and waited.

20

"I WAS IN a stall in the men's room one morning, feeling lousy because I'd stayed up all night. I snorted some coke, and my nose started to bleed. I had to sit on the toilet with my head back, holding toilet paper against my nose. Finally the bleeding stopped, and I decided to try to get through the day.

"I came out of the stall. Some little guy was going toward the sinks. I grabbed some towels and dried my hands, and this guy was messing with his hair, and I looked at his face in the mirror, and I almost had a heart attack."

"The little guy was a girl."

"How did you know that?"

"Because you almost had a heart attack."

"She was in the art department. She had short hair and she wore men's clothes. That's all I knew. I didn't even know her last name. Her first name was Paddi." He looked at her as if this were of enormous significance.

"Patty?"

"Paddi. Two *d*'s and an *i*. Okay, my nose started bleeding again. I grabbed another towel and held it up against my nose. Paddi was dumping two piles of coke on the sink in front of her. 'Try this,' she said. We're right in the middle of the men's room! I leaned over and snorted the stuff right off the sink, and bingo! I felt a thousand percent better. 'Get it?' she said. 'Always use good stuff.'

" 'What planet are you from?' I asked her.

"She smiled at me and said, *'I was born in a village at the foot of a great mountain. My father is a blacksmith.'*

"I almost passed out. She was quoting *Night Journey*. I said, *'I wander far and sometimes get lost. I own a purpose greater than myself, the saving of children from the darkness.'*

65

"And she chimed in, '*I conquer my own fear.*'

"We grinned at each other for a second, and I shooed her out-side before someone came in. She was waiting for me across the hall. 'I'm Paddi Mann,' she said. 'And you're Davey Chancel, of the famous Chancel House Chancels. Want to buy me a drink tonight?'

"Normally, assertive women put me off, and we're not sup-posed to go out with women from the office, but she could quote Hugo Driver! I told her to meet me at six-thirty at Hannigan's, a bar a couple of blocks away, and she said no, we should go to the Hellfire Club down on Second Avenue, great place, and let's meet at seven-thirty so she could take care of some things she had to do. Fine, I said, and she came right up in front of me and tilted up her head and whispered, '*His own salvation lay within himself.*'"

Nora had heard these words before, but she could not remem-ber when.

"You know what? I thought I could learn things from her. It was like she had secrets, and they were the secrets I needed to know."

"Sure," Nora said. "You needed to know the secret of how to score coke better than Bang Bang's."

Davey had gone home and changed into jeans, a black sweater, and a black leather jacket before walking to Second Avenue. The Hellfire Club was between Eighth and Ninth, on the East Side. He reached the corner of Ninth and Second only a minute or two past seven-thirty and walked down the east side of the avenue, passing a fast-food restaurant, a Mexican restaurant, and saw a bar farther down the block. He picked up his pace and went past a window that showed a few men huddled over a long, dark bar, put his hand on the door, and just below his hand saw the name MORLEY'S.

He had managed to miss the club. He went back up the east side of the avenue, checking the names on buildings, and missed it again.

A rank of three telephones stood only a few feet away. The first had a severed cord instead of a receiver, the second did not pro-vide a dial tone, and the third permitted six-sevenths of Davey's quarter into its slot and then froze.

Disgusted, Davey stepped away from the telephones and went to the corner to wait for the light to change. He glanced down the block and this time noticed a narrow stone stair-case with wrought-iron handrails between Morley's bar and a lighting-goods shop. The stairs led to a dark wooden door, which looked too elegant for its surroundings. Centered in the door's top panel was a brass plate slightly larger than an index card.

The light changed, but instead of crossing the street, Davey walked to the foot of the stairs and looked up at a five-story brownstone wedged between two apartment buildings. On either side of the door were two curtained windows. The lettering on the plaque was not quite legible from the bottom of the stairs. He climbed two steps and saw that the plate read HELLFIRE CLUB and, beneath that, MEMBERS ONLY. He went up the stairs and opened the door. Across a tiny entry stood another door, glossy black. Three commands had been painted on a white wooden plaque fixed just beneath the level of his eyes:

DO NOT QUESTION.
DO NOT JUDGE.
DO NOT HESITATE.

Davey opened the black door. Before him was a hallway with a floral carpet which continued up a flight of stairs. To his left an elderly woman stood behind a checkroom counter beside the opening into a dim barroom. Past the bar, a wide leather armchair stood beside an ambitious potted fern. A white-haired concierge at a glossy black desk turned to him with a diplomatic half smile. To eliminate the preliminaries, Davey peered into the barroom and saw only prosperous-looking men in suits seated around tables or standing in clusters of three or four. He noticed a few women in the room, none of them Paddi. In the instant before the man at the desk spoke to him, he saw—thought he saw—a naked man covered to wrists and neck with elaborate tattoos beside a naked woman, her back to Davey, who had shaved her head and powdered or otherwise colored her body a flat, dead white.

"May I assist you, sir?"

Startled, Davey looked at the concierge. He cleared his throat. "Thank you. I'm here to meet a woman named Paddi Mann." He glanced back into the bar and had the sense that the other people in the room had shifted their positions to conceal the surreal couple.

"Sir."

Davey looked back at the concierge.

"That was Miss Mann?"

When Davey said yes, the concierge told him to be seated, please, and watched him proceed to the leather chair, which provided a view of nothing more provocative than ·the wide mahogany doors and a row of hunting prints on the opposite wall. The concierge opened a drawer and drew out a ribbon microphone at least fifty years old, positioned it squarely in front of him, and said, "Guest for Miss Mann." The words reverberated from the barroom, from rooms upstairs, and from behind the mahogany doors.

One of the mahogany doors opened, and a Paddi Mann who looked less raffish and more sophisticated than her office persona stepped smiling into the hallway. The dark suit into which she had changed looked more expensive than most of Davey's own suits. Her shining hair fell softly over her forehead and ears.

She asked why he was dressed that way.

He explained that he thought he was going to meet her at a bar.

Bars were disgusting. Why did she think she had invited him to her club?

He hadn't understood, he said. If she liked, he could go home and put on a suit.

She told him not to bother and suggested they swap jackets.

He took off his leather jacket and held it out. Paddi slipped off her suit jacket and twirled herself into his jacket so smoothly that he barely had time to notice that she was wearing suspenders.

"Your turn," she said.

He was afraid he'd rip the shoulder seams, but the jacket met his back and shoulders with only a suggestion of tightness.

"You're lucky I like big jackets."

Paddi opened the mahogany door to a lounge in which groups of chairs and couches were arranged before a window. He saw the backs of several male heads, a white gesticulating arm, newspapers and magazines on a long wooden rack. A waiter with a black bow tie, a black vest, and a shaven head held an empty tray and an order pad.

Paddi directed him to a pair of library chairs before a wall of books at the right of the room. Between the chairs stood a round table on top of which lay a portfolio-sized envelope with the Chancel House logo. The waiter materialized beside Paddi. She asked for the usual, and Davey ordered a double martini on the rocks.

He asked what the usual was, and she said, "A Top-and-Bottom: half port and half gin." It was an outsider drink, she told him.

While he pondered this category, Davey took in that the owner of the naked arm he had glimpsed from the hallway was a middle-aged man seated in a leather chair near the center of the room. The arms of the chair cut his midsection from view, but there were no clothes on his flabby upper body, and none on the thick white legs crossed ankle to knee in front of the chair. A leather strap circled his neck. From the front of the strap, a chain, an actual chain, said Davey to Nora, like you'd use on a dog if the dog weighed two hundred pounds and liked to munch babies, hung between him and the bearded guy in a three-piece suit holding the other end. The man wearing the chain swiveled his head to give Davey a do-you-mind? glare. Davey looked away and saw that while most of the people in the room were dressed conventionally, one man reading a newspaper wore black leather trousers, motorcycle boots, and an open black leather vest that revealed an intricate pattern of scars on his chest.

He wondered how Paddi could have objected to his clothing when at least one person in the club wore no clothing at all.

"In here," she said, "people wear whatever is right for them. What's right for you is a suit."

"Some of these people must have a lot of trouble when they leave the club," he said.

"Some of these people never leave the club," she said.

"Is this stuff real?" Nora asked. "Or are you making it all up?"

"As real as what happened to Natalie," Davey said.

Paddi worked at Chancel House because it had published *Night Journey*. Her job gave her a unique connection to the book she loved above all others. And since she was on the subject, she drew out of the big Chancel House envelope a stiff, glossy sheet that Davey recognized as the reverse side of a jacket rendering.

"An idea of mine," Paddi said, turning the sheet over to display a drawing it took Davey a moment to understand; when he did, he wondered why the idea had never occurred to him. Paddi had drawn the jacket for an annotated scholarly edition of *Night Journey*. (Her design was based on the famous "GI edition" of the novel.) Every one of the hundred thousand Driver fanatics in America would have to buy it. Scholars would be able to trace the growth of the book over successive variations and discuss the meanings of the changes in the text. It was a great idea.

"But there was one problem," Davey told Nora. "In order to do it right, we needed the manuscript."

"What's the problem with that?" asked Nora.

The problem, Paddi said, was that the manuscript seemed to have disappeared. Hugo Driver had died in 1950, his wife in 1952, and their only child, a retired high school English teacher, had said in an interview on the twentieth anniversary of the book's publication that he had never seen any manuscripts of his father's books. As far as he knew, they had never come back from Chancel House.

Davey said he would try to find out what had happened to the manuscript. Lincoln Chancel had probably installed it in a bank vault somewhere. It certainly couldn't be lost. Nothing so important could have slipped through the cracks—it was the manuscript of the first Chancel House book, for heaven's sake!

"That would be unfortunate in light of the rumors," Paddi said.

"What rumors?"

"That Hugo Driver didn't really write the book," Paddi said.

Where did this stuff come from? She knew what it was, didn't she? It was what happened whenever somebody great appeared, a bunch of weasels started trying to shoot holes in him. Davey ranted on in this fashion until he ran out of breath, at which point he inhaled hugely and declared that after all it all made perfect sense; *Night Journey* was such a brilliant book that the weasels couldn't cope with it. It happened all the time. Somewhere, someone was saying that Zelda Fitzgerald was the real author of *Tender Is the Night*.

"Zelda *was* the real author of *Tender Is the Night*," Paddi said. "Sorry. Just kidding."

Davey asked her if she believed this crap.

"No, not at all," she said. "I agree with you. Hugo Driver should be on stamps. I think his picture should be on *money*. One of the reasons I like this club is that it seems such a Hugo Driver–ish sort of place, doesn't it?"

Davey guessed that it did.

Would he like to see more of it?

"I wondered when we were going to get to this part," Nora said.

21

AT THE LANDING above the curved staircase, Paddi did not take him down the dark corridor but led him up another flight of stairs. An even narrower version of the staircase continued upward, but Paddi took him into a corridor identical to the one below. Davey felt as if he were following Paddi through a forest at night.

Then she vanished, and he realized that she had slipped through an open door. The shade had been pulled down, and the room was darker than the corridor. After they undressed she led him to a futon. Davey stretched out against her, his body as hot as an oven-warmed brick, hers as cool as a stone drawn from a river. He hugged her close, and her cool hands ran up and down his back. When his orgasm came, he yelled with pleasure. They lay quiet for a time, then talked, and when they had established that neither of them was seeing anyone else, Davey fell asleep.

He woke up an hour later, hungry, light-headed, uncertain of his surroundings. He remembered that he was lying on a floor in the East Village. He was suddenly, shamefully certain that Paddi had stolen his money. He sat upright, and his hand touched a girlish shoulder. He looked down and made out the shape of her head on the pillow. Pillow? He did not remember a pillow. A sheet covered both of them.

"We should get something to eat," he said.

"I'll take care of that. Isn't there something else you'd like to do first?"

He stretched out beside her and once more felt that he was as hot as a potbellied stove and she as cool as a substance just extracted from a river. Davey surrendered to sensation.

Unimaginably later, they lay side by side, staring up. Davey had forgotten where he was. A slight, high-pitched buzzing sounded in his ears. The woman beside him seemed completely beautiful. Paddi rolled over, picked up an instrument like the mouthpiece of an old-fashioned telephone, and ordered oysters and caviar and other things he didn't quite catch and what sounded like a lot of wine.

Soon two young women entered the room carrying circular trays, from which they distributed around the futon a number of covered dishes. Two open bottles and four glasses appeared beside Davey's left shoulder. The women smiled at Paddi, who was sprawled on top of the sheet, but did not look at Davey. When they had put in place the last dish, they stood and turned to the door, where one of them said, "Shall I?"

"Yes," Paddi said. A low, rosy light spread through the room, and the women backed smiling through the door.

Plovers' eggs, dumplings, steaming sautéed mushrooms, eel, whitebait, rich finger-sized segments of duck, similar sections of roast pork, little steaming things like pizzas covered with fresh basil and glistening shreds of tomato, in a crisp transparent seal, round, pungent objects that must have been meatballs and tasted like single malt scotch, grapes, clementines; an excellent white burgundy and a better red bordeaux. Taking almost nothing herself, Paddi brought plate after plate before him. Davey sampled everything, and together they emptied half of each bottle. Paddi kept him amused with tales of the art department and gossip about people who worked at Chancel House; she quoted Hugo Driver and wondered at the friendship between the author and Lincoln Chancel. Did Davey know where this unlikely pair had met?

"Sure, at Shorelands," Davey said, "this estate in Massachusetts. They were put up in the same cottage." He thought that the owner of the place, Georgina Weatherall, who knew that Davey's grandfather was on the verge of starting a publishing company, had put them together in the hope that Lincoln Chancel would help Driver in some way. And exactly that had happened. Driver must have shown Chancel the manuscript of *Night Journey*, and Chancel had used it to make Driver's fortune and increase his own.

* * *

"Is that really how they met?" Nora asked Davey. "In a sort of literary colony?"

"Shorelands was a private estate where the hostess liked to feel that she was encouraging works of genius, but yeah, that's more or less right. And whether Georgina Weatherall had anything in mind or not, she did put Driver together with my grandfather, and things fell into place. Neither one of them had been at Shorelands before, so they probably spent a lot of time together, like the new guys at school."

A millionaire businessman and a penniless writer? Nora doubted that Lincoln Chancel, a ruthless acquirer of companies, had ever felt like a new boy in school. "Who else was at Shorelands at the same time? I bet, afterward, they all wished that they'd been put together with your grandfather. Did he ever go back?"

"God, no," Davey said. "Haven't you ever seen that *picture*?"

Davey began to laugh.

"What's funny?"

"I just remembered something. There's a picture from when my grandfather was at Shorelands—a photograph of all these guys sitting on the lawn. Georgina Weatherall's in it, and Hugo Driver, and all the people who were there that summer. My grandfather's squeezed into this rickety lawn chair, and he looks like he's about to strangle someone."

The rest of that night Davey lay with Paddi, sipping from a variety of drinks brought in by women he sometimes saw and sometimes did not, occasionally hearing music from the floors below, now and then catching a sob or a shout of laughter from rooms throughout the building.

And then, immediately it seemed, he was locking the door of his apartment, having showered, shaved, and changed clothes without any memory of returning home or performing these tasks. His watch said it was eight o'clock. He felt rested, sober, clearheaded. But how had he gotten home?

22

HE HAD PUSHED through the front doors of the Chancel Building with two appointments in mind, one still to be made, the other already fixed. At some time before he left the building today, he had to see his father to talk about Hugo Driver's manuscripts and doing a definitive edition of the novel, and this evening he was going back to the Hellfire Club. He was ready for both encounters. His father would welcome an idea sure to bring more prestige to the firm, and to his meeting with Paddi he could bring the good news from his father. If Alden Chancel had taken charge of the manuscript of *Night Journey*, Davey intended to take charge of its rebirth.

His ordinary duties devoured the morning until eleven, when he had to go to a meeting. After the meeting, he went up two floors to his father's office, where the secretary told him that Alden had left for lunch and would not be free until three-thirty.

At three twenty-five, Davey went back to see his father.

At first impatient, Alden grew interested in the project Davey described. Yes, it might be possible to publish such an edition as a paperback intended for classroom use. Yes, let's think about using the cover of the GI edition, we got a lot of mileage out of that. As for the manuscript, hadn't that gone back to Driver?

Davey said that an assistant in the art department, the person who had come to him with the idea, had already told him that Driver's son thought it was still with Chancel House. When he named the assistant, his father said, "Paddi Mann, interesting, the meeting I just came from was about an idea of hers, using two different covers on the new paperback of *Night Journey*. Bright girl, this Paddi Mann." But as for the manuscript, if the sole remaining Driver didn't know where it was, maybe it was lost.

For the next two hours, Davey searched the wrapped manuscripts on the conference room shelves and looked in broom closets and the windowless cubicles where copy editors toiled. He stopped only when he noticed that it was twenty minutes before he was to meet Paddi.

A low conversational buzz came from the bar, and Davey glanced through the arched opening as automatically as he had read the admonitions on the inner door. For a moment he thought he saw Dick Dart, but the man vanished behind the crowd. Dick Dart? Could he be in the Hellfire Club? Was *Leland*?

The voice of the concierge forced him to turn away from the bar. "May I assist you, sir?"

Davey placed himself in the chair beside the fern, the concierge opened the drawer, removed the heavy microphone, positioned it with excruciating exactness, and uttered his sentence. Paddi came through the mahogany door. She had her "Hellfire Club look," even though she seemed to be wearing exactly what she had worn to work. They ordered the same drinks from the same waiter. Davey described his searches, and Paddi told him it was important, crucial, to find the manuscript. Wasn't there a record somewhere of everything that came in and went out?

"Yes," Davey said, "but it didn't start until a month or two after the founding of the house. Before that, things were less formal."

"We'll think of something," Paddi said. "Think—what did you forget?"

"The storage area in the basement," Davey said. "I don't think anybody knows what's down there. My grandfather never threw anything out."

"Okay. What would you like to do tonight?"

There were some new movies, how about a movie?

"Or we could go upstairs. Would you like that?"

"Yes," he said. "Yes, I would."

23

AFTER THEY DRESSED and left the room, their arms around each other's waists, Davey felt that his life had undergone a fundamental change. His days and nights had been reversed, and his daytime self, which did boring things at Chancel House, was merely the dream of the more adventurous night-self, which bloomed under the ministrations of Paddi Mann.

They unclasped at the staircase, too narrow to permit them to walk down side by side. Paddi went before him, and he placed his hands on her shoulders. His shirt rode up on his wrist, uncovering his square gold watch. It was a few minutes past six. He wondered what they would do when they reached the street—it was scarcely believable that an outer world existed.

Davey followed her down the last of the stairs, past the empty desk, and outside into a world far too bright. Noises clashed and jangled in the air. Taxis the color of brushfire charged along Second Avenue. A drunken teenage boy in jeans and a denim shirt three times his size lolled against a parking meter; poisonous fumes of sweat, beer, and cigarette smoke came boiling through his skin and floated into Davey's nostrils.

"Davey—"

"Yes?"

"Keep looking for that manuscript. Maybe it's in the Westerholm house."

A bus the size of an airplane whooshed up to the curb, displacing thousands of cubic feet of air and pulverizing a layer of rubble. Davey clapped his hands over his ears, and Paddi waved and glided away.

Alden must have looked into the unused office and seen him leafing through a stack of forgotten manuscripts, some so old they

76

were carbons, because when Davey looked over his shoulder his father loomed behind him. Where the hell had he been the last two nights? His mother had been trying to get him out to Connecticut for the weekend, but the kid never answered his phone. What happened, had he found a new girlfriend or was he turning into a barfly?

Davey said he had been feeling antisocial. It had never occurred to him that it might be his parents who were calling. After all, he saw his father every day.

He was expected at the Poplars for the weekend, beginning Friday night. Alden turned and marched out of the little office, which had the dreariness of all empty spaces meant to be occupied by busy and productive people.

Paddi's trophy did not appear among the papers in the empty office. Davey took the elevator to the basement.

At two twenty-five, he emerged from the storage enclosure with blackened hands and smears of dust on his suit and his face. He had found boxes of letters from deceased authors to deceased editors, group photos of unknown men in square double-breasted suits and Adolphe Menjou mustaches, a meerschaum pipe, a badly tarnished silver cocktail shaker with a silver swizzle stick, but he had not found his trophy.

Two hours before he was to meet Paddi at an address she had printed on a slip of paper now in his jacket pocket, he returned to the basement and again attacked the boxes. He unearthed a carton of Artie Shaw seventy-eights and a deerstalker hat once likely paired with the meerschaum. In a jumble of old catalogs he came across copies of his mother's two early novels, which he set aside. A fabric envelope tied with a ribbon yielded a copy of the photograph he had described to Paddi, and this, too, he set aside. *Night Journey*'s precious manuscript declined to reveal itself. Paddi's final words came back to him, and he promised himself to have a good look through the closets and attic of the Poplars before coming back to town on Sunday.

24

AN ELEMENT OF disaster, however muted, was built into all of Davey's weekends at his parents' house. Daisy might appear for dinner too drunk to sit upright, or a lesser degree of intoxication might bring on a bout of weeping before the end of the soup course. Accusations, some so veiled Davey could not understand exactly who was being accused of what, might fly across the table. Even the uneventful weekends were tainted with the air of oppression, of mysterious but essential things left unsaid. This weekend, however, was an outright calamity.

The Italian girl's nephew, Jeffrey, had recently joined the Poplars household. At this point, his presence seemed an unnecessary affectation on Alden's part. Until Davey arrived in Westerholm on Friday evening, he had expected a younger male version of Maria, a cheerful, smiling person with the stout physique of a tenor hurrying forward to snatch away his weekend bag. But once Davey and Alden came in through the front door, Jeffrey was revealed to be a tall, middle-aged man in a perfectly fitted gray suit who showed no signs of hurrying forward, snatching bags or doing anything but nodding at them and continuing to pass through the rear of the hall, presumably on his way to the kitchen. His face seemed to suggest a quantity of thoughts and judgments held in check, and his eyes were hooded. Davey thought he must have been some foreign publisher his father had enticed into his web. Then Alden had introduced them, and the two had exchanged a look, Davey imagined, of mutual suspicion.

Friday's dinner had not been unusual. Alden had dominated the conversation, Daisy had agreed with everything he said, and Davey had been silent. When he mentioned the new edition of Driver's book, his father changed the subject. After dinner, Alden said that he hoped Davey would get some rest, he wasn't looking

78

very good, to be frank. By ten, despite the coffee, he was asleep in his old bed.

To his surprise, Davey did not wake up until eleven on Saturday morning. By the time he left his room, it was eleven-thirty. The irregular tap of typewriter keys and the smell of cigarette smoke, along with the faint drone of a radio, came through the door of his mother's studio. For a moment he considered going back for the books he had brought along from the Chancel House basement, but he decided to surprise his mother with them at brunch on Sunday, as he had originally planned.

Maria poured steaming coffee into a mug, uncovered golden toast in a silver rack, and asked if he would like a small omelette. Davey said that toast and jam would be fine and asked if she knew where Mr. Chancel was. Mr. Chancel had gone out shopping. Then, because she seemed to be preparing to leave, he asked her about Jeffrey.

Jeffrey was the son of her sister-in-law. Yes, he did enjoy very much to work for the Chancels. Before he come here? Well, before he come here, he do many things. College student. Soldier. Yes, officer in Vietnam.

Where college?

Maria struggled to remember. Harterford? Haverford? Davey supplied, aghast. In Massachusetts, said Maria, badly mangling the name. A terrible possibility occurred to Davey. *Harvard?* Maybe, could be, Maria offered. She untied her apron, and left him to wonder.

With at least an hour to squander before either parent appeared, Davey searched the basement without any luck. When he came back upstairs, he found his father removing groceries of various kinds, including scotch and vodka, from bags bearing the names of Waldbaum's and Good Grape Harvest.

"Doesn't Jeffrey do that sort of thing?" he asked.

"Jeffrey has the weekend off," his father announced. "Like you. What were you up to down there, that you got so dirty?"

"Trying to find some old books," Davey said.

During lunch, Alden abandoned the usual monologue to question his son about Frank Neary and Frank Tidball, their longtime crossword-puzzle makers. For decades Neary and Tidball had dealt with the company through Davey's predecessor, an amiable old alcoholic named Charlie Westerberg. Soon after Charlie had staggered cheerfully off into retirement, Neary and Tidball hired an agent, with the result that they were now paid a slightly higher fee for their puzzles. Most of the increase went in the agent's commission, but Alden had never ceased to blame Davey for the insurrection. For half an hour, he was forced to defend the two old puzzle makers against his father's implications that they were past their prime and should be replaced. Alden's real but unadmitted objections lay in the discovery, made soon after Westerberg's departure, that the two men shared an address in Rhinebeck. Neary and Tidball would be more difficult to replace than his father understood. There were only a few young crossword-puzzle makers, most of whom had adopted innovations undesirable to Chancel House customers, who did not long for clues about Moody Blues lyrics or the films of Cheech and Chong.

During this discussion, Daisy toyed with her food, at random intervals smiling to indicate that she was paying attention. As soon as Maria began clearing the plates, she excused herself in a little-girl voice and went back upstairs. Alden asked Davey a few questions about Leonard Gimmel and Teddy Brunhoven—he was always interested in the murderers—then wandered off to watch a baseball game on television. Within fifteen minutes, he would be dozing in his easy chair. Davey thanked Maria for the lunch and climbed the stairs to the attic.

The Poplars' attic was divided into three unequal areas. The old maid's rooms, the smallest of these, were a series of three chambers situated around a common bathroom and a narrow staircase at the north end of the house. These wretched rooms had been empty since early in the reign of Helen Day. (Davey's parents had ordered the construction of two large apartments over the garage, one for the Cup Bearer, the other for any overflow guests, and these apartments now housed Maria and her nephew.) The second, central portion of the attic, roughly the size of a hotel ballroom, had been floored and finished but otherwise unchanged. It was here that Lincoln Chancel's gifts to the first David Chancel had been preserved for the second, and for this reason the central section of the attic had always inflicted an oppressive, uncanny feeling of fraudulence upon Davey. The third section, reached by a door from the middle attic, had been floored but not otherwise finished.

Metaphorically holding his breath against the psychic atmosphere in the central portion of the attic, Davey walked through the jumble of old chairs, broken lamps, boxes upon boxes, and ratty couches to make sure that the old maid's rooms were as empty as he remembered.

The three little rooms contained nothing but spiderwebs, white walls blossoming with mildew, and dust-gray floors. Then he made another quick pass through the center of the attic to inspect the unfinished section. At last he could no longer postpone moving into the main area of the attic, jammed with Victorian furniture.

The old oppression came back to him in various forms as he lifted padded cushions and bent down to see far back into wardrobe closets. Davey experienced resentment. Why should he waste his time like this? Who was Paddi, anyhow, to set him prowling thieflike through his parents' house?

Davey's thoughts had reached this unhappy point when he heard footsteps on the stairs leading to the maid's quarters. He froze. His mind went empty, as though he were a burglar about to be discovered. He half-padded, half-ran to the light switch beside the main attic stairs, flicked it down, and crouched behind a Chinese screen in a heavy wooden frame.

The footsteps on the stairs reached the maid's rooms a few seconds after Davey had found shelter. Footsteps rang on the wooden floor. Peering around the side of the screen, Davey saw a line of light appear beneath the door separating the maid's quarters from the rest of the attic. He drew back. The footsteps advanced toward the door. He flattened his upper body over his knees and covered his head with his hands. The door swung open, and a shaft of light hurtled toward him. Then the entire room flared with light.

A voice he did not know called out, "Who's here?"

Footsteps came toward him. Davey found himself on his feet, fists raised against the shadow whirling to meet him. The shadow grunted in shock and surprise and struck out. The blow drove Davey's right hand into the bridge of his nose. Blood spurted out onto his clothes, and a bright, clear wave of pain made the world go dark. The side of his head crashed into the frame of the screen.

A hand caught his hair and pulled sharply, painfully, upward. "What the hell did you do that for?"

Puckered with consternation, Jeffrey's face stared down at him. "I thought you were someone else," Davey said.

"You attacked me," Jeffrey said. "You jumped up like a—"

"Wraith," Davey said. "I'm sorry."

"So'm I," said Jeffrey.

Davey clutched the standard of a tall lamp and tilted back his head. Sluggish blood ran down his throat. He said, "I guess I got scared. How did you know someone was up here? I thought you had the weekends off."

"I saw the lights go on from my windows."

Davey groped in his pocket for his handkerchief and swabbed his face before holding it to his nose. "Say, Jeffrey."

"Yes?"

"Did you go to Harvard?"

"If I did, I hope nobody finds out," Jeffrey said.

Davey swallowed. His entire face hurt.

He spent half an hour cleaning bloodstains from the attic floor, then went to his bathroom, washed his face and hands, and fell asleep stretched out on his covers with a cold cloth on the bruised parts of his face. He woke up in time to shower and put on fresh clothes for dinner. His nose was swollen, and a purple lump had risen on his right temple. When he explained at dinner that he had hit himself in the face with the bedroom door, his father said, "Funny, when you have kids nobody ever tells you how many lies you're going to have to listen to over the next thirty or forty years."

Daisy murmured, "Oh, Alden."

"If he hit himself in the face with his door, then he took a practice swing."

"Did someone hit you in the head, darling?" asked his mother.

"Since you ask, yes. Jeffrey and I had a little misunderstanding."

Alden laughed and said, "If Jeffrey ever hit you in the head, you'd be in the hospital for a week."

At twelve-thirty the next day, Davey brought down to the dining room the rescued copies of his mother's two novels and placed them under his chair. His father raised an eyebrow, but Daisy seemed not to notice. Unasked, Maria brought Bloody Marys to all three of them.

After the Bloody Marys came a bottle of Barolo and a soup in which streamers of egg, flecks of parsley, pesto sauce, and pasta circulated through a chicken broth. Davey took half a glass of the wine and nervously devoured the soup. A homemade mushroom and Gorgonzola ravioli followed the soup, and tender little filets of beef and potato croquettes followed the ravioli. Maria announced that in honor of Mr. Davey she had made a zabaglione, which would be served in a few minutes. Did they have these stupendous meals every weekend, did they eat this way every night? It was no wonder that Daisy was looking puffier than ever, although Alden seemed utterly unchanged. Davey said that he didn't remember the Italian girl's being such a great cook and Alden said, "*Vin ordinaire,* my boy."

The brief silence that followed his father's remark seemed the perfect time to produce his gift.

"Mom, I've got something for you."

"Goody, goody."

Unwilling to tell Alden that he had been prospecting in the Chancel House basement, Davey said that he had found two books in the Strand one day last week, and he hoped she would be pleased to see them again. He rose from his chair to bring the humble package down the table.

Daisy grasped the bag, tore out the books, smiled at their jackets, and opened them. Her eyes retreated into a band of red that appeared over her face like a mask. She set the books on the edge of the table and turned her face away. Still thinking that she was pleased by his gift, Davey said, "They're in such good shape." Daisy drew in a breath and let out a frightening sound that soon resolved into a wail. She shoved back her chair and ran from the room as the Italian girl entered with cups of zabaglione on a silver tray. Baffled, Davey looked inside the first of the two books and saw written in a hand more confident and decisive than his mother's, *For my heart's darling, Alden, from his dazzled Daisy.*

25

AT EIGHT O'CLOCK on the previous Thursday night, a flat package clamped under his left arm, Davey had stood uncertainly in front of a restaurant called Dragon Seed on Elizabeth

Street, looking back and forth from the restaurant's front door to a slip of paper in his hand. A row of leathery ducks the color of molasses hung across the restaurant window. The black numerals beside the menu taped to the door matched the number, 67, Paddi had written on the piece of paper.

A delicious odor of roast duck and frying noodles met him when he opened the door. Davey stepped inside, stood at the end of the counter for a moment to look over the room, then went to the only empty table and sat down.

All the men in the room ignored him. Davey looked around for the door that would lead to a staircase and saw two set into opposite ends of the rear wall, one of them marked RESTROOMS, the other PRIVATE. Then he was on his feet.

Two waiters in black vests and white shirts watched him from across the room, and a third set a platter of noodles before four stolid men in suits and began cutting toward him through the tables.

Davey tried to wave him off, and said, "I know it says Private, but it's all right."

"Not all right."

Davey put his hand on the knob, and the waiter's hand came down on his before he could open the door. "You sit."

The waiter pulled him away to his table and pushed him down. Davey placed his package on his lap and considered making a break for the door. He looked around and found that everybody in the restaurant was eyeing him.

The waiter came back through the tables carrying a tray with a teapot and a cup the size of a thimble. He set these before Davey nd spun away, revealing a small man in a zippered jacket behind m who rotated a chair and straddled it, and gave Davey a hor-ble smile. "You funny," the man said.

"I was invited." Davey withdrew from his pocket the paper on which Paddi had written her address and showed it to the man.

The man squinted at the paper. He looked straight into Davey's eyes, then back at the paper. Without any transition, he started laughing. "Come," the man said, and got on his feet. He led Davey to the front door, stepped outside, and motioned Davey to follow him. Davey came out. The man moved one step to his left and pointed at Dragon Seed's door. He pointed again, and this time Davey saw it.

Set back into the building between the entrance to Dragon Seed and a shop filled with souvenirs of Chinatown, at an angle that concealed it if you did not know it was there, was a plywood door with the number 67 spray-painted on it in black.

Grinning, the man prodded Davey's chest with his forefinger. "Dey go in, but dey don't come out." Davey settled the package under his elbow and knocked on the spray-painted door, and a faint voice told him to come in.

He found himself at the foot of a tenement staircase. "Lock the door behind you," the voice called down.

He came upstairs and passed through another door into a vast, darkened loft created by the removal of most of the tenement's walls. A few dim lights illuminated crude murals it took him a moment to see were illustrations of passages in *Night Journey*. Thick, dark curtains covered the windows. In the distance a high-backed sofa and two chairs stood in front of an ornate wooden fireplace frame and mantel affixed to a wall without a fireplace. Long bookshelves took up the wall at the front of the building. Rough partitions marked off two rooms, and one of these opened as Davey came deeper into the murk. Completely at ease, Paddi Mann emerged naked through the door.

"What is this place?"

"Where I live," Paddi said, not naked after all, but wearing a flesh-colored leotard. She gave him a smile and moved toward the sofa, swept up from a cushion a man's wing-collar formal shirt, slipped it on, and buttoned the last few buttons so that it covered her like a short white frock.

"What's that under your arm?"

"I had some trouble finding you." Davey's legs finally unlocked and permitted him to move toward her through the darkness.

"Looks like you had trouble finding the manuscript, too. Unless *that's* it."

"No."

Paddi shifted her position, drawing her legs up beside her and tucking them in. She gave three smart pats to the seat of the sofa.

He found that he was standing directly in front of her and sat down as ordered. Her feet insinuated themselves against his thigh as if for warmth. "Here," she said, and turned sideways to take from a tray and press into his hand a glass filled with ice cubes and a cloudy red liquid.

He drank, then jerked back his head at the pungent, unpleasantly sweet shock of the taste. "What's this?"

"A Top-and-Bottom. Good for you."

Davey let his eyes wander around the dark, jumbled spaces of Paddi's loft. Arches and openings led into invisible chambers from which came inaudible voices. "Are you going to show me what's in that package?"

Davey said, "Oh," because he had forgotten the package, and handed it to her. In seconds her fingers had undone the knots. In another second the wrapping lay in her lap like a frame around the frame and Paddi was gazing down at the long photograph with her mouth softly opened.

"Shorelands, July 1938."

"And here is your grandfather."

Warts and carbuncles jutting from nose and cheek, jowls bulging over his collar, eyebrows nearly meeting in a ferocious scowl above blazing eyes, hands locked on the arms of his chair, rage straining at the buttons, seams, and eyelets of his handmade suit, Lincoln Chancel appeared to have breakfasted on railroads and coal mines.

Davey regarded the phenomenon with the mixture of wonder, respect, and terror his grandsire invariably aroused in him. For the fifty years of his adult life, he had bullied his way south from Bridgeport, Connecticut, to New York and Washington, D.C., north to Boston and Providence, swallowing human lives. Before a massive stroke had felled him in a private dining room in the Ritz-Carlton Hotel, indictments and lawsuits had buzzed around the great man's head. After his death nearly all of the intricately pyramidal structure Lincoln had constructed had tumbled. What remained was a transient hotel in Rhode Island, a struggling woolen mill in Lowell, Massachusetts, both of which had soon folded into bankruptcy, and his last bauble, Chancel House.

"He looks so unhappy."

"He's the only one looking at the camera," Davey said, having noticed this for the first time. "See? Everybody else is looking at another person in the group."

"Except for her." Paddi delicately tapped the glass over the face of a small, strikingly pretty young woman in a loose white shirt, a half-mast necktie, and trousers. Seated on the ground beside Lincoln Chancel, she was gazing down at the grass, lost in thought.

"Yes," Davey said. "I wish I knew her name."

"Whose names *do* you know?"

"Apart from Driver and my grandfather, only her." He indicated a tall woman with a bulldog chin and a fleshy nose who sat upright staring at Lincoln Chancel from a wicker chair. "Georgina Weatherall. She and Hugo Driver are both staring at my grandfather."

"Probably wondering what they can get out of him," Paddi said. "Oh?"

"There have been a couple of books about Shorelands," Paddi said. "Georgina wanted to be the center of attention. Everybody made fun of her behind her back."

"Georgina couldn't have been too pleased about that girl."

Now Davey indicated an elongated, bearded gentleman in sagging tweeds gazing down at the young woman, his lips stretched so tightly that they looked like wires. "That's not a very friendly smile," Davey said. "I wonder who this guy was?"

"Austryn Fain," said Paddi. "In 1938 he had just published a novel called *The Twisted Hedge*. It was supposed to be wonderful and all that, but from what I gather people forgot about it in a hurry. He killed himself in 1939. January. Cut his wrists in a bathtub."

"Georgina wouldn't help him?"

"Georgina dropped him flat. But, Davey, look at this man. Merrick Favor was his name. He was murdered about six months after this photo was taken."

Paddi was pointing at the broad, handsome face of a man in an unbuttoned double-breasted blue blazer and white trousers who stood immediately behind Georgina. Like Austryn Fain, he was smiling at the girl seated on the grass.

"Murdered?"

"Merrick Favor was supposed to be a rising star. His first novel, *Burning Bushes*, got great reviews when Scribner's published it in 1937, and he was supposed to be working on something even better. One day his girlfriend showed up after trying to call him for a couple of days, and when she couldn't get him to come to the door, she climbed in a window, took a look around, and almost passed out."

"She found his body?"

"His house was torn up, and there were bloodstains everywhere. Favor had been stabbed to death, and his body was in his bathtub. They never found who killed him. The book he was working on was torn to scraps."

"Shorelands didn't bring much luck to these people," Davey said. "What happened to this guy?"

He was pointing at a long-haired young man with horn-rim glasses, a floppy bow tie, velvet jacket, soft eyes, short nose, and a witty mouth. This person seemed to be concentrating all of his thoughts on handsome Merrick Favor.

"Oh, Creeley *Monk*. Another sad story. A poet. His second book was called *The Field Unknown*, and the only reason anybody remembers it is that a lot of third-graders used to have to memorize the title poem."

"Oh," said Davey, "we had to recite that at the Academy. *The field unknown, the unknown field I thought I knew / In childhood days, my ways return me now to you.*"

"Creeley Monk killed himself, too. Shotgunned himself in the head. Right around the time Merrick Favor was killed."

Davey stared at her. "This guy blew off his head a few months after he left Shorelands?"

Paddi nodded.

Davey was staring at her. "Two of the guests at Shorelands that summer killed themselves?"

"It's even better than that. Three of them killed themselves. This man here, the one who looks like a bricklayer, he did, too." Paddi's finger was tapping the chest of a wide, sturdy man in a lumpy blue turtleneck sweater who was trying to smile at the camera and Lincoln Chancel at the same time.

"His name was Bill Tidy, and he'd published one book, called *Our Skillets*. It was a memoir of his childhood in the South End of Boston. Must have been the only really working-class guest Georgina ever had at Shorelands. *Our Skillets* is a beautiful book, but it went out of print right away and only came back into print in the late sixties. I don't know about this for sure, but I think Tidy had a lot of trouble getting to work on a new book after he got back to Boston. Anyhow, he jumped out of his fifth-floor window. In January 1939."

"When . . ."

"Right between Merrick Favor's murder and Monk's suicide, which happened a few days apart, and two days before Fain killed himself. It's like a curse or something, isn't it?"

"God, it's like they paid for Hugo Driver's success."

"You should write a book about all this," Paddi said.

"I thought you already read a book about all this."

"I read a lot of books about Shorelands because I'm interested in Hugo Driver, but this information is scattered all over the place. Actually, hardly anybody cares about what was going on at Shorelands after the early thirties. By the start of the war, it was all over. Georgina was drinking a lot and taking laudanum and her stories began smelling like fish. She told people that Marcel Proust used to stink up Honey House with his asthma powders, which is a nice story, but Proust never left France. Georgina finally retreated into her bedroom, and she died around 1950. The house rotted away until a preservation group bought it."

"What happened to the girl sitting on the ground next to my grandfather?"

"She was supposed to have disappeared during her stay, but even that isn't really clear."

The characters in the photograph on his lap, his grandfather and the great author, Austryn Fain and Merrick Favor and Creeley Monk, Georgina Weatherall and Bill Tidy and the abstracted young woman, seemed as familiar, as *known*, as his old schoolmates at the Academy. He saw into them so clearly that he could not understand why until now he had not seen the clearest thing in the picture. All he had really seen before was his grandfather's comic fury. What was clearest in the photograph was the reason for the universal discomfort.

As if the picture came equipped with a soundtrack and a flashback, it all but shouted that Lincoln Chancel had uttered a crude flirtatiousness to the attractive young woman at his feet, and that the young woman had swiftly, woundingly rebuffed him. While she looked inward and Chancel erupted, everyone else in the photograph took sides.

Davey said, "You know what? I don't know anything about you. I don't know where you were born, or who your parents are, or what college you went to, if you have brothers and sisters, anything like that. It's like you stepped out of a cloud. Where did you live before you walked into our offices?"

"Lots of places."

"Where were you born?"

"You really want to do this, don't you? Okay. I was born in Amherst, Massachusetts. My parents' names are Charles

Roland and Sabina. Sabina teaches German in a high school in
Amherst, and Charles Roland was an English professor at
Amherst College. I went to the Rhode Island School of Design.
After I got out of RISD, I went to Europe and traveled here and
there, but mainly lived in London, painting and taking art
courses, and after a couple of years I came back and lived in
L.A. and did some design work for a couple of small presses
and read everything I could about Hugo Driver, which is when
I learned about Shorelands, and after a while I came to New
York so I could get a job at Chancel. I just walked in, showed
my work to Rod Clampett, and he hired me."

"I should have guessed the RISD part," Davey said. Rod
Clampett, Chancel's art director, had gone to RISD and liked
hiring its graduates.

Paddi said, "Don't you think all this Shorelands business is like
some huge plot that you can't quite see?"

Davey began to laugh. "Well, if you're looking for a sinister
plot, Lincoln Chancel is your man. He was a tremendous crook,
I'm sure. It's like the big secret in my family—the thing we
don't talk about. On the way up, my dad's dad obviously
stabbed everybody he met in the back, he must have stolen with
both hands whenever he had the chance, he raped his way into
a huge fortune . . ."

Davey stopped talking for a moment, a meaningless smile stuck
to his face, as the crowded darkness in the center of the room
seemed to thicken. He glanced down, and his eye found propped
on the sofa the photograph from Shorelands. Lincoln Chancel was
suddenly before him, beaming undimmed fury, rage, and frustra-
tion into his soul.

Paddi stroked his cheek with a cool finger and then stood up,
held out her hand, and stepped back to lead him across the room.

"She insulted my grandfather, didn't she? That girl who
disappeared."

"Maybe your grandfather insulted her."

Moving backwards, she drew him toward a mural in which
Lord Night stood guard at the black opening of a cave, came up to
the wall, and instead of bumping into it, slipped into the cave.
Davey followed her through the opening.

And that, Davey said, was the end of his story.

26

"HOW CAN THAT be the end?" Nora was trying not to yell. "What happened?"

"This is the part that's hard to talk about."

Davey had not finished talking about Paddi Mann. He had merely finished talking in that way.

"You remember what we saw today? Where we went?"

Nora nodded, almost dreading whatever he would say next.

He gave her no help. "That's the point."

"Did you ever find the manuscript? What happened to her? Oh no, you're not going to tell me she was killed, are you?"

"I never did find the manuscript. Anyhow, my father told me that he'd decided against doing a scholarly edition of *Night Journey.*"

"That must have upset Paddi."

Davey went back to smoothing out the bedcover, and Nora tried again. "She was so committed to that project."

Davey nodded, looking down and pushing his lips forward in the way he did when forced into an uncomfortable situation.

"Just tell me what happened."

"We had that Thursday night, when I gave her the picture. On Monday, I never saw her at all, and when I got back to my apartment all the coke caught up with me and I slept for two straight days. I just conked out. Woke up barely in time to shower and put on new clothes before I went back to the office."

"Where Alden told you he wasn't going through with your pet project. And you had to break the news to Paddi."

"She was hanging around in the hallway when I got up to the fifteenth floor, like someone had told her what was going to happen. We didn't really have time to talk before I went in, and she said, 'Seven-thirty?' or something like that, and I nodded, and then I went in and saw Dad. She was still there when I came out, and I gave her the bad news. She didn't say a word. Just turned around and left. So at seven-thirty, I went to her place.

"When I got up to the loft, she wasn't there, so I walked around for a little bit. I thought she might have been asleep or in the bathroom or something. I looked at her books. You know what they were? Nothing but editions of Driver novels. Hardbacks, paperbacks, foreign languages, illustrated editions."

"That's not too surprising," Nora said.

"Wait. Then, of course, I had to go through the opening in the mural and look at the only other place in the whole loft I'd ever seen. So I walk into the cave. And my eyes bug out and my heart just about stops and I'm stuck. And after about a hundred years go by, I'm unstuck, I realize I'm not going to faint after all."

He looked at Nora, who did nothing but look back at him. This, too, had the tone of one of Davey's inventions.

"It was like a slaughterhouse. There was blood everywhere. I was so *scared.* I was pretty sure you couldn't lose that much blood and still be alive, and I was gritting my teeth until I saw her body. I got to the other side of the bed, where this big smear of blood went all the way across the floor and halfway up the wall. And that almost made me puke, because I'd been sure I was going to see her there. I even looked under the bed."

"Why didn't you call the police?" *And why do I want to believe this? He's describing Natalie's room.*

"I didn't know where the phone was! I don't even know if there was a phone!" Davey looked wildly around the bedroom and opened and closed his mouth several times, as if trying to swallow this remark.

"Weren't you afraid that whoever did it was still there?"

"Nora, if I'd even *thought* of that, I would have had a heart attack on the spot."

"Where did you find her body?"

"I didn't."

"Well, where was it? It must have been somewhere."

"Nora, that's what I'm saying. Nobody found it. It wasn't there."

"Somebody took it?"

"I don't know!" Davey yelled. He pressed both hands to his face, then let them drop.

"Oh. It was like Natalie, you mean. The body was gone, like Natalie."

He nodded. "Like Natalie."

Nora struggled to regain a sense of control, of a world in which things made sense. "But there can't really be any connection, can there?"

"You think I know?"

She tried again. "I don't suppose Natalie Weil quoted Hugo Driver at you and had you rummaging around for lost manuscripts . . ." In the midst of this, Nora remembered the books in Natalie Weil's bedroom, and the sentence trailed off.

"No, I don't suppose," Davey said, still not looking up.

The moment of silence which followed seemed extraordinarily crowded to Nora.

"What did you do when you realized that she wasn't there?"

Davey inhaled deeply and looked over her shoulder. "I was too scared to go home, so I walked all the way to midtown and took a hotel room under a phony name. Around noon the next day, I called Rod Clampett and asked if Paddi had turned up yet. He said he hadn't seen her all day, but he'd tell her to give me a call when she showed up. Of course, she never did."

"I guess you couldn't exactly look for her," Nora said. "But, Davey, excuse me, what's the point of all this?"

"I have to get up and move around a little. Could you make some coffee or something?"

"I could make decaf," she said, looking at the digital clock on the bedside radio. It was 2:00 A.M. She took from the couch a pale yellow robe, slipped it on, and tied its sash. Davey was sitting up in bed and staring at nothing. For a second, he looked like someone Nora had never seen before, an ineffectual man who would always be puzzled by life. Then he glanced up at Nora and was again her husband, Davey Chancel, trying to seem less distressed than he was.

"Nora," he said, "do you know where that blue silk bathrobe is, the one from Thailand?"

"On the hook in the bathroom," she said, and padded out to make coffee.

27

DAVEY SIPPED HIS decaffeinated French Roast and winced at the heat. "A little kümmel would go nicely with this mocha java, don't you think?"

Nora shook her head, then changed her mind. "What the hey."

Davey went to the cupboard and took out a bottle of Hiram Walker kümmel, all Nora had been able to find on her last visit to the liquor store. He frowned at the label to remind her that she should have gone to another liquor store, if not to Germany, to find decent kümmel, and filled his cup to the brim. Then he moved behind Nora and tipped perhaps half an inch of the liquid into her cup. A smell of caraway and drunken flowers filled the kitchen.

"Well?" she asked.

"Yes."

"Yes, what?" She sipped what tasted like a poison antidote with an accidental similarity to coffee.

"Yes, there is more. Yes, I'm kind of leery of telling you about it."

She found herself taking another sip of the mixture, which seemed less ghastly than before.

"I left out one thing about the last time I was in Paddi's loft."

"Oh, no."

"It wasn't anything I *did,* Nora. I'm not *guilty* of anything."

Then why do you look so guilty? she wondered.

"Okay, I did something." He drank again and tilted back his head as if, like a bird, he had to do that to swallow. Then he lowered his head and folded his hands around his cup. "I told you about looking under her bed."

Nora suddenly felt that whatever Davey said next would forever change the way she felt about him. Then she thought that his story about Paddi Mann had already changed the way she thought about Davey.

"I saw something under there."

"You saw something," she said.

"A book."

Is that all? Nora thought. *No severed head, no million dollars in a paper bag?*

"After I fished it out, I thought she might even have left it for me. What do you think it was?"

"The Egyptian Book of the Dead? The, uh, that Lovecraft thing, the *Necronomicon*?"

"*Night Journey.* A paperback."

"Forgive me," she said, "but that doesn't actually seem too startling."

Davey held her eyes with his own and took another swig of his doctored coffee. "Uh huh. I opened it up. You know, maybe there was a note or something in it for me. But there wasn't anything in it except what was supposed to be there. And her name."

"Her name," Nora said, feeling like an echo.

"Written on the flyleaf. At the top. Paddi Mann."

"She wrote her name in it."

"That's right. I shoved the book in my pocket and took it away with me. A few days later I tried to find it, but the damn thing was lost."

"It fell out of your pocket."

"Here we go," he said, and set his cup down. "Hold on. I'll be right back." Davey stood up and walked out of the kitchen, nervously straightening his blue robe.

Nora heard him return to the bedroom. A closet door opened and closed. In a moment, he reappeared holding a familiar black paperback. As if reluctant to surrender it, he sat down and held it up before him in both hands before offering it to Nora.

"Well, I don't suppose this is . . ." Nora noticed that she was as reluctant to take the book as he was to let go of it. She stopped talking and accepted it. Printed on the flyleaf, which had become slightly discolored, in small clear letters with a ballpoint pen, was PADDI MANN. Beneath her name, Davey had signed his own.

"So it turned up," Nora said.

"Where, do you suppose?"

"How should I know?" She took her hands off the book, thinking that she did not actually care where the book had surfaced, and for some reason hoping that she would not have to find out. She braced herself for another of Davey's inventions.

"Natalie Weil's bedroom."

"But—" Nora closed, then opened her mouth. No longer able to bear the expression in Davey's eyes, she looked down at her fingers spread on the edge of the table as if she were about to play the piano. "This book, the same book."

"This same book. I saw it when we went in, and after that big cop took us out, I went back, remember? I opened it up and just about passed out. Then I shoved it in my pocket."

"What made you go back in? Did you suspect that it might be—?"

"Of course not. I wanted to take a closer look at it." He shrugged his shoulders.

"You don't know how it got there."

"I didn't put it there, if that's what you mean."

"You never gave Natalie a copy of *Night Journey.*"

He looked at her in real exasperation. "Do I have to spell it out for you?"

Nora guessed he did.

"Someone took it from me. He killed Paddi and left the book for me to find. Later that week he stole it from me. And the same person killed Natalie and left it in her bedroom."

"The wolf killed Paddi Mann?" Nora asked, too confused to speak clearly.

"Lord Night? What does he have to do with it?"

"No, sorry, I mean *our* wolf—the Westerholm Wolf." She waved her hands in front of her, as if she were erasing a blackboard. "That's what I call the . . . the guy. The man who murdered Natalie and the others."

"*Our* wolf." Davey seemed disturbed, and Nora feared that his disturbance was caused by her appropriation of an animal sacred to Hugo Driver. "Yeah. It was the same guy. Okay. It has to be. He's not much like Lord Night, though."

"Davey," she said, "not everything is related to Hugo Driver."

"*Night Journey* is. Paddi Mann was certainly interested in Driver."

She had made him defensive. "Davey, all I meant is that he couldn't have left Paddi Mann's copy of *Night Journey* in Sally Michaelman's bedroom, or in Annabelle Austin's, or any of the others. And maybe he didn't steal yours. He probably found it."

Davey was vigorously shaking his head. "I bet there's some correspondence between the women he killed and certain parts of the book. In fact, that's obvious."

"Why is it obvious?"

"Because of Paddi," he said. "Paddi was obviously Paddy, don't you think?"

"Paddi was Paddi," she said. "I don't get it."

"In the book. The mouse. The mouse named Paddy, who tells Pippin Little about the Field of Steam. Jesus, don't you remember *anything*? Paddy is . . . Sometimes I wonder if you ever even read *Night Journey*."

"I read parts of it."

"You lied." He was looking at her in absolute astonishment. "You told me you finished it, and you were lying to me."

"I skipped around," she said. "I apologize. I realize that this is important to you—"

"Important."

"—but aren't you maybe a little upset that a man who killed five women is—"

"Is what?"

"—somehow connected to you? I don't know how to say it, because I don't really understand it." A flash of pain exploded behind the right half of Nora's forehead and sent a hot tendril down into her pupil. She leaned back in her chair and placed her hand over her eye.

"I'll never be able to get to sleep. I think I'll go down to the family room and put on some music."

Nora waited to be invited into the family room, so that she could refuse. She heard him push back his chair and stand up.

He told her that she could try lying down. He advised aspirin.

Nora removed her hand from her face. Davey tilted the square brown bottle over his cup and poured out several inches of amber liquid that reeked of caraway seed.

"You said you had that manuscript you found in the conference room, the Clyde Morning book? Would you mind if I took a look at it?"

"You want to read Clyde *Morning*?"

"I want to see the first new Blackbird Book," Nora said, but Davey acknowledged this conciliatory sally only with a frown and a shrug of his shoulders. "Would you get it for me?"

Davey tilted his head and rolled his eyes. "If that's what you want." He went into his "office." Nora could hear him talking to himself as he worked the catches on his briefcase. He came back into the kitchen, awkwardly holding a surprisingly slim stack of typing paper held together with rubber bands. "Here you are." He set the typescript on the table. "Tell me if you think it's any good."

She said, "You doubt the great Clyde Morning?"

Already at the kitchen door, Davey turned to give her a look that pretended to offer her sympathy for being left alone, and escaped.

She removed the rubber bands and tapped the bottom edge of the manuscript on the table. Then she folded over the last page and looked at the number in the top right-hand corner. Whatever miracles of the narrative art the hope of Blackbird Books had performed in *Spectre*, he had contained them within 183 pages.

From downstairs floated the eerie sound of Peter Pears singing words from a Britten opera Nora had heard many times but could not place. The voice seemed to come from an inhuman realm located between earth and heaven. *Death in Venice*, that was what Davey was listening to. She picked up the slim manuscript, carried it into the living room, switched on a lamp Sally Michaelman had sold her, and stretched out on a sofa to read.

BOOK III

AT THE
DEEP OF NIGHT

At last the child lost all hope and admitted to himself that this dark land was death, from which no release could be had. For a time he lost all strength and reason, and wept in panic and despair.

28

EARLY THE NEXT morning, Nora turned her back on Long
Island Sound, ran over the arched wooden bridge at Trap Line
Road, and came into the twelve acres of wooded marsh known
as the Pierce A. Gordon Nature Conservancy. The air was cool
and fresh, and behind her seagulls hopped along the long,
seaweed-strewn beach. She had reached the midpoint of
her run, and what lay before her were the pleasures of the
"Bird Shelter," as Westerholm natives called the Conservancy,
where for just under fifteen minutes she enjoyed the illusion of
passing through a landscape like that of the Michigan wilds to
which Matt Curlew had taken her on weekend fishing trips
during her childhood. These fifteen minutes were the secret
heart of her morning run, and on the morning after her first literally sleepless night in years, Nora wished no more than to
stop thinking, or worrying, or whatever it was that she had
been doing for the past four hours, and enjoy them. Familiar
trees filled with cardinals and noisy jays surrounded her. She
looked at her watch and saw that she was already nearly five
minutes behind her usual time.

Davey's crazy story had affected her more than she liked to
admit. In the past, Davey's embellishments, when not clearly self-
serving, had been in the service of either color or humor. Though
nothing if not highly colored, the tale of Paddi Mann had seemed
to conceal more than it gave away. Even if he had been trying to
emphasize the extent to which he had been seduced, he had overdone his effects.

Other things, too, had distressed her. Nora had read the first
twenty-odd pages of *Spectre* in such a swirl of doubt and anger
that the sentences had instantly disappeared from her memory.

What right did Davey have to demand that she be interested

101

in a second-rate author? For his benefit, Nora had absorbed a lot of information about classical music. She knew the difference between Maria Callas and Renata Tebaldi, she could identify fifty operas from their opening bars, she could tell when it was Horowitz playing a Chopin nocturne and when it was Ashkenazy. Why did she have to bow down to Hugo Driver?

At this point, Nora's conscience forced her to acknowledge that she had, after all, lied to Davey about reading Driver's book. She had closed the manuscript, gone downstairs, and paused outside the family room door. *Death in Venice* poured from the speakers. She slowly pushed open the door, hoping to see Davey sitting up and making notes or staring at the wall or doing anything at all that would prove he was at least as awake as she was. Covered to the throat by a plaid throw rug, eyes closed and mouth fluttering, Davey was lying on the couch. Exactly as she had foreseen, Mr. Sensitivity had loaded the two Britten CDs into the player, stretched out with the rug wrapped around him like a baby blanket, and trusted that she would be asleep before he was.

That was it, that *did it.* Nora took herself back to the living room and turned on the radio. She dialed until she reached a station pounding out James Cotton, blues with *wheels*, blues with *guts*, cranked up the volume, and sat down to start reading *Spectre* all over again.

Spectre was the second topic she wished to put out of her mind during the favorite part of her run. After about an hour's reading, a certain possibility concerning Clyde Morning had occurred to her. This possibility, if true, might mean something to herself and Davey, or it might not. Then there was a problem with the book itself. As she had feared, *Spectre* was a slight book. It read like a fictional skeleton barely fleshed out by a writer too tired or lazy to keep his characters' names straight. George Carmichael, the main character, had become George Carstairs by page 15, and by page 35 he had changed back to Carmichael. For the rest of the book, he switched back and forth, depending, Nora thought, on which name surfaced first in Clyde Morning's mind when he reported to his typewriter.

Even worse was the exhaustion which weighed down the writing. Three different characters said, "Too true." Far too many sentences began with the word "Indeed" followed by a comma. George Carmichael/Carstairs's eyes were invariably a "deep, soulful brown," and his shoes were always "crosshatched with scuff marks." Neither sense nor grammar was safe. As he ran down the stairs, the sun struck George in his eyes of deep, soulful brown. When he "gazed longingly" at his beloved, Lily Clark, his eyes adhered to her dress. Or they flew across the room to meet her "tigress' lips." Half a dozen times, George and other people "wore out shoe leather" by "pounding the pavement" or "double-jumping the stairs." After she had begun to notice these repetitions, Nora got up, found a pencil, and made faint check marks in the margin whenever one of them appeared.

When she had finished reading, pale light came slanting in through the windows at the front of the house. She returned to the kitchen for more coffee and discovered that she had ground beans from the package of French Roast that was not decaffeinated. Her radio station had pumped out blues all during the night and switched over to jazz while she read the manuscript's last pages. A tenor saxophone was playing some ballad so tenderly that individual notes seemed to float through her skin. "Scott Hamilton," said the announcer, "with 'Chelsea Bridge.' "

Scott Hamilton . . . wasn't that the name of an ice skater?

Nora had looked up from the manuscript, dazed and uncertain. It was as if along with the sound of the saxophone, some secret thought, one not to be admitted during normal hours, had swum into her mind, taken form, and floated out. Carmichael/Carstairs and Paddi Mann had been part of this thought, but it was gone. The experience had made her feel oddly like a visitor in her own life. She stood up, put her hands on her hips, and twisted her back twice sharply to the right, then twice to the left.

Davey had not left the family room during the night, but her irritation with him had passed. After nearly a week of keeping his fears inside him, he had finally blurted out his confession. Even if only a tenth of it was true, it was still a confession.

Nora went downstairs and peeked in on her husband. Above the rug, his face was tight with an anxious dream. She switched off the light and turned off the CD player. Upstairs, she put *Spectre* back in its rubber bands. She felt at once utterly tired and completely awake. Why not now, in the gift of these extra hours, take her run, and then make breakfast for them both before Davey left for New York? Inspired, she put on her shorts and running shoes, slipped into a tank top and a cotton sweater, pulled a long-billed cap on her head, and left the house. After a few minutes of stretching in the dew-soaked grass on a front lawn that looked exotic in the unfamiliar gray-blue light of dawn, Nora was loping past the sleeping houses on Fairytale Lane.

Tendrils of doubt and worry continued to prod at her concentration as she ran through the almost hallucinatory landscape of the Bird Shelter. Paddi Mann was not a problem; nor, really, was whatever Davey had been hiding. Davey's secrets invariably turned out to be less significant than he imagined. The problem was whether or not to tell him what she had inadvertently discovered about Clyde Morning.

29

NORA PICKED UP *The New York Times* from her doorstep, unlocked her front door, and automatically checked the signal on the security keypad. The green light burned; no one had touched the system since she had left the house. She carried the paper downstairs and opened the door to the family room. There, lost in untroubled sleep, was Davey, throw rug twisted around his hips, eyes closed, mouth open just wide enough for him to lick his lips.

She knelt in front of Davey and drew her hand down his cheek. His eyes fluttered open. "What time is it?"

She looked at the digital clock next to the CD player. "Seven-seventeen. You have to get up."

"Why? Jeez, did you forget it was Saturday?"

"It's *Saturday*? Good God," she said. "I'm sorry. I'm so mixed up, I guess I thought it was Monday."

He noticed what she was wearing. "You already did your run? It's so *early*." He sat up and took a closer look at her face. "Did you get any sleep?" He sat up and swung his feet to the floor. A faint smell of used alcohol clung to his skin. He drooped back against the wall and looked at her. "You really have this completely *wired* look. I didn't think *Spectre* was that exciting. In fact, from what I saw, it was kind of sucky."

This did not seem the time to risk telling him her theory about Clyde Morning. "Well, I had an idea or two, but I should take another look at the manuscript before I talk about them."

"Oh?" He tilted his head and looked wary.

"I just want to make sure of a few things. Do you want to go back to sleep?"

He rubbed his cheek. "Might as well get up. Maybe I can get in some golf before lunch. Would that be okay with you?"

"Good idea." Nora kissed his whiskery, slightly stale cheek and stood up. In the living room, she realized that she was still carrying the newspaper and tossed it onto a chair.

After a hurried shower, Nora turned off the water and left the compartment just as naked Davey entered the bathroom. When she reached for a towel, he grabbed one of her buttocks. She bunched the towel in front of his chest and pushed him toward the shower.

She toweled herself dry, wrapped the towel around her trunk, and came out into the bedroom to get dressed. Naked, pink, and rubbing his hair with a towel, Davey came out of the bathroom and said, "The only problem with going to the club so early is that you have to play with these old jock-type guys, and they all treat me like somebody's retarded grandson. They never pay attention to anything I say."

The telephone next to the bed rang. Both of them stared at it. "Must be a wrong number," Davey said. "Get rid of them."

Nora picked up the telephone and said, "Hello?"

A male voice she had heard before but did not recognize pronounced her name.

"Yes."

"This is Holly Fenn, Mrs. Chancel. I'm sorry to bother you so early, but in the midst of all the excitement down here, something came up that you might be able to help us with."

Davey appeared before her in a pale green polo shirt, boxer shorts, and blue knee-high socks. "So who is this idiot?"

She put her hand over the mouthpiece. "Holly Fenn."

"I don't know anybody named Holly Fenn."

"That cop. The detective."

"Oh, *that* guy. Swell."

Fenn said, "Hello?"

"Yes, I'm here."

"If you wouldn't mind performing a little public service for your local police, I wonder if you and your husband could come down here to the station. As friends of Mrs. Weil's."

Davey removed a pair of khaki pants from the dry cleaner's plastic bag and tossed the bag, now entangled with the hanger, toward the wastebasket, missing by a yard.

"I don't quite understand," she said. "You want to talk to us about Natalie?" Davey muttered something and thrust one leg into the trousers.

"I might have some good news for you," Fenn said. "It seems your friend may not be dead after all. LeDonne found her, or someone who claims to be Mrs. Weil, down on the South Post Road just a little while ago. Can you be in soon? I'd appreciate your help."

"Well, sure," she said. "That would be great news. But what do you need us for, to identify her?"

"I'll fill you in when you get here, but that's about it. You might want to come around to the back of the station. Everything's crazy around here."

"See you in about ten minutes," she said.

"In the midst of the pandemonium, I'm grateful to you," Fenn said. "Thanks." He hung up.

Still holding the receiver, Nora looked at Davey, who was now at his shoe rack, deliberating. "I still don't get it," she said. Davey glanced at her, made an interrogatory noise in his throat, and bent down to select penny loafers. "He wants us to come down to the station because that policeman who was at Natalie's house— LeDonne?—because he says LeDonne found a woman who said she was Natalie down on the South Post Road."

Davey slowly straightened up and frowned at her. "So why do they need us?"

"I'm not really sure."

"It's stupid. All they have to do is look at her driver's license. What's the point of dragging us in?"

"I don't know. He said he'd explain when we got there."

"It can't be Natalie. You saw her bedroom. People don't get up and walk away from a bloodbath like that."

"According to you, Paddi Mann did," she said.

His face turned a bright, smooth red, and he moved away to

slip on the loafers. "I didn't say that. I said she disappeared. Natalie was murdered."

"Why are you blushing?"

"I'm not *blushing*," he said. "I'm pissed off. You expect cops to be kind of dim and incompetent, but this is a new low. They pick up some screwball who says she's Natalie, and we have to waste the morning doing their job for them." He paced to the door, shoved his hands in his pockets, and gave her a guarded look. "I hope you know enough not to blurt out anything I told you last night."

Nora noticed that the receiver was still in her hand and replaced it. "Why would I?"

"I wish we had time to get something to eat," Davey said. "Let's get this over with, shall we?"

A few minutes later, the Audi was zipping beneath the trees that lined Old Pottery Road as Davey wondered aloud if he should tell the police about finding Paddi Mann's copy of *Night Journey* in Natalie Weil's bedroom. "The problem is, I took it. I bet I could get into trouble for that."

For Nora, the question represented another instance of Hugo Driver's amazing ability to go on making trouble long after his death. "There's no reason to bring it up."

Davey gave her an injured look. "This *is* serious, Nora. Maybe I shouldn't go in with you. This woman can't be Natalie, but what if she is?"

"If she can't be, she isn't. And if somehow she is Natalie, she'll have a lot more to talk about than a copy of *Night Journey*."

"I guess so." He sighed. "You said you had some idea about *Spectre*."

"Oh!" she said. "When I was running into the Bird Shelter, something about the writing occurred to me. But I could be wrong."

Davey accelerated downhill toward the green light on the Post Road, signaled for a turn, and swung north into the fast lane.

"You know how you used to joke about Clyde Morning and Marletta Teatime being the same person? I think they really could be."

He gave her an incredulous glance.

"Last month, I read a Marletta Teatime novel, remember? *The Grave Is Waiting?*"

"The Waiting Grave," Davey said.

"Right. Some things in the style struck me as funny. Marletta had people say 'too true' a couple of times when they agreed with something. Who says 'too true'? English people, maybe, or Australians, but Americans don't say it. In *Spectre*, people say 'too true' over and over."

"Obviously Clyde reads her books."

"But there's more. Marletta started half a dozen sentences with the word 'indeed.' The same thing happens in *Spectre*. And there's something about shoes. In the Marletta book, the gardener character, the one who kills the little boy, his shoes are crosshatched with scuff marks. That's how you find out later that he was impersonating a minister in the other town. Well, in *Spectre*, Morning keeps saying that George Whatshisname's shoes are crosshatched with scuff marks. It's not even a very good description."

"Oh great, now you're an editor."

Nora said nothing.

"You know what I mean. I don't think it's a bad description, that's all."

"Okay, look at their joke names," Nora said. "Morning and Teatime, it's like being called six o'clock and four o'clock."

"Hah," Davey said. "You know, maybe Morning invented Teatime as a pseudonym. It's not actually impossible."

"Thank you."

"If he had two names, he could unload twice as many books. God knows, he must have needed the money. All he had to do was set up Marletta's post office box and a separate bank account. Nobody ever saw either one of them, anyhow."

"So if they were the same person, it wouldn't cause any problems?"

"Not if we don't tell anybody," Davey said. "When *Spectre* is edited, we take out all the 'indeeds' and 'too trues' and the crosshatches, that's all."

"You could get a little publicity out of it," Nora said.

"And make us look like fools. No thanks. The best thing is to keep quiet and let the problem go away by itself. Which is what I wish we could do with this stupid Driver business."

"What Driver business?"

"It's so ridiculous I don't even want to talk about it."

"This is the problem your father told you about."

"The reason I had to watch that travesty. Okay, here goes."

Davey turned off the Post Road and drove toward the stone building of the Westerholm police station. The adjacent parking lot seemed unusually full to Nora.

"How can that movie be a nuisance for Chancel House?"

"It can't be," Davey said, sounding weary, "not in itself. What happened was, these two screwball women in Massachusetts went out to see that dumb movie right after they were going through some family papers in their basement." Davey came out of the main lot and turned into the police department lot, which was as crowded as the one they had just left. Cars and vans were parked in front of the station.

Nora said, "Look at those vans." She pointed at two long vans bearing the logos and call letters of network news programs in New York.

"Just what we need."

"These women found old family papers?"

"They thought they found a way to scare a lot of money out of my old man. Their greasy lawyer did everything but admit it."

Davey had now driven to the far end of the police lot without finding an opening, and he circled around toward the parking places reserved for police vehicles.

"I don't get it," Nora said.

"They found notes a sister of theirs was supposed to have made. Like *three pages*. In a suitcase." He pulled into an empty spot between two police cars.

"They're claiming that their sister wrote *Night Journey*?"

Whatever the women in Massachusetts were claiming was apparently not to be discussed, because Davey immediately got out of the car. Nora opened her door, stood up, and saw Officer LeDonne approaching. He looked like a man under a great deal of pressure.

"I'm not moving this car," Davey said. "You asked us to come down here."

"Will you follow me into the station, please? Mr. Chancel? Mrs. Chancel? I'll have to ask you to move pretty quickly, and not to talk to anyone until we're with Chief Fenn." He came toward them as he spoke and halted about two feet away from Davey. "Stick as close to me as you can." He looked at them both, turned around, and set off toward the front of the building.

When they came around the side of the station, Nora noticed

something she had not taken in earlier. Unlike the cars in the main lot, these were occupied. The men and women waiting in their cars watched LeDonne lead the Chancels toward the steps of the police station.

"Why, half the town is out here," she said.

"Been here since dawn," LeDonne said.

They hurried up the three long steps. Nora felt hundreds of avid eyes watching them from behind windshields and then was distracted by the commotion on the other side of the door. LeDonne sighed. "Up to me? We'd put 'em all in the holding pen and let 'em out one at a time." He faced the door, motioned them nearer, and lunged inside. Davey moved in behind Nora, put his hands on her hips, and pushed.

As Nora knew from her misadventure with the millionaire's child, the tall desk manned by a sergeant dominated one side of the space beyond the entrance, and on the other stood two long rows of wooden benches. A few steps ahead of her, LeDonne was pushing his way through a crowd surging forward from the benches. Two uniformed men behind the desk shouted for order. Davey's hands propelled her past an outheld microphone into a babble of questions and a sudden wave of bodies. Voices battered at her. Davey seemed to lift her off the ground and speed her along into the narrow vacancy behind LeDonne. From behind her right ear, Nora heard a reporter asking something about the Chancel family, but the question vanished as they turned into a wide hallway, where, abruptly, they found themselves alone.

"Chief Fenn's office is up ahead," LeDonne told them, seeming to promise that everything would be answered there, and started off again, leading them past a series of doors with pebbled glass windows. On the far side of a wide metal staircase he opened a door with the words CHIEF OF DETECTIVES written on the opaque window.

In the office stood a rolltop desk, a long, green metal desk facing two wooden chairs, and a gray metal table pushed up against a pale green cinder-block wall. Both the metal desk and the table were covered with papers, and more papers bristled from the open rolltop. A narrow window behind the green desk looked out on the police parking lot, where the Audi stood like a trespasser in the rows of black-and-white cars.

"Holly Fenn is a slob," Davey said, surveying the room with his arms crossed over his chest. "Are we surprised? No, we are not."

Nora sat on a wobbly wooden chair, and Holly Fenn charged through the door, carrying a thick, battered notebook before him like a weapon. "I suppose the press sort of closed in on you out there."

"They did," she said, and laughed. "What are they doing here, anyhow?"

Fenn stood up. "Our chief thought we could manage them a little better inside the station." He held his hand out toward Davey, who shook it. "Thanks for showing up like this, Mr. Chancel."

"I meant, what are they doing *here*?" Nora said. "I don't understand how they found out so fast about this woman who says she's Natalie."

Fenn paused halfway to his desk and turned to look at her. "You mean you really don't know?"

"Guess not," she said.

"Didn't you see the papers this morning?"

She saw herself tossing the newspaper toward a chair.

"Oh, my God." Davey put his hands on the top of his head. "You did it? You got him?"

"Looks like it." For a moment Fenn looked almost pleased with himself.

"Did what?" Nora asked.

"Brought in our murderer," Fenn said. "Been in custody since about ten last night. I think Popsie Jennings must have called the *Times* herself. You know Popsie, don't you?"

Both Chancels knew the notorious Popsie Jennings, who owned a women's clothing store on Main Street called The Unfettered Woman and lived in the guesthouse of her third husband's estate on the good side of Mount Avenue, about a quarter of a mile from the Poplars. A short, solid, blond woman in her mid-fifties with a Gitane voice and a fondness for profanity, Popsie looked as though she had been born on a sailboat and raised on a golf course, but she had lived unconventionally, even raucously, and was supposed to have named her dress shop after her conception of herself. She was rumored to have in her bedroom two paintings of horses by George Stubbs given her by her first husband, and to declare that all three were well hung—the paintings, the horses, and the first husband.

"He broke into *Popsie's* house?" Davey said. "He's lucky he didn't wind up tied naked to a bed and force-fed vodka."

"He almost was," said Fenn. "He came over to her house

around nine last night. She got suspicious, nailed him with an andiron, taped his hands and feet together while he was out, and then got a cleaver and said she'd castrate him if he didn't confess."

"Wow," Nora said. "Popsie was pretty sure of herself."

"Pretty damn mad, too."

"So who was the guy?" asked Davey.

"I suppose you know him, too. Richard Dart."

"Dick *Dart*?" Davey sat down clumsily on the chair next to Nora's and gave her a look of utterly empty astonishment. "I went to school with him. His brother, Petey, was in my class, and Dick was in the sophomore class when I graduated. We were never friends or anything like that, but I see him around town now and then. I introduced him to Nora a couple of months ago—remember, Nora?"

She shook her head, wondering why they were not talking about Natalie Weil and still not quite capable of taking in that she had actually met the man she had called the Wolf of Westerholm. "Where?"

"Gilhoolie's. Right after it opened."

And then she remembered the languid, drawling man in the awful bar, the man who had complimented her scent when she had not been wearing one. So she had spoken to, had looked into the eyes of, had been lightly touched by, the man she called the Wolf, who turned out to be a creepy, aging preppy with a drinking problem. The reason he acted as though he hated women turned out to be that he really did hate women. Still, Dick Dart did not at all match the vague mental images she had formed of Westerholm's murderer. He was too ordinary in the wrong ways, and not at all ordinary in other wrong ways. But maybe she should have guessed that the Wolf would have an ill-concealed sense of his own superiority.

"I still can't believe it," Davey said now. "You remember him, don't you, Nora?"

"He was awful, but I wouldn't have imagined he was *that* awful."

"His father is having a little trouble with that one, too." Fenn proceeded around to the front of his desk, thumped down the notebook, and sat to face them. "Leland sent over Leo Morris as soon as he heard what happened, and Leo has been in our face since two A.M. He's still back in the holding cell with your friend."

Though Leo Morris, the Chancel family lawyer who had hired

the *QE2* for his daughter's sweet-sixteen party, was one of the most powerful attorneys in Connecticut, he was not usually thought of as a criminal lawyer, and Davey expressed his surprise at this choice.

"Leo won't argue the case in court, they have a sharp young guy for that, but he'll stage-manage the defense. We'll have a fight on our hands."

"You're sure he's the guy," Davey said.

"He is the guy," said Fenn. "When we booked him, he had a silver cigarette case of Sally Michaelman's in his jacket pocket. She stopped smoking ten, twelve years ago, but her husband gave her the case a couple of years before they divorced. And when we searched Dart's apartment, we found lots of goodies. Jewelry, watches, little things that belonged to the victims. Some of this stuff was engraved, and we're checking the rest, but I'd bet you anything you could name we'll find that most of it came from the women's houses. Hell, he even took a book about Ted Bundy from Annabelle Austin's house—she wrote her name in it. Guess he wanted to pick up some pointers. Besides that, Dart had a scrapbook of articles about the killings, clippings from every newspaper for fifty miles around. And on top of *that*, while Popsie was threatening his manhood, he coughed up a detail we never told the press."

Davey, who had looked a little alarmed at the mention of the book, asked, "What detail?"

"I can't tell you that," said Fenn.

"What made Popsie suspicious in the first place?" asked Nora.

"Dart had no real reason for showing up at her house. He called to say he had to discuss something, but once he got there he just rattled off some gobbledygook about the inventory at the dress shop—stuff he didn't have anything to do with. Then he says it would be useful to have a look at the paintings in her bedroom, maybe she could will them to a museum for a tax deduction. He wants to look over the paintings before they go any further. Popsie tells him he's full of it, no tours of the bedroom tonight, junior, go home, but really what she thinks is, *This guy is lonely, he just wants to talk.* Popsie has been around enough men to understand that this guy isn't on the normal wavelength, it isn't about sex after all, so she figures she'll give him one more drink and throw him out. So she gets up, walks around him, and realizes that he's not just making her nervous, he's making her *really* nervous. She's standing next to the fireplace. And then she realized something that made her pick up the andiron and clout him in the head."

"What was that?" Nora asked.

"All the murdered women were Dart, Morris clients. Popsie referred Brewer, Austin, and Humphrey to Dart herself, and Sally Michaelman had referred *her*. They weren't on Dick's luncheon list, but they all knew him. She had what you could call a brain-storm, and because she's Popsie, instead of falling apart she got mad and brained him."

"Was Natalie a client of Dart's?" Nora asked.

Fenn tilted his head back and contemplated the ceiling for a couple of seconds. When he looked back at them he seemed almost embarrassed. "Thank you, thank you, thank you, Mrs. Chancel. I must be getting too old for this screwball job. Got so caught up in the excitement around here, I forgot the reason you came in." He slid the thick notebook closer to him and opened it to read the last page. From the other side of the desk, Nora saw that instead of the scrawl she might have expected, Fenn's notes were written in a small, almost calligraphic hand. He looked up at Nora, then back down at the page. "Let me tell you about this woman. Officer LeDonne was reporting to the station early, at my request. He was coming up the South Post Road when he noticed a woman behaving oddly on the sidewalk in front of the empty building that used to house the Jack and Jill Nursery, in the 1300 block there, just south of the old furniture factory?" He looked up at her.

"Yes." She felt a faint stirring of alarm.

"Officer LeDonne pulled over and approached the woman. She appeared to be in considerable distress."

"Did she look like Natalie?" Nora asked.

Fenn ignored the question. "The woman more or less begged to be taken to the police station. She was insistent on getting away from the old nursery. When LeDonne helped her into the patrol car, he saw a resemblance to the photographs he had seen of Mrs. Weil, and asked her if she was Natalie Weil. The woman responded that she was. He brought her here, and she was taken to the station commander's office, where she almost instantly fell asleep. We called her doctor, but all we got was his service, which said that he'd call us back. We'll take her to the hospital this morning, but in the meantime she's still asleep on the station com-mander's couch."

"She didn't explain anything about what happened to her? She just passed out?"

"She was asleep on her feet from the second she came into the station. I should mention this. LeDonne never met Mrs. Weil. I never met Mrs. Weil. Neither did the station commander. None of us knows what she looks like in person. So it seems as if the two of you can help us out again, if you don't mind."

"I hope it is Natalie," Nora said. "Can we see her?"

Holly Fenn came around the side of his desk with a half smile visible beneath his mustache. "Let's take a little walk."

"Hey, when Dick Dart was spilling his guts to Popsie and the policemen at her house, what did *he* say about Natalie?" Davey followed Nora and the detective toward the door.

"Said he never went near her."

"He never went near her?" Nora still had not quite separated Natalie's bloody disappearance from the fate of the other women.

"You believe him?" Davey stopped moving and let Fenn walk past him to get to the door.

"Sure." Fenn opened the door and turned toward them. "Dart admitted everything else to Popsie. Why would he lie about one more victim? But the real reason I believe him is that Natalie Weil didn't use Dart, Morris."

"He only killed his father's clients," said Davey, with a fresh recognition of this fact.

"Makes you think, doesn't it?" Fenn motioned them through the door.

Out in the hall he led them past dull green walls, bulletin boards, doors open upon rooms crowded with desks. They were approaching a metal door which stood open behind a uniformed policeman. Through the door a row of barred cells was visible. It struck Nora that the cells looked exactly the way they did in movies, but until you actually saw them you would not guess that they were frightening. "Your friend Dart is back there," said Fenn. "He'll stay until we move him to the county lockup. Leo Morris is with him, so it might be a while. We still have to take his picture and print him."

Nora imagined the languid, smirking man from the bar at Gilhoolie's penned up in one of these horrors. The image filled her with dread. Then she took another step, and the entire row of cells came into view. In the last of them, one man sat bowed over on the end of the cot and another, his face obscured by a row of bars, stood. They were not speaking. Nora could not look away.

Davey and Holly Fenn moved past the open door. Nora looked at the man hunched at the end of the cot, then took in his curly gray hair and realized that he was Leo Morris. Involuntarily she glanced at the man standing beside the lawyer, and at that second the man moved sideways and became Dick Dart, his face brightening with recognition. She felt an electric shock in the pit of her stomach. Dick Dart *remembered* her.

Dart looked relaxed and utterly unworried. His eyes locked on hers. He derived some unimaginable pleasure from the sight of her. He winked, and she pushed herself forward, telling herself that it was ridiculous to be frightened by a wink.

Farther down the hallway was a door marked STATION COM-MANDER. Nora forced herself to stop seeing the mental picture of Dick Dart winking at her and took a long, deep breath.

"Let's see what's happening." Fenn cracked open the door and peered in. A wide young woman in a police uniform immediately slipped out. Fenn said, "Folks, this is Barbara Widdoes. She's our station commander, and a good one, too. Barbara, these are the Chancels, friends of Mrs. Weil's."

"Holly gave me this job." Barbara Widdoes held out her hand and gave them each a firm shake. "He has to say I'm good at it. How do you do?" She was attractive in a hearty, well-scrubbed way, with friendly brown eyes and short, dark hair as fine as a baby's. Nora had misjudged her age by at least five years. The woman before her was in her late thirties but looked younger because her face was almost completely unlined. "Actually, all I do is keep everybody else out of this old bear's way. And rent my couch out to exhausted strays."

"Can we look in on her?" Fenn asked.

Barbara Widdoes glanced inside. She nodded and allowed Nora, Davey, and Holly Fenn to enter her office.

Covered to her neck by a blanket, a small old woman lay on a short, functional couch against the side wall of the dark office. Her eyes were deep in their sockets, and her cheeks were sunken. Nora turned to Holly Fenn and shook her head. "I'm sorry. It's someone else."

"Move a little closer," Fenn whispered.

When Davey and Nora took two steps nearer the woman on the couch, her face came into sharper focus. Now Nora could see why

LeDonne had mistaken her for Natalie. There was a slight resemblance in the shape of the forehead, the cut of the nose, even the set of the mouth. Nora shook her head again. "Too bad."

Davey said, "It's Natalie."

Nora shook her head. He was blind.

"*Look,*" Davey said, and instantly the woman opened her eyes and sat up, as if she had trained herself to spring out of sleep. She wore a filthy blue suit, and her bare feet were black with grime. Nora saw that this old woman was Natalie Weil after all, staring directly at her, her eyes wide with terror.

"*No!*" Natalie shrieked. "*Get her away!*"

Appalled, Nora stepped back.

Natalie screeched, and Nora turned openmouthed to Holly Fenn. Davey was already backing toward the door. Natalie pulled up her legs, wrapped her arms around them, and lowered her head, as if trying to roll herself up into a ball.

Fenn said, "Barbara?"

"I'll deal with her," said the policewoman, and moved across the room to put her arms around Natalie. Nora followed Fenn through the door.

"Sorry you had to go through that," said Fenn. "Do you both agree that she's Natalie Weil?"

"That's Natalie, but what happened to her?" Nora said. "She's so—"

"Why would Natalie react to you like that?" Davey asked.

"You think I know?"

"We'll get Mrs. Weil to the hospital," said Fenn, "and I'll be in touch with you as soon as I can make some sense out of all this. Can you think of any reason Mrs. Weil might be afraid of you?"

"No, none at all. We were friends."

Looking as perplexed as Nora felt, Fenn took them down the corridor, not back toward the entrance but in the same direction they had been going. "Can I ask you to stay home most of the afternoon? I might want to chew the fat later."

"Sure," Davey said.

Fenn opened a door at the back of the station, and the Chancels stepped outside into bright, hot light.

Davey said nothing on the way to the car and did not speak as he got in and turned on the ignition. "Davey?" she said.

He sped behind the station and into the little road that curved

away from the empty field and the river. It would take them
longer to get home this way, but Nora supposed that he wanted
to avoid the crowds and reporters at the front of the station.
"Davey, come on."

"What?"

Something unexpected leaped into her mind, and she heard
herself ask, "Don't you ever wonder what happened to all those
people from Shorelands? Merrick Favor and the others, the ones
that girl told you about?"

He shook his head, almost too angry to speak, but too contemptuous to be silent. "Do you think I care about what happened in
1938? I don't think you should start bugging me or anybody else
about stupid *Shorelands* in stupid *1938*. In fact, I don't think you
should have done anything you did. Whatever you did."

"Whatever I did?" This was really beyond her.

But Davey refused to say anything more on the ride home, and
when they returned to Crooked Mile Road, he jumped out of the
car, hurried into the house, disappeared into the family room, and
slammed the door.

30

AT TIMES LIKE this, Nora wished that her father were still alive to
give her advice about the male mind. Men were capable of
behavior explicable only to other men. Most conventional wisdom
on the subject was not only wrong but backwards, at least in
Nora's experience. Would Matt Curlew tell her to confront her
husband, or would he advise her to give him the temporary pri-
vacy he wanted? Some furious part of herself suggested that Matt
Curlew would remind her that these days even Catholics were
known to get out of bad marriages. Certainly Matt Curlew would
not have regarded Davey Chancel as a suitable son-in-law. In any
case, she could hear him advocating both courses with equal

clarity: *Get in there and make him open his yap* and *Back off and give the moody bastard a little time.*

Nora turned away from the door, remembering that her father had sometimes retreated to his basement workshop in a manner which indicated that he was to be disturbed only in case of emergencies on the order of fire or death. Davey was doing pretty much the same thing.

Nora went back upstairs to read about Richard Dart in the *Times*. On the bottom half of the front page, the headline SOCIALITE ALLEGED FAIRFIELD COUNTY SERIAL KILLER stood above a face-forward photograph of a barely recognizable grinning boy with shadowy eyes. Nora thought it must have been his law school graduation photo. According to the article, Dart was thirty-seven, a graduate of the Mount Avenue Academy of Westerholm, Connecticut, Yale University, and the University of Connecticut Law School. Since graduation, Dart had worked for the firm of Dart, Morris, founded by his father, Leland Dart, a significant figure in Republican politics in the state of Connecticut and a failed candidate for state governor in 1962. Richard Dart's specialty within the firm was estate planning. He had been brought in for questioning after Mrs. Ophelia Jennings, 62, widow of the yachtsman and racehorse owner Sterling "Breezy" Jennings, had rendered the suspect unconscious after becoming convinced of his guilt during a late-night legal consultation. Westerholm's chief of police expressed confidence in the identification of Richard Dart as the murderer of four local women, saying, "We have our man, and are fully prepared to offer conclusive evidence at the appropriate time." Did policemen ever really talk like that, or did reporters just pretend they did?

Leland Dart declined to speak to the press but said through a spokesman that the charges made against his son were completely without foundation.

Two long columns on page 21 gave the limited information the *Times* reporters had been able to unearth during the night. Mr. Dart's brother, Peter, a lawyer with a Madison Avenue firm, expressed conviction in his brother's innocence, as did several neighbors of the accused's parents. Roger Struggles, a currently unemployed boatmaker and close friend of the accused, told a reporter, "Dick Dart is a loose, witty kind of guy with a great sense of humor. He couldn't do anything like this in a million years." A bartender named Thomas Lowe described him as "laid-back and real charming, a sophisticated type." Mr. Saxe Coburg, his retired former English teacher, remembered a boy who "seemed remarkably comfortable with the idea of completing every assignment with the least possible effort." In his yearbook entry, Dart had expressed the surprising desire to become a doctor and chosen as his motto *As for living, our servants do that for us.*

At Yale, which both his grandfather and his father had attended before him, Dart was suspended during the second semester of his freshman year for causes undisclosed, but he managed to graduate with a C average. Out of the two hundred and twenty-four graduates in his law school class, Dart placed one hundred and sixty-first. He had passed his bar examinations on the second try and immediately joined Dart, Morris. The firm's spokesman described him as "a unique and invaluable member of our team whose special gifts have contributed to our effort to provide outstanding legal service to all of our clients."

The uniquely gifted lawyer lived in a three-room apartment in the Harbor Arms, Westerholm's only apartment building, located beside the Westerholm Yacht Club on Sequonset Bay in the Blue Hill area. His neighbors in the building described him as a loner who played loud music on the frequent nights when he returned home at 2:00 or 3:00 A.M.

This lazy, self-important pig had managed to slide through life, not to mention three good schools, on the basis of his father's connections. He had chosen to live in three rooms in the Harbor Arms. Blue Hill was one of the best sections of Westerholm, and the Yacht Club admitted only people like Alden Chancel and Leland Dart. But the Harbor Arms, which had been built in the twenties as a casino, was an ugly brick eyesore tolerated only because it provided convenient housing for the bartenders, waitresses, and other lower-level staff of the Yacht Club. What was Dick Dart doing in this dump? Maybe he lived there in order to irritate his father. Dick Dart's relationship with his father, it came to her, was even worse than Davey's with his.

She had a vivid, instantaneous flash of Dick Dart stepping sideways in his cell to freeze her with a gleaming wink. Nora folded the newspaper, sorry that she had met Dart even once and happy that she would never have to see him again. When the stories got worse, when the trial produced the torrent of ink and paper which

Alden had cheerfully predicted, she promised herself to pay as little attention as possible.

Then she wondered what it would be like to have actually known Dick Dart. How could you reconcile your memories with the knowledge of what he had done? Shuddering, she recognized the reason for Davey's distress. He had been given a moral shock. Someone he had seen every day for two years had been exposed as a fiend. Now sensible Matt Curlew could speak to her: *Let him think about it by himself for as long as he likes, then make him a good breakfast and get him to talk.*

Nora dropped the paper on the kitchen table and went into the kitchen to toast bagels, get out the vegetable cream cheese, and crack four eggs into a glass bowl for scrambling. This was no day to fret about cholesterol. She ground French Roast beans and began boiling water in a kettle. After that she set the table and placed the newspaper beside Davey's plate. She was setting in place the toasted bagels and the cream cheese when the music went off downstairs. The family room door opened and closed. She turned back to the stove, gave the eggs another whisk, and poured them into a pan as she heard him mount the stairs and come toward the kitchen. With a pretty good idea of what she was about to see, she forced herself to smile when she turned around. Davey glanced expressionlessly at her, then looked at the table and nodded. "I wondered if we were ever going to have breakfast."

"I'm scrambling some eggs, too," she said.

Davey entered the kitchen in a way that seemed almost reluctant. "That's the paper?"

"Page one," Nora said. "There's another long article inside."

He grunted and began reading while smearing cream cheese on a bagel. Nora ground some pepper into the eggs and swirled them around in the pan.

When she set the plates on the table, Davey looked up and said, "Popsie's real name is *Ophelia*?"

"Live and learn."

"Just what I was thinking," Davey said, concentrating on his plate. "You know, not that we have them that much, but you always made good scrambled eggs. Just the right consistency."

"Made?"

"Whatever. The only other person who got them just the way I like them was O'Dotto."

She sat down. "If her name was Day, why did you call her O'Dotto?"

"I don't know. It was what we did."

"And why did you call her the Cup Bearer?"

At last he looked at her, with the same irritated reluctance with which he had joined her in the kitchen. "Can I read this?"

"Sorry," she said. "I know it must be upsetting for you."

"Lots of things are upsetting for me."

"Go on," she said. "Read."

He placed the newspaper on his far side, so that he could glance from plate to print and back again without risking whatever he thought he would risk by looking at her. Behind Nora, the kettle began to sing, and she stood up to decant ground beans into the beaker and fill it with boiling water. Then she clamped on the top and carried the machine back to the table. Davey was leaning over the paper with a bagel in his hand. Nora put a forkful of scrambled egg in her mouth and found that she was not very hungry. She watched the liquid darken in the beaker as flecks of pulverized bean floated toward the bottom. After a while she tried the eggs again and was pleased to find that they were still warm.

Davey grunted at something he had read in the paper. "Geez, they got a statement from that cynical old fart Saxe Coburg. He must be about a hundred years old by now. I asked him once if he had ever considered putting *Night Journey* in the syllabus, and he said, 'I can trust my students to read drivel in their spare time.' Can you believe that? Coburg wore the same tweed jacket every day, and bow ties, like Merle Marvell. He even looked a little bit like Merle Marvell." Marvell, who had begun by editing the Blackbird Books, had been the most respected editor at Chancel House for a decade, and Nora knew that Davey's admiration of him was undermined by jealousy. From remarks he had let drop, she also knew that he feared that Marvell thought little of his abilities. The few times they had met at publishing parties and dinners at the Poplars, she had found him invariably charming, though she had kept this opinion from Davey.

She touched his hand, and he tolerated the contact for a second before moving the hand away from hers.

"This must be very strange for you. A kid you knew in school committed all these murders."

Davey pushed his plate away and pressed his hands to his face.

When he lowered them, he stared across the room and sighed. "You want to talk about what's upsetting me? Is that what you're trying to get at?"

"I thought we were getting at it," she said.

"I could care less about Dick Dart." He closed his eyes and screwed up his face. Then he put his hands on the edge of the table and interlaced his fingers and stared across the room again before turning back to her. The alarm in the center of her chest intensified. "Nora, if you really want to know what I find upsetting, it's you. I don't know if this marriage is working. I don't even know if it *can* work. Something really bizarre is happening to you. I'm afraid you're going off the rails."

"Going off the rails?" The thrilling of alarm within her had abruptly dropped into a coma.

"Like before," he said. "I can see it happening all over again, and I don't think I can take it. I knew you had some problems when I married you, but I didn't think you were going to go crazy."

"I didn't go crazy. I saved a little boy's life."

"Sure, but the way you did it was crazy. You stole the kid out of the hospital and put us all through a nightmare. You had to quit your job. Do you remember any of this? For about a month, actually more like two months before you capped things off by abducting that kid instead of going through channels, you got into fights with the doctors, you almost never slept, you cried at nothing at all, and when you weren't crying you were in a rage. Do you remember smashing the television? Do you remember seeing *ghosts*? How about *demons*?"

Davey continued to evoke certain excesses committed during her period of radioactivity. She reminded him that she had gone into therapy, and they had both agreed it had worked.

"You saw Dr. Julian twice a week for two months. That's sixteen times altogether. Maybe you should have kept going longer. All I know is, you're even worse now, and it's getting to be too much for me."

Nora looked for signs that he was exaggerating or joking or doing anything at all but speaking what he imagined was the truth. No such signs revealed themselves. Davey was leaning forward with his hands on the table, his jaw set, his eyes determined and unafraid. He had finally come to the point of saying aloud everything he had been saying to himself while listening to Chopin in the family room.

"I wish you'd never been in Vietnam," he said. "Or that you could just have put all that behind you."

"Swell. Now I'm talking to Alden Chancel. I thought you understood more than that. It's so dumb, the whole idea of putting things behind you."

"Going nuts isn't too smart, either," he said. "Are you ready to listen to the truth?"

"I guess I can hardly wait," she said.

31

"LET'S START WITH the small stuff," he said. "Are you aware of what you're like in the middle of the night?"

"How would you know what I'm like in the middle of the night? You're always downstairs drinking kümmel."

"Did you ever try to sleep next to someone who jerks around so much the whole bed moves? Sometimes you sweat so much the sheets get soaked."

"You're talking about a couple of nights last week."

"This is what I mean," he said. "You don't have any idea of what you really *do*."

She nodded. "So I've been having more bad nights than I thought, and that's been disturbing for you. Okay, I get that, but I'll sleep better now that Dick Dart is behind bars."

He bit his lower lip and leaned back in his chair. "When you're having one of these bad nights, do you sometimes look around under the pillows for a gun?"

For a moment Nora was too startled to speak. "Well, yes. Sometimes, after a really bad nightmare, I guess I do that."

"You used to sleep with a gun under your pillow."

"At the Evac Hospital. How did you ever figure out what I was looking for?"

"It came to me one night while you were sweating like crazy and rummaging under every pillow on the bed. You were hardly looking for a teddy bear. I'm just wondering, what would you do with a gun if you found one?"

"How should I know?" He was waiting for the rest of it. *Go on,* she told herself, *give him the rest of it.* "One night two guys raped me, and a surgeon gave me a gun so I'd feel more protected."

"You were raped and you never told me?"

"It was a long time ago. You never wanted to hear any more than about a tenth of what used to go on. Nobody does." Feeling that she had explained either too little or too much, Nora assessed Davey's response and saw equal quantities of injury and shock.

"You didn't think that this was something I ought to know about?"

"For God's sake, I wasn't deliberately keeping a big, dark secret from you. You weren't exactly in a hurry to tell me all about Paddi Mann and the Hellfire Club either, were you?"

"That's different," he said. "Don't look at me that way, Nora, it just is different." His eyes narrowed. "I suppose some of these nightmares of yours are about the rape?"

"The bad ones."

He shook his head, baffled. "I can't believe you never told me."

"Really, Davey, apart from not wanting to think about it all that much, I guess I didn't want to upset you."

He looked up at the ceiling again, drew in a huge breath, and pushed it out of his lungs. "Let's get to the next point. This Blackbird Books stuff is just a delusion. You had me going for a while, I'll grant you that, but the whole thing is ridiculous."

It was as if he had slapped her. "How can you say that? You can finally—"

"Stop right there. There's no way in the world my father would agree to it. If I went in there the way we planned, he'd bust me down to the mailroom. The whole thing was just a hysterical daydream. What got into me?" For a time he rubbed his forehead, eyes clamped shut. "Next point. You are not—I repeat, not—under any circumstances, to badger my mother into giving you her so-called manuscript. That is *out.*"

"I already told you I wasn't," she said. "Why don't you move on to the next point, if there is one."

"Oh, there are several. And we're still dealing with the little stuff, remember."

She leaned back and looked at him, inwardly reeling from the irony of the situation. When he finally displayed the confidence she had been trying to encourage in him, he used it to complain about her.

"I want you to show my father the respect he deserves. I'm sick and tired of this constant rudeness."

"You want me to keep quiet when he insults me."

"If that's how you hear what I just said, yes. Now, about moving out of Westerholm. That's crazy. All you want to do is run away from your problems, and on top of that you want to destroy my relationship with my parents, which I won't let happen."

"Davey, Westerholm doesn't suit us at all. New York is a lot more interesting, it's more diverse, more exciting, more—"

"More dangerous, more expensive. We hardly need any more excitement in our lives. I go to New York every day, remember? You want to deal with homeless people lying all over the streets and muggers around every corner? You'd go crazier than you already are."

"You actually think I'm crazy?"

He shook his head and held up his hands. "Forget about it. We're getting into the serious stuff now. Let's consider the way Natalie Weil reacted to you in the police station. She went nuts. And it wasn't because of me. It wasn't because of that cop. It was because she saw you."

"Something happened to her. That's why she acted like that."

"Something happened to her, all right. And where it happened was in the same nursery where you took that kid when you decided to play God. Do you want me to believe that's a coincidence?"

"You think *I* took her there?" The sheer unreasonableness of this idea made her momentarily forget to breathe.

"There's no other way to explain things. You locked her up in that empty building and kept her there until she managed to get out. Now I'm wondering whether or not you remember doing all this. Because you really did seem startled when Natalie started screaming, and I don't think you're that good an actress, Nora. I think you must have had some kind of psychotic break."

"I kept her locked up in an empty building. I guess I must have thrown all that blood around her bedroom, too. What else did I do? Torture her? Did I let her starve?"

"You tell me," Davey said. "But from the way she acted—the way she *looked*—I'd say both."

"You astound me."

"The feeling is mutual."

Nora regarded him during the silence which followed this exchange, thinking that he had somehow managed to become a person she did not at all know. "Would you mind telling me why I would do all this to Natalie Weil, whom I like? And whom I haven't seen, in spite of what you told Holly Fenn, for almost two years?"

For the first time during this confrontation, Davey began to look uncomfortable. He turned some thought over in his mind, and the discomfort moved visibly into anger. "Dear me, what in the world could it be? Wow, I wonder."

"Well, I do," Nora said. "Apparently it's staring me in the face, but I can't see it."

"Is this really necessary? At this point, I mean?"

"You bastard," she said. "You want me to guess?"

"You don't have to guess, Nora. You just want me to say it."

"So say it."

He rolled his head back and looked at her as if she had just asked him to eat a handful of dirt. "You know about me and Natalie. Satisfied now?"

"You and Natalie Weil?"

Wearily, he nodded.

"You were having an affair with *Natalie Weil?*"

"Our sex life was hardly wonderful, was it? When we did have sex, you were turned off, Nora. The reason for that is, you started going into the Twilight Zone. *I* don't know where you went, but wherever it was, there wasn't much room in there for me."

"No," she said, battling to contain the waves of rage, nausea, and disbelief rolling through her. "You cut *me* out. You were anxious about work, or so I thought, you had all this anxiety, and it began to affect you when we went to bed, and then you started getting even more anxious because of that, which affected you even more."

"It was all my fault."

"It was nobody's fault!" Nora shouted. "You're blaming me because you were sleeping with Natalie, damn her, and you know what that is? Babyish. I didn't tell you to stick your dick into her. You thought that one up all by yourself."

"You're right," he said. "You're not responsible. You hardly know what reality is anymore."

"I'm beginning to find out. When did this start? Did you drive up to her house one day and say, Gee, Natalie, old Nora and I aren't getting it on very well anymore, how about a tumble?"

"If you want to know how it started, I met her in the Main Street Delicatessen one day, and we started talking, and I invited her to lunch. It just sort of took off from there."

"How long ago was this wonderful lunch?"

"About two months ago. I'm just wondering how you found out about it, and when you started to hatch your crazy plan."

"I found out about two seconds ago!" she yelled.

"It's going to be interesting to hear what Natalie says when she's able to talk. Because from what I saw, you scare the shit out of her."

"I should," Nora said. "But because of what she did to me, not the other way around."

At an impasse, they stared at each other for a moment. Then a recognition came to Nora. "This is why you wanted to go to her house that day. You wanted to see if you left anything behind. All that stuff you told me last night was just another Davey Chancel fairy tale."

"Okay, I was afraid I might have left something at her house. If I saw something, I could say I left it behind the last time we visited her."

"And tell me some lie about how it got there."

He shrugged.

"How did Paddi Mann's book get into Natalie's house?"

He smiled. "Dick Dart didn't give it to her, that's for sure."

Nora felt like throwing every dish in the kitchen at the wall. Then, in a shivering bolt of clarity, she remembered Alden's talking to Davey on the terrace about Dick Dart, saying something like *I wonder what Leland's wife thinks about her son romancing the same women her husband seduced forty years ago.* Alden had said, *It'd be a strange boy who did that, wouldn't you think?* Alden had been the man Natalie called "the Prune." Alden had probably taken the photographs in Natalie's kitchen. No longer smiling, Davey gave her an uncertain, guilty glance, and she knew she was right. "Natalie had an affair with your father, didn't she?"

Davey blinked and looked guiltier than ever. "Ah. Well. She

did." He bit his lower lip and considered her. "Funny you should know about that."

"I didn't know. It just sort of hit me."

"I suppose she could have told you when it was going on. Didn't you meet Natalie in the supermarket a while ago?"

"Alden gave her those Blackbird Books," she said, having come to another recognition. "I wondered why they were separate like that on the shelf. They were a gift from a lover, and she kept them together."

"She never got around to them," Davey said.

"No wonder, given her active life. Did she cut him off when you turned up? Was it like a trade-in deal, a newer model, like that?"

"Their thing was over by then. It was no big deal in the first place."

"Unlike your grand passion. Stealing your old man's slut away from him must have perked the old ego right up. Kind of a primal victory."

"I didn't know about her and my father until later." Davey's left leg began to jitter, and he chewed on his lip some more.

"Did you get any comparisons? Length? Endurance? The sort of thing you boys worry about so much?"

"Shut up," he said. "Of course not. It was no big deal."

"Nothing is a big deal to you, is it? You have no idea what your feelings are. You just push them aside and hope they'll go away."

"Nora, I had a fling. People all over the world do the same thing. But if I'm as emotionally stupid as you say I am, why are we having this conversation? I'm worried about you, I know that much. The only way *I* know to explain these things is what I just said. And if you're going off the rails, I don't know what to do with you."

"But I didn't do it! You had this sneaky little affair, you *betrayed* me, and then you took your guilt and handed it over to me. If I'm crazy, your adultery is justified."

"Okay," he said. "Maybe there is some other explanation. I hope there is, because I really can't say I like this one very much."

"Oh, I love it," she said. "It shows so much trust and compassion."

"So I guess we'll wait and see."

"I can't stand this anymore," Nora said, electric with rage. "I can't stand *you* anymore. I'm furious with you for sleeping with

Natalie, yet if you can show me that you might begin to understand who I am, I could probably get over that eventually, but this
garbage is so much worse that I . . ." She ran out of words.

"If I'm wrong, I'll crawl over broken glass to apologize."

"Gee, it makes me so happy to hear that," she said.

He stood up and hurried from the room without looking at her.

32

AFTER THE DOOR to the family room had opened and closed, Nora
unclenched her hands and tried to force her body to relax. The
beginning of *Manon Lescaut* drifted up the stairs. He was going to
hide, presumably until a squad of policemen showed up to drag
her away in shackles to the lunatic asylum.

He had *reduced* her, *dwindled* her. In his version of their marriage, a criminally irrational wife tormented a caring, beleaguered
husband. Nora was not too angry to admit that their sex life had
been imperfect, and she knew that many marriages, perhaps even
most, had repaired themselves after an unfaithfulness. She could
acknowledge that her night terrors, apparently far worse than she
had imagined, might have played a role in what Davey had done.
She found herself ready to take on her share of guilt. What she
could not forgive was that Davey had *written her off*.

As soon as the difference in their ages had become a *difference*—Davey had started to panic. A woman's forty-nine lay
several crucial steps beyond a man's forty. Menopause, not nightmares and irrational behavior, was spooking Davey Chancel.

This was really bleak, and Nora pushed herself away from the
table. She piled their dishes and gathered the silverware, resisting
the impulse to hurl it all to the floor. She put the plates, cups, and
silver into the dishwasher, the pans into the sink. If Davey left her,
where would she go? Would he move into the Poplars while she
stayed in this house? The idea of living alone on Crooked Mile
Road made her feel almost dizzy with nausea.

She could remember what she had done every day since Natalie's disappearance. She had shopped, made the bed, cleaned the house, read, exercised. She had phoned agents on behalf of Blackbird Books. The afternoon of the day after Natalie's disappearance, when Davey would have had her tormenting the missing woman on the South Post Road, Nora had run into Arturo Landrigan's wife, Beth, in a Main Street café called Alice's Adventure. In spite of being married to a man so crass that he felt he should bathe in a golden tub ("Makes you feel like a great wine in a golden goblet," Arturo had confided), Beth Landrigan was an unpretentious, smart, sympathetic woman in her mid-fifties, one of the few women in Westerholm who seemed to offer Nora the promise of friendship, the chief obstacle to which was their husbands' mild mutual antipathy. Davey thought that Arturo Landrigan was a philistine, and Nora could imagine what Landrigan made of Davey. The two women had taken advantage of their chance meeting to share an unplanned hour at Alice's Adventure, and at least half of that time had been spent talking about Natalie Weil.

Maybe I really am crazy, she said to herself twenty minutes later as she drove her car aimlessly down Westerholm's tree-lined streets. Nora took another turn, went up a curving ramp, and found herself surrounded by many more cars than she had noticed before. Then she realized that she was driving down the Merritt Parkway in the direction of New York. Some part of her had decided to run away, and this part was taking the rest of her with it. They had covered about fifteen miles; New York was only twenty-five more away. In half an hour she could be ditching the car in a garage off the FDR Drive. She had a couple of hundred dollars in her bag and could get more from an automatic teller. She could check into a hotel under a false name, stay there for a couple of days, and see what happened. *If you're going to change your life, Nora,* she said to herself, *all you have to do is keep driving.*

So there were presently two Noras seated behind the wheel of her Volvo. One of them was going to continue down the Merritt Parkway, and the other was going to get off at the next exit and drive back to Westerholm. Both of these actions seemed equally possible. The first had a definite edge in appeal, and the second corresponded far more with her own idea of her character. But why should she be condemned always to follow her idea of what was right? And why should she automatically assume that turning back was the only right course of action? If what she wanted was to flee to New York, then New York was the right choice.

Nora decided not to decide: she would see what she did and add up the cost later. For a few minutes she sped down the parkway in a state of pleasantly suspended moral freedom. An exit sign appeared and slipped past, followed by the exit itself. The two separate Noras enjoyed their peaceful habitation of a single body. Ten minutes later another exit sign floated toward her, and she remained in the left-hand lane and thought, *So now we know.* Several seconds later, when the exit itself appeared before her, she flicked her turn indicator and nipped across just in time to get off the parkway.

33

NORA PULLED HER Volvo into the empty garage. That she would not have to explain herself to Davey came as a relief mixed with curiosity about what he was doing. At first she thought that he must be visiting his parents, but as she moved to the back door, she realized that Holly Fenn might have called with news of Natalie. A vision of her husband murmuring endearments to Natalie Weil made her feel like getting back into the Volvo and lighting out for some distant place like Canada or New Mexico. Or home, her lost home, in upper Michigan. She had friends back in Traverse City, people who would put her up and protect her. The notion of protection automatically evoked the image of Dan Harwich, but this false comfort she pushed away. Dan Harwich was married to his second wife, and neither groom nor bride would be likely to welcome Nora Chancel into their handsome stone house on Longfellow Lane, Springfield, Massachusetts.

She glanced into the family room and continued on upstairs. She wondered if Davey had gone out to look for her. The most likely explanation for his absence was that he had been summoned to the police station, in which case he would have left a note. She went to the usual location of their notes to each other, the section of the kitchen counter next to the telephone, where a thick pad stood beside a jar of ballpoint pens. Written on the top sheet of the pad were the words "mushrooms" and "K-Y," the beginning of a shopping list. Nora went to the second most likely place, the living room table, which held nothing except a stack of magazines. Then she returned to the kitchen to inspect the table and the rest of the counter, found nothing, and went finally to the fourth and least likely message drop, the bedroom, where she found only the morning's rumpled sheets and covers.

Feeling as if she should have become the irresponsible Nora who had disappeared into New York, she was moving toward the living room when the telephone rang.

She lifted the receiver, hoping in spite of herself to hear Davey's voice. A woman said, "I made up my mind, and I want you to do it."

"You have the wrong number."

"Don't be silly," said the woman, whom Nora now recognized as her mother-in-law. "I want to go ahead with it."

"Is Davey there?"

"Nobody's here. I can shoot right over and give it to you. I've been alone with the thing so long, I think it's *crucial* that you read it. I won't be able to sit still until I hear from you."

"You want to bring your book over here?" Nora asked.

"I want to get out and around," Daisy said, misunderstanding Nora's emphasis. "I haven't been out of this house in I don't know how long! I want to see the streets, I want to see everything! Ever since I made up my mind about this, I've been absolutely *exalted*."

"You're sure," Nora said.

"I bless you for offering, I bless you twice over. You can bring it back to me Tuesday or Wednesday, when the men are at work."

"You're going to drive?" Daisy had not undertaken to pilot a car as far as the end of the driveway in several decades.

Daisy laughed. "Of course not. Jeffrey will drive me. Don't worry, Jeffrey is *completely* dependable. He's like the *Kremlin*."

Nora gave up. "You'd better do it fast. I don't know when Davey's coming home."

"This is so *exciting*," Daisy said. She hung up.

Nora released a moan and slumped against the wall. Davey could never know that she had seen his mother's book. The entire transaction would have to be conducted as if under a blanket in deepest night. Daisy would give her the manuscript, and after a few days, she would give it back. She did not have to read it. All she had to do was give Daisy the encouragement she needed.

Nora straightened up and went to the living room window, not at all comfortable with the idea of treating Daisy so shabbily.

When she thought that Daisy's car would soon be turning into Crooked Mile Road, she left the house and walked down to the end of the drive. A Mercedes came rolling toward her. Daisy began to open the door before the car came to a stop, and Nora stepped back. Daisy leaped out and embraced her. "You darling genius! My salvation!"

Daisy leaned back to beam wildly at Nora. Her eyes were wet and glassy, and her hair stood out in white clumps. "Isn't this wonderful, isn't this wicked?" She gave Nora another wild grin and then turned around to wrestle from before her seat a fat leather suitcase bound with straps. "Here. I place it in your wonderful hands."

She held it out like a trophy, and Nora gripped the handle. When Daisy released her hands from the sides, the suitcase, which must have weighed twenty or thirty pounds, dropped several feet. "Heavy, isn't it?" she said.

"Is it finished?"

"You tell me," Daisy said. "But it's close, it's close, it's close, and that's why this is such a brilliant idea. I can't wait to hear what you have to say about it. My God!" Her eyes widened. "Do you know what?"

Nora thought that Daisy had read about Dick Dart in the morning paper.

"They've gone and put up this hideous *fortress* on the Post Road, right where that lovely little clam house used to be!"

"Oh," said Nora. Daisy was talking about a cement-slab discount department store which had occupied two blocks of the Post Road for about a decade.

"I think I should write a letter of complaint. In the meantime, Jeffrey is going to expand my horizons by driving me hither and yon, as you are going to do, also, my dear, by talking to me about my book. While I'm taking in the sights, you'll be peering into my *cauldron.*"

"Enjoy yourself, Daisy," Nora said.

"You must enjoy yourself, too," Daisy said. "Now I think Jeffrey and I had better make our getaway. I will be calling you this evening for your first impressions. We need a code word, to announce that the coast is clear." She closed her eyes and then opened them and beamed. "I know, we'll use what you said when I called you. If Davey's in the room, you say 'wrong number.' That's perfect, I think. I do have a gift for this sort of thing. Perhaps I should have been a spy." She climbed back into the car and whispered through the open window, *"I can't wait."*

Nora bent down to see what Jeffrey made of all this. His face was rigidly immobile, and his eyes were dark, shining slits. He leaned forward and said slowly, "Mrs. Chancel, I don't mean to be presumptuous, but if I can ever do anything for you, call me. My last name is Deodato, and I have my own line."

Nora stepped back, and the car moved forward. Daisy had turned around in her seat, and Nora tried to return her smile until Daisy's face was only a pale, exulting balloon floating away down the street.

34

NORA HOISTED THE case onto the sofa and undid the straps. Scuffed and battered, variously darkened by stains, the suitcase appeared to be forty or fifty years old. When Nora finally yanked the zipper home, the top yawned upward several inches, the mass of pages beneath it expanding as if taking a deep breath.

Thousands of pages of different sizes, colors, and styles rose up. Most of these were standard sheets of white typing paper, some of them yellow with age; some of the remainder were standard pages shaded ivory, gray, ocher, baby blue, and pink. The rest, amounting to about a third, consisted of sheets torn from notebooks, hotel stationery, Chancel House invoice and order forms used on their blank sides, and the sort of notepaper that is decorated with drawings of dogs and horses.

Where could she hide this monstrosity? It would probably fit

under the bed. She knelt to get her arms under the bottom of the
case, lifted it off the sofa, and staggered backwards, barely able to
see over the top. A faint odor of dust and mothballs hung about the
weight of paper and leather in her arms.

The first sheet floated along in front of her and resolved itself
into a title page which had never managed to make up its mind.
Over the years Daisy had considered an ever-growing number of
titles, adding new inspirations without rejecting the old ones.

In the bedroom Nora cautiously made her way toward the
couch, then bent down to lower the case onto an outflung leg of
a pair of jeans and a blouse she had been intending to iron.
Holding her breath, she put one hand on top of the suitcase while
with the other she tugged the jeans to one side, the blouse to the
other. Then she sat beside it. She looked at it for a moment,
regretting that she had ever offered to read this unwieldy epic,
then grasped it front and back and lowered it to the floor. Yes, it
might just, it probably would, fit under the bed.

Nora regarded the bright double window in the wall to her left.
She stood up to raise the bottom panes as far as they would go and
returned to the couch. She looked down at the untidy stack of
pages at her feet, sighed, picked up sixty or seventy pages, turned
over the title, or nontitle, page, and read the dedication. Typed on
a yellowing sheet with the letterhead of the Sahara Hotel, Las
Vegas, complete with an idealized front elevation of the building,
it read: *For the only person who has ever given me the encouragement necessary to any writer, she who alone has been my companion and without whose support I would long ago have
abandoned this endeavor, myself.*

On the next page, also liberated from the Sahara Hotel, Las
Vegas, was an epigraph attributed to Wolf J. Flywheel. *The
world is populated by ingrates, morons, assholes, and those
beneath them.*

Nora began to enjoy herself.

PART ONE: How the Bastards Took Over.

She began reading the first chapter. Through a maze of crossed-
out lines, arrows to phrases in the margins, and word substitutions,
she followed the murky actions of Clementine and Adelbert
Poison, who lived in a decrepit gothic mansion called The Ivy in
the town of Westfall. A painter whose former beauty still shone
through the weight she had put on during the course of an unhappy
marriage, Clementine drank a bit, wept a bit, pondered suicide,

and had a peculiarly ironic, distant relationship with her son, Egbert. Adelbert made and lost millions playing with the greater millions left him by his tyrannical father, Archibald Poison, and seduced waitresses, secretaries, cleaning women, and the Avon Lady. When he was home, Adelbert liked to sit on his rotting terrace scanning Long Island Sound through a telescope for sinking sailboats and drowning swimmers. Egbert was a boneless noodle who spent most of his time in bed. Some vague but nasty secret, possibly several vague but nasty secrets, fouled the air.

When she reached the end of the first chapter, Nora looked up and realized that she had been reading for half an hour. Davey had still not returned. She looked back at the page, the last line of which was *"You know very well that I never wished to reclaim Egbert," said Adelbert.* Reclaim him? Egbert did resemble something reclaimed, like a lost dog.

The telephone rang. Hoping to hear her husband's voice, Nora picked it up and said, "Hello?"

"Goody goody, you didn't say 'Wrong number,' so you can talk." Daisy's voice, slightly slurred. "What do you think?"

"I think it's interesting," Nora said.

"Poop. You have to say more than that."

"I'm enjoying it, really I am. I like Adelbert and his telescope."

"Alden used to spend hours looking for topless girls on sailboats. How far are you?"

"The end of chapter one."

"Umph." Daisy sounded disappointed. "What did you like best?"

"Well, the tone, I suppose. That sort of black humor. It's like Charles Addams, in words."

"That's because you've only read the first *chapter*," Daisy said. "After that it goes through all kinds of changes. You'll see, you're in for a real treat. At least I *hope* you are. Go on, go back to reading. But you really like it so far?"

"A lot," Nora said.

"Whoop-de-do!" Daisy said. "Stop wasting time talking to me and *surge ahead*." She hung up.

Nora went back to the couch and began the second chapter. Adelbert stood beside a tall, bony, blond woman and signed a hotel register under a false name. In their room Adelbert ordered the woman to undress. *Honey, can't we have a drink first?* He said, *Do what I say.* The woman undressed and embraced him.

Adelbert pushed her away. The woman said she thought they were friends. Adelbert took a revolver from his jacket pocket and shot her in the forehead.

Nora read the line again. *Adelbert raised the revolver, squeezed the trigger, and put a bullet through her stupid forehead.* This was a new side of Adelbert. Nora smiled at the idea of Daisy's turning Alden into a murderer. She was killing off her husband's conquests.

The telephone rang again. Groaning, Nora got up and answered it by saying, "Daisy, please, you have to give me more time."

A male voice asked, "Who's Daisy?"

"I'm sorry," Nora said. "I thought you were someone else."

"Obviously. I hope she gives you all the time you need, whoever she is."

"Holly," Nora said. "Chief Fenn, I mean. How embarrassing. I'm glad you called, actually. You must have some news."

"It's Holly, and the reason I'm calling is that we don't have any news yet. We finally got Mrs. Weil's doctor off the golf course, and he shot her full of sedatives and put her in Norwalk Hospital. According to him, the earliest we can get a straight story out of her is probably Monday morning. I thought I'd pass that along, so you can relax for one night, anyhow."

She thanked him and said, "I guess if I'm going to call you Holly, you ought to start calling me Nora."

"I already do," he said. "I'll be in touch Monday morning around nine, ten at the latest."

A wave of relief loosened the muscles in Nora's back. Holly Fenn assumed her innocent of whatever had happened to Natalie, that sow. Holly Fenn wanted to *clear things up.*

She returned to Daisy's epic. Adelbert parked in front of his crumbling mansion and went inside to pull Egbert out of bed. Egbert got off the floor, crawled back into bed, and pulled the covers over his head. Adelbert went downstairs to order a cringing servant to bring a six-to-one martini to the library. By the time the servant appeared with his drink, Adelbert was deep into a volume called *The History of the Poison Family in America.*

A new chapter, apparently from a much older version of the novel, began. On yellowed pages, the letters rose above and sank beneath the level of the lines, every *e* tilting leftwards, every *o* a bullet hole. After a battle with the style, far more congested than that of the first two chapters, Nora saw that Adelbert was reading about the history of his father during the period immediately after the birth of Egbert. A secret Nazi sympathizer, Archibald had made millions by investing in German armament concerns and was presently diverted from his covert attempts to consolidate a group of right-wing millionaires into a Fascist movement by a maddening personal problem. After rereading several pages three times over, Nora gathered that Adelbert and Clementine had perhaps produced the grandson Archibald passionately desired. Either the child had died or they had put him up for adoption. Archibald's tirades, lengthily represented, had not convinced them to repair the loss. When his orders and ultimatums came to nothing, Archibald informed his son that he would be cut out of his will if he did not provide an heir.

All of this lay half hidden beneath a furious explosion of exclamation points, tangled grammar, and backwards sentences. Archibald's fantasies about American Fascism clouded whole pages with descriptions of Nazi uniforms and other regalia. Hitler appeared, confusingly. She could not be certain if the new child had been reclaimed, adopted, or even resurrected.

Nora turned to a page typed on a sheet of Ritz-Carlton stationery and skimmed through three paragraphs before the first two sentences chimed in her head. She went back and reread them and then reread the sentences again. *Adelbert's shoes were crosshatched with scuff marks. Indeed, Adelbert's were not the shoes of a fastidious man, and such secret stains and stinks permeated his entire character.*

"Oh, my God," Nora said. "It was Daisy."

35

SHE LOOKED UP in astonishment. Not only were Clyde Morning and Marletta Teatime the same person, but both were Daisy Chancel. After Blackbird's initial authors had deserted Chancel House, Alden had replaced them with his wife, who had churned out piecework horror novels while she labored on her grim monstrosity. Blackbird's two stalwarts had never been seen or heard from because they were phantoms. *Spectre* had been hidden on a conference room shelf because Daisy had lost interest and written it when tired, drunk, or both. Alden would never revive Blackbird. Davey had been right about that, though he did not know why.

She wondered how he would react if she presented him with her discovery, then realized that she could not. Nora knew exactly how Davey would respond, by frothing at the mouth for twenty minutes before disappearing downstairs to hide behind Puccini. A more urgent question was whether or not to tell Daisy what she had discovered. Once again, for a time two separate Noras inhabited a single body, which stood up to move into the kitchen and make a ham sandwich. Daisy's instability made it equally possible that she would be enraged or delighted to have her pseudonyms known. Nora carried the sandwich back into the bedroom and realized that Davey had been gone for hours. At least he was not in Norwalk Hospital cooing over Natalie Weil. She decided to do precisely what she had done on the parkway, postpone any decision until it made itself. Daisy's manner would dictate her choice.

Nora bit into her sandwich and began skipping through the pages, trying to learn where this story was going.

After another hour, she decided that if this story was going anywhere, it was in some Daisyish direction unknown to the normal world. Scenes concluded, and then, as if an earlier draft had not been removed, repeated themselves with slight variations. The tone swung from dry to hysterical and back. At times Daisy had broken up a straightforward scene to interpolate handwritten passages of disjointed words and phrases. Some scenes broke off unfinished in midsentence, as if Daisy had intended but forgotten to return to them later. There was nothing faintly like a conventional plot. One chapter read in its entirety: *The author wants to have another drink and go to bed. You idiots should do the same.*

After following these confusions through a maze of arrows and crossings-out, Nora began to feel sick to her stomach. She decided to see what happened at the end and dug the last thirty pages out of the pile. Cleanly typed on fresh white bond, they were free from alterations, insertions, or marks of any kind. Nora leaned back, resumed reading, and soon found herself once more entangled in barbed wire.

The ending of Daisy's book described an argument between

Clementine and Adelbert ranging over the whole of their marriage. At various moments, they were in their twenties, their forties, fifties, and sixties. The site of the argument shifted from different rooms in their house to train compartments, hotel dining rooms, and terraces in European cities. They lounged on the grass in a London park and propped up the bar of a Third Avenue gin mill at two in the morning. The ending was a compilation of the occasions of their dispute. What Nora did not understand was the nature of the dispute itself.

Clementine spewed accusations, and Adelbert responded with irrelevancies, most of them about music. *I have kept your business going, you bastard, but instead of thanking me you kicked me in the teeth.* (Adelbert: *I never liked Hank Williams all that much.*) *Your entire existence is based on a lie, and so is our son's.* (Adelbert: *Cheap music sounds good on car radios.*) *You're not merely a fraud, but a fraud soaked in blood.* (Adelbert: *Most people would rather go to a ball game than a symphony, and they're correct.*) Bile soaked the paragraphs, a bitterness evoked by a subject as familiar to Clementine and Adelbert as it was opaque to Nora.

The last paragraph drew away from the protagonists to describe the terrace of a restaurant in the Italian Alps. Glasses sparkled beside white plates and shining silverware arrayed on pink tablecloths. Snow gleamed on the peaks beyond the terrace. A distant bird sang, and a diner answered with an imitation as exact as an echo. A white cloud of cigar smoke arose from a far table and dissolved into the air.

"Fraud," Clementine said, *and the moron sun, having no choice, shone down upon the Poisoned world.*

Nora placed the last page atop the others and heard the sound she had most been dreading, the ringing of the telephone.

36

"THANKS BE TO God, I did not hear the most hateful phrase on the face of the earth, 'Wrong number.' Haven't I been good? Haven't I been the most restrained little thing on the face of the earth? I am proud of myself, unto the utmost utmost. I have been circling this phone, picking it up and putting it down, I have several times dialed the first three numerals of your phone number only to put the blasted thing down again, I promised you hours of peace and quiet untroubled by little me, and by my count three hours and what's more twenty-two minutes have passed, and so what did you think? Tell me, speak, discourse, dearest Nora, please say something."

"Hello, Daisy," Nora said.

"I know, I'm too nervous to shut up and let you speak, listen to me babble! How far are you? What do you think? You like it, don't you?"

"It's really something," Nora said.

"Isn't it ever! Go on."

"I've never read anything like it."

"You got through the whole thing? You couldn't have, you must have *skimmed*."

"No, I didn't," Nora said. "It isn't the kind of book you can skim, is it."

"What do you mean by that?"

"For one thing, it's so intense." Daisy uttered a satisfied grunt, and Nora went on. "You have to pay attention when you're reading."

"I should hope so. Go on, Nora, *talk* to me."

"It's a real experience."

"What kind of experience? Be more specific."

Confusing? Irritating? "An intense experience."

"Ah. I think you already said that, though. What *kind* of intense experience?"

Nora groped. "Well, intellectual."

"Intellectual?"

"You have to think when you're reading it."

"Okay. But you keep saying the same things over and over. A little while ago, when you were talking about how it wasn't the kind of book you could skim, you said, 'for one thing,' so you must have another reason in mind, too. What was it?"

Nora struggled to remember. "I guess I meant the condition of the manuscript."

An ominous silence greeted these words.

"You know what I mean, all those changes and deletions."

"For God's sake, the whole thing has to be retyped, but you asked to see it, remember, so I gave it to you as is, this is so obvious, but anybody can read a book after it's published, that's hardly the point, I want to hear what you have to say, and you're talking about something completely irrelevant."

"I'm sorry. All I meant was that you have to read it more slowly this way."

"Yes, you have been abundantly clear on the subject, trivial though it is, and now that we have that out of the way I wish to sit back and soak up your observations."

Nora could hear Daisy's impatience compounding itself several times over. "Some of it is very funny," she said.

"Goody goody. I meant for parts to be *ecstatically* funny. Not all of it, though."

"Of course not. There's a lot of anger in it."

"You bet. Anger upon anger. Grrr."

"And you took a lot of chances."

"You wonderful girl, you saw that? Blessings on your head. Tell me more."

"So it seemed very experimental to me."

"Experimental? What could possibly seem *experimental* to you?"

"The way you repeat certain scenes? Or how you end some sections before they're finished?"

"You're talking about the times when the same things happen all over again after they happened the first time, but differently, so the real meaning comes out. And the other thing you're talking about is when anyone with half a brain can see what's going to happen, so there's no point in writing it all down. My God, it's a novel, not journalism."

"No, you're right. It's a wonderful novel, Daisy."

"Then tell me why it's wonderful."

Nora groped for the safest comment that could be made about the book. "It's bold. It's daring."

"But why do you think so?" Daisy shouted.

"Well, a lot of books start in one place and tell you a story, and that's that. I guess what I mean is, you're willing not to be linear."

"It's as linear as a clothesline. If you don't see that, you don't see anything at all."

"Daisy, please don't be so defensive. I'm telling you what I like about your book."

"But you're *making* me be defensive! You're saying these stupid things! I spent most of my life laboring over this book, and you sashay up to me and tell me it doesn't even have a story."

"Daisy," Nora said, "I'm trying to tell you that it's much richer than the books that only tell you a story."

Slightly mollified, Daisy asked, "What's your favorite part so far?"

Nora tried to remember something she had liked. "I have lots of favorite parts. Adelbert killing the women. The way you present Egbert. Your descriptions of Adelbert's clothes."

Daisy chuckled. "How far are you? What's happening now?"

Nora tried to remember what had been going on at the point she had skipped ahead. "I'm at the part where Archibald is carrying on about Nazi uniforms and talking to Hitler while he's making Clementine and his son give him a grandson."

"The fantasia? You're only as far as the fantasia? Then you can't possibly see the pattern, you're not entitled to speak about it at all. I trusted you with my soul and you're walking all over it with your big dirty feet, I give you a masterpiece and you spit on it."

Nora, who had been uttering Daisy's name at intervals during this tirade, made a desperate effort to placate her. "Daisy, you can't twist everything around this way, I am not lying to you, I understand what you have put into your book, and I know how special it is because I know you wrote those Clyde Morning and Marletta Teatime novels, and this is so much more adventurous and complex."

During the long silence which followed she thought that she

might have reversed the trend of this conversation, but Daisy had been gathering herself to scream. *"Traitor! Judas!"*

The line went dead.

Nora dropped the receiver in its cradle and blindly circled the bedroom, hugging herself. When she reached the telephone again, she sat on the bed and dialed the Poplars' number. She heard the phone ring three times, four times, five. At the tenth ring, she hung up, fell back on the bed, and groaned. Then she sat up and dialed the Poplars' number again.

After the second ring, Maria picked up and spoke a cautious "Hello?"

"Maria, this is Nora," she said. "I know Mrs. Chancel doesn't want to talk to me, but could you please tell her I have important things to say to her?"

"Mrs. Chancel doesn't want," Maria said.

"Say whatever you have to, but get her to talk to me."

Nora heard the telephone clunk down, then a few nearly inaudible words from Maria followed by a series of howls.

"Mrs. Chancel say you not family, her son family, not you. No good. Not talk." She hung up.

Nora fell back onto the bed and contemplated the ceiling. After an indeterminate time, one small consolation offered itself. Daisy would never speak to Alden of what had occurred. From this certainty grew a larger consolation. Because Daisy would not trouble Alden, Alden would not trouble Davey. Over time, the issue of Daisy's novel would vanish into the established pattern. In a week or two she and Nora could work out a reconciliation.

She got off the bed to reassemble the manuscript and stuff it back into the suitcase.

37

STILL ANXIOUS, NORA wandered into the kitchen and wiped down the counter. The problem was that if something could go wrong, it usually did. For Daisy, the manuscript was in enemy territory as long as it remained with Nora. She thought about dragging the suitcase from under the bed and driving it to Mount Avenue, but this prospect immediately induced exhaustion and despair.

Without considering what she was doing, Nora went to the sink, turned on the hot water, squirted soap into the palm of her hand, and began washing her hands. Then she washed her face. When she was done, she washed her face and hands again. The fourth time she scrubbed soap into her cheekbones and the flanges of her nose, Nora became conscious of these actions. Hot water stung her skin. She turned on the cold tap, rinsed herself, and reached for a dry dish towel. Her face stung as if she had sandpapered it. Blotting herself dry, Nora realized that she still felt appallingly dirty— no, not *still*, but rather as though someday very soon she *would* be appallingly dirty. Fighting the urge to turn the water back on and scrub herself all over again, she drifted into the living room, lay down on the sofa, and closed her eyes until the sound of Davey's car turning into the driveway awakened her. She wondered where he had been for the previous nine or ten hours and decided she didn't care. The Audi pulled into the garage.

Here was an interesting problem: would he slip into the family room and pretend she was not there, or would he come upstairs to confront her? Davey opened and closed the back door. His footsteps brought him toward the stairs. However slowly, he was moving in her direction.

Davey reached the top of the stairs and glanced into the kitchen before turning to the living room. He was looking for her, definitely a good sign. Was this what was called grasping at straws? *Go on,* she thought, *grasp away.* He came into the living room. His eyes locked with hers and slid away. He dropped into the chair most distant from Nora, leaned back, let his arms fall, and closed his eyes.

Nora said, "Welcome back."

"Did the police call?"

"Natalie's under sedation."

He was still collapsed into the chair as if thrown into it, and his eyes were closed.

"It might be nice if you said something."

Davey opened his eyes and leaned forward, catching her eyes yet again and then quickly looking down. "When I heard you leave, I bounced around the house like a Ping-Pong ball. Finally I went for a drive, got on the expressway and headed north. No idea where I was going. I had to think. That's what I've been doing all this time, driving and thinking. When I got to New Haven, I got off the highway, went to the campus, and walked around for about an hour."

"Eli, Eli," Nora said. She wondered if Davey had ever associated with Dick Dart in New Haven.

"Don't be sarcastic, all right? Nora, I was thinking about you. This morning everything seemed so clear. About ten minutes after you left, I began to wonder. Did that sound like you? You can do some rash things, but I thought you'd draw the line a long way short of kidnapping and torture."

"What do you know?" Nora said.

"I thought about what you said—that I was putting my guilt on you. But all the pieces fit together so perfectly, the whole pattern was so convincing, that it seemed like it had to be the truth. It was like one of those crossword puzzles Frank Neary and Frank Tidball do! The only part that didn't fit was you."

"You debated with yourself."

He nodded. "The more I thought, the idea that you kidnapped Natalie got more and more ridiculous. I got back in my car and drove around New Haven. New Haven is a crummy town, once you get away from Yale." Here he looked up at Nora, as if the irrelevance of the sentence had released him.

"I got completely lost, if you can believe that. I spent four years in New Haven, and it isn't that big. You know what happened? I got scared. I thought I'd never find my way out. I kept driving past the same little diner and the same little bar, and it was like I was under a curse. I almost had a *breakdown*." He wiped his forehead. "After about an hour I finally drove past this pizza joint I used to go to, and I knew where I was. No kidding, I almost cried from relief. I got back on I-95. My hands were still shaking. It felt like my whole life was up in the air."

"Good thinking," Nora said.

He nodded. "I was so *tired* and so *hungry*. When I got to Cousin Lenny's, I drove in. I grabbed a booth and ordered meat loaf and mashed potatoes. When it came, I dumped ketchup all over the meat loaf like a little kid, and when I was eating, this idea opened up in my head like a giant scroll: If I could get so lost in New Haven, you could be telling the truth. Who says all the pieces have to fit, anyway? One thing I knew for sure. Even if you did find out about me and Natalie, you could never kidnap her. That's not you."

"Thank you."

"You really didn't, did you?"

"I said that three or four times this morning."

"I was just so *convinced*. I . . ." He shook his head and looked down again, then back up. Complicated feelings, all painful, filled his eyes. "Will it do any good if I apologize?"

"Try it and see."

"I apologize for everything I said. I wish with all my heart for you to forgive me. I'm sorry that I let myself get into that thing with Natalie Weil."

"That thing is commonly called a bed," Nora said.

"You're mad at me, you must despise me and detest Natalie."

"That's about right."

"This morning, didn't you say that we could eventually work things out? I want to do that, Nora. I hope you'll forgive me. Will you take me back?"

"Did you leave?"

"God bless you," said Davey, uncomfortably reminding Nora of his mother. He pushed himself out of the chair and came forward. Nora wondered if he intended to kneel in front of her. Instead, he kissed her hand. "Tomorrow we start over again." He placed her hand on her lap and began caressing her leg. "What did you do all day?"

"I almost drove to New York." She moved her thigh away from

his hand. "I was thinking about not coming back. Then I turned around and came back."

"I would have gone crazy if you hadn't been here when I got back."

"Here I am."

He kissed the top of her head. "I have to lie down and get some sleep. I can barely stand up. Do you mind?"

"Of course not."

He went toward the hallway, turned to give her a grateful look and a sketchy wave, and was gone.

Nora leaned back against the sofa. If she had any feelings, they were like the little, black, shriveled husks left behind by a fire. She supposed that someday they would turn back into feelings.

38

HUNGER EVENTUALLY FORCED Nora off the sofa. Her watch said it was ten minutes to eight. Davey slept on. Nora thought he would probably wake up around midnight, fumble his way out of his clothes, and climb right back into bed to finish digesting his meat loaf and mashed potatoes, another example of Davey's habit, when under stress, of regressing to the age of training wheels. A search of the kitchen shelves yielded a can of mushroom soup, hot diggity. She plopped the congealed gray-brown cylinder into a pot, turned on the heat, and waited for it to melt while she toasted two slices of whole-wheat bread.

As soon as she began to spoon soup into her mouth an inner rheostat dialed itself upward, and a sense of well-being came to life within her. She'd return Daisy's book, and that would be that. She could get over Natalie Weil, though she would never trust her again. Nora didn't have to trust her; she never had to see or speak to the platinum cockroach again. If they met over the dairy counter at Waldbaum's, in a nanosecond Natalie's frisky little cockroach heels would skitter her away behind a mountain of toilet paper until Nora was in the parking lot. Pleased by this image, Nora took the last spoonful of soup, crunched the final inch of toast, and stood up to rinse the dishes.

The telephone went off. Nora abandoned the dishes and hastened to pick it up before it awakened Davey. She said "Hello?" What followed froze her stomach before it reached her mind. A man ice cold with rage said something about an unimaginable breach of trust, something about an unspeakable intrusion, something else about devastation. At last she recognized the ranting voice as Alden Chancel's.

"And what I will never understand," he was saying now, "besides the unbelievable pretension of imagining that you could offer advice about writing, is your persistence in following a course you knew to be dangerous. Didn't it ever occur to you that your recklessness might have *consequences*?"

"Alden, stop yelling at me," Nora said.

"You refuse to listen to people who know better than you, you pick up an axe and start swinging. You burrow in like a termite and eat away at other people's lives. You are an outrage."

"Alden, I know you're upset, but—"

"I am not *upset*! I am *furious*! The person who is going to be upset is *you*!"

"Alden, Daisy wanted me to read her manuscript. She insisted on bringing it here, she wouldn't have let me say no."

"She has been laboring over this god-awful thing for decades, but until you came sidling up to her, did it ever occur to her to show it to anyone else? Daisy doesn't solicit comments on unfinished work. You weaseled into her like you weaseled into this family, and you planted a virus inside her. You might as well have killed her outright."

"Alden, I was trying to help her."

"Help? You picked up a knife and stuck it in her heart."

"Alden!" Nora shouted. "None of that is true. When Daisy called me to see how I was getting on with her book, I said it was a wonderful book. She kept twisting everything I said into an insult."

"This surprised you? You must be feebleminded. Daisy knows her book is a chaotic mess. It can't be anything else."

"I don't know if it's a chaotic mess or not, and neither do you, Alden."

"You're a destructive jackass, and you should be horse-whipped."

"*Alden!*" she shouted again. "Unless you calm down and try to understand what really happened, you're going to—"

Hair flattened on one side, clothes crisscrossed with wrinkles, Davey came into the kitchen and stared at her openmouthed.

"That's Dad? You're talking to my father?"

Nora held the telephone away from her ear. "I have to explain this to you," she said to Davey. "Your mother misunderstood something, and now your father's going crazy."

"Misunderstood what?"

Alden's voice bellowed from the receiver.

"You have to stick with me on this," Nora said. "They're both flipping out."

Alden tinnily bawled Nora's name.

She put the receiver to her ear again. "Alden, I'm going to say one thing, and then I'm going to hang up."

"Let me talk to him," Davey said.

"No!" Nora told him. "Alden, I want you to calm down and think about what I said to you. I would never deliberately hurt Daisy. Let things quiet down, please. I'm not going to talk to you until you're willing to listen to my side of the story."

"Nora, I want to talk to him."

"I hear my son's voice," Alden said. "Put him on."

Davey put his hand on the receiver, and Nora reluctantly surrendered it.

"He called me a termite. He called me a jackass."

Davey waved for silence. "What?" He clutched his hair and fell against the counter. His fingers burrowed farther into his hair, and he gave Nora an agonized look of disbelief. "I *know* that, how couldn't I know that?" He closed his eyes. Though he had clamped the receiver to his ear, Nora could still hear the clamor of Alden's voice. "Well, she says she wanted to help Mom . . . I know, I know . . . Well, sure, but . . . Yeah. Okay, fifteen minutes." He hung up the receiver. "Oh, God."

He looked around the kitchen as if to reassure himself that the cabinets, refrigerator, and sink were all still in place. "We're going over there. I have to wash my face and brush my teeth. I can't show up like I am now."

"Call him back and tell him we'll come tomorrow night. We can't go over there now."

"If we don't show up in fifteen minutes, he'll come over here."

"That'd be better," Nora said.

"If you want to piss him off even more." Davey came across the kitchen and glowered at her. "Where is that blasted manuscript, anyhow?"

"Under the bed."

"Oh, God." Davey hurried into the hallway.

39

BY THE TIME they reached the Post Road, Nora had described the conversations she had had with Daisy before and during her reading of the book, and by the time the barred iron fence in front of the Poplars came into view, she had finished telling him about the telephone call which had led to the present difficulty. What she had not described was the book itself. She also left out one other detail. Emitting noxious fumes, the suitcase sat in the trunk.

"She forced it on you," Davey said.

"If I hadn't agreed, she would have started screaming at me then."

"It doesn't sound like she gave you any way to say no."

"She didn't."

Davey turned into his parents' drive. Looking at the gray stone facade of the house, Nora experienced even more tension than the sight of the Poplars usually aroused in her.

"We ought to be able to make Dad understand that," Davey said.

"You're going to have to do most of the talking."

When they got out of the car, Davey looked up at the house and rubbed his hands on his trousers. For a couple of seconds, neither of them moved.

"Was the book any good, anyhow?"

"I have no idea," Nora said. "It's mostly a furious attack on Alden. His name in the book is Adelbert Poison."

Davey closed his eyes. "What's her name in the book?"

"Clementine."

"Clementine Poison? Am I in there, too?"

"Afraid so."

"What's my name?"

"Egbert. You almost never get out of bed."

"I want to get this over with and go home." He went to the back of the car and, grunting, lifted out the suitcase. "It must be one elephant of a manuscript."

"You have no idea," Nora said. "Davey, I was serious about what I said before. You're going to have to speak up, because if I say anything, Alden is going to yell at me."

"He'll yell at me, too." Davey closed the trunk and lugged the case toward the steps. "No matter what you think you want, Nora, you can't stay out here."

She and Davey slowly ascended the steps. He pushed the brass-mounted button beside the huge walnut door.

Maria opened the door before Davey's hand left the button. Evidently she had been posted at the entry. "Mr. Davey, Mrs. Nora, Mr. Chancel say you go to library." She gave the suitcase an uneasy glance.

"Is my mother in there, too?"

"Oh no, oh no, your poor mother she can't leave her room." Maria stepped back and held the door.

"When I was a little kid, he always chewed me out in the library." In the living room, a water stain twice the size of the suitcase darkened the carpet at the foot of an empty pedestal intended for a Venetian vase. A second large stain dripped down the wall beside the fireplace.

At the far end of the living room, the door to the library was closed. "Here goes nothing," Davey said, and opened it.

Wearing a blue pin-striped suit he had put on for the occasion, Alden stood up from a red leather chair at the far end of an Oriental rug bursting with violent blues and reds. "I think the first order of business is the surrender of the manuscript."

Davey walked toward his father as a man armed with a Swiss Army knife approaches a hungry tiger. Alden accepted the suitcase and put it down. He pointed at a tufted leather couch behind a leather-topped coffee table. "Sit."

"Dad—"

"Sit."

They moved around the table and sat. Alden placed himself on the chair and moved his foot to press a raised button set into the floor amid the fringes of the rug.

"Dad, none of this is—"

"Not now."

The door opened to admit Jeffrey.

"The object is now returned," Alden said. "Take it upstairs to Mrs. Chancel and place it in her hands."

Jeffrey bent to pick up the suitcase and turned around to carry it off as if he were disposing of a dead animal. On his way out, he gave Nora a dark, unreadable glance. The door closed behind him.

"You have nothing to say in this matter," Alden told his son. "Unless, that is, you encouraged either your wife or your mother in their actions."

"Of course I didn't," Davey protested. "I told Nora to stay away from Mom's work. I knew something terrible would happen."

"As it did. Now we must deal with the fallout. Your mother is in great emotional extremity. When I came home this evening, I found her weeping and hoarse from screaming. The living room was littered with broken glass. Maria was too frightened to cope, and Jeffrey, who must have understood that his role in this unhappy matter would rebound on him, was cowering in his apartment."

"Jeffrey?" Davey said. "What role did Jeffrey have?"

Alden ignored him. "Of course Jeffrey was responding to a request on the part of his employer. I have spoken to him, and we can all be sure that Jeffrey will never again be involved in any transaction of this kind. But nothing like this is ever going to happen again."

"What did he do?" Davey asked.

"He drove her," Nora said.

"Yes. He drove Daisy to the house you share with this viper."

"Please, Dad, don't call her names. I want you to understand what really happened. Mom called Nora and insisted that she read the book. She didn't give her a chance to say no."

"Really." Radiating contempt, Alden turned to Nora. "You have no free will? You don't have the excuse of being on our payroll, except indirectly, and you cannot be said to be a friend of Daisy's. Daisy doesn't have friends. Were you being a dutiful little daughter-in-law?"

"In a way, that's right," Nora said. "I did think I might be able to help her in some way."

"So you suggested that you read what she had written in order to offer editorial advice."

"No, just to give her someone to talk with about her book. Give her support."

"We see how well that worked. But you don't deny that this evil suggestion came from you?"

"I wanted to be helpful."

"I repeat. The suggestion was yours?"

"Yes, but Davey and I talked about it, and I agreed not to pursue it. Today Daisy called me and said it was crucial that I read her book and she was coming over right away."

"At which point you could have told her that you were too busy, or any one of a hundred other things."

"She wouldn't have accepted any excuses. If I had tried to back out, she would have been terribly insulted."

"You encouraged her mania instead of dampening it. But that wickedness is nothing beside the unspeakable obscenity of claiming that my wife is the author of Clyde Morning's and Marletta Teatime's novels."

"What?" Davey whirled to stare at Nora.

"She is," Nora told him. "In her book, there are those cross-hatched scuff marks and sentences starting with 'Indeed.' "

"Why didn't you tell me before this?"

"I forgot," she said, which was the truth. "There was so much else, it just slipped my mind."

Alden said, "Are you starting to see the kind of woman you married? Is a bit of light beginning to dawn?"

"He doesn't want you to know," Nora said. "He doesn't want anyone to know."

"Shut your vile mouth," Alden shouted, pointing at Nora. "Not only does this lie insult my wife, who considers herself an artist and has never even *read* one of our horror novels, it throws mud at my firm and myself. You are endangering our reputation and mine. It's scandalous, and I won't stand for it."

"Oh, God," Davey said.

"Davey, stop moaning and pay attention to me." Alden inhaled. "Your marriage was a mistake. This creature has brought discord into our family from the moment she appeared. She has injured you in ways you can't even begin to comprehend." Alden, who had begun to shout again, brought himself under control. "Maybe we share a taste for erratic women."

"I'm leaving," Nora said, and stood up.

"You generally run away when you hear the truth, don't you?"

"I don't take orders from you, Alden. Davey, let's go."

Looking only half awake, Davey began to stand up.

"Sit down," Alden said.

Davey sat down.

"I am going to make this very simple for you, Davey. I am presenting you with a choice. If you divorce this woman and get your life in order, you stay on at Chancel House and remain in my will. If you refuse to see reality and stay in your marriage, you're out of both your job and my estate. You'll have to find a way to support yourself—if you can, which I'm sorry to say I doubt."

"That's not a choice, it's an ultimatum," Nora said.

"As far as I'm concerned, you are no longer in this room. Davey, I want you to think about your decision. Think hard. Do you want to stay with the madwoman you married, or do you want the life you deserve? We would be more than delighted to have you back with us."

"Do you really mean all this?" Davey asked.

"You have a week to think things over. I want you to do the right thing, and I think you will see that I am acting in your best interests."

Nora said, "You're using your money like a club. If you stick to this sadistic plan, you'll wind up losing your son. Do you want that to happen?"

Alden stood up. "Davey, you may leave. I have to go upstairs and deal with your mother."

Davey obediently stood up. Alden marched to the door and held it open.

"Dad," Davey said.

"I'll speak to you next Sunday."

Davey moved toward the door. "Boy, are you going to be sorry," Nora said. Pretending that he could not see or hear her, Alden patted Davey on the back as he went through the door. Nora suppressed the impulse to slap away his hand.

Clutching a white cloth in a distant corner of the living room, Maria quivered and began to move toward the entry. Alden said, "My son can let himself out of the house." She froze in midstep.

"Good-bye, Maria," Nora said, but Maria was too terrified to speak.

40

THEY CAME OUT of the house into abrupt night. Davey went down a step and looked back at the door. "Maybe we should go back in."

"What for? He gave his speech."

"I guess you're right. He's too angry."

"Phooey. He's happier than he has been in years. He thinks he's got you right where he wants you."

Davey shook his head and went down the rest of the stairs, fumbling in his pocket. "Would you drive? I feel kind of scrambled."

Nora took the keys. By the time she got into the driver's seat and moved it forward, he was leaning back with his eyes closed, his body so limp it seemed lifeless. "Come on," she said. "He'll never go through with it. All you have to do is call his bluff."

"He doesn't bluff."

Nora started the car and drove toward the distant gate in a cocoon of darkness. After a moment she turned on the headlights. "Do you think he's really willing to cut you out of his life forever?"

"I don't *know*," Davey moaned.

"Of course he isn't," Nora said. "He's trying to bully you. This time, you can't let him get away with it." She turned onto Mount Avenue, accelerated, and the car shot forward like a nervous horse.

"What are you talking about?"

Usually an excellent, even a bold driver, Nora made a small adjustment to the wheel, and the Audi twitched sideways over the broken yellow line. She steered back into the proper lane and deliberately relaxed her hands. "The last thing in the world he wants is to lose you. That's what this is all about."

Davey moaned again, whether at his plight or her handling of his car she could not tell. "He's going to do everything he said."

"So what? After a couple of weeks he'll come nosing around to see how you're doing. If you don't have a new job, he'll give you your old one back. If you accept, he'll offer you a higher salary or a better position."

"Suppose he doesn't. Suppose it isn't a strategy."

An odd sense of familiarity as strong as déjà vu took possession of Nora. Hadn't she been reading a book in which a character presented an ultimatum much like Alden's? What scene, what book? Then it came to her: Alden had reminded her of Archibald Poison forcing Adelbert and Clementine to provide him with a grandson.

"Don't have an answer, do you?"

"What?"

"What happens if he really means it?"

"Every publishing house in New York would take you on. Some of them would hire you just to spite Alden. In fact . . ." She grinned sideways at Davey, who had flattened both hands on top of his head. "Screw the week. Call the people you know at other houses. Take the best offer you get, then go into your father's office and resign. He'll go nuts."

"No, he won't," Davey said. "Why would anybody give me a job? I edit crossword puzzle books. I send out form letters on behalf of the Hugo Driver Society. Besides, you don't know what's going on in publishing. Nobody quits anymore. It's not like the eighties, when people hopped around all over the place."

"Davey, you don't need this crap. Make some calls and see what happens."

They drove the rest of the way home in silence.

In the dark, Nora felt her way to the light switch and realized that Davey was still in the Audi. She spoke his name. He slowly left the car. When Nora opened the back door, he began moving zombielike to the front of the garage.

"It's going to be all right," she said, struggling to maintain her optimism. She closed the door behind them and saw him glance at the family room. "Come on upstairs," she said.

He dragged himself toward the stairs. Nora followed him into the kitchen, turning on lights as Davey advanced before her. "Let me make something for you," she said.

"Who can eat?"

Nora watched him take the bottle of kümmel from the shelf, select a lowball glass, and fill it to within an inch of the rim. He sat down opposite her and began revolving the glass on the table. At last he looked up at her.

"You're letting this get to you too much."

"There's one big difference between us, Nora. He's not your father."

"Thank God," Nora said, perhaps unwisely. "My father would never have treated you like that."

"I forgot, the great Matt Curlew was perfect. According to you, my father is the scum of the earth."

"I never said that," Nora protested. "I hate the way he treats you, and this ultimatum is the perfect example. He's using Daisy's tantrum to drive us apart."

"Gee, thanks. In case I don't understand what my father is doing, you have to explain it three or four times." He took a gulp of his drink, and a delicate shade of pink rose into his cheeks.

"Oh, Davey, maybe I've been talking too much, but he made me incredibly angry. And you were so silent."

"You keep forgetting he's my *father*. This guy you say has mistreated me all my life sent me to the best schools in America—something the sacred Matt Curlew never did for you—he gave me a job and pays me a lot more money than I deserve, he runs an important company—another thing Matt Curlew didn't do—and in case you forgot, see this table? He paid for it. He paid for everything in this house, including the light-bulbs and the toilet paper. I think he deserves some gratitude, not to mention respect."

"In other words, he owns you."

"He doesn't own me, he loves me. Even though I don't like some of the stuff he does, you can't order me to hate him."

"I don't want you to hate him," Nora lied. "But I love you, too, and I'd like you to get out from under his thumb." Davey lifted his glass and drank. "In a way he was right. You have to decide which one you want more, him or me. But if you choose him, you lose me for good, and if you choose me, you'll get him back in about a second."

"I'm married to you, not my father," he said.

"Thank God, I was beginning to get worried."

"But I don't want to lose either one of you. I think you're nuts to imagine that he'll change his mind."

"He won't change his mind, he'll just wait for another chance."

"How can you be so sure? If he cans me and I can't find another job, we're going to run out of money in about three months. Then what? Welfare? A cardboard box?"

"He'd never let that happen. You know he'd—"

"If I do get a job with another publisher, do you know what my salary would be? About a third of what I'm making now. We move out of here, okay, but all we could afford would be some dinky rathole of an apartment."

"Who says you have to work in publishing? The world is full of jobs."

"Don't you read the newspapers? Okay, maybe I could get a job as a clerk, but then we'd get half of a rathole."

"I can get a job," Nora said. "That way we get the whole rathole."

"God, it's like being married to Pollyanna."

"But you will make the calls, won't you?"

Davey pursed his lips and gave the refrigerator a considering glance. "Actually, there might be another way."

"What other way?"

"I could tell him that I'll move back into the house if he lets you stay here as long as you want. I think he'd go for it."

"We'd have lawyers all over us before you stopped talking. Good old Dart, Morris would build a wall between us six feet thick. How does that help us?"

"Once I'm there, I can talk to him, and if I can talk to him, I can soften him up. Sooner or later, he'll listen to reason."

"Davey, the Trojan horse."

"That's right."

Nora leaned back in her chair and looked at him steadily for what seemed a long time.

"I knew you wouldn't like it," he said. "But he has to calm down sooner or later."

"Davey, your father is doing his damnedest to turn you back into a child, and you want to give him a helping hand. Once he has you locked up in there, he's going to keep hammering away. By the time he's finished, you'll be wearing diapers and eating pureed carrots, and we'll be divorced."

"What a high opinion you have of me." His face had turned a brighter shade of pink.

"I know what happens when you're around your father. You turn mute, and you do everything he says."

"Not this time." He frowned at his glass, then looked back up at Nora in a way that seemed almost challenging. "Where did you find that garbage about my mother writing the Morning and Teatime books, in the astrology column?"

"It's true," Nora said. Davey grimaced. "I was reading along, and there they were, the crosshatch scuff marks and a sentence starting with 'Indeed.' I was flabbergasted."

"Not as flabbergasted as my mother. She's never even read novels like that. You heard my dad. Why would she do it in the first place?"

"Because Alden talked her into it. He thought he could make a lot of quick money out of horror novels."

He put on a disgusted expression and gazed at his drink. "Nora, even if this crazy idea came to you, why did you decide to tell her about it? Didn't you realize what would happen? I don't get how . . ." He threw up his hands.

"She was already ranting at me about spitting on her masterpiece, and I tried to rescue myself by telling her that it was so much better than those books. I guess I thought she'd be flattered."

"Smart," he said. "You throw a bomb into the living room and expect her to take it as a compliment."

Nora pushed herself away from the table. "I have to go to bed. Will you come, too?"

"I'm going to stay up. I won't be able to get to sleep for hours."

"But you will make those calls?"

"I don't need another bully in my life."

"I'm sorry, I won't say any more about it, I promise." Nora backed toward the door. "I'll see you later, then."

"I suppose."

She forced herself to smile as she left the room.

41

ABOUT HALF AN hour after Davey had left for work on Monday morning, Nora cried out aloud and woke herself up. Sweat covered her body and dampened the sheets. A small, trembling pool lay between her breasts. She groaned and wiped her face with her hands, then grabbed a dry portion of the top sheet on Davey's side of the bed and blotted her chest. "Holy cow," she said, an expression inherited from Matt Curlew. As soon as she wiped away the moisture, more of it rolled from her pores. Her body radiated heat. "Oh, hell," she said. "A hot flash." She had not known that you could get a hot flash while sleeping. An insect of some kind began crawling up her right thigh, and she raised her head to look at it. Nothing was on her thigh, but the sensation continued. Nora tried to rub it away. The invisible bug moved another two inches up her leg and ceased to be. She lay back on the damp sheets, wondering if phantom insects were common occurrences during hot flashes, or if this were some little treat all her own. A few seconds later the moisture on her body turned cold, and it was over.

After she had showered and out of habit put on a dark blue T-shirt, white shorts, and her Nikes, Nora realized that she had dressed for a run. She padded into the kitchen for a glass of orange juice and realized that she knew at least one person sufficiently down-to-earth not to mind being asked what some would consider an intrusive question. She pulled the telephone directory toward her and looked up Beth Landrigan's number. Only when she heard the telephone ringing did she wonder if she might be calling too early.

Beth's untroubled greeting dispatched this worry. "Nora, how nice, I was just thinking about you. Our lunch last week was so much fun that we should do it again. Just us, no noisy husbands. Let's cut loose and go to the Château."

"Great," Nora said. "I love the Château, and Davey never wants to go there."

"Arturo practically lives at the Château, but he never goes there for lunch, so we'd be safe. Wednesday?"

"You're on. Twelve-thirty?"

"Could you wait until one? I have a Japanese lesson at eleven-thirty on Wednesdays, and it lasts an hour."

"Sure," Nora said. "Wow, Japanese lessons. I'm impressed."

"So am I. I'm getting to speak it like a native . . . of Germany, unfortunately. Anyhow, you didn't call me to talk about my language difficulties. What's on your mind?"

"I wanted to ask you a question, and I hope it won't offend you."

"Fire away."

"It has to do with menopause."

"Offended, are you kidding? Everybody I know is menopausal, including me. It's all the rage. What's the question?"

"I had my first hot flash this morning."

"Welcome aboard."

"This strange thing happened. In the middle of it, I felt a bug crawling up my leg, but there wasn't any bug. I could really *feel* it. Did that ever happen to you?"

Beth was laughing. "Oh God, the first time that happened I almost jumped out of my skin. They tell you about the flashes, they tell you about night sweats and lots of other unpleasant things, but they never get around to telling you about the bug."

"I'm glad it's not just me."

"There's even a name for it. I can't remember the word, but it's something like masturbation. Maybe I'll ask my tutor what it's called in Japanese. On second thought, I'd better not. He'd probably run out of the house. He's an intellectual lad, but he probably doesn't know a thing about menopause."

"Probably knows a lot more about masturbation," Nora said, and the two women laughed and talked another few minutes before saying good-bye.

Cheered by this conversation and delighted by the promise of a friendship with funny, smart, levelheaded Beth Landrigan, Nora settled her long-billed blue cap on what she hoped was her own level head and left the house.

Forty-five minutes later, Nora heard the telephone ringing as she opened her front door, and she rushed up the stairs to answer it.

Sweat darkened the blue T-shirt and shone on her legs. She snatched up the receiver and said, "Hello."

"Nora, this is Holly. I'd like you to get down to the station right away. Can you do that?"

"Did Natalie say something?"

"We have a lot of things to talk about, and that's one of them. If you don't have a car, I can send a man for you."

"I came in from my run just this second, and I'm dripping. Let me take a quick shower and change clothes, and I'll be right in."

He hesitated. "Okay, but some folks here are going to get nervous if you don't show up soon, so make it as quick as you can."

"Holly, you sound so . . . kind of abrupt. Should I be worried about anything? My life has gone so haywire lately, I wouldn't be surprised."

"It isn't quite that simple," he said. "Do what you have to do and get here as fast as you can."

"I'll see you in twenty, twenty-five minutes."

"Come around to the back. This place is a zoo."

Nora said, "Okay, good-bye," and Fenn hung up without speaking.

42

NORA PARKED IN the slot Davey had taken behind Fenn's office, and saw through his window the back of his head and shoulders as he talked to Barbara Widdoes, who was wandering back and forth in front of his desk. Several other people, dark shapes in the back of the room, also seemed to be present. Through the humid air, Nora rushed past the row of police cars. She had put on a blue chambray shirt, jeans, and brown loafers. Wet hair clung to her ears. Her heart pounded.

It isn't quite that simple. What did that mean?

The back door swung open as she hurried up the concrete path. A red-haired, acne-pitted fullback in a tight uniform shirt stepped out. He looked from side to side before turning his corrugated face to her.

"Mrs. Chancel, okay? I'm going to take you down the hall to Chief Fenn's office, and we're going to have to do this fast. Things are real complicated here today."

"They're real complicated here, too," she said. The policeman gave her a neutral look. She moved through the door into relative coolness. A chaos of voices came from the front of the building. "This way," the policeman said, moving past her to walk briskly down the cement-block corridor. It occurred to Nora that she spent a great deal of time following men. They passed the door marked STATION COMMANDER and approached the metal door to the double row of cells. A vivid memory of Dick Dart's winking at her reminded Nora to look straight ahead, and she took in no more than that men in the tribal uniforms of police officers and lawyers crowded the passage between the cells. An intense, quiet conversation was going on among the lawyers, but she could not, and did not wish to, make out their words. The babble from the front of the station increased as she double-timed behind the officer. At last they came to Fenn's office.

The policeman knocked on the door and leaned in. He said, "Mrs. Chancel." Several people moved into different positions. A chair scraped. Fenn said, "Show her in."

Behind his desk Fenn was standing with his arms at his sides, looking at her in a distinctly unsmiling fashion echoed by Barbara Widdoes, who stood at attention at the far corner of his desk. Nora felt panic's icicle jab her stomach. Two men in dark suits and white shirts, one wearing black-framed sunglasses, stepped forward from the adjacent wall: Slim and Slam, the FBI men who had been in Natalie Weil's house.

"Hello, Mrs. Chancel," said Fenn. So Nora was no longer Nora. "I think you've met all the people in this room. Barbara Widdoes, our station commander, and the federal agents assigned to this case, Mr. Shull and Mr. Hashim." Mr. Shull, the taller of the two, wore the sunglasses. They gave him a vaguely hipsterish air which suddenly struck Nora as hilarious.

"Nice to see you again," she said, and a second of silence greeted her remark.

"I guess we can get this thing straight," Fenn said, and became Holly once again. "Let's try to figure out what we have here."

"About time," said Mr. Shull, speaking either to himself or to

Mr. Hashim, who crossed his arms and watched Nora take one of the chairs. Holly sat down, and Barbara Widdoes perched herself on the edge of the chair next to Nora's and put her fat knees and calves together. The two federal agents stayed on their feet.

Mr. Shull folded the sunglasses into the top pocket of his suit jacket.

"Well now, Nora," Holly said, and smiled at her. "The people in this room have differing opinions on various matters, one of them being what to do with you, but with your help we might work out a consensus. It's going to be important for you to be completely frank and open with me. Can you do that?"

"What did Natalie say?" Nora asked. Behind her, one of the FBI men made a little popping sound with his lips.

"Mrs. Weil said a lot of things, which we'll get to in a minute. I want you to go back to the time we met on her front lawn. We had a little discussion there that made me think you and your husband might be able to help us. Do you remember that?"

"I remember," Nora said. "We said we'd been there a couple of times."

"Six, if I recall. The last time being two weeks before her disappearance."

Nora nodded, silently condemning Davey for his self-serving lie.

"Do you want to stand by that statement, or have you had second thoughts about it?"

"Well, the truth is, I hadn't been in that house in over two years."

Barbara Widdoes clasped her hands on top of her knees, and Mr. Hashim and Mr. Shull slowly moved to the other side of Holly's desk.

"That agrees with what Mrs. Weil told us. If there was some point to misleading me as to the nature of your relationship with Mrs. Weil, I'd certainly like to hear it."

Nora sighed. "Actually, it was Davey, my husband, who said we'd been there all those times, and that we had dinner at her place two weeks before. Remember? He said we had Mexican food and watched wrestling on TV, but that was what we did about a month before we bought our house, the time we did go there."

"Do you have any idea why he'd say all that?"

She sighed again. "He has this, I don't know, habit of stretching the truth. Almost always, it isn't anything more than exaggerating—like decorating the facts."

"As I remember, you went along with this particular decoration."

"We'd just had a quarrel, and I didn't want to irritate him, especially by contradicting him in front of you. Now that I'm thinking about this, I thought you knew he was lying right away."

"Didn't take Sherlock Holmes," Holly said. "From our point of view, this made the two of you kind of interesting. So I decided to let you into the house and see if any other interesting things might come up."

"Are we getting to it now?" asked Mr. Shull. "Can we skip the cracker-barrel stuff?"

"It?" Nora looked at Mr. Shull, who smiled at her.

"There's something all of us find puzzling," Holly said. "It has to do with the physical evidence at the crime scene, and also a couple of remarks made by you and your husband. Do you recall your husband telling me that you didn't think Mrs. Weil was dead?"

"I don't know where he got that from. I was sure she was dead."

"Your husband's comment showed considerable foresight, wouldn't you say?"

"To tell you the truth, I think he was just trying to make me look foolish."

"Because of your quarrel?"

"I suppose."

"What was your quarrel about?"

"He thinks I don't show his father enough respect, and I think his father's a bully. We go round and round."

"The argument isn't important," said Mr. Shull. "If you don't get to it right now, I'm taking over."

"We're there," Holly said. He smiled at Nora again, but not vindictively, as Mr. Shull had done. "Let's get to when we were standing outside Mrs. Weil's bedroom. Do you remember the condition of the room?"

Nora nodded.

"Do you remember what I said to you?"

"I didn't have to go in if I didn't want to."

"Do you remember what I said right after that?"

"No, I don't. I'm sorry."

"I suggested that you might want to reconsider the idea that Mrs. Weil was not dead."

"I don't remember that," Nora said.

"You don't remember your response? It concerned the blood in the room."

"It did?"

"You said, 'Maybe it isn't her blood.' Do you remember now?"

"Oh, you're right, I did, I remember. But that just popped into my mind because of Davey, what he told you outside." She glanced up at Mr. Shull, who, smiling, looked back. "Of course it was her blood, it couldn't have been anything else." She turned to Holly Fenn. "It wasn't her blood? It was some kind of blood."

"Yes, it was some kind of blood."

"What kind?"

"Animal blood," Holly said. "Pig, most likely. You see why we're interested in your remark."

"I guess I do," Nora said. "But it was just this dumb thing I said."

"We're in sort of a quandary here, Nora."

"You're in a quandary," said Mr. Shull.

"So you weren't speaking with any real knowledge when you told me that the stains in that room might not have been Mrs. Weil's blood."

"None at all. But everything connected to Natalie's disappearance is strange."

"Yes, let's turn to Mrs. Weil at this point. Mrs. Weil said a lot of contradictory things, but she did give us one new bit of information."

Barbara Widdoes spoke for the first time. "You were aware that your husband and Mrs. Weil were having an affair, weren't you?"

"I only found out on Saturday afternoon."

"How did that happen?"

"Davey told me. He was very distressed about what had happened to her, and he blurted it out."

"You deny any involvement in Mrs. Weil's abduction and mistreatment?"

"It still isn't clear that abduction occurred," Holly said.

"Holly, you were in my office Saturday morning," said Barbara Widdoes. "You saw the woman go into hysterics when she saw Mrs. Chancel and stay that way until she was sedated. What occurred is pretty clear to me, and it ought to be clear to you, too.

Mrs. Chancel learned about her husband's affair, removed the victim from her bedroom, and kept her prisoner in her old stamping grounds, the former nursery. I'm sure you remember the incident. She detained her there until the victim managed to escape. I don't like all these coincidences. We have a pattern here, and I don't think Mrs. Chancel should be permitted to leave this station until she is read her rights and booked on a variety of charges."

"Somebody finally came out with it," said Mr. Shull.

"You want to arrest me?" Nora asked. "I didn't do anything to Natalie. I wouldn't treat my worst enemy that way." She looked across the desk at Holly Fenn. "Didn't you say Natalie contradicted herself? About me?"

"Didn't she, Barbara?" Holly said. "You think about this, too, Mr. Shull. We have a victim one step away from saying she was abducted by little green people from outer space. She says Mrs. Chancel forced her out of her house and locked her up in the old nursery, but is there anything in all that about the animal blood in the bedroom?"

He focused on Nora again. "Here's the situation with Mrs. Weil. The first thing she said when we went in there this morning was that you went to her house, threatened her with a knife, drove her to that building, and chained her up. Two minutes later we want her to repeat her story so we can take a statement, and she says she has no idea what happened to her. She looks back at the past week, and it's all a fog. She thinks she found her own way to the South Post Road but couldn't say how or why. So we write that down all over again and read it back to her and we say, Is that what happened? and she says, I don't remember. Then she lies there for a while, and after that she can respond to questions again, and we ask her about you, and she cries and says you took her to the building, and the whole thing starts all over again." He looked over at Barbara Widdoes. "Is that accurate? Have I exaggerated anything?"

"Holly, our victim is considerably disordered. But she keeps returning to the accusation, and that's enough for me. Give her another day or two, she'll be able to connect the dots."

"Barbara, Mrs. Weil keeps returning to the kidnapping story, yes, but she also keeps returning to wandering away by herself. Unless Mrs. Chancel gives us a confession and pleads guilty, we'll have to put our victim on the stand. Do you think we really have a case here?"

Barbara Widdoes glanced at Mr. Shull. "We have the grandmother of all motives, she had nothing but opportunity, and we'll come up with physical evidence in about ten seconds. In the old nursery where Mrs. Chancel took a child the first time she experimented with kidnapping."

Nora and Holly Fenn both began to protest, but Barbara Widdoes stood up and said, "I want to move on to the next phase. As soon as we process Mrs. Chancel, she can get in touch with her lawyer." She looked down at Nora. "In fact, your lawyer is probably here. Aren't you a Dart, Morris client? Leo Morris is waiting for charges to be filed against Mr. Dart, and we'll be doing that after we finish with you. If you like, I could advise him of your situation and tell him you have asked to see him."

Nora swiveled in her chair to look at Holly. "This is really happening? I'm going to be arrested for something I didn't do?"

"Barbara's our station commander. This is her call. Get your lawyer on it."

The entirety of her situation burst upon her, and its sheer, improbable hopelessness caused her to slump against the back of the chair and laugh out loud. Everybody in the room stared at her, exhibiting emotions from concern to contempt.

"Mrs. Chancel, are you all right?" asked Barbara Widdoes.

"I wish you knew what else is going on in my life."

Holly looked at his watch as he came around the side of his desk. "I'd let you use my phone to call your husband, but we're running out of time. I want to get you through our procedures before the Dick Dart circus gets out of hand. When we're done, I'll take you around to one of the interview rooms. You can use the phone there while you wait for Leo Morris."

She stood up.

"We need a little time with Mrs. Chancel, too," said Mr. Shull.

"How could I forget?" Holly placed his hand between her shoulder blades and urged her forward. "If we don't get this done fast, it'll take hours. Everything's going to go crazy around here in about ten minutes."

"Everything already has gone crazy," Nora said.

Holly opened the door with one hand while keeping the other on her back, moved her into the corridor, and followed immediately behind. Voices and the tramp of feet came from the front of the station, and before Barbara Widdoes and the FBI men were out of the office, a crowd of men burst around the corner and came hurrying toward them. At the front of the crowd, Officer LeDonne was a few paces in front of Leo Morris, who gave Nora a look of intense, unfriendly curiosity. Next to the lawyer, Dick Dart, in a gray suit and a white shirt but without a necktie, caught sight of Nora and grinned.

"What's this?" said Holly. "Cripes, they're taking him around the back to keep him away from the reporters. I'll send them back to the cells so we can take care of you first."

Officer LeDonne slowed down at the sight of Holly Fenn, and the other two men bumped into him.

"LeDonne, take this man back to the holding cell. I want my other business out of the way before we deal with him. Is that okay with you, Counselor?"

Leo Morris gloomily inspected Nora with his dark-rimmed eyes.

Nora tried to back through the door so that Dick Dart would stop grinning at her, but Barbara Widdoes pressed against her and gripped her arms.

"Davey Chancel's lovely spouse," Dart said. Nora closed her eyes.

Holly turned to LeDonne. "Take them back and keep the reporters away."

Before LeDonne could respond, a second group burst around the corner and filled the corridor, bawling out questions. Two or three men with video cameras on their shoulders forced their way to the front of the crowd.

"Everybody stop!" Holly shouted. "People, stop moving. LeDonne, wait a second before you lead the prisoner around the back. I want our station commander to take these men into her office. Mrs. Chancel and I will wait here."

Barbara Widdoes released her grip on Nora and squeezed out of the office, followed by the FBI men. They escaped down the corridor.

Holly raised his voice. "Media people, go back to the front of the station, this is not permissible, am I understood?"

"Nora-pie," said Dick Dart, and she looked up at the eyes sparkling in his grinning face.

Leo Morris and Holly Fenn suggested in their various fashions that Dart refrain from speaking, but he held Nora's eyes with his own and said, "What an interesting day." Then he wrapped his left arm around Officer LeDonne's neck and snatched his revolver from its holster so quickly that LeDonne was straining against the arm clamped over his throat, and the revolver was aimed at his temple before Nora was aware that Dart had moved at all.

LeDonne stopped struggling, and Holly stepped forward. The reporters fell silent. Dart tightened his finger on the trigger. "Now, now," he said. "Be a good boy."

Holly held up his hands. "Mr. Dart, you are in a police station. Release the officer and surrender his weapon."

"Do what he says," said Leo Morris. The lawyer's voice came out in a high-pitched squeak.

"Leo, isn't it obvious that I am in charge here?"

"Not for long," Holly said.

"Move against the wall."

Holly slowly began going to the other side of the hall, and Nora followed.

"No, Nora, you go back into the doorway." Dart pushed the gun barrel into LeDonne's head and walked the policeman toward her like a doll. LeDonne's face was mottled scarlet, and rage and panic filled his eyes. Nora glanced at Holly Fenn, who frowned and nodded. She stepped backwards.

"What do you think you're doing?" Holly asked.

"Simple exchange of prisoners," said Dart. "Followed by a daring escape and a successful flight, that kind of thing."

Holly opened his mouth, but before he spoke, Dart sent LeDonne reeling toward him and immediately materialized beside Nora. LeDonne collided with Holly, and Dart circled Nora's neck with his arm and pressed the barrel of LeDonne's revolver to her temple. The metal felt cold and brutal, and Dart's arm cut off her breath. "Ready?" he asked. "Bags packed? Passport in order?" He pulled her into Holly's office and slammed the door with his foot.

BOOK IV

GENTLE FRIEND

THE OLD MAN TURNED TO THE TREMBLING BOY AND SAID, "YOU HAVE ENTERED MY CAVE FOR A PURPOSE. IN THIS DARKNESS SHALL YOU LEARN ABOUT FEAR."

43

DICK DART BENT Nora back over his knee to turn the lock on the office door. "You and I are going out that window. If you give me any trouble I'll kill you on the spot. Do you understand?" She nodded, and he propelled her across the room. "Where's your car?" She pointed through the window at the Volvo. Holly Fenn shouted from the other side of the door, and the knob rattled. "I lead a charmed life," Dart said. "Open the window. Now. Jump out and get into the driver's seat. I'll be right behind you."

Nora's hands moved to the bottom of the window, efficient little hands, and pushed it up. She thrust her left leg through the frame and saw it outlined against the grass below, her slim leg encased in blue denim, her ankle, her narrow, sockless foot in a brown basket-weave loafer. Her leg seemed entirely surreal, suspended above the grass. What would it do next, this entertaining leg?

The entertaining leg strained toward the strip of green between the building and the concrete path, and, when she pushed her bottom over the windowsill, abruptly landed on the grass. Awkwardly, she pulled her right leg through the window. As soon as she hopped backwards, Dick Dart flew face first through the empty space, the revolver clutched to his chest. He got his feet under him in midair, landed so close to her that she felt the shock in the earth, spun her around, and jabbed the gun into her back.

"Keys," Dart said. She reached in her pocket and pulled them out as she trotted toward the car. "Get in and drive. *Go!*" He was already sliding into the passenger seat.

Sweating, Nora backed out of the parking space. "You want me to take that little road?"

"What a piece of shit you drive. We're going to have to

trade up. Faster, faster. When you get to the end of this street, turn left and get to I-95."

Nora slowed down for the stop sign at the end of the road, and Dart swore and held the gun to her head. Nora pressed the accelerator, rocketed past the stop sign, and turned left. Holding the gun to her head, Dart checked the rear window and whooped. "They're not behind us! Those dummies are still talking to the door!" He lowered the gun and slapped his knee. "Hah! They couldn't get through the reporters. Shows you how shitty the press in this country is." He grinned at her. A stench of sweat, oil, bad breath, and secret dirt floated out of him. "Brighten up, you're on the road with Dick Dart, it's an adventure."

Traveling at sixty miles an hour down a tree-lined, completely foreign street she knew she had seen dozens of times, Nora barely took in his words. Her hands had clamped to the wheel, her teeth were gritted, and her eyes felt peeled. She ran two more stop signs. Where *was* I-95?

"I knew we were connected the first time I saw you. I'm protected, I'm guided, and nothing bad is ever going to happen to me. What the fuck are you *doing*?" He rammed the revolver's barrel into her ear. "Stop, damn you."

Nora slammed her foot on the brake. Her hands shook, and her throat had constricted.

"Where are you going? Hardly the time for the scenic route." Metal ground into her ear.

"I don't remember how to get there," she said.

"Cool under fire, are we?" He glanced at the rear window, then removed the gun. "Back up past the stop sign, turn right. Go to Station Road, turn left. We want north, toward New Haven."

She backed up and made the turn toward Station Road. In the distance, sirens wailed.

"Step on it, bitch, you cost us about thirty seconds. Move it!"

Nora hit the accelerator, and the Volvo jolted forward. At the next stop sign, she nipped past a Dodge van just entering the intersection. The driver hit the horn and held it down. "Asshole," said Dart. "Blow these guys off, run around them."

Two cars proceeded down the road ahead of them. The sirens seemed to get nearer. A man in cycling shorts and a helmet rode a bicycle toward them in the center of the opposite lane. "What about—"

"Go through the dumb fuck."

Nora accelerated into the cyclist's lane. The man driving the car in front of them turned his head to stare, the surprise on his face nothing compared with the astonishment on the cyclist's. Nora honked. The man, who had something like five seconds in which to decide what he wanted to do, wasted two of them on wagging his index finger and shouting. Nora locked her elbows, stretched her mouth taut, and uttered a high-pitched, panicked whine.

"Bye-*byeee*," Dart sang.

The cyclist wrenched himself sideways and disappeared from the windshield a moment before being struck by the Volvo. Nora twisted her head. She had a momentary glimpse of man and bicycle entangled at the bottom of a shallow, grassy ditch, then blew past the second car at seventy miles an hour.

"Hope he broke his dumb neck," Dart said. "Good work, kiddo. But if you stop for the Station Road light, I'll shoot off your right nipple, am I understood?"

Nora blasted up a little rise, and at the top felt the car leave the road for a second before thumping back down. Dick Dart yipped and waved the revolver. Two blocks away, at the end of the empty road, the traffic light burned red. Cars streamed in both directions through the intersection.

"I can't do this."

"Poor baby, you'll miss that nipple. Gonna smart, too. But you know what?" He patted her on the top of her head. "I bet it turns green before we get there. If I win, you have to tell me everything you did to Natalie Weil."

"If you lose, we get turned into tomato soup." She roared through an intersection, and one block separated them from the traffic light.

"*C'est la vie.*"

Making a low sound in her throat, Nora straightened her arms and locked her elbows.

"Slow down a little for the turn." Dart sounded completely calm.

Nora slammed her foot on the brake, and her chest bumped the wheel. Dick Dart, who had been lounging back in his seat, slipped forward and down until his knees hit the dashboard. The car slewed halfway around and shot out into the intersection just as the light turned green. Dart pushed himself back into his seat and grabbed the door handle. Nora hauled on the wheel and brought the car into line.

"Hooray! Nora keeps her nipple," Dart shouted. "Personally, I'm very happy about that."

He's happy about that? Nora thought. She said, "I have to slow down—look at all these cars." A line of automobiles was strung out in packs of two and three on the long four-lane straightaway of Station Road.

"Pass 'em, crank it up and pass 'em, I'm not kidding. We get on the expressway, we're outta here. Then you can tell me about Natalie Weil."

The next four minutes were a blur of honking horns, startled faces, waving fists, and accidents averted only by the last-second recognition on the part of other drivers that, yes, the woman driving the Volvo wagon in the oncoming lane really did intend to keep moving. Several times, Nora's insistence on forward progress caused some minor fender damage to the vehicles of the drivers who had to accommodate the drivers who had to accommodate her. Finally, she crossed laterally over the right lanes in another outraged din and twirled onto the ramp to the northbound lanes of the expressway. What seemed to be four solid lanes of cars and trucks racing in the direction of Hartford and New Haven appeared before her. Nora closed her eyes and kept her foot down on the accelerator. When she opened them three long seconds later, she found herself about to smash into the rear end of a sixteen-wheeler with huge BACK OFF, DUMMY mud flaps. She backed off.

A state police car with a flashing light bar screamed toward them on the other side of the divider and flew past.

"You want to continue your criminal career, you could always get a job as a getaway driver. Now we want to move along a little less conspicuously before we turn into Cousin Lenny's."

This was the restaurant where Davey had convinced himself of her innocence while eating meat loaf submerged under ketchup.

"Why there?"

"Every cop in the state—fuck, every cop in the Northeast—is looking for this Swedish piece of shit. Nora, sweetie, if you're going to be a getaway artist, you have to learn how to think like one."

I'm not your sweetie, she thought.

"Okay, tell me what you did to Natalie Weil."

He was leaning against the passenger door, smirking.

"How do you know about her? You were in a cell for two days."

"When I wasn't discussing my *hobbies* with nauseating Leo Morris, that dishonest squirrel-eyed fart, I spent a lot of time talking with Westerholm's fine young officers. They told me about the *other* interesting matter taking place in the station. I heard that the station commander thought you kidnapped Ms. Weil and the chief of detectives thought you were innocent."

"They told you that?" asked Nora, aghast.

"If I happened to be the murderer of several of Westerholm's most notable bitches, a matter I strenuously denied, though not to you, of course, *if* I happened to be the celebrity in question, I would undoubtedly be interested in learning that I had inspired a copycat. Not just any old copycat, no no, but the delightful Nora Chancel, wife to pretty but ineffectual Davey Chancel. Needless to say, I was honored. Leo Morris, on the other hand, did not take the news as happily as I did."

"Leo Morris knew?"

"I told him. He was not delighted by the prospect of mounting your defense. In fact, he dislikes you, your husband, and the entire Chancel clan."

"Leo Morris?"

"Let us not wander from the point. You did it, didn't you? You beat the crap out of that little asshole. You locked her up and did nasty stuff to her."

Nora did not respond for a second, and then said, "Yes. I beat the crap out of her, and then I dragged her into a filthy room and did nasty stuff to her."

"What did she do to *you?*"

"She slept with my husband."

"Were you going to kill her?" Dart had become less offhand.

"I could hardly let her go, could I?"

"What an event! My opposite number, my female self! It doesn't mean I won't kill you, but I'm thrilled."

"Why break me out of jail if you're going to kill me?"

"If you're a good girl I might keep you around."

"You could travel faster on your own."

"What would you do if I let you go?"

"Get some money from a cash machine, I guess, and go to New York. Figure out a way to get in touch with Davey."

"You wouldn't last a day. You'd be standing in a phone booth a block away from the cash machine, trying to sweet-talk nebbishy Davey Chancel into sending you your favorite Ann Taylor dress, and all of a sudden a hundred cops would be aiming guns at you. Listen, you have to learn to think in a whole new way. In the meantime, I can keep you out of trouble."

"This is your idea of staying out of trouble?"

"This is my idea of staying out of prison," he said. "There's one other reason I want to keep you around for a while."

The skin on the nape of her neck contracted. She glanced sideways to see him leaning against the door, his hands folded on one knee and his mouth in a twist of a smile. "What would that be?"

"Unlike you, I have a plan. You have this quality—what to call it?—a sort of a peasant forthrightness, which I see opening necessary doors."

"Which doors?"

He placed his index finger to his smiling lips.

"What's this plan?"

"I suppose I can give you the broad outlines. We are going to go to Massachusetts and kill a couple of old farts. Here comes that disgusting restaurant. Turn into the lot."

Nora flicked the turn indicator and changed lanes. The huge sign, COUSIN LENNY'S FOOD GAS, floated toward them.

"Can I ask you another question?"

"Ask."

"How did you know I wear Ann Taylor dresses?"

"Nora, my love, I spend my entire life doing nothing but talking to women. I know everything."

"Can I ask you another one?"

"As long as it isn't tedious."

Nora turned onto the access road into Cousin Lenny's parking lot. "Holly Fenn said one detail about those murders was never released to the press. What was it?"

"Ah, my little signature. I cut them open and took out most of their internal organs. Let me tell you, you learn a lot more doing that than you do from anatomy books. Okay, go over there to the far side, and we'll wait for the right donor to come along."

Nora advanced down a row of parked cars to the far end of the lot. Concrete barriers stood before a line of green Dumpsters. Behind the Dumpsters a weedy field extended toward a distant windbreak of gaunt trees.

"Back in," Dart said. "We want to be able to see our prospective benefactors. Weigh their advantages and disadvantages."

"You know how to do that thing with the wires?"

"If I knew how to hot-wire a car, we'd already be *in* a car on our way to Fairfield. But we're not, are we, dearest Nora? No no, no no. We desire the keys to our new vehicle, and therefore we must take them from the hands of the temporary owner. We prefer an elderly person who trembles at the prospect of violence." He leaned forward, put his hands on the dash, and looked from side to side. His right hand held the revolver, index finger inside the trigger guard. "The constables are bound to show up soon. We need our benefactor, and we need him now."

"Don't kill anybody," Nora said. "Please."

"Little Miss Failed Executioner. Excuse me." He scanned the lot again. "Hello, hello. What do we have here? A definite possibility." A long, black Lincoln driven by an elderly man with a round, bald head moved toward them through the sunlight. Beside the driver sat a young woman with shoulder-length dark hair. "Daddy Warbucks and his trophy bimbo," said Dart. "Two-for-one sale."

"Everybody in the restaurant would hear the shots."

"And pretend they didn't."

The Lincoln backed carefully into the second of three empty spaces. "The man loves his vehicle," said Dart. He fastened his hand around Nora's wrist. "My side." He pulled her toward him and slid the hand holding the revolver into his jacket pocket.

"You're hurting me."

"Diddums widdums hurtum booboo?" He kept his hand around her wrist as Nora squirmed out of the car, and pulled her along behind him toward the Lincoln. "I start to run, you start to run, got it?"

She nodded.

Dart dragged her another two yards, then stopped moving. "What the hell?"

The bald man was gazing at the young woman with an expression of absolute innocence. The woman gestured; the man smiled. Pulling Nora behind him, Dart walked slowly toward the Lincoln. The woman smacked her palm against her forehead, opened her door, got out, and resolved into a fourteen-year-old girl in a tight white jersey, cutoff jeans, and platform espadrilles. Without bothering to close her door, she loped toward the entrance to the restaurant. In a seersucker suit, a starched white shirt, and a navy blue necktie, the old man sat peacefully behind the wheel of his car.

"Allah is good, praise be to Allah." Dart jerked Nora across the asphalt to the open door. He bent down and said, "Greetings."

The old man blinked his shining blue eyes at Dick Dart. "Greetings to you, sir. Can you help me?"

"I intend to do just that," Dart said. His hand hung suspended within his pocket, the revolver bulging the fabric.

"I do not remember who I am. Also, I have no idea where I am or how I got here. Do you know if this is my car?"

"No, old buddy, this one's mine," Dart said. The hand came out of his jacket pocket, and the bottom half of his suit jacket swung forward. "But I saw you come in, and I can tell you where yours is."

"Goodness, I do apologize. I can't imagine how I came to . . . I hope you didn't imagine that I intended to steal your car." The old man got out and stood blinking benignly in the sun. "I have a granddaughter, I know that much, and I seem to have the impression that she was with me just now."

"She went into the restaurant," Nora said.

"Goodness. I had better go in and look for her. Where did you say my car was?"

"Other end of the lot." Dart glared at Nora. "Can't miss it. Bright red Cadillac."

"Oh, my. A Cadillac. Imagine that."

Dart took Nora's hand and pulled her toward the open door. "Miles to go before we sleep. Better find your car before you look for your granddaughter."

"Yes." The old man marched a few paces across the lot, then turned around, smiling. "Miles to go before I sleep. That's Robert Frost."

Dart got into the Lincoln. For a moment, the old man looked disappointed, but the smile returned, and he waved at them before resuming his march toward a nonexistent red Cadillac.

Dart spun the car toward the expressway. "God, it's even full of gas." Then he snarled at Nora. "Why did you tell the old zombie about his granddaughter?"

"I—"

"Don't bother, I already know. You felt sorry for him. We're the two most wanted people on earth, and you take time off to do social work."

He moved smoothly out into the traffic. Cool air streamed from vents on the dashboard. "That was so beautiful I can't stay mad. *'Can you help me?'* I almost fainted. He asked me if this was his car!" Dart tilted back his head and released a series of laughs abrupt as gunfire. "He gave it to me!" More laughter. "See that big goofy face? Old fuck looked like a blank tape."

"You're right," Nora said.

"Check the glove compartment and find out his name from the no-fault slip."

Nora opened the glove compartment and stared at what was within. A fat, shiny, black leather wallet sat beside a tall stack of bills held together by a rubber band. "You're about to get a lot happier."

"Why?" Nora removed the wallet and the money from the glove compartment. "Oh. My. God. Look at that. How much is it?"

A wad of bills distended the wallet's money compartment. She riffled them, hundreds and fifties and twenties. Then she pulled the rubber band off the stack. "An amazing amount."

Dart yelled at her to count it. Nora began adding up denominations—twenty thousand in hundreds, a thousand in fifties, and five hundred in twenties.

"Twenty-one thousand, five hundred dollars? Who the hell was this guy?"

Nora raised a leather flap and looked at the driver's license. "His name is Ernest Forrest Ernest. He lives in Hamden."

Dick Dart started laughing as soon as he heard the name. "That was the great Ernest Forrest Ernest?" He gave a whoop of joyful disbelief. "This day is right up there with the greatest, most supremo, days of my entire life. You don't know who he is?" Ticking and rumbling with suppressed laughter, he slanted his head to look at her. "No, you're too out of it to know about him. Alden would know him, though. In the great man's presence, Alden Chancel would stain his Polo trousers."

"Who is he?"

"Twenty years ago he was the lieutenant governor of Connecticut, and now he's like the grand old man of the Republican party in this state. The distinguished pile of shit I'm proud to call my father worships him. What can I say? The man is a god."

At first faintly, then gaining in volume, the sound of a police siren came to them. Dart checked the rearview mirror, gave Nora a warning look, took the revolver out of his pocket, and held it in his right hand. "They can't know about this car already."

Nora clenched her fists and forced herself not to scream. Disgust, hatred, and fear washed through her body. She looked back, saw that the flashing light bar was still a quarter of a mile behind them, and turned to inspect Dick Dart, for the first time really to examine him with the intensity of her loathing. Two years younger than Davey, he appeared to be at least five years older. His skin had a gray pallor. Many shallow wrinkles creased his forehead. Two small, vertical lines, now barely visible beneath dark stubble, ran down his cheek. Above the stubble fine red veins rode on his cheekbones, and larger red and blue veins had surfaced at the base of his long, fleshy nose. Dick's liver had been putting in a good deal of overtime. His long, oval face would have had an unremarkable handsomeness except for the sneering self-regard which permeated its every inch. His eyebrows were permanently arched above his light, alert eyes, and his lashes were a row of pegs. An untrustworthiness, a sly disregard for rules and orders came like an odor from his face. If his hair had been recently washed, it would have been perfect prep hair, slightly too long, falling in soft, natural curves on the sides of his head, and flopping boyishly over his forehead. His wide, blunt hands had enjoyed a manicure a few days earlier. The tired-looking gray suit had clearly cost a lot of money, and he wore a gold Rolex watch. His old ladies had one and all found him delightful.

"What are you doing, taking a fucking inventory?"

"No," Nora said hastily. "I was thinking about something."

"Give me that wallet and the rest of the money."

The wallet lay forgotten in her lap, and she was still holding the bills. She stuffed as much as she could into the money compartment and handed it all to him, and he shoved it into various jacket pockets. "Thinking about what, exactly?"

"I was wondering how you got suspended during your freshman year at Yale."

"How did you—oh, the newspaper. Well, what I did, I beat up this pig of a townie. Lucky for me, she really was a pig, and all that ever came out of it was the suspension." He glanced at the rearview mirror. "Here he comes. He's gotta be looking for your crappy Volvo wagon."

Nora braced herself.

The screech of the siren grew louder and louder. If Dart started shooting, she would crouch in the well before her seat. Could she grab the gun away from him? Nora remembered how he had jumped through the window and discarded the notion of trying to snatch the gun. For a person in lousy shape, Dick Dart was amazingly strong. She was in excellent shape, and she knew she could not have made that catlike leap.

The patrol car slipped into the next lane and sped past. Neither of the policemen in the car glanced at them. In seconds, the flashing lights and the noise were five cars away, and Dart applauded himself with yips and hoots.

"Did I call it, or what?" He held the barrel of the pistol up to his mouth. "I want to thank the members of the Academy, my mother and father, all my colleagues at the office, you guys know who you are, Leo, Bert, Henry, Manny, I couldn't have done it without your support, and I must not fail to mention those lovely ladies, my special clients, Martha, Joan, Leslie, Agatha—love those eyes, Agatha!—dear JoAnne, who never fails to order the best Margaux on the Château's wine list, Marjorie, Phyllis, sparkly little Edna of the pudgy ankles, and last but not least, the enchantress Olivia, who makes liver spots look like beauty marks. I wish to thank the Creator for the gifts He has lavished upon this unworthy being, and the Westerholm police force for all their assistance. But above all, I wish to thank my good-luck charm, my rabbit's foot, my four-leaf clover, my shining star, my hostage and partner in crime, the delectable Mrs. Nora Chancel. Couldn't have done it without you, babe, you make the magic, you are the wind beneath my wings." He blew her a kiss with the revolver.

"You're even crazier than I thought you were," Nora said.

"Most people can never be their real selves, they could never let themselves do what you did to Natalie Weil. The difference between you and me is that when you call someone crazy you think it's an insult, and I understand that it's a compliment."

"I don't think I have a real self anymore," Nora said.

"I'll show you your real self," Dart told her. "Remember, you make the magic."

Nora groaned, but only inwardly, with her real self, and Dick Dart smiled his mockery of a human smile as he drifted onto the off ramp for the Fairfield exit.

44

DART STEERED THROUGH a series of narrow streets lined with two-story houses on small lots sprouting lawn furniture, plastic pools, and brightly colored children's toys. A dancing gleam kindled in his eyes. "Dear Nora, to me has fallen the serious responsibility of freeing you from your illusions." He rolled up to a stop sign and turned right onto nearly empty Main Street toward Fairfield's small business district.

"You'll see what I see, see through my eyes. I sense—I sense . . ." He turned into an angled parking spot in front of the hardware store and leaned toward Nora, his right hand three or four inches from her face, thumb and index finger nearly touching. "You're *this* close."

His odor coated her like a mist. Dart lowered his hand and leaned back, eyes gleaming and mouth compressed. Nora tried not to show the nausea she felt.

"I'm going into the hardware store," he said. An incandescent sliver of hope sparked into life within her.

"You're coming with me, Nora. Any appeal for help, any attempt to get away from me, will be dealt with very seriously." He was still gleaming, as if saying these words in this way amused him enormously. "I have to make some purchases, and as yet I cannot leave you alone in the car. This is a test, and if you fail it you'll certainly never have to face another one."

"You could leave me in the car," Nora said. "I won't go anywhere. How could I? I'm one of the two most wanted people on earth."

"Bad girl." Dart patted her lightly on the knee. "There will come a time when you are allowed various freedoms, but we have to know you will not abuse them."

He got out and walked around the front of the car to open her door. She said, "Aren't you afraid of being recognized?"

"I've been in this store maybe once. Besides, nobody has a good photograph of me." He leaned down smiling and whispered, "And should some unfortunate happen to recognize me, I have Officer LeDonne's mighty thirty-eight."

Dart wrapped a hand around her elbow and propelled her into the hardware shop.

The dim, cool interior instantly reminded Nora of the hardware stores of her childhood. At the far end a man in shirtsleeves stood between a wooden counter and a wall covered with battery displays, coiled hoses, ranks of scissors, rolls of tape, and a hundred other things. On the soft wooden floor between the counter and the front door stood rows of shelves and bins, each as chaotic as the rear wall. Matt Curlew had drifted entranced through such places. Unlike Matt Curlew, Dick Dart moved quickly through the aisles, snatching up ropes, two differently sized screwdrivers, a roll of duct tape, pliers, a hammer. He had released Nora's elbow as soon as they entered the store, and she trailed after him, noting his purchases with increasing alarm.

"You could set all that on the counter and let me begin totaling it up," said the clerk. When he glanced at Nora, whatever he saw in her eyes caused him to step back from the counter.

"Great idea," said Dart, and moved to the counter. "Need some items from your knife case. Open it for me?"

"Sure thing." The owner glanced again at Nora but now apparently saw nothing to alarm him. Pulling a fat key ring from his pocket, he led Dart toward the glass case. He unlocked the metal ratchet at the front of the case, slid back one of the panels, and said, "Anything in particular?"

"Just a good knife or two."

"We're no fancy knife shop, but I got some good German stag handles, that kind of thing."

"I like a nice knife," Dart said.

The man stepped back, and Dart slid the panel farther along and reached in to pick up a brutal-looking, foot-long knife with a curved blade and a thick black handle.

"You got one serious knife there," said the owner.

Dart scuttled along the case to select an eight-inch knife which folded into a handle carved from an antler.

"That's the one I told you about, that one there's a real collectible."

"Pop for one more." Dart stood up to inspect the smaller knives at the top of the case. Humming to himself, he danced his fingers over the glass without actually touching it. After a few bars, Nora recognized the song he was humming, "Someone to Watch Over Me." "Here we go." He bent down to remove a short, double-edged knife with a utilitarian black handle. "Got a sheath for this?"

"A belt sheath? Yep."

The owner placed the knives and a black leather case beside the other purchases, looked up the tax on a chart, and added the column of numbers. "Well, sir, that comes to two hundred twenty-eight, eighty-nine. Cash or charge?"

"Hey, I'm an old-fashioned American, cash on the barrelhead." Dart took the bulging wallet from his jacket pocket and put two hundred and forty dollars on the counter.

The owner grunted and began bagging the items on the counter.

"Separate bags for the knives," Dart said.

"Didn't do too badly, Nora baby." Dart was driving up a side street toward the Fairfield railroad station, the smallest of the knives concealed under his jacket in the leather sheath, which he had clipped to his belt. The other two knives were in a bag on the backseat, the rest of the purchases in the trunk. "You gave that old dodo one hell of a look, though. Have to watch out for that, have to control yourself."

"I did control myself," Nora said. "What are you doing? I don't suppose we're going to take the train."

"Daddy is looking for something, and, wonder of wonders, I believe he has just found it. You're a fucking rabbit's foot." He slid past a dark blue sports car with tinted windows and swerved into the curb next to an empty lot. "Get out of the car and stand next to me."

She joined him at the back of the Lincoln. While Dart leaned into the trunk and removed a screwdriver from the bag, Nora glanced up and down the street, praying for the arrival of a police car. Before them, on the other side of a long, narrow parking lot, lay the railroad station; back toward Main Street, beyond the empty lot, stood the flowered walkway and green-striped canopy of a restaurant called Euphemia's Diner.

Dart closed the trunk without latching it. "Stand between me and the street. Don't let anybody see what I'm doing." He grinned at her, and with his right hand reached around to the small of his back.

"What are you going to do?"

"Buy a little time." He led her toward the rear of the little blue car. "You're not going to take a stupid pill, are you?"

"No," she said. A small, bright blade projected from his palm.

He knelt beside the rear bumper and jabbed the blade into the tire. The blade slipped out, and the tire hissed and softened. "If anybody happens along, we're inspecting our flat. Don't look at me, watch the street and tell me if anybody comes along." He slipped the little knife back into its sheath.

Nora moved to shield him from the sidewalk. "I don't get what you're doing."

"Swapping plates. It's not as easy as it used to be. All these idiots treat their plates like oil paintings. This was the first one that didn't have a *frame* around it." The screwdriver clicked against metal. Dart grunted, then began humming "Someone to Watch Over Me" again. Heat poured down on them. The police car for which Nora continued to pray neglected to appear.

"Now the front." She followed him and stood in the road as metal rubbed against metal. "Want to hear a little-known fact about our old pal Ernest Forrest Ernest? This great man fancied the Nazis during the Second World War, though it was of course a deep dark secret, and afterward he was part of a splendid little group of ultrawealthy men who tried to promote Fascism right here in our good old cradle of liberty. . . . All right!"

He went two paces to the rear of the Lincoln and started to remove the screws in its license plate. "They didn't use the nasty F-word, of course. They called it the Americanism Movement, which lasted about five minutes until Joe McCarthy came along and put them in his pocket and they had to pretend they liked it. But the point of this"—he slapped the other car's plate into position and fit the screws into place—"is that little Davey's grandfather was behind the whole show."

Nora remembered the passages about Fascism in the chapter of Daisy's book she called "the fantasia."

"Lincoln Chancel was the badass's badass."

"So I gather."

Dick Dart looked up at her in amused surprise. "I don't think Davey knows a quarter of the stuff the old man did."

"He knows he wasn't a saint."

Dart stood up, went to the front of the Lincoln, and knelt down while Nora posted herself to shield him from the empty street. She had been in Fairfield perhaps thirty times during the two years of her marriage, she had shopped on Main Street for her jeans and Ann Taylor dresses, she had bought veal chops and crown roasts from the excellent butcher, enjoyed lunches and dinners at three different restaurants, and in all that time, it came to her now, she had never seen a single policeman.

"We behold an unhappy degeneration in the Chancel line," Dart said. "Lincoln Chancel wouldn't have used Davey for a toothpick. Lincoln was one dangerous son of a bitch, and Davey doesn't have the guts of a teddy bear. Alden is sort of halfway between them, a thug and a bully, but not a *real* thug or a *real* bully."

"He has his moments," Nora said.

"You never met the real thing. Alden thinks he's a big shot and he prances around talking tough, but I think his old man cut his nuts." He stood up and motioned for Nora to follow him to the rear of the sports car.

They were walking side by side down the street like any ordinary couple. The man beside her looked like a stockbroker or lawyer after a rough night, and she probably looked like his wife.

The old plate came off, the new one went up. "If Alden Chancel hadn't inherited Chancel House, what would he be doing? He has one great editor, Merle Marvell, and a lot of blockheads. One dead writer, Hugo Driver, keeps the company solvent. His royalties bring in about forty percent of the company's total revenue, and almost all of that is generated by one book, *Night Journey*. Alden's a disaster. Right now he's negotiating a deal to sell the company to a German publisher—to get a lot of money out of the business before he runs it into the ground. The only reason the German publisher is interested is *Night Journey*."

"Alden's trying to sell the company? How do you know about this?"

"We're the lawyers, baby. Remember? As we go along putting dents in dear old Dart, Morris, I am going to give you an education. Before I begin, I have to *do* something, but after that, tutorials in the real world are in session. Okay, let's wrap up this tedious bullshit."

He stood up and shook out his arms, then produced a wrinkled,

distinctly unclean handkerchief from a trouser pocket and
swabbed his forehead.

"He's selling the company?"

"Trying to." Dart pulled her up the street and knelt in front of
the Lincoln. "I'm going to tell you something little Davey never
heard about his grandfather. The guy wasn't born rich, you know,
he got there by himself. Did many, many nasty deeds. Even murdered someone once."

"I don't believe that," she said, although what she knew of Lincoln Chancel nearly made it possible.

"Old Lincoln was a brute, baby. My sainted daddy, who has
been privy to the real history of the Chancels for the last forty
years, told me in a moment of imperfect sobriety that Lincoln
Chancel once tore a man to pieces—turned him into hamburger
with his bare hands. Lincoln was caught short playing too many
ends against the middle, threat of scandal, and the only way out
was the removal of one man. He arranged a confidential appointment with the guy, canceled it on the morning of the day they were
supposed to meet, and showed up unannounced around the time of
the meeting he canceled. Nobody knew he was supposed to be
there, and the guy was all alone. Got away scot-free."

Dart said, "Good for another day, anyhow. Let's go to Main
Street and pick up a couple of bottles."

45

POLICE CARS SWEPT past them, most of them silently, several
flashing and wailing. Dart amused himself by pointing the
revolver at drivers and passengers in other cars and pretending to
shoot them. Hartford loomed up alongside the expressway, and
Nora sped upward to fly through the office towers at seagull
height. Dart lolled, half in his seat, half against the door, and
sneered his smile at her.

"Why do you have your window down? What happened to air-conditioning? Save-the-planet kind of thing?"

"I don't want to pass out from your stink."

"My stink?" He opened his jacket and sniffed his armpits. "You're probably having some feminine disorder."

"You hate women, don't you?"

"No, I hate my father, women I actually adore. They're physically weaker than men, so they had to work out a million ways to manipulate them. Some of these stratagems are fantastically ornate. Guys who don't understand that women are incapable of psychological straightforwardness don't stand a chance. One morning they wake up beside some cash register who has a big fat diamond ring and a gold band on her finger, and she controls the pussy. If he wants any, he has to hand over the credit cards. If he complains, she makes him feel so small and selfish he makes her breakfast for a week. But is he allowed to say no? Uh uh, baby. And think about this. She can hit him, that's fine. Brute like him deserves to be hit. But can a man hit a woman? If he does, she whips his ass in divorce court and takes all his money without even having to give him sex. He's completely under the control of a capricious, amoral being with a tremendous capacity for making trouble. Remember the Garden of Eden? Great place until this woman came along, whispering, *Come on, take a bite, the Big Guy isn't paying any attention.* Been the same way ever since. If the woman's really good, this poor sucker with a noose around his neck, a perpetual hard-on, and someone else's hand in his pocket is convinced that he's running the show. He's so tangled up he thinks his wife is this sweet little thing who isn't very good at practical matters but sure is great, damn it, a goddamned pearl for putting up with him. Once a year she gives him a blow job, and he's so grateful he races out to buy her a fur coat. Those fur coats in a restaurant, where women don't want to put them in the check-room? Every single one of those coats? A blow job, and every woman in the place knows it. And here's something else—the older the woman, the better the coat."

"And you claim to adore women," said Nora.

"I didn't make this stuff up. Spent the last fifteen years of my life taking my Marthas and Ednas and Agathas to the Château and listening to them talk. I hear the things they're telling me and I also hear what they're *really* saying. And sometimes, Nora, more often than you would imagine, they are the same thing. An eighty-five-year-old woman who has had three face-lifts, two husbands, at least one of them seriously rich, both currently dead, also a couple of glasses of wine with a rakish, good-looking young lawyer, is likely to let down her guard and tell you how she got through a long and pampered life without ever working a single day. Once they see that I already know how it works, they can start having a good time. These ladies are generally pissed off, they used to be fascinating, the whole male world used to stand in line to get into their pussies, and all of it went away when they turned into old ladies. Husbands are dead. Nobody on earth is interested in listening to them. Except me. I could listen to them all day long. Love those soft, elegant, smoky voices full of hidden razor blades, but even more I love their stories. They're so corrupt. They don't even begin to know how corrupt they are, can't, don't have the moral machinery for it. The only thing they regret is that the good part didn't last another ten years, so they could have gotten their hooks into one more rich sucker who got off on hearing about his great big cock. I love the way they look—hair all stiff but made to look fluffy and soft, makeup put on so well you can hardly see their wrinkles, their hands covered with rings so you won't notice the brown spots and the veins and lumpy knuckles. Nobody can tell me I don't like women."

"Did you sleep with your old ladies?"

"Haven't had sex with a woman under sixty-five in at least nine or ten years. No, sixty-two, I forgot about Gladys."

"But you *killed* women," Nora said.

"Wasn't personal."

"It was to them," Nora said.

"I was killing clients, understand? Every time I murdered someone, another chunk fell off the old man's business. Along about the time I did Annabelle Austin, that book agent, he spent two days saying, Couldn't somebody else's clients get killed? If I could have done another ten, he'd be tearing his hair out."

"But you always chose women clients, and always a certain kind of woman."

Dart's eyes went flat and two-dimensional.

"Oh. You didn't like the way they lived."

"Could put it that way," Dart said. "Those people went around acting like men."

His tone gave her an insight. "Did they behave well around you?"

"The times they came into the office, when I came up to them and said something flattering, they could barely bring themselves to speak to me."

"Unlike your old ladies."

"I would never have murdered my old sweethearts . . . unless they were the only clients left."

"What about me?"

He smiled, slowly. "Do you mean, am I going to kill you?"

Nora said nothing.

"Dear Nora-pie. We'll know more after our reality lesson."

"Reality lesson?"

He patted her knee. "Lots of motels in Massachusetts. We want one with a nice big parking lot."

46

ON THE FAR side of Springfield, Dart pointed at a three-story, sand-colored building with white balconies outside the windows. "Bingo!" It stood at the far end of a half-filled parking lot the size of a football field. A vast blue-and-yellow sign stretching across the roof said CHICOPEE INN. A Swiss ski lodge called Home Cooking faced the lot from the left. "Get over, we don't want to miss the exit."

Nora crossed two lanes and left the highway. "Forgot I was talking to Emerson Fittipaldi," Dart said.

She drove a short distance down the street and turned into the lot.

"Darling, we'll always have Chicopee. And home cooking, too! Don't you love home cooking? Mom's famous razor blade soup, that sort of thing?"

"Should I park in any particular place?" Nora was weary with dread.

"Right in the goddamned middle. Do you have some favorite alias, my dear?"

"Some what?" She drew the Lincoln into an empty space approximately in the center of the lot.

"Need new names. Have any suggestions, or shall I choose?"

"Mr. and Mrs. Hugo Driver." She closed her eyes and slumped back against the seat. "The Drivers."

"Love the concept, tremendously appropriate, but using the names of well-known people is usually an error." He turned sideways and tried to reach the bags on the backseat. "Hell." Dart knelt on his seat and leaned over, almost touching the top of the car with his buttocks. Nora opened her eyes and saw the pocket containing the gun hanging a foot away from her face. She considered the energy and speed necessary to snatch it out of his pocket. She wondered if she knew how to fire a revolver. Dan Harwich had instructed her in the operation of the safety on the pistol he had given her, but did revolvers have safeties, and if so, where were they? By the time this baffling question had occurred to her, Dart was pulling himself and two brown paper bags back over the top of the seat. He pushed the bag containing the bottles into her lap. "You carry this one and the one in the trunk. One more thing: please refrain from giving people these bone-chilling looks of anguish, okay? World loves a happy face. Come to think of it, I don't think I've ever seen you smile, and I smile at you all the time."

"You're having a better time than I am."

"Smile, Nora. Brighten up my day."

"I don't think I can."

"Rehearsal for the wonderful smile you're going to give the moron behind the desk."

Nora faced Dart, pulled back her lips, and exposed her teeth.

He gave her a long, considering look. "Call on some of the old fire, Nora-pie. Let's see the blazing figure who beat the shit out of Natalie Weil."

"Too scared to come out."

He gave an exasperated sigh. "This is a *project*." He made the sign of the cross over his heart.

"A project?"

"Inside." He took the keys and got out. She waited for him to pull her across the seat, but instead he walked to the front of the car and looked back at her, eyebrows raised. Nora left the car and looked around at a vibrant blur. She blotted her eyes on her sleeve and moved toward Dart.

A young man with shoulder-length blond hair lowered a half-liter Evian bottle to an invisible shelf in front of him, smiled across the desk as they came into the chill of the lobby, and stood up. His lightweight blue blazer was several sizes too large for him, and the bottoms of the sleeves were rolled. A silver tag on his lapel said that his name was Clark. "Welcome to the Chicopee Inn. Can I help you?"

"Need a room for the night," Dart said. "Sure hope you got one for us. Been driving two days straight."

"Should be no problem." His eyes moved to the bags they were carrying, then from Dart to Nora and back again. His smile vanished. He sat down in his chair again, pulled a keyboard toward him, and depressed random-seeming keys. "One night? Let me set you up, and then we'll take some information." He brushed his hair back with one hand, exposing a circular gold ring in his ear. Keys clicked. "Three twenty-six, third floor, double bed. Is that okay?" Dart agreed. Nora slumped against the counter and regarded the bright, unreal green of the carpet. "Name and address, please?"

"Mr. and Mrs. John Donne, Five eighty-six Flamingo Drive, Orlando, Florida."

At the boy's request, he spelled out Donne. Then Dart spelled Orlando for him. He supplied a zip code and a telephone number.

"Orlando's where they have Disney World, right?"

"No need to leave America, you want to see exotic places."

"Uh, right. Method of payment?"

"Cash."

Clark paused with his hands on the keyboard and looked up. He flicked back his hair again. "Sir, our policy in that case is to request payment in advance. The rate for your room is sixty-seven dollars, forty-five cents, tax included. Is that all right?"

"Policy is policy," Dart said.

Clark returned to the keyboard. The tip of his tongue slipped between his lips. A young woman in a blazer identical to his came through a door behind him to his right and gave Dart a double take as she walked past the desk to another door in the wall to his left.

"I'll get your keys and take the payment." He opened a drawer to remove two round-headed metal keys. He put them into a small brown folder and wrote 326 in a white space at the top of the folder. The boy stood up and slid the folder across the desk. Dart placed a hundred-dollar bill beside it. "You can swing your car right up in front here to bring in your bags," the boy said, his eyes on the bill.

"Everything we need in the world is right here."

The boy picked up the bill and said, "One minute, sir." He went through the door from which the young woman had emerged.

Dart began humming "I Found a Million-Dollar Baby."

A few seconds later, the boy reappeared, smiled nervously at Dart, unlocked a cash drawer, and counted out change.

"Good business demands vigilance," said Dart, shoving the bills and coins into a trouser pocket.

"Yeah. I should explain, we don't have a restaurant or room service, but we serve a complimentary continental breakfast from seven to ten in the Chicopee Lounge just down to your right, and Home Cooking—right outside in our lot—they give you good food there. And checkout is at twelve noon."

"Point me toward the elevators," Dart said. "You behold a pair of weary travelers."

"Past the lounge, on your left. Enjoy your stay."

Nora jerked herself upright, and Dart took a step back from the desk, opening a path to the elevators. She plodded past him, trying not to hear the cajoling voices in her head. The bottles took on weight with every step. She barely noticed the small, open room outfitted with couches, chairs, and tables into which Dart slipped to extract a folded newspaper from a rack. He placed a hand in the small of her back and urged her toward the elevators, where he punched a button. "Every little bird must find its branch."

Upstairs in a hazy corridor, Dart fit one of the keys into the lock of room 326. "Nora, look." It took her a moment to notice the three round holes, puttied in and clumsily retouched with paint, in the brown door. "Bullet holes," Dart said.

Nora walked in. Every little bird must find its branch. You didn't have to leave America to see exotic places. As she moved past the bathroom and the sliding panel of a closet, she heard Dart close the door and slide a lock into place. A window leading onto a narrow white balcony overlooked the parking lot. She put her bags on the table. Dart brushed past her, clicked the lock on the window, and moved a metal rod to draw a filmy curtain. He shrugged off his jacket, hung it over the back of a chair, and took his knives from their bag. "Lookee, lookee." He was pointing at discolored blotches on the lampshade. "Bloodstains. *Our* kind of place."

Nora glanced at the queen-sized bed jutting out into the room.

Dart unpacked the purchases from the hardware store and arrayed them in a straight line on the table. He moved the coils of rope from first place to second, after the roll of duct tape, and made sure everything was straight, bottom ends lined up. "Forgot scissors," he said. "We'll survive." He laid the two larger knives at the end of the row, then fussed with the alignment. "Shall we begin?"

She said nothing.

He picked up a vodka bottle, untwisted the cap, and swished vodka around in his mouth before swallowing, then recapped the bottle and set it gently on the table. "Take your clothes off, Nora-pie."

"I don't feel like doing that."

"If you can't do it yourself, I'll have to cut them off."

"Please," she said. "Don't do this."

"Don't do what, Nora-pie?"

"Don't rape me." Soundlessly she began to cry.

"Did I say something about rape? What I said was, take off your clothes."

She hesitated, and through her tears saw him pick up the larger of the two knives, the one Matt Curlew would have called an Arkansas pigsticker. He stepped toward her, and she began unbuttoning her shirt. A small, separate part of her mind marveled at the quantity of tears spurting from her eyes. She placed the blue shirt uncertainly on the chair and glanced at the blurry figure of Dick Dart. The blurry figure nodded. Nora undid her belt, unbuttoned her jeans, pulled down the zip, and stepped out of the brown loafers. Hatred and disgust penetrated the cloud wrapped around her emotions. She made a small, high-pitched noise of outrage, pushed down her jeans, and, one leg after the other, stepped out of them. She draped the jeans over the arm of the chair and waited.

"Not really *into* underwear, are you? Dear me, look at that bra. Your basic no-frills Maidenform Sweet Nothings, isn't it? A thirty-four B? You should try one of those new uplift bras, not just an underwire, but the new kind, do wonders for you, give you a nice contour on top. Well? Let's unhitch Nora's pretty mammaries, shall we?"

Nora closed her eyes and reached up to unhook the bra, which was, as Dart had said, a Maidenform Sweet Nothings, size 34 B. She let the straps slip backwards over her shoulders, exposing her breasts, pulled it away from her body, and dropped it onto the chair.

"Don't really hang up our clothes at home, do we? You've got, ummm, you've got an overstuffed chair with layers of T-shirts and blouses draped over the back and jeans folded on the seat. No, I take it back. For you I see a nice long couch, hardly visible under all those clothes. What you do is grub around in these clothes, wear them a few times, and then dump them into the hamper and start all over again."

This was, in fact, exactly what Nora did, except that she did it less consistently than Dart had suggested.

"Oh my, look at that. Hanes Her Way undies—purple, what's more, to, go with your tired white Maidenform. Nora, you shouldn't buy your dainties at the drugstore. At the very least, your bra and undies should match. With your body, you'd look good in Gitano. They make pretty matching bras and underpants, and they're cheap. You want to spend more money, try Bamboo or Betty Wear. Myself, I'm crazy about Betty Wear, it's nice stuff. Listen, do yourself a favor and stop throwing out those Victoria's Secret catalogs. I know you think they're cheesy, but if you'd just *look* at them at least as thoroughly as Davey undoubtedly does, you'd see that they're very useful. Above all, you owe it to yourself to look at *Vogue* now and then. Great magazine, I never miss an issue. I bet you've never even bought one."

"I bought one once."

"When? In 1975?"

"Around then," she said, her arms folded over her chest and her hands on her shoulders.

"Written all over you, especially those Hanes Her Way spanky-pants. Should take better care of yourself. Take the dumb things off."

She pushed down the waistband on her underpants, shoved them to her knees, and stepped out.

"Nora's got a great big bush! God, Nora, you've got this *clump,* get out the Weedwacker!"

She had gradually been convincing herself that no man who spoke in this way to a woman would rape her—a rapist would never advise the purchase of Betty Wear, much less be able to identify a Maidenform Sweet Nothings bra and Hanes Her Way underpants—but his next words undermined her shaky hope that Dart wished to do no more than inspect her body.

"Sit on the bed," he said.

She walked to the end of the bed as if over broken glass and sat down with her hands on her shoulders and her legs clamped together. A sudden mental flash of Barbara Widdoes's plump knees and fat calves above her heavy shoes brought with it the surprising thought that Barbara Widdoes was probably a lesbian.

"Have to restrain you for a while," Dart said, and picked up one of the coils of rope to slice off two sections, each about four feet long. These he carried toward Nora, along with the knife and the roll of duct tape. "Might be a little uncomfortable, but it won't actually hurt." He knelt in front of her, looked up into her eyes, winked, and wound one of the sections of rope around her ankles. "You have a nice body," he said. "Maybe just the teeniest bit stringy, and your skin could use a moisturizer." The rope bit into her skin, and she said, "Ouch."

"Doesn't pinch, isn't tight enough," Dart said, tying the ends of the rope into an elaborate knot. He put his hands on her knees and looked directly at her breasts. "Small, and they kind of sag, but still pretty, if you want my opinion." He reached for the tape, unpeeled a strip three feet long, tore it off the roll, and wound it over the rope around Nora's ankles. Then he stood up, touched her chin with the tips of his fingers, and tilted her face toward his. "You're the kind of person who thinks she's above makeup, apart from a little lipstick now and then, but you're wrong. You ought to try Cover Girl Clean Make-up, or maybe Maybelline Shine Free. That's all you need, a little blush. Plus one of those nice new mascaras, like Cover Girl Long 'N Lush. And you really do need a good scent. You have a teeny-tiny little bottle of Chanel No. 5 on your dresser, right, and you put on a dab or two when Davey takes you out somewhere fancy. Right?"

She nodded.

"You're not really the Chanel No. 5 type, but nobody ever knew enough to tell you. You should wear Chanel Coco, if you want Chanel, or L'Air du Temps, if you're feeling a little more feminine. You ought to wear a good scent every day, *all* day, no matter what you're doing."

He took his fingers from her chin and moved behind her. The bed sank under his weight. "Hands," he said. She put her hands behind her back, and he grasped her wrists and lashed them together. "This is a disgrace. You need a manicure more than anyone I've ever met. Pedicure, too. And you have to start using some really good nail polish, I don't care what kind. We're going to have to shop for some essentials, and after we get toothpaste and stuff like that, I'll get you some female equipment. It'll help our project."

She heard him rip off a length of tape and felt him coil it around her joined wrists. "Why are you doing this? Are you going somewhere?"

"Don't want you to run away while I wash the Westerholm slammer off me. Want to come in with me?"

"No, thanks."

He cackled. "You can have one after."

"After what?"

He patted her shoulder and hitched himself off the bed to carry the tape and the knife to the table, where he placed them in their old positions and made sure they were properly aligned.

"Are the two of us going to sleep in this bed?"

He looked over his shoulder in mock surprise. Slowly, as if pondering the question, he revolved to face her. "Since there's only one bed, I suppose I presumed . . . And twin beds are so Ozzie and Harriet . . . But if you have strong objections, I guess I could sleep on the floor." His drawl ridiculed his own words. "All right?"

She nodded.

"All right, then." Dick Dart stripped off his shirt, dropped it on the floor, and undid the top of his trousers. His tasseled black loafers came off, and he bent down and skipped out of his trousers. His arms and shoulders were flabby, and a crust of black hair covered his chest. The shapeless slab of his stomach pushed out the waistband of boxer shorts decorated with a fly-fishing pattern. "But I don't expect to have that problem." He pushed down the shorts, exposing a nest of brown curly hair and a long, thick cucumber penis ridged with prominent veins. He tossed the shorts onto the chair and unselfconsciously walked to the table to pick up the roll of tape. His buttocks were flat, almost absent, and his heavy thighs and calves ended in wide, oddly primitive-looking feet, like those of dinosaurs. Tufts of black hair grew alongside his spine at the small of his back.

He ripped a four-inch section off the tape and came toward Nora, penis swinging before him like a pendulum. "We'll work things out." Then he was standing in front of her, the ridged gray cucumber at the level of her eyes radiating stinks like a swamp. She began to shake. Tears slipped from her eyes. He pushed up her chin, smiled down over the bulge of his belly, and flattened the tape over her mouth. "Breathe through your nose. Don't panic."

He pushed her shoulders and sent her flopping backwards onto the bed. Dart disappeared. She tried to gasp, and coarse tape clamped against her lips. Her body demanded oxygen, immediately. Pain blazed in her shoulders, and the rope chewed on her wrists and ankles. She rolled from side to side, choking on tape, and finally remembered to breathe through her nose. Dimly she heard a chuckle, then the closing of the bathroom door. The shower hissed and rattled against the tub. Dart's unmelodious voice began singing "Them There Eyes." Nora rotated her hands and wrists the quarter inch permitted by the rope handcuffs. She lay collapsed against the bedspread, too terrified to cry.

Nora had a sudden vision of herself as seen from above: naked, bent across the bed, trussed like a roaster for the oven. She looked like a corpse in a crime-scene photograph. The woman in the photograph was nothing, an emptiness, less than pathetic. Some deaths might be preferable to the madness waiting within her, but not that one.

Dart came out of the bathroom, hair plastered to his head, water shaping the hairs on his legs into vertical lines. "What a picture you make." He unfurled a towel and systematically began rubbing it over his arms, chest, gut, genitals, legs.

"Back in a second." He vanished into the bathroom and reappeared with a fresh towel. Instead of returning to the bedside, he closed the bathroom door and stepped back toward the closet. Nora watched his reflection in the mirror on the bathroom door. He scrubbed his hair until it floated about his head, and then lightly ran the towel over his neck, his chest, his penis. He clutched himself with the towel, pulled himself roughly several times, and manipulated his testicles. After reaching a satisfactory stage of self-arousal, he stood sideways, held in his belly, gave himself an encouraging pat, as much a slap as a caress, and twitched upward another half inch. Dart had forgotten all about her. His beloved, the cucumber, jutted out before him. Dart clutched it in his fist and jerked up and down, causing the entire structure to darken to purple, bloat out another half inch, and raise itself in an upward curve. This accomplished, Dart turned to face himself head-on. Excited by the sight of itself, the thing in front of him stiffened into a curved rigidity ending in a red-blue knob the size of a small apple. Dart's eyes were glazed, and his mouth was open. Nora thought he was about to ejaculate. He hefted his testicles and groaned. *Go on*, she said to herself, *spurt all over the mirror*.

The eyes in the mirror met hers.

47

DART STRODE BACK into the room. "Hope you appreciate my consideration in showering. Did it for me more than for you, but wouldn't want any unseemly body odors distracting you from what most women find a deeply enjoyable experience." He straddled her legs, bent over her, pushed the head of his penis into her stomach, and rubbed it back and forth across her stomach. "Like that?" He stroked one of her breasts with his free hand. Nora closed her eyes, and he pinched her nipple. She uttered a sharp sound of protest into the tape over her mouth. "Pay at-*ten*-tion," he sang, twirling the nipple painfully between his thumb and index finger. "We are going to perform an introduction, and it isn't polite to close your eyes." Smiling, he hitched himself up onto the bed and settled his knees on either side of her rib cage. "Nora's titties, meet the Big Guy." He leaned forward and ran the Big Guy along first one nipple, then the other. He lowered himself between her breasts, squeezed them around himself, and pumped back and forth. Dart released her breasts and hitched himself forward to thrust his beloved before her eyes. "Don't call me Dick for nothing, right? Never saw one like that before, did you?"

The object four inches from Nora's eyes looked like something pried out of calcified mud at an archaeological dig, something offered for half price at an Arabian bazaar, something carved from an enormous root. Granddad had brought it home from his travels and shown it to Grandma, and after she stopped shouting at him he had taken it upstairs to the attic and buried it in a steamer trunk.

Varied in texture from corrugation to a dangerous, slick smooth-ness, lumpy with veins, a goiter stuffed with rocks—was this what most men wanted to have? Would Davey wish to swap his nice, willing member for this? She knew the answer. He would, absolutely.

She shook her head, *No.*

"Going to go places hubby could never take you, Nora-pie."

He moved off the bed, went to the table, and picked up the largest knife. Then he knelt in front of Nora and peeled the tape off her legs. Instead of cutting the rope, he laboriously untied the knot. Her legs loosened and sagged. Nora instantly closed them, and Dart chuckled and stood up. "Move up on the bed," he said.

She hesitated, and Dart brought the point of the knife into con-tact with her left thigh.

She got her feet on the bed and levered herself up to the pillows. Her arms and shoulders ached, and her wrists burned. Dart walked up beside her on his knees. When he reached her groin, he slapped the knife on the pillow, thrust his hand between her legs, and rum-maged around until he inserted a blunt fingertip. Nora's body shuddered and went cold.

Humming to himself, Dart withdrew his finger and slid on top of her. He pushed her legs apart, planted his knees between them, and moved down to take aim. Nora made a high-pitched sound muffled by the tape. Her face was covered with tears.

Dart maneuvered a portion of himself into her and grunted. He shoved forward. Nora felt as though she were being torn apart. She screamed and heard only a thin, weightless wail. Smiling, Dick Dart propped himself on his elbows and held the knife to her throat. "What we have here is a reality lesson. All sex is rape, pure and simple. I am going to put my cock into your pussy. This act has been known to send women out of their minds, even then it was rape . . ." He pushed himself another quarter inch forward.

". . . and do you know why? Because when it was all over, I owned them. That's the secret." He hoisted himself up, withdrew a tiny bit, and then rammed himself into her. Nora screamed again and rolled to one side.

Dart shoved her back down.

"Better relax, or there's going to be a lot of blood. Have to stretch you out, and you'll get there as long as you loosen up." He withdrew and plunged ahead again, invading her. "Do you know the secret?" Nora had been hiding within herself with her eyes closed, her body clamped in revulsion, and when Dart slapped her cheek she realized that he was talking to her. "Didn't think so." He shoved forward again. "Women, who run rings around men all the time, who can outthink any man ever born, have one weakness. They love being fucked more than anything else on earth." His voice seemed to come from a distant professorial source completely unrelated to what he was doing.

"Money, cars, fur coats, jewelry, houses, they're smart enough to know those things are just toys. Give them all away for a guy with a johnson big enough to turn them inside out. Trouble is, most women never find that guy. But if they do, they're *his*. Every guy is trying to do this, because deep down every guy knows how it's supposed to be, and every woman is secretly hoping he'll turn her inside out, because deep down she knows that's the way it's supposed to be. So it's always a rape."

Nora opened her eyes to a curious sight. Dick Dart's upper portion hung over her. His mottled face had hardened around his concentration, and another face, a secret face, seemed to surface beneath the public one. His lips had drawn back from his yellow teeth. His nose had sharpened, and a suggestion of hair darkened his cheeks. She closed her eyes and heard distant artillery fire.

Eternities later, a quickening in her torture returned Nora to the world. Dick Dart's sweat plopped on her in great tears. He groaned; his hands locked on her shoulders. His body froze, his legs turned to iron bars. Her mind seemed to burst into flame. He arched his back and slammed into her twice, three times, four, five, so forcefully her head banged the headboard.

Dart collapsed on top of her. She felt extraordinarily defiled, so dirty that she could never again be clean. When he rolled off, she felt as though he had broken each of her bones systematically. She would never open her eyes, never again. A hand crawled over her thigh.

"Was it good for you, darling?"

He left the bed and padded into the bathroom. Everything hurt everywhere. She was afraid to open her eyes.

Little voices hissed and chattered. Her demons had found her again. The demons were fond of room 326, and presently they were fond of Nora also, because once more she had been pushed through the bottom of the world into the devastation where they flourished. Nora hated and feared the demons, but she was much more fearful of what she would see if she opened

her eyes; therefore she had to endure them. She remembered
from her last exposure that although demons did not wish to be
seen, you occasionally caught sight of those who crept up to
impart a morsel of demon knowledge. Some of them were tiny
red devils with toothpick pitchforks, some looked like animals
created by mad scientists: long-toothed badgers with rat's tails,
hairy balls with darting eyes and heavy claws. Some demons
looked like moving smudges.

An indistinct, winged thing flapped past her head whispering,
"He isn't a wolf."

Nora wondered if she would have the demons if she had been
raised in some sensible religion, like Buddhism.

The thing circled around and flew past again. *"He's a hyena."*

"You belong to a hyena," giggled something invisible but near.
A tinny ripple of demon laughter greeted this remark.

"Wasn't it fun, wasn't it fun?" sang another. *"And now you're
back with us again!"*

Most of the information imparted by demons was true, for if
they told lies they would be lunatic annoyances, not demons.

She heard them rattling up to her, whispering to each other in
their rapid-fire voices, and drew into herself as tightly as possible,
though she knew that the elated demons would never touch her.
If they touched her, her mind would shatter, and then she would
be too crazy to be interesting.

A demon who looked like a rat with small blue wings and
granny glasses whispered, *You can't get out of this one, is that
clear? You passed through and now you're on the other side, is
that clear?*

When she nodded, the ratlike demon said, *Welcome to the Hellfire Club.*

"It's not as bad as it looks," said Dick Dart. Nora opened her
eyes, and the demons scattered under the bed, behind chairs, into
drawers. Her pain bounded back into her body and stretched like a
big cat. Naked, smiling, his hair combed, Dart stood beside the
bed, idly tugging at himself. His free hand held a damp white
towel. The secret face moved toward the surface of his public face.
Nora saw that it was true; he was a hyena. "Take a gander. You
have to sit up anyhow, so I can get the rope off your wrists."

She shook her head.

Dart told her in an equable, good-humored fashion that like it or
not she was going to sit up, grasped an upper arm, and jerked her

forward. The room swung before and beneath her. Grimacing, she looked down and nearly fainted.

"Okay, let's get this off." Dart reached across the pillow for the knife and expertly nicked the tape around her wrists. He ripped off the tape and worked on the knot until the rope released her wrists. "Now the gag. I'm going to do this fast. Make any noise louder than a peep, I'll ram this knife in you, understand?" She closed her eyes. The chattering demons crowded around. Her lips and a good deal of skin seemed to rip away with the tape, but she managed not to whimper.

He tossed the damp towel onto her legs. "Wipe yourself off. Have to strip the bed. I don't want to sleep in this mess."

Nora obediently passed the towel down the tops of her thighs and realized that if he was going to strip the bed, she would have to get off. She moved her right leg half an inch to the side, and her various pains held steady. Gritting her teeth, Nora swung both legs off the bed and forced herself to stand up. Her head swayed, and a bolt of pain shot upward in her groin.

"Girl's a trouper," said Dart, reclaiming the knife. "To prove I'm not completely evil, I did you a favor. Try to guess what it is."

"Can't," she muttered.

He smiled at her and tugged out the bedclothes. "Ran you a bath, Nora-pie. Aren't you grateful?"

"Yes." At that moment she wanted a bath more than she wanted freedom.

"Pop yourself in that tub." In a single gesture, he jerked the bloody cover and sheets off the bed, balled them up, and threw them into the corner.

She walked, knees trembling, to the bathroom. The casket-sized tub was three-fourths filled with water. The soap dish held a tiny plastic bottle of shampoo and a cake of soap the size of a commemorative stamp. Two curling black hairs adhered to the soap.

Nora's stomach contracted, and she turned to the toilet in time to vomit pinkish drool into the bowl. She wrenched a tissue out of the dispenser, tottered over to the tub, picked up the soap as she would have a dead spider, then dropped the wrapped obscenity in the toilet and flushed it away. From a shell-shaped dish beside the sink she took another minuscule bar of soap and, stepping as gingerly as a stork, at last got into the tub.

Ah, yes. She never wanted to be anywhere at all except the

inside of the tub. A pink cloud swam into the water from the center of her body. Delicately Nora explored herself. She was still bleeding, not seriously, and she had a lot of sore tissue. Various little fires continued to burn along the path of Dart's invasion. She soaped her arms and legs and realized that she would have to wash again under the shower to remove the film of blood deposited by the water in the tub. She was bending forward to open the drain when Dick Dart sauntered into the bathroom. She leaned back and sank up to her neck in the cloudy water, and her knees rose like islands.

"Comfy?" Dart grinned down at her, then inspected his face in the mirror. "I hate the way your teeth feel when you haven't brushed. Being unshaven doesn't exactly fill me with joy, either. On our way to lunch, we can see if this place has a gift shop."

Dart moved forward and peered into his eyes in the mirror, twirled around, and sat on the toilet, regarding her almost paternally. "Couldn't help but notice you experienced some discomfort during our encounter." He put a sarcastic stress on the last word. "To facilitate matters I'm going to do what I do with my old dears and buy some K-Y. Lubrication will eliminate about half of your problem, but if you don't relax, you're going to keep on getting hurt."

Nora closed her eyes. A demon flapped up and hissed, *"You're going to get hurt!"*

She opened her eyes.

"Embarking on the great adventure of menopause, aren't we?"

"Yes," she said, startled.

"Irregular periods, vaginal dryness?"

"Yes."

"Irritability?"

"I suppose."

"Hot flashes?"

"Just started."

"Formication?"

"What's that?"

"Sensation of an insect crawling on your skin."

She astounded herself by smiling.

"Doing any hormone replacement therapy? You should, but you have to experiment with the dosage levels before you get it right."

She closed her eyes.

"I suggest a shower and a shampoo before we visit Home Cooking. Time for the next step in your education."

He bestowed another hyena smile upon her and walked out. Moving as if in a trance, Nora dialed a disk at the end of the tub, and the bathwater gurgled into the drain. She pulled herself to her feet, waded through the froth, and twisted both dials at once. Water shot from the faucet. She flipped the lever directing the water to the showerhead, and freezing water shattered against her body.

BOOK V

LORD NIGHT

THE HUGE BLACK ANIMAL MIGHT HAVE BEEN GRINNING AT HIM.
"WHY, NOW THAT YOU HAVE LEARNED ABOUT YOUR FEAR, YOU
MUST LEARN TO TRUST IT, OF COURSE."

48

"OF COURSE IT'S about money." Dart put down his fork and grinned. He had taken her to the hotel's gift shop, where he bought toothbrushes and toothpaste, a pack of disposable razors and shaving cream, two combs, mouthwash, a deodorant stick, a black polo shirt with MASSACHUSETTS stitched across the left breast in small red letters, and a copy of *Vogue*. His teeth were no longer so yellow, and without the stubble his cheeks were almost pink. Nora had heard only something like half of what Dart said, and half of that had disappeared into the demonic buzz filling her head. "Hey, this is America! Bid'ness is bid'-ness. When you see the other side is likely to rake in a hell of a lot more money than you are, what do you do? Switch sides. Here, what we have on the table adds up to four or five million smackers. Put that against a pissy billing of maybe ten thousand tops, you've got what the boys call a no-brainer."

"From *Night Journey*." This, along with the name of the young woman who had mysteriously disappeared from Shore-lands, was most of what she had been able to retain from Dick Dart's explanation.

"Absolutely. You prove that Hugo Driver stole the manuscript, fifty-four years' worth of royalties, not to mention all future royal-ties, go to the real heirs. And if you can prove that the publishing house cooperated in this fraud, all of their profits from the book, plus a whopping payment in damages, go into the pot. On top of that, there's all the money from foreign editions."

Nora's legs felt like rubber, and the center of her body sent out steady waves of pain. She looked at her plate. Beside a nest of french fries glistening with grease, a rectangle of processed cheese drooped over a mound of whitish paste on a slice of toast.

"So the old man cut a deal with this Fred Constantine, the old

213

ladies' lawyer. Constantine knows he's in over his head, little practice in Plainfield, does a few penny-ante divorces and real estate closings, sixty-five years old, hasn't seen the inside of a courtroom since he got out of law school. Imagine his relief when after making him piss blood for a couple of weeks the great Leland Dart suggests—suggests, mind you—that an accommodation might be arranged. Whoopee! If Mr. Constantine could settle for a payment of something on the order of a hundred thousand dollars, Dart, Morris might be willing to render some assistance to his poor defrauded clients, who would no doubt be delighted to receive fifty percent of the ultimate proceeds. Mr. Constantine, who has no idea how much money is at stake, thinks he's getting a great deal!"

A bitten-off portion of a french fry lay on Nora's tongue like a mealworm. She spat it into her hand and dropped it on her plate. "How can they do something like that?"

"Very carefully." His eyes glowing, he pushed the remains of his first cheeseburger into his mouth and wiped his fingers with his napkin. "Operative word? Buffers. By the time you're done, you're in a fortified castle a thousand miles away, and, baby, the drawbridge is up."

"I mean, how can they *do* it?"

Holding his second cheeseburger a few inches from his mouth, Dart looked away and giggled. "Nora-pie, you're so touching. I mean that sincerely. Bid'ness is bid'ness, I told you. What's the name of our economic system? Isn't it still called capitalism?" He shook his head in mock incredulity and took an enormous bite out of the cheeseburger. Frilly lettuce bulged from the back of the bun, and pink juice drooled onto his plate.

Nora closed her eyes against a wave of nausea. Alden Chancel and Dick Dart thought alike. This discovery would be amusing, had she the capacity to be amused. Leland Dart, who shared Alden's moral philosophy, used it to justify betraying his own client. Presumably this moral philosophy reached its fulfillment in the lunatic cheerfully demolishing a cheeseburger across the table.

Nora remembered a detail from the Poplars' terrace. "I heard Alden tell Davey that your father might be playing both ends against the middle."

Dart swallowed. "Do the Chancel boys talk about this in front of you?"

"Davey was taking notes on the movie of *Night Journey*, and when I asked him why, he said there was some problem with the Driver estate." The night in the family room seemed to have taken place on the other side of an enormous hole in time. "A little while later, he told me something about two old ladies in Massachusetts who found some notes in their basement."

She realized that she was having a civil conversation in a restaurant with Dick Dart as if such occasions were absolutely normal.

"Notes on the movie. What a schlump. Katherine Mannheim's sisters never read the book, of course, they remembered the movie when they found the notes, but I mean really . . ."

"I suppose you want to kill the sisters." Nora poked her fork into the white paste and transported a portion the size of a pencil eraser to her mouth. It seemed that she had ordered a tuna melt.

"Absolutely not. The people I want to kill might help the case against Chancel House. We'll be protecting Hugo Driver's name, something I am pleased to do because I always liked Hugo Driver. Not the last two, you know, only the good one."

"You like *Night Journey*?" That Dick Dart had enjoyed any book surprised her.

"Favorite book, bar none," he said. "Only novel I ever really liked. To keep up with some of my old ladies, I had to pretend to swoon over Danielle Steel, but that was just work. Agatha had a pash for Jane Austen, so I plowed through *Pride and Prejudice*. What a waste. Literally about nothing at all. But I reread *Night Journey* every couple of years."

"Amazing." Nora ate another forkful of her tuna. If you peeled off the plastic cheese and avoided the bread, it was edible after all.

"Amazing? *Night Journey* is one twisted motherfucker of a book. Whole thing takes place in darkness. Almost everything happens in caves, underground. All the vivid characters are monsters."

It was like a warped echo of Davey; for the thousandth time she was listening to a man rave about the book. In asking him to research the case against Chancel House, Leland Dart had exploited his son's one conventional passion. The recognition that Alden Chancel had done the same thing with Davey brought with it an upwelling of her nausea.

"I never read it," she said.

"Davey Chancel's wife never read *Night Journey*? You lied

to him, didn't you? You told him you'd read it, but you were lying."

Nora turned her head to stare at the two elderly couples at separate tables in front of the window. The big reversed letters on the window arched over them like a red rainbow.

"You did, you lied to him." Another dirty explosion of laughter. He went back to work on the second cheeseburger. "Don't suppose you ever heard of a place called Shorelands."

"Hugo Driver was there. And Lincoln Chancel. In 1938."

"Bravo. Do you remember who else was there that summer?"

"A lot of people with funny names."

"Austryn Fain, Bill Tidy, Creeley Monk, Merrick Favor, Georgina Weatherall. The maids. A lot of gardeners. And Katherine Mannheim. Did Davey tell you anything about her?"

Nora thought for a moment. "She was good-looking. And she ran away."

"Upped and vanished."

"What do you think happened to her?"

"Her sisters say she had a 'weak heart,' whatever that means. Supposed to avoid exertion, but she refused to be an invalid. Rode bikes, went on trips. If she'd lived like Emily Dickinson, she might still be alive."

"You read Emily Dickinson?"

He made a sour face. "Florence. One of my ladies. Besotted with Emily Dickinson. Had to put up with reams of that stuff. Even had to read a *biography*. Bitch makes Jane Austen look like Mickey Spillane." He closed his eyes and recited.

> *"There's a certain Slant of light,*
> *Winter Afternoons—*
> *That oppresses, like the Heft*
> *Of Cathedral Tunes—*
>
> *Heavenly Hurt, it gives us—*
> *We can find no scar,*
> *But internal difference,*
> *Where the Meanings, are—"*

He opened his eyes. "It's not even actual English, it's this gibberish language she made up. Read page after page of that vapor for Florence, and now it's stuck in my mind, along with everything else I ever read."

The lines had swept into Nora like an inexorable series of waves. "That's too bad," she said.

"You have no idea. Anyhow, I guess the Mannheim girl croaked, and in the confusion Driver swiped her manuscript. *Night Journey* was published the next year, and what do you know, pretty soon every other person in the world was reading it."

"I saw soldiers carrying it in Vietnam," Nora said.

"You were in Nam? Excuse me, *the* Nam. No wonder you have this wild streak. Why were you there?"

"I was a nurse."

"Oh, yes, I recall a certain adventure involving a child, yes, yes."

She looked down at her plate.

"Nora fails to demonstrate excitement. Very well, let us return to our subject. Most, I repeat, most unusually, Mr. Driver makes over the copyright to his book to his publisher in exchange for an agreement that he shall be paid all royalties due during the course of his and his wife's lifetime, all rights thereafter to revert to said publisher, who agrees to remit a smaller portion to Driver child or children for the course of their lives. This was supposed to be a gesture of gratitude, but doesn't it seem a bit excessive?"

"You've been doing a lot of work." Acting on its own instructions, her hand detached another wad of tuna and brought it to her mouth.

"Made stacks and stacks of notes, none of them currently available, due to the interference of our local fuzz. Fortunately, I retain all of the essentials. I'd like to visit a library during our busy afternoon, continue my research, but let me distill our mission for you." He looked sideways to ensure that the waitress was still seated at the counter. "You know three of these scribblers offed themselves."

She nodded.

"Austryn Fain. No wife, no little Fains. Creeley Monk was a perv, so of course he left behind no weeping widow or starving children. But luck is with us, for in the summer of 1938 Mr. Monk was sharing his life with a gentleman still with us, a doctor in fact, named Mark Foil. Dr. Foil, bless him, still lives in Springfield, the very same city in which he dwelt with our poet. I very much want to think that he occupies the same house, along with lots and lots of Monk memorabilia. Unfortunately, I couldn't find an address for him, but once we get to Springfield, I'm sure we will be able to unearth it."

"Then what?" Nora asked.

"We telephone the gentleman. You explain that you are doing research for a book on the events at Shorelands in 1938. You feel that the other guests, Creeley Monk in particular, have been unfairly overshadowed by Hugo Driver. Since you happen to be in Springfield, you would be extremely grateful if Dr. Foil could give you an hour of his time to discuss whatever he remembers of that summer—anything Monk might have said to him, written to him, or put in a diary."

Even in her present condition, encased within a tough, resistant envelope which at the cost of prohibiting any sort of action protected her from feeling, Nora remarked upon the oddity of this creature's obsessions so closely resembling Davey's. What Dart was asking her to do seemed as abstract as the crossword puzzles concocted by Davey's two old men in Rhinebeck. She filled in a square with a question. "What if Monk never even mentioned Hugo Driver?"

"Very unlikely, but it doesn't matter. After we get inside I have to kill the old boy."

The hyena within Dick Dart displayed its teeth. "He'll see us, baby. If we get lucky down the line, the old guy is going to put things together. Next stop is Everett Tidy, son of Bill. Everett lives in Amherst, he's an English professor. Don't you think the name Tidy in a headline will catch Foil's eye? Gots to cover our tracks."

The smell of cigarette smoke floated toward them, and Nora turned to see the waitress approaching their table.

Dart said, "Let's shop and do the library while we can still use the Lincoln."

49

MAIN STREET, OF what town? Dart pulled her into women's clothing stores, shooed away the clerks, and hand in hand drew her up and down the aisles, flicking through dresses, blouses, skirts. Here a sand-colored linen suit, skirt knee-length, jacket without lapels ("Your interview suit," Dart said), in the next shop brown pumps and a cream silk jersey, short sleeves, collarless. No, she did not have to try them on, they would fit perfectly. And they would; without asking, he knew her sizes. Into a barn where summer-school students with lumpy backpacks prowled the long aisles and Dart heaped up jeans, hers and his, T-shirts, ditto, a dark blue cotton sweater, hers. A minimalist boutique, a conference with another charmed clerk, the production of six Gitano bras, white, six pairs of Gitano underpants, white, six pairs of Gitano pantyhose. Around the corner, his and hers low-cut black Reeboks.

Two wheeled carry-on black fabric suitcases. Into Main Street Pharmacy for quick selections under the eye of a blond-gray mustache with granny glasses: L'Oréal Performing Preference hair color, Jet Black and Starlight Blonde; LaCoupe sculpting spritz; Always ultra plus maxi with wings, her brand, though Dart had not asked; Cover Girl Clean Make-up, Creamy Natural; Cover Girl Lip Advance, Poppy; Maybelline Shine Free Sunset Pink eye shadow ("Glimmer, don't glitter," said Dart); K-Y; Cover Girl Long 'N Lush mascara; Vidal Sassoon Ultra Care shampoo and conditioner; Neutrogena bath bars; Perlier Honey Bath and Shower Cream; Revlon emery boards and cuticle sticks; OPI Nail Lacquer, a smooth, quiet blush she could not catch before he tossed it into the basket; a dram of Coco by Chanel; a jug of Icy Cool Peppermint Scope mouthwash; Hoffritz finger- and toenail clippers, styling scissors, tweezers, nail cleaner. From behind the digital register where the numbers mounted past one hundred dollars, the mustache declared, "Mister, I've seen savvy husbands before, but you take the cake."

Back to the car. Dart angled in before a bowfront shop, Farnsworth & Clamm, and drew Nora into an air-conditioned club room where another mustache marched smiling toward them through glowing casements hung with suits. Yes, Dart murmured, 46 extra long—this one, this one, a double-breasted blue blazer, four blue shirts, four white shirts, cotton broadcloth, spread collars, 17 neck, 36 sleeves, eight boxer shorts, 38 waist, eight pairs calf-length black socks, a dozen handkerchiefs, pick out some ties too, please. Alterations immediately, if poss. Nora deposited in a stiff leather chair near the tall mirror, a stooping man with a tape measure around his neck summoned from the depths, Dart disappeared into the changing room for an eye blink before emerging in the first of his new suits. Another stooping figure materialized to whisk away the suit while Dart twinkled into number two. Dart and his reflection preened. The fittings completed, Dart inhabited another club chair and the mustache presented a bottle of Finnish vodka, two glasses, a bucket of ice. While you wait, sir. The presentation of the bill. Nora looked over and saw that Dart had purchased six thousand dollars' worth of clothes.

"Nearest really good library?" Dart asked.

He swung the Lincoln into the exit near the Basketball Hall of Fame, and Nora realized that, wherever they had been before, now they were in Springfield, where Dr. and Mrs. Daniel Harwich lorded it over Longfellow Lane. If she could escape from Dick Dart, would the doctor and his wife give her shelter in their basement? Answer cloudy, ask again. Three years before, a semi-radioactive Nora had whirled into Springfield on what she imagined was a sentimental visit, wound up in a bar, then a motel, with a strange, embittered Dan Harwich, who afterward talked her into coming home with him. Ten-thirty at night. The Mrs. Harwich of the time, Helen, who had microwaved her half of dinner an hour earlier and dispatched it with several vodka tonics, started shouting as soon as they came through the door. Nora had attempted an exit, but Harwich had settled her in a chair, presumably as a witness. What she had witnessed had been an old-time marital title bout. Helen Harwich ordered them both out, Dan to return the next morning to pick up some clothes and depart for good. Back to the motel, Harwich uttering evil chuckles. The next morning, he promised to call her soon. Soon meant two days later, another call a week later, a third after another two weeks. After that, intermittent calls, intermittently. Two years later, a wedding announcement accompanied by a card reading, *In case you wondered.* The new Mrs. Dr. Harwich was named Lark, née Pettigrew.

"I have to use the bathroom when we get to the library," Nora said.

Dandy, he'd go with her, fact was, he had to bleed the lizard. Dart parked across the street from a long stone building resembling the Supreme Court, complete with Supreme Court steps. In a wide marble hall on the second floor, the ladies' room, like the reading room downstairs, was empty. Dick Dart lounged in behind her. Nora took one stall, he another. They left together, startling a pop-eyed, quavery woman whose mouth opened and closed like a molly's until they had passed out of sight on the stairs.

Dart pushed Nora not ungently into a chair before a long wooden table, sat beside her, and opened a fat volume entitled *Shorelands, Home to Genius.* She sat beside him, now and then hearing tiny, metallic voices like the voices of insects. She was within the envelope, the envelope excluded feeling, she was fine. Dart grinned at his book. She pulled toward her *Muses in Massachusetts* by Quinn W. S. Dogbery, opened it, and read a random paragraph.

Due to the erratic nature of the artistic personality, any community like Shorelands will produce scandal. On the whole, Georgina Weatherall's colony of gifted personages ticked peacefully along, producing decade after decade of significant work. Yet problems did arise. There are those who would list the "strange" disappearance of the minor poet Katherine Mannheim among these, though the present writer is not of their number. This young woman had alienated both staff and fellow guests during her brief residence. There can be no doubt that her hostess was resolved to issue her walking papers. Miss Mannheim, who did not wish to face an humiliating expulsion, departed in a fashion calculated to cause a maximum of confusion.

Shorelands' true scandals, as we might expect, are very different in nature.

Dart thumped two telephone directories on the table and patted her on the back.

Perhaps most distressing to Georgina Weatherall was the disappearance, not of a troublesome young malcontent, but of a favorite work of art from the dining room, a drawing by the Symbolist Odilon Redon of a strapping female nude with the head of a hawk upon her shoulders. There can be no doubt that Georgina's desire for the Redon drawing had its origin in its title, identical to that of a central Shorelands tradition. The works in the dining room were typically of a more traditional nature. The Redon drawing, measuring some eight by ten inches, hung far up on a wall filled with more notable works. A guest with a particular interest in Redon first noted its absence in 1939. An immediate search of the rooms and cottages yielded no result. Georgina Weatherall remarked several times to guests during the succeeding years that it would not surprise her to discover that Miss Mannheim had absconded with it during her "midnight flit," and while the matter may never be resolved, it may be not uncharitable to acknowledge that the drawing did then and does now possess considerable monetary value.

Dart said, "Out of here," gripped Nora's arm, and pulled her outside into the heat and light.

They made three trips to get all the bags and packages into the hotel.

"Clark, my old friend, could you spare a moment to help us convey these essentials up to our charming room?"

Clark licked his lips. "Whatever." He leaned into the office behind him and said something inaudible to whoever was in there. Then he emerged through the lobby door, glanced at Dart, and moved toward the suitcases. He was shorter than he had seemed behind the counter, four or five inches over five feet.

"I'll get the suitcases," Dart said. "Help my wife."

"Whatever." Clark picked up as many bags as he could. Nora took up three others, leaving one on the floor. Clark looked up at Dart, who smiled, opened his mouth, and chopped his teeth together. The boy glanced at Nora, and bent over, bit down on the twine handles of the remaining bag, and jerked it upward.

The three of them crowded into the elevator.

"I'm interested in your use of the word 'whatever,' " Dart said. "Mean something, or merely verbal static?"

The boy grunted and clutched his armful of bags. Sweat ran down his forehead.

"Is it as rude as it sounds? Sort of a hint that the person who says 'Whatever' feels a mild disdain for the other party. Is that accurate, or am I being paranoid?"

Clark shook his head.

"A great relief, Clark."

The elevator reached the third floor, and Dart led them down the hall. "Clark, old dear, deposit those shopping bags in front of the closet and hang the suit bags."

Dart motioned Nora through the door. Clark bent over to deposit on the floor the bag he held with his teeth, exhaled a shaking breath, and lowered the shopping bags. He succeeded in getting the hanger wires over the rail in the closet and backed out into the corridor.

Dart locked the door and came into the room to stand smiling in front of her. Nora drew up her knees and hunched her back. He moved away, and she looked up. He was selecting a length of rope. "Do I have to tell you everything?"

She kicked off her shoes. Her fingers, which did not have to be told what to do, began unbuttoning her shirt. Dart went to the bathroom for the pharmacy bag and carried it to the table as she undressed. One by one, he took the items out of the bag and arranged them on the table. When everything had been satisfactorily aligned, he took the scissors from their plastic case and beckoned Nora into the bathroom.

"Straddle the toilet," he said. Quivering, Nora positioned herself over the bowl, and Dick Dart hummed to himself as he cut off most of her pubic hair and flushed it away.

"Okay," he said, moved her backwards like a mannequin, turned her around, planted a hand between her shoulder blades, and urged her back into the bedroom, where he tied her hands behind her back and taped her mouth shut.

She looked up at the flat white ceiling. Dart hiked himself up onto the bed. "It's not going to be as bad this time, see?" She turned her head to see him brandishing a tube of K-Y.

It was slightly less painful than before, but every bit as bad.

50

"KEEP YOUR HEAD upright. You have to cooperate with me, or you'll end up looking like a ragamuffin." Bath cream scented the air in the bathroom, and her hair, still wet, hung straight and flat. Dart lowered his head alongside hers so that the mirror framed their faces. "Tell me what you see."

Nora saw a terrorized version of herself with shocked eyes, parchment skin, and wet hair, posing with a hyena. "Us."

"I see a couple of fine desperadoes," said the hyena in the mirror. "You needed me to open your eyes, and along I came. Wasn't any accident, was it?"

"I don't know what it was, but—"

Before she could add *I wish it had never happened,* the eyes in the mirror charged with an illumination. "Used to do this with hubby dear, didn't you? Put your heads together and looked at yourselves in the mirror. I know why, too."

She did not have to tell him he was right; he already knew that. "Why?"

"Until now, I hadn't seen how much you and Davey resemble each other. Bet there's a nice little erotic charge in that— probably helped Davey get it up. Like making it with who you'd be if you were the opposite sex. But Davey isn't your male self. The biggest risk Davey-poo ever took was getting into bed with Natalie Weil, and the only reason he did that was his old man made him so insecure about his manhood that he had to prove he could use it."

Nora clamped her mouth against agreeing, but agree she did.

"I'm your real male self. Only difference is, I'm more evolved. Which means that eventually we are going to have tremendous sex."

The hyena surged into his face once more. "In fact, Nora-boo, didn't you have a bit of an orgasm that time?"

"Maybe," she said, thinking it was what he wanted to hear.

He slapped her hard enough to snap her head back. A broad, hand-shaped red mark emerged on her cheek. "I know you didn't come, and so do you. Goddamn it, when I make you come, they'll hear you howling in the next county. Shit."

He slammed his fist against the bathroom door, then turned around and pointed at her face in the mirror. "I bust you out of jail, I buy you clothes, I'm going to give you the best haircut you ever had in your life, after that I'm going to do what your mother should have done and teach you about makeup, and you *lie* to me?"

She trembled.

"I have to keep remembering what women are like. No matter how much a man does for them, they stab you in the back first chance they get."

"I shouldn't have lied," she said.

"Forget it. Just don't do it again unless you want to hold your guts in your hands." He wiped his face with a towel, then draped it over her shoulders. "Stop shaking."

Nora's eyes were closed, and in some world where the demons did not exist she felt a comb running through her hair. "This is going to be an inch or two shorter all over, but it'll look completely different. For one thing, I cut hair a lot better than the last guy who did this. Also, I know how you ought to look, and you don't have the faintest idea. It's too bad we have to turn you into a blonde, but that'll be okay too, believe me. You'll look ten years younger."

He positioned her head and started cutting with small, precise movements of the scissors. Dark hair fell onto the towel and drifted down to her breasts. He said, "Hold still. I'll get the hair off you later." Wisps of hair landed on her forearms, her stomach, her back. Dart was humming "There'll Be Some Changes Made." "Good hair," he said. "Nice full texture, good body."

She opened her eyes and beheld exactly what he had promised, the best cut of her life. It was too bad that she should be given such a cut when she was a corpse being prepared for the coffin. His hands flew about her head, fluffing, cutting.

"Pretty good, if I do say so myself." He snapped the towel

away from her shoulders and brushed hair from her body.
"Well?"

Nora snatched the towel and wrapped it around her chest.
Dart grinned at her in the mirror. She ran her fingers through her
short, lively hair and watched it fall perfectly back into place.
Apart from the fading red mark on her cheek, the only problem
with the woman in the mirror was that beneath the cap of beautifully cut hair her face was dead.

Dart opened the box of hair coloring and removed a white
plastic bottle with a nozzle and a cylinder of amber liquid. He
snipped off the tip of the nozzle. "You won't be as blond as the
picture, but you'll be blond, anyhow." He wiggled his hands
into the transparent plastic gloves from the inner side of the
instruction sheet. After pouring in the amber liquid, Dart shook
the bottle.

"Bend forward." She leaned over the sink, and Dart squeezed
golden liquid into her hair and worked it in with his fingers.
"That's it for twenty-five minutes." He looked at his watch. "Sit
here so I can use the mirror." She dragged her chair in front of
her as she backed toward the toilet.

Dart leaned forward and began cutting his own hair. He did a
better job with the back of his head than Nora had expected,
missing only a few sections where long hair fanned over the
rest. "How's it look?"

"Fine."

"In the back?"

"Fine."

He snorted. "Guess that means close enough for jazz." He
opened the box of black hair color and mixed the ingredients.
"I'm going to have to close my eyes, so I want you to put your
hand on me. If you take it off, I'll smash your head open on the
bathtub."

"Put my hand where?"

"Grab anything you like."

She hitched herself forward and, shivering with revulsion,
placed her hand on his hip.

Dart squeezed the fluid into his hair. "I wish I were a woman,
so I could have me do this for myself. Without doing it like
this, I mean."

"You wish you were a woman," Nora said.

He stopped massaging the lather into his hair. "I didn't say that."

Goose bumps rose on Nora's arms.

"I didn't say I wanted to be a woman. That's not what I said."

"No."

Violence congealed about Dart's heavy body and sparkled in the air. He lowered his hands and faced her.

"I mean, I would enjoy having these things done to me by me. The women who get my special treatment are *extremely* lucky people. I think it would be nice to be pampered, like I pamper you. Anything strange about that?"

"No," she said.

He turned back to the sink and shot her a simmering glance. She settled her hand on his hip. "You're tied down by the crappy little conventions that inhibit melon-heads like your husband. The truth is, there are two kinds of people, sheep and wolves. If anyone should understand this, it's you."

He peeled off the smeary gloves. "That's that." She lowered her hand and looked at the door. "Nope, we're staying in here. Sit on the side of the tub."

Nora moved. Dart frowned, tossed the gloves into the basket, checked himself in the mirror, and sat on the toilet. "We have some time to kill. Ask me something, and try not to make it too stupid."

She tried to think of a question that would not infuriate him. "I was wondering why you live in the Harbor Arms."

He held up his finger like an exclamation point. "Very good! First of all, my parents will never come there—the place gives them hives. Secondly, nobody gives a shit what you do." For fifteen minutes, he described the advantages of living in a place where the fellow residents willingly supplied drugs, sex, and gossip—the members of the Yacht Club universally assumed that their waiters and busboys, Dart's confidants, chose not to overhear their private conversations.

If she were alive, Nora thought, most of what she would feel about this vain, destructive, self-important man would be contempt. Then she realized that what she was now feeling actually was contempt. Maybe she was not entirely dead after all.

"Anyhow," Dart said, "time to wash that gunk out of your hair and do the conditioner."

"I'd like to do it by myself."

He held up his hands. "Fine. Use a little warm water, lather up, and rinse. Then take that tube on the side of the sink and massage the whole thing into your hair. After two minutes we'll rinse it out."

Nora worked her fingers through her hair until a cap of white foam appeared, then lowered her head beneath the tap and washed it away.

"Amazing," Dart said.

Nora looked up.

A drowned sixteen-year-old blonde stared at her from the other side of the mirror. Short, wet hair only slightly darker than Natalie Weil's lay flat against her head.

"I didn't think it'd be *that* good," Dart said. "Don't forget the conditioner."

Nora took her eyes from the drowned girl's and unscrewed the cap, then faced the strange girl again and squeezed the contents of the tube over the top of her head in a long, looping line. Together she and the girl worked their fingers through their hair.

"My turn." Soon a black-haired Dick Dart was grinning at his image in the mirror. "Should have done this years ago. Don't you think I look great?"

A greasy crow's wing flattened over his head. Stray feathers adhered to his temples and forehead.

"Great," she said.

He pointed at the sink, and she came forward to rinse out the conditioner.

"Okay, next step." Dart pulled her toward the bedroom and sat her at the table. "Watch what I'm doing so you'll be able to do it for yourself, later." He flipped open a mirrored case and handed it to her. He smoothed a dab of makeup across her cheekbones and feathered it down her cheeks, stroked mascara into her eyelashes, brushed lipstick onto her mouth. "When we're all done, I want you to clean up your nails and cuticles and put on that polish. I suppose you *have* done that before?"

"Of course." She could not remember the last time she had applied nail polish.

"One last touch," Dart said, putting a dime-sized dab of the sculpting spritz on his palm. Behind her, he began massaging her scalp. He combed, patted, combed, tugged at her hair. "Impress myself. Go in the bathroom and take a look."

Nora slipped into her blue shirt.

"You won't believe it."

Nora stood in front of the mirror and lifted her eyes. A woman just beginning her real maturity, the second one, a woman who should have been selling expensive shampoo in television commercials, looked back at her. Her glowing gamine's hair had been teased into artful ridges and peaks. She had perfect skin, a handsome mouth, and long, striking eyes. She was what the lacquered twenty-somethings who lived on mineral water from Waldbaum's wanted to be when they grew up. For some reason, this woman wore Nora's favorite blue shirt.

Nora moved her face to within three inches of the mirror. There, lurking beneath the blond woman's mask, she saw herself. Then she pulled back and disappeared beneath the mask. A howl of rage came from the bedroom.

Dick Dart was seated at the table with the newspaper he had taken from the lounge. The bottle of Cover Girl Clean stood open on the bottom half of the paper, and he was jabbing the brush at a story, spattering the paper with tan flecks. "Know what these idiots are saying?" He turned toward her a face from a trick photograph, its left half smoothed into a younger, unlined version of the right. "I should sue the bastards."

Nora went past the row of shopping bags outside the closets. "What's wrong?"

"The *Times*, that's what. They got everything wrong, they fouled up in every possible way."

She sat on the bed.

"Know what you are, according to this rag? A socialite. If you're a socialite, I'm the Queen of Sheba. 'To abet his escape, Dart seized a hostage, Westerholm socialite Nora Chancel, 49, wife of David Chancel, executive editor at Chancel House, and son of the current president and CEO of the prestigious publishing company, Alden Chancel. Neither David nor Alden Chancel could be reached for comment.'" He read this in a mincing, sarcastic drawl which made every word seem a preposterous lie.

She said nothing.

"If you go by this article, the only criminal in Westerholm is me, and can you guess what they say I am? Go on, take a stab at it."

"A murderer?"

"A *serial killer*! Are they so brain-dead they can't tell the difference between me and some psycho who goes around killing people at random?" Indignation brought a flush to the side of his face he had not made up. "They're insulting me in print!"

"I don't really—"

Dart pointed the makeup applicator at her like a knife. "Serial killers are scum. Even Ted Bundy was a nothing from a completely insignificant family of nowhere Seattle nobodies."

He was breathing hard.

"I see," Nora said.

"What's the point of doing anything if they're going to twist it around? What about credit where credit is due?"

She nodded.

"Here's another lie. They say I'm an *accused* serial killer. Excuse me, but when did that happen? I was brought into the station because of the allegations of a drunken whore, I spent about twelve hours with Leo Morris, but when during all that time was I accused? This is libel."

She kept her eyes on his.

"Work like mad, put yourself in constant danger, accomplish things the ordinary jerk couldn't even dream of, and they go out and peddle these *lies* about you. It makes me so *mad*!"

"Do they have any idea of where we are? What about the car?"

"For what it's worth, it says here that the fugitive and his hostage—hostage, that's a good one—fled in the hostage's car, which was later discovered in the parking lot of a restaurant stop on I-95. Probably they do know about that old asshole's Lincoln. I was going to get a new car tonight anyhow." He picked up the makeup bottle and threw the newspaper at her. *"Serial killer."*

She sat back on her haunches. "What are you going to do?"

He dipped the applicator back into the jar of makeup, positioned the mirror in front of him, and started working on the right side of his face. "We're going to change into new clothes and pack up. Early tomorrow, we're going to await the arrival of a weary traveler, kill him, and steal his car. Move to another motel. Sometime before noon tomorrow, we'll locate Dr. Foil. After that, we'll journey on to Northampton and pay a call on Everett Tidy, son of poor Bill."

He replaced the cap on the bottle and offered his face for inspection. "What do you think?"

From the neck up, he was a different, younger man who might have been a doctor. Nurses would have flirted with him, gossiped about him. "Remarkable," she said.

He reached across the table for the rope and the duct tape.

51

NORA RETURNED TO her body. Perhaps her body returned to her. The process was unclear. From an indefinite realm, she had fallen into a damp bed already occupied by a large male body sweating alcoholic fumes. Her body was sweating, too. She raised a tingling hand to wipe her forehead, and the hand jerked to a halt before it reached her face, restrained by a tight pressure encircling her wrist. On examination this proved to be a rope. The rope extended beneath the inert body of the man, whom Nora could remember linking them wrist to wrist as she passed through the interior of cloud after cloud. She was back with Dick Dart, and she was having the second hot flash of her life. A nice mixture of demons in high good humor squatted around the bed, sniggering and muttering in their rat-tat-tat voices.

A man half visible in the darkness crossed his legs ankle to knee in a chair near the window. She looked more closely at the man and saw that her father had found a way to join her in this netherworld.

Daddy, she said.

This is a pretty pickle you're in, said her father. *Seems to me you could use a little good advice from your old man right about now.*

Don't wake him up. You're talking too loud.

Hey, this clown can't hear me. He drank most of that bottle of vodka, remember? That guy's out cold. But even stone-cold sober, he wouldn't be able to hear either one of us.

I miss you.

That's why I'm here.

Nora began to cry. *I need you.*

Honey, the person you need is Nora. You got lost, and now you have to find yourself again.

I don't even have a self anymore. I'm dead.

Listen to me, sweetie. That pile of horse manure did the worst thing to you he could think of because he wants to break you down, but it didn't work, not all the way. Forget this dead business. If you were dead, you wouldn't be talking to me.

Why not? You're dead, too.

You're not as easy to kill as Dick Dart thinks you are. You're going to get through it, but to do that you have to go through it. It's hard, and I wish it didn't have to be this way, but sometimes you have to take an awful bitter pill.

The form facing her in the chair, one ankle on the opposite knee, had been gradually coming clearer in the darkness, and now she could make out his plaid shirt open over the flash of a white T-shirt, the vertical red stripes of his suspenders, his work boots. His close-cropped white hair glimmered. She fastened on his beloved, familiar face, the clear eyes fanned with deep wrinkles and the heavily lined forehead. Here was Matt Curlew, her strong capable steady father, looking back at her with a mixture of tenderness and authority which pierced her heart.

It's too much, she said.

You can come through. You have to.

I can't.

He folded his hands together on top of his raised leg and leaned forward.

Okay, maybe I can. But I don't want to.

Of course not. Nobody wants to go all the way through. Some people, they're never even asked to do it. You might say those are pretty lucky people, but the truth is, they never had the chance to stop being ignorant. You know what a soul is, Nora? A real soul? A real soul is something you make by walking through fire. By keeping on walking, and by remembering how it felt.

I'm not strong enough.

This time, you get to do it right. Last time you got hurt as bad as this, you closed your eyes and pretended it didn't happen. Inside you, there are a lot of doors you shut a long time ago. What you have to do is open those doors.

I don't understand.

Just let yourself remember. Start with this. Remember one summer when you were nine or ten and I taught you all those knots? Remember doing the half hitch? The slipknot?

Tying knots when she was ten years old? The present Nora had never been ten years old.

You were sitting on that stump in the backyard, the one from the oak that fell down during that hellacious storm.

Then she did remember: the smooth white surface of the stump, her tomboy self fooling with a length of rope she had unearthed in the garage, her father wandering up to ask if she wanted to learn some fancy knots. Then the pleasure of discovering how a random-seeming series of loops magically resolved into a pattern. She had badgered him for weeks, showed off at the kitchen table, impressed various boys, absorbed by one of those childish fascinations which last a season and then disappear for good.

I remember.

What was the best one? You used it to tie up Lobo.

The witch's curse?

The guy who taught it to me called it the witch's headache. Probably has a dozen names. If you tie it right, nobody who doesn't know the trick can ever undo it. From what I can see, your friend Dick Dart tried to put a witch's headache on your wrist, but he doesn't know as much about knots as he does about cosmetics.

Nora looked down at the complication on her wrist, as solid as a bracelet and intricate as a maze. Something about the pattern was misshapen.

You can get out of that contraption in a couple of seconds. You see how?

Nora tugged here and there with her free hand, gently loosening the web, then slowly drew the end of the rope from under a strand, unwound it from around her wrist, and passed it beneath another strand. The knot sagged into a series of loops from which she could easily slide her hand.

Now tie it all back up again with that stupid mistake where he missed the choke.

But I can get away!

You're not done yet, honey. You have to stick with this animal for a while, then you'll be able to go through with what you have to do.

I don't know what you're talking about!

I wish I could guarantee you it'll all turn out the way it

*should, but can anybody ever promise that? Don't worry about
the knot—it'll tie itself, and miss the choke, too.*

I suppose you think this is easy.

*Nothing about this is easy. Go all the way through it, honey.
This time go all the way through.*

Nora watched the rope slither twice around her wrist, create a
loop, wind around, slip beneath a strand and through the loop,
miss the essential hitch, and tuck itself into the web. When she
looked up, her father said, *I love you, Sunshine. You're one hell
of a girl.*

Help me, she said, but the chair was empty.

52

FAINT GRAY LIGHT touched the edge of the curtains. The last time
she had looked at them, she had seen darkness, so she had slept.
Dart had planned a busy day, and she was supposed to stop him.
She could not stop Dick Dart. A thick membrane made of transparent rubber surrounded her, stealing her will, robbing her of the
power to act. Within the membrane, she could do no more than
follow orders and utter occasional remarks. Matt Curlew had
come to her in a dream and shown her that Dart couldn't tie the
witch's headache, but he knew nothing about the membrane.

Dart lay on his side, turned away from her. Experimentally,
she put her hand on his shoulder. He rolled over to face her, his
bloodshot eyes gleaming. "Need an early start today. Get any
sleep?" His breath smelled like burning tires.

"A little, I guess."

He sat up and pulled her wrist onto his broad thigh. "Don't
suppose you made any little efforts to untie that knot while I
was out."

"I touched it, that's all."

"Ooh, Nora, you excite me." He giggled. "This knot, you try
to get out of it, it tightens up on you. Called the devil's conun-

drum. Watch this." He tugged at a strand, passed it beneath another, and the knot dissolved. "Need two hands to make it work. If you try it, you'll cut off most of the circulation to your hand."

If you tied it right, that is, she thought. Inside the bubble, she made a ghostly smile.

He looked at his watch. "The first thing I want you to do is pack everything in your suitcase, leaving out one of the new T-shirts and jeans. I have to fix your face and hair. Then we're going to keep our eyes on the parking lot." He patted her face. "If I say so myself, I improved your looks about a thousand percent. Don't you agree? Don't you have to admit that your rescuer from Durance Vile is a genius?"

"You're a genius," Nora said.

Dart jumped out of bed and spun around. "I'm a genius, I was born a genius, I always will be a genius, and I have never done anything wrong! Ladies and gentlemen, please put your hands together for a man who can truly be said to be one of a kind, the great one, the maestro, Mr. RIIICH-ARD *DART*!"

He flapped a hand at Nora, and she clapped twice.

"Hustle your fine little buns into the bathroom and brush your teeth. Void your bowels. Enjoy a lengthy urination. While I do the same, get your shit packed. Time's a-wasting."

Nora had folded all the new clothes into the suitcase, slid the unopened packets of soap and bath cream down the sides, jammed in the mouthwash, and begun placing all the makeup and beauty-care equipment on top of the pile. After packing his own clothes twice as well as she in half the time, Dart stopped admiring himself in the mirror to check her progress. "Didn't your mother teach you *anything*? You can't put that stuff in your suitcase, for God's sake."

"Where do you want me to put it?"

He winked at her. "Little surprise." He opened the closet door, took from the shelf a black leather handbag with a golden snap, and danced toward her. "Gucci, you will observe. Testimonial to your invaluable assistance."

"I didn't see you buy this."

"Took advantage of the trusting inattention of the salesladies at our second stop. Fit neatly into the bag from the first emporium."

Nora scooped the bottles, cases, and containers into the bag and snapped it shut.

"Let's find our victim," Dart said.

53

"A LOT OF people think traveling salesmen died out with Willy Loman, but the world is full of guys with their backseats full of sample cases and catalogs. Travel these huge territories, two or three states, the whole Northeast. Drive high-end Detroit iron and pull into joints like this too tired to fight."

Standing on the balcony a few feet from Dart, Nora rubbed her bare arms. Condensation shone on the empty cars beneath them, and the windows of Home Cooking were dark. The headlights of a dark green sedan on the side of the lot shone on a cement planter in which geraniums wilted in a carpet of cigarette butts.

"Idiot's battery is going to die before he gets his ass out of bed," Dart said. "Some people shouldn't be allowed to drive."

"You're sure someone's going to come in?"

"Dick Dart's word is his bond," he said in a booming voice. "If Dick Dart tells you something, you can take that motherfucker to the motherfucking bank."

A car veered into the exit. "What did I tell you?" Dart pulled her into the room and looked back at the car, which drove past the entrance to the lot. "Cheapskate's looking for a place costs five bucks less a night." He dropped Nora's arm and stepped back out onto the balcony. "Let's see some action here, people. Haven't got all day."

He shoved his hands in his pockets and rose onto the balls of his feet. He patted the top of the balcony rail with his fingertips. "Still can't get over that serial killer thing." For a minute or two, he paced up and down on the narrow balcony. "Let's take our bags downstairs."

Nora carried her suitcase in one hand, and with her other arm clutched to her chest the bags from the hardware store and liquor store. Draped over these was Dart's bulging suit bag.

They carried their things past an empty desk. "No conception of service left in this country. We're turning into *Nigeria.*" He crammed himself into the revolving door, swore, swung it around, and disappeared from view, leaving Nora to solve the problem of the revolving door by herself. She had to struggle around twice to move everything outside. Once, she would have fled through the hotel and escaped, but the person she was now could not do that; she had been punished too much, and the transparent membrane protected her from further punishment.

Dart was standing beneath the marquee. "Get over here in case one of those morons actually *deigns* to work the desk." He pulled keys from his jacket pocket and displayed them on his palm. "These things cost something, but hey, they just work here, it's not their money." He tossed them into the cement planter. "That thing is supposed to add some beauty to the place, and what do people do? Turn it into an ashtray. First of all, they *smoke*, as if nobody ever told them they're begging for lung cancer, and then they throw their butts into a planter. Anybody can stop smoking. Used to smoke four packs a day, and I stopped. What happened to self-control? Fuck self-control—what happened to simple consideration for others?"

Nora watched dark outlines speed down the highway against the brightening sky.

"Isn't there any work ethic left in this country?"

Nora looked at the car with its lights burning and made out a shape behind the wheel.

"Come on, Nora. Can't do everything by myself. Wind it up, cross your fingers, turn the key, do whatever the hell you do."

"I don't do anything."

"Do you . . ." He stopped talking and looked at her, blinking rapidly. "If that dodo left his lights on, maybe he left his keys in his car."

He walked out from under the canopy, bent to look into the car, and ran toward it, pulling the revolver from his jacket pocket.

Nora pressed the heavy suit bag to her eyes and waited for the explosion. Dart's shoes thudded on the asphalt and came to a stop. She heard his dirty bow-wow-wow laugh.

She lowered the bags. Dart was blowing her a kiss from beside the open car door. "Goddamn it, Nora, you deserve a bonus."

She moved toward him.

"Ta da!" Dart stepped aside to reveal an obese male body slumped behind the wheel. A yellow tie had been yanked sideways, and the first four buttons of the shirt had been torn off.

"Heart attack, wouldn't you say?"

"Looks that way," Nora said.

"Butterball here's about fifty pounds overweight, and the inside of his car reeks of cigarettes." He touched the corpse's flabby cheek. "This bag of shit drove in about a minute before we went out onto the balcony, turned off his car, and dropped dead before he could switch off his lights. He's been here all along! Put down that stuff and give me a hand."

Dart kneeled on the passenger seat, wrapped his arms around the dead man's chest, and yanked him sideways. Nora bent down and pushed. Her hands sank into the soft body.

"Jesus, Nora, you've handled dead bodies before. You can't wimp out on me now."

Nora put her shoulder into the dead man's side. "Push!"

The body tumbled into the passenger seat.

Dart tossed the keys over the top of the car. "Put the bags in the trunk."

Obedient Nora opened the trunk and laid the suit bag across cartons and boxes. Then she got in the backseat and Dart accelerated backwards, braked, and shot toward the front of the hotel. The dead man's head rolled sideways. They jammed the rest of the bags into the trunk and backseat. The knives between his feet, Dart rolled chuckling toward the exit. Then he braked and leaned toward the corpse.

He tugged a wallet from the dead man's jacket. "Check out these business cards. Playtime Enterprises, Boston. Gumbo's Goodies, Boston. Satisfaction Guaranteed, Waltham. What are these places? Hot Stuff, Providence. The Adults Only Parlor." Dart started laughing. "Jumbo sells sex toys! What a gem! Let's find out his name."

He held up a license displaying a photograph of a pudgy face with distended cheeks and close-set eyes. "We have the pleasure of being in the company of Mr. Sheldon Dolkis. Mr. Dolkis is, let's see, forty-four years of age, weight two hundred twenty-five pounds, height five feet, eight inches. He claims to have hazel eyes, and he has declined to be an organ donor. We shall see about that, I believe." Dart grasped the corpse's right hand.

"A treat to make your acquaintance, Shelley. We'll paint the town red."

He drove into the southbound lanes of the highway. "We want a Mom and Pop motel redolent of the two quintessential Normans, Rockwell and Bates. A shabby little office and a string of depressing cabins."

"Why is that what we want?"

"Can't leave our new friend in the car, now, can we? Shelley is part of our family."

"You're going to *keep* him?"

"I'm going to do a lot more than that," Dart said.

54

"DELIGHTFUL PLACE, SPRINGFIELD," Dart said. "Pay attention now, Shelley. Even a lowlife like you must have heard of the Springfield rifle, but did your education cover the Garand? Wonderful weapon for its time. For two hundred years, both of these rifles were manufactured in Springfield. It may be the only city in America with a weapons museum. Now, *there's* a museum worth visiting. Of course it also has that Basketball Hall of Fame, if you can believe that. Have to throw the yokels a crumb now and then.

"Basketball was okay when white people still played it, but look what happened. Overgrown glandular cases took over, and now it's all exhibitionism. Sportsmanship? Forget it, there's no sportsmanship in the ghetto, and basketball is only the ghetto with big paychecks. All part of the decline in public morality. My father—you think he cares who really wrote *Night Journey*? His idea of good literature is a copy of *American Lawyer* with his picture on the cover. You should see what goes on at Dart, Morris— the bill padding, the Concorde flights we charge to the client. What gets me, they don't see the humor in this stuff, they chug down two bottles of Dom Pérignon and stuff themselves with caviar at what they call a conference, bill the client five hundred bucks for the dinner, and don't even think it's funny! No wonder people hate lawyers. Compared to the other guys, I'm a paragon. I take care of my old ladies. If I bill them for lunch, it's because during that lunch, we talked about business. It isn't all Danielle Steel and Emily Dickinson, you know."

They had been driving aimlessly through the outskirts of Springfield, Dart scanning both sides of the streets for a motel as he talked.

"Take Shelley Dolkis here. Delivered dildos and inflatable dolls to guys too feeble to have sex with other people. Even the sex industry has a hierarchy, and Shelley was on the bottom end—the jerk-off end. But if he could talk, he'd tell you he provided a necessary service. If people didn't have access to his products, why, they'd go out and commit rape!"

"I suppose you're right," Nora said.

"Whole thing comes down to having the balls to be completely straight about being crooked. The guy who runs for the Senate and says he wants the job so he can screw the aides, stuff his pockets with payoff money, take a lot of drugs, and swim naked with a couple of strippers, that's the guy who gets my vote. This country founded on fairness? A bunch of other guys owned it, and we *took* it. Wasn't there a little thing called the Boston Tea Party? Suppose you came to Connecticut in 1750 and happened to see a nice plot of land on the Sound with half a dozen Pequot Indians living on it. Did you say, too bad, guess I'll move inland? You killed the Indians and got your land. You lived in Westerholm a couple of years. Ever see any Pequots? The same things happen over and over. History books lie about it, teachers lie about it, and for sure politicians lie about it. Last thing they want is an educated public."

"Yes."

"This is a happy time for me. I'm a lot more sensitive than most people think I am, and you're beginning to see that side of me."

"That's true," Nora said.

"And here's a place that will suit our little family just fine."

A shabby row of cabins stood at the top of a rise. Numbered doors lined a platform walkway. A neon sign at the entrance to the parking lot said HILLSIDE MOTEL.

"Hillside, like the strangler," Dart said. He pulled up in front of the last unit and patted the corpse's cheek. "Relax for a moment, Shelley, while Nora and I secure our accommodations."

An ancient Sikh accepted twenty-five dollars and shoved a key across the counter without leaving his chair or taking his eyes off the Indian musical blaring from the television set on his desk.

"Nora, Nora," Dart said as they walked on creaking boards back toward their car and Sheldon Dolkis. "As they say in beer commercials, does it get any better than this?"

"How could it?" Nora said.

"You and me and a big fat dead man." He slid the key into the door of the last room. "Let's have a look at our bower."

An overhead light in a rice-paper bubble feebly illuminated a bed covered with a yellow blanket, a battered wooden dresser, and two green plastic chairs at a card table. Worn matting covered the floor. "Nora, if this room could talk, what tales it would tell."

"Suicides and adulteries," Nora said, and felt a dim flicker of terror. This was not the kind of thing the person inside the bubble was supposed to say.

But she had not displeased Dick Dart. "You get more interesting with every word you say. When you were in Vietnam, were you raped?"

She collapsed against the wall. *Davey couldn't figure it out in two years of marriage, and Dick Dart saw it in about twenty-four hours.*

He glanced outside. "After we escort Shelley into this lovely room, I have a story to tell you."

Back outside, Dart opened the passenger door and put his hand on Dolkis's shoulder. The dead man was regarding the roof of his car as if it were showing a porn movie. "Shelley, old boy, time for a short stroll. Nora-sweetie, what I am going to do is pull him toward me, and I want you to get up behind him and catch him under the other arm."

Dart leaned into the car and pulled the dead man's head and shoulders into the sunlight. "Get set, don't want to drop him." Nora wedged herself next to the car and bent down. The dead man's suit was the oily green of a Greek olive and stank of cigarette smoke. "Here we go," Dart said. The suit jerked sideways. She lifted the arm and edged in close to the body. "Good hard pull," said Dart. The body lifted off the car seat, and its feet snagged. A soft noise came from the open mouth. "Don't complain, Shelley," Dart said. He reared back, and Dolkis's feet slid over the flange. One of his shoes came off. "Walky walky," Dart said.

They dragged him inside. At the far end of the bed, Dart

lowered his side of the body and let go. The weight on Nora's back slipped away, and the body's forehead smacked against the rattan carpet. Dart rolled the corpse over and patted the bulging gut. "Good boy." He untied the twisted necktie and threw it aside, then unbuttoned the shirt and pulled it out of the trousers. A thin line of dark hair ran up the mound beneath the sternum and down into the dimple of the navel. Dart unbuckled the belt and undid the trouser button.

"What are you doing?" Nora asked.

"Undressing him." He yanked down the zipper, moved to the lower end of the body, pulled off the remaining shoe, and peeled the socks off the plump feet. He yanked at the trouser cuffs. The body slid a couple of inches toward him before the trousers came away, exposing white shorts with old stains on the crotch. Dart reached into the left front trouser pocket and extracted a crumpled handkerchief and a key ring, both of which he threw under the table. From the right pocket he withdrew a brass money clip and a small brown vial with a plastic spoon attached to the top.

"Shelley took coke! Do you suppose he actually *tried* to get a heart attack?" He unscrewed the cap and peered into the bottle. "Selfish bastard used it all up." The bottle hit the floor and rolled beneath Nora's chair. "I have to get some things out of the car."

Dart strode out into the dazzling light. Grateful to be powerless, to feel nothing, Nora heard the trunk of the car open, the rustle of bags, a lengthy silence. A blue jay screamed. The trunk slammed down. A dignified, doctorly man carried a lot of bags into the room and became Dick Dart.

He hitched up his trousers, knelt beside the body, and arranged the bags in a row beside him. From the first he dumped out his knives. From the second he removed a pair of scissors. He took the half-empty vodka bottle from the third, removed the cap, winked at Nora, and took a long pull, which he swished around in his mouth before swallowing. He shuddered, took a second drink, and replaced the cap. "Anesthesia. Want some?"

She shook her head.

Dart walked up the body and levered the trunk upright. "Give me a hand."

When the body was naked except for underpants, Dart rummaged through the suit pockets: a ballpoint pen, a pocket comb gray with scum, a black address book. He threw these toward the wastebasket, then noticed the money clip on the floor beside him. "My God, I forgot to count the money." He pulled out the bills. "Twenty, forty, sixty, eighty, ninety, a hundred, a hundred and ten, four singles. Why don't you take it?"

"Me?"

"A woman's incomplete without money." He folded the bills into the clip, scooped coins from the floor, and dropped it all into her palm. "Nora-pie, would you be so kind as to go into the bathroom and tear down the shower curtain?"

She went into the bathroom and groped for the switch. Glaring light bounced from the walls, white floor, and mirror. A translucent curtain hung down over the side of the white porcelain tub. Nora reached up and tore at the curtain. One by one, plastic rings popped off the rail.

When she carried the sheet into the bedroom, the light from the bathroom fell across the floor. "Perfect." Dart cut away the dead man's underpants and spread the shower curtain next to the body. A flap of underwear lay across Sheldon Dolkis's groin. "Let's see how our boy was hung." He ripped away the cloth. "Had to jerk off with tweezers."

Dart draped his suit jacket over the back of a chair. He rolled his sleeves halfway up his biceps and tucked his necktie in between the third and fourth buttons of his shirt. Kneeling beside the body, he slid his arms under the back, grunted, and rolled it onto the shower curtain. He moved up and rolled it over again, so that the body faced upward. He fussed with it, centering it on the plastic sheet. "All righty." He rubbed his hands together and looked fondly down at the corpse. "Do you know what I wanted to be when I grew up?"

"A doctor," Nora said.

"A *surgeon*. Loved cutting things up. *Loved* it. What did the great Leland Dart say? 'I'm not wasting my money on some medical school that'll flunk you out in a year.' Thanks a bunch, Dad. Lucky me, I found a way to be a surgeon despite him."

He lowered himself to his knees and picked up the stag-handled knife. "You've seen a million operations, right? Watch this. Tell me if I'm any good." She watched him slide the knife beneath the breastbone and draw it down the mound of the belly, bisecting the line of hair. Yellow fat oozed from the wound. "I don't suppose, when reminiscing about his dear old Yale days, your husband ever mentioned an organization called the Hellfire Club?"

55

SHE GAVE A start of surprise and said, "You did that very well."

"Of course," he said, annoyed. "I'm a born surgeon. What's the essential quality of a born surgeon? A passion for cutting people up. Used to practice on animals when I was a kid, but I didn't want to be a *vet*, for God's sake." He cut away wide semicircles of flesh on either side of the incision, then carved off soft yellow fat and dropped it onto the shower curtain. In a few seconds, he had exposed the lower part of the rib cage and the peritoneum. "Want to take a look at Shelley's liver—a real beauty, I bet—and his pancreas, check him for gallstones and anything else that might turn up, but I have to get this huge, ugly membrane, the greater omentum, out of the way. Look at that fat. This guy could keep a soap factory running for a month."

"You've been doing your homework."

"Medical books are much more enjoyable than the nonsense I read for my old darlings." He sliced through the thick, fatty membrane and peeled it back, then began probing the abdominal cavity.

"The Hellfire Club?" Nora asked.

"You know about the secret societies at Yale, don't you? The *secret* secret societies are a lot more interesting. The Hellfire Club is one of the oldest. Used to be you could only get in through heredity, but during the forties they started taking in outsiders. Lincoln Chancel was buddy-buddy with some old sharks who were members, and they bent the rules to get Alden in, so Davey was eligible, and he joined. I came in when I was a sophomore, so we were there together for a year. Jesus Christ, look at this."

He sliced the peritoneal attachments and pulled the liver out of the body. "Right lobe is about half the size it's supposed to be. See all this discoloration? A decent liver is red. Here, around the vena cava, this big vessel, it's turning black. The texture is all wrong. I don't know what the hell old Shelley had, but his bad habits were killing him." Dart placed the severed liver on the plastic sheet and cut it in half. "What a mess. Hepatic artery looks like a tooth-pick. . . . I don't know why Davey stayed in the club. Probably his old man thought it would toughen him up. He was all wrong for the place. It was about cutting loose, getting down and dirty. Sex, drugs, and rock 'n' roll."

This was interesting, even within the comforting membrane. Most of what Davey had said to her had been a lie. "Where did you meet?"

"Used to rent a couple of floors in the North End. When the neighbors got suspicious, we'd move into another building. Point was, once you got inside the club, you could do whatever you liked. Nobody was allowed to criticize anything another member chose to do. Don't question, don't hesitate, don't judge. Naturally, we had a few ODs. No problem, dump the body in a vacant lot. People in your generation think they invented drugs. Compared to us, you were pussies. Hash, LSD, angel dust, speed, heroin, ben-nies, lots and lots of coke. Now, that's one area where little Davey felt right at home. He'd go three and four nights without sleeping, shoving blow up his nose with both hands, babble about Hugo Driver until he finally passed out."

Nora watched his hands working inside the gaping body.

"Hate the smell of bile. If people think shit smells bad, they ought to take a whiff of the stuff that goes through their gall-bladder." Dart brought a roll of toilet paper from the bathroom to mop up a dark brown stain spreading across the sheet. He sliced the pear-shaped sac of Dolkis's gallbladder in half and crowed. "What did I tell you? Gallstones. At least ten of 'em. If his liver didn't kill him first, Shelley was in line for some painful surgery." He wrapped the mutilated gallbladder in toilet paper and set it aside, but the wet, dead stench still hung in the air.

"I want to check out this guy's pancreas and look at his spleen. The spleen is a gorgeous organ."

"Did you bring girls to the Hellfire Club?" asked Nora.

"Any woman who walked into that place was fair game. Even Davey's crazy girlfriend, Amy something or other, came there once. Made her even crazier than she was before. Then Davey started turning up with this chick. If Amy was strange, this babe was *completely* weird. Men's clothes. Short hair."

Dart was severing connective tissue and ducts with quick, accurate movements of his knife. "You'd see this cute little thing sitting alongside Davey and think *Yeah, I'll jump her bones,* and then for some reason you realized no, no way. Also, every word she said about herself was a lie. *Hello.*"

Dart held up a dripping, foot-long pancreas with a gray-brown growth the size of a golf ball drooping from its head. "I've seen tumors before, but this baby is something special. Shelley, your body should be on display in a glass case. I can't wait to see what his heart looks like."

"She was a liar?"

"Have you noticed your hubby has a tendency to expand upon the truth? This girl was even worse. I guess little Davey had a propensity for crazy ladies." He put down the diseased pancreas and gave her a twist of a smile.

"What was her name?"

"Who knows? She even lied about that. As you may have noticed, I can tell when people are lying. She was about the best liar I ever met, but she was a liar, all right. According to Davey, she went to New Haven College, and came from some little town up around here, I forget which. Chester, something like that. Granville, maybe. I checked her out. She wasn't registered at New Haven College, and no family with her last name lived in that town."

"Could it have been Amherst?"

"Amherst? No. Why?"

"Davey once told me a story about an old girlfriend of his who said she came from Amherst. I thought it might be the same girl."

He gave her a long, straight look. "The lad probably reeled in wacko ladies by the hundreds. He's very pretty, after all. Anyhow, he spent almost all his free time with this one. I don't suppose they spent the whole time talking about Hugo Driver, but whenever *I* saw them together she was after him to get his father to do something or other with *Night Journey.* She was totally focused on that book. The girl was after him to let her see the manuscript—something like that. I know he tried, but it didn't work."

Dart manipulated the knife and held up a purple, fist-shaped organ. "Looks surprisingly okay, considering the company it kept."

"What happened to the girl?"

He placed the spleen beside the oozing liver. "One night I happened to walk into our favorite pizza place, and who should I see in the back of the room but Davey and his friend. Your husband-to-be was polluted. I was hardly sober myself, but I wasn't nearly as bad as Davey. He waved me over to their table, pointed at me, and said, 'There's your answer.' The girl said no. It had to be the two of them, no one else. I was the answer. No, I wasn't. The girl was stone-cold sober. Finally I figured out that until he got loaded, she'd wanted him to drive the two of them someplace, and he still wanted to do it. She kept saying they could wait until the next day. That fool you married was insisting on going that night—to Shorelands. She wanted to see the place, so tonight was the night. I could drive. All this without asking me if I had the slightest interest in driving across Massachusetts at night.

"The girl refused to have me drive them, so naturally I decided to do it. Along the way I planned to inform Davey of his girlfriend's inventions. *Then* we'd have an entertaining scene, wouldn't we?

"Davey was too drunk to see that the girl was furious. He couldn't drive, and she didn't have a license. I solved their problem. 'It's no good anymore,' the girl kept saying, but he wouldn't listen to her. Well, off we go. Davey passed out in the backseat. The girl sat up front with me, but she wouldn't say any more than it took to give me directions. We got about a hundred miles down the highway, and Davey woke up and started quoting from *Night Journey*. I wish I had whatever you're supposed to use to cut through ribs, because this knife isn't making it. I got through the cartilage and stripped away a lot of the intercostal muscle, but I'm going to have to break 'em off with my hands."

Dart grasped a rib and pulled, swearing to himself. The curved bone gradually moved upward and then snapped in half. "Good enough, I guess." He sliced through more cartilage.

"I tried to drown him out with the radio, but all I could find was disco shit, which I *hate*. Know what I like? Real music. Kind of singers you never hear anymore. Give me a good wop baritone and I'm a happy camper. Ah, getting a good view of the heart now.

"There we are, a hundred miles into the middle of nowhere,

Davey spouting Hugo Driver, the girl sitting like a marble statue. All of a sudden she has to pee. Which makes me see red, because we just *passed* a rest stop, why didn't she pipe up then? Like a peek into this girl's mind? 'Whenever possible,' she says, 'I like to pee in the woods like Pippin Little, because I *am* Pippin Little.' This seemed like the moment to tell Davey what I know about the bitch, so I do. I have to repeat it two or three times, but he does finally get it. She may be Pippin Little, but she sure as hell isn't who she told him she was. In fact, it hits him, drunk as he is, that what she was calling herself was a hell of a lot like the name of *another* character in *Night Journey*. The girl doesn't turn a fucking hair. She says, 'Turn off at the next exit. I can get out there.'

" 'If you won't tell me who you really are, you can get out and stay out,' Davey yells.

"We're so far in the country it's like a coal mine. I get off the highway, and we're at the edge of these woods. Davey makes a grab for the girl, but she zips out and runs into the trees. Davey starts swearing at me—now it's *my* fault she's a liar. After ten delightful minutes, I finally suggest that his friend is taking an extremely long time to finish her business. He piles out and charges around in the woods for about half an hour. The hell with this, he says, let's go back to New Haven and this time I'm driving. He gets behind the wheel and guns the car around. All of a sudden the bitch is right in front of the car, and then she disappears. Our hero starts crying. Then he whips a gram out of his pocket, snorts about half of it, and drives away."

"He left her there?"

"Drove away. Eighty miles an hour all the way back to dear old Yale, that maker of men, not to mention hit-and-run drivers."

"What happened after that?"

"Crazy Amy got out of the locked ward, and Davey went straight back to mooning over her. Never came back to the Hellfire Club. Boo hoo, we all sure missed him."

"Is there a Hellfire Club in New York?"

Dart looked up at her, eyes narrowed. "As a matter of fact, yes. In the twenties, a group of alums decided there was no reason the fun should stop on graduation day. More formal than the New Haven thing—servants, a concierge, great food. The dues are high enough to keep out the riffraff, but the essential spirit remains the same. Why do you ask?"

"I was wondering if Davey ever went there."

His eyes shone. "Might have spotted that gutless hit-and-run artist within the hallowed halls a time or two. Avoided him like the plague, of course."

"Of course."

"Darling heart, would you do me a favor? The hammer I bought in Fairfield is in a bag on the backseat. If I'm going to break these ribs, I might as well do it a little more efficiently."

Entirely amused, Dart stood up and watched her move toward the door. Nora went outside, where the air was of an astonishing sweetness. She looked back and saw Dart just inside the door, holding his arms, stained red to the elbows like a butcher's, out from his sides. Amusement radiated from his eyes and face. "You should smell the air out here," she said.

"I prefer the air in here," Dart said. "Funny old me."

Heat shimmered off the top of the car. Nora leaned into the oven of the interior and opened a bag on the laden backseat. The long wooden shaft of the hammer met the palm of her hand. Her heart leaped in her chest, and her face grew hot beneath the makeup. She became aware that the thick balloon filled with emotional exhaust fumes was no longer about her. She had not noticed its departure, but it had departed all the same. Dart beckoned her back into the room with a courtly wave.

"Close the door, my dear. Only a tiny test, but you passed it beautifully."

"You're a fun guy."

"I am!" He pointed a red finger at Sheldon Dolkis. "I want you right beside me. You're a nurse, you can assist. Kneel on a pillow, so as not to hurt your knees. Considerate me. Take one off that scabby bed."

Nora knelt on the pillow and set the hammer down next to her right thigh. Dart squatted and pointed into the body cavity. "That aortic arch looks more like a slump, and the old pulmonary trunk is like a worn-out inner tube. I want to see his superior vena cavity. Bet it's a terrible mess." He leaned forward to peer between the ribs on the far side of the chest, clearly expecting her to do the same.

Nora's heart jumped like a fish. She picked up the hammer, still wondering if she could actually go through with it. Then she planted her left hand in the middle of his back as if for support and smashed the hammer into the side of his head.

Dart exhaled sharply and almost fell into the open body. He caught himself by sinking his hands into the cavity and tried to get to his feet. Nora leaped up and battered the back of his head. Dart sagged to his knees. She cocked back her arm and whacked him again. He toppled sideways and struck the floor.

Nora crouched over him, the hammer raised. Her heart beat wildly, and her breath came in quick, short pants. Dart's mouth hung open, and a sliver of drool wobbled from his lower lip.

She dropped to one knee and thrust her hand into his pocket for the car keys. A second later, she was running through the sunlight. She started the car and backed away from the motel. Through the open door, she saw Dick Dart rising to his knees. She jolted to a stop and tried to shift into drive but in her panic moved the indicator to neutral. When she hit the accelerator, the engine raced, but the car slid downhill. She pressed the brake pedal and looked back at the room. Dart was staggering toward the door.

Her hand fluttered over the shift lever and moved the car into drive. Waving his red arms, Dick Dart was racing toward her.

The car shot forward. She twisted the wheel, and the right front fender struck him with an audible thump. Like the girl in the story, he disappeared. Nora fastened her shaking hands on the wheel and sped downhill.

BOOK VI

FAMILIAR MONSTERS

PIPPIN UNDERSTOOD THE NATURE OF HIS TASK. THAT WAS NOT THE PROBLEM. THE PROBLEM WAS THAT THE TASK WAS IMPOSSIBLE.

56

STREETS, BUILDINGS, STOPLIGHTS flew past her, other drivers honked and jolted to standstills. Pedestrians shouted, waved. For a lengthy period Nora drove the wrong way down a one-way street. She had escaped, she was escaping, but where? She drove aimlessly through a foreign city, now and then startled by the stranger's face reflected in the rearview mirror. She supposed that this stranger was looking for the expressway but had no idea of where to go once she got there.

She pulled to the side of the road. The world outside the car consisted of large, handsome houses squatting, like enormous dogs and cats, on spacious lawns. It came to her that she had seen this place before, and that something unpleasant had happened to her here. Yet the neighborhood was not unpleasant, not at all, because it contained . . .

Sprinklers threw arcs of water across the long lawns. She was in a cul-de-sac ending in a circle before the most imposing house on the street, a three-story red-brick mansion with a bow window, a dark green front door, and a border of bright flowers. She had arrived at Longfellow Lane, and the house with the bow window belonged to Dr. Daniel Harwich.

Her panic melted into relief. She had reached the end of the street before she realized that Mrs. Lark Pettigrew Harwich might not welcome the sudden appearance of one of her husband's old girlfriends, however desperate that old girlfriend might be. At that moment, coffee mug in one hand, Dan Harwich emerged from the depths of the room and stood at the bow window to survey his realm. A fist struck her heart.

. Harwich gave Nora's car a mildly curious glance before taking a sip of coffee and raising his head to look at the sky. He had changed little since she had last seen him. The same weary,

witty competence inhabited his face and gestures. He turned
and disappeared into the room. Somewhere behind him,
pouring coffee for herself in a redesigned kitchen, very likely
lurked wife number two.

Nora cramped the wheel and sped out of the circle, wondering how on earth she was going to find a telephone. She
turned left onto Longfellow Street, another treeless length of
demi-mansions old and new, all but identical to Longfellow
Lane except for being a real street instead of a cul-de-sac and
the absence from any of its numerous bay windows of Dr.
Daniel Harwich. At the next corner, she turned left onto Bryant
Street, another stretch of wide green lawns and sturdy houses,
and began to feel that she would spend the rest of her life
moving down these identical streets past these identical houses.

At the next corner she turned left again, this time onto Whit-
tier Street, then onto Whitman Street, another replica of Longfellow Lane, the chief difference being that instead of an asphalt
circle at the end of the block there was a stop sign at an intersection, and directly beside the stop sign stood the metal hood
and black rectangle of a public telephone.

57

THREE FEET FROM a chintz sofa piled with cushions, Nora felt
herself slip into a collapse. She sank a quarter of an inch, then
another quarter of an inch, taking Dan Harwich's unresisting hand
with her. Then an arm wrapped around her waist, a hand gripped
her shoulder, and she stopped moving.

Harwich pulled her upright. "I could carry you the rest of the
way."

"I'll make it."

He loosened his grip, and Nora stepped around the side of a
wooden coffee table and let him guide her to the sofa.

"Do you want to lie down?"

"I'll be okay. It's letting go of all that tension, I guess." She slumped back against the cushions. Harwich was kneeling in front of her, holding both her hands and staring up at her face.

He stood up, still staring at her face. "How did you get away from this Dart?"

"I hit him with a hammer, then I ran into him with the car."

"Where?"

"Outside some motel, I don't remember. Don't call the police. Please."

He looked down at her, chewing his lower lip. "Back in a sec."

Nora put an arm behind her back and pulled out a stiff round cushion embroidered with sunflowers on one side and a farm-house on the other. There was still an uncomfortable number of cushions back there. She did not remember the chintz sofa or this profusion of cushions from her earlier visit to Longfellow Lane. Helen Harwich's living room had been sober and dark, with big square leather furniture on a huge white rug.

Now, apart from the mess, the room was like a decorator's idea of an English country house. Dirty shirts lay over the back of a rocking chair. One running shoe lay on its side near the entrance to the front hall. The table on which she had nearly cracked her head was littered with old newspapers, dirty glasses, and an empty Pizza Hut carton.

Harwich came back with a tumbler so full that a trail of shining dots lay behind him. "Drink some water before it slops all over the place, sorry." He handed her the wet tumbler and knelt in front of her. Nora swallowed and looked around for a place to put the glass. Harwich took it and set it on the table.

"You're going to leave a ring," she said.

"I don't give a shit." He grasped her right hand in both of his. "Why don't you want me to call the police?"

"Right before I got abducted by Dick Dart, I was about to be charged with about half a dozen crimes. It sounds a little funny, given what happened, but I'm pretty sure that kidnapping was one of them. That's why I was in the police station."

Harwich stopped kneading her hand. "You mean if you go to the police you'll get arrested?"

"Think so."

"What did you do?"

She pulled her hand away from his. "Do you want to hear what happened, or do you just want to call the FBI and have me hauled away?"

"The FBI?"

"Couple of real charming guys," she said. "They had no trouble at all assuming I was guilty."

Harwich stood up and moved to the other end of the sofa.

"If this is too much for you, I'll get out of here," Nora said. "I have to find this doctor. If I can remember his name."

"You're not going anywhere," Harwich said. "I want to hear the whole story, but before that, let's see if we can take care of Dick Dart." He stood up and took a cellular phone from the mantel. Nora started to protest. "Don't worry, I won't say anything about you. Try to remember the name of that motel." He went across the room and pulled a telephone book from beneath a stack of magazines and newspapers.

"I can't."

"Did it have a sign?" He held his finger over a number.

"Sure, but . . ." She saw the sign. "It was called the Hillside. 'Like the strangler,' Dart said."

"Like the strangler?"

"The Hillside Strangler."

"Jesus." Harwich punched numbers. "Listen to me. I'm only going to say this once. The escaped murderer Dick Dart checked into the Hillside Motel in Springfield this morning. He may be injured." He turned off the phone and replaced it on the mantel. "I suppose you'll feel safer once Dart is off the streets."

"You have no idea."

"So talk," Harwich said.

She told him about Natalie Weil and Holly Fenn and Slim and Slam, she told him about Daisy's book and Alden's ultimatum, she described the scene in the police station, Natalie's accusation, her abduction, Ernest Forrest Ernest, the Chicopee Inn. She told Harwich that Dart had raped her. She told him about the library and the shopping spree and being made up; she told him about Sheldon Dolkis.

While she spoke, Harwich scratched his head, squinted, circled the room, flopped into a chair, bounced up again, interjected sympathetic, astounded, essentially noncommittal remarks, and finally urged her into the kitchen. After gathering up the dirty glasses and utensils and stashing them in or around the sink, he made an omelette for them both. He leaned forward, his chin on his elbow. "How do you get yourself into these situations?"

She put down her fork, her appetite gone. "What I want to know is, how do I get out of it?"

Harwich tilted his head, raised his eyebrows, and spread his hands in a pantomime of uncertainty. "Do you want me to take a look at you? You should have an examination."

"On your kitchen table?"

"I was thinking that we could use one of the beds, but if you prefer, I could take you to my office. I have an operation this afternoon, but I'm free until then."

"There's no need for that," Nora said.

"No serious bleeding?"

"I bled a little, but it stopped. Dan, what should I *do*?"

He sighed. "I'll tell you what baffles me about all this. This woman, this Natalie Weil, accuses you of beating her, starving her, God knows what, and the FBI and most of your local police force believe her. Why would she lie about it?"

"Screw you, Dan."

"Don't get mad, I'm just asking. Does she have anything to gain from having you put away?"

"Can we turn on the radio?" Nora asked. "Or the TV? Maybe there'll be something about Dart."

Harwich jumped up and switched on a radio beside the silver toaster at the end of a counter. "I guess I don't have the fugitive mind-set." He moved the dial to an all-news station, where a man in a helicopter was describing a traffic slowdown on a highway.

"The fugitive mind-set," Nora said.

"I'm only a jaded old neurosurgeon. I lost all my old wartime instincts a long time ago. But I'd better hide your car."

"Why?"

"Because about a minute after they show up at the motel, they're going to be looking for an old green Ford with a certain license plate. And it's in my driveway."

"Oh!"

The telephone rang. Harwich glanced at the wall phone in the kitchen and then back at Nora before pushing himself away from the table. "I'll take this in the other room."

No longer certain of what she made of Dan Harwich or he of her, Nora turned back to the radio. An announcer was telling Hampshire and Hampden counties that the temperatures were going to stay in the high eighties for the next two or three days, after which severe thundershowers were expected. In the next room Harwich raised his voice to say, "Of course I know! Do you think I'd forget?"

She stood up and carried her cup to the coffeemaker. Dishes and glasses filled the sink, and stains of various kinds and colors lay on the counter. Then she heard the words "Richard Dart" come from the radio.

".... this vicinity. Police in Springfield discovered a mutilated male corpse and signs of struggle in a room at the Hillside Motel on Tilton Street. Springfield police have indicated the possibility that the fugitive serial killer has been injured, and are conducting a thorough search of the Tilton Street area. Residents are warned that Dart is armed and extremely dangerous. He is thirty-eight years old, six feet, two inches tall, weighs two hundred pounds, has fair hair and brown eyes, and was last seen wearing a gray suit and a white shirt. The fate and whereabouts of his hostage, Mrs. Nora Chancel, are likewise unknown."

Smiling an utterly mirthless smile, Dan Harwich came back into the kitchen and stopped moving at the sound of Nora's name.

"Mrs. Chancel is described as being forty-nine years of age, five-six in height, slender, weighing approximately one hundred and ten pounds, with short, dark brown hair and brown eyes, last seen wearing blue jeans and a long-sleeved dark blue shirt. Anyone seeing Mrs. Chancel or any person who appears to be Mrs. Chancel should immediately contact the police or the local office of the FBI.

"Police have not yet been able to identify Dart's latest victim.

"In other local news, State Senator Mitchell Kramer resolutely denies recent charges of mishandling of . . ."

Harwich switched off the radio. "Give me the keys." Nora handed them over.

"Your life is a lot more adventurous than mine." He smiled almost apologetically.

"I'm making you uncomfortable, so I'll go," she said. "You don't have to keep me around out of charity because we used to be friends."

"We were a lot more than that. Maybe I ought to be uncomfortable now and then." He grinned at her, and his eyes flickered, and for a second the old Dan Harwich shone through the surface of this warier, more cynical version. "Back in a flash."

"In the meantime, try to think about what I ought to do, will you? Can you?"

"I'm thinking about it already," Harwich said.

58

WHEN HARWICH CAME back, Nora said. "I get the feeling your wife isn't expected anytime soon."

"Don't worry about her." Harwich arched his back. "Lark's not in the picture anymore."

"I'm sorry. When did that happen?"

"The disaster took place on the day we got married. I think I got involved with her to get away from Helen. You remember Helen, I suppose?"

"How could I forget Helen?"

"Probably the only time you were thrown out of somebody's house." Harwich laughed. "In the end, she didn't want to live here and I did, so I bought her out. *Bought* is the word, believe me. Two million in alimony, plus ten thousand a month in support payments. Thank God, last year she suckered some other poor bastard into marrying her. At least I covered my ass when I married Lark. She signed a prenuptial—two hundred fifty thousand, all her clothes and jewelry and her car, that's it. On the whole, I should have been smarter than to marry someone named Lark Pettigrew. I let her redo the whole place, and now I'm living in this dollhouse." He gave Nora a rueful, affectionate look. "The woman I should have married was you, but I was too stupid to know it. There you were, right in front of me."

"I would have married you," Nora said.

"That last time? You turned up here like Vietnam all over again, I mean, you were *wild*. And I was already seeing Lark, anyhow. What I'm saying is, I should have married you instead of that miserable witch Helen."

"Why didn't you?"

"I don't know. Do you know? It's probably better we didn't. I don't seem to be very good at marriage." He made a wide gesture with one arm and laughed. "Lark took off about three weeks ago. and the week after that I fired the cleaning woman. I don't mind the mess. Damn woman used to rearrange all my books and papers. Excuse me, but I never understood why I should have to learn my *cleaning woman's* filing system."

She smiled.

"Christ, what's the matter with me?" He clamped his eyes shut. "All this stuff happening to you, and I'm talking about bullshit instead of helping you."

"You're already helping me," Nora said. "You don't know how often I think about you."

He leaned over the top of his chair and closed one hand around one of hers, squeezed, and released it. "I think you should stay here at least a day or two, maybe more. I have that operation this afternoon, but I'll come back around four or five, get some food, we can see if they picked up Dart, talk things out. Let me pamper you."

"That sounds wonderful," Nora said. "You'd really let me stay?"

Harwich leaned forward and took her hand again. "If you even try to get away, I'll lock you in the attic."

Her pulse seemed to stop.

"I can't believe I said that." He gripped her hand, which wanted to shrink to a stone. "Nora, you're like a godsend, you remind me of real life, can you understand that?"

"I remind you of real life."

"Yeah, whatever that is. You do." Harwich let go of her hand and wiped his eyes, which had suddenly filled with tears. "Sorry. I'm supposed to be helping you, and instead I come unglued." He tried to smile.

"It's okay," Nora said. "My life is a lot messier than yours."

He rubbed his finger beneath his nose and withdrew into himself for a moment, gazing unseeing at the plates stacked at the edge of the table. "Let's make up your bed." He stood up, and she did too, returning his smile. "Do you want to bring in your bags, or anything?"

"Right now, all I want to do is rest."

"Sounds good to me," Harwich said.

59

AFTER STOPPING AT the linen closet for paisley sheets and matching pillowcases so new they were still in the package, they went into a front bedroom with flowered blue wallpaper and knotty pine furniture disposed around the edges of a pink-and-blue hooked rug. A rocker made of lacquered twigs sat in front of the window. Harwich ripped the sheets from their wrappers before flipping the dark blue duvet off the bed.

"The bed's comfortable, but stay out of that chair." Harwich nodded at the rocker. "One of Lark's inspirations—a two-thousand-dollar chair that tears holes in your sweaters."

He snapped a fitted sheet across the bed. Nora slid the top corner over the mattress as Harwich did the same on his side. They moved down the bed to fit the sheet over the bottom corners. Together they straightened and smoothed the top sheet and tucked it under the foot of the bed.

"Hospital corners," Harwich said. "Be still, my heart." They began stuffing pillows into the cases.

"Dan, what am I going to do?"

He shoved his hands in his pockets and stepped toward her, the playfully ironic manner instantly discarded. "First of all, we have to see if the police pick up Dart, or, even better, find his body. Then we want to find out if the FBI is still after you." He put his right hand on her shoulder.

"You don't think I should try to see this doctor?"

"Aren't I good enough for you?" He tried to look wounded.

"The one Dick Dart wanted to kill."

"The only thing you should do, if you still care about Davey, is tell him the Chancel House lawyers are selling them down the river. That might straighten out your problems with the old man."

261

Dan Harwich seemed to have admitted fresh air and sunlight into a dank chamber where Nora had been spinning in darkness.

"If I were you," Harwich said, "I'd take his father for everything I could get. That tough old number from up the road in Northampton, Calvin Coolidge, wasn't wrong: the business of America is business."

Nora closed her eyes against a wave of nausea and heard the shufflings of a gathering of demons. "Don't do this to me," she said. "Please."

Harwich put an arm around her waist and guided her to the side of the bed. "Sorry. You need rest, and I'm talking your ear off."

"I'll be okay." She clasped her hand on his wrist, feeling completely divided: one part of her wanted Harwich to stay with her, and another, equal part wanted him to leave the room. "I should apologize, not you."

"Stretch out."

She obeyed. He went to the foot of the bed, untied her shoes, and pulled them off. "Thanks."

"You remember this doctor's name?"

She shook her head. "Something Irish."

"That narrows the field. How about O'Hara? Michael O'Hara?"

She shook her head again.

"The man you want is gay, isn't he?" He began kneading the sole of her right foot with his thumbs. "I can't think of more than three gay doctors in the whole town, and they're all younger than I am." What he was doing to her foot set off reverberations and echoes throughout her body. "Did you hear his first name?"

She nodded.

"What letter did it start with?"

Without any hesitation at all, Nora said, "M."

"Michael. Morris. Montague. Max. Miles. Manny. Mark. What else? Monroe."

"Mark."

"Mark?" He dug his thumbs into her left foot, and a tingle wound all the way up her backbone. "Mark. With an Irish last name, and gay to boot. Let's see. Conlon, Conboy, Congdon, Condon, Mulroy, Murphy, Morphy, Brophy, O'Malley, Joyce,

Tierney, Kiernan, Boyce, Mulligan, this isn't easy. Burke. Brannigan. Sullivan. Boyle.'"

"Hold on. That was close. Sounds like Boyle." She held her breath and closed her eyes, and a name floated toward her out of the darkness. "Foyle. His name was Mark Foyle."

"Mark Foil?"

"That's the name."

He laughed. "Yes, but you were thinking F-o-y-l-e, which is why you thought it was an Irish name. Mark Foil is about as Irish as the queen of England, and his name is Foil as in *tinfoil*. Or as I heard him say once, Foil as in *fencing*." He spoke the last phrase in a mincing, affected voice.

"You know him."

"Foiled again," Harwich said, using the same swishy voice.

"Is he like that?"

"He couldn't afford to be. The man was a GP for upwards of forty years, and this isn't the most liberated place on the face of the earth."

"Where does he live?"

"The good part of town," Harwich said. "Unlike we lesser mortals, Dr. Foil can behold a great many trees when he glances out of his leaded windows." He patted her foot. "Look, if you want to see the guy, I'll take you over there. But the guy's one of those patrician queers."

The word *queers* chilled Nora. It sounded ugly and wrong, especially coming from Dan Harwich, but she pushed aside her distaste. "You think he wouldn't have time for me?"

"Foil never had time for *me*, if that's any indication. God, you should see his boyfriend."

The telephone down the corridor began ringing. "You could probably use a nap," Harwich said.

"I could try."

Released, he gave her foot a last pat, went smiling toward the door, and closed it behind him. Nora heard his footsteps racing toward the telephone, which must have been in his bedroom. A moment later, in a voice loud enough to be overheard through the door, he said, "Okay, I know, I know I did."

She thought she might as well take a bath. On the marble shelf beside the antique sink in the bathroom lay three new toothbrushes still in their transparent pastel coffins and a pump dispensing baking soda and peroxide toothpaste. Nora struggled with one of the toothbrush containers until she managed to splinter one side. Above the tub, modern fittings protruded from the pink-tiled wall. Checking for the necessary supplies, Nora saw a tall, half-filled bottle of shampoo and a matching bottle of conditioner, both for dry or damaged hair, surrounded by a great number of hotel giveaway containers. A used shower cap lay over the showerhead like a felt mute over the bell of a trombone.

Lark had moved out of Harwich's bed before she had moved out of his house. On a shelf above the towels Nora saw a deodorant stick, a half-empty bottle of mouthwash, a Murine bottle, a nearly empty aspirin bottle, an emery board worn white in a line down the middle, a couple of kinds of moisturizer and skin cream, and a tall spray bottle of Je Reviens, almost full. She began pulling the T-shirt out of her jeans.

Someone behind her said, "Hold it," and she uttered a squeak and jumped half an inch off the ground.

"Sorry, I didn't mean to . . ."

She turned around, her hand at the pulse beating in her throat, to find an apologetic-looking Dan Harwich inside the bathroom door.

"I thought you heard me."

"I was getting ready to take a bath."

"Actually," Harwich said, "maybe we ought to get in touch with Mark Foil. In case Dart did get away, as unlikely as that is, we have to make sure Mark is protected."

"Well, fine," Nora said, unsure what to make of this sudden reversal.

"We might be able to go over there this morning." His whole tempo had sped up, like Nora's pulse. Smiling in an almost insistent way, he went sideways through the bathroom door, silently asking her to come with him.

"You changed your mind in a hurry."

"You know my whole problem? I can't get out of my stupid patterns. I think Mark Foil looks down on me, and I resent that. An egotistical voice in my head says I'm a hotshot and he's only a retired GP, who does he think he is, screw him. I shouldn't let that kind of crap keep me from doing what's right."

Nora followed him into a huge bedroom with a four-poster bed and a big-screen television set. Clothes lay scattered across the floor. "What was Dart going to say to these people? How was he going to get into their houses?"

"I was supposed to be writing something about that summer at Shorelands—the summer of 1938. Everybody knows about Hugo Driver, but the other guests have never been given their due. Something like that."

"Sounds good," Harwich said. "If I have a talent for anything besides surgery, it's for bullshit. Who do you want to be?" He kicked aside a pile of old socks and sweat clothes on his way to a bookcase.

"Gosh, I don't know," Nora said.

"What's a lady-writer kind of name? Emily Eliot. You're my old friend Emily Eliot, we went to Brown together, and now you're writing a piece about whatsit, Shorelands. Let's see, you got a Ph.D. from Harvard, you taught for a while, but quit to be a freelance writer." He was paging through a fat directory. "We have to make you a respectable citizen or Mark Foil won't give you the time of day. You published one book five years ago. It was about . . . hmm . . . Robert Frost? Was he ever at Shorelands?"

"Probably."

"Published by, who? Chancel House, I guess."

"And I was edited by Merle Marvell."

"Who? Oh, I get it, he's the big gun there."

"The biggest," said Nora, smiling.

"The whole point about lying is to be as specific as possible." He flipped a page and ran his finger down a list of names. "Here we go. Since this is Mark Foil we're talking about, he might be spending the summer on a Greek island, but let's give it a try. What was his boyfriend's name, Somebody Monk, like Thelonious?"

"Creeley," she said.

Harwich dialed the number and held up crossed fingers while it rang.

"Hello, I wonder if I could speak to Mark, please. . . . This is Dan Harwich. . . . Yes, of course, hello, Andrew, how are you? . . . Oh, are you? Wonderful. . . . Provincetown, how nice for you. . . . Well, if you think you could. . . . Thanks."

He put his hand over the receiver. "His boyfriend says they're going to Provincetown for the rest of the summer. Doesn't sound too good." He attended to the telephone again.

"Mark, hello, this is Dan Harwich. . . . An old friend of mine from Brown, a writer, showed up here in the course of doing research for a book, and it turns out that she wants to get in touch with you. . . . That's right. Her name is Emily Eliot, and she's completely house-trained, Harvard Ph.D. . . . A poet named Creeley Monk? . . . Yes, that's right. She's interested in the people who were at a place called Shorelands with him, and it seems she came across your name somewhere. . . ."

He looked at her. "He wants to know where you saw his name."

Dart had not explained how he had heard of Mark Foil. "Doing research on Creeley Monk."

He repeated the phrase into the telephone. "No, she did a book before this. Robert Frost. . . . Yes, she's right here."

He held out the receiver. "Emily? Dr. Foil wants to talk to you." When she took it from him, he pretended he was working a shovel.

A clipped, incisive voice nothing like Harwich's effeminate parody said, "What is going on, Miss Eliot? Dan Harwich doesn't have any serious friends."

"I was a youthful mistake," Nora said.

"You can't be writing a book about Creeley Monk. Nobody remembers Creeley anymore."

"As Dan said, I'm working on a book about what happened at Shorelands during the summer of 1938. I think Hugo Driver's success unfairly eclipsed the other writers who were there."

"Do you have a publisher?"

"Chancel House."

A long silence. "Why don't you come over and let me take a look at you? We're going out of town this morning, but we still have some time."

60

A SLENDER, SMILING young man in a lightweight gray suit and black silk shirt opened the door of the stone house amid the oak trees and greeted them. Harwich introduced his friend Emily Eliot to the young man, Andrew Martindale, who looked straight into Nora's eyes, widened his smile, and instantly changed from a diplomatic male model into a real person filled with curiosity, humor, and goodwill. "It's wonderful that you're here," he said to Nora. "Mark is tremendously interested in your project. I wonder if you know what you're in for!"

Nora said, "I'm just grateful that he's willing to talk to me."

"*Willing* is hardly the word." Martindale let them pass into the house and then stepped backwards onto a riotous Persian rug. A broad staircase with shining wooden treads stood at the end of a row of white columns. "I'll take you into the library."

At the end of the row of columns, he opened a door into a book-lined room twice the size of Alden Chancel's library. In a dazzle of sunlight streaming through a window, a white-haired man in a crisp dark suit who looked unexpectedly familiar to Nora was standing beside an open file box on a gleaming table. He grinned at them over the top of his black half-glasses and held up a fat volume bound in red cloth.

"Andrew, you said I'd find it, and I did!"

Martindale said, "Nothing ever gets lost in this house, it just goes into hiding until you need it. And here, just in time to share your triumph, are Dan and Ms. Eliot. Would you like some coffee? Tea, maybe?"

This was addressed to Nora, who said, "If you have coffee ready, I'd love some."

The white-haired man tucked the red book under his arm, twinkled the half-glasses off his nose and folded them into his top pocket, and came loping across the room with his right hand extended. He was as smooth as mercury, and though he must have been in his mid-seventies, he looked as if he had undergone no essential physical changes since the age of fifty. He shook Harwich's hand, then turned, all alertness, interest, and curiosity, to Nora, who felt that with one probing glance Mark Foil instantly had comprehended all that was important within her, including a great deal of which she herself was unaware.

Harwich introduced them.

"Why don't we sit down so that you can tell me about yourself?" Foil indicated a plump sofa and two matching chairs near the bright window. A glass table with a neat stack of magazines stood within reach of the furniture. Nora took one end of the sofa, and Mark Foil slid into the other. As if he were cutting her loose, Harwich moved around the glass table, sat down in the chair beside the far end of the sofa, and lounged back.

"You haven't been sleeping very well, have you?" Foil asked.

"Not as much as I'd like," she said, surprised by the question.

"And you've been under a good deal of stress. If you don't mind my asking, why is that?"

She looked across at Harwich, who looked blandly back.

"The past few days have been kind of strange," she said.

"In what way?"

Looking at the kind, intelligent face beneath the white hair, Nora came close to admitting she was here under false pretenses. Mark Foil took in her hesitation and leaned forward without altering his expression.

Nora looked up from Foil to Harwich, who was staring at her in unhappy alarm.

"To tell you the truth," she said, "I've just become menopausal, and my body seems to have turned against me."

Foil leaned back, nodding, and behind him, unseen, Harwich flopped back into his chair. "Apart from your looking much too young, it makes a lot of sense," Foil said. "You're seeing your gynecologist, keeping a watch on what's going on?"

"Yes, thanks."

"I'm sorry if I seemed to pry. I'm like an old firehorse. My reflexes are stronger than my common sense. You and Dan were friends at Brown?"

"That's right."

"What was our eminent neurosurgeon like in those days?"

Nora looked across at our eminent neurosurgeon and tried to guess what he had been like at Brown. "Ferocious and shy," she said. "Always angry. He improved once he got into medical school."

Foil laughed. "Wonderful thing, the memory of an old friend. Keeps us from forgetting the cocoons from which we emerged."

"Some old friends remember more than you imagine possible," Harwich said.

"When I was that age, I read Browning and Tennyson until they came out of my ears. Not very up to date, I'm afraid. I suppose part of what I liked about Creeley's work was that although he was much better than I ever would have been, he wasn't very up to date, either. In medicine you have to be up to the minute to be any good at all, but I don't think that's true in the arts, do you?"

Andrew Martindale backed through the door holding a wide silver tray with three cups and a silver coffeepot in time to hear Foil's last sentence. He turned around to carry the tray toward the glass table. "Not again."

"But this time we have a Harvard Ph.D. and professional writer to consult. Emily, what do you think? Andrew and I have an ongoing argument about tradition versus the avant-garde, and he's completely pigheaded."

Martindale slid the tray onto the table, almost clipping the stack of magazines. Nora looked at them and knew she was lost, out of her depth, about to be exposed as a fraud. *Avec*, *Lingo*, and *Conjunctions*, which almost certainly represented Martindale's taste in literature, might as well have been written in Urdu, for all she knew of their contents.

"Settle our argument," Foil said.

Harwich said, "You shouldn't—"

"No, it's all right," Nora said. "I don't think you can settle it, and I don't think you want to, because you get too much fun out of it. Speaking for myself, I like both Benjamin Britten and Morton Feldman, and they probably hated each other's music." She looked around at the three men. Two of them were gazing at her with undisguised friendly approval, the third with undisguised astonishment.

Martindale smiled at them all and vanished.

As if following stage directions, the three of them picked up their cups and sipped the excellent coffee.

"You're right, we enjoy our ongoing argument, and part of what I like in Andrew is that he keeps trying to bring me up to date. And although Creeley's work is not the sort of thing he generally likes, he's been supportive of my efforts to publish a Collected Poems." Foil smiled at her. "It would be nice if your work finally permitted me to do him justice."

Nora felt like crawling out of the house.

"Merle must be your editor."

"Excuse me?"

"Merle Marvell. At Chancel House. Isn't he your editor?"

"Oh, yes, of course. I didn't realize you knew him."

"We've met him a half dozen times, but I don't really know him except by reputation. As far as I know, Merle is the only person at Chancel who'd have enough courage to take on a project which might turn out less than flattering to Lincoln. In fact, I have the idea that Merle is the *only* real editor at Chancel House."

Nora smiled at him, but this conversation was making her increasingly uncomfortable.

"Do you think Chancel House would be willing to publish something which puts Driver in a different light? Creeley didn't think much of him to begin with, and by the end of the summer, he positively detested the man."

"I think they're willing to present a balanced viewpoint," Nora said.

"Well, then." Foil placed his cup in its saucer. "I don't see why I shouldn't share this with you." He picked up the thick red book. "This is the journal Creeley kept during the last year of his life. I read it when I went through his papers after his death. Read it? I *studied* it. Like every suicide's survivor, I was looking for an explanation."

"Did you find one?"

"Does anyone? He had been disappointed the day before he killed himself, but I wouldn't have thought . . ." He shook his head, the memory of defeat clear in his eyes. "It still isn't easy. Anyhow, if you're interested in bringing the celebrated Hugo Driver down a peg or two, this will be useful to you. The man was a weakling. He was worse than that. It took a while for Creeley to convince anybody of the fact, but he was a thief."

61

NORA'S BLOOD SEEMED to slow. "Are you saying that he stole other writers' work?"

"Oh, they all do that, starting with Shakespeare. I'm talking about *real* theft. Unless you're saying that Driver actually plagiarized *Night Journey*. But if that was your story, I hardly suppose Chancel would be backing you." He grinned. "Instead of giving you a contract, they'd be more likely to put one out on you, Merle Marvell or no Merle Marvell."

Harwich chuckled, and Nora silenced him with a murderous glance. "Are you saying that Creeley Monk saw him steal things from the other guests?"

"Not just Creeley, thank goodness. You're interested in all of them, aren't you? In everything that went on that summer?"

She nodded.

"This is what I'm prepared to do." He gestured with the book. "I'll describe some of the contents of this journal. You continue your research while Andrew and I are on Cape Cod. When I get back, I'll talk to Merle Marvell and hear what he has to say about you and your project. I'd do that now, but we have limited time this morning. You have the most—ah, colorful—neurosurgeon in the state vouching for you, so I'm willing to go farther than I normally would, but I want to be as cautious as is reasonably possible. You have no objections, I assume?"

She thought hard for a moment while both men looked at her, Harwich shooting sparks of wrath and indignation, Foil calmly. "Why don't I send you the chapters after they're written? If you let me borrow the journal, I could have more time to sort through all the information, and I can get it back to you at the end of the summer."

He was already shaking his head. "I hold Creeley's papers in

271

trust." Seeing that Nora was about to object, he raised an index finger. "However! When Merle tells me that you are indeed what you say you are, as I'm sure he will, I'll give you a copy of all the relevant pages from this diary. Do we have an agreement?"

Harwich gave her a grim, unhappy glance. Nora said, "I think that will be fine."

"Okay, then." A suppressed vitality came into his features, and Nora saw how eager he had been all along to do justice to his dead lover. "Let me tell you something about his background, so you'll be able to appreciate what sort of person Creeley was." He paused to gather his thoughts. "He was a year behind me at the Garand Academy, on a scholarship. We were all alike—except Creeley. Creeley was as conspicuous as a peacock in a field of geese.

"Creeley's father was a bartender, and his mother was an Irish immigrant. They lived in a little apartment above the bar, and he had to take two buses to get to school. Creeley turned up wearing big black work shoes, a hideous striped suit far too big for him, and a Buster Brown collar with a *velvet* bow tie. Of course, the older boys beat him up, and that was that for the Buster Brown collars, but he kept the velvet bow tie. That had been *his* idea. He'd read that poets wore velvet bow ties, and Creeley already knew he was a poet. He also knew, at the advanced age of fourteen, that he was sexually attracted to other males, although he pretended otherwise. In order to survive, he had to. But he didn't see any point in pretending about anything else.

"By his second year he resembled the rest of us. Because he was absolutely fearless, because he was such a *character*, he already had a place in the school. Everybody cherished him. It was remarkable. Here was this utterly philistine school, and Creeley Monk single-handedly made them—us—respect a literary vocation. In his junior year, he published a few poems in national magazines.

"I went to Harvard, and he came on a full scholarship a year later. It didn't take us long to become close. Creeley and I lived together while I was at medical school, and he moved to Boston when I had my internship and residency there. He got a job writing catalog copy for a publishing house, and we had separate apartments in the same building, which was his choice. He didn't want to do anything that might compromise my career. But in every other way we were an established couple, and when I moved back here, he did, too. Again, we had separate apartments, and I went into practice with two older men. During this time, Creeley and I were like people in an open marriage. He was devoted to me, and God knows I was devoted to him, but he was promiscuous by nature, and he was commuting to Boston almost every day, so that was how it was.

"He began publishing in all kinds of journals and magazines, gave readings, won a few prizes. In 1937 *The Field Unknown* came out, and I'm happy to say it was nominated for a Pulitzer Prize. Georgina Weatherall invited him to Shorelands for the following July, and we both saw this as a great sign.

"In the end, he was disappointed. None of the writers he most admired were present, and two people there had not even published books—Hugo Driver and Katherine Mannheim. He had seen one story by Katherine Mannheim in a literary magazine, and rather liked it, but she had published a fair amount of poetry, which he liked a lot more. In person, she turned out to be a very pleasant surprise. He had imagined her as a kind of a lost, waif-like little thing, and her sharpness and tough-mindedness came as a surprise. There was something else he liked about her, too. I'll read you some of that from the diary. Hugo Driver was another matter. Creeley had read some of his stories in little magazines and thought they were weak tea. Even before Creeley became aware of his thieving, Driver made him uncomfortable. In his first letter back to me, he said Driver was 'dank and desperate,' which turned into a running joke. After a while, he was referring to Driver as 'D&D' in the diary, and then that became 'DD,' which became 'DeDe,' like the girl's name.

"The others were a mixed bag. Austryn Fain struck him as a clever nonentity, a sort of literary hustler who spent most of his time trying to charm Lincoln Chancel into giving him a lot of money for his next book. Then there was Bill Tidy. Creeley respected Tidy, and he loved his book, *Our Skillets.* They had a lot in common. So he went to Shorelands anticipating a kind of meeting of minds, but Tidy put up a rough-spoken, workingman front and refused to talk to him.

"And then there was the rising star of the gathering, Merrick Favor. Creeley was instantly attracted to him, but it was hopeless. I could see what was coming when he wrote that the first time he went to dinner in Main House and saw Favor talking to Katherine Mannheim in a corner, he thought he was seeing me!"

Suddenly Nora realized that the reason Mark Foil had seemed like a known quantity to her was that he was an older version of the handsome young writer in the famous photograph. She managed to say, "Yes."

"I suppose he really did look like me, but that was all we had in common. Favor was straight as a die and a compulsive womanizer to boot. He and Austryn Fain both flirted with Katherine Mannheim, but she wouldn't have either one of them. She made fun of them. Even Lincoln Chancel made some kind of crude pass at her, and she demolished him with a joke. But you know the lure of what you can't get. Creeley developed a hopeless crush on Favor. It drove him crazy, and he enjoyed every frustrating second of it."

"You didn't mind?" Nora asked.

"If I'd minded that sort of thing, I couldn't have put up with Creeley for a week, much less all those years. He wasn't designed to be celibate. Do you know how the place was set up, how they lived, what their days were like?"

"Not in much detail," Nora said. "They lived in different houses, didn't they, and they had dinner together every night?"

Foil nodded. "Georgina Weatherall lived in Main House, and the guests were assigned to cottages scattered through the woods around the gardens. These were one- and two-story affairs originally built for the staff, back when the family who owned the place had an army of servants. Creeley was in Honey House, one of the smallest cottages, all by itself on the far side of the pond. He had only two tiny rooms and a saggy single bed, which made him very grumpy. As the only woman guest, Katherine Mannheim was put by herself in the next-largest guest house, Gingerbread, stuck back in the woods past the gardens. Austryn Fain and Merrick Favor shared Pepper Pot, and Lincoln Chancel and Dank and Desperate were installed in the biggest cottage, Rapunzel, which had a stone tower on one side and was halfway between Gingerbread and Main House. Chancel had the tower for himself. I suppose he commandeered it."

"I still don't really understand why Lincoln Chancel wanted to go there in the first place," Nora said, having just realized this. "He had his businesses to take care of, and he hardly had to spend a month in a kind of literary colony for the sake of Chancel House."

Foil started to answer and checked himself. "I always took his being there for granted, but he didn't have to subject himself to Georgina's selection of writers, did he? He wasn't there for the entire month, though, he showed up only for the last two weeks."

"The answer's obvious," Harwich said. The other two waited. "Money."

"Money?" Nora said.

"What else? The Weatheralls owned half of Boston. Lincoln Chancel was supposed to be richer than God, but didn't his whole empire turn belly-up pretty soon after all this? He was looking for cash to start up his publishing company."

"Anyhow," Foil said, "to get back to Shorelands, even the normal guests had no formal daily schedule. During the day they could do as they pleased as long as they stayed on the estate. If they wanted to work, the maids carried box lunches to the cottages. If they wanted to socialize, Georgina held court on the terrace. You could swim in the pond or play tennis on the courts. The gardens were famous. Guests wandered around the different areas, or sat on the benches and read. At six everyone gathered in Main House for drinks, and at seven, they went into the dining room. Let me read you something. This is what Creeley wrote when he got back to Honey House on his first night."

He opened the red book and flipped through pages until he found the entry he wanted.

"The gods in charge of railways having seen to my arriving at this longed-for destination five hours late, thereby postponing the death of my illusions, I was escorted in haste by the alarming Miss W., an apparition in blazing, ill-assorted colors (purple, red, orange, and pastel blue) distributed among layers of scarves, shawls, gown, stockings, and shoes, also in a not-to-be-ignored profusion of monstrous jewels, also in ditto face paint, down a narrow path through the gardens—all splendid so far—to a narrower path leading at weary length to my abode, Honey House, a name which had implied rustic charm to susceptible me. In reality, rustic Hovel House is charmless. Miss W. pointed with a ring-encrusted finger to a tiny prison bedroom, a squalid kitchen alcove, a clunky desk where I am to Create! Create! Cawing, she 'left me to my devices.'

"Whom do I see upon first entering the Baghdad of the Main House lounge but, sensibly engaged with a pretty boy, my life's ever-sensible companion? Salvation! He had arrived to rescue me from the Hovel! Down flaps Milady, attired in even gaudier rags, face a-glow with fresh paint, to screech introductions to my own, yet not my own MF but his virtual doppelgänger, MF2, who in fact is last year's literary darling, Merrick Favor, and the boy, an actually not-terribly-androgynous young woman revealed to be Katherine Mannheim, whose work appeals to me. As does Katherine herself, due to her prickly unsentimental good nature, her stylish unstylishness, her caustic wit, and, not least, her readiness to admit dismay at our hostess and her realm. And also, alas, to the Favored one, due no doubt to all of the above save the last, Well-Favored being too polite for words, but more than these to her physical attractions. MF2 tolerates my intrusion, and we three discuss our current projects, I already in thrall to 2, he eyeing the girl. 2 at work on a novel, of course, at which KM declares herself 'unwriting' a novel. I ask about unwriting, and she replies, 'Just like writing, only in reverse.' We murmur admirations of Georgina, which 2 sweetly takes at face value. Among the others I recognize Bill Tidy from publicity photos—awkward, shy, and out of sorts, I must make common cause with him soon—and a bearded string bean who must be Austryn Fain. (At dinner I will be across from him, and yep, he is, fain would I lament he is a talentless lunkhead intent on buttering up Milady, even unto exclaiming over her tacky collection of 'art,' which consists of a jumbled crowd of earnest daubs all but obliterating her prize, a fine Mary Cassatt, and her only other decent piece, a moody Redon vastly preferred by me.) 2 shares lodgings with Lunkhead and pretends not to be displeased, and Lunkhead, as misguided as his roommate, shares 2's yearnings for KM. In a corner lurks a bedraggled soul later revealed to be one Hugo Driver, of whom the better must remain less said. Invited to drink, I strike a blow for the proletariat by requesting an unposh Wine Spo-dee-o-dee, half red wine, half gin, oft served at the paternal inn, and KM delights by putting down her bubbly and asking for a lethal Top-and-Bottom, equal parts port and gin. These are wincingly delivered.

"Dinner likewise consists of sweet and raw in equal portions, for while KM coruscates and gorgeous 2 is resolutely amiable, our hostess utters dilations upon the Germanic Soul. I deflect attention to the paintings. Mary Cassatt receives her due, and the earnest daubers are praised to the skies, creepy Fain chiming in. I remark upon the little Redon, which displeased Milady screeches she installed only because of its name. What does Miss Mannheim think of the wondrous Lockesly portrait of yon peasant before his sheepfold? enquires Georgina, seeking to restore the proper moral tone. 'I think,' said KM, 'of Aristotle Contemplating the Home of Buster.' 'Oh my dear,' smirks Georgina, 'you mean, you surely intend to say . . .' 'That bellwether is a Buster if I ever saw one,' said KM, and sharply we returned to the magnificence of all things Teutonic.''

Mark Foil looked up from the diary and gave Nora an almost apologetic glance. "Creeley fell into this tone when he was rattled or insecure, and alcohol always encouraged his showy side. He mentions only one Wine Spo-dee-o-dee, something he only drank when he wanted to offend people he thought were being pretentious, but I'm pretty sure he had at least three of them. Of course he loved the girl's ordering a Top-and-Bottom. it proved they were two of a mind. They used to talk about their 'outsider drinks.' ''

"Outsider drinks," Nora said, jolted by another reference to Paddi Mann.

"Creeley learned about them from the musicians who used to come to the family bar. But he also meant that the two of them were outsiders at Shorelands. The joke about Aristotle Contemplating the Bust of Homer took care of *her*, and Georgina wasn't completely obtuse, she at least *sensed* that Creeley thought she was absurd, so he was on the outs, too. Which meant we have this little situation here."

"What did Driver steal?" Nora asked.

Two loud thumps came from the other side of the door. Andrew Martindale walked in, tapping the face of his watch with a satisfied expression on his face. "Thirty-three minutes, a world record. How are we doing?"

"As usual, I've been talking too much," said Foil. He pulled up his sleeve to glance at his own wristwatch. "We still have plenty of time if we don't dawdle on the way."

Martindale went to a wing chair on the far side of the room, where he crossed his legs and composed himself.

"Where were we?" Foil asked.

"Stealing," Nora said.

"We were stealing something?" said Martindale.

"Hugo Driver was stealing something." Foil opened the red diary and turned pages. "This was a few days before Lincoln Chancel's arrival, and all sorts of trunks and boxes, even furniture, had been delivered to Rapunzel and set up in the tower. Chancel insisted on his own bed, so it came on a truck and was carried up into the tower, and the old one went into the Main House basement. He had a ticker tape machine put in, so he could keep up with the stock market. A big carton of cigars arrived from Dunhill. A catering company installed a mahogany bar in one room and stocked it with bottles."

Foil examined a page. "Here we are, the day before Chancel's arrival. Like good outsiders, Creeley and Katherine Mannheim had been indulging in Top-and-Bottoms, and in the middle of dinner he had to leave the table to visit the bathroom. Who should he spot acting fishy in the lounge but good old D&D, Hugo Driver, who had left the dining room without anyone's noticing.

"I did not even see him at first, and I might not have seen him at all if he hadn't sucked in enough air to fill a balloon and followed that by kicking one of the legs of the sofa. When I looked toward the source of these noises, I observed KM's embroidered bag sliding down the back of the sofa and coming to rest on the seat with a distinct rattle. D&D, whom I had thought wrapped in his usual nervous gloom back at the table, emerged around the side of the sofa and slid something into the right pocket of his shabby houndstooth jacket. He twitched the flap over the pocket and tried to face me down. What a pathetic creature it is. I stopped moving and smiled at it and in a very quiet voice asked it what it was doing. I believe it all but fainted. I said that if it replaced the stolen object at once, I would keep silent. The nasty sneak bared its teeth and informed me that Miss Mannheim had requested that it bring her a pillbox from an inner compartment of the bag, and that had I not been fixated on Rick Favor, I would have overheard the exchange. I had observed KM whispering to D&D, and its dank desperate glee at having been so favored, but that had been all. It produced the proof of its innocence, a small silver pillbox. Soon after my return from the bathroom, another laborious dinner and its hymns to Nietzsche and Wagner happily in the past, I inserted myself into the scented region between 'Rick' (!!) and KM and described what I had seen and said. KM brandished the pillbox, and 2 unsubtly implied I had imagined the theft. I implored her to look through the bag, and when she complied I saw, though 2 did not, an amused expression cross her features. 'Who steals my purse steals trash,' she said. Excited now, dear 2 prepared himself to assault D&D, but was stayed by KM's saying that no, nothing was missing, certainly nothing of value, and he had after all produced the invaluable box, from which she then extracted a minute ivory pill and lodged it like a sweet beneath her pointed tongue.

"But two weeks later," Foil said, "while everyone else paid court to Lincoln Chancel, Driver slipped a pair of Georgina's silver sugar tongs into his pocket, and Creeley saw him do it. The first person he told was Merrick Favor, and Favor called him a degenerate and said that if he didn't stop slandering Hugo Driver, he'd punch him in the face."

"Speaking of degenerates," Andrew Martindale said from his distant chair, "the lunatic who escaped from jail in Connecticut is on the loose in Springfield, what about that? Dick Dirt?"

"Dart," Nora croaked, and cleared her throat. "Dick Dart."

"He was in a motel on the other side of town. When the police got there, all they found was a corpse cut to pieces in one of the rooms. No sign of Dart. The reporter said the body looked like an anatomy lesson."

Nora's face felt hot.

Foil was watching her. "Are you all right, Ms. Eliot?"

"You have to drive to Provincetown, and we're keeping you."

"Let me worry about getting us to Cape Cod in time. Are you sure you're all right?"

"Yes. It's just . . ." She tried to invent a reasonable-sounding explanation for her distress. "I live in Connecticut, in Westerholm, actually, and I knew some of Dick Dart's victims."

Andrew Martindale looked sympathetic, Mark Foil concerned. "How terrible for you. Did you ever meet this Dart person?"

"Briefly," she said, and tried to smile.

"Would you like to break for a couple of minutes?"

"No, thank you. I'd like to hear the rest."

Foil looked down again at the book open in his hands. "Let's see if I can boil this down. Lincoln Chancel arrived on schedule and almost immediately turned Hugo Driver into a kind of servant, sending him on errands, generally exploiting him in every way. Driver seems to have gloried in the role, as if he expected to keep the job when the month was over. Poor Creeley was left out in the cold. I gather that Merrick Favor mentioned his accusations to one or two people, and after that both he and Katherine Mannheim were out of favor with their hostess. She more than Creeley, actually, because she quickly became absorbed with her 'unwriting,' whatever that meant, and even skipped a few dinners to work on it. This put her in such disfavor that everybody began to feel that it was only a matter of time before Georgina booted her out, as she'd been known to do when a guest seriously disappointed her.

"One night they all took part in a ceremony called 'the Ultimate,' which took place in an area called Monty's Glen. I don't know any more about it, except that it was boring. All Creeley said in his diary was *the Ultimate, yawn, glad that's over.'* But the next day all the excitement began. After lunch, Creeley was out walking through the gardens. Merrick Favor came up behind him and tapped him on the shoulder, and Creeley all but passed out. For a second, he thought Favor had boiled over and wanted to hit him, but instead he apologized to Creeley. Hugo Driver really *was* a thief, or so he strongly suspected. Then he explained himself.

"Favor had been trailing after Katherine Mannheim through the gardens, hoping to have a word alone with her, but every time she sat down for a moment, one of the other men popped through an opening in a hedge and sat down beside her. The last one had been Driver, and Favor had watched them say a few words to each other until Miss Mannheim got up and walked away through a gap in the hedges. Favor had started to go toward her when he saw Driver notice that she had left her bag lying half open on the bench, and he stopped to watch what would happen. Driver glanced around"—Foil imitated the quick movements of a man who wishes not to be observed—"and moved closer to the bag. From where he was standing, Favor couldn't see Driver dip into the bag, and Driver was clever enough not to look at his hands. Favor was pretty sure what was going on, anyhow, and he was almost certain that he *did* see Driver slide some kind of object into his jacket pocket, so he came out of hiding and confronted the little weasel. Driver denied everything. He even said he'd had enough of these accusations and intended to complain to Georgina. Off he went. Favor took the bag to Miss Mannheim and told her what he'd seen. When she looked in the bag, she laughed and said, 'Who steals my trash steals trash.' That night she disappeared."

"After Favor thought he saw Driver stealing something from her bag," Nora said.

"Right. She didn't show up for dinner. Georgina was irritated and foul to everyone, even Lincoln Chancel. Late at night, Creeley went out for a walk and came across Chancel and Driver near Bill Tidy's cottage, and Chancel was extraordinarily rude to him. He told him to stop sneaking around. The next night, again no Katherine Mannheim, and after dinner, Georgina led the entire party to Gingerbread on the pretext of seeing whether Miss Mannheim was ill. Everybody could sense that unless they found Katherine Mannheim in a high fever and too weak to get out of bed, Georgina was going to throw her out on the spot. Instead, she was gone. She'd taken off sometime between the previous afternoon and that night. Georgina didn't even seem surprised, Creeley wrote. She behaved as though she expected to find an unlocked door and empty cottage. 'I am sorry to say,' she said, 'that Miss Mannheim appears to have jumped the wall.' And that was that. She had a number for one of Miss Mannheim's sisters and called her to ask her to remove the few things left behind in the bungalow, and the next day the sister arrived. She had no idea where Miss Mannheim could have gone. She wasn't in her apartment in New York, and she hadn't spoken to anyone in her family. She was unpredictable, and she'd previously disappeared from places where she'd felt uncomfortable. But her sister did have one huge worry."

"That she was dead," Nora said.

"You've heard about her weak heart. The sister was afraid that she might have wandered into the woods and suffered heart failure, so she insisted on calling in the police. Georgina was furious but gave in. For a couple of days, the Lenox police questioned the guests and staff at Shorelands. They searched the grounds and the woods. In the end, it seemed pretty clear that she had run off, and a week later, the summer was over."

"And then all these deaths," Nora said.

"Like a plague. Georgina must have felt some sort of renewal was called for, because she immediately paid for a lot of extensive renovations, but all those deaths cast a long shadow over the place."

"There's going to be a long shadow over *us*," Andrew Martindale said.

"One more minute." Foil consulted his watch and skipped over a thick wad of pages. "I want you to hear something from the end, so you'll know as much as I do about Creeley's death." He looked up again. "If you learn anything at all that might shed light on this, I'd appreciate being let in on it. I know it isn't likely, but I do want to ask."

"I'll tell you about anything I find," Nora said.

"It's so enigmatic. Here's what Creeley wrote in his journal three days before he killed himself.

"All at once, a beam of light pierces the depression I've been in since leaving Shorelands. It seems there is hope after all, and from a most Unexpected Quarter. Interest in high places! What a blessed turn, if all goes as it should.

"Then this, the next day.

"Nothing, nothing, nothing, nothing, nothing. Done. Finished. I should have known. At least I did not babble to MF. How cruel, to be written only to be unwritten.

"And that's it, that's all, that's the last entry. I didn't hear from him on either of those days. When I tried to call, the operator told me his phone was off the hook, and I assumed he was working. I knew he'd been unhappy for a long time, so it was good to think he was working hard. But he never let three days go by without at least talking to me, and the next day, when I still couldn't get through to him, I drove to his apartment after my last patient."

Foil paused for a moment. "It was a dark, miserable day. Freezing. We'd had a terrible winter. I don't think we'd seen sunlight for a month. I got to his building. Creeley had the top floor of a duplex, with a separate entrance to his part of the house. After I got out of the car, I climbed over a snowbank and looked up at his windows. All his lights were on. I went up the steps to the porch and rang his bell. His downstairs neighbors, the owners, were both out, and I could hear their dog barking. They had a collie named

Lady—high-strung, like all collies. That's a desolate sound, you know, a dog barking in an empty house. Creeley didn't answer. I thought he'd turned up his radio to drown out the sound of the dog, which he had to do off and on during the day. He didn't mind, Creeley played music all the time when he was writing, and the only problem with turning it up was that sometimes he couldn't hear the bell. I rang it a few more times. When I still didn't hear him coming down the stairs, I took out my key and let myself in, just like a hundred times before.

"As soon as I got in, I heard his radio going full blast. 'Let's Dance,' Benny Goodman's theme song. It was one of the remote broadcasts they used to do in those days. I went up the stairs calling out his name. Lady was going crazy. Before I got to the top of the stairs, I started smelling something. I should have recognized the smell right away. I opened his living room door, but he wasn't there. I hollered his name and turned the radio down. That blasted collie got even louder. I knocked on the bathroom door and looked in the kitchen. Then I tried the bedroom.

"Creeley was lying on his bed. Blood everywhere. Everywhere. He'd used the shotgun his father had given him for his sixteenth birthday, when he still had hopes of normal male hobbies for his son. I went into shock. I just *shut down*. It seemed like I stood there for a long time, but it could only have been a couple of minutes. After a little while, I called the police and waited like a robot until they came. And that was that. Try as I might—and I tried, all right—I never understood why he did it."

62

"WELL, I UNDERSTAND why he did it." Harwich turned out of the driveway onto Oak Street and rotated his shoulders several times, as if trying to shake off the atmosphere of the past thirty minutes. He leaned sideways to see himself in the rearview mirror and ruffled the tight gray curls on the side of his head. "Mark is an okay guy, but he doesn't want to see the truth."

Nora pointed at a driveway a little way ahead of them on the other side of the street. "Pull in there."

He stared at her. "What?"

"I want to see them leave."

"You want—oh, I get it." He pulled up slightly ahead of the driveway between two wings of a stone wall, and backed in. "See? You think I don't know what this is about, but I do."

"Good," Nora said.

"You want to make sure they get away safely."

"I'm glad you don't mind."

"I didn't say I didn't mind. I'm just a very agreeable person."

"So tell me why Creeley Monk killed himself."

"It's obvious. This guy reached the end of his rope. First of all, he was a working-class kid who pretended to be high society. From the second he got into that school, his whole life was an act. On top of that, he couldn't sustain his initial success. Shorelands was supposed to raise him to a new level, but no one wanted to publish his next book. One flutter of interest sends him into ecstasies, and when it doesn't pan out, he's devastated. He takes the shotgun out of his closet and ends it all. Simple."

This clever, rapid-fire dissection, as of a corpse under a scalpel, irritated Nora unreasonably; Harwich had reduced Mark Foil's account to the empty diagram of a case history.

"Anyhow, you did a good job in there," Harwich told her. "But there is this little issue about that editor who turns out to be part of the Homintern. Did you get that? *We've* met him a couple of times? Pretty soon Mark is going to know this book is just a smoke screen, and then he's going to have a lot of questions for me."

"It's no big deal. I said I had a book contract, and it turns out I don't. I'm writing the book before I take it to a publisher."

"I'm still in a tricky position. Anyhow, there they are, safe and sound." He nodded toward a long, graceful-looking gray car moving down Oak Street in front of them. "Not a care in the world, as usual."

"You don't like them, do you?"

"What's to like?" he burst out. "These two guys live in a world where everything's taken care of for them. They're so smug, so lovey-dovey, so pleased with themselves, tooling off to Cape Cod in Martindale's new Jaguar while his patients climb the walls."

"I thought he was retired."

"*Mark's* retired, except from all the important stuff, the state boards and the national committees. Andrew has about six jobs, as far as I can make out. Head of psychiatry here, professor of psychiatry there, chief of this and that, a great private practice full of famous painters and writers, plus his books. *The Borderland of the Borderline Patient. The Text of Psychoanalysis. William James, Religious Experience, and Freud.* I forget the others." He pulled out of the drive, enjoying her amazement.

"I thought . . ." Nora did not want to admit what she had thought. "How can he take a month off? Oh, I forgot. It's August, when all the shrinks go to Cape Cod."

"That's right, but Andrew spends *his* month off running a clinic in Falmouth. And writing. He's a busy lad." He gave her a sidelong, appraising look. "Hey, why don't you take some time off yourself? You shouldn't run around on your own while your madman is on the loose. And there's no point in trying to find this Tidy character."

"What do you think happened to Katherine Mannheim?"

"Easy. Everybody thought either she ran away or died in the woods, so they couldn't see that both things were true. She's carrying her suitcase through the woods at night, the weight is too much for her, an owl scares her, blooey. A couple of nitwit cops pretend to search the woods, and surprise, surprise, they don't find her. I've never been inside Shorelands, but I've seen it, and even now we're talking about two square miles of wilderness. An army couldn't have found her."

"You're probably right," she said, idly watching suburban houses grow closer together as the lots shrank and sprouted the swing sets, wading pools, and bicycles in the driveway she had seen while Dick Dart drove them into Fairfield in Ernest Forrest Ernest's car. "Oh, my God."

Harwich gave her a look of concern.

"I know why Lincoln Chancel went to Shorelands."

"Money, I told you."

"Not for the reason you think. He was trying to recruit Georgina Weatherall for his Fascist cause, the Americanism Movement. Lincoln Chancel secretly supported the Nazis. He got together a bunch of sympathetic millionaires, but they had to keep quiet during the war. In the fifties, Joe McCarthy roped them into anti-Communism, I guess, and they had to go along."

He looked at her suspiciously. "I have to say, you do liven things up. Let me take you out for dinner tonight, I know a great French place out near Amherst—a little bit of a drive, but it's worth it. Amazing food, candlelight, the best wines. Nobody'll see us, and we'll be able to have a good long talk."

"Are you worried about somebody seeing us?"

"We have to keep you under wraps. In the meantime, I'll order a pizza. There's not much food in the house. You can get a nap, and I'll go to the hospital. Don't answer the phones or open the door for anyone, okay? We'll keep the world at arm's length for a while and get reacquainted all over again."

Nora leaned back against the seat and closed her eyes. Instantly, she was standing in a forest clearing ringed by tall standing stones. Counting money into neat stacks at a carved mahogany desk placed between two upright stones, Lincoln Chancel glanced up and glared at her. Misery and sorrow overflowed from this scene, and Nora stirred and awakened without at first recognizing that she had fallen asleep. Longfellow Lane rolled past the windows like a painted screen.

"Right now you need to be taken care of," Harwich said.

He pressed a button clipped to his visor to swing up the garage door and drove inside to park beside Sheldon Dolkis's green Ford. As soon as he got out of the car, he moved to the wall and flipped a switch to bring the heavy door rattling down. A bare overhead light automatically turned off, and the door clanked against the concrete. Nora felt almost too tired to move. Harwich's dim form moved past the front of the car toward the right side of the garage. "You okay?" he said, and opened an interior door. A panel of gray light erased the front of his body and turned his hair to silver fuzz.

"Guess I didn't know how tired I was." She dragged herself out of the remarkably comfortable seat and noticed that a small figure like a white sparrow had perched atop the car's hood. No, not a bird, a winged woman, poised for flight. This had a meaning, but what meaning? Oh yes, what do you know, Dan Harwich numbered among his possessions a Rolls-Royce. How odd; the deeper into the world she descended, the further up she went. The car door closed with a bank vault's serious thunk, and Nora went past the waiting Harwich into the house.

"Everything caught up with you," he said from behind her. He put a sympathetic hand on her shoulder and squeezed past in the narrow space of the rear entry, lightly kissed her, and took her with him through the kitchen to the living room, where she stood embarrassed in the midst of a yawn while he darted forward and drew down on a cord which advanced dark curtains across the bow window. "Let's get you settled," he said, and ushered her gently up the stairs, past the linen closet, and into the guest room, where he conducted her toward the bed and removed her shoes once she had stretched out. She yawned again, hugely.

"You fell asleep in the car for about ten minutes."

"I did not." The protest sounded childish.

"You did," Harwich said in an amused echo of her tone. "Not very peacefully, though. You made a lot of unhappy noises." He began massaging the sole of her right foot.

"That feels wonderful."

"Why don't you take off that T-shirt and unbutton your jeans? I'll help you slide them off."

"No." She shook her head back and forth on the pillow.

"You'll be more comfortable. Then you can slide under the covers. Hey, I'm a doctor, I know what's best for you."

Obediently she sat up and yanked off the white V-necked shirt, turning it inside out in the process, and flipped it toward him.

"Cute bra," he said. "Do the top of those jeans."

Protesting, she flattened out and undid the button, pulled down the zip, and wiggled the jeans over her hips. Harwich yanked them down, and in one quick movement they whispered over her thighs, knees, feet. "Matching panties! You're a fashion plate." He raised the sheet and the cover so that she could wriggle under and then lowered them over her, not without a little tucking and patting. "There you are, sweetie."

"What a guy," she heard herself say, and roused herself to add, "Give me about an hour, okay?" The words sounded distant in her ears, and soft, slow-moving bands of color began to spill from the few objects visible through the slits of her eyes, one of them being Dan Harwich as he drifted toward the door.

The broad circle of grass within the tall stones looked like a stage. Nora moved forward as Lincoln Chancel wrapped bands around the stacks of bills before him and one by one placed them in a satchel as carefully as if they were raw eggs. He gave Nora a sharp, disgruntled look and returned to his task. "You don't belong here," he said, seeming to address the satchel.

His ugliness outdid the famous photograph, in which it had seemed a by-product of rage. It was an entire ugliness, domineering in its force.

"No sand in your craw. A few setbacks and you're on your knees, whimpering *Daddy, help me, I can't do it on my own.* Pathetic. When people talk to you, all you hear is what you already know."

"I understood why you went to Shorelands," she said, doing her best to mask the fear and impotence she felt.

"Consider yourself fired." He sent her a cold, ferocious glance of triumph and pulled a thick cigar from his top pocket, bit off the end, and lit it with a match which had appeared between his fingers. "Go home. It's not a job for a little girl."

"Screw you," Nora said.

"Gladly." He grinned at her like a dragon through a flag of smoke. "Even though you're too scrawny for my taste. In my day we liked our women ample—womanly, we used to say. Tits like bolsters, buttocks you could sink your hands into. Women to make your pole stand up and beg for it. One other kind I liked, too—small ones. Every big man wants to roger a little thing. Get on top, you feel like you'll either snap their bones or split 'em in half. But you're not that type, either."

"The Katherine Mannheim type."

He drew on the cigar and blew out a quivering ring of smoke that smelled like rotting leaves. "The runaway." Instead of losing its shape and drifting upward, the trembling smoke ring widened and began shuddering toward Nora. "Little bitch didn't have the manners of a whore."

The smoke ring floated into the middle of the grassy circle, paused, and twisted into nothingness. Pretending that she had already followed orders and left, Chancel snapped the lock of the satchel over the last wad of bills, and her question spoke itself in her head. *What did she say . . .*

"What did she say to you while the photograph was being taken?"

He looked over at her and mouthed the cigar. "Who?"

"Katherine Mannheim."

"I graciously invited her to sit on my lap, and she said, 'I've already seen your warts, I don't have to feel one, too.' Tidy and that blockhead Favor both laughed. Even the pansy smiled, and so did that poser with the funny name. Austryn Fain. What kind of a handle is Austryn Fain?" He aimed the astonishing nose at her like a gun. "You don't know anything. You don't even read the right books. Get out of here. Lose yourself in the woods."

She cried out and found Harwich's shadowy, reassuring face inclining toward her. "Ow, that hurt," he said, maintaining his smile. "You walloped me!"

"Sorry. Bad dream." A long leg brushed hers, and she squinted at his face.

"Do you always make so much noise in your sleep?"

"Get out of this bed. What are you *doing* here?"

"I'm trying to calm you down. Come on. There's nobody here but me."

Nora dropped her head back on the pillow.

"Nobody's going to hurt you. Dr. Dan is right here to make sure of that." He slid closer to her and inserted an arm between her head and the pillow. A smooth cotton shirt encased the arm. "In my medical opinion, you need a hug."

"Yeah." She was grateful for this simple kindness.

"Close your eyes. I'll get out of here when you fall asleep again."

She turned into his arms and tugged a corner of the pillow between her head and his shoulder. He caressed the side of her head and began stroking her bare arm. "Your operation," she murmured.

"Long way off."

"I never sleep during the day," Nora said, and in seconds proved herself a liar.

When she opened her eyes again, Harwich passed a warm hand up her arm and tugged the sheet over her shoulder. Various, not entirely subjective internal dials and gauges informed her that she had spent a significant time asleep. What time was it? Then she wondered if Dick Dart had been arrested since they had left Mark Foil's house. Harwich circled her waist with an arm.

"Don't you have an operation pretty soon?" she asked.

"Took less time than I thought it would."

"It went all right?"

"Except for the demise of the patient."

She whirled around to face him and found him propping his head on one hand, smiling down. "Joke. Barney Hodge will live to tear another thousand divots from the country club greens."

"How long have I been asleep?"

"Most of the day. It's about five-thirty."

"Five-thirty?"

"When I got back, I checked on you, and there you were, out cold, even quiet. I was getting the feeling that you refought the war every time you fell asleep."

"I just about do, according to Davey."

"Not in my house." He leaned forward and brushed his lips against her forehead. "My house is good for you."

"So are you," she said.

"I like to think so." He raised her chin with his hand and kissed her gently on the lips.

"The perfect host."

"The perfect guest." He kissed her again, for a longer time and far more seriously.

"I'd better get out of bed before we do something foolish," she said, relieved that he was in his clothes, and then noticed his bare shoulder visible above the sheet. "You took your shirt off."

"More comfortable. Fewer wrinkles. Besides, a shirt seemed so unfriendly." He circled her waist and pulled her toward him to whisper, "Pants did, too." She stiffened, and he said, "We're alone here. We don't have to answer the phone or open the door. Why don't we spend a little time together? I want us to be nice to each other. You're this spectacular person, and we really care for each other."

"Whoa, hold on," she said. "What are you doing?"

He smiled at her. "Nora, one of the best things about this lovely relationship of ours is that we always wind up in bed. You go out and raise hell all over the place while I stay here in my hole, marrying the wrong people out of boredom, I guess, but sooner or later you always explode back into my life and we charge our batteries all over again. Isn't that right?"

"Jesus," Nora said.

"It's always the same, and this time you show up more gorgeous than ever! You're out of your mind with worry . . ."

"Hardly just worry."

". . . and come right here because you knew you belonged with me. We're in this little bubble of time made just for us.

Inside that bubble we help each other, we heal each other. When we're healed, we go on and tackle all the other crappy parts of life."

"I'm not so sure about that," Nora said. "Hold it, I have to tackle the bathroom before I make any decisions here."

"All the decisions were made a long time ago," Harwich said. "This is the follow-through."

Some fierce emotion she could not begin to identify gripped her, lifted her out of bed, and carried her toward the bathroom. Harwich said, "I'll be here when you get back," but she hardly heard him. She locked the door and sat on the toilet, her face blazing. The enormous feeling within her refused to speak its name even as it sent tears brimming in her eyes. He wanted to take care of her, she needed his care. This had seemed to be true. "But I don't need to get *laid*," she whispered to herself. "I don't *need* him to *fuck* me." She flushed the toilet and looked around at the objects on the bathroom shelves, the dangling shower cap, the lush hotel bathrobe, the shampoo and conditioner, the perfume. "Oh, my God," she said to herself, "I'm an idiot."

She stood up, washed her hands, and wrapped the thick robe around herself, all the while watching her feelings align themselves into new positions. The largest of these feelings—not humiliation, chagrin, regret, not even the ghost of her old attachment to Dan Harwich, but simple anger—sent her back into the bedroom to face him.

"What's that for?" he asked, referring to the robe.

"My self-respect," she said. "Battered as it is."

"Uh oh. Come on, Nora, sit down and talk to me. I want to help you."

"You did help me," she said, moving toward the chair where he had deposited her clothes. His own jeans lay folded over the top of the chair, his shirt unfurled like a jacket across the back. "You took me in, you fed me, you let me see Mark Foil. I'm grateful, so thanks, Dan."

"You're not grateful, you're upset. I understand, Nora. You went through a terrible experience, and it's still affecting you. You don't think you can trust anybody, and when I try to comfort you, all the bells go off. You suddenly think you can't trust even me. Part of the fault is mine, I can see that."

Halfway to the chair, she turned around and faced him, wrapping her arms around her chest. "What part is that, Dan?"

"I take too much for granted."

"Christ, you said it."

"I mean, I didn't think you could misunderstand me that much. I promise you, Nora, I had no intention of doing anything you didn't want to do."

"And one of the best things about our relationship is that we always wind up in bed, so after I felt good and safe, you'd really help me out and have sex with me."

"Let's face it, Nora, we do go to bed together, and we do feel better afterwards."

"You feel so much better afterwards you go out and get married. You always have girlfriends, don't you, Dan? When one wife finally figures you out and gets fed up, you have her replacement lined up to put her name on the prenuptial agreement. The first time I turned up here, you brought me home from the motel to meet Helen and give her a really good reason to get out quick so you could marry Lark. You couldn't marry me, I'm too crazy."

"Nora, you don't want my life. There isn't enough excitement here for you."

She turned away, went to the chair, and stepped into her jeans with her back to him.

"I'm crazy about you. I think you're an amazing woman."

"You don't have any idea who I am. I'm your shipboard romance." She fastened the jeans and threw the robe aside, let him gape. "You're tantalized by the chaos I bring to your tedious, self-important existence, but you want to keep it at bay. It's whoopee time with the emotional bag lady, and when party time is over, back to the girl in the on-deck circle, right?" She had been wrestling the T-shirt, trying to pull it right side out but in her agitation only bundling the body of the shirt into one of the sleeves. She pulled fabric out of the sleeve and tugged the shirt on inside out. "The girl whose things are all over the bathroom, the one who called you twice this morning, the girl who swipes little mementos from the hotels the two of you stay in when you go away together."

"All the fiction in the world isn't in novels," he said, marveling.

"This is the same girl who told you she was coming over here this morning, when you suddenly changed your mind and decided to whisk me off to Mark Foil's house. You figured you could fend off the third Mrs. Harwich for a day or two. I'm too much of a risk to keep around longer than that, aren't I?"

Harwich was sitting up in bed with his arms around his raised knees, watching her with an expression of mild, half-amused perplexity. He hesitated for a conspicuous beat before speaking, as if assuring himself that she had finished at last. "Would you like to stop fantasizing and listen to the truth?"

"The only thing I don't understand," she said, "is why she doesn't sleep in your bedroom. I really don't get that part. Does she snore like a pig, or are the two of you saving a whole night together in the master's bedroom for after the wedding, like a reward kind of deal?"

Harwich inhaled deeply, leaned forward, and opened his hands, palm up, the image of beleaguered reason. "This whole picture you're describing is *all made up*. It isn't *real*. Dick Dart knocked you for a loop, remember? As long as you can keep in mind who I am, the real me and not this monster you just invented, I'll be as patient and supportive as I know how. Maybe you can't accept that right now, but it's the God's truth."

This spoke to all of her old feelings about Dan Harwich, and his reasonableness, his steady, kind, affectionate regard, filled her with doubts. This was *Harwich*, she reminded herself. Three years ago she had thrown herself at him. Could she blame him for catching her? It was true. She had willingly helped him speed up the wreckage of his first marriage. "Say more," she said.

"I don't blame you for feeling strange about Lark. But I was honest about her. I told you I was already seeing her when you came here last time. I can't pretend I've ever been a faithful husband, because I haven't. Okay? I confess. I mess around. I get bored. I need what you have, that . . . spirit. But honest, this is the truth, I don't have a new bride waiting in the wings."

"Then whose stuff is that in the bathroom?"

He looked sideways for a moment, considering, then again met her eyes. "Okay. But bear in mind that I don't really have any reason to explain this or anything else. You see that, don't you?"

"So explain." Her angry certainty was ebbing away.

"What the hell, Nora, I'm not a monk. During the course of

my tedious, self-important life, it has now and then come to my attention that some women really do prefer having their own separate bathroom. So I put some toothbrushes and other stuff in there just in case."

"You didn't change your mind about taking me to see Mark Foil because your new girlfriend said she was coming over?"

"I don't blame you for letting the past few days make you suspicious of men. And I know it looks bad, my getting into bed with you, but cross my heart, I had no intention of coercing you into having sex. I hope you believe me."

She sighed. "Honest to God, Dan, I almost—" The telephone in the bedroom down the hall rang once, twice, and Harwich's face modulated from earnest entreaty to a spasm of irritation and back to a close approximation of innocent indifference before it rang a third time. "Don't you want to get that?"

"This is more important."

"It might be the hospital."

"Trust me, it's just some pest."

The distant telephone continued to ring: a fifth time, a sixth, a ninth time, a tenth.

"Don't you have an answering machine?"

He held her eyes expressionlessly for a moment or two. "I turned off the machine on that line."

"Why would you do that?" Nora watched calculation, annoyance, and something alert and wary appear in his face. "Why, Dan?"

The telephone stopped ringing.

"I guess it wasn't such a good idea," he said. "But hell, nobody's perfect."

"You bastard." She felt as though she had been punched in the stomach. "You slimy, self-serving, lying creep." The feeling in her stomach intensified. "You almost had me talked into getting back into bed with you."

"Do it anyhow. What's the difference? This is about you and me. To hell with anybody else."

"You still think you have a chance, don't you?"

"Consider this. I was protecting your feelings. Okay, I have a woman friend, I've known her for a couple of months, and she stays here from time to time. *I* don't know if I'm going to marry her. If I'm not willing to let her destroy our relationship, why should you?"

She looked at him in outright amazement. "You really are an absolute bastard. Boy, I wonder what you . . . No, I already know."

"You know what I think of you? I doubt that very much. But don't waste time brooding about it, just get in your car and go. At this point, I don't see much point in prolonging the situation. Take off. Nice to know you, kind of."

She considered throwing some heavy object at him but then realized with a sad, final thump of defeat that he was not worth the effort. "Answer one question for me, will you?"

"If you insist."

"Why does this woman sleep in here instead of your bedroom? I don't get it."

"Because of the pillows," Harwich said. "If you really want to know."

"The pillows?"

"She's allergic to down pillows, and they're the only kind I can stand to sleep on. These are foam. I think sleeping on a foam pillow is like having sex with a condom."

She found she could smile. "Dan, I don't see much of a future for your third marriage."

His eyes hardened, and his mouth thinned like a lizard's. "The truth is, Nora, you were always a little nuts. Being nuts was okay in Vietnam—it probably helped you make it through—but it sure as hell doesn't work anymore."

"I'm beginning to understand that you have a lot in common with Dick Dart." She walked down the side of the bed toward the door. Harwich slid an inch or two away, trying to pretend that he was merely finding a more comfortable position. "On the whole, I prefer Dick Dart. He's a lot more upfront than you are."

"See what I mean?" he said, smirking, now that he was out of reach.

She opened the door and looked at him as calmly as she could. "Aren't you a little worried?"

"Why don't you just leave? Do I have to tell you never to come back, or have you figured that out for yourself?"

"That old Ford is parked *really* close to your car," she said, and closed the door behind her. She could hear his shouts as she went down the stairs, and they followed her through the kitchen. By the time she had raised the garage door and started the car, he was standing naked in the back door, no more than an absurd figure with a potbelly, stork legs, and graying pubic hair, yelling but too afraid of being seen by his neighbors to come any closer. She backed out without touching the Rolls.

63

"D-E-O-D-A-T-O," NORA SPELLED.

During the seconds while the telephone reported a dense silence, she regretted the impulse to call the Chancels' man-servant. Why had she imagined that Jeffrey would not go imme-diately to Daisy, or Alden if Alden was home, or even the police? When the need to talk to someone in Westerholm had seized her, enigmatic Jeffrey had seemed the most likely candidate, although for an irrational moment she had imagined consulting Holly Fenn. She *still* wished she could talk to Fenn, absolute proof, if after Harwich she needed proof, of her rotten taste in protective men. A telephone began to ring, and she realized that she had not con-sidered what she would do if an answering machine picked up. Nora moved the receiver away from her head and heard a metallic voice say "Hello." Was this voice Jeffrey's? Nora envisioned a room full of cops in headphones leaning over a tape recorder. She moved the receiver back to her ear, more uncertain than ever.

A male voice, Jeffrey's, repeated the greeting as a question.

She spoke his name.

Silence. Then, "Nora." She had never before heard him speak her name without calling her "Mrs." Most often, he had never called her anything but "you." "Where are you?"

"In Massachusetts."

He paused for a moment. "Would you prefer me to keep quiet about this? Or would you like me to speak privately to anyone in particular?"

"I don't know yet," she confessed, understanding that "anyone in particular" meant Davey. Jeffrey's tact extended to his private life.

He weighed this. "Are you all right?"

"I think that remains to be seen. I guess I'm trying to decide what to do. Everything's so *complicated.*" She fought the desire to break down into tears. "Jeffrey, I'm sorry to do this to you, but I don't exactly feel safe right now."

"No wonder," he said. "All sorts of people are trying to find you."

"Don't make me ask a lot of questions. Please, Jeffrey."

Nora could all but hear him thinking. "I'll try to tell you what I know, but don't hang up and disappear on me, okay? Nobody's listening, I'm alone in my room, and you're fine as long as you stay where you are, at least for now. You're at a pay phone?"

"Yes." Her anxieties ebbed.

"All right. It's a good thing you called on this line. The other ones are all tapped."

"Oh, God," she said. "They still think I kidnapped Natalie Weil."

"They're acting that way." An ambiguity hung in the air while he hesitated. "From what I overhear, Mrs. Weil isn't making a lot of sense." There was another brief silence. "For what it's worth, I don't think you went near her."

"What about Davey?"

"Davey's under a lot of pressure."

"He's staying with his parents?"

"Yes. Pretty soon he'll be right *here.*"

"With you?"

"In my apartment. In what used to be my apartment. Until yesterday he was staying in your house, at least at night, but with all the excitement, Mr. Chancel persuaded him to move back here. He put his foot down about staying in his old bedroom, but after Mr. Chancel . . . um, temporarily changed the conditions of my employment, he agreed to take over my place."

"Alden fired you?"

"Mr. Chancel called it a provisional suspension. He was very sorry about it. Our salaries will be paid through the end of the month, and if conditions are right, we can return. If not, he'll give us two months' severance pay and sterling recommendations."

"Us?"

"My aunt and me. I'm packed up, and when she finishes we'll be leaving."

Nora discovered that she could be shocked. "But Jeffrey, where will you go?"

"My aunt is going to stay with some cousins on Long Island. I'd drive her out there, but she won't let me, so I'm dropping her at the train station, and I'll stay with my mother for a while."

Nora had never considered that Jeffrey might have a mother. He seemed to have arrived on the planet fully formed, without the customary mediation of parents. "He ordered you and Maria out so that Davey could stay in your apartment?"

"Mr. Chancel told us that his business was not doing as well as it should, and that for the time being he had to make certain sacrifices."

It sounded to Nora as though the German deal Dick Dart had mentioned had fallen through. Good. She hoped that Chancel House would dwindle and starve. For a time, her attention wandered from whatever Jeffrey was saying.

". . . but still. Here's Merle Marvell asking about that time, that place, and right away we get suspended, or fired, or whatever it is."

"I'm sorry, Jeffrey, I faded out for a little bit. What happened?"

"Merle Marvell asked Mr. Chancel if the firm had signed up a woman to do a book about . . . a certain subject. A few writers. Someone had just called *him* asking about it, and he thought it sounded funny because he'd never heard of it."

"Hold on, hold, on." Nora tried to grasp what he had said. "Merle Marvell told Alden someone was asking about a woman who claimed to be writing a book?"

"I'm sorry for bringing it up. I wondered . . . sorry. Forget it."

"Jeffrey—"

"My aunt would jump down my throat if she knew I brought this up. The Chancels have always been very generous to us. Look, is there anything I can do for you? Do you need money? I'm coming up to Massachusetts anyhow, so I could bring you whatever you need."

"Jeffrey," Nora said, and then thought that she probably would be in need of money before long. But that was not Jeffrey's problem; his problem sounded closer to home. "Did this

woman's book have to do with a place called Shorelands? And
what went on there in 1938?"

Jeffrey did not respond for a moment, and then said, "That's
an interesting question."

"I'm right, aren't I?"

Again he considered his words. "How do you know?"

"Well, I hope you'll keep this to yourself," she said, "but I'm
the woman."

Jeffrey managed a partial recovery. "The woman pretending
to be writing the book about Shorelands in 1938 was you."

"Why does it matter to you?"

"Why does it matter to *you*?"

"That's a long story. I think I'll get off now, Jeffrey. I'm getting nervous."

"Don't hang up," he said. "This might be straight out of left
field, but have you ever heard of a woman named Katherine
Mannheim?"

"She was at Shorelands that summer," said Nora, more baffled than ever.

"Were you looking for information about her? Was Katherine Mannheim why you cooked up this story about a book?"

"What's all this to you, Jeffrey?" Nora asked.

"We have to talk. I'm going to pick you up and take you
somewhere. Tell me where you are and I'll find you."

"I'm in Holyoke. At a pay phone on a corner."

"Where?"

"Ah, this is the corner of Northampton and Hampden."

"I know exactly where you are. Go to a diner or something,
go to a bookstore, there's one down the street, but wait for me.
Don't run away. This is important."

The line went dead. Nora stared at the receiver for a second
and then dropped it on its hook. No longer quite aware of her
surroundings, she stepped away from the telephone and tried to
make sense of what she had just learned. Jeffrey had overheard
Alden's half of a conversation with Merle Marvell. Mark Foil,
no fool, had called Marvell to check on "Emily Eliot," and the
puzzled editor had immediately telephoned his boss at home.
Why was Alden at home? Because the president of Chancel
House had to face the unpleasant task of firing two long-
standing employees? Or because Daisy had not recovered from

her fit, and the great publisher had to deal with the consequences of dismissing her caretakers? Nora could not imagine
Alden fetching drinks and bowls of soup to his stricken
wife . . . Ah, of course: tricky Alden, getting, as usual, exactly
what he wanted. Daisy's weakness had forced Davey back to
the Poplars. Alden had put him under his thumb by linking his
concern for his mother to the hypothetical independence of
separate living quarters over the garage. Getting what you
wanted was easy if you had the morals of a wolverine.

Nora's satisfaction at having worked out this much evapo-
rated before the remaining mystery, that of Jeffrey. Why should
he care about an obscure, long-dead poet?

64

NORA WALKED SLOWLY to the edge of the pavement. There,
side by side in the next block, stood the plate-glass window of
Unicorn Books and a dark blue awning bearing the words
Dinah's Silver Slipper Café. As if on cue, her stomach told her
that she was ravenous.

Into the bookstore she sailed, for the moment holding her
hunger at bay. She moved along toward *Night Journey* and its less
celebrated siblings, pulled all three paperbacks from the shelf, and
carried them to the counter.

"Driver, Driver, Driver," the man said. "Dark, darker, darkest."

"I gather you don't approve," Nora said.

He rang up the total, and she gave him twenty of Sheldon
Dolkis's dollars.

"I have a few doubts about *Night Journey*."

"What kind of doubts?"

"Not my cup of tea," he said, and handed her the bag.

"I want to know more about your doubts," she said, fending off
her hunger. "People keep telling me I have to read it."

"The Driver people are like Moonies. They're worse than authors, worse even than authors' *wives*."

"I know two people who read it once a year," Nora said.

"All kinds of people get the bug. A lot of them never read anything else. They love it so much that they want to read it all over again. Then they think they've missed something, and they read it a third time. By now they're making notes. Then they compare discoveries with other Driverites. If they're tied into computer discussion groups, that's it; they're gone. The really sick ones give up on everything else and move into those crazy houses where everybody pretends to be a different Driver character." He sighed and looked away. "But I don't want to spoil the book for you."

Within the pastel interior of Dinah's Silver Slipper, an efficient young woman led Nora to a table by the window, handed her a three-foot-high menu, and announced that her waitress would be right with her.

Nora lined the books up in front of her. The later two were each several hundred pages longer than *Night Journey*. Nora turned them over and read the back jackets. *Night Journey* was the classic, world-famous, much-beloved, et cetera, et cetera. Readers everywhere had blah blah blah. The manuscripts of *Twilight Journey* and *Journey into Light* had been discovered among the author's papers many years after his death, and Chancel House and the Driver family were pleased to grant his millions of admirers the opportunity to blah blah blah.

"Hold on," Nora said. "Author's papers? What papers?"

An alarmed female voice said, "Excuse me?"

A college-aged girl in a blue button-down shirt and black trousers stood beside her. "I'll have the seared tuna and iced coffee, please."

She opened *Night Journey*, leafed past the title page, arrived at Part One, entitled "Before Dawn," and began grimly to read. The waitress placed a basket of bread sticks at the far end of the table, and Nora ate every one before her meal appeared before her. She fed herself with one hand while propping up the book with the other. The landscapes were cardboard, the characters flat, the dialogue stilted, but this time she wanted to keep reading. Against her will she found that she was *interested*. The hateful book had enough narrative power to draw her in. Once she had been drawn in, the characters and the landscape of caverns and stunted trees through which they wandered no longer seemed artificial.

She knew the reason for her anger, and it had nothing to do with *Night Journey* or Hugo Driver's unfortunate influence on susceptible readers. Jeffrey had told her that Davey was moving back to his parents' house. He had succumbed to Alden's gravitational pull.

More than an hour had passed while she consumed the seared tuna and nearly a third of *Night Journey*. Jeffrey was close to the Massachusetts border, speeding toward Holyoke to pick her up and take her somewhere.

BOOK VII

THE GOLDEN KEY

"You shall find it, Pippin," said the old man. His beard rustled along the ground. "I promise you that. But will you recognize it when you find it? And do you imagine that if you succeed in claiming it, it will make you happy?"

65

NORA WENT BACK down the sidewalk and sat facing Northampton Street on a wrought-iron bench in the shade of an awning. Shelley Dolkis's Ford stood at a parking meter on the far side of the pay telephone, some ten or fifteen feet away. A few cars drove past, none containing Jeffrey. At five-thirty on an August afternoon in Holyoke, most people had already reached the places they were going.

Nora had forgotten to put another set of quarters in the meter, which now displayed a red violation band. She had no desire to get back into that car. Then she remembered the suitcase on the backseat and darted over to it. She leaned into the airless oven of the interior, grabbed the handle of her suitcase, and tossed the keys onto the front seat.

At first she placed the carry-on bag on the bench beside her, then tucked it under the bench and gave herself a gold star for criminal cunning. Jeffrey failed to appear. Two or three minutes later, a dark blue vehicle with the sobriety of a hearse drew near. Nora straightened up and waited for it to pull to the curb behind the Ford, but at a steady fifteen miles an hour it proceeded toward the corner of Northampton and Hampden. The driver, a gaunt old party in sunglasses and a fishing hat, stared straight ahead as the car crept past her.

Now the only two cars on the street were a block away to the north, the wrong direction. Nora leaned back into the bench and closed her eyes. She counted to sixty and opened them. A muddy pickup with a Red Sox pennant dangling from the antenna chugged in from the south. She sighed, opened her bag, and took out *Night Journey*. Pippin was hiding in a crumbling old house where an evil crone dragged herself from room to room searching for him. The door creaked, and Pippin heard the crone's hairy feet whispering on the rotting floorboards. She looked up. The old man in the fishing hat had pulled into a parking spot in front of Dinah's Silver Slipper and was now stepping cautiously toward the restaurant's entrance. Behind him, like an ocean liner following a tug, came an old woman in a bright print dress. Nora looked the other way, and a police car with HOLYOKE P.D. on its door was swinging out around the mud-splashed truck.

Nora dove back into the book. *"Where, oh, where can my pretty be? I want to stroke my pretty boy."*

The police car drove past, and the tingling in her scalp receded. She kept her head tilted toward the book, watching the car move toward the end of the block. It veered left and made a wide U-turn in front of the pickup. She moved the book closer to her face. The police car cruised to a stop in front of the blue hearse. She peeked at the policemen. The officer in the passenger seat got out, walked across the sidewalk, and went into the Silver Slipper.

The police were looking for Nora Chancel, a woman with dark brown hair who never wore makeup. She opened her bag, found the Cover Girl Clean, and snapped it open to examine herself in the mirror. Far too much of Nora Chancel had surfaced through her disguise. She smoothed on a layer of makeup and erased the more prominent lines, applied mascara and lip gloss, tweaked and ruffled her hair into an approximation of what Dick Dart had accomplished. She risked another glance at the policemen and felt half the tension leave her body. They were leaning against the car and drinking coffee.

Far off to the south, a siren rose into the air, at first barely audible, gradually growing more insistent, finally becoming the distant explosions of red and yellow from the lights across the top of a state police car. Nora rammed the bag under her arm, stood up, and took a step forward. One of the Holyoke cops looked at her. She stretched her arms, twisted right and left, and went back to the bench. Where's the book, get the book, it's in here somewhere. She pulled a book from the jumble in the bag, opened it, and pretended to read.

The two cops gulped the last of their coffee, strolled to the corner, and dropped their cups into a wire basket. Fiddling with their shirts and ties, they moved off the sidewalk to walk down the street toward the Ford. When they passed Nora, the officer who had looked at her turned his head and made a flapping, downward gesture with his hand. Stay put.

She nudged the suitcase farther back under the bench and watched the flamboyant arrival of the state police.

The car wailed to the front of the Ford and turned off its lights and siren a second before another highway patrol car came screaming into Northampton Street. Two big men in flat-brim hats left their car angled in front of the Ford. One of them began questioning the two policemen while the other walked past the green car and waited for the second state vehicle. The clamor of the siren shut off in mid-whoop, but the light bar stayed on. One of the big troopers consulted with the driver of the second car, who got out along with his partner and matched the plate with a number in his notebook. Both men from the second car walked crouching around the Ford to peer through the windows. They pulled gloves from their belts and opened the front and rear doors on the driver's side. One of them leaned in and brandished the keys. He gestured to the local cops. The younger of the two jogged back toward his police car while the trooper opened the trunk and began poking through bags and boxes.

His partner walked back to their vehicle and rapped on a rear window. The window rolled down, and the state policeman put his hands on the sill and leaned forward to talk to two men in the backseat. The troopers who had arrived first were talking to the remaining Holyoke cop, who pointed across the street, then at the Ford, and finally at his own car. Nora bent forward and groped for the handle at the top of her suitcase.

One state policeman looked up, grinning, from the trunk. The rear doors of the second state car opened, and two men in dark suits, white shirts, and dark ties, one of them taller and fairer than the other, got out. The taller man wore heavy black sunglasses. Nora froze, her case halfway out from under the bench. Mr. Shull and Mr. Hashim, Slim and Slam, idled up to the trunk and inspected a box proffered by the grinning trooper. Nora pushed her suitcase back under the bench and tried to vanish into the shadow of the awning.

Slim looked inside the box, and the corners of his mouth jerked down. He displayed its contents to Slam, who nodded. Slim handed the box back to the trooper, and the trooper allowed himself a final smirk before returning it to the trunk. Mr. Hashim began rooting through the Ford's glove compartment. Mr. Shull wandered away, thrust his hands in his pockets, and regarded the surface of Northampton Street through his hipster sunglasses.

The trooper who had shown Mr. Shull the box came up beside him, attended to a few words, and then signaled to one of the big troopers from the first car. After another brief exchange, he waved at the local cop, who bounced forward and answered a few questions. He nodded, shrugged, nodded again, then turned to point at Nora.

The trooper glanced at her, asked a question, got another nod in return, and planted his hands on his hips as the policeman began walking toward Nora. Mr. Shull lifted his head and looked at Nora, then at the cop, then back at Nora. He drifted to the passenger door and said something to Mr. Hashim. Mr. Hashim leaned forward and gave her a skeptical glance through the windshield of the Ford.

The policeman coming toward her had concerned brown eyes and a wispy mustache, and his belly was beginning to roll over his belt. Nora swallowed to loosen her throat and sat up straight. She found that she was still holding the book open somewhere in the middle, and inserted a finger to look as if she had been interrupted while reading. "Hi," she said.

The policeman moved into the shade. He took off his hat. "Hot out there." He wiped his forehead with a hand and wiped the hand on his trousers. "I'd like to ask you a few questions."

"I don't know what I can tell you."

"Let me ask the questions and we'll find that out." He put his hat back on his head and took a notebook and ballpoint from his shirt pocket. "How long have you been out here, ma'am?"

"I'm not too sure."

The policeman put his foot on the bench and flattened the notebook on his knee. "Could you give me a rough estimate?"

"Maybe half an hour."

He made a note. "Did you observe any activity taking place in or around the vehicle under investigation? Did you observe anyone in contact with the vehicle?"

She pretended to consider the question. "Gee, I don't think so."

"Would you give me your name and address, please?"

"Oh, sure. No problem. My name is . . ." Her mind refused to supply any name but Mrs. Hugo Driver. "Dinah," she said. Shorelands? "Dinah Shore." As soon as the words were out of her mouth, she felt like holding out her hands for the cuffs.

The policeman looked up from his notebook. "That's your name, Dinah Shore?"

"I got teased about it all the time in school. For a long time I had to listen to all these Burt Reynolds jokes, but that stopped a couple years ago. Thank God." She forced herself to stop babbling.

"I can imagine," said the policeman. "Address?"

Where did Dinah Shore live? "Boston." She groped for a Boston street name. "Commonwealth Avenue. Four hundred Commonwealth Avenue. I just moved there about a week ago. Half my stuff is still in storage."

"I see." Another note. "What brings you to Holyoke, Dinah?"

"I'm waiting for a friend. He's picking me up."

"You don't have a car, Dinah?"

Of course she had a car. Every American had a car. "I have a Volvo station wagon, but it's in the garage." The policeman stared down at her, waiting for Dinah Shore, a resident of Boston, to explain her presence on a bench in Holyoke. "A friend gave me a ride this far, and my other friend is coming along to pick me up. He should be here soon."

"And you've been here how long, Dinah?"

What had she said earlier? "I'm not too sure. Maybe forty-five minutes?"

"You bought your book in the Unicorn?"

How did he know that? The policeman nodded down at the brown paper bag printed with a picture of a unicorn and the name of the bookstore beside her bag. "Oh, yes. I knew I'd have to wait for a while. So I went into the bookstore, and then I had something to eat at that restaurant next to it."

"Dinah's?"

"Is it called Dinah's? What a coincidence."

He stared at her for a moment. "So you went into the Unicorn, you looked around, you bought a book—"

"Three books," she said. She looked away from the policeman's troubled gaze. A red MG convertible driven by a man in a blue Eton cap was cruising past the patrol cars and officers taking up most of the southbound lanes in the region of Sheldon Dolkis's Ford. Another Holyoke squad car had joined them, and two burly men in sports jackets were talking to the troopers. A tow truck turned the corner of Hampden Street and came to a halt. The man in the Eton cap pulled to the curb across the street from Nora. Her heart gave a thump of alarm; the face under the blunt visor of the cap was Jeffrey's. He looked back at the crowd of policemen and their vehicles. One of the highway patrol cars was moving out of the way, and the tow truck was making beeping sounds as it backed up toward the Ford.

"You bought three books, and you went into Dinah's. You had something to eat. You did all that in forty-five minutes?"

"It was probably more like an hour. My friend just showed up."

The policeman twisted his body to look across the street. "That's him in the MG?"

She raised her arm and waved. Jeffrey was looking at the corner where she had said she would meet him. "Jeffrey!" He snapped his head in her direction and took in the spectacle of an unknown blond woman waving at him from a bench while a policeman glanced back and forth between them. It was dawning on him that the unknown blond woman had called him Jeffrey. He bent over the top of the door and peered at her. Nora prayed he would not utter her name.

The cop said, "That guy doesn't look like he knows you."

"Jeffrey's a little nearsighted." She spread her arms and shrugged, miming her good-humored inability to leave the bench.

"Oh, *there* you are," Jeffrey said. He opened the door and put one leg out of the car, but she waved him back.

The policeman faced her again and hitched himself back into position. "Where did your friend from Boston drop you off?"

"On the corner. Where all the people are."

"Did you happen to notice if the vehicle was parked there at the time?"

"Yes. I saw it parked right there."

"How long were you in the bookstore?"

"Maybe five minutes."

"And then you go into Dinah's. They give you a table, you look at the menu, right? Somebody takes your order, right? How long did that take?"

"About another five, ten minutes."

"So we have forty to forty-five minutes in Dinah's. And in that time, you ate lunch and managed to read half of that book?"

"Oh." Nora held up the book. Her finger was still inserted between the pages.

"Dinah, we have a big problem here." He adjusted his cap.

He put his hands on his hips. Nora prepared herself for imminent arrest. The cop sighed. "Do you have any idea at all of what time it was when your friend dropped you off on the corner?"

She looked up at his cynical young face. "Around four-thirty," she said.

"So you've been in this vicinity for more like two hours, isn't that about right, Dinah?"

"I guess it must be."

"We don't have much of a sense of time, do we?"

"Apparently not."

"Apparently not. But that's how long you have been wandering around this part of Holyoke. In all that time, did you happen to see a woman who would be, say, about ten years older than you are, about your height and weight, with chestnut-brown hair down to just below her ears?"

"Are you looking for her?"

"She might have been wearing a long-sleeved, dark blue silk blouse and blue jeans. Five six. A hundred and ten pounds. Brown eyes. She probably came here in that car that was towed away."

"What did she do?" Nora asked.

"Let me try one more time. Have you seen the woman I described to you?"

"No. I haven't seen anyone like that."

He took his foot off the bench and flipped the notebook shut. "Thank you for your cooperation, Dinah. You can go."

She stood up. "Thank you." She went across the curb, and Jeffrey got out of the MG. When she stepped down into the street, the policeman said, "One more thing, Dinah."

She turned around, half-expecting him to handcuff her. He shook his head, then bent down to pull her case from beneath the bench. "Good luck in all your endeavors, Dinah."

66

JEFFREY DID NOT speak until they were out of Holyoke and accelerating onto I-91. With her legs stretched out before her and the rest of her body tilted back at a surprisingly relaxed angle, Nora felt as if she were being carried along on a conveyance more like a flying carpet than an ordinary car.

"I was worried about you back there." Jeffrey shifted gears to overtake a moving van bulling along at a mere ten miles over the limit, and the magic carpet lengthened out and sailed into the wind.

"Me, too."

"I didn't recognize you. This . . . transformation. It's quite a surprise."

"There have been a lot of surprises lately."

"I must say, if you're anything to go on, more women ought to be—"

"Don't. Please? Just don't." Jeffrey looked abashed, and to mollify him she said, "I'm glad you didn't yell my name."

"All I really meant was, it's a relief to see you like this. You know, apart from the . . ." He drew a circle around his face with an index finger.

"The transformation."

"Better disguise than a hat and a pair of dark glasses."

"Dick Dart has strong feelings on the subject of cosmetics." Saying his name out loud made her chest feel tight. "He's still out there somewhere."

"You're sure of that?"

"Pretty sure. The cop who was questioning me while you were being so sensible said they were looking for an old dame with brown hair. No, he didn't, don't look dismayed. But Dart couldn't have told them about the new me, or right now the FBI would be dragging me away in leg irons."

Jeffrey nodded while levitating into a new lane. "I noticed Hashim and Shull, those two human andirons. Charming couple."

"They were at Mount Avenue?"

"For a couple of hours yesterday and this morning, while they were setting up the phone equipment and talking to Mr. and Mrs. Chancel—and your husband." He glanced at her with the consciousness of introducing a new and difficult subject. "The old manse has been a little chaotic the past few days."

For the moment, she avoided the topic of her husband. "Weren't you afraid they'd see you?"

"I would have been if they'd ever seen *me*. Mr. Chancel had me bring him lunch in the library because he had to do a lot of business over the phone. The andirons were in the kitchen, so I just got a glimpse of them as I went past the door."

"Tell me about Davey. Is he moving back to the Poplars because the FBI wanted him there?"

"Or was it his father's idea, you mean? A little of both. The agents did want to keep an eye on him, and Mr. Chancel was after him to help take care of his mother. To tell you the truth, I did wonder if Mr. Chancel was getting rid of us in order to pressure Davey back into the Poplars." Jeffrey looked over at Nora to see if this had been too critical of his employer.

"Could you put your radio on, Jeffrey?"

"Sorry." He reached for the dial. "I should have thought of that earlier."

With another smooth change of gears, the magic carpet flew around a brace of plodding cars. An announcer with a buttery voice said it was a glorious evening in Hampden, Hampshire, and Berkshire counties, and proceeded to go into details.

"How bad is Daisy?" Nora asked.

"She discovered *All My Children*, and it seems to have cheered her up. Someone named Edmund kidnapped someone named Erica in Budapest and kept her in a wine cellar, but then the Erica person decided she wanted to stay kidnapped in order to get back at someone named Dmitri. My aunt told me all about it. I gather that Mrs. Chancel feels that your story is similar to the Erica person's. You're a romantic heroine."

"Lovely."

"She's reconsidered whatever you said to her about her book. My aunt has been bringing her sections, and she rewrites them, propped up in bed."

"Before and after *All My Children*."

"During, too. It's inspirational."

"Is Alden helping her?"

"Mr. Chancel isn't allowed in her room." Jeffrey paused; apparently he had said all he wished to say about the Chancels. "Could you tell me why you claimed to be writing a book about Shorelands?"

"Dick Dart has this mission. He wants to keep anybody from proving that Hugo Driver didn't write *Night Journey*, so he wants to eliminate people connected to writers who were at Shorelands that summer. The man I talked to left for Cape Cod right after he called Merle Marvell, so he's safe, but that still leaves one. A professor in Amherst. I'd better get in touch with him soon. Dart has his address."

"You said two men. The writers they had connections to were . . . ?"

"Creeley Monk and Bill Tidy. Why?"

"Not Katherine Mannheim."

"No, but her sisters started all the trouble, I guess."

Jeffrey nodded. "Would you fill me in on this mission of Dart's, and tell me whatever you know about Shorelands and *Night Journey*?"

"Jeffrey, who *are* you? Why do you care?"

"I'm taking you to someone who'll be able to answer most of your questions, and I don't want to say anything first. I can tell you about me, though, if you're interested, but I'm not very important."

"Who are you taking me to?" An entirely unforeseen possibility occurred to her. "Katherine Mannheim?"

He smiled. "No, not Katherine Mannheim."

"Did she write *Night Journey*?"

"To tell you the truth, I hope she didn't. I'm one of the few who can resist that book."

"I never even gave it a serious try until a couple of hours ago."

"And?"

"Jeffrey, I'm not going to say any more until you tell me about yourself. You've always been such an *enigma*. How can someone like you be happy working for Alden and Daisy? Did you really go to Harvard? What's your *story*?"

"My story, well." He looked more self-conscious than she had ever seen him. "It's a lot less interesting than you make out. My mother wasn't prepared to raise a child after my father died, so I was raised by my father's relatives, all those Deodatos on Long Island. For a couple of years, I was moved around a lot—Hempstead, Babylon, Rockville Centre, Valley Stream, Bay Shore. I saw my real mother on her holidays, but I had plenty of other mothers, and they all doted on me. Went to Uniondale High School. Got a scholarship to Harvard, which was a big deal, majored in Asian studies, got halfway proficient in Chinese and Japanese, graduated magna cum laude. Instead of going to graduate school, I disappointed everybody and enlisted in the army. After I got through officers' training and the Vietnamese course in Texas, I pulled a lot of strings and got into the military police in Saigon. I did some good there, and the work was interesting. Continued the karate lessons I started in Cambridge.

"When I came back, I took the test for the Long Beach police and got in despite being ridiculously overqualified. One of my uncles was a detective in Suffolk County, and that helped. For three years I did that, took more Japanese at Hofstra, private calligraphy lessons, got my black belt, took a lot of cooking classes, and then I sort of fell apart. Quit the force. Did nothing but kill time on the boardwalk and sit in my apartment. After six or seven months, I took all my money out of the bank and went to Japan to polish up my Japanese and live in a Zen monastery. It took two years, but I was accepted into a monastery—long story—and stayed there about eighteen months. Very satisfying, but I had this problem: I wasn't Japanese and never would be. I came back so broke that I had to teach karate on a cruise liner for my passage. No idea what I was going to do. I decided to take the first job anyone offered me and devote myself to it as selflessly as possible. When my aunt told me the Chancels wanted to hire a male housekeeper, I moved to Connecticut and tried to do the best job I could."

Nora was gaping at him in unambiguous astonishment. "And you say that's not *interesting*? My God, Jeffrey."

"It's just a series of anecdotes. Spiritually I never got anywhere until I moved in with the Chancels. I have no actual

ambitions, obviously, apart from that, and helping the Chancels
was a lot more satisfying than a lot of other things I could have
done."

Nora, who had been marveling at the disparity between her
fantasies about Jeffrey and his reality, suddenly heard what the
announcer was talking about and turned up the volume on the
radio. "I have to hear this."

Jeffrey seemed startled but not at all offended. "Certainly."

What had snagged in her ear was an account of a fire in
Springfield. ". . . as we have been informed, no fatalities have
been reported as yet, though according to our most recent
reports, the blaze has spread to several other houses in the
exclusive Oak Street residential area."

"It's him," Nora said.

"Him?"

"Shh."

"To repeat, arson is now assumed to be the cause of the fire
in Springfield's Oak Street region first reported shortly after
five o'clock this evening by neighbors of Dr. Mark Foil, in
whose residence the blaze originated. Area residents are advised to keep in touch with the Fire Department's emergency
hotline, which is providing minute-by-minute—"

Nora turned off the radio. "Do you know who Mark Foil is?"

"I'm completely in the dark."

"Mark Foil is the man who called Merle Marvell." Jeffrey
still did not quite seem to take it all in. "Which was why Marvell called Alden." The appalled expression on Jeffrey's face
made it clear that he understood what had happened.

"You're convinced it was Dart who torched that house."

"Of course it was him."

Jeffrey looked at his watch, made some rapid mental calcula-
tions, then hauled down on the steering wheel and without bothering to signal rocketed across two lanes of moderately heavy
traffic. Horns blared. He spun the car into Exit 18 at the last possible second. The MG squealed down the ramp and blasted
through a stop sign to turn right on King Street in Northampton.

Nora unclenched her hands from the door handle. "What the
hell was *that* all about?"

Jeffrey pulled over to the side of the road and stopped the car.
"I want you to explain why Dick Dart is willing to murder

people and burn down houses in order to protect Hugo Driver's reputation. Start at the beginning and end at the end."

"Yes, sir," Nora said.

67

ONCE NORA BEGAN, she found that talking to Jeffrey Deodato was very different from telling the same story to Harwich. Jeffrey was *listening* to her. By the time she finished, she felt as if her story, initially as confused as Daisy's novel, had in the act of telling reshaped itself into a coherent pattern, at least within Jeffrey.

"I see," he said, with the sense of having seen more than she had. "So now that Dick Dart has done what he could to hurt Dr. Foil, he'll move on to Everett Tidy. And he probably has a car."

"Cars sort of give themselves to him."

"We'd better see Professor Tidy. All I need is a telephone."

"You're going to call him?"

Jeffrey pulled away from the curb. "I'm going to call a friend of his."

"You know him?"

"I've known him forever." Jeffrey turned right at the end of the block and rolled up to a telephone. "I'll just be a minute," he said, and jumped out of the car, fishing in his pocket for change.

Nora watched him dial a number and speak a few sentences into the receiver. He turned his back on her and spoke another few inaudible sentences. He hung up and came back.

"Who was that?" Nora asked, and Jeffrey smiled but did not answer. He spun the MG around in a tight circle and zipped back out onto King Street. "How do you know Bill Tidy's son?"

"I met him a long time ago."

"*Now* where are we going?"

"Amherst, where else?" Jeffrey turned right into a parking lot and continued straight through it into another parking lot, from which he emerged onto Bridge Street and accelerated back toward the distant parade of cars and trucks on the highway. "Just out of curiosity," he said, "do you remember if Davey told you the name of that girl who was so interested in Hugo Driver? The one who did or did not work for Chancel House, and was or was not a member of something called the Hellfire Club?"

"Paddi Mann."

"I was afraid of that."

It took her a moment to gather herself. "You know Paddi Mann, too?"

"Paddi's dead now, but I used to know her. Her real name was Patricia, but she turned into Paddi after she fell in love with Hugo Driver. The person we're going to see in Amherst, the one who knows Everett Tidy, is Sabina Mann, her mother."

"How do you know Sabina Mann? *Why* do you know Sabina Mann?" Nora wailed. "What is *going on*?"

Jeffrey would not answer.

Davey had not made up the whole story. It had really happened, but five years earlier, in New Haven. Or it had happened twice.

"Don't tie yourself into knots," Jeffrey said.

"And you won't tell me how you know them."

"First we'll take care of Everett Tidy."

"Then tell me who you were taking me to in Northampton. I'm going to be meeting him anyhow when we leave Amherst."

"Not him," he said. "Her."

"Who is it?"

"It's about time you met my mother," Jeffrey said.

68

ON THE WAY into Amherst, Nora idly inspected a bronze sign and saw that the comfortable-looking two-story brick house on a little rise had been the residence of Emily Dickinson. She heard Dick

Dart saying, "*We can find no scar, But internal difference, Where the Meanings, are—*" and her mouth went dry and goose pimples rose on her arms.

Uphill into a commercial section with bookstores and restaurants, left past a pretty commons like a green pool, uphill again past Amherst College's weathered brown and red buildings.

Jeffrey turned into a side street lined with handsome old houses, some of them surrounded by white fences, others nearly hidden by gardens of vibrant, nodding lilies and lush hydrangeas. He pulled up in front of a house barely visible behind its front garden.

Nora followed him up a path through waving pink and yellow lilies as high as her head. Three brick steps led up to a gleaming wooden door with a brass bell. The perfume of the lilies surrounded her and drifted off in a breeze she could barely feel. When the door swung open, a tall, gray-haired woman in half-moon glasses and a loose, long-sleeved smock the yellow of daffodils gave her a spine-stiffening glance and pulled Jeffrey into an embrace.

"Jeffrey, you horrible beast, sometime I hope you'll give me more than fifteen minutes' warning before you decide to favor me with a visit. I suppose you're staying with your mother, that's the only reason I ever get to see you!"

"Hello, Sabina, now let go of me before you break something."

She stepped back and grasped his upper arms. "You look very dashing in that *cap*."

"You look wonderful yourself, but you always do."

"I trust your mother's fine? She's so busy all the time, I never get to talk to her. I know she did the Trustees' Banquet at the start of the summer, and of course the reception at the President's House, but that's nothing to her, food for two hundred, is it?"

"Piece of cake. Lots of pieces of lots of cakes."

"And how are things with you?" She had kept her grip on his arms. "Still happy working for your inferiors?"

"I'm fine. Sabina, this is my friend Nora."

She released him and extended a hand to Nora. "You're the mysterious person who had to see Ev Tidy?"

Nora took Sabina Mann's hand and met her intelligent, commanding eyes, a few shades bluer than glacier water. "Yes, thank you, I hope I didn't put you to any trouble."

"No trouble, Ev came right over. Jeffrey knows he can get anything he wants. The only problem is he doesn't want enough."

Sabina Mann was making rapid assessments of Nora's age, marital status, social position, and role in Jeffrey's life. "I'm sworn to silence and secrecy, Jeffrey won't tell me why, but I suppose I might be allowed to ask if you have known him long?"

Nora thought that she had been given a passing grade on the first test. "I've known Jeffrey for a couple of years, but actually I hardly know him at all."

Sabina Mann continued her silent assessment. She was far more annoyed than she would let Jeffrey see. "Let's explore what our mutual friend has told you. I suppose you know about that ridiculous job he's so pleased with, but has he told you about—"

"Now, now, Sabina."

"Indulge me, dear. Has our friend mentioned his wonderful success at Harvard?"

"He has."

"Good. Do you know about the Silver Star and Bronze Star he got in Vietnam, or his tenure in a monastery in Japan?"

"No to the first, yes to the second," Nora said with a glance at Jeffrey.

"Since you have been so *favored*, you must know that he's fluent in Mandarin, Cantonese, and Japanese, but I wonder if he's told you—"

"Please, Sabina, be fair."

"Has Jeffrey ever told you, my dear, that he has written two plays which were produced off Broadway?"

Nora turned to stare at him.

"Pseudonymously," he said. "Weren't nothin'."

"Now I know something about you, Nora."

"Don't, Sabina."

"Be quiet, Jeffrey. You're using my house for your own private reasons, so I'm entitled to all the information I can unearth. And what I have unearthed is that this lovely young woman is an employee at Chancel House, because that awful Mr. Chancel is the person from whom you most wanted to keep that particular secret. I'm sure she shares my distaste for your employer and his entire family, including his peculiar wife, his useless son, and the son's unsuitable wife, sufficiently to keep it safe. Isn't that right, my dear?"

"I didn't know the son's wife was as bad as the rest of them," Nora said.

"She isn't, that's why she's unsuitable. The only thing wrong with her is that she was foolish enough to marry into that family. But you're under Alden Chancel's thumb just like Jeffrey, so you can't be expected to comprehend the trail of destruction left behind by the Chancels."

"Are you finished, Sabina?" Jeffrey asked.

"I'd better be. Everett never enjoyed being kept waiting."

69

A STOCKY MAN with a steel-gray Vandyke beard and short, silver gray hair abruptly closed the book in his hands and looked up frowning. "Twenty minutes, Sabina. Twenty *full* minutes."

"It was only fifteen minutes, Ev. As I am to be excluded from this gathering, I needed a little time by myself with Jeffrey and his companion."

One side of Everett Tidy's frown tucked itself into his cheek in what might have been amusement.

"Would you like some coffee or tea, Jeffrey? Nora?"

"No, thank you," Jeffrey said, and Everett Tidy said, "Tea. Gunpowder."

"Gunpowder tea, then." She closed the door behind her.

Nora glanced back at Tidy and caught him looking at her. Unembarrassed, he held her eyes for a moment before turning to Jeffrey. "Hello, Jeffrey."

"Thank you for coming on such short notice."

Tidy nodded, turning over the book in his hands as if puzzled to be still holding it. He moved toward a high-backed velveteen sofa, placed the book on an end table, and looked up at Nora again. A cold, brisk wind, as much a part of him as the crease in his khaki trousers and the brutal little brush of his beard, seemed to snap toward her.

"Sabina thinks I'm impatient," he said. "The reason for this misperception is that my awareness of the many tasks which

immediate obligations keep me from fulfilling makes me testy."
The temperature of his private breeze dropped by several
degrees. .

"Until my retirement, I lived in college housing, which
means that for twenty-two years I had an extremely pleasant
house with plenty of room for my family and my library. I could
have *remained* in my extremely pleasant house, but my wife is
dead and my children are gone, and other faculty members had
much more need of the space than myself. Therefore I bought
an apartment, and when I am not writing two books, one about
Henry Adams, the other about my father, I am weeding out
books so that I can fit the remainder of my library into three
rooms. Half an hour ago Sabina told me that an acquaintance of
Jeffrey's wished to speak to me on a matter of the gravest
importance. This matter concerned my safety." He inhaled, and
his chest expanded. "Well, here I am, and I must insist that you
tell me what the ragtag *hell* is going on here."

Jeffrey said, "Ev, you should know that—"

"I am talking to your companion."

The abyss between this man's experience and hers momentarily silenced Nora. She would never be able to convince
Everett Tidy that someone wanted to kill him.

Tidy conspicuously looked at his watch, and Nora at last registered why he had to sort through his books. "How long ago did
you move into your apartment?"

He lowered his arm with exaggerated slowness, as if he
thought sudden movement might startle her. "Six weeks. Is
there some point to your question?"

"If someone came looking for you at your old house, would
the new people tell him where you are? Do they know your new
address?"

He turned to Jeffrey. "Are we to go on in this fashion?"

"Please answer her question, Ev."

"Fine." He swung back to Nora. "Does Professor Hackett
know the street address of my apartment building? No, he does
not. In any case, the Hacketts are spending the month in the
upper valley of the Arno—the Casentino. Who are you, and
what are you after?"

"Her name is Nora Chancel," Jeffrey said.

Tidy blinked rapidly several times. "I know that name."

"Have you been watching the news the past few days?"

"I don't own a television set. I listen to the radio." He was talking to Jeffrey but keeping his eyes on Nora. His entire body seemed to lose its stiffness. "My God. Nora Chancel. The woman who was . . . Heavens. Until now I didn't connect the name to . . . Good Lord, and to think . . . So that's you."

"That's me."

Sabina Mann backed through the door carrying a tray and stopped moving as soon as she turned around. "I seem to be interrupting you." She looked at each of them in turn. "It must be an extraordinary conversation." She put the tray on the end table and fled.

Tidy had not taken his eyes from Nora. "Are you all right? You don't appear to have been injured, but I can't even begin to imagine the psychic trauma of such a thing. How are you doing?"

"I can't really answer that."

"No, of course not. What a thoughtless question. At any rate, you escaped that fellow and had the good sense to summon Jeffrey. If I were in trouble, I'd want Jeffrey's help, too. Please, let's sit down."

He patted the sofa, and Nora sat on the worn plush. He added milk to a cup of tea and gave it to her. She felt slightly dizzied by the reversal of his manner. Jeffrey slid into an overstuffed chair on the other side of the fireplace. Tidy remained on his feet, fingering his beard. There was no trace of the arctic wind.

"I apologize for blustering. I got in the habit when I discovered that it was useful for intimidating my students."

Nora said, "I'm glad that you're willing to hear me out."

He perched on the edge of the sofa. "I can only suppose that what you want to say to me concerns the man who abducted you. Please remind me of his name."

"Dart," she said. "Dick Dart. You wouldn't ever have heard of him."

He considered the notion for a few seconds. "No. On the other hand, I gather that he has heard of me. I'm right in saying he is a murderer, aren't I? There is no doubt about that?"

"No."

"And he wishes me ill."

"Dick Dart wants to kill you."

He straightened his back and gave her the benefit of his fine blue eyes. "What an extraordinary thing, to hear such a sentence. I find myself at a loss."

"Everett," Jeffrey said, "would you please shut up and let her talk?"

"Let me ask one more question, and then you can fill in the details, if there are any. Is there a motive, or did this man pick my name out of a hat?"

Nora looked at Everett Tidy, visibly restraining himself, all but biting his tongue. "He wants to kill you because you're Bill Tidy's son."

Tidy brought his hand to his cheek as if he had been slapped. Making a monumental effort to remain silent, he nodded for her to continue.

When she had finished, Tidy said, "So Dart assumes my father kept journals, which he did, that they deal with his stay at Shorelands, which they do, and that I am in possession of these journals, which I am. Tell me, do I have the honor of being first on Dart's list? I suppose I must."

"You're the second. This afternoon he started in Springfield with a doctor named Mark Foil. Foil was the longtime companion of Creeley Monk, and now he's his literary executor. I saw Foil just before he went out of town. Dart got there a little while later."

"Dart set the fire in Springfield?"

"He isn't very subtle," Nora said.

Tidy sat perfectly still for a moment. "Might I ask why you and Jeffrey did not go to the police before arranging to see me?"

"I can't talk to the police."

Tidy faced Jeffrey. "Is that so? She cannot?"

"Leave it alone, Ev," Jeffrey said.

"I don't imagine this fellow will have any luck finding my apartment, but I cannot allow him to destroy Professor Hackett's house under the impression that I still live there. I do not have to give my name or mention you in any way. All I have to say is that I saw a man resembling Mr. Dart in the area, and they will do the rest. Then I have some things to tell you, if you have the time."

"Good," she said.

Tidy stood up and gazed at her for a moment, biting his lower lip. "I won't let Sabina overhear my call." He bustled out of the room.

"Oh, I brought you some money." Jeffrey stood up, digging his wallet from his back pocket as he came toward her. "Three hundred dollars. Pay me back anytime, but take it. You're going to need money." He offered her what seemed a large number of bills.

Here she was, Nora Chancel, about to accept the offer of Jeffrey's money. She did not want to take it, but she supposed she had to. She was the object of other people's whims, some of them kindly, others malign. "Thank you," she said, a little stiffly, and accepted the money. "I'm grateful." She bent down for her bag and snapped it open. "I'll pay you back as soon as I can."

"There's no rush." He glanced at the door. "I hope Ev isn't saying too much."

The door opened just as he finished speaking, and Tidy walked in, frowned at him, and closed the door with theatrical care. "I had to persuade Sabina to go upstairs before I placed the call. She isn't very happy with us, I'm afraid." He watched Nora fasten her bag, then looked back up at her face. "Would you mind going somewhere with me? You too, of course, Jeffrey."

"Another trip," Nora said. "Where this time?"

"Amherst College Library, where I deposited my father's papers. It's closed, but I have all the keys we'll need. Jeffrey, it might help if you picked up that tray."

Sabina Mann was stationed on her bottom stair as the three of them came out of the living room. Everett Tidy did not see her until he was almost directly in front of her, and then he stopped short. Nora, right behind, almost bumped into him. Jeffrey fell into place beside her, and an awkward moment passed.

"Sabina," Tidy began, but she interrupted him.

"They come, they confer, they make clandestine telephone calls, and then, en masse, they depart. It's like a play."

Jeffrey held out the tray, and she reluctantly stepped down to accept it. "I promise to explain everything as soon as I can."

"The Lord knows what that means. Everett, may I ask where you are going, unless that is another state secret?"

"Sabina," he said, "I understand that all of this must be very puzzling to you, and I regret the necessity of rushing out without an explanation. However, I—"

"Why don't you try telling me, in simple words, where you are taking them?"

He tilted his head. "How do you know that I'm taking them somewhere?"

"You're holding your car keys," she said.

With all the dignity he could summon, Tidy said, "We have to go to the college library, Sabina. I'll come back in half an hour or so, shall I?"

"Don't bother. Call me tomorrow, if you have anything to say. Jeffrey, will you be returning?"

"I'm sorry, but I'll have to get to Northampton. I'll see you soon, I promise."

"You are the most maddening person." She gave Nora a look in which outright disapproval threatened to appear. "I'll see you to the door."

70

THERE WAS SO much space in front of the long backseat that the two men seemed to be twice the normal distance from her. "That woman isn't happy with me."

"It isn't just you," Jeffrey said. "Sabina's used to being unhappy with *me*."

"Your aunt hasn't been happy with me since I dropped out of the Emily Dickinson Society," Tidy said.

"Your aunt? Sabina Mann is your aunt?"

"You really do talk too much, Ev."

Tidy swung his head sideways to stare at him, then looked forward again. "Excuse me, Jeffrey, but I naturally assumed that your friend knew who you are. Why would she get in touch with you if—"

"That's enough."

"Damn you, Jeffrey, let him talk," Nora said. "I tell you everything, and all you do is move me around like a puppet. I don't care if you won the Congressional Medal of Honor and the *Nobel Prize*, you hear me? You're not my golden boy. I'm really, really sick of this."

What she really wanted to do, what every cell in her body *told* her to do, was open the door and jump out. If she didn't get out of the car soon, she would have to flail out, scratch their faces, bite whatever she could bite, because if she didn't something worse would happen to her.

"I don't blame you for being annoyed with me, Nora."

"Stop the car."

"I want you to think about two things."

"I don't care what *you* want, Jeffrey. Let me out."

"Calm down and listen. If you still want to get out afterwards, fine, do it."

"To hell with you." She gripped the door handle.

"You were fed up back at the house, too, weren't you? That was when this started—when we were alone in the living room."

Nora opened the door, but before she could jump out, Jeffrey had scrambled over the seat and was lunging toward her. Tidy shouted something from the front. As Nora leaned out of the door, Jeffrey caught her around the waist and pulled her back in. Holding her tight while she fought to get free, he slammed the door and locked it. She hit him in the arm, but he fastened his hands around her elbows and pushed her down into the seat.

"Let *go* of me!"

His face was a few inches from hers. She kicked at his ankle, missed, and tried again. Her foot banged against his leg. "Ow," he said, and his face came closer. "Tell me why you're mad. It isn't because of me."

She kicked out again, but he had shifted his leg and her foot shot into empty air. She tried with the other foot and missed again. He pressed her arms against her body and pinned her to the seat. "Come on, tell me why you're mad."

She yelled, "Let go of me!"

"I'm letting go." Little by little, his grip loosened as his face drew back, until finally he was no longer holding her at all. She raised her right hand, but it was too late to hit him. Her mind was already working. She lowered her hand and glared at him. Jeffrey fumbled with something beneath him which floated upward and became a jump seat.

"What kind of car is this, anyhow?" she said, collapsing back into the seat. "A taxi?"

"A Checker," said Everett Tidy. He had pulled over to the side of the road and was staring back at them with one arm over the top of his seat. "My father used to drive one, and they're all I've ever owned. Had this one since 1972. Are you all right?"

"How could I be all right?" Nora said. "People keep grabbing me and moving me from one place to another without ever telling me the truth. Even before the FBI showed up, my life turned into a catastrophe, and then horrible things happened to me and I just about lost my mind. People lie to me, they just want to use me, and I'm sick of all these secrets and all these plots."

She stopped ranting and drew in a large breath. Jeffrey was right. She was not angry with him. It had come to her that she was still furious at Dan Harwich, or if not at the real Dan Harwich, the loss of the man she had imagined him to be. This loss felt like an enormous wound, and part of her fury was caused by the knowledge that the wound had been self-inflicted.

"Excuse me," Tidy said.

"Wait a second," Jeffrey told him. "It's Dick Dart, isn't it? Plus Davey moving out of your house. You *have* been mistreated, of *course* you feel like you have no control over your life. Anybody would."

"I suppose." Another recognition moved within her: that her real resentment had to do with an almost impersonal aspect of her predicament. From the beginning, she had been forced to concentrate on a matter far more important to everyone else around her than to herself. A cyclone had smashed her life and whirled her away. The cyclone was named Hugo Driver, or Katherine Mannheim, or Shorelands, or *Night Journey*, or all of these together, and even though Dick Dart, Davey Chancel, Mark Foil, and the two men in the Checker cared enough about the cyclone to open their houses, ransack papers, battle lawsuits, drive hundreds of miles, risk arrest in its name, it had been she, who cared not at all, who had been taken over.

Tidy said, "Jeffrey, I must—"

"Please, Ev. Nora, I didn't feel I could speak for my mother, so I had to postpone certain things until she could meet you. What would you like to do? It's up to you."

She leaned back against the seat. "I'm sorry I got wild. Why don't we just forget about it and go back to what we were doing?"

"I'm sorry," Tidy said, "but I can't do that until somebody tells me what you meant about the FBI."

Jeffrey said, "You heard her say she couldn't go to the police. You took that in stride, I remember."

"I want to know why the FBI is involved. I'm not going anywhere until I do."

"Nora?" Jeffrey said, and put a hand, one of the hands which had recently held her down, on her knee.

She jerked the knee from under his hand. "No problem. I don't have any secrets, do I? You want to hear the story, Professor? Fine, I understand, you want to know if you'll be morally compromised by associating with me."

"Nora," Jeffrey said, "Ev is only—"

"A neighbor of mine was kidnapped. We thought she was murdered, but she wasn't. When she turned up, she claimed that I kidnapped her. At least that's one of the things she says. She isn't very rational. Because it turned out my husband was sleeping with her, which was news to me, the FBI took her seriously. Is there anything else you'd care to know?"

Tidy scratched his beard. "I think that will do. Are we still going to the college library, then?"

"I wouldn't dream of going anywhere else," Nora said.

71

NORA TOLD EVERETT Tidy what she had learned about Creeley Monk in a monastic room on the top floor of the Amherst library. Beside her at a long wooden table, Tidy had listened with a gathering excitement which finally had seemed to freeze him into the inability to look at anything but the old upright typewriter at the end of the table and the photograph on the wall of his father seated before the same typewriter.

After Nora had finished, Tidy slid a file box forward and said, "I'm grateful to you for sharing your information with me."

"You're welcome," she said, waiting to hear what the story had meant to him.

"My father did distrust Creeley Monk, and I should explain that first. He simply did not believe Monk's story of being a working-class boy from Springfield, the son of a barkeep, and so on. Monk had attended Harvard and wore expensive clothes, and my father, who was almost completely self-taught, thought he was being laughed at. Almost everything about Shorelands made him uncomfortable. He would not have accepted Georgina's invitation at all if he had not seen it as a way through his difficulties with his second book. He knew he'd made a mistake almost as soon as he got there, but he thought he had no choice but to stick it out. He was not a person at ease with the notion of giving up."

"I understand," Nora said.

"He was depending on the book to earn enough so that he would never have to drive a cab again. And within a day, he knew that Lincoln Chancel was coming, presumably to scout out writers for his new publishing house."

Nora wanted to steer the conversation toward whatever had aroused the enormous quantity of feeling beating away within this disciplined man, a matter presumably related to Katherine Mannheim, but one question about the admirable Bill Tidy troubled her. "Didn't he more or less abandon your mother and you when he went to Shorelands?"

Tidy shook his head vehemently. "There was no question of abandonment. We had a standing invitation to Key West, where an old friend of my father's named Boogie Ammons owned a small hotel. When the invitation to Shorelands came, my father arranged for my mother and me to stay there. That entire month, we lived better than we would have at home. We missed him, of course, but he wrote two or three times a week, so we had some idea of what he was doing."

"Did you keep the letters?"

"I have most of them. They tend to be noncommittal about his stay there. It wasn't until years after his death that I could face reading his journals, and then I learned how much he had hated Shorelands."

Tidy opened the file box and took out a dark green, cloth-bound volume. "I also saw how uncomfortable he was with himself. Do you understand? He was on a kind of high wire, gambling that he wouldn't fall."

"I don't think I do understand," Nora said.

Tidy nodded. "Think of his situation. My father was really struggling with a new book. If everything worked, he would finally be set free to do nothing but write. Lincoln Chancel was a crude, grasping monster, but he represented a way out. My father was so desperate that he could not keep himself from playing up to the man. Against his own moral sense. Unfortunately for him, another guest was even more desperate. Hugo Driver capitalized on the accident of being in the same house as Chancel by turning himself into a human barnacle."

"So he must have envied Driver," Nora said.

"Which made him feel even worse about himself. He couldn't trust his own instinctive dislike of the man. Therefore, my father never joined the group on the terrace, where Chancel appeared almost every afternoon, because Hugo Driver would be there. And, because he questioned his antipathy toward Driver, he forced himself to suspend judgment when he heard gossip, all the more so since he distrusted the source."

"He already thought Creeley Monk was a liar," Nora said.

"Monk struck him as exactly the sort of person who made up stories about other people. Especially if it might help his own cause. In this instance, with Merrick Favor."

Here at last was a chance to move into the center of his concerns. "What did your father think of Katherine Mannheim?"

Everett Tidy puzzled her by looking across the table at Jeffrey, who shrugged. He ran his fingers across the top of the book in front of him, clearly considering his words.

"Mostly for the reasons I've explained, my father actually had little contact with the other guests. The other part of his isolation was physical. Georgina put him in Clover House, off in the woods behind Monty's Glen, so far away from Main House that poachers sometimes wandered through in the middle of the night. He heard poachers even on the night Miss Mannheim vanished."

Tidy fell silent, and Nora waited for him to work out a way to speak of whatever had ignited him.

"There's nothing in my father's journals to suggest that Driver stole a manuscript from Miss Mannheim."

"I see," Nora said, feeling that she did not at all see.

"But you ask me what my father made of Miss Mannheim, and this information might still be useful to you—and through you, to me. My entire life, I can say, has been haunted by whatever happened at Shorelands that summer." His mysterious excitement seemed to intensify. "There is still one great matter to discuss, and it may be as critical to you as it is to me. If it's at all possible, will you let me know whatever you manage to discover?"

"Of course."

"Thank you. Now to Katherine Mannheim." He said this with the air of deliberately postponing his "great matter." "Clearly she was an attractive, interesting presence, utterly self-reliant. She could be intentionally rude, I gather, but what really struck my father, apart from her independence, was what he called her serenity."

"Serenity?"

"That surprises you, doesn't it? He meant a combination of self-confidence, instinctive goodness, courage, and compassion. Initially her prickliness, her willingness to be indifferent to conventional manners, misled him, but after the first week, he began to see these other qualities."

Tidy opened the journal. "Listen to this.

"I have been thinking about this curious person, Katherine Mannheim. She has never had any money and lives simply and without complaint. Where she seems bohemian and reckless, she is utterly focused. She writes slowly, with great care, publishing little, but what is published shines. To her, recognition, acclaim, every sort of public reward, mean nothing. I wonder if I would be as foolish as Merrick and Austryn if I were not so gladly married to my darling Min."

"Min and Bill?" asked Nora. "Wasn't there a movie—"

"Family joke," said Tidy. "My mother's real name was Leonie.

"Even the monstrous Lincoln Chancel, thirty years older than Katherine, and who wears his gluttony on his face, desires her. Merrick and Austryn are attracted to her inner being but imagine they want her body, so do not see that Katherine is chaste. It is not warm, this chastity; it is icy and determined.

"Katherine Mannheim never expected to live to old age. All her life she was aware of her weak heart, but she refused to live like an invalid except in this one regard. What I've always imagined is that where she considered activities like bicycle riding, drinking wine, and taking long walks potentially dangerous, she was certain that sex could kill her. And in any case, her instincts led her to a modest way of life."

"Did your father know what she was working on?" asked Nora.

"Not at all. What Georgina called the Ultimate, a kind of end-of-term tradition, should have explained it, but she didn't play along."

"What was the Ultimate?"

"At the end of the third week of their stay, all the writers met at dusk for a kind of round-robin in Monty's Glen, inside the ring of standing stones known as the Song Pillars. The gardener who had created the clearing, Monty Chandler, had noticed that a number of boulders dug out of a nearby field were all roughly twelve feet high, flat on both ends, and he had gone to a lot of trouble to upend them in the clearing. The guests sat in a circle inside the pillars. Georgina delivered some set pieces about Shorelands' history. When she finished, the guests described what they were working on, how it was developing, and so on. Of course, they were expected to pay tribute to Georgina's hospitality and describe the ways in which Shorelands had inspired them. They were also supposed to be amusing. Georgina Weatherall expected to be entertained as well as praised. As you might expect, Katherine Mannheim refused to play the game."

He turned over a few more pages. "Here it is.

"After Merrick's song of praise to Miss Weatherall's hospitality, the wonders of Shorelands, and his own talents, it was Katherine Mannheim's turn to speak. She smiled. She was sure, she said, that we would understand her decision to obey her usual practice of choosing not to speak of work in progress. Those who had preceded her were braver and less superstitious than she, qualities for which she admired them greatly. As for Shorelands, its magnificence was so great as to defy description, but she was pleased to mention the services of Agnes Brotherhood, the maid who every morning cleaned her kitchen and made her bed. Upon leaving Shorelands, she would sorely miss the domestic assistance of Miss Brotherhood."

"She refused to talk about her work and thanked the maid," Nora said. "Sounds like she knew she was going to be asked to leave."

"Or wanted to be," said Tidy. "Georgina was outraged. Here's what my father says:

"Miss Weatherall tugged her layers of purple and crimson around her shoulders. Her face turned bright red beneath her makeup. She muttered that she would convey Miss Mannheim's compliments to the maid. Hugo Driver, next in line, began by praising Miss Weatherall's generosity and went on to speak at such length of the meals, the gardens, the conversations, that by the time he finished with a panegyric to our hostess, a genius whose greatness lay in this, that, and the other, no one noticed that he had never bothered to mention his writing.

"As a result," Tidy concluded, "we don't actually know what either one of them was working on during that summer."

"Driver saw a chance to hide behind a smoke screen," Nora said.

"Maybe because he wasn't making much progress, which would mean that he was more and more dependent on Lincoln Chancel. Anyhow, when it was my father's turn, he spoke as much to Chancel as to Georgina Weatherall. My father continued to hold out hope even after he came back home."

"Did he ever finish his book?" Nora asked.

Tidy inhaled sharply, then swiveled his chair to face her with all of his suppressed intensity visible in his eyes. "Let me ask you this. Have you been told what happened to the novel Merrick Favor was working on?"

"It was torn to pieces."

"As was my father's book. Shredded, carbon and all."

Jeffrey spoke for the first time since they had come into the library. "What are you saying, Ev?"

With what seemed to Nora a deliberate and momentary relaxation of his iron self-control, Tidy looked up at his father's photograph. "So here we are, at the serious matter."

"Don't keep us in suspense," Jeffrey said.

"I'll try not to." Tidy glanced at Nora, then back up at the photograph. "The winter after he came back from Shorelands, my father told my mother that he was pretty sure he could finish his book in two or three weeks if he could work without interruptions. The upshot was that we were invited back to Key West—when my father was done, he was invited down, too, to celebrate. Boogie Ammons said, 'It's worth a few hamburgers to finally get that book out of you.' A little more than two weeks later, a policeman came to the hotel and told my mother that my father had killed himself.

"I couldn't read anything he wrote until I was teaching here and had a family of my own. His journals were in a trunk in my basement. One night when everyone else was in bed, I drove to this library, took out *Our Skillets*, brought it home, opened a bottle of cognac, and stayed up until I finished the book. It was an incredibly emotional experience. Then I had to read his journals. When I finally felt strong enough to face the last one, I found something completely unexpected. A week before we went to Florida, his agent had written to tell him that he'd been approached by Lincoln Chancel, who was interested in making a confidential exploration of my father's situation. Chancel had liked what he'd heard of the new book, wondered how close the book was to completion and whether my father might be willing to consider his publishing it. My father wrote back, saying that he was close to finishing the book and wanted to show it to Chancel. He didn't mention any of this to my mother.

"About a week later, he got some exciting news. Since he was writing for himself, he wasn't very specific about this in his journal. See what you make of this.

"I left my typewriter to answer the telephone. I spoke my name. What a great change came then. There is to be a royal visit. The Royal Being will come alone. I am to tell no one, and if I violate this condition by so much as hinting about this matter, even to my wife, all is off. Only He and I are to be present. The great event is to take place in three days. I don't know what I expected, but THIS, well, THIS beats all."

He looked over at Nora. "Well?"
"It's like Creeley Monk," she said. "Was the visit called off?"
"Here's the last thing my father wrote."

"Cancellation. No explanation. I can hardly pick myself up off the floor. Can I continue? Do I have a choice? I have no choice, but how can I continue when I feel like this?

"It's exactly what happened to Creeley Monk a few days later. Do you think it can be a coincidence?"

"I guess not," Nora said, "but that would mean . . ."

"That Monk got the same kind of call as my father. Doesn't it seem likely that Merrick Favor and Austryn Fain were approached in the same way? And doesn't it seem even likelier that the person who arranged a private meeting and then canceled it was Lincoln Chancel?"

"Good God," Jeffrey said. "You think it was a setup."

"It would have taken more than rejection from Lincoln Chancel to make my father throw in the towel."

Nora stared at him. Then she gave a wild look across the table at Jeffrey, who had evidently seen where all this was going sometime before. "You think Lincoln Chancel murdered your father and Creeley Monk. And Merrick Favor and Austryn Fain, too."

"I think Chancel pushed him out of the window and tore his manuscript to bits, just like Favor's."

"Maybe this is obvious, but why would he do it?"

"I suppose he had something to hide," said Tidy.

"The real authorship of *Night Journey.*"

"Of course," said Jeffrey. "Monk knew that Driver was a thief. He told Merrick Favor, and both your father and Fain overheard, but nobody believed him. Later Favor told them both that Monk was right. He was convinced he'd seen Driver steal something from Katherine Mannheim. Everybody knew that Driver was having trouble with whatever he was writing, but six months later he produces this stupendous book, and gives the copyright to Chancel House."

"There you are," Tidy said. "Chancel was as ruthless with Driver as with everyone else. All he had to take care of was the possibility that Katherine Mannheim had spoken about her work to one of the other guests."

"He made these confidential appointments," Nora said, "and canceled them. Then he showed up on their doorsteps and waited for them to turn their backs."

For a second, the three people in the room at the top of the library said nothing.

"Now what?" Nora asked.

"It seems the rest is up to you," said Tidy.

72

"WHAT AM I supposed to do?" Nora asked. "I can't prove that Davey's grandfather murdered four people fifty-five years ago. It makes sense to Everett Tidy and you and me, but who else is going to believe all this?"

"I think Ev meant that you should continue what you're already doing." The sky was still bright, and vibrant green fields lay on either side of the long, straight road to Northampton. Warm wind streamed into Nora's face and ruffled her short hair while seeming to slip past Jeffrey without touching him.

"What am I doing?"

"Taking one step after another."

"Brilliant. After all that, do you think that Katherine Mannheim wrote *Night Journey*?"

"I think it's more likely than I did this morning."

"Why is it so important for me to meet your mother?"

"I always forget how pretty this part of Massachusetts is."

He would not be drawn. "All right. Let's try another subject. What did your father do?"

"He was a cook, or maybe I should say chef. My whole family, on that side anyhow, were all great cooks. My great-grandfather was the head chef at the Grand Palazzo della Fonte in Rome. His brother was the head chef at the Excelsior. Despite the handicap of not being Italian, my mother was as good as all the rest of them. Before my father died, they were going to open a restaurant. She still loves it, in fact."

"And now she keeps herself busy cooking for the Trustees' Banquet and the President's Reception."

Jeffrey gave her a sidelong look.

"Your aunt Sabina said something about it."

"You have a good memory."

"Is Sabina your mother's sister?"

Jeffrey tugged the Eton cap an eighth of an inch lower on his forehead. For the first time, the breeze buffeting Nora seemed also to touch him.

"I see. That's the end of the line. Can you at least tell me about Paddi?"

"I can tell you part of it, but the rest will have to wait. You remember how Sabina feels about the Chancels. She blames them for a lot of things, but the main one is what happened to her daughter. She was a nice girl before she went off the tracks. Maybe she was a little like me, and that was why I liked her. Patty, which was her name then, was a lot younger than I, but I always enjoyed her company. Of course, I was gone a lot, so I wasn't around when she discovered *Night Journey*. The book took over her life. She changed the spelling of her name. Sometimes she pretended to be other characters in the book. I guess Patty got deeper and deeper into her obsession, to the point where she would disappear from home to visit other Driver people. There was a lot of drug abuse, fights at home, her entire personality changed, she wouldn't spend time with anyone who wasn't capable of spending day after day talking about nothing but Driver and the book, and when she was sixteen she ran away.

"One Driver person told her about another, and she floated through this seedy underworld devoted to Pippin Little, living in Driver houses. These people spend their lives acting out scenes in the book. Nobody knew where she was. A couple of years later, she managed to fake her way into the Rhode Island School of Design, I can't imagine how, and Sabina sent her money, but Patty refused to see her. She was there maybe a year, then she vanished again. Sabina got one postcard from London. She was in another art school and living in another Driver house. Lots of drugs. Then she moved to California—same situation—and wound up in New York, moving back and forth between the East Village and Chinatown, completely submerged in this crazy Driver world. That must have been when she zeroed in on Davey. Anyhow, she took off again, and nobody knew where she was until she died of a heroin overdose in Amsterdam and the police got in touch with Sabina."

There had been less decoration in Davey's story than Nora had thought. "Thanks for telling me," she said. "But I still don't understand why she was so fixated on the manuscript and Katherine Mannheim."

"Stop asking questions, and tell me about your childhood or how you met Davey. Tell me what you think of Westerholm." He would go no further.

"I can't stand Westerholm, I met Davey in a Village bar called Chumley's, and my father used to take me on fishing trips. Jeffrey, where am I going to sleep tonight?"

"There's a nice old hotel in Northampton. You can stay there as long as you like."

A few minutes later they passed beneath the highway and came into Northampton from the east. Rows of shops and grocery stores lined the street. At the bottom of a hill, the buildings became taller and more substantial, and the MG moved slowly amid a lot of other cars. They passed beneath a railway bridge, and young people moved along the broad sidewalks and stood in clusters at the immense intersections. Jeffrey pointed down a wide, curving street at the Northampton Hotel, an imposing brown pile with a flowery terrace before a glassy new addition.

"When we're all through at my mother's place, I'll bring you back, get you a room. Over the next couple of days we can talk about what you ought to do. We can probably have lunch and dinner together most of the time, if you like."

"This great cook doesn't feed you?"

"My mother isn't very domestic."

Nora looked out at pleasant, pretty Main Street with its lampposts and restaurants advertising wood-fired brick oven pizzas, tandoori chicken, and cold cherry soup; at galleries filled with Indian art and imported beads; at the pretty throngs and gatherings of the attractive young, mostly women, strapped into backpacks in their sawed-off jeans and halter tops or T-shirts; and said to herself: *What am I doing here?*

"Almost there," Jeffrey said, and followed a flock of young women on bicycles out of the traffic into a quieter street running alongside a tract like a parkland where dignified oaks grew alongside well-seasoned brick buildings connected by a network of paths. The young women on bicycles swooped down a drive with a Smith College plaque. Jeffrey executed a smooth U-turn in front of a large, two-story, brown clapboard building with a roofed porch wide enough for dances on the front and left side. It looked like a small resort hotel in the Adirondacks. A sign set back from the sidewalk said HEAVENLY FOOD & CATERING.

Jeffrey turned to her with an apologetic smile. "Just let me go in and prepare her, will you? I'll be back in a couple of minutes."

"She doesn't know I'm coming?"

"It's better that way." He opened his door and put one leg out of the car. "Five minutes."

"Fine."

Jeffrey got out, closed the door, and leaned on it for a moment, looking down at her. If he had been tempted to say something, he decided not to.

"I won't run away," she said. "Go on, Jeffrey."

He nodded. "Be right back." He went up the long brick walkway, jumped up the steps, and glanced back at Nora. Then he walked across the porch and opened the front door. Before he went inside, he took off his cap.

Nora leaned back, stretched her legs out before her, and waited. An insect whirred in the grass beneath the sign. Across the street a dog woofed three times, harshly, as if issuing a warning, then fell silent. The air had begun faintly to darken.

After five minutes, Nora looked up at the porch, expecting Jeffrey to come through the door. A few minutes later, she looked up again, but the door remained closed. Suddenly she thought of Davey, at this moment doing something like arranging his compact discs on Jeffrey's shelves. Poor Davey, locked inside that jail, the Poplars. She got out of the MG and paced up and down the sidewalk. Could she call him? No, of course she couldn't call him, that was a terrible idea. She looked up at the porch again and felt an electric shock in the pit of her stomach. An extraordinarily beautiful young black woman with a white scarf over her hair was looking back at her from the big window. The young woman turned away from the window and disappeared. A moment later, the door finally opened and Jeffrey emerged onto the porch.

"Is there a problem?" Nora asked.

"Everything's all right, it's just sort of hard to get her *attention*."

"I saw a girl in the window."

He looked over his shoulder. "I'm surprised you didn't see a dozen."

She preceded him up the slightly springy wooden steps and walked across the breadth of the porch to the front door. Jeffrey said, "Here, let me," and leaned in front of her to pull it open.

Nora walked into a big open space with a computer in front of an enormous calendar on the wall to her right, and a projection-screen television and two worn corduroy sofas on its other side. At the far end a wide arch led into an even larger space where young women in jeans bent over counters and other young women carried pots and brimming colanders to destinations farther within. One of the pot carriers was the striking black woman she had seen in the window. A slender blonde in her mid-twenties who had been watching a cartoon looked up at Nora and said, "Hi!"

"Hello," Nora said.

"You're the first woman Jeffrey ever brought here," the blonde said. "We think that's cute."

On the other side of the arch, ten or twelve young women chopped vegetables and folded dumplings on both sides of two butcher-block counters. Copper pots and pans hung from over-head beams. In front of two restaurant ranges, more women, most of them in white jackets and head scarves, attended to sim-mering pans and bubbling vats. One briskly stirred the contents of a wok. A stainless-steel refrigerator the size of a Mercedes stood beside a table at which two young women were packing containers into an insulated carton. Beyond them, a long window looked out onto an extensive garden where a woman in a blue apron was stripping peas. All the women in the kitchen looked to Nora like graduate students—the way graduate stu-dents would look if they were all about twenty-five, slim, and exceptionally attractive. Some of the women at the counters glanced up as Jeffrey led her toward the cluster in front of the nearest range.

Slowly, like the unfolding of a great flower, they parted to reveal at their center a stocky woman in a loose black dress and a mass of necklaces and pendants stirring a thick red sauce with a wooden spoon. Her thick, iron-gray hair had been gathered into a tight bun, and her face was unlined and imposing. She looked at Jeffrey, gave Nora an appraising, black-eyed glance, and turned to the woman Nora had seen at the window. "Maya, you know what to do next, don't you?"

"Hannah's mushrooms, *then* the other ones, and then it all goes into the pot with Robin's veal, five minutes, and bang, out the door."

"Good." She slapped her hands together and took two steps away from the range. "Let's get Sophie doing something useful. How's the packing going?"

"Almost done with this one," said one of the girls at the table.

"Maribel, get Sophie to help you carry them out to the van." A tall, red-haired girl with round horn-rim glasses moved toward the arch. The older woman looked at her watch. "Jeffrey picked a busy day to drop in. We're doing the Asia Society at nine, and a dinner party in Chesterfield just before that, but I *think* everything is running on schedule." She made another quick inspection of her troops and turned to Nora. "So here you are, the woman we've all been reading about. Jeffrey says you want to talk to me about Katherine Mannheim."

"Yes," Nora said. "If you can spare me some of your time."

"Of course. We'll get out of here and sit in the front room." She held out her hand and Nora took it. "Welcome. I gather that you may have to conceal yourself for a time. If you like, you could pitch in here. I can't give you a room, but you could sleep on a sofa until we find something nicer for you. I can always use another hand, and the company's enjoyable for the most part."

"I think I'll get her a room at the Northampton Hotel," Jeffrey said.

Jeffrey's mother had not taken her eyes off Nora. "Do whatever you please, of course, but if you're at loose ends, you can always pitch in here."

"Thank you. I'll remember that."

"I'd be happy to help the woman who married Davey Chancel."

Nora looked in surprise at Jeffrey, and his mother said, "I take it that my son left the explanations to me."

"Would I dare do anything else?" Jeffrey asked.

Sophie and Maribel had paused on their way to the table to help themselves to Swedish meatballs from a steaming platter, and the older woman said, "Pack the van, my little elves." Chewing, they hurried across the kitchen. "Let's go to the front room and sit down. I've been on my feet all day."

She gestured toward the sofa where Sophie had sprawled in front of the television. Nora sat, and Jeffrey put his hands in his pockets and watched his mother switch off the set. She placed herself at the end of Nora's sofa and rested her hands on her knees. "Jeffrey didn't introduce us, and I gather that you have no idea of who I am, apart from being this person's mother."

"I'm sorry, but I don't," Nora said. "You knew Katherine Mannheim? And you know the Chancels, too?"

"Naturally," she said. "Katherine was my older sister. I met Lincoln Chancel at Shorelands, and before I knew what was what, he hired me to work for him. I was still there when your husband was just a little boy."

Nora looked from the older woman to Jeffrey.

Jeffrey cleared his throat. "Mr. Chancel disliked the sound of Italian names."

"When Mr. Chancel hired me, I was Helen Deodato, but you may have heard of me as Helen Day," his mother said. "I got so used to it that I still call myself Helen Day. When Alden Chancel and his wife took over the house, they used to call me the Cup Bearer."

BOOK VIII

THE CUP BEARER

FOR A LONG TIME, PIPPIN SAT IN THE WARMTH AND THE FLICK-ERING LIGHT OF THE FIRE WITHOUT SPEAKING. HE GAZED INTO THE OLD WOMAN'S FACE. AFTER ALL SHE HAD TOLD HIM, THE WHITE WHISKERS SPROUTING FROM HER UPPER LIP AND POINTED CHIN NO LONGER FRIGHTENED HIM. NOT EVEN THE SKULL FROM WHICH SHE DRANK HER FOUL BROWN POTION, NOR THE HEAP OF SKULLS BEHIND HER, FRIGHTENED HIM NOW. HE WAS TOO INTERESTED IN HER STORY TO BE AFRAID. "I DON'T UNDER-STAND," HE SAID. "YOU ARE HIS MOTHER, BUT HE IS NOT YOUR SON?"

73

FOR WHAT SEEMED to her an endless succession of seconds, Nora could not speak. She could not even move. The decisive old woman before her, her necklaces of antique coins, of heavy gold links, of pottery beads, silver birds, silver feathers, and shining red and green stones motionless on her chest, her broad hands planted on her knees, sat tilted slightly forward, taking in the effect of her announcement as Nora stared at the firm black eyebrows, clever black eyes, prominent nose, full, well-shaped lips, and rounded chin of Helen Day. The Cup Bearer, O'Dotto—Day and O'Dotto, the two halves of her last name—unknown to Davey because his grandfather had thought Italian names too proletarian to be used in his house.

The woman said, "Jeffrey, you should have told her *something*, at least. Springing all this on her at once isn't fair."

"I was thinking about being fair to you," Jeffrey said.

"I'll be all right," Nora said.

"Of course you will."

"It's a lot to take in all at once. I've heard so much about you from Davey. You're legendary. They still talk about your desserts."

"Whole family has a sweet tooth. Old Mr. Chancel could eat an entire seven-layer cake by himself. Sometimes I had to make two, one for him and one for everyone else. Little Davey was the same way. I used to worry about his getting fat when he grew up. Did he? No, I suppose not. You wouldn't have married him if he'd been a great lumbering bag of guts like his grandfather."

"No, I wouldn't have, and he isn't."

"Who am I to talk, anyhow?" Helen Day seemed almost wistful. "Davey must have missed me after his parents got rid of

347

me. Poor little fellow, he'd have had to, with those two for parents."

Nora said, "He once told me he thought you were his real mother."

"His real mother hardly spent much time with him. Hardly knew he was in the house, most of the time."

"And of course even *she* wasn't his real mother," Nora said. "You must have been at the Poplars when the first child died."

Helen Day put a forefinger to her lips and gave Nora a long, thoughtful look. She nodded. "Yes, I was there during the uproar."

"Daisy and Alden didn't even want a child, did they? Not really. It was Lincoln who made them adopt Davey."

Another considering pause. "The old man let them know he wanted an heir, I'll say that. There weren't too many quiet nights on Mount Avenue during that time." She looked away, and her handsome face hardened like cement. "According to Jeffrey, you wanted to talk to me about my sister."

"I do, very much, but can I ask you a few questions about other people in your family first?"

She raised her eyebrows. "Other people in my family?"

"Is Sabina Mann your sister?"

The old woman flicked her glance toward Jeffrey.

"We had to see Ev Tidy," Jeffrey said. "His number is unlisted, so I called Sabina and asked her to invite him to her house."

"Which she was delighted to do, I'm sure. I bet she bustled in and out with lots of cheap cookies and cups of Earl Grey."

"It was Gunpowder, and she only bustled in once. I have to admit that she was peeved with me."

"Gunpowder," said Helen Day. "Dear me. She'll get over it. You wanted to talk to Everett about Shorelands because of his father, I suppose."

"That's right," Nora said.

"And was he helpful?"

"He had some ideas," Jeffrey said, with a warning glance at Nora which did not escape his mother's notice.

"I won't pry. It isn't my business, except for what concerns my sister. But from what I remember of Everett's father, he couldn't have had much to say about Katherine. It was my impression that he'd scarcely talked to her. Couldn't be much there to excite poor old Effie and Grace." When Nora looked confused, Helen Day added, "My sisters. They're the fools who saw that movie and hired a lawyer."

"You're right," Jeffrey said. "Bill Tidy had no idea what Katherine was writing."

"Hardly a surprise. The whole idea is mad. Now I am informed that this madness has infected the wretched man who stole you out of a police station." She shook her head in disgust. "Let me answer your question. No, Sabina Mann is not my sister, thank the Lord. She was Sabina Kraft when she married my brother Charles. Thereby completing the severing of relations between my brother and myself which began when he changed his name."

"Why did he change his name?"

"Charles hated my father. Changing his name was no more than a way to cause him pain. He did it as soon as he turned twenty-one. The disgrace nearly cost Effie and Grace what little minds they have. Katherine didn't care, of course. It didn't mean anything to *her*. Katherine was like a separate country all her life."

Nora was thinking that Helen Day, who had apparently not protested Lincoln Chancel's desire to change her own last name, was no less idiosyncratic than her sister.

"You weren't close to Charles or your two other sisters?"

"I got along with the Deodatos a lot better than my own family, if that's what you're after. Good, sensible, warmhearted people, and they were delighted to take Jeffrey in when it became obvious that I couldn't cope with being a single mother. I certainly wasn't going to subject my little boy to *Charles*, never mind Sabina, and Effie and Grace could scarcely take care of themselves. But here was this glorious clan, full of cooks and policemen and high school teachers. I was so fond of them all, and they had no problems with my way of life, so there was never any difficulty about my seeing Jeffrey whenever I could. When I left the Chancels, I knew I had to come back to this part of Massachusetts. This was my home, and it was where my husband died. It's the one place in the world I've ever really loved. Jeffrey understood."

"I did," Jeffrey said. "I still do."

"I know you do. I just don't want Nora to judge me harshly. Anyhow, between us all, we did a pretty good job with Jeffrey, didn't we? He's done a lot of interesting things, even though his Mannheim half meant that other people had a lot of trouble understanding them. There's a lot of me in Jeffrey, and a lot of

Katherine, too. But Jeffrey is much nicer than Katherine ever was. Or me either, come to that."

"Katherine wasn't nice?"

"Am I? You tell me."

"You're beyond niceness," Nora said. "I think you're too good to be nice."

Tiny pinpoints of light kindled far back in the old woman's eyes. "You just described my sister Katherine. I'd like you to remember my offer. If you ever find yourself in need of a safe place, you'd be welcome here. You would learn to cook every sort of cuisine, and you'd be able to put away some money. We operate on a communal basis, and everybody shares equally."

"Thank you," said Nora. "I'm tempted to sign up on the spot."

"I should have known," Jeffrey said. "The famous Helen Day Halfway House, Cooking School, Intellectual Salon, and Women's Shelter strikes again."

"Nonsense," the old woman said. "Nora understands what I mean. Now we are going to talk about my sister Katherine, so you can stop fretting."

"Halleluiah." Jeffrey went to the other sofa and sat down facing them.

"Did Katherine ever talk to you about her writing?" Nora asked.

"I can remember her reading some poems to me when she was twelve or thirteen and I was about nine. It was an occasion, because Katherine was always very private about her writing. Not her opinions, mind you. If she thought something was absurd, she let you know. Anyhow, as I was saying, I used to see her writing her poems all the time, and once I asked her if I could read them. No, she said, but I'll read some of them to you—and she did, two or three short poems, I forget. I didn't understand a word, and I never asked again."

"But later on? When you were both grown up?"

"By that time, we didn't talk to each other more than once every couple of months, and all she said about her writing was that she was doing it. She did call to tell me she was going to Shorelands. She was pleased about that, and she was going to stay with me for a couple of nights when she left. I was up here, and Katherine lived in New York—by herself, of course, in Greenwich Village, a tiny apartment on Patchin Place. I went there two weeks after I came back home from Shorelands. I knew she was dead, I hope you take my word for that."

"What did you think had happened to her?" Nora asked.

"Years later, that silly old windbag Georgina Weatherall pretended to think Katherine had run away with some drawing of hers and changed her name to keep out of sight. What a story! Katherine never stole anything in her life. Why should she, she never wanted anything. It just made Georgina look better than having one of her guests die so far off in the woods that you could never find her body."

"You're positive that's what happened."

"I knew it the second I saw that ridiculous woman. Katherine would have known just how to ruffle her feathers, and the last thing that kind of woman can stand is the thought that someone is laughing at her. It was exactly like my sister to provoke a fool like that, and then decamp a split second before she was ordered off the premises. It was just her bad luck to die in the midst of this particular jaunt, so that we could never give her a burial. Her heart caught up with her at the wrong time, that's all."

"How did Georgina know to call you after she disappeared?"

"Katherine gave her my number. Who else's? She wouldn't have given her Charles's number, or Grace and Effie's, heaven knows. Katherine always liked me more than any of the rest of them. I want to show you some things."

She stood up with a rattle and rustle of the necklaces and went through the arch. Nora and Jeffrey heard her giving orders in the kitchen, then the slow march of her footsteps up a staircase.

"What do you think she wants to show me?" Nora asked.

"Do you think I ever know what my mother is going to do?"

"What's wrong with Grace and Effie?"

"They're too normal for her. Besides, they were scandalized that she went off and worked for Lincoln Chancel. They thought it wasn't good enough for her. My aunts don't much like what she's doing now, either. They don't think it's very ladylike."

"Hard to see how it could be any more ladylike," Nora said.

He smiled. "You haven't met Grace and Effie."

"How did they wind up with this notebook, or whatever it was, the one that caused all the trouble?"

"My mother used to keep her sister's papers in the basement here, but after she had a couple of bedrooms put in downstairs, she didn't have much room left. Grace and Effie agreed to take them—four cardboard boxes, mostly drafts of stories and poems. I looked through them a long time ago."

"No novel."

"No." He looked back toward the arch and the kitchen full of women. "By the way, despite the way she talks about Lincoln Chancel, or even Alden and Daisy, my mother's still loyal to them. Don't mention what we were talking about with Ev Tidy, okay? She'd just get angry."

"I saw the look you gave me."

"Remember, when she stopped working for them, she recommended Maria, who was about eighteen and just off the boat. Maria hardly even spoke English then, but they hired her anyhow. They hired me, too. She thinks the Chancels have done a lot for our family."

"I never did understand why Alden and Daisy fired her," Nora said. "She was like a member of the family."

"I don't think they did. She quit when she had enough money saved up to start this business."

The treads of the staircase creaked.

"I'm sure Davey told me that they fired her. Losing her was very painful for him."

"How old was he, four? He didn't know what was really going on." He gave her a tight little smile as his mother's footsteps came down the stairs. "Too bad they didn't send him out to Long Island. It might have done him some good."

"Might have done him a lot of good," Nora said, and turned toward the kitchen to see Helen Day, flanked by three of her assistants, leaning over a copper vat. She inhaled deeply, considered, and spoke to an anxious-looking girl who flashed away and returned with a cup of brown powder, a trickle of which she poured into the vat.

The long day caught up with Nora, and she felt an enormous yawn take possession of her. "How rude," she said. "I'm sorry."

Helen Day marched back through the arch, apologizing for the delay. She sat a few feet away from Nora and lowered two objects onto the length of brown corduroy between them. Nora looked down at a framed photograph on top of a spring binder so old that its pebbled black surface had faded to an uneven shade of gray. "Now. Look at that picture."

Nora picked it up. Two little girls in frocks, one of them about three years old and the other perhaps eight, stood smiling up at the photographer in a sunny garden. The smaller girl held a doll-sized china teacup on a matching saucer. Both girls, clearly sisters, had bobbed dark hair and endearing faces. The older one was smiling only with her mouth.

"Can you guess who they are?" asked Helen Day.

"You and Katherine," Nora said.

"I was playing tea party in the garden, and wonder of wonders, Katherine happened along and indulged me. My father came outside to memorialize the moment, no doubt to prove to Katherine at some later date that she was once a child after all. And she *knows* what he's doing, you can see it in her face. She can see right through him."

Nora looked down at the intense self-sufficiency in the eight-year-old girl's eyes. This child would be able to see right through most people. "Did you find this picture in her apartment?"

"No, that's where I found the manuscript. This picture was on her desk in Gingerbread, and it was the first thing I saw when I went there. *Good heavens,* I said to myself, *look at that.* You know what it means, don't you?"

Nora had no idea what it meant, but Helen Day's eyes and voice made clear what it meant to her. "Your sister felt close to you," she said.

The old woman reared back with a rustle of necklaces and pointed a wide pink forefinger at Nora's throat. "Grand-slam home run. She felt closer to me than anyone else in our whole, all-balled-up family. Whose address and telephone number did she give in case of emergency? Mine. Whose picture did she bring to Shorelands and put right in the place of honor on her desk? Mine. It wasn't a picture with stuffy Charles, was it?"

Because the finger was still aimed at her throat, Nora shook her head.

"No. And it wasn't a picture of those two idiots who never read a book in their lives, Effie and Grace, not on your life. She never felt any closer to those three than she did to strangers on the street. At first, I couldn't understand Katherine going off and leaving our picture behind, but when I noticed she had left her silk robe and a bunch of books, too, I saw what she was doing. She knew I'd be coming to get everything for her. She left those things behind for me, because she knew I'd take care of them for her. And I bet you can guess why."

Again Nora gave the answer Helen Day waited to hear. "Because you understood her better than the others."

"Of course I did. She never made any sense to them her whole life long. It was like Jeffrey with the Deodatos. I love them, and they're wonderful people, but they never could figure out some of the things Jeffrey did. People like Jeffrey and my sister always color outside the lines, isn't that right, Jeffrey?"

"If you say so, Mom," Jeffrey said. "But you've colored outside the lines a few times yourself."

"That's what I'm saying! A couple of times in my life people said I was crazy. *Charles* told me I was crazy. Going with Lincoln Chancel! Giving up my son, and not even to him, but to people he thought were inferior! You must be as crazy as Katherine was, he said. Well, I said, in that case I'm not doing too badly. You can bet he changed his tune when Jeffrey got his scholarship to Harvard and did so well there. When people don't have a prayer of understanding you, the first thing they do is call you crazy. Grace and Effie *still* think I'm crazy, but I'm doing a lot better than they are. They thought Katherine was crazy, too. She embarrassed them, just like I did when I went to work for the Chancels."

She folded her arms over her chest in a clatter of coins and beads and gave Nora a flat black glare. "My sisters actually thought Katherine ran away with that drawing, changed her name, and lived off the money she got for it. Know what they told me? They said Katherine never had a bad heart in the first place. Dr. Montross made a mistake when she was a little girl, and she's had special treatment ever since. Stole that drawing and took off, changed her name, now she's laughing at us all. They said Charles changed his name, didn't he? Didn't you? they said. Wasn't Mr. Day you married, was it? I said I never changed my name, man I worked for did that, and when he spoke, you *listened*. All I did was get used to it, and it was only my married name anyway. All that writing, they said, that was crazy, too, but it wasn't, was it, Jeffrey?"

"Not at all," Jeffrey said.

"She was invited to Shorelands. Nobody says those other people were crazy. And Dr. Montross wasn't a fraud. Katherine had rheumatic fever when she was two, and her heart could have given out at any time. We all knew that. She *died*. Grace and Effie said, You never found her, did you, and neither did all those policemen, but they didn't see what it was like. You could have sent twenty men into those woods for a month, and they wouldn't find everything."

"If she wanted to get out, why go through the woods instead of taking some easier way?"

"Didn't want to go past Main House," said Helen Day. "Katherine didn't want anyone to see her. And you know, maybe she did get to the road. Maybe she even got a ride and a room for the night, or took the train somewhere, but her heart stopped and she died. Because she never got in touch with me about her things. I waited two weeks, but neither Katherine nor anyone else called me, and I *knew*."

"But your brother and your two older sisters didn't agree? They thought she might still be alive?"

"Charles didn't. He was sure Katherine had died, just like me. Dr. Montross told our parents that it would be a miracle if Katherine lived to be thirty, and she was twenty-nine that year."

"And Grace and Effie?"

"They knew it, too, but they changed their minds when that book came out, almost saying in black and white that Katherine took that picture from the dining room. Katherine couldn't do anything right, as far as they were concerned. They never had a good word to say for her until they started going through her papers before throwing them out—papers I gave them for safekeeping— and saw some scribbles on a few pieces of paper that reminded them of a movie they didn't even like! They still thought she was crazy, but they didn't mind the idea of making some money off of her. Old fools. Katherine didn't write that book, Hugo Driver did. If you want to know what my sister was writing, look in that folder."

74

WITH A RUSH of expectant excitement, Nora opened the spring binder. Jeffrey stood up to get a better look.

UNWRITTEN WORDS
by
Katherine Mannheim
15 Patchin Place, #3
New York, New York
(copy 2)

She turned over the title page to find a poem titled "Dialogue of the Latter Days," heavily edited in green ink. Her heart sank. *This* was what Katherine Mannheim had been writing? The poem continued on to the second page. She flipped ahead and saw that it took up twenty-three pages. "Second Dialogue," also heavily edited, ran for twenty-six pages. Two more "dialogues" of thirty to forty pages apiece filled out the book.

"It's one long poem, or so I've decided, divided up into those dialogues. She had two copies, and made changes to both of them. She must have taken the first copy to Shorelands to spend the month revising it there, and I think she was planning to type up a third and final copy with all the revisions when she got back."

She had been "unwriting" the *Unwritten Words* through a lengthy, painstaking series of revisions. "This was on her desk?"

"In her apartment, right next to her typewriter, along with a big folder full of earlier versions. The one she took to Shorelands was lost along with everything else she put into her suitcase."

"You never showed it to me," Jeffrey said.

"You weren't here all that often, and I wasn't done looking at it. I always had trouble understanding the things Katherine wrote, and this was harder than anything else, especially with all those scribbles. After a couple of years, I began to find my way. I saw— I think I saw—that she was writing about her death. About living with her death, the way she did for so long. If you had asked me, I would have said that she never thought about it because she didn't seem to. Katherine wasn't a brooding sort of person at all, but of course she thought about it all the time. That's why she wrote the way she did, and why she lived the way she did. What I think is, my sister Katherine was a saint. A real-life saint."

Startled, Nora looked up from the book. "A saint?"

Helen Day smiled and glanced down at the photograph. "Katherine was the most sensitive, most intelligent, most dedicated person I've ever known, and deep down inside herself the *purest.* What most people call religion didn't affect her at all, even though we were raised Catholic. You'll find more spiritual people outside churches than in them. Katherine couldn't be bothered with the unimportant things most people spend their whole lives worrying about. She knew how to have a good time, she sometimes shocked ordinary-thinking people, but she had *focus.* When I take on new girls here, I look to see if they have at least a little bit of what Katherine had, and if they do, welcome aboard. You do, you have some of it."

"Well, a lot of ordinary-thinking people might think I'm a little bit crazy," Nora said, thinking of her gleeful demons.

"Don't you believe it. You've been *hurt.* I can see that. No wonder, considering what happened to you. Here you are, chasing around Massachusetts instead of going back home, if you still have a home to go back to." She looked over at her son. "Alden Chancel might not think you're the right wife for his son, but you're hardly crazy. In fact, what *I* think, you're one of those people who take in more than most of us."

"You're giving me too much credit," Nora said.

"You're a person who wants to know what's true. When I look back, it seems to me that most of what I learned when I was little was all wrong. Lies were stuffed down our throats day and night. Lies about men and women, about the proper way to live, about our own feelings, and I don't believe too much has changed. It's still important to find out what's really true, and if you didn't think that was important, you wouldn't be here right now."

Yes, Nora thought, *I do think that it's important to find out what is really true.*

Helen Day checked her watch. "I have to make sure everything's all right before I put in an appearance at the Asia Society. I hope you'll think about everything I said."

"Thank you for talking to me."

All three stood up. "You'll be at the Northampton Hotel?"

"Yes," Jeffrey said.

Helen Day had not taken her eyes off Nora. "If you're still up around ten, would you give me a call? I want to talk about something with you, but I have to think it over first."

"Something to do with your sister?"

The old woman slowly shook her head. "While I'm thinking about my question, you should think about your husband. You're stronger than Davey, and he needs your help."

"What's this 'question' of yours?" Jeffrey asked.

She turned to him and took his hand. "Jeffrey, you'll come here tomorrow, won't you? We'll have time for a real conversation. If you turn up around eight, you can help with the driving, too. We have to pick up a lot of fresh vegetables."

"You want me to drive one of the vans while Maya and Sophie sit in the back and make fun of me."

"You enjoy it. Come over tomorrow."

"Should I bring Nora?"

Helen Day had been moving them slowly toward the front door, and at this question she met Nora's eyes with a look as significant as a touch. "That's up to her." She let them out into the warm night.

75

"YOU LIKED HER, didn't you?"

"Who wouldn't like her?" Nora asked. "She's extraordinary."

Jeffrey was driving them down Main Street, where restaurant windows glowed and gatherings of three and four drifted in and out of pools of light cast by the streetlamps.

"I know, but she drives a lot of people up the wall. She makes up her mind about you as soon as she meets you, and if she takes to you, you're invited in. If not, you get the big freeze. I was almost certain she'd warm to you right away, but . . ." He glanced at her. "I guess you see why I couldn't say much about her beforehand."

"I suppose I do," she said.

"What would you like to do?"

"Go to bed," she said. "After that, maybe I'll spend the rest of my life chopping celery for your mother. I'd have to change my name, but that's all right, everybody else already has. After a couple of years maybe I'd get to be as perceptive as your mother thinks I am."

Jeffrey gave her one of his sidelong looks. "I thought you seemed unhappy back there. Disappointed, I guess."

"Well, you're already perceptive enough for both of us. Yes. I guess I was expecting too much. I thought that even if everything was falling apart around me, at least I could help prove that your aunt was the real writer of *Night Journey*. Instead, all I managed to find out was that Hugo Driver was a nasty little creep who stole things. But if he didn't steal *Night Journey*, then everything we thought we knew was all wrong. What did your aunts see in those pages, anyhow? What excited them so much?"

"Phrases. Descriptions of landscapes, fields and fog and mountains. Most of them were sort of like Driver, but not close enough to justify calling a lawyer. There was something about death and childhood—how a child could see death as a journey."

"That makes a lot of sense for Katherine Mannheim, but it hardly proves anything about the book."

"Two other phrases got them excited, mainly. One was about a black wolf."

"That doesn't mean anything."

"The other was 'the Cup Bearer.' They did get excited about that." The front of the hotel floated past them. A guitarist played bossa nova music on the terrace.

"I don't get it. That's what Davey used to call your mother."

"You saw that picture of the two of them as little girls, where my mother is holding a cup. After that, Katherine started calling her the Cup Bearer." He rolled the MG down into the lot. His smile flashed. "I forgot, you never read *Night Journey*."

"I still don't get it."

"Book Eight of *Night Journey* is called 'The Cup Bearer.' That's what really got Grace and Effie going, that and the wolf." He pulled into an empty spot and switched off the engine.

"But Davey was calling your mother the Cup Bearer before he could even read. How did he ever hear about it?"

"He must have seen the photograph in her room," Jeffrey said. "He went there looking for her sometimes, when Alden and Daisy left him alone. If he'd asked her about it, she would have told him about the nickname. That would have been another reason why the book meant so much to him later on. It reminded him of my mother."

Now she knew why Davey had been irritated with her when

she had asked him about the origin of the nickname. Jeffrey was waiting patiently for her to finish asking questions so that they could leave the car. "Is the Cup Bearer in the book anything like your mother?"

"Well, let's see." He propped his chin in his hand. "She makes this foul-smelling brew. She had no children of her own, but she raised someone else's child. On the whole, she's pretty fearsome. I'd have to say she's a lot like my mother."

"Hugo Driver never saw that picture. Where did he get the phrase from?"

"You got me."

In the warm evening air they moved toward the concrete steps, washed shining white by the lights, leading to the hotel's back door. Half his face in shadow, the Eton cap tilted over his forehead, Jeffrey more than ever resembled a jewel thief from twenties novels. "Maybe this is none of my business," he said. "But if she leans on you to call Davey, think hard before you do it. And if you do decide to call him, don't tell him where you are."

He turned away and led her up the gleaming steps.

76

WITHIN A SMALL, wary portion of her mind, Nora had been awaiting the news that the hotel had only a single unoccupied room, but Jeffrey had not turned into Dan Harwich. He had returned from the desk with two keys, hers for the fifth-floor room overlooking the terrace and the top of King Street where she had taken a long bath and now, wrapped in a white robe, occupied a grandmotherly easy chair, the radio playing Brahms's Alto Rhapsody and the air conditioner humming, reading her husband's favorite novel as an escape from thinking about what to do next.

Pippin Little wandered from character to character, hearing stories. Some of these characters were human and some were monsters, but they were fine storytellers one and all. Their tales were colorful and involved, full of danger, heroism, and betrayal. Some told the truth and others lied. Some wanted to help Pippin Little, but even they were not always truthful. Some of the others wanted to cut him up into pieces and turn him into tasty meat loaf, but these characters did not always lie. The truth Pippin required was a mosaic to be assembled over time and at great risk. Nearly everybody in *Night Journey* was related to everybody else; they made up a single enormous, contentious family, and as in any family, its members had varying memories and interpretations of crucial events. There were factions, secrets, hatreds. Pippin had to risk entering the Field of Steam to learn its lessons, or he had to avoid its contagion; if he stood among the Stones of Toon, he would acquire a golden key vital to his search, or he would be set upon by the fiends who pretended to possess a golden key.

It was just past nine-thirty, half an hour before she had been invited to call Helen Day. Did she want to call Helen Day? Not if Jeffrey's mother was going to do no more than try to make her feel sorry for Davey. She already felt sorry for Davey. Then she remembered that Helen Day had spoken of having to think about some matter before she could discuss it. Probably the old woman was considering telling her something she had already guessed, that the Chancels had never wanted their son.

She might as well get as far as she could with *Night Journey*. If she skipped here and there, she could just about finish the hundred pages remaining. Or she could go straight to the last twenty-five pages and see if Pippin ever made it to Mountain Glade. On the night her life had started to go wrong, she had come awake in time to see Pippin racing downhill toward a white farmhouse, which she had made the mistake of calling "pretty." *Pretty, so what if it's pretty,* Davey had said, or something close; *it's all wrong, Mountain Glade isn't supposed to be pretty. Does that place look like it contains the great secret?*

So what *did* this all-important place look like? Lord Night said it was "an unhallowed haunt of baleful spirits revealed by the Stones of Toon"; the Cup Bearer described it as "a soul-thieving devastation you must never see"; even less satisfactorily, Gentle Friend called it "the locked prison cell wherein you have interred your greatest fear." Nora turned over most of the pages remaining before the end of the book and skimmed down the lines before finding this paragraph:

The great door yielded to the golden key and revealed what he had most feared, yet most desired to see, the true face of Mountain Glade. Far down the stony, snow-encrusted mountain, he beheld a misshapen cottage, a bleak habitation of lives as comfortless as itself.

Pippin had come back home.

A few minutes before the appointed time, Nora found the Northampton telephone directory in a drawer and sat on the bed to use the telephone.

"Heavenly," said a female voice.

Nora asked for Helen Day, and the phone rapped down on a counter. She heard a buzz of cheerful female voices.

"Hello, this is Helen Day."

Nora gave her name and added, "Sounds like you're having a party over there."

"Some of the elves got home early from the Asia Society. I have to change phones." Nora held the dead receiver while time ticked on. She moved the telephone closer to the side of the bed, stretched out, yawning, and closed her eyes.

"Are you there? Nora? Are you all right?"

The ceiling of a strange room hung above her head. She lay on an unfamiliar bed slightly too soft for her taste.

"Nora?"

The strangeness around her again became the room at the top of the Northampton Hotel. "I think I fell asleep for a second."

"I have at least half an hour before anybody's going to need me again. Can you talk for a bit, or do you want to forget about it and go back to sleep?"

"I'm fine." She yawned as quietly as possible.

"I often think about Davey. He was such a darling little fellow. I want to hear whatever you can tell me about him. What is he like now? How would you describe him?"

"He's still a darling little fellow," Nora said.

"Is that good?"

Nora did not know how honest she should be, nor how harsh an honest description of Davey would be. "I have to admit that being a darling little fellow at the age of forty has its drawbacks."

"Is he kind? Is he good to people?"

Now Nora understood what Helen Day was asking. "He isn't

anything like his father, I have to say that. The problem is, he's insecure, and he worries a lot, and he's frustrated all the time."

"I suppose he's working for his father."

"Alden keeps him under his thumb," Nora said. "He pays Davey a lot of money to do these menial jobs, so Davey is convinced he can't do anything else. As soon as his father raises his voice, Davey gives up and rolls over like a puppy."

Helen Day said nothing for a moment. "Do you and Davey go to the Poplars often?"

"At least once a week. Usually on Sundays."

"How are relations between Alden and you?"

"Strained? Rocky? He put up a good front for about six months, but then he started to show how he really felt."

"Is he civil, at least?"

"Not anymore. He despises me. I did this stupid thing and Daisy went out of her mind, so Alden called Davey on the carpet and said that unless he left me, he'd fire him from Chancel House and cut him out of his will."

Helen Day was silent. "I had the feeling that you had something else in mind when you asked me to call," Nora said.

"Alden is blackmailing Davey into leaving you."

"That's the general idea. I tried to convince him that we didn't need Alden's money, but I don't think I did a very good job."

"What was this thing that gave Alden his excuse?"

"Daisy talked me into reading her book. When she called me up to talk about it, she went on a kind of rampage. Alden blamed me."

"He's a terrible bully. I respect the man no end, but that's what he is."

"I don't respect him. He never wanted Davey, but he can't let him go. All Davey's life he's suffered from the feeling that he's not the real Davey Chancel, so he'll never be good enough."

"I was afraid of this," Helen Day said. "Alden's making him *pay*."

"Lincoln did the same thing, didn't he? He forced Alden and Daisy to adopt a grandson, and they went along for the sake of the money. Isn't that what you were thinking about telling me? You didn't want to say it in front of Jeffrey."

Again Helen Day waited a long time to speak. "I wish I could discuss that subject, but I can't."

"I already know. There was something just like it in Daisy's book."

"Daisy was furious with both of them."

"She didn't want him, either. I'm surprised they ever had a child in the first place."

Helen Day said, "I suppose they were surprised, too."

"You were at the Poplars when the first one was born. You saw them go through all that."

"I did."

" 'The uproar,' you called it."

"That's exactly the right word. Noise day and night, shouting and yelling."

"And you think Davey ought to know why his parents have always treated him the way they do. That he was only a way for Alden to stay in his father's will."

Silence.

"Alden made you promise, didn't he? He made you promise never to tell Davey about this." Another recognition came to her. "He made you leave, and he gave you enough money to start up your own business."

"He gave me the chance I needed."

"You've been grateful ever since, but you've never felt right about it."

After a pause, the old woman said, "He shouldn't be playing the same dirty trick on his son that his father played on him. That makes me very unhappy."

"Did they even want the *first* child? They must have had it because of Lincoln."

"If you guess, I'm not telling you. Do you understand? Keep guessing. You're doing an excellent job so far."

"So they didn't. How did the first one die?"

"I thought you said that Daisy wrote about this in her book."

"She did, but she changed everything." An amazing thought flared in Nora's mind. "Did Daisy kill the baby? It's a terrible thing to say, but she's almost crazy enough to have done it, and Lincoln and Alden wouldn't have had any trouble hushing it up."

"The only thing Daisy Chancel ever killed was a bottle," said Helen Day. "What would you do with an unwanted baby?"

"You gave yours to your relatives."

"But what would most people do?"

"Give it up for adoption," Nora said.

"That's right."

"But then why make up a story about it dying? It doesn't make sense."

"Keep guessing."

"You give up one child and then adopt another one? I don't even know if that's possible. No agency would give a child to a couple that had given their own away."

"Sounds right to me," said Helen Day.

"So the first one died. It must have been a crib death. Unless Alden murdered it."

"What did Daisy put in her book?"

"It was all mixed up. There was a child, and then it was gone. The Lincoln character rages around, but half the time he's in a Nazi uniform. Lincoln Chancel didn't wear Nazi uniforms, did he?"

"Mr. Chancel collected Nazi flags, uniforms, sashes, armbands, things like that. After he died, Alden asked me to burn them. You have to *guess,* Nora. Do you guess the baby died?"

"I guess it didn't die," Nora said. "I guess it was adopted."

"That's a good guess."

"But . . ." A moment from Daisy's book played itself out in her mind: Adelbert Poison squabbling with Clementine on his rotting terrace. Nora tried to remember what he had said about Egbert—some word Daisy had written. What had actually happened to Davey, the only sequence of actions which made sense out of these uproars, came to her an instant before she recalled the word, which was *reclaim.* It felt as though a bomb had gone off in her chest.

"Oh, no," she said. "They couldn't have."

After she said what was in her mind, she had no doubt that she was right. "They had Davey adopted, and then Lincoln made them take him back. There was no first Davey. *Davey* was the first Davey."

"Sounds like a pretty good guess to me," said Helen Day. "The Chancels have grand imaginations. Everyday truth doesn't stand a chance."

Nora let her idea of their crime speak for itself. "Neither one of them ever wanted him. They had to take him back for the sake of the money. They would have been happier if he *had* died."

"And Alden's been making him pay ever since."

"He's been making him pay ever since," Nora echoed.

"I was right about you. You do see more than most other people."

"They lied to him all through his life. How old was he when they got him back?"

"About six months. The other family didn't want to lose him, but Lincoln made Alden and Daisy go up to New Hampshire, and they said all the right things and got him back."

"Everybody believed that their child had died. The only person who knew what had happened was you. When Davey got older, they were afraid you'd tell him the truth, so they made you leave."

Helen Day sighed. "One of the hardest things I ever did in my life. I could *see* Jeffrey whenever I wanted, and I knew he was with people who loved him. But Davey was all alone. When Mr. Chancel died, they just ignored him. They're fine people, but they didn't want to be parents."

Nora was still reeling. "How can you say they're fine people when you know what they did?"

"It isn't so easy to judge people when you understand them. Alden has a cold heart and he's a bully, but I know why. His father. That's the pure and simple truth."

"I bet that's right," said Nora.

"You never knew Lincoln Chancel. Mr. Chancel had more energy, brains, and drive than any other six men put together. He was a *fighter*. Some of the things he fought for were wrong and bad, and he didn't give a hoot about the law unless it happened to be on his side, but he didn't pussyfoot through life—he *roared*. There were times when I was angrier at him than I've ever been at anyone, but there was something magnificent about him. I always thought Mr. Chancel was a lot like my sister, with everything turned inside out. Neither one of them was very nice, but if they'd been nice people they wouldn't have been so impressive."

"But he was a monster."

"You have to have a saint inside you to be a monster. Mr. Chancel caused a lot of damage, but his heart wasn't cold, not at all. When I went to Shorelands, who do you suppose tried hardest to find my sister? Who talked Georgina into letting me stay four days? Mr. Chancel. Who went out into the woods with me and the policemen? He had his businesses to run, he had his ticker tape and his telephone calls, but he did more to help find Katherine than any of those writers."

"I see," said Nora.

"I hope you do. And he saw what kind of shape I was in, with my husband dead and my son gone and my heart broken over poor Katherine, and he offered me a job at twice what I was getting, plus room and board."

"You feel strongly about him."

"Some things you don't forget. If Mr. Chancel had lived, he would have told Davey the truth, I know that."

"Should I?" Nora asked.

"You do whatever you think is best, but that's the kind of person you are anyhow. I just want you to remember that *I* didn't tell you, because I do what I think is best, too, and I don't go back on my promises."

"Look, didn't they have to have some kind of burial? There was supposed to be a *body*."

"Private burial. In the graveyard behind St. Anselm's. Just Alden, Mr. Chancel, and the rector. Short and sweet, and the only man crying at the funeral was Mr. Chancel, because Alden knew damn well that what they were burying was a couple bricks packed in a shroud so they wouldn't slide around in the coffin."

"God, what a devil," Nora said.

"His father said a lot worse than that when he found out." Helen Day surprised Nora by laughing out loud.

77

DAVEY WAS IN Jeffrey's apartment, where the telephone line was untapped. If she called him, she was under no obligation to reveal his father's treachery. He would believe her in time, she knew, but if she troubled him with Helen Day's revelation while he was still under Alden's spell, he would accuse her of lying. Once she accepted the truth, he would have to burst out of the Poplars, out of Chancel House, out of Alden's life forever.

Nora reached out and touched the receiver. The plastic seemed warm and alive. She pulled back her hand, then reached out again. The bell went off like an alarm, and she jumped. *Davey*.

She picked up the receiver and said hello.

"Nora, is that you?" The man at the other end was not Davey.

"It's me," she said.

"This is Everett Tidy. I tried to call you before, but you were on the phone. It's not too late to talk, is it?"

"No."

"I thought you ought to know about something. I don't mean to worry you, but it's got me a little disturbed."

She asked him what had happened.

"I got two calls. The first was from a lawyer named Leland Dart. He's the father, isn't he?"

Nora asked what Leland Dart had wanted.

"He apologized for taking my time and all of that. He explained that he was the counsel for Chancel House and asked if I was aware that there had been some recent discussion about the authorship of one of their properties. I told him I knew nothing about it. Then he told me the property was *Night Journey*, and that, as I undoubtedly knew, my father had once had some contact with its author, Hugo Driver. He wanted to know if I was in possession of any papers of my father's which could demonstrate Driver's authorship. If I didn't have the time, he'd be happy to send one of his staff up to Amherst to go through everything for me."

"What did you say?"

"That nothing my father had written could prove anything about *Night Journey* one way or the other. Had I examined everything? Yes, I said, and he'd have to take my word for it, there wasn't anything he could use. Then he asked how many journals or diaries my father had left, and where I kept them. Were they on deposit in a library somewhere, or were they in my house? The Amherst College Library, I told him. If he sent a young fellow up to Amherst, would I agree to let him inspect the papers? Not on your life, I said. Then he said that he might need to be in correspondence with me, and he wanted to verify my address. He read out the address of my old house. Was that right? I said that as far as I was concerned, we had no more to talk about."

"Good," Nora said.

"Then he asked if I had been discussing this matter recently with any other parties. I told him that was none of his business, either. Had I heard of a woman named Nora Chancel, he asked. Had Nora Chancel come around making inquiries related to Hugo Driver?"

"He asked about *me*?"

"Right. I said no, I hadn't had any contact at all with you, and if he wanted to have a sensible business discussion, why didn't he call at a sensible hour? Well, he as good as called me a liar, and said you were a fugitive from justice, I should refuse to have anything to do with you, and there would be serious consequences if I ignored his advice."

"Why would Leland Dart—"

"The next thing he said was that he had a young lawyer already in the Amherst area, and wouldn't I agree at least to meet with the man? No. I would not. He argued with me a little while, and then I heard it."

"It?"

"The background. People talking. Voices. This strange ringing noise. Then I recognized it, that bell sound a cash register makes when a total is rung up."

"A cash register?"

"So I said, 'Are you calling me from a bar?' and he hung up."

"Oh, no."

"Are you thinking what I'm thinking?"

"That it was Dick pretending to be his father?"

"I thought about all the stress the man is under. If your son is Dick Dart, maybe you'd be tempted to do some of your business in bars. But after the next call, it occurred to me that it might have been Dick."

No more than twenty minutes after the man calling himself Leland Dart had hung up on him, Tidy had heard from a Captain Liam Monoghan of the Massachusetts State Police. Everett Tidy was on the verge of being taken in for questioning, perhaps even charged with various crimes, and if he had one hope in the world of escaping these humiliations, that hope was in Captain Monoghan. Monoghan said, *I don't think you were aware that this woman was a fugitive from the FBI,* and, *We have information that Mrs. Chancel has altered her appearance. We also have information that she may be in the Northampton area. Is that correct?*

"If he'd named any other town, I wouldn't have said anything at all, Nora. I would have thought he was bluffing. But you have to appreciate my position. I want to help you in any way I can, but

I am not willing to go to jail. That man *promised* that I'd spend at least one night in jail if I didn't come across, and if that happened, I was afraid I'd involve Jeffrey and his mother."

"Professor Tidy, Dick Dart cut and dyed my hair, but the police don't know that. The only way they *could* know it is if Dick Dart told them."

There came a silence nearly as long as one of Helen Day's. "I don't think the man I talked to was a policeman," he finally said.

"What did you tell him?"

"He said he'd be satisfied that I was acting out of innocent motives if I could confirm or deny the information that you were in Northampton. If I continued to obstruct the police, there were people down at State Police headquarters who wanted to bring me in for the night. It seemed to me that the way to do as little damage as possible was to confirm what they already knew, so I told him that I did have the feeling that you had intended to go to Northampton, but I didn't know any more than that. He thanked me for my cooperation and said an officer would be coming over soon to take a statement. I called you as soon as I got off the phone."

"No officer turned up at your apartment."

"No. I suppose one could still show up. What do you think?"

"It was Dick Dart both times," Nora said. "When he was pretending to be his father, he learned enough to be pretty certain that I'd visited you, so he made the second call to see if he could bluff more information out of you."

"I'm so sorry." He groaned. "Nora, I had no idea I was putting you in danger. How did he figure out where you were?"

"He didn't," Nora said. "Northampton was just an educated guess. If he guessed wrong, he'd just have to keep naming towns until he got it right."

"Do you think I should call the police—the real police?"

"No, don't do that."

"Get out of there," Tidy said. "Go to Boston and hide out until you can be sure you're safe. If you can get there tonight, call me and I'll wire you enough money to hold you for a while. Get Jeffrey to take you."

"I want to find out if I'm still in trouble, but if I am, I might take you up on that."

"I have a little house up in Vermont which is looking very attractive right about now. Do you think Dart might still be trying to find out where I live? I hate to think of him being in Northampton, but I have to say that I don't like the thought of him in Amherst, either."

There was a silence Nora chose not to fill.

"I've been learning a very unhappy truth, the past hour or so."

"What's that?"

"It is extremely unpleasant to be afraid," Tidy said.

78

"DAVEY?"

The shocked silence, which rode atop a swell of violins and horns, continued until Nora filled it herself. "Davey, it's me."

"Nora?"

"Can you talk to me?"

"Where are you?" His voice sounded a little slower than usual. "Is it safe to talk?"

"How did you know I was here?"

"That's not important. Is this line tapped?"

"How should I know? No, I don't think it is. My father got rid of Jeffrey and the Italian girl, so that's why I'm in Jeffrey's apartment." A blast of music obliterated his next few words.

"Davey, please turn down the music. I can't hear you."

He must have waved a remote control, because the music instantly subsided. "So how are you? Are you okay? You *sound* okay."

"It's a little complicated. How are you?"

"Lousy," Davey said. "I've been worried sick ever since Dart grabbed you out of the police station. I thought he was going to kill you. You know how I found out? The receptionist saw it on television on her break! She called me, and I ran downstairs. There were about twenty people around her desk. For half an hour they were showing stuff about you and Dick Dart, and then Dad took me back to Westerholm. Ever since, all we do is watch the news channel and talk to cops. And Mr. Hashim and Mr. Shull, boy, do we ever talk to those guys. Mr. Shull is sort of cool in a dumb kind of way. They both really hate Holly Fenn. They'd like to skin him alive."

Nora heard the sound of ice cubes chiming against glass. "Holly Fenn should get canned, he messed up big-time on this one. Hey, Nora, are you really all right?"

"In some ways, Davey."

"When Mr. Shull told us you got away, I was really glad."

"Glad."

"I was relieved. Don't you think I was relieved?"

"Davey, can I come home?"

"What do you mean?"

Her heart sank at the suspicion in his voice. "Is Natalie still accusing me of kidnapping her?"

"From what I hear, Natalie still isn't saying anything at all. Mr. Hashim and Mr. Shull still think you're guilty." He hesitated. "Natalie took a lot of drugs, did you know that?"

"No."

"One of those cops found a coke stash taped to the back of a drawer in her bedroom. Remember her refrigerator magnets? I guess they should have told us something." Again she heard ice cubes rattling in a glass. "Were you in Holyoke?"

"Yes," Nora said.

"You drove to Holyoke and ditched that dead man's car?"

"I didn't intend to. I went into a restaurant and had something to eat, and when I came out the police were all over the place."

"You went into a *restaurant*? You *had something to eat*? What is this, a field trip?"

"I have to eat now and then," Nora said.

"But you could have come home. It makes you look so guilty when you hide out like this."

"Come home where—to the Poplars?" Nora asked. "I suppose Alden would greet me with shouts of joy."

"Come home and face the music, I mean. My father doesn't have anything to do with that. He didn't do anything wrong."

"Neither did I," Nora said. "But I bet your father is trying his damnedest to make you think I did." Another chink of ice cubes. "What are you drinking, Davey?"

"Vodka. Did you know that Jeffrey supposedly wrote plays that were put on at the Public Theater? I asked him about these posters he has up in his living room, and he claimed he wrote these plays, under the name Jeffrey Mannheim. I don't think he did, do you? They got awfully good reviews."

"Jeffrey has hidden depths," Nora said.

"He's the Italian girl's nephew, for God's sake! What kind of hidden depths could *he* have?" He took another chiming mouthful of the drink. "Yeah, forget Dad. Of course my father is running you down all over the place. Mom is even worse. She thinks you *arranged* to be kidnapped by Dick Dart. She wishes she'd thought of it. I think Mr. Hashim almost sort of believes her."

"Wonderful."

"I tell you, Nora, I've been really worried about you, but I have no idea what you think you're doing."

This had the ring of an accusation. "Mainly, Davey, I've been trying to stay away from Dick Dart and avoid the police until it's safe to come back home."

"The cops found a lot of new clothes from a fancy men's store in that car, and when they went to the shop, the salesman remembered the two of you very well. Dick Dart tried on a bunch of new suits, and you just sat there and watched him. Then the cops went up and down the street, and they find out that the two of you have been in half the shops in town. *Everybody* remembers this nice lovey-dovey couple."

"Dick Dart is a lunatic, Davey. Do you think I cooperated with him because I *like* him? I hate him, he makes my skin crawl. If I had done anything to call attention to myself, he would have killed me."

"Not if he couldn't see you," Davey said. "Like if he was in a changing room."

"I wasn't feeling all that confident, Davey. Just before we went on our shopping expedition, he raped me. I wasn't actually thinking too clearly. I felt like I'd been broken in half, and I wasn't up for any heroics."

"Oh God, oh no, I'm so sorry, Nora."

"I didn't cooperate with him, in case you're wondering. I was trying too hard not to pass out. Besides, my hands were tied behind my back and my mouth was taped shut."

"You must have been scared to death."

"It was even worse than that, Davey, but I'll spare your feelings."

"Why didn't you tell me before?"

"Because you didn't ask me any real questions. You went on and on about Jeffrey and watching the receptionist's television. Also because you didn't sound too sympathetic, and now I know why. You imagined that I was having all that fun with Dick Dart. You want to know how I got away from him? I hit him on the head with a hammer. I thought I'd killed him. I got outside and started the car, but what do you know, I didn't kill him after all, because he came charging out of the motel room, and I steered toward him and hit him with the car."

"My God. That's terrific."

"It would have been terrific if I'd killed him, but I didn't. He's still wandering around trying to find people who might help prove that your beloved Hugo Driver didn't write *Night Journey*."

Davey made a strangled sound of protest and outrage, but Nora ignored it. "He just found out where I am, and now he's probably sharpening his knives so he can do a really good job on me."

"Where are you?"

"If I tell you, you can't tell anyone else. You can't even tell them we had this conversation."

"Sure."

"I'm serious, Davey. You can't tell anyone."

"I *won't*. I just want to know where you are."

"I'm in Northampton, in a room in the Northampton Hotel."

"Hold on a sec."

She heard him put down the receiver. A refrigerator door opened, and ice cubes chinked into a glass. Liquid gurgled from a bottle. He came back to the telephone. "What are you doing in Northampton?"

"I'm *hiding*, what do you think I'm doing?"

"Hold on, does this have anything to do with Jeffrey? Did he tell you I was staying in his apartment? Are you with Jeffrey? What the hell are you doing with Jeffrey?"

"I needed help and I called him."

"You called *Jeffrey*? That's crazy."

"I couldn't call you, could I? All the lines are tapped. And once Jeffrey realized that I'd been asking questions about Katherine Mannheim, he insisted on picking me up."

"I'm lost. Jeffrey is a servant, he's Maria's goddamned nephew, what can he possibly have to do with Katherine Mannheim?" A slosh, a chinking of ice cubes. "I'm beginning to hate the sound of that woman's name. I hope she died a horrible death. Why are you asking questions about her?"

"Dick Dart is doing more than buying new clothes." For a little while she explained Dart's mission, and Davey responded with moans of disbelief. "I don't care if you don't believe it, that's what's going on, Davey. As for Jeffrey, he's Katherine Mannheim's nephew because his mother, Helen Day, was her sister."

"His mother? Helen Day?"

"She met your grandfather at Shorelands when she went there to see if she could find Katherine. Her husband had died, and she wasn't happy in her work, and he hired her." She went on to explain the connections between Helen Day, Jeffrey, and Maria.

"Do these people think Katherine Mannheim wrote *Night Journey*? That could ruin us!"

"But Chancel House is in plenty of trouble even without a scandal about Hugo Driver. According to Dick Dart—"

"That expert on the publishing industry."

"He knows a lot about Chancel House. Your father is running it into the ground, and he's been trying to sell it to a German firm. This Katherine Mannheim business is driving him crazy, because it could wreck the German deal."

"There is no German deal. Dick Dart made it all up."

"He passed along another interesting story, too. About the Hellfire Club."

"Oh," Davey said. "Well, okay."

"'Well, okay'? What does that mean?"

"Okay, I didn't exactly tell you the truth."

"You belonged to the Hellfire Club."

"There was no Hellfire Club, not really. That was just what we called it."

"But there's a branch in New York, isn't there? And you're a member."

"It isn't *like* that. You keep making it sound like a real club, when it's just these guys who get together to mess around. They do hire a good chef now and then, or they used to, and they did have a concierge and a coat-check woman. There was a bar, and you could take girls to the rooms upstairs. I only went a couple of times after Amy and I broke up."

"Who was the girl you took to the Hellfire Club in New Haven?"

"The same little menace who turned up in the art department. At Yale she called herself Lena Ware. Every time I saw her, she was reading *Night Journey*. I think she came to New Haven *looking* for me."

"Why didn't you tell me you'd met her twice?"

"It would have sounded so strange. And I didn't want to tell you about . . . you know . . . about what Dart probably told you."

"About hitting her with the car."

"I *didn't* hit her. Well, I *thought* I did, but I didn't. When I met her at Chancel House a couple of years later, and she was calling herself Paddi Mann, she said she was so mad at me that she wanted to scare me. Nora, she was nuts. I love Hugo Driver, but she never thought about anything else. You should have seen her friends! There are Driver houses, did you know that? I went to one with her. It was in a tenement over a restaurant on Elizabeth Street. It was really bizarre. Everybody was high all the time, and they had cave rooms, and people who dressed up like wolves, and all this stuff."

"That was what you described to me, wasn't it?"

"Uh huh. Anyhow, she kept trying to get me to go to Shorelands because she had this screwball theory that Shorelands was in *Night Journey*."

"How?"

"She said she thought you couldn't understand the book unless you went to Shorelands, because Shorelands was in it. Something about the places, but that's all she said. The whole idea was goofy. I got a book about Shorelands by a guy with a funny name, and it didn't say anything new about *Night Journey*."

"Just out of curiosity, what really happened the last time you went to her place?"

"I found the book under her bed, and I really did think that something bad had happened to her, because she just disappeared. Her room was completely empty. The other Driver people who lived there didn't know where she had gone, and they didn't care. She wasn't a girl to them, she was Paddi Mann, the real one, the one in the book. When I left, I felt so depressed that I couldn't stand the thought of going home, so I did check into a hotel for a couple of nights. When we moved into our house, the book turned up in a carton I took out of the Poplars."

"It was in our house?"

"I remember opening it up and seeing her name. For a second,

Nora, I almost fainted. Every time that girl turned up, my life went haywire. I put it in the Chancel House bookcase in the hallway. The day I met Natalie in the Main Street Delicatessen, she mentioned that she'd never read *Night Journey*. She liked horror novels, but Driver always seemed too much like fantasy to her, so she'd never tried him. The next day I pulled one of the *Night Journey*s out of the bookcase and gave it to her, and it turned out to be that one."

"Oh, Davey," she said. He took another swallow of his drink. "So you wanted to get it before the cops saw it."

"I told you that. It had my name in it, too."

"So to cover up your affair, you told me this story instead of saying, 'Well, Nora, after we bought the house I gave this book to Natalie.' "

"I know." He groaned. "I was afraid you'd figure out that I was seeing her. Anyhow, why are you asking me all this stuff? You don't care about Hugo Driver."

"I bought all three of his books today."

"No kidding. After you finish the first one, you have to read *Twilight Journey*. It's really great. God, it would be wonderful to talk to you about it. Want to know what it's about?"

"I have the feeling you want to tell me," Nora said.

As ever, Davey instantly became more confident when given the opportunity to talk about Hugo Driver. "Like in the first book, he has to go around talking to all these people and piece together what really happened out of their stories. He learns that his father killed a bunch of people, and almost killed *him* because he was afraid he'd find out. Anyhow, early in the book he hears that his parents aren't his real parents, they just found him in the forest one day, which in some ways is a tremendous relief, so off he goes in search of his real parents, and a Nellad, which is a monster that owns a gold mine and looks like a man but isn't, slices him with its claws, and the old woman who dresses his wounds tells him that his mother really is his mother. His parents left him in the forest when he was a baby, but she went out that same night and brought him back. He says, '*My mother is my mother.*' "

79

FOR THE SECOND time that night, an enormous recognition seemed to gather in the air around Nora's body, cloudy, opaque, awaiting the moment to reveal itself. "Incredible," she said.

"It's a fantasy novel—what do you want, realism?" The ice cubes rang in the glass, and music rustled in the background. "It's so strange. You've been through all this terrible shit, and we're talking about Hugo Driver. I'm pathetic. I'm a joke."

"No, what you're saying is interesting. Tell me what happens in the third one."

"*Journey into Light*? Pippin learns that the real reason they're living way out in the forest at the foot of the mountains is that his grandfather was even worse than his father. He tried to betray his country, but the plot failed, and they escaped into the woods before their part in it was discovered. The Nellads are some other descendants of his grandfather's, and they have all his evil traits. They're so bad they turned into monsters. Pippin's grandfather killed a whole lot of people to gain control of a gold mine, but that was a secret, too. The gold mine has to be taken back from the Nellads, and Pippin has to reveal the truth, and then everything is all right."

It was not merely incredible; it was stupefying: Hugo Driver had structured his last two novels around the best-kept secrets of his publisher's family. *No wonder they were published post-humously,* Nora thought, and then wondered why they had been published at all. She marveled at the grandeur of Alden Chancel's cynicism; certain that no one but himself and his wife would understand the code, he had cashed in on Driver's popularity. Probably his audacity had amused him.

"Your father published these books," she said, as much to herself as to Davey.

"They don't sound like his kind of thing, do they? But you know how proud he is of never reading the books he publishes. He always says he wouldn't be able to publish them half as well if he actually had to read them."

Davey was right. Alden took an ostentatious pride in never reading Chancel House books. He had not known the contents of Hugo Driver's posthumous novels.

"Why are we talking about this?" Davey asked. "Nora, come home. Please. Come here, and we'll settle everything." With these words, he had produced his own golden key. He wanted her back; he would not abandon her during the ordeal of Slim and Slam. "I'll drive up there and bring you back. You could stay the night in the house, and I'd come over in the morning to take you to the station. Everybody's going to be pissed as hell at me, but I don't care."

He wanted her to stay in the house while he returned to the Poplars. He wanted her back, but only so that he wouldn't have to worry about her. "You can't drive, Davey," she said. "You've been drinking."

"Not that much. Two drinks, maybe."

"Four, maybe."

"I can drive."

"No, don't do it. I don't want to come back until I know I'm not going to be arrested."

"What about not getting killed? Isn't that a little more important?"

"Davey, I'll be fine." Nora promised herself to leave Northampton early the next morning. "Listen, I was looking at those books I bought today, and there's something I can't figure out. On the paperbacks of the last two, the copy on the back cover says that the manuscripts were discovered among the author's papers."

"Where else do you find manuscripts?"

"Hugo Driver's haven't exactly been easy to find, have they? Hugo Driver is about the only writer in history who didn't leave any papers behind when he died."

"Well, they didn't just drop down out of the sky."

The recognition hovering about Nora streamed into her in a series of images: a baby left in a forest, then reclaimed by his mother; an old man, the baby's grandfather, wearing a Nazi uniform; Daisy Chancel exhaling smoke as she fondled a copy

of Driver's last book. *You're not one of those people who think*
Journey into Light *is a terrible falling off, are you?*

The last two Driver novels had not fallen from the sky; they had
flowed from the busy typewriter just off the landing of the
Poplars' front staircase. Twenty years before he had turned to
Daisy to produce the Blackbird Books, Alden had cajoled her into
giving him two imitation Hugo Driver novels. He had needed
money, and sly Daisy, knowing he would never read the books,
had vented her outrage while she saved his company. Alden—
Adelbert—was a fraud in more than one way. This was the real
reason for her hysteria and his rage at Nora's discovery that Daisy
had written the Blackbird books.

"What's going on?" Davey asked. "I don't like this. I know
you, you have something up your sleeve. You could have come
home this afternoon, and instead you get *Jeffrey* to drive you
around the Berkshires so you can meet the Cup Bearer and ask a
lot of questions about Hugo Driver. Are you trying to help these
Mannheim people destroy my father?"

"No, Davey—"

"Jeffrey is like a spy, he came here to burrow around for proof
his aunt wrote *Night Journey*, Helen Day was probably doing the
same thing, they both wanted the money, only my father figured
out what the Cup Bearer was up to and he fired her, but he's such
a good guy he hired half her family anyhow."

"That's wrong. Neither one of them wants anything from
you. Helen Day is convinced that her sister didn't write *Night
Journey*."

"They're using you. Can't you see that? God, this is horrible. I
used to love the Cup Bearer, and she lied to my parents, she lied to
me, and she lied to you. Her whole goddamned life is a lie, and so
is Jeffrey's. I'm coming up there tonight and taking you away
from these people."

"No, you're not," she said. "Helen Day is not a liar, and you're
not coming up here just to drive me back to the police."

"Hold on, I'll be right back." The clunk of the telephone against
the desk, the opening of the refrigerator. The rattle of ice cubes,
the gurgle of vodka. "Okay. Now. Helen Day, damn her to hell.
Can't you see that if she was Katherine Mannheim's sister, she's
also the sister of these two old bats who are suing us?"

"She never even liked her other sisters. She won't have anything to do with them."

"Sure, that's what she told you, and you're so naive you believed her. What's this 'Day' business, anyhow? That can't be her name. She came here under an alias. I suppose that isn't suspicious."

Nora explained how and why his grandfather had shortened her name.

"But she's still a liar."

"Helen Day isn't the liar in this story, Davey." She immediately regretted having been provoked into making this statement.

"Oh, it's me, isn't it? Thank you so much, Nora."

"I didn't mean you, Davey."

"Who's left? I was right the first time, you have something up your sleeve. Oh God, what else? You hate my father and you'd like to ruin him, just like these Mannheims or Deodatos or whatever their real names are. I should hang up and tell the cops where you are."

"Don't, Davey, please." She drew in a large breath. "You're right. There is something I'm not saying, but it doesn't have anything to do with *Night Journey*."

"Uh huh."

"I found out something about you tonight, but I'm not sure I should tell you now because you won't believe me."

"Swell. Good-bye, Nora."

"I'm telling you the truth. Helen Day knows this *thing*, this *fact* about you. She kept it secret all her life, but now she thinks you ought to know it."

Davey abused and insulted Helen Day for the space of several sentences, and then asked, "If this information is so important, why didn't she tell it to me?"

"She promised not to."

"Then why did she tell you? I hear the faint sound of tap dancing, Nora."

"She didn't tell me. She made me guess until I got it right."

He gave a weary chuckle.

"Why do you think Helen Day left the Poplars?"

After another couple of abusive sentences, he said, "At the time, what my parents told me was that she decided to go away and open her own business. Which I guess is what she did, right?"

"On her savings? Do you think she could have saved up that much money?"

"I see. The story is that my father paid her to keep quiet, right?

This secret must be right up there with the key to the Rosetta stone."

"For you it *is* the Rosetta stone," Nora said.

"I know, *I'm* the real author of *Night Journey*. No, too bad, it was published before I was born. Nora, unless you spit out this so-called secret right now, I'm going to hang up on you."

"Fine," she said. "I just have to work out a way to say it." She thought for a moment. "Do you remember what your mother did all during your childhood?"

"I do believe we're about to go to Miami by way of Seattle here. Fine. I'll play along. Yes, I remember. She sat up there in her office and she drank."

"No, when you were a child, she wrote all day long. Your mother got a lot of work done in those days, and not all of it was put into the book she asked me to read."

"Okay, she wrote the Morning and Teatime books. You're right about that. I went through four or five of them, and all those things you mentioned were there. It's kind of funny, because I also found some expressions I must have heard her say a thousand times. They just never registered before. Like 'sadder than a tabby in a downpour'—stuff like that. 'We wore out a lot of shoe leather.' That's one reason the old man came down on you so hard. He overreacted, but he doesn't want anybody to know. I can see why. It wouldn't make him look very good."

"Thank you."

"But she wrote those books in the eighties, and we're talking about the sixties."

"Do you have copies of the last two Driver novels with you?"

"No way, you hear me? If you're trying to tell me my mother wrote the later Drivers, you belong in a loony bin."

"Of course I'm not," she lied. "The whole point is in the difference between the two styles."

"I am really not following you."

"I'm going to Miami by way of Seattle, remember? Unless I do it this way, you'll never believe me. So humor me and get the books."

"This is nuts," Davey said, but he put down the receiver and came back in a few seconds. "Boy, I haven't read these in probably fifteen years. Okay, now what?"

Nora had pulled the two books from her bag, and now she

opened *Twilight Journey*, looking for she knew not what, with no assurance of finding it. She turned over some thirty pages and scanned down the paragraphs without finding anything useful.

"What do you want to show me?"

Some lines on page 42 rose up to meet her eye. *"Too true,"* said *the wrinkled creature squatting on the branch. "Too true, indeed, dear boy."* She had to get Davey to notice these Daisyish sentences without seeming to point them out. "Turn to page forty-two," she said. "About ten lines down from the top. See that?"

"See what? *'He looked up and scratched his head.'* There?"

"A few lines down."

Davey read, " *'Pippin turned slowly in a circle, wishing that the path were not so dark, nor the woods so deep.'* That?" This was the sentence immediately below those with Daisy's trademarks.

"Read that paragraph out loud, and then read the whole page to yourself."

"Fine by me." He began reading, and Nora frantically searched through random pages.

"Now I should read the page to myself?"

"Yes." She scanned another page and saw a second *indeed.*

"All right, what about it?"

"That didn't sound a lot like your mother's writing, did it?"

"No, not really," Davey said, sounding uneasy. "Of course not. How could it? What's your point, Nora?"

"Look on page eighty-four, right below the middle of the page."

"Huh," Davey said. "That long paragraph, beginning with *'All the trees seemed to have moved'*?"

She told him to read it aloud, then read the whole of the page to himself, as before.

"I'm getting a funny feeling about this."

"Please, just do it."

He began reading, and Nora turned to the back of the book and found, just above the final paragraph, the proof she needed. *"With a shock, Pippin remembered that only a day before he had felt as bereft as a long-haired cat in a rainstorm."* She waited for Davey to finish reading page 84.

"Are you being cute or something?" he asked. "You told me you weren't trying to tell me that my mother wrote this. A few piddly coincidences don't prove anything. I'm starting to get highly ticked off all over again."

"What coincidences? Did you see something in those paragraphs you didn't mention?"

"I'm getting fed up with your games, Nora."

Time to raise the ante: she had to give him part of the truth. "I don't think Hugo Driver wrote this book," she said. "It really did appear out of nowhere, didn't it? There were no papers. You would have seen them long ago, if they existed."

"Are you ever on thin ice. What's next? Hugo Driver was my mother in male drag?"

Nora seized on a desperate improvisation. "I think Alden wrote these books."

"Oh, come on. I never heard anything more ridiculous."

"Just consider the possibility. Alden knew he could make a whopping amount of money in a hurry if he brought out posthumous Driver novels. Because there weren't any real ones, he had to provide them." Nora continued improvising. "No one could know that they weren't real, so he couldn't farm them out. He couldn't even trust Daisy. Haven't you always thought these were different from the first one?"

"You know I have. They're good, but not like *Night Journey*. A lot of writers never come up to their first successes."

"The same person wrote these two, isn't that right?"

"And the same person wrote *Night Journey*. Who sure as hell wasn't my father."

"What's the name of that monster who cuts Pippin with his claws?"

"He doesn't have a name. He's a Nellad."

"Nellad. Remind you of anything?"

"No." He considered it for a moment. "It does sort of sound like Alden, if that's what you mean." He laughed. "You're telling me he put his own name in the book?"

"Wouldn't it be just like him to thumb his nose at everybody that way?"

"I have to give you credit for ingenuity. All these other people are trying to show that Driver didn't write *Night Journey*, and you're saying, yes, he did write that one, but not the other two. Which is almost possible, Nora. I'll grant you that much. If you weren't all wrong you could actually be right."

"Some of this really does sound like Alden to me. Look at the last page."

"All right." He read in silence for a time. "Come on. You mean that cat?"

Nora said that she meant the entire page. "I think Alden wrote this. I didn't even notice about the wet cat until you mentioned it."

"Well, it sounds more like my mother than my father, because my father never wrote anything except business letters."

"I don't think it sounds like your mother's writing," Nora said.

"God damn, you haven't been *listening* to me. I told you, someone's as sad as a wet cat in a couple of those Blackbird Books, and she used that phrase all the time when I was a kid. She still does sometimes."

"I had no idea."

"It still can't be true. My *mother*?"

"Alden used some of her favorite phrases. He wouldn't trust her that much."

"She's about the only person he would trust. I have to look at more of this." She heard him turning pages, breathing loudly, now and then taking a sip of his drink. "It can't be, can it? There are a million different ways to explain . . ." He let out a noise halfway between a wail and a bellow. *"NO!"*

"What?"

"One of the villagers, right here, page one fifty-three, says, '*You may ask me twenty-seven times, and the answer will never change.*' Twenty-seven times! My mother used to say that all the time. It was her expression for infinity. Holy shit."

"Your mother wrote it?"

"Holy shit, I think she did," Davey said. "Holy shit. She really did. Holy shit. It's no wonder they were so freaked when you accused her of writing the horror novels. This could absolutely finish us off."

"I don't see why," Nora said. "Doesn't it put your mother in a good light? If she did write those books, that is."

"God, you're naive. If this gets out, my father gets accused of fraud, and *Night Journey* immediately becomes suspect. There'll be lawyers all over the place."

"If it gets out."

"It better not. This has to stay secret, Nora."

"I'm sure it does," she said.

"At least we finally got to Miami. If the Cup Bearer knew my

mother wrote those books, I guess I'm not surprised that they had
to buy her off and get rid of her. Wow."

"Hold on to your hat," Nora said.

80

As SHE TOLD Jeffrey early the next morning in the restaurant off
the terrace, the rest of their long conversation had lasted half an
hour, and in the course of it Nora had felt Davey's universe spin
and wobble. His past had been yanked inside out; Nora had questioned the central theme of his life. He ridiculed, protested,
denied. He had hung up after ten minutes and picked up the telephone again only after it had rung a dozen times. "Think about
what she *wrote*," Nora had said, and listening to her account
while spreading damson preserves on a croissant, Jeffrey shook
his head. He, too, at first had been suspicious of the night's discoveries. "Think about what your grandfather was like and what
your father did to us, but first of all, think about what Daisy put in
that book. That's your story, Davey. It's a message to you." No,
no, no. Helen Day had lied. Nora had brought him back again and
again to the child abandoned in and rescued from the forest, to
My mother is my mother. "If it's true, I'm Pippin," Davey had
said, sounding the first note of the awe which follows all great
revelations. Nora had told him, "You've always been Pippin,"
and she had not added what she told herself: *Me, too.* "I feel like
Leonard Gimmel or Teddy Brunhoven," he had said. "There is a
code, and I can read it."

"Yes. There is a code, and it's about you."

"She wanted me to know. Even though she couldn't tell me."

"She wanted you to know."

"Should I confront him? Should I go over there and tell him I
know?"

For the first time in their marriage, Nora advised Davey not to confront his father. "You'd have to tell him how you found out, and I don't want anybody to know where I am."

"That's right. I'll wait until whenever. Until I can."

This had left unspoken more than Nora liked. "You believe me, anyhow, don't you?"

"It took me a while, but, yeah, I do. I guess I really ought to thank you. I know that sounds funny, but I am grateful, Nora."

Fine, but gratitude isn't enough is what she had said to herself when the conversation had limped to an inconclusive end.

She tore a flaky section off a croissant and put it in her mouth. Less than a quarter of the pastry, her second, now remained on her plate, and she was still hungry. Three tables away, a pair of heavyset men in windbreakers stoked in enormous breakfasts of scrambled eggs, bacon, and fried potatoes. Nora felt as though she could have eaten both of their meals.

On the other side of the window wall to her right, a tall boy in a blue shirt was washing the terrace flagstones with a bucket, a long broom, and a hose. Rivulets sparkled and gleamed between the shining stones. Another boy was flapping pink tablecloths over the tables like sails and smoothing them out with his hands. It was as humble as the two men and their breakfasts, but to Nora this scene suddenly seemed to overflow with significance.

"To change the subject, you think Dart called Ev Tidy," Jeffrey said.

She nodded and reached for another section of croissant, but she had eaten it all.

"Let me get you some more of those." In a few seconds, Jeffrey returned carrying a plate heaped with sweet rolls, croissants, and thick slices of honeydew. Nora attacked the melon with her knife and fork.

"Do you think Ev is safe?"

"He said he was going to a house he owns in Vermont." Nora finished the melon and began on the Danish. She felt as energetic as if she'd had a full night's sleep, and she had an idea of how to fill the next few days.

"You can't be as casual as you seem about Dart being in town," said Jeffrey.

"I'm not casual about it at all. I want to leave Northampton this morning."

"I was thinking about a nice little inn not far from Alford. If you like, we could see my mother for a bit, and then I could run you over there. It's charming, and the people who own the place were friends of my parents. Besides, the food is great."

For a secular monk, Jeffrey placed a sybaritic degree of importance on meals. "I do want to see your mother, but I'd like to go somewhere else after that, if you don't mind."

"You want to stay with Ev in Vermont?"

"That's not quite what I had in mind. Don't they rent out the old cottages at Shorelands?"

He gave a doubtful nod. "You want to go to Shorelands?"

Nora groped for an explanation that would make sense to him. "I've spent days listening to people talk about that place, and I'd like to see what it looks like."

Jeffrey folded his arms over his chest and waited.

She glanced outside at the boys, one of them sluicing away the last of the soapy water, the other arranging chairs around the tables, and moved a step nearer the truth. "I'm in a unique position. I've talked to Mark Foil and Ev Tidy, but they've never talked to each other. Foil knows what Creeley Monk wrote in his journal, and Tidy knows what his father wrote, but the only person who really knows what's in both journals is me, and I have the feeling that there's a missing piece. Nobody ever tried to put everything together. I'm not saying I can, but last night and this morning, when I was thinking about all these conversations I've been having, it seemed to me that I at least had to look at the place. Half of me has no idea what's going on or what to do, but the other half is saying, *Go to Shorelands, or you'll miss everything.*"

" 'Miss everything,' " Jeffrey said. " 'A missing piece.' Is it just me, or are you talking about Katherine Mannheim?"

"She's at the center of it. I don't know why, but I almost feel responsible for her." Jeffrey jerked up his head. "All these people had conflicting views of her. She was rude, she was impatient, she was a saint, she was a tease, she was truthful, evasive, dedicated, frivolous, completely crazy, completely sane. . . . She goes to Shorelands, she gets everybody worked up in a different way, and she never comes out. What comes out instead? What's the only thing that really comes out of that summer? *Night Journey.*"

Jeffrey regarded her with what looked like mingled interest and doubt. "The way you put it, you make it sound like the book is a kind of substitute for her." He thought for a second. "Or like she's in it."

"Not directly, nothing like that. But a phrase of hers is: the Cup Bearer." Jeffrey opened his mouth, and Nora rushed to say, "I know we've talked about this before, but it still seems like an enormous coincidence. Davey saw that photograph of the sisters in your mother's apartment at the Poplars, but Hugo Driver couldn't have seen it. It's part of the missing piece."

"If you want to play detective, I'll cooperate. It is possible to stay there. Five or six years ago, a French publisher, a great Driver admirer who wanted to stay there for a night, had some trouble getting accommodations. Alden asked me to take care of it for him. Which I did. The Shorelands Trust runs the estate, and some of the old staff is put up in Main House, but Pepper Pot and Rapunzel have rooms for people who want to stay the night. I got the French guy a room in Rapunzel, and he was delighted. So was Alden."

"Will you call them?"

"While you pack, but first I want to ask you a question."

"Go ahead." She braced herself, but Jeffrey's question was milder than any she had expected.

"Why did you want to tell me the family secrets? I came to the Poplars so late that I didn't even know Davey was supposed to have been adopted."

"I didn't want to be the only other person who knew." She stopped short of adding, *In case anything happened to me.*

"I'm sorry to hear that," he said, and signaled the waitress for their check.

81

WHEN THE TELEPHONE rang, she was in the bathroom, considering the question of makeup. On the fourth ring she picked it up and heard Jeffrey answer her question.

"I hope you don't mind waiting about half an hour," he said. "I called my mother to tell her we were coming over, and she's in a high old state. Apparently I agreed to drive some of the girls over to a market this morning, and I'm already late. It'll take forty minutes at the most, and I'll swing by to pick you up as soon as we're back."

"Perfect," she said. "I was just thinking that I'd be safer if I put my disguise back on."

"Your ... ? Oh, the war paint. Good idea. You're checked out of the hotel, and I booked you into Pepper Pot as Mrs. Norma Desmond. I thought you were probably tired of being Dinah Shore."

They agreed to meet in the lobby in forty minutes. Jeffrey would call up to her room if he returned before that. "Do me a favor," he said. "Wait for me in the lobby, okay? I don't want to be responsible for all the skeletons in the Chancel closets."

Half an hour later the young woman at the desk glanced at Nora as she came out of the elevator and then returned to explaining the hotel's charges to a flustered old couple complaining about their bill. A soft pinkish light suffused the otherwise empty lobby. Nora wheeled her case to an armchair next to a table stacked with brochures and sat down to read "The 100 Most Popular Tourist Sites in Our Lovely Area." The white-haired couple were still wrangling over their room charges, but now it was the clerk who was flustered. The husband, a pipe-stem with a natty blazer, ascot, and shining wings of white hair, was loudly explaining that the telephone charges *had* to be mistaken because neither his wife nor himself ever used the telephones in hotel rooms. Why pay a surcharge when you could come down to the lobby and use the pay phone?

The clerk spoke a few words.

"Nonsense!" the old man bellowed. "I've just explained to you that my wife and I don't *use* telephones in hotel rooms!"

His wife backed away from him, and the young woman behind the desk spoke again.

"But this is an error!" the man shouted. The clerk disappeared, and the old man whirled on his wife. "You've done it again, haven't you? Too lazy to take the elevator, and what happens? *Two dollars* wasted, and here I am, making a scene, and it's all your fault."

His wife had begun to cry, but she was too frightened to raise her hands and wipe her eyes.

Nora saw an echo of Alden Chancel in the domineering little dandy and could not bear to be in the same room with him. She left the suitcase beside the chair and went down the hallway to the exit onto the terrace. Through the windows, she saw half a dozen cars, none of them Jeffrey's, driving down King Street. Sunlight glittered on the washed flagstones, and yellow lilies nodded beside the steps down to the pavement. She pushed through the door into fresh, brilliant morning.

When she reached the top of the steps, she looked up King Street for the MG, wishing that she could have taken a run that morning. Her muscles yearned for exercise; her breakfast seemed to have vaporized into a need for work and motion. She looked back at the hotel and through the glass wall saw the elderly husband spitting invective as he put down his suitcase to open the door for his wife. He was a gentleman of the old school, complete with all the tyrannical courtesies, and he had parked on the street because he thought he might be charged for using the hotel lot. Gripping the strap of her handbag, Nora marched down and walked five or six feet up the block, looking for Jeffrey.

The MG did not appear. Nora glanced over her shoulder and saw the couple coming down the steps onto the sidewalk. The man's face was pink with rage. She put them out of her mind and concentrated on the pleasures of walking briskly through the air of a beautiful August morning, still nicely cool and scented with lilies.

When she reached Main Street she looked left toward the row of shops extending toward the Smith campus and Helen Day's house, by now expecting to see Jeffrey tooling along in the sparse traffic. Half the shops on both sides of Main had not yet opened, and none of the few cars was Jeffrey's. With the blunt abruptness of a heart attack, a police car appeared from behind a bread truck and came rolling toward Nora. She forced herself to stand still. For a long moment the police car seemed aimed directly at her. She swallowed. Then it straightened out and came with no great urgency toward the intersection. Nora pretended to search for something in her bag. The car drew up before her, rolled past, and turned into King Street. She watched it move, still in no apparent haste, in the direction of the hotel. She decided to forget about exercise and wait for Jeffrey in the lobby.

Down the block, the dandy was standing beside an antique touring car with sweeping curves, a running board, and a massive grille decorated with metal badges. He opened the passenger door and extended his hand to his wife. Quivering, she hoisted herself onto the running board. The police car slid past them. The old man strutted around to the driver's side, giving the hood a pat. Down the street, the police car pulled up in front of the hotel, and two officers began moving up the steps.

King Street remained empty. When Nora turned back, the policemen were striding across the terrace toward the glass doors. Telling herself that they were probably after nothing more than coffee and apple turnovers in the café, she stepped into the street and began walking toward the shelter of a movie theater. The old man started up his extravagant car and pulled away from the curb. Standing near the middle of the street, Nora waited for him to go past. The car came to a halt before her, and the window cranked down. The old woman sat staring at her lap, and her husband leaned forward to speak. "The crosswalks are designed for use by pedestrians," he said in a pleasant voice. "Are you too good for them, young lady?"

"I've been watching you, you brutal jerk," she said, "and I hope your wife kills you in your sleep one night."

His wife snapped up her head and stared at Nora. The old man jolted away with a grinding of gears. Either a laugh or a scream came through the open window. Nora hurried to the other side of the street and moved beneath the theater marquee to the concealment of an angled wall next to the ticket booth. She looked at the hotel without seeing the policemen, then back at the antique car, which sat waiting for the light to change at the top of the street. A red car, not Jeffrey's but familiar all the same, swung around the antique vehicle onto King Street, followed by an inconspicuous blue sedan. *It isn't, it can't be,* Nora said to herself, but the Audi moved steadily toward her, and it was. She saw Davey's dark hair and pale face as he hunched over the wheel to stare at the Northampton Hotel.

She stepped out of the angle in the wall, then moved back. Davey drove by. The blue sedan followed him to the hotel. Both cars pulled into the lot and disappeared.

Nora hovered in the shelter of the wall, praying for the policemen to leave the hotel. If Jeffrey came by, she'd wave him down and explain that her plans had changed, she was going to go back to Westerholm after all. Shorelands represented someone else's past, and she had to tend to her present. The policemen stayed inside the hotel, and she hugged herself, watching the glass doors at the edge of the terrace.

Children ran back and forth on the flagstones, weaving around the waiters. The glass door swung open, and a waiter with a tray balanced on his shoulder and a folding stand in his hand came outside. Before the door could swing shut, Davey rushed out and looked over the tables. When he did not see Nora, he walked across the terrace and came to the steps to the sidewalk.

Nora moved forward. Another police car turned onto King Street. Davey scanned the sidewalk in front of him. The police car approached. Nora left the angle of the wall and began walking back up toward Main. The patrol car went past without stopping. She turned around on the sidewalk to see Davey making his way back through the tables. When the car reached the front of the hotel, it made a U-turn and pulled up behind the first one. Two officers got out and jogged up the steps, and a third patrol car came up from the bottom of King Street and turned into the hotel parking lot.

Her only hope was that Davey would return to the terrace alone. She moved a little farther up the street and watched him go back into the hotel. The two policemen were pushing through the tables under the curious gazes of most of the people eating breakfast. Davey disappeared, and the policemen reached the door a few seconds after it closed.

Come back out, she said to herself. *Get out of there and walk up the street.*

Two hefty parents and three even larger teenagers crowded toward the door. Davey came out just as they reached it, moved to one side, and held the door. Nora began walking toward the hotel. When the last of the family had waddled through, Davey held it open for two men in business suits. One of them wore black sunglasses. Davey shrugged and put his hands in his pockets. Nora's breath caught in her throat, and she took a step backwards. The men in suits were Mr. Hashim and Mr. Shull.

Conversing like old friends, Davey and the FBI men were walking around the street side of the tables, going toward the steps.

Too shocked to process what she had just seen, Nora began

moving up the street. About twenty feet away was a parking lot for shops fronting on the lower end of Main. If she could get into the lot without being seen, she could walk through one of the shops and work her way to Helen Day's house.

She looked over her shoulder. Mr. Shull was jabbing his thumb toward the hotel and talking to Mr. Hashim, who glanced at Nora. Her heart struck her ribs, and her knees seemed loose. She marched past faded posters of handsome old buildings and trees in their fall colors in the windows of an empty information booth. A big black-and-white CLOSED sign, spotted brown by the sun, had been taped to the inside of its door. Nora turned into the lot and risked another glance over her shoulder.

Davey and Mr. Shull were moving toward Main Street. Mr. Shull was ticking off points on his fingers, and Davey was nodding.

You worm, you weasel, how could you do this to me?

An arm wrapped itself around her neck. Shock and terror locked her heart, and the arm tightening around her throat turned her scream into a croak. The man bent her backwards and dragged her into the lot.

82

"LOVE THESE REUNIONS of ours," said Dick Dart. "So important to keep up with old friends, don't you agree?" Nora pulled at the arm cutting off her breath, and her feet scrabbled on the dirty asphalt. "Especially those who have reached out and touched you." She tried to kick him, and then her balance was gone. Dart circled her waist with his free arm, lifted her off the ground, and carried her deeper into the lot.

"You'll love the car," he said. "As soon as I saw it, I knew that the time had come to gather in my little Nora-pie, and if you don't stop thrashing around I'll slit your throat right here, you stupid piece of shit." He let go of her waist, and her body sagged against his chest. Beneath his forearm, a sharp point jabbed into her neck. "Don't want that, do we?"

She shook her head the eighth of an inch his grip would allow. A dry rattle came from her throat.

"I'm a forgiving person," Dart announced into the rush of blood filling her ears. "Understand your distress, your confusion. Gosh golly gee, you're a human being, aren't you? I bet you'd love to take a breath right about now."

She did her best to nod.

"Let me get us out of sight, and we'll take care of that."

He carried her between two vans and pulled her to the wall. His arm loosened. A single breath of burning air rushed into her lungs, then he tightened his grip again. "There, now. Like another one?"

Braced against the wall, Dart held her back over his knee. If she struggled she would drop to the ground. Her feet dangled on either side of his bent leg. She nodded, and the arm relented for the length of another gasping inhalation.

She twisted her head and looked at him out of the side of her right eye. He was grinning, his eyes alight with pleasure below the brim of a black poplin cap which revealed a strip of white bandage above his ear. She could just see the shining edge of the knife where it met the hilt.

"I've missed you, too," he said. "To prove it, I'm going to let you breathe again." His arm dropped. "We'll be nice and quiet now, won't we?" Gulping air, she nodded. "Darling Davey turned you in, didn't he? Thrill for the boy, hanging out with the big, bad FBI. Think he's bonded with the one in sunglasses." He yanked her farther up his leg and closed his arm around her throat a little less tightly than before. "Over the initial shock of joy? Adjusted to the delightful reappearance of an old friend? Do we understand that any outburst will result in a little rough-and-tumble throat surgery?"

Nora came as close as she could to saying yes.

"I'm going to prove something to you." He stood up and deposited her on the ground. She was standing with her back to Dick Dart in the three feet of space between a battered brown van and an even more battered blue one painted with the words MACMEL PLUMBING & HEATING. At the end of the tunnel formed by the vans lay an asphalt parking lot scattered with crumpled candy wrappers and cigarette butts. Amazed to be alive, she turned around.

Dart was leaning against the side of the tourist center, one leg
bent under him and his arms crossed over his chest. The black
cap came down to just above his glittering eyes. A faint stubble
covered his cheeks and chin, and in his right hand was the stag-
handled German knife he had bought in Fairfield.

"Do you see?"

"See what?" Her hands trembled, and something in her stomach trembled, too.

"You're not running away."

"You'd kill me if I did."

"There is that. But I'm your best bet for getting out of this mess.
You're afraid of me, but you're beginning to believe that I'm too
interested in you to kill you out of a simpleminded motive like
revenge, and you're furious with Davey. As long as I seem reasonable and calm, you'd rather take your chances with me than let
that weak sister see you get arrested."

She stared at him—this was almost right.

"The difference between Davey and me is that I respect you.
Am I going to lose my mind because you acted like a woman
when I let my guard down? Not at all. You hurt me, but not that
much. I have a truly hard head, after all. I'll have to take more pre-
cautions with you, but don't we still have things to do together?
Let's do them."

"Okay," Nora said, thinking fast and hard. "Whatever you say."

"I suppose you did your best to make yourself up, but that's
ridiculous. You smeared it on with a trowel."

"Are you going to get me out of here or not?"

Dart uncoiled from the wall, gripped her arm, and led her out
between the vans. Two uniformed policemen ambled past the
entrance. "You're responsible for my acquiring this wonderful
work of art." She turned from the policemen to see the antique car
owned by the tyrant in the ascot and blazer. "We'll even be able to
keep it for a while."

He led her to the driver's door and helped lever her up onto the
running board. "Know how to drive stick shift?"

"Yes."

"The perfect woman." Dart sighed. He trotted around the back
of the car to get in on the passenger side. Nora looked at the seats
and floor carpeting and was relieved not to see bloodstains.

BOOK IX

MOUNTAIN GLADE

THE HEART'S GLADE, WHERE THE GREAT SECRET LAY BURIED.

83

"NICE AND EASY, now. This is an actual Duesie, treat it with respect."

"A doozy?"

Dart rolled his eyes, and Nora backed smoothly out of the parking spot, shifted into first, and drove toward the King Street exit. "A Duesie. A Duesenberg, one of the greatest cars ever made. An aristocrat. It's really delicious, the way these plums fall into my hands when you're around."

Davey and the two FBI agents stood at the center of a group of uniformed policemen in front of the hotel. Some of the men looked at the Duesenberg as Nora turned toward Main Street.

"People are so busy looking at the car that they don't pay any attention to who's driving it."

Out of habit, she turned right on Main. Two college-aged young women crossing Gothic Street watched them go by with smiles on their faces. Dart was right, people stared at the car, not the people in it.

"You've had time to consider things, see what the world is like without me, so all you need is some consistent supervision and we'll be back on the right track. How'd you learn to work a gearshift, anyhow? Most women don't have a clue."

"I learned to drive in an old pickup." Dart was leaning against a walnut-paneled door, smirking at her and fondling the pistol he had taken from Officer LeDonne. "How did you get this car?"

"Nora magic. If not for this evidence of your ability to smooth my passage, I might have treated your moment of rebellion a good deal more harshly. But here *you* are, and instantly, here's the *Duesie*. Kismet. Though I did have my eye on your friend's MG. Is he an ex-cop?"

"He's an ex–lots of things." She glanced again at his twist of a smirk, unwilling to let him see her dismay. "Including a cop. He was the housekeeper at the Poplars."

"Devoted manservant," Dart said. "Deeply attached to the young lord's beloved. A romantic dalliance, perhaps?"

"No."

He raised his eyebrows and grinned. A stream of pedestrians moved staring past the front of the car.

"Last night, I asked some questions of the local citizens. An MG fancier who had observed the two of you pointed me toward the hotel, and there I came upon the vehicle in question. I thought I'd collect your friend when he came back for you this morning, but you came out and had your encounter with the previous owners of the Duesie. The old black magic has them in its spell, I says to myself, I says. Give me a little peek into the workshop, Nora-pie, tell me what you said to them."

"I said I hoped his wife would kill him in bed one night."

Dart barked out his ugly laugh and patted his fingertips against the barrel of the gun in applause. "Struck a nerve, magic one, struck a nerve. By the time they got to the corner, the old waffle was screeching at him. When you ducked into the front of the theater, I hustled across the street and followed them, acting on faith, always the proper thing to do, and before they went ten feet, Douglas Fairbanks pulled over to chastise her. The waffle got out and walked away. Doug took after her, so angry he forgot his keys. He trotted along, screaming at her, collapsed, bang—the old boy's flat out on the sidewalk. Another victim of an unwise marriage. I got in the Duesie and drove it right past the commotion, and do you know what? I think the waffle saw me. Bet she experienced one of the great moments of her life. When Douglas Fairbanks wakes up in the hospital, he'll take one look at the monitors at his bedside, the tubes coming from his every orifice, and he'll say—*What happened to my car?* And the waffle will say, *Dear, I was too worried about you to think about the Duesie.* This is the most important thing in his life, but can he criticize her for letting it get stolen? He wants to tear her heart out and fry it over an open fire, but instead he has to be grateful to her!"

Dart smiled to himself. "Sometimes I doubt myself. Sometimes I stop and wonder if I'm wrong and everybody else is right. And then something like this happens, and I know I can relax. Men are just dogs, but women are lions."

He reached over what seemed a much greater distance than would have been the case in any other car and patted her knee.

"You, Nora, are still a baby lion, but you're a *great* baby lion, and you've grown by leaps and bounds. When we started on our odyssey, you didn't know enough to last five minutes. But after twenty-four hours at the feet of the great Dick Dart, you're able to figure out a way to see Dr. Foil and Everett Tidy."

Nora pulled up at the stop sign before the Smith campus at State Street, and the usual backpacks and blue jeans gave the car the usual appreciative stares.

"Thought we'd get out of Massachusetts for a couple of nights, find a nice motel somewhere up in Maine. Safest place in America. Half of Maine hasn't even heard of television yet. They're still waiting to see if that moon-landing thing worked out." He opened the glove compartment. "Must be some maps here. Assholes with medals on their cars always have a million maps. Right again, Dick, we knew we could count on you."

Smith College rolled past the side of Dart's head. Nora glanced up Green Street and saw Jeffrey sprinting across the sidewalk to his car. "Would you consider another possibility?"

He tilted his face toward her as he sorted through the maps. "Maine sound a little primitive? I have a better idea. Canada. Don't need passports, they just wave you in and out. Our charming cousins to the north. Most self-effacing people on earth. You know what a Canadian says when you're about to kill him? 'May I floss first?' "

"I have a reservation in one of the cottages at Shorelands."

"Shorelands?" He fell back against the leather seat. "Idea has a decided sparkle. Continuation of our original quest. I trust this reservation is in some suitably neutral name."

"Mrs. Norma Desmond."

"Lovely. I can be Norman Desmond. My character takes shape about me even as we speak. Norm, husband of Norm. Lawyer by day, devotee of the written word by night. All my talks with my old dears very useful. Every now and then I could reel off some verse to impress the shit out of the guardians of culture. Wouldn't have to be Emily, I can quote lots of other idiots, too. Keats, Shelley, Gray—all the greats."

"Can you?"

"I told you, as soon as I read something, it's in there for good. Let me win a couple of bets in bars, but after a while, I couldn't get anybody to wager that I wasn't able to recite all of 'To a Sky-Lark.' Want to hear it?"

"Not really."

"Good. It's terrible. Now, were you going there by yourself?"

"Jeffrey was going to drive me there and drop me off."

He nodded. "Pull over to the side, so I can look at one of these maps and figure out how to get there."

She coasted to a stop. Dart removed a folded map from the pile. "Okay, here's Lenox and here's us. No problem. We go back into town, take 9 all the way to Pittsfield, and go south on 7. On the way, you can tell me what you got out of Mark Foil and Everett Tidy. But before that, do explain why you decided to go to this broken-down literary colony. Documents hidden under the floorboards? Katherine Mannheim's draft of *Night Journey* salted away in the bole of a tree?"

"I want to see where they all met each other."

"And?"

"Get a better idea of the layout."

"Piece together their comings and goings, that sort of thing? What else?"

She remembered the boys arranging the terrace in the lemon light of the morning; she remembered Helen Day. "I thought I might be able to talk to some of the maids."

"You mystify me."

"Some of the old staff is still around. The other night I realized that servants know everything. Like those boys you told me about, the ones who work at the Yacht Club."

"Deeply flattered, but the hag who changed Hugo Driver's sheets fifty-five years ago isn't likely to know what he wrote or didn't write, even if she's still alive."

"Katherine Mannheim didn't write *Night Journey*. That isn't the issue anymore."

He took it in. "Then why didn't Alden Chancel tell the old ladies to cram their lawsuit up the old rectal valve? He could have told their lawyer to go to hell at the beginning, but he put Dart, Morris on the case. If he's in the clear, why fork out money to his law firm?"

Nora remembered how she had felt when she had seen Davey on the hotel terrace with his new pals, Mr. Hashim and Mr. Shull. Dart was going to love what she was about to tell him.

"Alden doesn't want anybody to question Driver's authorship of his books. That's a sensitive point."

He became instantly attentive. "Do tell. I mean, do. Tell."

"The horror novels weren't the first books Daisy wrote for Alden under a phony name. The other name she used was Hugo Driver."

Dart blinked, then laughed. "That boozy old pillowcase wrote *Night Journey*?" For a second he was the nice-looking man he would have been if he were not Dick Dart, and he laughed again. "No wonder Alden got rid of the manuscript! No, it can't be. She's too young. You're riding the wrong horse, babycakes."

"She didn't write the good one," Nora said. "She wrote the other two."

Dart opened his mouth as if to make a point. Then he regarded her in pure appreciative amazement. "Bravo. They came out in the sixties. How'd you find out?"

"You'd never see it unless you compared the Driver books with her horror novels, but once you do it's obvious. Daisy has certain trademark expressions she uses over and over. There was never any reason for anyone to read her horror books side by side with the last two Drivers, so no one ever noticed."

Dart grinned. "Hate poetry, love poetic justice. Once you start questioning Hugo Driver, everything he owns is up for grabs. *That's* why he called my old man." He tapped the gun barrel against his lips. "If Driver wrote *Night Journey*, why did he give the copyright to Lincoln Chancel?"

"I think something went on at Shorelands that nobody but the two of them knew about. After they came back, they were partners. Chancel even had Driver stay overnight at the Poplars a couple of times. Ordinarily, he wouldn't have bothered to spit on a weasel like Hugo Driver, even one who made a lot of money for him."

"So Driver had something on him."

"Or he had something on Driver, and he wanted to make sure that Driver didn't forget it."

"Could only be one thing," Dart said. "Tell me what it is. Get it right, I'll do you a big favor."

"Hugo Driver killed Katherine Mannheim. Maybe he didn't mean to, but he killed her anyhow, and Lincoln Chancel knew it. Chancel helped him hide the body in the woods, and Driver was in his power ever after."

Dart nodded. "Desperate man, desperate act. Why? What happened?"

"One day Bill Tidy spotted Driver doing something fishy with her bag. Maybe he stole a notebook and found enough to realize that all he needed to pull himself out of his hole was a little more of the story. Driver was a thief; he did what came naturally to him, he stole her ideas. Maybe he broke into Gingerbread looking for more material, and Katherine surprised him. She said something cutting to him—she was good at that, you wouldn't have liked her at all. Maybe he hit her. Whatever he did, she died. Driver wasn't ruthless enough to be a killer, like Lincoln Chancel."

Another thought came to her. "It almost has to have been something like that. She would never have invited Driver into Gingerbread, but he was inside it because in the book he used a photograph she kept on her desk."

Dart smiled up at the roof of the car and hummed a few bars of "Too Marvelous for Words." His smile broadened. "Turn this buggy around and pick up 9. I've just had a particularly lovely idea."

"Didn't you say something about a favor?"

"I believe I did. This is going to mean a lot to you."

She glanced at his gleeful face.

"The time ever comes I have no choice but to kill you, I'll do it quickly. Goes against the grain, making a sacrifice here, but I guarantee you won't suffer."

"You're quite a guy, aren't you, Dick?"

"Go to the wall for my friends," he said.

84

WHEN THEY GOT to Pittsfield, Dart manacled a hand to her elbow and guided her through shops for shaving supplies, a toothbrush, a glossy silk tie, boxer shorts, and over-the-calf socks. Outside of town, he asked her to drive into a gas station and pulled her into the men's room. Nora looked away as he filled the tiled cubicle with a fine sea-spray. "If cars could run on piss, I'd be a national resource." Dart removed his cap and leaned over the sink to inspect the bandage wound around the sides of his head. "Cut this off me." Nora found the scissors and worked the tip of one blade under the topmost layer of cloth. Soon she was unwinding a long white strip from around his head.

"Who did this for you?"

He gave her a glance of weary irony.

When the last of the bandage came away, Dart tilted his head and probed his hair with his fingers while scrutinizing himself in the mirror. "What's a couple of lumps to an adventurous soul, eh? Hurt pretty good at the time, though. Distinct memory of pain. Flashes of light behind my eyes. Second biggest headache of my life."

"What was the biggest?"

Dart lowered his hand and his suddenly expressionless eyes met hers in the mirror. In the hot little box of the bathroom, Nora went cold. "Popsie Jennings. Old whore landed a solid one with her andiron. Still hurts worse than either of yours." He looked away and fingered a spot on the back of his head. "I have to shave, brush my teeth, make myself pretty for Shorelands. What's my name again?"

It took her a moment to understand what he meant. "Norm. Norm Desmond."

He smiled at her and took the razor and shaving cream from a paper bag. "Tonight Mrs. Desmond is going to bestow upon Mr. Desmond a particularly deep marital pleasure. At least twice. You have to work off your debt." He squirted shaving cream onto his fingers and began working it into his stubble.

"I want to tell you about the fun we're going to have at Shorelands. Going to be a great pleasure for both of us." He rinsed his fingers and began drawing the razor down the right side of his face. "You want to talk to the old ladies, right? Win them over, pump them for information?"

"That's right."

"Let's do it the stand-up way. Scare the shit out of some old dame, she'll spill everything she knows. You did it to Natalie Weil, so do it to one of them."

Nora watched him shave. Unlike any other man she had

known, Dart cleared an area of foam and whiskers, then ran the razor back over the same patch of skin in the opposite direction, in effect shaving himself twice. "You want me to kidnap one of the maids."

"Tie her up, beat the crap out of her, whatever. Get her out of the house and into the car. She says whatever she says, and then I kill her. Be interesting. Lot of entertainment in an old lady." He threw out his arms, splattering foam on the tiles. "I award myself the Dick Dart Prize for Superior Achievement in Twisted Thinking. I'll be your support group, give you all the help you need to do your thing." He finished shaving his face, ran water over the head of the razor, and began on his neck. "Afterwards, we have to trust each other. It'll be you and me, babe, the Dream Team. After the first one, cops don't care how many murders you commit. In death-penalty states they don't bring you back to execute you all over again. Shows how fucked up they are, the low value they put on life." He ran the razor over a few patches of foam, reversed direction and shaved the same places again, then rinsed his face with cold water and reached for a handful of paper towels.

"How do you see us ending up? If you don't mind my asking."

Dart blotted his face, threw the wadded towels on the floor, and looked meditative for a moment before taking the new toothbrush from the bag. He snapped the case in half and tossed it aside. "Toothpaste."

Nora rooted in her bag and brought out her toothpaste. "Well?"

"Roadblock. A million cops and us. Hey, if we get to Canada, we might have a whole year. Essential point is, we do not under any circumstances allow ourselves to be arrested. We broke out of one jail, we're not going to wind up in another one. Live free or die." He bent forward and attended to his teeth.

85

At the bronze Shorelands Trust sign, they drove between overgrown stone pillars into a tangle of green. "The drums, the beastly drums," Dart intoned, "will they nevah cease, Carruthers?"

Crowded on both sides by trees, the path angled right and disappeared. Nora reached the curve and saw the path divide at a wooden signpost standing on a grass border. One branch veered left, the other right, into a muddy field. As they approached the sign, the words grew legible. MAIN HOUSE. GINGERBREAD. HONEY HOUSE. PEPPER POT. RAPUNZEL. CLOVER. MONTY'S GLEN & THE SONG PILLARS. MIST FIELD. All of these lay somewhere up the left-hand path. VISITOR PARKING pointed to the field.

Nora drove out of the woods and turned right. A man in khaki work clothes pushed himself out of a lawn chair next to a trailer on a cement apron and came forward, admiring the car.

"What a beauty," he said. "Godalmighty." He had furrowed cheeks and small, shining eyes. Dart snickered.

"We like it," Nora said, giving Dart a sharp look.

The man stepped back and licked his lips. "Don't make them like this baby anymore."

"By gum, they shore don't, Pops," Dart said.

The man glanced at Dart and decided to pretend he wasn't there. "Ma'am, if you're here on a day visit, there's a ten-dollar entrance fee. If you're an overnight guest, pull right into the lot there and check in at Main House after I find your name on the list."

"We're staying overnight. Mr. and Mrs. Desmond."

"Back in a jiffy." After another lingering look at the car, he went into the trailer.

"Did a little prison time, but not for anything interesting," Dart said.

"You don't know that."

"Wait."

The man came out of his trailer holding a clipboard with a pen dangling from a string. He thrust it through the window and pointed at a blank space on a form. "Sign right there, Mrs. Desmond. Hope you enjoy your stay."

Dart leaned forward with a wicked smile. "What did they put you in for, old-timer?"

"Pardon?"

"Knife a guy in a bar, or was it more like stealing bricks off a construction site?"

Nora handed him the clipboard. "I apologize for my husband. He thinks he's a comedian."

"Not all comedians is funny." The man's face had gone rigid, and the light had disappeared from his eyes. He grabbed the clipboard, stamped across the cement, climbed into his trailer, and slammed the door.

"This may come as a surprise to you," Nora said, "but you have an unpleasant streak."

"Now you want to bet that I can't quote all of 'To a Sky-Lark'?"

The field squished under the Duesenberg's oversized tires. "No."

"How about every third word? Slightly adjusted for effect?"

"No." She put the car in a spot at the far right end of the field.

"Too bad. It's a lot better my way.

> *Thee, bird wert—*
> *Heaven it full profuse unpremeditated*
> *still from thou a fire.*
> *Deep and still and singest.*

There are a lot of ways to be a genius. I'm going to feel right at home here."

Nora picked her way across the field, stepping over the muddy patches. "I'm not sure it's an act of genius to hang on to that car."

Dart moved along behind her. "After you perform your kidnapping stunt, we'll liberate another one. In the meantime there isn't a safer place in the whole state for the Duesie than right here. This was a *brilliant* idea."

Nora circled a mudhole and realized with a sinking of her heart that she had brought this madman into a private playpen. After the trust had decided to rent out cottages, they must have put in telephones. Dart could not watch her every minute; by now, he didn't even feel that he had to. They were partners. As soon as possible, she would call the local police and escape into the woods.

The path leading into the center of Shorelands held long, slender pockets of water, and the raised sections gleamed with moisture. Sometime during the night it had rained. While the sidewalks and highways had dried in the sun, open land had not. She looked up. Heavy clouds scudded across a mottled sky.

"Going to be good for both of us," Dart said.

"Imagine how I feel," Nora said.

Her short heels sank into the earth, and she moved onto a wet, stony ridge. The trees on either side seemed to close in. Dart began humming "Mountain Greenery." They came out of the trees and moved toward a gravel court surrounded by a low stone wall topped with cement slabs. The wall opened onto a white path between two narrow lawns, and the path led up four wide stone steps to the centerpiece of this landscape, a long stone building with three rows of windows in cement embrasures, some dripping water stains like beards. At every second window the facade stepped forward, so that the structure seemed to spread its wings and fold out from the entrance. Near the far end, a workman halfway up a tall ladder was scraping away a section of damaged paint, and another was repairing a cracked sill on the ground floor. Dick Dart linked his arm in hers and led her up the path to Main House.

86

WHITE-HAIRED MEN AND WOMEN lingered inside a gift shop across from a black door marked PRIVATE STAFF ONLY. Beyond, marble steps ascended to a wide corridor with high peach walls broken by glossy plaster half columns. In the big lounge across the corridor, a group of about twenty people, most of them women, listened to an invisible guide. French doors opened onto a terrace. Dart pulled Nora up the steps. At the left end of the hallway, a knot of tourists emerged from a room at the front of Main House and pursued a small, white-haired woman into another across the corridor. To their right, a curved staircase led past a gallery of paintings to the second floor. Nora thought of screaming for help, and words thrust up into her throat until she realized that if she released them, Dart would yank the revolver from his pocket and murder as many of these people as he could. The group in the lounge began shuffling after their guide through an interior arch on the far side of the fireplace.

Dart tilted his head to admire the plaster palmettes and arabesques spread across the barrel-vaulted ceiling. "Hell with the roadblock and the violent demise. We lie low for a while, then I touch my old man for a couple million dollars. We go to Canada, buy a place like this. I put in a couple hidden staircases, state-of-the-art operating theater, big gas furnace in the basement. Have a ball."

The short, white-haired guide led her party into the big room across the corridor and spread her arms. "Here we have the famous lounge, where Miss Weatherall's guests gathered for cocktails and conversation before their evening meal. If you're wishing you could listen in, I can tell you one thing that was said in this room. T. S. Eliot turned to Miss Weatherall and whispered, 'My dear, I must tell you . . .' "

410

In a carrying voice, Dart announced, "That stuffed shirt Eliot stayed here exactly two days, and all he did was complain about indigestion."

Most of the tourists who had been listening to the guide turned to look at Dart.

" *'The breeding of land and dull spring, us, earth, snow, life, tubers.'* Every third word of the beginning of 'The Waste Land,' with certain adjustments for poetic effect, *'Us, the shower; we went sunlight. Hofgarten coffee.'* Heck of a lot punchier, don't you think? My 'Prufrock' is even better."

The guide was trying to shepherd her charges into the next room.

"Can you do that with everything?" Nora asked.

"Everything. *'Go, and the spread, the patient upon; Let through muttering, restless hotels, restaurants, shells insidious. Lead an . . . Oh, ask it.'* "

A voice behind them asked, "Are you a poet?"

A tall woman in her late twenties, her face strewn with freckles and her strawberry-blond hair hanging straight to her shoulders, stood behind them, one foot on the top of the stairs. She wore a simple off-white suit, and she looked charming.

Dart smiled at her. "How embarrassing. Yes, I hope I may claim that honor."

The young woman came toward them, holding out a deeply freckled hand. "Mr. and Mrs. Desmond?"

Dart enfolded her hand in both of his. "I'll tell, if you will."

"Marian Cullinan. One of my jobs here is being in charge of Guest Services. Tony let me know you were coming, and I'm sorry to be late, but I had to take care of a few things at my desk." Dart released her. "You had no trouble finding us, I hope?"

"None at all," Dart purred.

"Good. And please, don't be embarrassed that we inspired you to think about your work. We hope we have that effect on all the writers who visit us. Are you published, Mr. Desmond?"

"A fair bit, I'm happy to say."

"Wonderful," said Marian. "Where? I should know your name. I do my best to keep up with people like you for our reading series."

Dart glanced at Nora and presented Marian with a shy, modest face. "Here and there."

"You can't get out of it that way. I'm interested in contemporary poetry. I bet your wife will tell me where you've placed your work."

Nora struggled to remember the magazines on Mark Foil's coffee table. "Let's see. He's published quite a bit in *Avec* and *Conjunctions*. And *Lingo*."

"Well!" She looked up at Dick Dart with a quick increase of interest and respect. "I'm impressed. I thought you must be a Language poet. I'd love to ask you about a thousand questions, but I don't want to be rude."

"Might be enjoyable," Dart said. "Poets don't get a great deal of attention, all in all."

"Around here they do. We'll have to make sure you get our VIP treatment. When good writers do us the honor of visiting, we like to extend our hospitality a little further than we can with the usual guest."

"Isn't that sweet as all get out?" Dart looked at Nora with dancing eyes.

"This is *wonderful*. I can show you Miss Weatherall's photo archive, her private papers—really anything you might care to see—and tonight you must have dinner with Mrs. Nolan, Margaret Nolan, the director of the trust, and me in the dining room. It would be such a treat for us. We'll have a splendid dinner, we do that for our literary guests, something off the original Shorelands menu. Margaret and I love the opportunity to re-create the old atmosphere. Does that sound like something you'd like to do?"

"Honored," Dart said.

"Margaret will be thrilled." Marian looked as if she wanted to give Dart a hug. "We'd better take care of the paperwork so I can start organizing matters. Would you come into my office?"

"Putty in your freckled little hands," Dart said.

She gave him an uncertain glance before deciding that what he had said was hilarious. "My freckles used to make me feel self-conscious, but I don't think about them anymore. Sometimes, I confess, I'd still like to cover them up, if I could find a cosmetic that worked."

"I could help you with that," Dart said. "No problem at all."

"Do you mean that?"

Dart shrugged and nodded. The young woman looked at Nora.

"He means it," Nora said.

"Artists are so . . . *extraordinary*. So . . . *unexpected*."

"I'm a little more in touch with my feminine side than the average guy," Dart said.

Marian brought them through the door marked PRIVATE, down a functional hallway to an unmarked door, and into a tiny office with a window on the entrance. A photograph of a young soldier in uniform had been pinned to the bulletin board. She moved behind the desk, took a form from the top drawer, and smiled at Dart. "Mr. Desmond, since I suppose you will be filling this out, perhaps you should take the chair? I wish I had two, but as you can see, there's no room."

Dart examined the form. Grinning, he took a pen from her desk and began writing.

Marian looked brightly up at Nora. "Now that I know who you are, I'm so glad we're putting you and Mr. Desmond in Pepper Pot. Pepper Pot is where Robert Frost stayed when he was Miss Weatherall's guest in 1932."

"And where Merrick Favor and Austryn Fain stayed in 1938."

Marian tilted her chin, and her hair swung to the back of her neck. If the poetic Mr. Desmond appreciated freckles, she intended to give him a good view. "I don't think I know those names."

"My wife has a special interest in the summer of 1938." He smiled as if to suggest that wives must be expected to have their foibles, and Marian smiled back in indulgent understanding.

"We'll have to see what we can do to help you." She read what Dart had written on the form. "Oh, isn't that cute. Your names are Norma and Norman."

"Language poetry strikes again."

She smiled and gave her head a flirtatious shake. Norman Desmond was a hoot. "There's a tour beginning in forty minutes, which would give you more than enough time to settle in. Afterwards, I'll take you into the parts of the house normally off-limits. We're not really a hotel, so we can't provide valet or room service, but if you have any special needs, I'll do my best."

Dart turned a rueful smile to Nora. "We're gonna have to tell her, Norm."

Nora had no idea what he thought they had to tell Marian Cullinan. "I guess so."

"Truth is, we don't have our bags. Stolen out of our car at a rest stop this morning. All we have is in Norma's handbag and what we're wearing."

Marian looked stricken. "Why, that's terrible!" She ripped a sheet off a yellow pad. "I'll have Tony pick up some toothbrushes and toothpaste in town, and whatever else you need. A razor? Shaving soap? Tell me what you need."

"Thankfully, we have all the toiletries we need, but there are some other items I'd be grateful for."

"Fire away," Marian said.

"We enjoy a nightcap in the evenings. Could your lad pick up a liter of Absolut vodka? And we'd like an ice bucket to go with that."

"Sounds sensible to me." She wrote. "Anything else?"

"I'd like two more items, but I don't want you to think they're strange."

She positioned her pen.

"A twelve-foot length of clothesline and a roll of duct tape."

She looked up to see if this was another of his little jokes.

"Doesn't have to be clothesline," Dart said. "Any smooth rope about a quarter inch in diameter is dandy."

"We aim to please." She wrote down his requests. "We do have a lot of rope coiled up in the bathroom down the hall. The workmen store it there, even though I've asked and asked . . ."

"Too rough," Dart said.

"Would you mind if I asked . . . ?"

"Medical supplies," Dart said. "Repair work."

"I don't quite . . ."

He tapped his right knee. "Not the leg I was born with, alas."

"*Excuse* me. It should all be in your room by the time you're finished with the tour." She looked stricken again. "Unless you need something right away."

"No hurry. The old joint's had a bit of a workout, little loose, little floppy, and I want to stiffen it up later."

"Our pleasure. And you, Mrs. Desmond? Is there anything I can do for you? I hope I might call you Norma." She gave Nora a closer look. "Are you all right?"

"Are some of the people who were at Shorelands at the end of the thirties still here? If so, I'd like to speak to them."

Brilliant smile. "Lily Melville is a fixture here, and she was a maid in those days. When the trust came into being, Lily was so helpful that we put her on the staff. You might have seen her leading a group through the lounge."

"White hair? Five two?" Dart asked. "Pink Geoffrey Beene knockoff, cultured pearls?"

"Why, yes." She was delighted with him. "Norman, you are an amazing man."

"Sweet old darling," Dart said.

"Well, she's going to get a kick out of you, but don't let on you know it isn't a real Geoffrey Beene."

Dart held up his hand as if taking a vow. Nora broke in on their rapport. "Is Lily Melville the only person left from that time?"

"Another former maid, Agnes Brotherhood, is still with us. She's been under the weather lately, but it might be possible for you to talk to her."

"I'd like that," Nora said.

"Hugo Driver," Marian said, pointing at Nora. "I *knew* there was something about 1938. So you are a Hugo Driver person." She smiled in a way which may not have been entirely pleasant. "We don't see as many Driver people as you might expect. As a rule, they tend not to be much like ordinary readers."

"I'm not only a Driver person," Nora said. "I'm a Bill Tidy, Creeley Monk, and Katherine Mannheim person, too."

Marian gave her a doubtful look.

"Fascinating group," Dart said. "Class of '38. Tremendous interest of Norma's."

"You're involved in a research project."

"According to Norma," Dart said, "*Night Journey* wouldn't exist without the Shorelands experience. Essential to the book."

"That is incredibly interesting." Marian pushed herself back from the desk and folded her hands in front of her chin. "Given Driver's popularity, we ought to be doing more with him anyhow. And if we can claim that Shorelands and these people you mention are central to *Night Journey*, that's the way to do it." She stroked her perfect jawline and gazed out of the window, thinking. "I can see a piece in the Sunday *Times* magazine. I can certainly see a piece in the book review. If we got that, we could put on Hugo Driver weekends. How about an annual Driver conference? It could work. I'll have to run this past Margaret, but I'm sure she'll see the potential in it. To tell you the truth, attendance has been suffering lately, and this could turn things around for us."

"I'm sure Leonard Gimmel and Teddy Brunhoven would be delighted to participate," Nora said.

Marian swung toward her and raised her eyebrows.

"Driver scholars," Nora said.

"With luck, we could have everything in place by next spring. Let's discuss these matters with Margaret during dinner, shall we? Now, the rate for your accommodations is ninety-six twenty with the tax, and if you give me a card, you can be on your way to Pepper Pot."

"Always use cash," Dart said. "Pay as you go."

"*That's* refreshing." She watched Dart take his wallet from his trousers and marveled at the number of bills.

Marian made change from a cash box and handed him two keys attached to wooden tabs reading PEPPER POT. "You'll meet Lily outside the lounge, and I'll be waiting for you when the tour ends. I think we'll all have a lot of fun during your stay."

"My plans exactly," Dart said.

87

"SHOULD HAVE BECOME a poet a long time ago. If the spouse hadn't been present, I could have planked our new friend right there in her office."

"You made a big impression on her," Nora said.

"I bet Maid Marian has freckles in her armpits. For sure she has freckles on the tops of her udders, but do you think she has them on the undersides, too?"

"She probably has freckles on the soles of her feet."

They had left Main House by the front door and taken the path angling into the woods on the far side of the walled court. Tall oaks interspersed with birches and maples grew on either side of the path. A signpost at a break in the wall pointed to GINGERBREAD, PEPPER POT, RAPUNZEL.

"Isn't it wonderful how everything falls into place when we're together? We show up as ordinary slobs, and two minutes later we're VIPs. We have the run of the place, and on top of that, they're giving us one of the historic old-time Shorelands dinners. Do you understand why?"

"Marian thinks you're hot stuff."

"That's not the reason. Here's this big place, four or five people in it full-time, tops. Night after night, they have soup and sandwiches in the kitchen, complaining to one another about how business is falling off. Rope in someone they can pretend is a VIP, they have a pretext for a decent meal. These people are starved for a little excitement. In the meantime, we get to see how many people are in the house, find out where their rooms are, check the place out. Couldn't be better."

Another wooden signpost came into view on the left side of the path. A brown arrow pointed down a narrow lane toward GINGERBREAD.

She looked over her shoulder. "I wish you hadn't asked for the rope and the duct tape. There's no need for those things."

"On the contrary. I'll need them twice."

They reached the sign. Nora looked to her left and saw the faint suggestion of a gray wooden building hidden in the trees. A window glinted in the gray light.

"Twice?"

His mouth twitched. "In your case, we can probably dispense with the tape. But our old darling is another matter. Physical restraint adds a great deal to the effect. Which one do you fancy, Lily or Agnes?"

She did not reply.

"Like the sound of Agnes. Touch of invalidism, less of a fight. Thinking of your best interests, sweetie."

"Very kind of you."

"Let's press on to dear old Salt Shaker or Pepper Grinder or whatever the place is called."

Wordlessly Nora turned away from Gingerbread, where Katherine Mannheim had probably died in a struggle with Hugo Driver, and began moving up the side of the path. Dart patted her shoulder, and she fought the impulse to pull away from his touch. "You're going to do fine." He ruffled the hair at the back of her head.

The path curved around an elephant-sized boulder with a rug of moss on its rounded hips. On the other side of the path a double signpost at the edge of the trees indicated that RAPUNZEL lay beyond a wooden bridge arching over a narrow stream, and PEPPER POT at the end of a narrow trail leading into the woods to their right.

Dart hopped neatly over four feet of glistening mud onto a flat rock, from there onto the grassy verge. He rattled the heavy keys in the air. "Home, sweet home!"

Nora moved a few feet along her side of the path and found a series of stones and dry spots which took her across.

The trail slanted upward through Douglas firs with shining needles. A small hewn-timber cottage gradually came into view at the end of a clearing. Extending from a shingle roof, a canopy hung over a flat porch. A brick fireplace rose along the side of the cottage, and big windows divided into four panes broke the straight lines of the timbers on both sides of the front door. An addition had been built onto the back by workmen who had attempted to match the timbers with machine-milled planks. No telephone lines came into the house.

"Hear the banjo music?" Dart said. "The Pinto put me in a shit-kicker's cabin."

"Two or three people made this place by hand," Nora said. "And they did a good job."

Dart drew her up two hewn-timber steps onto the porch. "Your simple midwestern values make me feel so decadent. In you go."

They entered a dark room with double beds and pine desks against the walls at either end. In the center of the room a brown sofa and easy chair flanked a coffee table. Along the far wall were a counter, kitchen cabinets, a sink beneath a square window, and an electric range. Heavy clothespresses occupied the far corners of the room, and the apron of the stone fireplace jutted into the wooden floor. Dart locked the door behind them and flipped up a switch, turning on a shaded overhead light and the lamps on the bedside tables.

"Fucking Dogpatch." He wandered into the kitchen and opened and closed cabinets. "No minibar, of course."

"Aren't you getting a bottle?"

"If you don't have choices, you might as well live in Russia. How much time do we have? Twenty-five minutes?"

"Just about," said Nora, grateful that it was not enough for Dick Dart's idea of an enjoyable sexual experience.

"Do you suppose this dump has an actual bathroom?"

She pointed at a door in the rear wall. "Through there."

"Let's go. Take your bag."

Nora questioned him with a look.

"Want to repair your makeup. I can't stand the sight of that mess you made of my work."

88

THE SHORT, WHITE-HAIRED guide trotted up the steps and bustled forward. She was energetic and cheerful, and she seemed to know several of the people in the group.

"Hello, hello!" Two men in their sixties, like Dick Dart in jackets and ties, one with a gray crew cut, the other bald, greeted her by name. Her smile congealed for a moment when she noticed Dart.

"Here we are," she said. "I don't usually lead groups back to back, but I was told that we have a promising young poet with us, and that he specifically asked for me, so I'm delighted to be with you." She turned her smile to a dark-haired young man who looked like an actor in a soap opera, one of Daisy's Edmunds and Dmitris. "Are you Mr. Desmond?"

Edmund/Dmitri looked startled and said, "No!"

"I'm afraid that's me," Dart said.

"Oh, now I understand," she said. "You have strong opinions, that's only natural. From time to time, Mr. Desmond, please feel free to share your insights with the rest of us."

"Be honored," Dart said.

She smiled at the group in general. "Mr. Norman Desmond, the poet, will be giving us his special point of view as we go along.

I'm sure we'll all find him very interesting, but I warn you, Mr. Desmond's ideas can be controversial."

"Little me?" Dart said, pressing a hand to his chest. Some members of the group chuckled.

"I also want to inform you that two other creative people, old friends of ours, are with us today. Frank Neary and Frank Tidball. We call them the two Franks, and it's always a pleasure when they join us."

The two older men murmured their thanks, mildly embarrassed to have been identified. Their names sounded familiar to Nora. Frank Neary and Frank Tidball, the two creative Franks? She didn't think that she had ever seen them before.

"You might be interested in how this old lady in front of you learned so much about Shorelands. My name is Lily Melville, and I've spent most of my life in this beautiful place. Lucky me!"

One of those people capable of saying something for the thousandth time as though it were the first, Lily Melville told them that Georgina Weatherall had hired her as a maid of all work way back in 1931, when she was still really just a child. It was the Depression, her family's financial situation meant she had to leave school, but Shorelands had given her a wonderful education. For two years sne had helped cook and serve meals, which gave her the opportunity to overhear the table talk of some of the most famous and distinguished writers in the world. After that, she took care of the cottages, which put her into even closer contact with the guests. Regrettably, in the late forties Miss Weatherall had suffered a decline in her powers and could no longer entertain her guests. During the years following her departure from Shorelands, Miss Melville frequently had been sought out by writers, scholars, and community groups for her memories. Soon after the trust had acquired the estate in 1980, she had been hired as a resident staff member.

"We'll begin our tour with two of my favorite places, Miss Weatherall's salon and private library, and proceed from there. Are there any questions before we begin?"

Dick Dart raised his hand.

"So soon, Mr. Desmond?"

"Isn't that very attractive suit you're wearing a Geoffrey Beene?"

"Aren't you sweet! Yes, it is."

"And am I wrong in thinking that I caught a trace of that

delightful scent Mitsouko as you introduced yourself so eloquently?"

"Mr. Desmond, would you join me as we take our group into the salon?"

Dart skipped around the side of the group and took her arm, and the two of them set off down the hallway ahead of Nora and the others.

They had visited the salon, library, lounge, and famous dining room, where a highly polished table stood beneath reproductions of paintings either owned by Georgina or similar to those in her collection. Like her library, her paintings had been sold off long ago. They had strolled along the terrace and descended the steps to admire the view of Main House from the west lawn. Lily spoke with the ease of long practice of her former employer's many peculiarities, representing them as the charming eccentricities of a patron of the arts; she invited the remarks, variously startling, irreverent, respectful, and comic, of the poet Norman Desmond, who now accompanied her down the long length of the west lawn toward the ruins of the famous gardens, restoration of which had been beyond the powers of the trust.

Nora fell in step with the two Franks and wondered again why their names seemed familiar. Certainly their faces were not. Without quite seeming to be academics, both Franks had the bookish reserve of old scholars and the intimate, unintentionally exclusive manner of long-standing collaborators or married couples. They had been amused by some of Dick Dart's comments, and the Frank with the gray crew cut clearly intended to say something about Mrs. Desmond's interesting husband.

Here are your telephones, Nora told herself. *You can get these guys to go to the police. But how to convince them?*

"Your husband is an unusual man," said Gray Crew Cut. "You must be very proud of him."

"Can I talk to you for a second?" she asked. "I have to tell you something."

"I'm Frank Neary, by the way, and this is Frank Tidball." Both men extended their hands, and Nora shook them impatiently. "We've taken Lily's tour many times, and she always comes up with something new."

Tidball smiled. "She never came up with anything like your husband before."

Dart and Lily had paused at the edge of a series of overgrown scars, the remains of one section of the old gardens. Past them, an empty pedestal stood at the center of a pond. Lily was laughing at something Dart was saying.

"You can hardly be a poet if you don't have an independent mind," said Neary. "Where we live, in Rhinebeck, up on the Hudson River, we're surrounded by artists and poets."

Nora took an agonized look across the lawn. Dart spoke to Lily and began walking quickly toward the group moving in his direction, Nora and the two Franks a little apart from the others.

"Wasn't there something you wanted to say?" Neary asked.

"I need some help." Dart advanced across the grass, smiling dangerously. "Would you please take my arm? I have a stone in my shoe."

"Certainly." Frank Neary stepped smartly up beside her and held her elbow.

Nora raised her right leg, slipped off her shoe, and upended it. "There," Nora said, and the two men politely watched the fall of a nonexistent stone. "Thank you." As Neary released her arm, she watched Dart striding toward her with his dangerous smile and remembered where she had heard their names. "You must be the Neary and Tidball who write the Chancel House crossword puzzles."

"My goodness," Neary said. "Frank, Mrs. Desmond knows our puzzles."

"Isn't this *lovely,* Frank?"

Nora turned to smile at Dart, who had noticed the tone of her conversation with the Franks and slowed his pace.

"You know our work?"

"You two guys are great," Nora said. "I should have recognized your names as soon as I heard them."

Dart had come within hearing distance, and Nora said, "I love your puzzles, they're so clever." Something Davey had once said came back to her. "You use themes in such a subtle way."

"Good God, someone understands us," Neary said. "Here is a person who understands that a puzzle is more than a puzzle."

Dart settled a hand on Nora's shoulder. "Puzzles?"

"Norman," she said, looking up with what she hoped was wifely regard, "Mr. Neary and Mr. Tidball write those wonderful Chancel House crossword puzzles."

"No," said Dart, instantly falling into his role, "not the ones that keep you up late at night, trying to think of an eight-letter word for smokehouse flavoring?"

"Isn't that great?"

"I'm sure you three have a lot to discuss, but we should catch up." Dart smiled at the two Franks. "I *wondered* what you were talking about. Do you have an editor over there at Chancel House?"

"Yes, but our work doesn't need any real editing. Davey makes a suggestion now and then. He's a sweet boy."

The four of them came up beside the rest of the group, and Lily said that after viewing the pond, they would be going on to Honey House, at which point the official tour would conclude. Anyone who wished to see the Mist Field, the Song Pillars, and Rapunzel was free to do so.

"You gentlemen come here often?" Dart asked.

Together, swapping sentences, Neary and Tidball told their new friends that they tried to visit Shorelands once a year. "Five years ago, we stayed overnight in Rapunzel, mainly so we could walk through Main when it wasn't filled with tourists. It was tremendously enjoyable. Agnes Brotherhood was full of tales."

"What kind of tales?"

Neary looked at Tidball, and both men smiled. Neary said, "There's a big difference between Lily and Agnes. Agnes never liked Georgina very much, and back then she was willing to gossip. Frank and I heard stories that will never be in the history books."

Lily had begun to speak from the raised flagstone ledge surrounding the pond. Frank Neary raised a finger to his lips.

After telling two mildly prurient anecdotes about the accidental unclothed encounters of writers of opposite sexes, Lily hopped off the ledge and declared that their final stop, Honey House, the only cottage restored to its original condition, was the perfect conclusion to their tour.

An overgrown stone path curved away from the pond and led into the trees. At the rear of the group, Nora and Dart walked along just behind the puzzle makers, and the others strung out in pairs behind Lily's pink suit. The air had darkened.

"Might rain," Dart said.

"It will," Tidball said. "It's getting here a little ahead of schedule, which is good for them. Rain cuts into attendance quite a bit. Shorelands gets muddy when it rains. If it's going to happen, they'd rather have it now instead of on the weekend."

"Cuts into attendance?" Neary asked. "I should *say*. Rain has the same effect on attendance that the fellow in the papers, Dart, had on his victims."

Lily and the couple behind her stepped onto a bridge over the stream which wandered through the northern end of the estate. Their shoes rang on the bridge, *trip trap, trip trap*, like the three billy goats gruff in the fairy tale.

"Heard anything new about good old Dart?" Dart asked. "What a story! We couldn't make much sense out of it. Fellow was accused of murder but never charged. What was the woman doing in the police station? More there than meets the eye. Still on the loose, this odd couple?"

"Oh, yes," said Neary. "According to the radio, Dart is supposed to be in Northampton, and that's not far from here." His eyes had become large and serious. "I agree that more is going on than meets the eye. Frank and I have a connection with the woman." He leaned in front of Nora to look into Dart's face. "You asked about our editor, Davey Chancel. Well, she's his wife. If you ask me, Nora Chancel had something going with this Dart."

"I should say that's a definite possibility," Dart said. "What do you know about this woman, your editor's wife?"

The others had crossed over the bridge, and now the two Franks, followed closely by Nora and Dick Dart, stepped onto it. *Trip trap, trip trap.*

"We've heard rumors," Tidball said.

"Go on," said Dart. "I'm absolutely riveted."

"Apparently the woman is an unstable personality. We think they were in cahoots. When he got arrested, she went to the police station and staged her own 'kidnapping,' quote unquote, to get him out. She's probably more dangerous than he is."

Neary laughed, and a second later Nora laughed, too.

They followed the others toward a cabin tucked away at the base of the trees. Lily stood at the front door facing them.

"Quite a saga, isn't it?" Dart asked.

"I can hardly wait for the movie," Nora said.

Lily held up a hand as if taking an oath. "We here at Shorelands are very proud of what you are about to see. The planning began four years ago, when our director, Margaret Nolan, said to us at dinner, 'Why don't we make it possible for our guests to walk into one of our cottages and experience the world created by Georgina Weatherall? Why not re-create the past we celebrate here?' We all fell in love with Margaret Nolan's vision, and for a year we assembled records and documents in order to reassemble a picture of a typical cottage interior from approximately 1920 to approximately 1935. We vowed to cut no corners. Let me tell you, when you begin a project like this, you find out how much you don't know in a hurry!"

Polite laughter came from everyone but Nora and Dart.

"You are wondering how we chose Honey House. I'll be frank about that. Expense had to be a consideration, and this is one of the smallest cottages. Our last great general renovation was in 1939, and the task before us was enormous. With the help of Georgina Weatherall's records, we covered the walls with a special fabric obtained from the original manufacturer. It had been out of production since 1948, but several rolls had been preserved at the back of the warehouse, and we bought all of them. We learned that the original paint came from a company which had gone out of business in 1935, and nearly lost hope, but then we got word that a paint supplier in Boston had fifteen gallons of the exact brand and color in his basement. Donations poured in. About a year and a half ago, it all came together.

"This should go without saying, but I must insist that you touch none of the objects or fabrics inside. Honey House is a living museum. Please show it the respect it deserves, and allow others to enjoy this restoration for many years to come. Am I understood?"

Dart's cry of "Absolutely!" rang out over the mutter of assent from the group.

Lily smiled, turned to the door, took a massive key from a pocket of the pink suit, and looked over her shoulder. "I love this moment." She swung the door open and told the young couple directly in front of her to switch on the lights.

The boy led the first of the group through the door. Soft sounds of appreciation came to those still outside.

"They all do that," Lily said. "As soon as the lights go on, it's always *Ooh! Aah!* Go on, Norman, get in there. It'll knock your eyes out."

Dart patted her shoulder and followed Nora through the door.

89

EVERY POSSIBLE SURFACE had been covered with porcelain figurines, snuffboxes, antique vases, candles in ornate holders, and lots of other things Nora instinctively thought of as gewgaws. Paintings in gilt frames and mirrors engulfed in scrollwork hung helter-skelter on the aubergine-colored walls.

Lily addressed the group. "I will leave you to feast upon this splendid re-creation. Feel free to ask me about anything that strikes your eye." The couples separated into different portions of the interior, and she came up to the Franks with a proprietary swagger. "Isn't it wonderful?"

Nora said, "I had no idea the guests lived in this kind of splendor."

"Nothing was too good for the people who came here," said Lily. "To Miss Weatherall, they were the cultural aristocracy. Mr. Yeats, for example." She pointed across the room at a photograph of a man with a pince-nez on the bridge of his nose. "He was a great gentleman. Miss Weatherall loved his conversation."

"A writer named Creeley Monk stayed here, too," Nora said.

"Creeley *Monk*? I don't seem to recall . . ."

"In 1938."

Lily's eyes went flat with distaste. "We like to dwell on our triumphs. And here we have one example, standing right next to you! Frank and Frank are published by Chancel House, which was born that very summer, when Mr. Driver met Mr. Lincoln Chancel. Now, *he* was a great gentleman."

"I guess it wasn't such a bad summer after all," Nora said.

Lily gave a ladylike shudder.

"Is this a reconstruction of what would have been here during the thirties?"

"No, not at all," Lily said, untroubled by the contradiction of her earlier remarks. "We wanted to represent the estate as a whole, not just a single cottage. When you put it together like this, you get a real feel of the times." A man who apparently wanted to question her about a collection of paperweights waved to her, and she scampered away.

"Nineteen thirty-eight isn't their favorite year," said Tidball.

"I wonder if you know anything about a poet named Katherine Mannheim," Nora asked.

Tidball rolled his eyes upward and clasped his hands in front of him.

"It seems you do," Nora said. Dart looked on, indulgent, pleased to sense the presence of trouble ahead.

The Franks exchanged a brief glance. "Let's wait until the tour is over," Neary said. "Were you going to look at the Mist Field and the Song Pillars?"

"You haven't seen the Song Pillars, you haven't seen Shore-lands," said Dart.

Half an hour later, the four of them lagged behind the others on the path threading north through the woods. Dart was walking so close behind Nora that he seemed almost to engulf her.

"Where did these airy-fairy names come from?" he boomed out.

"Georgina," Neary said, striding along at the head of their column of four. "When her father owned the estate, the only cottage that had a name was Honey House, after an old butler who lived there, Mr. Honey. After her father turned it over to her, all of a sudden everything had a new name." He looked back, grinning at the others. "Georgina's romantic conception of herself extended to her domain. These people tend to be dictatorial."

Frank Neary was a clever man. Dart could not keep his eye on her all afternoon, and she needed only a few seconds.

"That's where your poet went wrong," Neary said. "We got all this from Agnes Brotherhood, so you have to take into account that she never really cared for Georgina. Lily, on the other hand, worshiped her. Lily detested Katherine Mannheim because she didn't give Georgina the proper respect. Agnes told us that Katherine Mannheim saw right through Georgina the first time she met her, and Georgina hated her for it."

Tidball said, "According to Agnes, Georgina was jealous. But the entire subject still seemed to make her nervous."

The path curved around the left side of a meadow and disappeared into the trees on its far side, where several large, upright gray stones were dimly visible. "Here it is, the famous Mist Field."

"Mist Field," Nora said. "Why does that sound familiar?"

"Mr. Desmond, do you write every day?" Tidball asked.

"Only way to get anything done. Get up at six, scribble an ode before going to the office. Nights, I'm back at it from nine to eleven. By the way, please call me Norman."

They began moving up the path again.

"Are you part of a community of poets?"

"We Language poets like to get together at a nice little saloon called Gilhoolie's."

"How would you define Language poetry?"

"Exactly what it sounds like," Dart said. "Language, as much of it as possible."

"Have you ever read Katherine Mannheim's poetry?" asked Neary.

"Never touch the stuff."

Neary gave him a puzzled look.

"Why did Agnes think Georgina was jealous of Katherine Mannheim?" Nora asked.

"Georgina was used to being the center of attention. Especially with men. Instead, they were drooling over this pretty young thing. Being the kind of person she was, it took her a couple of weeks to understand what was going on. Lily Melville set her straight."

"Should have thrown the bitch out right then," Dart said.

Neary seemed startled by his choice of words. "Eventually she decided to do that, but she didn't want to act in any way that might injure her reputation. She was worried about finances, and sending away a guest could look like a distress signal. Here are the Song Pillars and Monty's Glen. Impressive, aren't they?"

A short distance from the path, six tall boulders with flat ends had been placed in a circle around a natural clearing. The other members of Lily Melville's group were already drifting back to the path, and a sixtyish woman in a turquoise exercise suit came up to them and introduced herself as Dorothea Bach, a retired high school teacher. She wanted to know all about Mr. Desmond's poetry.

"My odes and elegies were originally inspired by my own high school English teacher." He began spouting nonsense which thrilled Dorothea down to her bright blue running shoes. Fascinated, Tidball moved a step nearer.

Nora hurried up beside Neary, who was moving toward the boulder. He turned to her with a conciliatory smile, apologizing in advance for what he had to say. "To hear your husband talk, you'd think he didn't know anything about poetry at all."

"I need your help."

"Another imaginary stone?" He held out his arm.

"No, I—"

Dart stroked the back of her neck. "Don't let me break up this private moment, but I couldn't bear that woman a second longer."

Neary turned to Nora with a questioning look. She shook her head.

They passed through the Pillars and walked to the center of the clearing. "Every single time I come here, I think about going back in time to one of the great summers and listening to the conversation here. I get goose bumps. Right here, great writers sat down and talked about what they were working on. Wouldn't you like to have heard that?"

"Must have been a stitch," Dart said.

"You're a piece of work, Norman," Neary said.

"Humble laborer in the vineyards," Dart said.

"All in all, Norman, I wouldn't say that humility is your strong suit."

"Maybe you boys should leave us alone," Dart said. "After a while, little old swishes start to get on my nerves."

Frank Tidball looked as if he had been struck on the back of his head with a brick, and Frank Neary was enraged and weary in a manner to which he had clearly grown accustomed long ago. "That's it. This man is a lunatic, and he frightens me."

"I *should* frighten you," Dart said, glimmering with pleasure.

Neary held his ground. "Good-bye, Mrs. Desmond. I wish you luck."

Dart laughed at him—every word he said was ridiculous.

"Frank, I know my husband has offended you, but what were you saying about Georgina's money troubles? It might be very important to me." Nora had seen the money problem like the hint of a clue to an answer, and it was too important to be allowed to escape.

"I have no problem with you, Mrs. Desmond." He gave a contemptuous glance at Dart, who briskly stepped forward and grinned down at him.

Neary refused to be intimidated. "Georgina's trust fund wasn't large enough to pay for all the servants and upkeep or the food and drink for the guests. Her father indulged her for a long time, but in 1938 he lost patience. He cut her off, or seriously cut her back, I'm not sure which. Georgina was almost hysterical."

"Lily Melville told us that she had the whole place renovated the next year," Nora said.

"He must have relented. I'm sure that he was used to giving her whatever she wanted."

"Tale of Two Bitches," Dart said.

"I've spent enough time with this madman," Neary said. "Let's go." Tidball was staring at Dick Dart. Neary touched his elbow as if to awaken him, and Tidball spun away and marched toward the edge of the clearing. Neary followed him without looking back. They passed through the Pillars and moved toward the path with a suggestion of flight.

"Let's amble back to the house and meet the dear little Pinto. Something has occurred to me. Can you guess what?"

Before Nora could tell Dart that she could not read his mind, she read his mind. "You want Marian Cullinan."

He patted her head and grinned. "Probably time for me to bid farewell to older women. And Maid Marian has two great advantages."

She began to walk over the matted grass toward the boulders. "Which are?"

"One, you don't like her. She's fair Natalie all over again, wants to steal your man. Let's punish the cow—hey, it's what you want to do anyhow."

"And the second advantage?"

"Marian undoubtedly owns a nice car."

Heads down, moving a little faster than was necessary, Neary and Tidball were already most of the way across the meadow. Dart indulgently watched them wade through the long grass. "Lots of fun in store for us tonight, sweetie-pie."

90

MARIAN CULLINAN'S EAGER face appeared at her window as they approached the front of Main House, and when they came inside she was waiting for them, taking in Dart with theatrical awe. "Norman, you made Lily's day. She wants to take you on all of her tours."

"Entirely reciprocated. Reminds me of some of my dearest friends."

"Isn't he off the scale when it comes to charm, Mrs. Desmond?"

"Completely," said Nora. This dopey woman, so bored that she made passes at married male guests, probably represented her last hope of getting the police to Shorelands. "But please, call me Norma."

"Why, *thank* you!"

"Maybe you could join us for a nightcap up at good old Salt Shaker after dinner," Dart said. "So much to talk about, so many avenues to explore."

Marian's freckles slid sideways with a knowing twitch of the mouth. "That depends on how much paperwork I can get done. I used to have an assistant, but the Honey House restoration ate up most of our budget." Most of her bright, spurious eagerness reappeared. "And of course we're very proud of the result. Didn't you just love it?"

"Who wouldn't?" Dart said. "Can we get you up there tonight, Marian, or are we going to have to abduct you?"

"You'd be doing me a favor." She sighed and pantomimed exhaustion. "Would you like to see the rooms upstairs?"

Nora asked if they could talk to Agnes Brotherhood.

Marian closed her eyes and pressed a hand to her forehead. "I

431

forgot to check on that. I'd have to look in to see how she's doing. Why don't we go upstairs?"

"Does this VIP treatment extend to a sandwich before we start laying our hands on history?"

"A sandwich? Now?"

"Circumstances deprived me of my usual healthy breakfast. Could gobble up the Girl Scouts along with their cookies."

Marian laughed. "In that case, we'd better take care of you. How about you, Norma?"

Nora said she could wait for dinner.

Dart grasped her wrist, killing her hopes of getting to a telephone while he gobbled up any nearby Girl Scouts. "When it comes to appetite, Norm Desmond has never been found wanting."

"I wouldn't think so," Marian said. "Let's see what damage you can do to our kitchen." An unmarked door at the right side of the marble stairs opened onto a steep flight of iron steps. "You'll be all right on these, with your . . . ?" She touched her knee.

"All is well."

Marian started down the staircase. "Would you mind if I asked how . . . ?"

" 'Nam. Pesky land mine. Your brother was there, wasn't he?"

She looked back up at him. "How did you know about my brother?"

"Handsome picture on your bulletin board. I gather he was killed in action. Hope you will accept my condolences, even after all this time. As a former officer, I regret the loss of every single man in that tragic conflict."

"Thank you. You seem so young to have been an officer in Vietnam."

He barked out a laugh. "I'm told I was one of the youngest officers to serve in Vietnam, if not the youngest." He sighed. "Truth is, we were all boys, every one of us."

Nora felt like pushing him down the stairs.

"I'm going to make you the best sandwich you ever had in your life," Marian said.

"I have the distinct impression that you went to a Catholic girls' school. Please don't tell me I'm mistaken."

"How can you tell?" Marian began to descend the clanging stairs again, looking up at him with the smile of a woman who had never heard a compliment she didn't like.

"Two kinds of women hatch out of Catholic girls' schools. One is sincere, hardworking, witty, and polite. Best manners in the world. The other is unconventional, intellectual, bohemian. They're witty, too. Tend to be a bit rebellious."

At the bottom of the stairs Marian waited for Dart and Nora to come down into a good-sized kitchen with a red-tiled floor, a long wooden chopping block, glass-fronted cabinets, and a gas range. There was a teasing half smile on her face. "Which kind am I?"

"You fall into the best category of all. Combination of the other two."

"No wonder Lily enjoyed your tour." Smiling, Marian opened a cabinet, took down a plate and a glass, and opened the refrigerator. "Dinner is going to be one of our specials, so I'd better let that remain a surprise, but here's some roast beef. I could make you a sandwich with this whole-wheat bread. Sound good?"

"Yum yum. You got some mustard, mayo, maybe a couple slices of Swiss cheese to go with that?"

"I think so." She bent down to root around on a lower shelf, giving Dart a good view of her bottom.

"Any soup?"

She laughed and looked at Nora. "This man knows what he wants. Minestrone or gazpacho?"

"Minestrone. Gazpacho isn't soup."

Marian began pulling things out of the refrigerator.

Dart was wandering around and inspecting the kitchen. "Norma can give you a hand."

"Once an officer . . ." Nora said.

Marian told her where to find the can opener. Nora picked up a saucepan and poured the soup into it. After she had set the pan on the stove, she looked up to find Dart staring into her eyes. He glanced at her bag, which she had dropped on the counter, back at her, and then at a spot above the counter behind Marian's back. The handles of at least a dozen knives protruded from a wooden holder fastened to the wall. Dart smiled at her.

Marian took a bag of leftover lettuce from the refrigerator and dropped it on the counter. "Men are amazing," she said. "Where do they put it all?"

"Norman puts it in his hollow leg," Nora said. Standing

behind the other woman, she looked at the knife holder and shrugged. She could not steal a knife without Marian's noticing.

Nearly undressing Marian with a smile, Dart said, "Might some beer have found its way into the refrigerator?"

"That's a distinct possibility."

"Don't like invading strange refrigerators. Let's hunker down, survey the vintages."

Marian glanced at Nora, who was stirring the soup. She set down her knife and moved toward the refrigerator, where Dart beamed at her, rubbing his hands.

" *'Open thy vault most massy, most fearsome, Madame Ware,'* " Dart said, quoting something Nora did not recognize.

"I know that!" Marian cried. "It's from *Night Journey*, the part near the end where Pippin meets Madame Lyno-Wyno Ware. He has to talk that way because, um . . ."

"Because the Cup Bearer told him he had to, or she wouldn't tell the truth."

"Yes! And the vault disappoints him because it's only a metal box, but when she opens it up he sees that inside it's the size of his old house, and Madame Ware says . . . something about a book, the mind . . ." She snapped her fingers twice. "They're bigger on the inside."

" *'My vault, like a woman's heart or reticule, is larger within than without. Even a little pippin was once held within a seed.'* "

Nora had been backing away from the stove and was now nearly within reaching distance of the knife rack.

"Right! That's it!" Marian spun around and pointed a shapely, freckled finger at Nora. "See? I'm not completely ignorant about Hugo Driver. We can work together."

"Marian," Dart said, an impatient edge in his voice, "open the massy vault, will you?"

She turned her back on Nora and made an elaborate business of opening the refrigerator.

"Hunker, Marian. Can you hunker?"

"With the best of them." She squatted down before the crowded shelves knee to knee with Dart. "Behold the beer."

"I don't see any beer."

She leaned over to point, in the process brushing a breast against Dart's arm. "Are you a Corona kind of guy?" Marian asked.

Dart glanced at Nora over the top of the other woman's head, and she stepped back and lifted the first knife out of the holder.

"In weak moments." Dart looked at the hefty, workmanlike carving knife in Nora's hand, nodded minutely, and glanced again at the holder.

"What are your feelings about Budweiser?" She leaned into him more firmly.

"I think I like the looks of the one beside it."

Nora pulled a cleaver from the rack, and Dart's eyes crinkled. "Yes, that's a lovely shape. Pull it out, so I can get a good look at it."

Marian reached into the refrigerator, bringing herself into closer contact with Dart. "Grolsch does have a nice shape, doesn't it?"

Nora carried the knife and the cleaver to the counter. While Dart and Marian Cullinan admired different sorts of vessels, she opened her bag and slipped them inside. She moved over to stir the soup, and the other two stood up. Marian gave her an uncertain smile. Her face seemed a little flushed along the tops of her cheekbones.

Nora poured the soup into a bowl, and Marian found a soupspoon and a bottle opener in a drawer.

Dart raised the Grolsch bottle and took a long swallow.

Nora slid her bag off the counter and took it to a chair beneath a wall-mounted telephone.

"Don't hang back, darling spouse. Join the party."

Nora considered her bag. Dart still had his back to her. "Are you abandoning us?" Marian asked, smiling at Nora as she assembled beef, Swiss cheese, and lettuce on top of a slice of toast. Dart waved her forward, and she walked away from the fantasy of ramming a carving knife into his back.

Nora patted a spot beneath his left shoulder blade. "Are you happy now?"

Dart sang the first phrase of "Sometimes I'm Happy" and pushed away the empty bowl. "Bring on the meat."

"I didn't imagine you could actually quote Hugo Driver," Marian said to him.

Dart said something unintelligible through a mouthful of food, apparently quoting more of *Night Journey*.

"Don't get him started," Nora said.

"Could we get him to recite some of his poetry during dinner?"

Dart uttered a gleeful *"Ungk!"* around the sandwich. His eyes sparkled.

Forced to deal directly with Nora, Marian fell back on cliché. "What was your favorite part of the tour?"

"Can I ask you about the restorations?"

"That's practically an obsession with us. Lily must have told you about how hard we worked to put Honey House together. I could tell you lots of horror stories."

"I wasn't thinking so much of Honey House."

"Main House is a more interesting problem, I agree. As great as Georgina Weatherall was, she had been going downhill for some time before her death, and toward the end she pretty much retired into one room on the second floor. Which meant that the roof leaked in a hundred places, and there was water damage just about everywhere. As you probably saw when you came in, we're still having work done. The next big project is restoring the gardens, and that's a *huge* job."

"Are any of the former gardeners still around?"

"No. Georgina had to let everyone but Monty Chandler, the head gardener, go. You saw the Song Pillars and Monty's Glen?"

"We did."

"When you were up there, did you hear the stones singing?"

"They sing?" Nora asked.

"When there's any kind of a wind, you can hear them make this *music*. Eerie."

"I suppose Monty Chandler is dead."

"He passed away a couple of years before Georgina, which was another reason things got out of hand. Monty Chandler kept things in line by being a sort of handyman–carpenter–security force. There used to be problems with poachers and people breaking into the cottages, but Monty scared them all off. And when he wasn't overseeing the gardens, he was patching roofs and doing other repairs. That's why Georgina could get by for so long without bringing in workmen. I know she spent a lot of money fixing the place up when her father gave it to her, but she didn't have to do that again until the late thirties!"

"I understand she was having some money troubles then," said Nora.

Footsteps sounded on the metal staircase.

"Margaret and Lily are coming down to start dinner. We'd better do the second floor."

Heavy lace-up brown shoes topped with swollen ankles appeared on the stairs, followed by a long, capacious navy blue cotton dress buttoned up the front, then a wide arm, and finally an executive face, broad in the cheeks and forehead, and gray hair clamped into place with a tightly wound scarf, also navy blue. Margaret Nolan reached the bottom of the stairs and stopped, her hand on the railing, taking them in with an alert curiosity which did not completely disguise her mild irritation. Lily Melville smiled at Dart from over her shoulder.

"Our special guests have an interest in the kitchen, Marian?"

"One of them had a special interest in a snack," Marian said.

Margaret inspected Dart with a level glance. "Looking at Mr. Desmond, I don't suppose it will affect his performance at dinner." She pushed herself away from the stairs and came puffing toward them.

"Margaret Nolan." She extended a wide, firm hand to Dart. "I run this madhouse. We are delighted to have your company, Mr. Desmond, though I must confess that I've never read your work. Marian tells me that it's very exciting."

Dart said, "We do what we can, we can do no more."

Margaret turned to Nora with the air of having chosen to ignore this remark. Her handshake was quick and dry. "Mrs. Desmond. Welcome to Shorelands. Are you happy with Pepper Pot?"

"It's great," Nora said.

"I'm pleased to hear it. But now, if we are to meet our schedule, we must begin. You'll forgive us, I hope?"

"Certainly," Nora said. Here before her, five feet, eight inches tall, weighing one hundred and eighty pounds, chronically short of breath, radiating decisiveness, common sense, and strength of character, was her answer. This woman would take in Nora's situation and figure out a way to resolve it in three seconds flat. She would need half as much explanation as Frank Neary, and a tenth as much as Marian Cullinan. But when could she get her aside? After dinner she would volunteer to carry the plates down to the kitchen—something, anything—to be alone with Margaret Nolan and whisper, *He's Dick Dart. Call the police.*

"All right, then." Margaret smiled as briskly as she had shaken Nora's hand. "Lily?"

Lily trotted to the side of the kitchen to take two white aprons from a hook on the far side of the wall telephone, and paused at the chair on the way back. "Isn't this your bag, Mrs. Desmond?"

"Oh, it is, I'm sorry." Nora took a step toward Lily and the chair, but Margaret stopped her with a touch. "Bring it to her, Lily."

Lily picked up the bag. "What do you have in here, brass knuckles?"

"I never go anywhere without my weapons collection," Nora said.

Marian said, "We should go upstairs and let them work their wonders."

"Where *is* that carving knife?" Margaret asked. "It couldn't have just walked away."

"I'm so curious," Dart said. "What treat are you two wonderful ladies going to whip up?"

Looking at Dart as if she were a second-grade teacher faced with an impertinent student, Margaret turned from the rack and put on her apron. "We are going to prepare one of Ezra Pound's favorite meals."

"Georgina liked Ezra, didn't she?"

"She did."

"Real-world politics," Dart said. "None of that guff about equality our leaders spout while they plunder the till. I'm on their side. Let's call a jackboot a jackboot, okay?"

Both Lily and Margaret were staring at him. Dart held up a hand. "Hey. What was good enough for Ez is good enough for me." Smiling at the two women frozen behind the chopping block, he pulled Nora toward the stairs.

91

Marian closed the door with a bang. "Norman, don't you understand that I could lose my *job*?"

"Solemn promise," Dart said. "By the time we finish dessert, they'll be begging me to come back."

"But you practically called Georgina Weatherall a Nazi!"

"Wasn't the old girl a tad gone on the majesty of the Fatherland? Doesn't make her a bad person."

Marian shook her head and checked to make sure that no one could overhear their conversation. "Norman, you can't go around saying these things in front of Margaret."

"Try to stop him," Nora said.

"I understand," Dart said. "Divine handmaiden to the diviner arts. Natural aristocrat. *My* problem is, I can't stand women like that."

Marian calmed down enough to say, "We don't admit it very often, but I'm sure Georgina Weatherall could be hard to deal with."

"Not her, Madame Director," Dart said. "Women like that might as well grow beards and smoke cigars. Nonetheless, I promise you a tremendously entertaining evening." He touched a finger to her chin. "I want you to have a glorious time. Still depending on you to drop in for that nightcap."

"This man," Marian said. "You can't stay angry with him."

Portraits lined the broad staircase. "This one used to hang in Georgina's bedroom." Marian was pointing at an oil painting of an elderly man in a business suit coiled in a leather chair. He had a tight, fanatical face dominated by a heavy nose and a protruding chin. "George Weatherall."

"'My Heart Belongs to Daddy.'"

439

Marian smiled at him from the top of the stairs, then conducted them down a hallway darker and narrower than the one below. Despite the framed book jackets and photographs of Main House in various stages of restoration on the walls, the second floor was more utilitarian and domestic than the first. They had moved from the public life into the private.

Nora asked, "Why don't you let people into her bedroom?"

"Wait'll you see it. That's not the way we want people to remember Shorelands."

"I thought you were after historical accuracy."

"*Accurate* accuracy is too raw for the public. The longer I stay in this job, the more I wonder if there is any such thing as historical accuracy. But I can't say that's very helpful when you have a painting contractor standing in front of you who wants to know right now what exact shade of purple to put on the wall."

"I thought Lily said that you were given a lot of the original paint. How could there be a problem with the shade?" Nora asked.

"We did have the original paint, but only about half the amount we needed, and it had turned into glue. The whole thing was a nightmare. In the end, we mixed whatever we could salvage in with new paint."

"How did you know what shade it was supposed to be?"

"From Georgina's room."

"The paint you got for Honey House was actually the kind used in Main House?"

"Nobody really knows what kind of paint was used in the cottages." Marian gestured at the doors lining the hallway. "The two rooms on the left are Margaret's bedroom and office, and she'd rather not have us go in there. In the old days, Georgina Weatherall kept this entire floor for her personal use. Emma Brotherhood, Agnes's sister, her personal maid, lived in this first room. The second was a wardrobe and changing room, and it's connected to the bathroom, the third door along, directly across from Georgina's bedroom. Next to that was the morning room, where Georgina wrote her letters and planned the menus. These days, that's where we store all the donations we can't use."

Marian smiled at Dart. "Anyhow, behind the door on the other side of the stairs is the staircase to the third floor. I have the two rooms immediately across the hall at the top of the stairs, and Lily has the two rooms next to me. Margaret's secretary, who's on her vacation this week, has the room next to Lily's. All the other rooms up there are empty. This room on the right, which we use for meetings, was where Georgina met special guests." She opened the door to a small, efficient chamber dominated by a boardroom table. "This was where Miss Weatherall would complain, gossip, get recommendations about new writers. And in here, people like Lily and Agnes could pass along anything she ought to know."

"KGB," Dart said. "Ears at the keyhole."

"We had a thief here once, you know."

"You surprise me," Nora said.

"A young woman took off with a valuable drawing just before she was to be asked to leave. Can you imagine? It was worth a fortune. By Rembrandt, or maybe Rubens, I don't remember."

"Neither one," Nora said. "It was by an artist named Redon."

"Somebody with an R name, anyhow," Marian said. "Georgina's bedroom is next. During the last two years of her life, she almost never left it. It's cleaned and dusted twice a week, but we never go in there ourselves. Personally, I think it's a little creepy."

She ushered them into a dark space where dull glints of glass and metal and a sense of hovering presences suggested a spectacular jumble of objects. "Georgina never opened her curtains, so we keep them closed. I always have a little trouble finding the light, because the switch is in back of . . . Here we go."

Layer after layer, the room emerged into view. In delirious profusion, silks, faded tapestries, worn Oriental rugs, and swags of lace dripped from the top of the canopied bed and over the backs of chairs, and hung on the crowded walls, folding behind and draping over a riot of ornate clocks, mirrors, framed drawings, and photographs of a woman whose face, a replica of her father's, had been softened by enthusiastic makeup and a surround of shapeless dark hair. An impressively ugly Victorian desk lay buried beneath a drift of papers lapping against porcelain animals and glass inkwells. A gramophone with a bell-like horn stood on an ormolu table. Other small tables draped with lace held stacks of books, silver-backed hairbrushes, and much else.

The room reminded Nora of a more chaotic Honey House. A

second later, she realized that she had it backwards: Honey
House was a more presentable version of this room. As her eyes
adjusted to the clutter, she began to take in the real condition of
Georgina's bedroom. Ancient water stains had leached the
purple to blotchy pink. The fabrics strewn over the furniture
were ripped and discolored, and the lace canopy hung in tatters.
Stains mottled the white ceiling. Beside the bed, in front of an
anachronistic metal safe with a revolving dial, brown threads
showed through the pattern of the rug.

"I'd better see if Agnes is up to company," Marian said, and
disappeared.

Here was the real Shorelands, the one room in all of the estate
where real history was still visible. Concealed at the center of
the house, it was a shameful secret too important to erase.
Georgina Weatherall, whose greatest advantages had been
wealth, vanity, and illusion, had risen day after day to admire
herself in her mirrors, brushed her hair without ever managing
to push it into shape, painted on layers of makeup until the mirrors told her that she was as commanding as a queen in a fairy
tale. If she noticed a flaw, she submerged it beneath rouge and
kohl, just as she buried the stains on her walls and the rents in
her lace beneath layers of fabric.

Monty Chandler had never entered this room to repair the
water damage: no one but Georgina and her maid had been
allowed here. The maid had loved Georgina, who had so
demanded love that she had seen it in people who mocked her.
This monolithic ruthlessness was what was meant by a romantic
conception of oneself.

Nora could almost respect Georgina Weatherall. Georgina
had been sick with self-importance, and if Nora had met her at
a party, she would have fled from the airless closet such people
always create around themselves. But Georgina Weatherall had
worked heroically in the service of her illusions. In her, perhaps
for the first time in his life, Lincoln Chancel had met his match.

Marian opened the door and said, "Wonder of wonders, you
could have a word with Agnes now, if you like."

92

"SHE REALLY IS SICK, I know, but boredom makes her cranky, and when Agnes gets cranky she lays it on a little too thick. I can't promise you more than a couple of minutes." Marian paused. "A couple of minutes will probably be enough."

An irritated voice came through the door. *"Are you talking about me?"*

"Why don't you let us see her alone?" Nora said. "I know you have work to do."

"I shouldn't." Marian looked up and down the hallway. "You might need help getting away."

"We'll manage."

"Maybe just this once. Margaret doesn't . . ." She bit her lower lip.

Margaret doesn't want strangers left alone with Agnes?

"Margaret doesn't have to know."

"All right. If I can get my work done, I'll be able to come up for that nightcap." She knocked once and opened the door. "Here they are, Agnes. I'll look in on you later."

"Bring me some magazines. You know what I like."

Marian moved back, and Nora and Dart stepped into the doorway.

The old woman lying in the bed was about as thick around as a kitchen match. The straight hair, dyed black, falling from a center part on either side of her shrunken face, looked like a doll's wig. Her eyes were bright, lively, and suspicious. She had inserted one twiglike finger into the book in her lap, as if she had to see who these people were before deciding how much time to give them.

Marian introduced them and left.

"Come in, close the door."

They walked up to the bed.

"I'm surprised she left. You'd think I was a mad dog, the way they carry on." She examined Dart. "You're this fellow who's supposed to be a poet? Norman Desmond?"

"And you're the historical monument, Agnes Brotherhood."

She gave him a close inspection. "You don't look much like a poet."

"What *do* I look like?"

"Like a lawyer who spends a lot of time in bars. Should I know your name?"

"I wouldn't go that far," Dart said. He was enjoying himself.

"Don't pretend to be modest. You don't have a modest bone in your body." Agnes turned her eyes on Nora. "Does he?"

"Not a one," Nora said.

"Marian wouldn't be wasting her time on you if you were a nobody. Have you published a lot of books?"

"Alas, no."

"Who's your publisher?"

"Chancel House."

Agnes Brotherhood waved a hand in front of her face as if to banish a bad smell. "You'd leave them in a hurry if you'd ever had the misfortune of meeting the founder."

"In a class by himself," Dart said. "Villainy personified."

"You might as well stay a while. Move those chairs up to the bed." She nodded at two folding chairs against the wall and slipped a card into her book, the Modern Library edition of Thoreau.

Agnes noticed Nora's interest. "I reread *Walden* once a year. Do you like *Walden*, Mr. Desmond?"

Dart lifted his chin and recited, " *'When I wrote the following pages, or rather the bulk of them, I lived alone, in the woods, a mile from any neighbor, in a house which I had built myself,'* so on and so forth. Does that answer your question?"

"Let's hear the rest of the sentence."

". . . *'on the shore of Walden Pond, in Concord, Massachusetts, and earned my living by the labor of my hands only.'* "

"Not quite the truth, I believe, but lovely all the same. Now what would you like me to talk about? The great hostess and her noble guests? What D. H. Lawrence ate for breakfast? That kind of thing?"

Dart glanced at Nora. "You're not as reverent about the great hostess as Lily Melville, are you?"

"I knew her too well," Agnes snapped. "I had a job, and I did it. Lily had a *cause,* the adoration of Georgina Weatherall. I used to laugh at her sometimes, and she didn't like it one bit."

"You used to laugh at Georgina?"

"At Lily. Nobody laughed at Georgina Weatherall. She had her qualities, but a sense of humor wasn't one of them. If you were going to make fun of Miss Weatherall, you had to do it behind her back, and a lot of them did, but that isn't something you're going to hear about these days. Were you on Lily's tour?"

Nora said they had been.

"Tour of the shrine, that's what you get with Lily. When the mistress got sick and she was let go, she went around being the Shorelands expert in front of all these groups." She laughed. "It's a lot more fun meeting people without Freckle Face listening in. She used to interrogate people from my groups to see if I'd said anything I shouldn't. Hah! As if I didn't know my job. I know more than they like, that's what bothers them. I know things they don't know."

"Reason they keep you around," Dart said.

Agnes frowned at him. "I devoted my life to Shorelands. They know that much." She nodded at a pitcher and a glass on the window ledge. "Could you get me a glass of water? I keep asking them to get me a table on wheels, like in hospitals, but do I get one? Not yet, and it's been days."

"Would you mind if I asked what's wrong with you?" Dart said. "Do you have an illness?"

"My illness is called old age," Agnes said. "Plus a few other disorders."

Dart peered into the pitcher. "Empty."

"Take it into the bathroom and fill it up, please?"

"Well . . ." Dart drawled. "Can I do that, honey? Dare I leave you alone? Hate to miss anything."

"I'll fill you in," Nora said.

Dart shook a warning finger at Nora and carried the pitcher from the room.

Agnes fixed Nora with bright, suspicious eyes. When Dart's footsteps had crossed the hall, Nora leaned toward her. "Do you have a telephone?"

Agnes shook her head.

"Have you ever heard of a man named Dick Dart?"

Agnes shook her head again. Across the hall, water splashed noisily into a container.

"Can you get to a phone?"

"There's three or four in the director's office."

"As soon as we leave, go to the office and call the police." The water cut off. "Say that Dick Dart is having dinner at Shorelands. Agnes, this is extremely important, it's life and death." Footsteps left the bathroom. "Please."

Dart surged into the room, and water splashed out of the pitcher. "Filled to overflowing. What have we been talking about, my dears?"

"My health," Agnes said. "Present and future." She turned her puzzled, now decidedly alarmed, gaze to him.

"What *are* your health problems, sweetheart?" He poured several inches of water into her glass. "Dehydration?" She reached for the glass and he pulled it back, laughed, and allowed her to take it. "Little joke."

"Arrhythmia. Sounds worse than it is." She took two swallows and handed him the glass. "Put it on the floor beside my bed. I'm going to be back on my feet in a couple of days. I can still lead a tour as well as Lily Melville."

"Of course you can, lots better than that old fool," Dart said. He sat down, crossed his legs, and patted Nora on the back. "Did you miss me, my sweetie?"

"Horribly," Nora said.

Agnes was staring at him as if she were trying to memorize his face. "What are the names of your books, Mr. Desmond?"

He looked, smiling, toward the ceiling. "The first one was called *Counting the Bodies*. *Surgical Notes* was the name of the second."

Her hands twitched. "What are you especially interested in, Mrs. Desmond? You don't want to waste time listening to me complain."

"The summer of 1938." Agnes held herself utterly still. "I'm interested in whatever happened that summer, but especially in a poet named Katherine Mannheim."

The old woman was staring at her with even more concentration than she had given Dart. Nora could not tell what she was thinking or feeling.

"I'm also interested in the renovation that happened the year after that."

"Who are you? What do you want?" Her voice trembled.

"I'm just an interested party."

"What is this about?" Agnes looked back and forth between Dart and Nora.

"History," Dart said. "Flashlight into the past. What Honey House is supposed to be." He grinned. "'Fess up now, did it ever look like that antique shop we saw today?"

Agnes was silent for a time. "I went in and out of the cottages every day of my life, and the only one that ever had what you could call a lot of *stuff* in it was Mr. Lincoln Chancel's Rapunzel, and he put all of it in there himself. If our guest-houses had been like that, some of these noble individuals would have waltzed off with whatever they could stuff into their suitcases. The trust people, they don't care, as long as it looks pretty."

She turned her gaze to Nora. "By and large, this was a fine, decent place. I won't say otherwise. And the things I think, I'm not going to say to any policeman, that's for sure."

"We mentioned policemen?" Dart asked.

"Not at all." Nora tried to communicate silently with Agnes and saw only anxiety in her eyes.

"I don't understand what's going on," Agnes wailed.

Nora leaned forward. "All I want to talk to you about is that summer. That's all. Okay?" She saw a looming panic. "What-ever you have to do afterwards is fine. You can do whatever you want." She waited a beat, and Dart turned his entire body in her direction. "Call down and talk to Margaret. Call anyone you like. Do you understand?"

The dark eyes seemed to lose some of their confusion. "Yes. But I don't know what to say."

Nora remembered her conversation with Helen Day. "I know this is difficult for you. Let me tell you what I think. I think you don't want to be disloyal, but at the same time you've been keeping something secret. It isn't pretty, and people like Marian Cullinan and Margaret Nolan wouldn't want it to come out. But they don't even know about it, do they?"

"They're too new," Agnes said, looking at her in mingled wonder and suspicion.

"Lily knows part of it, but not as much as you do, isn't that right?"

Agnes nodded.

"And here come two people you never saw before. I think part of you wants to get this thing off your chest, but you don't see why you should tell it to *us*. I'd feel the same way. But I'm interested in what happened that year, and almost no one else is. I'm not a cop or a reporter, and I'm not writing a book."

Agnes glared at Dart.

"He doesn't care what happened to Katherine Mannheim," Nora said.

To indicate his indifference to the disappearances of female poets, Dart faked a yawn.

"I might be the only person you'll ever meet interested enough in this to talk to people who knew Bill Tidy and Creeley Monk."

"Those poor men," Agnes said. "Mr. Tidy was a good, honest soul, and Mr. Monk, I liked him, too, because he could make you laugh like anything. Didn't matter to me if he was a . . ."

"A wagtail?" Dart said. "A prancer? A tiptoe boy?"

Agnes gave him a disdainful glance. "There's a lot of ways to be a good person." She returned to Nora. "Those two didn't know anything. They were here, that's all. Even if they heard anything, they wouldn't have thought twice about it."

Nora remembered something Everett Tidy had told her. "On the night Katherine Mannheim disappeared, Bill Tidy thought he heard poachers."

Agnes shook her head. "Wasn't a poacher in a hundred miles who'd risk his hide at Shorelands, not in those days. Monty Chandler gave one a load of bird shot and caught another in a mantrap, let him starve for two days, and that was it for poachers."

"So he heard something else."

Agnes pulled her robe closer to her neck. "Guess he did."

Almost against her will, Nora pushed forward. "I have some ideas. What if I tell you about them, and you tell me if I'm right?"

Agnes squinted at her and nodded once. "I could do that." She took in a great breath and pushed it out. "After all this time . . ." She began again. "That girl had a little sister. Kept her picture on her desk. The sister came here. Fine young lady. If she's still alive, she deserves to know the truth." She gave a flickering, almost frightened glance at Nora.

Nora tried to look as if she knew what she was doing. "I don't think Katherine Mannheim ran away from Shorelands. I think she died. Is that right?"

"Yes." Agnes's upper lip began to tremble.

"I think Hugo Driver had something to do with her death. Am I right?"

"What do you mean?"

"Didn't she come into Gingerbread and find Driver looking through her papers? Wasn't there a struggle?"

"No! That's all *wrong*." Agnes's chin began to tremble.

Nora's impersonation of confident authority began to evaporate. Her favorite theory had just been destroyed. "She died that night. Her body had to be hidden."

A tear slipped from Agnes's right eye.

"She's buried somewhere on the estate."

Agnes nodded.

"And you know where."

"No, I don't. I'm *glad* I don't." She glanced at Nora. "I have to do tours, you see. Couldn't go where they put her."

"Hugo Driver and Lincoln Chancel."

"Did everything together, those two."

"That's why you still hate Lincoln Chancel."

Agnes shook her head with surprising vehemence. "I hated Mr. Chancel from the beginning. That man thought he had a right to touch you. Thought he could do anything he wanted and then make it all right with money."

"He offered you money?"

"I told him he was trying his dirty tricks with the wrong girl. He laughed at me, but he kept his hands to himself after that."

As interesting as this digression was, Nora wanted to get back to the main subject. She tried another approach. "Georgina knew that Katherine Mannheim hadn't just disappeared, didn't she? When she led everyone up to Gingerbread after dinner the next night, she already knew that the girl was dead."

"I hate to say it, but she did."

"She knew the door was unlocked even before she opened it."

"I wasn't there," Agnes said miserably. "But Miss Weatherall knew."

"How did you know her door was unlocked? Did you tend to Gingerbread?"

She nodded. "When I went to do the cleaning that morning, the door was unlocked and she wasn't inside. I hoped she was probably out in the gardens. At noon I put her box lunch in front of her door, because that was what we did, and it was still there the next morning."

"You didn't know that she was never going to come back."

"How could I? The mistress told me she'd run away. 'Climbed the wall,' she said. Made me feel funny. Especially after . . . after what happened."

A hint of understanding came to Nora. The reason that Georgina Weatherall had known her troublesome guest was gone before she opened the door to Gingerbread was directly in front of her, becoming more troubled with every second. "Did you say something to her, Agnes? Did you see something that disturbed you and tell Georgina about it?"

"I wish I never had." She held herself stiffly for a moment, and then another bolt of emotion went through her, and she began to cry.

Perfectly at ease, Dart twisted his mouth into a smile.

Nora tried to work out what Agnes had seen and remembered that Creeley Monk had seen Driver and Lincoln Chancel on the grounds late that night. "Tell me if I'm right. Did you take walks at night?" Agnes glanced fearfully at her, then nodded. "The night Katherine Mannheim died, you took one of your walks. You went up the path toward Gingerbread." Agnes lifted her head and gave her another frightened glance. "Were they carrying her body? Is that what you saw?"

"*No! No!*" She covered her eyes with her hands. "Then I would have known right away, don't you see? I saw . . . you have to tell *me*."

"You saw them."

Agnes shook her head.

"You saw Hugo Driver."

Agnes looked at her in furious disappointment. "No!"

"Lincoln Chancel," Nora said. A great deal of what was as yet unspoken fell into place. "You saw Lincoln Chancel leaving Gingerbread. My God, Lincoln Chancel killed her."

Dick Dart took his hands from behind his head and leaned forward, malicious delight alive in his face.

Nora said, "He was going back to Rapunzel to get Driver. I'm right, aren't I, Agnes? You saw him going through the woods, but you didn't know why."

Agnes forced herself to take a deep breath. "He was *running*. I couldn't tell what the noise was. I thought it was some animal. I was by the big boulder up on the path. We used to have bears in our woods back then, and sometimes we still do. I hid behind the boulder, and the noise got closer and closer. Then I heard a man swearing. I knew it was Mr. Chancel. I peeked out. Here he comes out of the path, racing like a crazy man up toward Rapunzel. He went over the bridge, *bang! bang! bang!* I was so *afraid*. I wished it was a bear! I should have . . ." She drew up her knees and buried her face in the covers.

Nora moved onto the bed and embraced her.

"Female bonding," Dart said.

"You thought you should have gone to the cottage," Nora said. Agnes sighed in her arms. "But you were afraid. You were right to be afraid. They might have caught you."

"I *know*." Agnes leaned into Nora's chest and took another deep breath. "I started back to Main House, and then I decided I had to look in on Miss Mannheim after all, but I heard Mr. Chancel and Mr. Driver coming down from Rapunzel, so I stayed behind the boulder. They came over the bridge, clump clump clump, and went up the Gingerbread path."

She pulled away from Nora and patted her face with the bed-covers. "You can sit down again."

"Are you sure?" Agnes shrank from another attempt at an embrace, and as Nora got off the bed, she collapsed onto her pillow. "I went flying back to Main House. I got upstairs, and the mistress was standing in the hallway. What's going on, Agnes, she says, why are you running around in the middle of the night, I demand an explanation. I told her. She says, Agnes Brotherhood, you leave this to me. She slapped on her big red hat and out she went. The mistress loved that big red hat, but it was the silliest thing you ever saw." Agnes glowered at the ceiling.

"You waited for her to come back," Nora said.

"Waited and waited. After a long time she looks around my door and says, Agnes, Miss Mannheim is one of those women who require male companionship when their spirits are low.

Mr. Chancel chose to protect himself from scandal. Put the entire matter out of your mind, she says."

"And you tried to do that."

Agnes gave an unhappy nod. "I asked if Miss Mannheim was all right, and she said to me, Women like that are always all right." Dart grunted in approval. Agnes scowled at him. "I'm not saying there aren't women like that, but Miss Mannheim was a fine person."

"The next day you must have thought that she'd run away."

"I thought she *left*. There's a big difference between running away and leaving. Miss Mannheim wouldn't have run away from anything."

Agnes tugged her robe around her and looked at Nora with frustrated defiance. She had told her story, but at the center of the story was a vacuum.

A knock at the door cut off whatever she might have said next. Marian Cullinan peeked in. "We must be having a wonderful time, you've been in here so long."

"High point of the tour," Dart said. "Fantastic tales of the good old days."

"*Wonderful.*" She approached the bed.

Nora looked at Agnes to see if she remembered what she had been asked to do, and the old woman dipped her head a fraction of an inch.

Marian stepped between them. "Agnes, you know the rules. I bet your blood pressure is through the roof."

"I want to say something to Mrs. Desmond, Marian."

"One little teeny-tiny thing, and then I have to take these nice people away."

Agnes reached for Nora's hand. "You have to hear the rest."

Marian laughed. "You want to tell these people your life story, Agnes? Mrs. Desmond will stop in again, I'm sure."

"Tonight," Agnes said, clutching Nora's hand.

Marian displayed a trace of impatience. "That won't be possible, Agnes. We have to protect your health."

Agnes dropped Nora's hand. "You're not my doctor."

"Well, on that note." Marian smiled at Nora. "Shall we?"

She bustled them out with a complicitous glance at Dart and a pained smile for Nora. "I hope that wasn't too awful."

"You kidding?" Dart said. "That was better than *Psycho.*"

Shaking her head, she took them toward the staircase. "I

don't know how we're going to tell her that she can't lead any more tours. I mean, look at her, would you want to follow Agnes around the estate?"

A door clicked open behind them.

"Now what?" Marian said.

Clutching her bathrobe about her, Agnes hobbled out of her bedroom.

Marian put her hands on her hips. "I see it, but I don't believe it."

"Last roundup," Dart said.

Marian hurried up to the old woman and whispered to her. Agnes tottered forward another step. Roughly, Marian turned her around and marched her back to her room. Agnes shot Nora a look of bleak humiliation. A few seconds later, Marian came out and locked the door.

"Honestly. I've had my difficulties with Agnes, but I never had to lock her in her room before. She said she had to go to the office, can you imagine?"

"It can't really be necessary to lock her up," Nora said. "What if she has to go to the bathroom?"

"She can hold it until she gets her dinner. Margaret's already in a fine old state, thanks to Norman and his jackboots. By the time dinner is over, I'm going to need that nightcap." Marian took them to the staircase. "I'm not sure what to suggest. Ordinarily you'd want to go back to Pepper Pot or walk around Lenox, but it looks like we're building up to a rainstorm, and when that happens our paths turn into mudslides. Let's go down and see what it's doing outside."

A gust of wind slammed against the building. Somewhere beneath them, windows rattled in their frames. "As we speak," Marian said. Rain struck the front of the house like buckshot, fell away for a second, and then came back in a stronger, continuous wave.

The lights had been turned on in the lounge. The windows showed a dark sky sheeting down rain onto a sodden lawn. "At least the last tour ended before we had a lot of would-be lawyers demanding their money back." In the distance, trees bent before the wind. "It's a wild one." She turned to Dart. "What do you want to do? We have umbrellas, but they wouldn't last a second out there. You could make a run for

Pepper Pot if it dies down, but you'd be covered with mud by the time you got there."

"Screw that," Dart said. "I hate getting wet. Mud drives me up the wall."

Beyond the splashing lawn, the trees threw up their arms. "It looks like you're stuck here until the end of dinner. We might be able to scrounge some boots for you, Norma, but Norman, what do we do about you?" Marian rubbed her forehead. "I'll get Tony to bring up a slicker and a pair of boots after dinner. Norma can use a raincoat of mine. And don't worry if the lights go out. We have lots of candles. Besides, our power company may be run by a bunch of hicks, but they always get the lights back on about an hour after the storms end. I promised you a special dinner, and that's what you're going to get."

"Goody."

"What would you like to do? I have to get some more work done in my office, and then I have to help in the kitchen, so you'll be more or less on your own."

"I'd like to talk to Agnes some more," Nora said.

"We'll have to save that for another day." Three short dashes bracketed by outturned parentheses appeared in the middle of Marian's forehead, then melted away. "Weren't you interested in Georgina's papers?"

"I'd love to see them." The records were bound to be in the office on the second floor, and Dart had to go to the bathroom sometime.

"Can a thirsty man get a drink around here?" Dart asked.

"Absolutely," Marian said. "Come with me and I'll set you both up."

Tossing back her hair, she took them into the main corridor, went down the marble steps, and looked back up at Nora. "Don't you want to see the records?"

"Aren't they upstairs?" Nora asked.

"They were, but after a couple of writers invaded Margaret's office, we moved everything into the little room my secretary used to have, when I *had* a secretary."

Marian led them to a windowless cubicle fitted with a desk, a schoolroom chair, and metal shelves half-filled with bound ledgers, files of correspondence, and boxes marked PHOTO-GRAPHS. "Norman, I'll be right back with your drink. Vodka, is that right? On the rocks?"

"Drink to build a dream on."

If there had ever been a telephone in the cubicle, it had vanished along with Marian's secretary.

93

TEN MINUTES LATER, Dart repeated the first thing he had said after Marian had left them. He was leaning back in the chair with his feet up on a shelf, stirring the ice cubes in what was left of his drink with a finger. "That story was even worse than Jane Austen's garbage."

Nora closed one ledger and took another from the pile in front of her. Throughout the twenties and early thirties Georgina had spent a great deal of money on champagne acquired through a bootlegger named Selden, who after the repeal of the Volstead Act in 1933 had apparently opened a liquor store. Models of order in one regard, the ledgers were chaotic in most others. In a hand which degenerated over the years from a Gothic upright to a barbed-wire scribble, Georgina had recorded every dollar which had entered and left Shorelands, but she'd made no distinctions between personal expenses and those of the estate. A five-dollar outlay for a new fountain pen appeared beneath one for three hundred dollars' worth of Dutch tulip bulbs. Nor had she been rigid as to dates.

"Maybe Agnes saw Chancel running down the path. Maybe she made the whole thing up one night after nipping too much amontillado, but *we'll* never know. You know why? Shorelands is the Roach Motel for reality. The truth goes in, but it never comes out, and the reason for that is Georgina. Do you think Georgina Weatherall was ever capable, even way back in the days before she swapped sherry for liquid morphine, of giving you an accurate account of what took place on any given day?"

"Judging by the state of her records, not really."

"Those novelists must have felt right at home. This whole place is fiction." He laughed out loud, delighted by his own cleverness. "Even the name is a lie. It's called Shorelands, but it isn't on any shore. Old George thought she was beautiful and grand and universally adored, but the truth is, she was a horse-faced joke in circus clothes who got people to show up by giving them free room and board. Having famous writers suck up to her made her feel important. She couldn't stand reality, so she went around pretending the run-down shacks her servants used to live in were 'cottages.' She handed out these fancy names. 'I dub thee Gingerbread, I dub thee Rapunzel, and while I'm at it, I think I'll dub that mangy swamp up there the Mist Field.' What does that tell you? Pretty soon a little girl with an apron is going to show up trotting after a rabbit on its way to a tea party."

"I think I'm the little girl," Nora said.

"There you are. Why should Agnes be any different? She spent her whole life in this illusion factory. She has no idea what really happened to that girl."

"I think she does," Nora said, "and something you said a little while ago gave me an idea."

Dart looked pleased with himself again. "I don't believe it for a second, but how did she find out?"

"Georgina told her what happened to Katherine."

"That makes a lot of sense. The great lady tells a servant that she helped conceal a murder? If it *was* a murder, which I also doubt."

"You heard Agnes."

"Agnes is stuck in bed while her archrival, Lily Melville, is bouncing around handing out lies to tourists. She's alone up in that room with Henry David Thoreau, and she thinks he's a liar, too."

"They do need a little more reality around here," Nora said.

"About eleven or twelve tonight, they'll get more than they can handle. In the meantime, find anything in those books?"

"Not yet." She took another ledger from the pile. The entries began in June of an unspecified year with the receipt of a five-hundred-dollar check from G.W., presumably Georgina's father, and the expenditure of $45.80 for gardening supplies. The next entry was *18 June, $75—, Selden Liq., Veuve Clicquot,* so the ledger had been filled sometime after 1933. The handwriting had only just begun its deterioration.

"What a diligent little person you are, Nora-pie." He lounged

over to the shelves and pulled down a box marked PHOTO-
GRAPHS. Nora flipped pages of the ledger, and Dart began
sifting through the box. She worked her way through another
three or four pages without finding mention of any sum larger
than a few thousand dollars. "Agnes wasn't bad-looking way
back then," Dart said. "No wonder Chancel groped her."

He handed her a small black-and-white photograph, and she
looked at the pleasant face of the young Agnes Brotherhood,
whose prominent breasts plumped out the front of her black uniform. Undoubtedly the maid had been forced to swat away any
number of male paws. She passed the photograph back to Dart,
and the instant he took it from her, she knew how Katherine
Mannheim had died. She had known all along without knowing:
her own life gave her the answer.

Shaken, she turned a few pages at random, scarcely taking in
the cryptic entries. A case of gin and two bottles of vermouth
from the liquor store owned by Georgina's former bootlegger.
*Meds., $28.95. Disc, $55.65. Whl.Mt., $2.00. Mann & Ware,
phtgrs., $65.*

"Hold on," Nora said. "Did professional photographers take
any of those pictures?"

"Sure. The big group photos."

Dart rooted through the box and handed her an eight-by-
twelve photograph of the usual group of men in suits and neck-
ties surrounding a regal Georgina. Stamped on the back was the
legend "*Patrick Mann & Lyman Ware, Fine Portraiture, Mann-
Ware Studios, 26 Main St., Lenox, Massachusetts.*"

Patrick Mann, Paddy Mann, Paddi Mann.

Lyman Ware, Madame Lyno-Wyno Ware, Lena Ware.

Shorelands, *Night Journey*, Davey Chancel.

Two photographers who took the group portrait every year,
two fictional characters, a troubled Driver fanatic who had pursued Davey.

"A little bee is buzzing around up there."

She handed the photograph back to him. A girl named
Patricia Mann, Patty Mann, had immersed herself in the Driver
world and become first Lena Ware, then Paddi Mann. Part
of her entry into the world of lunatic Driver fans had been
the coincidence of her name resembling that of a Lenox
photographer.

Then it came home to Nora that Paddi Mann had been

Katherine Mannheim's niece: family rumor had pushed her even deeper into the Driver world. She had been convinced that her father's unconventional sister had written her sacred book and had twice tried to rescue her aunt from oblivion. She had even dressed like Katherine Mannheim.

Nora riffled the pages of the ledger, and a name and a number seemed to leap up toward her. *Rec'vd L. Chancel: $50,000.* "Lincoln Chancel gave her fifty thousand dollars."

Dart ambled over to look at the entry. "Isn't even a date there. It sure as hell doesn't prove she blackmailed him. Nobody could blackmail that old bastard."

Nora turned another few pages. "Here are the renovations. Look, five hundred dollars to a roofer, two hundred to a painter. About a week later, the same painter gets another two hundred. Fifteen hundred to a building contractor. Six hundred to B. Smithson, electrician. The painter again. Then down here at the bottom of the page, the contractor is getting another thousand. It goes on and on."

"The old scorpion guzzled a lot of the widow, didn't she?"

"The widow?"

"The widow Clicquot, you ignoramus. All right, he gave her a lot of money, and she used it to spruce up the place. Chancel was greedy, but he sure as hell wasn't a miser. Made a lot of money and threw half of it away. 'Georgina, you old ratbag, here's fifty thou, whip those hovels into shape, and get yourself a couple cases of the widow while you're at it.' That's what happened."

"Lincoln Chancel voluntarily gave fifty thousand dollars to a woman he probably despised? At a time when fifty thousand was about three or four hundred thousand in today's money?"

"The man was hardly petty. Besides, he had two other reasons for being generous to Georgina. He wanted to enlist her in his movement, and he met Driver because of her. I bet he had some idea of how much he was going to make out of *Night Journey.* Fifty thousand was chump change."

Nora smiled at him. "You don't want to think that your hero could have been blackmailed."

"The man *was* a hero," Dart said. "The more you learn about the guy, the better he gets. Anyone tried to blackmail him, he'd start up the chain saw. Trust me."

Dart adored monsters because he was one himself, but about

this he was right: it would not have been easy to extort money out of Lincoln Chancel. Someone knocked at the door.

"Refill," Dart said. "Love that woman."

Marian Cullinan peeped inside. "Sorry to interrupt, Norma, but you have a phone call. A Mr. Deodato?"

Dart looked lazily down at her.

"I'll wait in here until you're done," Marian said.

94

DART CLOSED MARIAN'S door and whispered, "Be a smart girl, now." Smiling, he waved her to the telephone. When Nora picked up the receiver, he came up beside her and pressed his head next to hers.

Nora said, "Jeffrey? It's nice of you to call."

"That's one way to put it," Jeffrey said. "I called before, but some woman told me you were on a tour. Why didn't you phone me?"

"There are hardly any telephones in this place, and I've been pretty busy. I'm sorry you were worried, Jeffrey."

"What did you think I'd be? Anyhow, I made it most of the way there before the rain stopped me. How did you manage to get to Shorelands?"

"It's not important. Once I saw all those policemen at the hotel, I went out by a side door and ran into a friend who gave me a ride. I'm sorry I couldn't get in touch with you. Where are you now?"

"A gas station outside Lenox. It looks like I'll have to stay here a couple of hours. Look, Nora, I have some important things to tell you."

"You must have walked into all those cops."

"Did I ever. I spent most of the day at the police station. I was sure I was going to be arrested, but they finally let me go."

"I saw Davey just before I left. Did he meet your mother?"

"That's one of the things I want to tell you. He came to her house with a couple of FBI agents. It was quite a scene. Davey broke down and cried. Even my mother was touched. From what she told me, all hell broke loose in Westerholm this morning. Davey went to his father with what you told him last night, and Alden threw him out of the Poplars. Davey's falling apart. He wants you back. I didn't know how you'd feel about that, so instead of calling him after I talked to my mother, I wanted to get in touch with you. I'd prefer to be doing it in person, but from here on the road is underwater."

"Instead of calling him? Why would you call Davey?"

"To tell him you might have gone to Shorelands. Or, what I was afraid of, that Dick Dart had managed to get ahold of you again."

"I don't understand."

"That's because you don't know the rest of my news. After I get to Shorelands, you'll probably want to come back to Northampton with me. Or I could drive you back to Connecticut, if that's what you want to do."

Dart pulled the knife from his belt sheath and held it in front of her face.

"Jeffrey, slow down. I have to stay here tonight, and I don't want you to come until tomorrow. I'm sorry, but that's how it is. How could I go back to Connecticut, anyhow?"

"Well, it's kind of strange, but everything's cleared up," he said. "You're not wanted anymore."

Dart's eyes flicked toward her.

"What happened? How do you know, anyhow?"

"My mother. Nobody really understands this yet, but one of the FBI men said that Natalie Weil has completely recanted. She told the police that you didn't kidnap her after all."

"I'm in the clear?"

"As far as I know. The whole thing seems very confused, but I guess Natalie did say that she was wrong or mistaken or something, and she's sorry she ever involved you."

Dart's gaze had become flat and suspicious. Nora said, "I don't understand that."

"I get the impression that Natalie has everybody a bit baffled, but it's certainly good news as far as you're concerned. The only thing the police want to talk to you about now is Dick Dart. He got out of Northampton by stealing an antique Duesenberg, if you can believe that."

"Did he really?" Nora asked.

"Why don't I pick you up as soon as I can and take you wherever you want to go?"

"I know it's a tremendous inconvenience, but I want to stay here and wrap up the work I'm doing."

"You want me to wait at this gas station until the rain stops and then drive back to Northampton?" He seemed almost dumbfounded.

"I wish there were a way to do this that would be easier on you."

"So do I. Can you call me tomorrow? After about eight in the morning, I'll probably be at my mother's house." His voice was flat.

"I'll call you."

"You want me to call Davey and tell him you're okay?"

"Please, no."

"You must be on to something pretty interesting, to want to stay there."

"I know you deserve better than this, Jeffrey. You're a good friend."

"Have I earned the right to give you some advice?"

"More than that."

"Leave him. He'll never be anything but what he is right now, and that isn't good enough for someone like you."

"So long, Jeffrey."

Dart set down the telephone. "I think you broke his heart. Jeffrey wanted to spend the night with my own Nora-pie. But let's consider a more crucial matter. Little Natalie has recanted. You never kidnapped the whore after all." He waved his hands in circles at the sides of his head. "The curse of Shorelands strikes again; we're wading through lies." Dart put the point of the knife under her chin and brushed it against her skin. "Help me out here."

"I can't explain it." Nora raised her chin, and Dart jabbed her lightly, indenting her skin without breaking it. "You heard him. Nobody understands what Natalie's doing."

"Give it your best shot."

"Natalie's been medicated for days. I don't think she can even remember what happened. And she takes drugs. Davey told me the cops found a bag of cocaine somewhere in her house."

"Adventurous Natalie."

"Maybe she can't remember what I did. Maybe she has some other reason for lying. I don't know, and I don't care. I was going to kill her."

He stroked her cheek. "These threats of unexpected visitors make me uncomfortable. Let me tell you what I want to do tonight. Everything is going to work out fine. Daddy has a new plan."

95

AT A LITTLE past six, Marian returned to say that dinner would be ready in a few minutes. She had applied a pale pink lipstick and a faint eyeliner and put on a necklace of thin gold links which drooped over her clavicles like a pet snake. "I hope you're hungry again," she said to Dart, who was bored and grumpy because he had not been offered a second drink.

"I'm always hungry. I tend to be on the thirsty side, too."

"Could that be a hint? Margaret opened a bottle of wine, and I think you'll enjoy her selection."

"Only one?" Dart held out his glass. "Why don't you do your best to guarantee high spirits by arranging at least one more bottle to go with our feast?"

Her smile slightly strained, Marian took the glass and stepped behind Nora. "Find anything useful?"

Nora had seen two more entries of payments from Lincoln Chancel, one for thirty thousand dollars, the other for twenty thousand. Each had been followed by outlays to dressmakers, milliners, fabric shops, and the ubiquitous Selden. After spending most of the first fifty thousand on the estate, Georgina had devoted the second to herself.

"I'm getting there," she said.

"You could come back here after dinner, if you like."

This suggestion dovetailed with Dart's new plans for the night, and Nora forced herself to say, "Thank you, I might want to do that."

"I'd better tend to your thirsty husband or he won't be in a good mood."

"Damn right," Dart said. "Speaking of moods, how's Lady Margaret's? Has she bounced back?"

"Margaret doesn't bounce," Marian said. "But I'd say there's still hope for a civilized evening."

"Boring. Let's get down and dirty."

"I'd better hurry up with that drink."

The chandelier had not been turned on, and all the light in the room came from sconces on the walls and candles in tall silver holders. Five places had been set with ornate blue-and-gold china. Reflected candle flames shone in the silver covers of the chafing dishes and the dark windows. Invisible rain hissed onto the lawn. Margaret Nolan and Lily Melville turned to Dart and Nora, one with an expression of neutral welcome, the other with an expectant smile. Lily danced up with her hands folded before her.

"Isn't this storm *terrible*? Aren't you happy this didn't happen when we were on our tour?"

"Rain was invented by the devil's minions."

"Big storms always scare me, especially the ones with thunder and lightning. I'm always sure something awful is going to happen."

"Nothing awful is going to happen tonight." Margaret came toward them. "Except for the usual power failure, and we're well equipped to deal with that. We're going to have a lovely evening, aren't we, Mr. Desmond?"

"Are we ever."

She turned to Nora. "Marian says that you've been roaming through our old ledgers in aid of a project related to Hugo Driver. I hope you'll share your thoughts with us."

Margaret was willing to overlook Dart's provocations for the sake of the business to be brought in by Hugo Driver conferences. Nora wondered what she could say to her about the importance of Shorelands to Driver's novel.

"What became of Marian? We expected her to come in with you."

"Arranging a libation," Dart said.

Margaret raised her eyebrows. "We have a good Châteauneuf

for the first course, and something I think is rather special, a 1970 Château Talbot, for the second. What did you ask Marian to bring you?"

"A double," Dart said. "To make up for the one she forgot."

"You are a poet of the old school, Mr. Desmond. Mrs. Desmond? A glass of this nice white?"

"Mineral water, please," said Nora.

She went to the bottles as Marian hurried in with the refilled glass. "Margaret, I hope you won't mind," she said, handing off the drink, "but Norman felt that one bottle of the Talbot might not be enough, so I looked around and opened a bottle of Beaujolais. It's down on the kitchen counter."

Margaret Nolan considered this statement, which included the unspoken information that the second bottle was perhaps a tenth the price of the first, and cast a measuring glance at Dart. He put on an expression of seraphic innocence and swallowed half his vodka. "Very intelligent, Marian. Whatever our guest does not drink, we can save for vinegar. Please, help yourself."

Marian poured herself a glass of white wine. "I called Tony and asked him to bring up rain clothes for Norman and leave them inside the front door. The telephone lines might go down, and the poor man has to get back to Pepper Pot. I can loan Norma some things of my own."

"Another intelligent decision," said Margaret Nolan. "Since you are on a first-name basis with our guests, all of us should be. Is that agreeable?"

"Completely, Maggie." Dart raised his glass to his mouth and gulped the rest of the vodka.

With elaborate ceremoniousness, Margaret indicated their seats: Norman to the right of the head of the table, Nora across from him, Marian next to Norman, Lily beside Nora. "Please go to the sideboard and help yourselves to the first course. Once we are seated, I will describe our meal, as well as some aspects of this wonderful room not covered during the normal tours. Lily, will you start us off?"

Lily skipped to the sideboard, where she lifted the cover from an oval platter next to a basket of baguettes. On either side of a mound of pale cheese strips lay broiled peppers, sliced and peeled, red to the left, green to the right, flanked with black olives and topped with anchovies. Quarters of hard-boiled eggs had been arranged at either end of the platter. An odor of garlic and oil rose from the peppers. Lily took a salad plate from the stack next to the platter and held it up before Dart. "This is Georgina's own china. Wedgwood."

" 'Florentine,' " Dart said. "One of my personal faves."

"Norman, you know everything!"

"Even beasts can learn," Dart said.

Lily gave herself minute portions of both kinds of peppers, a few olives, and a single section of hard-boiled egg. Dart took half the red peppers, none of the green, most of the olives, half of the eggs and cheese, and all but three of the anchovy slices. Atop it all he placed a six-inch section ripped from the French bread. The others followed, choosing from what was left.

Dart sat down, winked at Lily, and filled his wineglass with white wine from the bucket.

Margaret took her seat and gave his plate a lengthy examination. "This is what Miss Weatherall called her 'Mediterranean Platter.' Monty Chandler grew the peppers, along with a great many other things, in a separate garden north of Main House."

While she spoke, Dart had been shoveling peppers into his mouth, demolishing the hard-boiled eggs, loading strips of cheese onto chunks of bread and chomping them down. As she finished, he bit into the bread and tilted in wine to moisten it all. His lips smacked. "Weird cheese."

"Syrian." Margaret gravely watched him eat. "We get it from a gourmet market, but Miss Weatherall ordered it from an importer in New York. Nothing was too good for her guests."

Dart waggled the bottle at her. "Yes, please." He gave her half a glass and then filled Marian's.

A blast of wind like a giant's hand struck the house. Lily crushed her napkin in her hands. "Lily, you've lived through thousands of our storms," Margaret said. "It can't be as bad as it sounds, anyhow, because the power's still on."

At that moment the wall sconces died. The reflections of the candle flames wavered in the black windows, and again the wind battered the windows.

"Spoke too soon," Margaret said. "No matter. Lily, stop *quivering*. You know the lights will come on soon."

"I know." Lily thrust her hands between her thighs and stared at her lap.

"Eat."

Lily managed to get an olive to her mouth.

"Marian, perhaps you'd better take a candle up to Agnes. She has eaten, hasn't she?"

"If you can call it eating," Marian said. "Don't worry, I'll take care of it. And I'll bring back more candles, so we can see our plates."

"And will you check the phones?" She turned to Dart. "One of the few drawbacks of living in a place like this is that when the lights go out, fifty percent of the time the phones do, too. They're too miserly to put in underground phone lines."

"Curse of democracy," Dart said. "All the wrong people are in charge."

Margaret gave him a look of glittering indulgence. "That's right, you share Georgina Weatherall's taste for strong leaders, don't you?"

Lily looked up, for the moment distracted from her terror. "I've been thinking about that. It's true, the mistress did say that powerful nations should be led by powerful men. That's why she liked Mr. Chancel. *He* was a powerful man, she said, and someone like that should be running the country."

Dart beamed at her. "Good girl, Lily, you've rejoined the living. I agree with the mistress completely. Lincoln Chancel would have made a splendid president. We need a man who knows how to seize the reins. I could do a pretty good job myself, I venture to say."

"Is that right," Margaret said.

Dart took the last of the white wine. "Death penalty for anyone stupid enough to be caught committing a crime. Right there, give the gene pool a shot in the arm. Public executions, televised in front of a live audience. Televise trials, don't we? Let's show 'em what happens after the trial is over. Abolish income tax so that people with ability stop carrying the rabble on their backs. Put schools on a commercial basis. Instead of grades, give cash rewards funded by the corporate owners. So on and so forth. Now that the salad part of the meal has been taken care of, why don't we dig into whatever's under those lids?"

Margaret said, "It occurs to me that a playful conversation like this, with wild flights of fancy, must be similar to those held here during Miss Weatherall's life. Would you agree, Lily?"

"Oh, yes," Lily said. "To hear some of those people talk, you'd think they'd gone right out of their heads."

"One of the paintings in this room was actually here in those days. Along with the portrait of Miss Weatherall's father on the staircase, it's all that survives from her art collection. Can you tell which one it is?"

"That one." Nora pointed to a portrait of a woman whose familiar face looked out from beneath a red hat the size and shape of a prize-winning pumpkin.

"Correct. Miss Weatherall, of course. I believe that portrait brings out all of her strength of character." Marian came back into the room with a candlestick in each hand and two others clamped to her sides.

"I think you might remove the hors d'oeuvres plates, Marian, and give me the others so that I can serve up the main course. How is poor Agnes?"

"Overexcited, but I couldn't say why." Marian began collecting the plates. "The phones are out. I suppose they'll be working again by morning."

"I'd love to see Agnes once more," Nora said.

Margaret lifted a silver cover off what appeared to be a large, round loaf of bread. Flecks of green dotted the crust. "Norma, I'm sure that Lily and I can be at least as helpful as Agnes Brotherhood. What is this project of yours? A book?"

"Someday, maybe. I'm interested in a certain period of Shorelands life."

Margaret cut into the crust. With two deft motions of the knife, she ladled a small section of the dish onto the topmost plate. Thin brown slices of meat encased in a rich gravy slid out from beneath the thick crust. To this she added glistening snow peas from the other serving dish. "There are buttermilk biscuits in the basket. Norma, would you please pass this to Lily?"

Dart watched the mixture ooze from beneath crust. "What is that stuff?"

"Leek and rabbit pie, and snow peas tossed in butter. The rabbit is in a *beurre manié* sauce, and I'm pretty sure I got all the bay leaves out."

"We're eating a rabbit?"

"A good big one, too. We were lucky to find it." She filled another plate. "In the old days, Monty Chandler caught three or four rabbits a month, isn't that what you said, Lily?"

"That's right." Lily leaned over and inhaled the aroma.

"Marian, would you bring us the Talbot?" She arranged the remaining plates, and Marian poured four glasses of wine.

As soon as she sat down, Dart dug into his pie and chewed suspiciously for a moment. "Pretty tasty for vermin."

Margaret turned to Nora. "Norma, I gather that the research you speak of concentrates on Hugo Driver."

Nora wished that she were able to enjoy one of the better meals of her life. "Yes, but I'm also interested in the other people who were here that summer. Merrick Favor, Creeley Monk, Bill Tidy, and Katherine Mannheim."

Lily Melville frowned at her plate.

"Rather an obscure bunch. Lily, do you remember any of them?"

"Do I ever," Lily said. "Mr. Monk was an awful man. Mr. Favor was handsome as a movie star. Mr. Tidy felt like a fish out of water and kept to himself. He didn't like the mistress, but at least he pretended he did. Unlike *her*. *She* couldn't be bothered, sashaying all around the place." She glared at Nora. "Fooled the mistress and fooled Agnes, but she didn't fool me. Whatever happened to that one, it was better than she deserved."

The hatred in her voice, loyally preserved for decades, was Georgina's. This too was the real Shorelands.

Margaret had also heard it, but she had no knowledge of its background. "Lily, I've never heard you speak that way about anyone before. What did this person do?"

"Insulted the mistress. Then she ran off, and she stole something, too."

A partial recognition shone in Margaret's face. "Oh, this was the guest who staged a mysterious disappearance. Didn't she steal a Rembrandt drawing?"

"Redon," Nora said.

"Made you sick to look at. It was a woman with a bird's head, all dark and *dirty*. It showed her private bits. Reminded me of *her*, and that's the truth."

"Norma, perhaps we should forget this unfortunate person and concentrate on our Driver business. According to Marian, you feel that Shorelands may have inspired *Night Journey*. Could you help me to understand how?"

Nora was grateful that she had just taken a mouthful of the rabbit pie, for it gave her a moment's grace. She would have to invent something. Lord Night was a caricature of Monty Chandler? Gingerbread was the model for the Cup Bearer's hovel?

A gust of wind howled past the windows.

Sometime earlier, following Lily on the tour, she had sensed . . . had half-sensed . . . had been reminded of . . .

"We should visit the Song Pillars," Marian said. "Can you imagine how they sound now?"

Lily shuddered.

A door opened in Nora's mind, and she understood exactly what Paddi Mann had meant. "The Song Pillars are a good example of the way Driver used Shorelands," she said.

Dart put down his fork and grinned.

"He borrowed certain locations on the estate for his book. The reason more people haven't noticed is that most Driver fanatics live in a very insular world. On the other side, Driver has never attracted much academic attention, and the people who know Shorelands best, like yourselves, don't spend a lot of time thinking about him."

"I never think about him," Margaret said, "but I think I am about to make up for the lapse. What is it you say we haven't noticed?"

"The names," Nora said. "Marian just mentioned the Song Pillars. Driver put them into *Night Journey* and called them the Stones of Toon. Toon, song? He changed the Mist Field into the Field of Steam. Mountain Glade is—"

Margaret was staring at her. "Mountain Glade, Monty's Glen. My Lord. It's true. Why, this is wonderful. *Think* of all the people devoted to that book. Norman, help yourself to more of that wine. Your wife has earned it for you. Marian, get the bottle of Beaujolais you opened before dinner, and bring it up with the champagne in the refrigerator. We were going to have a Georgina Weatherall celebration, and by God, we shall."

Marian stood up. "You see what I mean about the Driver conference?"

"I see more than that. I see a Driver *week.* I see Hugo Driver T-shirts flying out of the gift shop. What cottage did that noble man stay in when he was here?"

"Rapunzel."

Lily mumbled something Nora could not catch.

"Give me three weeks, and I can turn Rapunzel into a shrine

to Hugo Driver. We'll make Rapunzel the Driver center of the universe."

"He wasn't noble," Lily muttered.

"He is now. Lily, this is a great opportunity. Here you are, one of the few people living actually to have known the great Hugo Driver. Every single thing you can remember about him is worth its weight in gold. Was he untidy? We can drop some socks and balled-up typing paper around the room. Did he drink too much? We put a bottle of bourbon on the desk." Lily took a sullen gulp of wine. "Come on, tell me. What was wrong with him?"

"Everything."

"That can't be true."

"You weren't here." She looked at Margaret with a touch of defiance. "He was sneaky. He was nasty to the staff, and he stole things."

Marian appeared, laden with bottles and a second ice bucket. "Who stole things?"

"We may have to rehabilitate Mr. Driver a bit more than our usual luminaries," Margaret said.

"You knew he was a thief," Nora said.

"Of course I knew. Stole silver from this room. Stole a marble ashtray from the lounge. Stole two pillowcases and a pair of sheets from Rapunzel. Books from the library. Stole from the other guests, too. Mr. Favor lost a brand-new fountain pen. The man was a plague, that's what he was."

The cork came out of the Veuve Clicquot with a soft, satisfying pop. "Maybe we should rethink our position on Mr. Driver," Marian said.

"Are you serious? We're going to polish this fellow up until he shines like gold, and if you're not willing to try, Lily, we'll let Agnes do it."

"She won't." Lily drank the rest of her wine. "Agnes was the one who told me half of what I just said. I want some champagne, too, Marian."

"What else did he steal, Lily?" Nora asked.

The old woman looked at a spot on the wall above Nora's head, then pushed her champagne flute toward Marian.

"He stole that drawing, didn't he? The missing Redon. The one you never liked."

Lily glanced unhappily at Nora. "I didn't tell you. I wasn't supposed to, and I didn't."

Margaret took a sip of champagne and looked back and forth from Nora to Lily in great perplexity. "Lily, two minutes ago you said that the Mannheim girl stole the drawing."

"That's what I was supposed to say."

"Who told you to say that?"

Lily swallowed more champagne and closed her mouth.

"The mistress, of course," said Nora.

Dart chuckled happily and helped himself to rabbit pie.

Lily was gazing almost fearfully at Nora.

"She knew because she saw the drawing in Rapunzel the night Miss Mannheim disappeared," Nora said.

Lily nodded.

"When did she tell you about this? And why? You must have asked the mistress if it was really Hugo Driver and not Miss Mannheim who had stolen the drawing," Nora said.

Lily nodded again. "It was when she was sick."

"When there were no more guests, and she almost never left her room. Agnes Brotherhood spent a lot of time with her."

"It was *unfair*," Lily said. "Agnes never loved her the way I did. Agnes's sister Emma used to be her maid, and then Emma died, and the mistress wanted Agnes next to her. She didn't know the *real* Agnes, it was only that the sisters looked alike. I would have taken better care of her. I tried to watch out for her, but by that time it was Agnes, Agnes, Agnes."

"So it was Agnes who told you about the drawing first."

Margaret put her chin on her hand and followed the questions and answers like a spectator at a tennis match.

"She came out of the mistress's bedroom, and I looked at her face, and I said, 'What's wrong, Agnes?' because anyone could see she was upset, and she told me to go away, but I asked was something wrong with the mistress, and Agnes said, 'Nothing we can fix,' and I kept after her and after her, and finally she put her hand over her eyes and she said, 'I was right about Miss Mannheim. All this time, and I was right.' That trampy little thing, I said, she made fun of the mistress, and besides she stole that picture. 'No, she didn't,' Agnes says, 'it was Mr. Hugo Driver who did that.' She started laughing, but it wasn't like real laughing, and she said I should go upstairs and ask the mistress if I didn't believe her."

"So you did," Nora said.

Lily finished her glass and shuddered. "I went in and sat down beside her and touched her hair. 'I suppose Agnes couldn't keep quiet,' she said, and it was like before she got sick, with her eyes alive. I said, 'Agnes lied to me,' and I told her what she said, and she calmed right down and said, 'No, Agnes told you the truth. Mr. Driver took that picture,' and she knew because she saw it in his room at Rapunzel. 'Why would you go to his room?' I asked, and she said, 'I was being my father's daughter. You could even say I was being Lincoln Chancel.' So I said, 'You shouldn't have let him take it,' and she told me, 'Mr. Chancel paid for that ugly drawing a hundred times over. Send Agnes back to me.' So I sent Agnes back to her room. The next day, the mistress told me that she couldn't afford my wages anymore, and she would have to let me go, but I was never to tell anyone about who stole that picture, and I never did, not even now."

"You didn't tell," Nora said. "I guessed."

"My goodness," said Margaret. "What a strange tale. But I don't see anything that should trouble us, do you, Marian?"

"Mr. Chancel bought the drawing," Marian said. "Hugo Driver borrowed it before payment had been arranged, that's all."

"Love it," Dart said.

"If we could arrange for the loan of the drawing from the Driver estate, we could hang it in Rapunzel and weave it into the whole *Night Journey* story." Margaret sent a look of steely kindness toward Lily. "I know you didn't like the man, Lily, but we've dealt with this problem before. Together, you, Marian, and I can work up any number of sympathetic stories about Mr. Driver. This is going to be a windfall for the Shorelands Trust. More champagne, Norman? And we do have, as a special treat, some *petits vacherins*. Delicious little meringues filled with ice cream and topped with fruit sauces. Mr. Baxter, our baker in Lenox, had some fresh meringue cases today, wonder of wonders, and Miss Weatherall loved *vacherins*."

"Count me in," Dart said.

"Marian, would you be so kind?"

Marian once again left the room, this time patting Dart on the back as she went past him. As soon as she had closed the door, Lily said, "I don't feel well."

"It's been a long day," Margaret said. "We'll save you some dessert."

Lily got unsteadily to her feet, and Dart leaped out of his chair to open the door and kiss her cheek as she left the room. When he took his chair again, Margaret smiled at him. "Lily had some difficulties tonight, but she'll do her usual splendid job during our Driver celebrations. I see no hindrances, do you?"

"Only acts of God," Dart said, and refilled his wineglass.

Marian returned with a tray of *petits vacherins* and another bottle of champagne. "Despite Lily's qualms, I thought we had something to celebrate, so I hope you don't mind, Margaret."

"I won't have any, but the rest of you help yourselves," Margaret replied. Yet, when the desserts had been given out and Marian danced around the table pouring more champagne, she allowed her glass to be filled once more. "Mr. Desmond," she said, "I've been wondering if you would be so kind as to recite one of your poems. It would be an honor to hear something you have written."

Dart gulped champagne, took a forkful of ice cream and meringue, another swallow of champagne, and jumped to his feet. "I composed this poem in the car on the way to this haven of the literary arts. I hope it will touch you all in some small way. It's called 'In Of.' "

> *"Farewell, bliss—world is, are,*
> *lustful death them but none*
> *his can I, sick, must—*
> *Lord, mercy us!*

> *"Men, not wealth, cannot*
> *you physic, must all to are*
> *the full goes I sick must—*
> *Lord, mercy us!*

> *"Beauty but flower*
> *wrinkles devour falls the Queens*
> *died and dust closed eye;*
> *am I die?*
> *Have on!*

"Strength unto grave feed Hector swords,
not with earth holds her
Come!
the do, I,
sick, must—
Lord, mercy us!"

He surveyed the table. "What do you think?"

"I've never heard anything quite like it," Margaret said. "The syntax is garbled, but the meaning is perfectly clear. It's a plea for mercy from a man who expects none. What I find really remarkable is that even though this is the first time I've heard the poem, it seems oddly familiar."

"Norman's work often has that effect," Nora said.

"It's like something reduced to its essence," Margaret said. "Have you spoken to Norman about our poetry series, Marian?"

"Not yet, but this is the perfect time. Norman, can we talk about your coming back to do a reading?"

Once again Marian had unknowingly assisted Dart's plans for the night. He pretended to think it over. "We should take care of that tonight. The only problem is that I'm going to need my appointment book, and it's in the room. But if you decide you want that nightcap, you could come up later."

"And let my appointment book talk to your appointment book? Yes, why don't I do that?"

"You young people," Margaret said. "You're going to have hours of enjoyment talking about all sorts of things, and I'm going to fall asleep as soon as I fall into bed. But before that, Marian, you and I have to see to the kitchen."

"Let me help," Nora said. "It's the least I can do."

"Nonsense," Margaret said. "Marian and I can whip through everything in half an hour. Anyone else would just get in our way."

"Margaret, dear," Dart said. "It's only seven-thirty. You can't mean you're really going to go to bed as soon as the dishes are done."

"I wish I could, but I have an hour or so of work to get through in the office. Marian, let's take the dishes down and attack the kitchen."

Dart glanced at Nora, who said, "Marian, I'd like to spend more time with the records and photographs, but I want to rest for a little bit first. So that you won't have to jump up and down answering the door, do you think you could give me a key?"

"Why don't we just leave the door unlocked?" Margaret said. "We're completely safe here. When were you planning on coming back?"

"Nine, maybe? The storm should be over by then. I could get some work done while Norman and Marian match their schedules."

"Oh?" Marian glanced at Dart. "That works for me. I'll leave the downstairs lights on and come over to Pepper Pot about nine. Does that sound all right to you?"

"Perfect," Dart said. "Did I hear a promise of rain gear?"

"Let's take care of that right now." Marian left the room, and Nora helped Margaret stack the dishes. Soon Marian returned with green Wellingtons, a shiny red raincoat with snaps, and a wide-brimmed matching hat. "My fireman outfit. Don't worry, I have lots of other stuff to get me over there dry. And Norman, Tony's gear is just inside the door."

Nora removed her shoes and pulled on the high boots. Marian had big feet. She put on the shiny coat and snapped it up, and Dart put down his empty glass. "Very fetching."

The sound of the rain was stronger at the front of the building. Dart examined Tony's dirty yellow slicker with revulsion, and he wiped his handkerchief around the interior of the hat before entrusting his head to it. His shoes would not go into the boots, so he too took off his shoes and jammed them into the slicker's pockets. "Almost rather get wet," he muttered.

"Wait! Don't go yet!" Marian called from behind them, and appeared at the top of the marble steps with Nora's bag and four new candles. "You'll find matches on the mantelpiece. Good luck!"

96

THE WORLD PAST the front door was a streaming darkness. Chill
water slipped through Nora's collar and dripped down her back.
Water rang like gunfire on the stiff hat. Dart grasped her wrist
and began running toward the gravel court. When they reached
the path, she nearly went down in the mud, but Dart wrenched
her upright and tugged her forward. Water licked into her
sleeves. The trees on either side groaned and thrashed, and hallucinatory voices filled the air.

Nothing had worked; she had been unable to speak to any of her
possible saviors, and Dart was going to kill Marian Cullinan and
spend a happy two hours dissecting her body while waiting for the
older women to sink into sleep. Then he would pull her back
through the deluge to Main House, where he looked forward to
watching her murder Agnes Brotherhood. As he had said to her,
genius was the capacity to adapt to change without losing sight of
your goal. "Let's face it," he had said, "we're stuck here for the
night, so the kidnapping is out. We have to take care of them all—
those three old Pop-Tarts, too. They're calling me a serial killer, I
might as well have a little fun and act like one. First of all, we convince everybody that you'll be coming back here by yourself.
When we're through with the Pinto, we trot back here and visit the
bedrooms so kindly pointed out to us. No alarms or telephones.
Safety, ease, and comfort. When we're done, we enjoy a cham-
pion's breakfast of steak and eggs in the kitchen, and depart in the
Pinto's car."

Trying to match her pace to Dart's, Nora bent over and ran,
able to see no more than the rain sheeting off the brim of the red
hat and the mud rising to her ankles. Dart yanked at her hand,
and she lost her grip on the bag, which dropped into the mud.
The cleaver, the carving knife, and much else tumbled out. Dart

yelled something inaudible but unmistakable in tone, dragged her back, and bent down to scoop what had fallen out into the bag. Off to the right, a branch splintered away from a tree and crashed to the ground. Dart rammed the bag into her chest, whirled her around, and pushed her through the mud to the PEPPER POT sign and the ascending path. Her feet slipped, and she slid backwards into him. He pushed her again. Rain struck her face like a stream of needles. Nora tried to walk forward, and her right foot slipped out of the lower part of the boot. Dart circled her waist and lifted her off the ground. Her foot came out of the boot. Dart kicked it aside and carried her up the path.

He set her down on the porch and unfastened the clasps of the slicker to pull the key from his jacket pocket. Rain drummed down onto the roof. An unearthly moaning came from the woods. *Hell again,* Nora thought. *No matter how many times you go there, it's always new.* Dark puddles formed around them. A film of water covered her face, and her ribs ached from Dart's grip. He opened the door and pointed inside.

His hat and slicker landed on the floor. Nora put down the bag and fished the candles from the pockets of Marian's coat. Dart took the candles, locked the door, and made shooing motions with his hands. Nora hung Marian's things on a hook beside the door and lifted her foot out of the remaining boot. "Hang up that garbage I had to wear and find the matches. Then put your bag in the bathtub and get back here to help me pull off these disgusting boots."

"Put my bag in the tub?"

"You want to destroy a Gucci bag? I have to clean it off and try to dry it."

Nora carried the dripping bag across the lightless room into the bathroom. Was there a window in the bathroom, a back door? A gleaming black rectangle hung in the far wall. She moved forward until her legs met the bathtub, stepped inside, dropped the bag, and ran her hands along the top of the window. Her fingers found a brass catch. The slide refused to move. "What are you doing?" Dart shouted.

"Putting down the bag." She pulled at the slide, but it was frozen into place.

"Get back in here."

A column of darkness against a background of lighter darkness ordered her to the fireplace on the far side of the room.

Holding her hands before her, Nora put one foot in front of another and made her way across the room.

Apparently able to see in the dark, Dart directed her to the fireplace and matches, then told her to walk fifteen paces forward, turn left, and keep walking until she ran into him.

Dart grabbed the matches out of her hands, lit a candle, and walked away. She could see nothing but the flame. He jammed the candle into a holder from the windowsill, lit the other two, and put them into the candlesticks on the table in the center of the room. The rope and duct tape lay beside an ice bucket and a liter of Absolut. Dart took two gulps of vodka and drew in a sharp breath. Muddy bootprints wandered across the floor like dance instructions. "Sounds like the inside of a bass drum." He dropped into a chair and stuck out one leg. "Do it."

Nora put her hands on the slimy boot. "Pull." Her hands slipped off. "Take your clothes off."

"Take my clothes off?"

"So you can prop my legs against your hip and push. Don't want to wreck that suit."

While she was undressing, Dart sent her to the kitchen for a glass. He blew into it, held it up to the flame for inspection, and pulled a dripping handful of slivers from the bucket. Before drinking, he drew a circle in the air with the glass, and Nora walked back to the bed and removed the rest of her clothes. "Hang up your things. Have to look good until we can get new clothes." He followed her with his eyes. "Okay, get over here, and put your back into it this time."

She pulled his outthrust leg into her side. His trousers were sodden, and an odor of wet wool came from him. She held her breath, gripped his leg with her left hand, pushed at the heel, and the boot came away. "Let my people be!" Dart swallowed vodka. "One down, one to go."

When the second boot surrendered, Nora staggered forward and felt an all too familiar surge of warmth throughout her body. Dizziness, a sudden sweatiness of the face, a hot necessity to sit down. "Oh, no," she said.

"Mud washes off," Dart said. Then he bothered to look at her. "Oh Christ, a hot flash. God, that's ugly. Wipe off the mud and lie down."

She got to the bathroom and splashed water on her face before erasing the clumps and streaks from her body.

When she came out, Dart pointed to the bed. "Women. Slaves to their bodies, every one." She was vaguely aware of his giving her another disgusted look. "Seven-hundred-dollar Gucci bag, covered with mud. Here I go, doing your work for you again."

He poured more vodka. "And wouldn't you know it, the ice is all gone." Nora watched the ceiling darken as he carried a candle into the bathroom.

Her body blazed. Water ran. Dart spoke to himself in tones of complaining self-pity. Nora wiped her forehead. She could feel her temperature floating up. Bug, where are you, little bug? A hot flash is hardly complete without a touch of formication. Shall we formicate? Come on, let's try for the brass ring. Dick Dart is repulsed by female biology, let's have the whole menopausal circus. Give me an F, give me an O, give me an R. Formication, of thee I sing. The riot in her body swung the bed gently up and back. A rustle of leathery wings and a buzz of glee came from beyond the fireplace. Begone, fiends, I don't want you now. She wiped her face with a corner of the sheet, and it came away slick with moisture.

Dart poked his head through the bathroom door and announced that if she wasn't ready by the time the Pinto came, she'd be sorry. *I'm plenty sorry right now, thank you very much.*

Having enjoyed itself for some three or four minutes, the hot flash subsided, leaving behind the usual sense of depletion. From the bathroom came swishing sounds accompanied by Dartish grumbles. Nora remembered that he had put the gun in his desk drawer. Surprise, surprise! She wiped her body with her hands and swung her legs off the bed. The sounds of running water and exclamations of woe testified to the absorption of Mr. Dart in his task. Despite her ignorance of revolvers and their operation, surely she could work out how to fire the thing once she got her hands on it. She moved silently toward the middle of the room and observed that the desk drawer appeared to have been pulled open. Another six tiptoe steps brought her to the desk. She lowered her hand into the drawer and touched bare wood. What's the matter, Dick? Don't you trust me?

She moved to the door, put on the slicker, and snapped it shut. In the bathroom, Dart was bent over the tub, his sleeves pushed up past his elbows. A candle stood at the bottom of the tub, and flickering shadows swarmed over the walls. Dye dripping from Dart's hair had stained the top of his shirt collar black. A thick line of grit ran from the middle of the tub to the drain, and limp bills had been hung over the side to dry. The cleaver and the carving knife lay encased in mud beside the bag. Various bottles and brushes and other cosmetic devices had already been washed and placed atop the toilet.

He took in the slicker with contempt. "Grab a towel. One of the little ones."

She gave him a hand towel, and he passed it under the running tap. "Wipe up the mud out there before it dries."

"Aye, aye, sir." Nora took the towel into the room to swab muddy footprints. By the time she returned, Dart was holding the bag out before him.

"This thing might survive after all." He handed her the wet bag. "Get it as dry as you can. Tear the pages out of one of those books, wad a towel into the center of the bag, and cram the pages between the towel and the inside of the bag. Don't forget the corners. Do it in here, so I can make sure you do it right."

She brought the paperbacks into the bathroom and placed them on the floor beside the toilet to buff the handbag with the towel.

"Blot up as much water as you can. Ram it into the bottom corners."

Nora pushed the towel around the inside of the bag, and Dart bent over the tub to rinse the towel she had used on the floor under hot water, rub soap into it, and begin washing the cleaver.

"You memorize everything you read, and you never forget it?"

He sighed and leaned against the tub. "I told you. I don't *memorize* anything. Once I read a page, it stays in there all by itself. If I want to see it, I just *look at* it, like a photograph. All those books I had to read for my old ladies, I could recite backwards if I wanted to. Let me feel that."

He swiped his fingers on her towel and ran them across the lining of the bag. "Wad toilet paper down in there. Would you like to hear the complete backwards *Pride and Prejudice*? Austen Jane by? Almost as bad as the forward version."

Nora stuffed toilet paper into the corners of the bag and began ripping pages out of *Night Journey*.

Dart ran the cleaver under hot water and soaped it again. "How do you think I got through law school? Name a case, I could quote the whole damn thing. If that was all you had to do, I'd have made straight A's."

"That's amazing." She plastered the first pages against the sodden silk lining.

"You'll never know how relieved I was when I got assigned someone like Marjorie West. Seventy-two years old, rich as the queen of England, never read a book in her life. Four dead husbands and never happier than when talking about sex. Ideal woman."

Nora had met Marjorie West, whose Mount Avenue house was even grander than the Poplars. She was herself a structure on the grand scale, though much reconstructed, especially about the face. Nora found that she did not wish to think about Marjorie West's relationship with Dick Dart. These days, Marjorie West probably did not want to think too much about it, either. Nora tore another twenty pages out of *Night Journey*. "So you could quote from this book, too."

"You heard me quote from that book." He placed the cleaver on the rug and addressed the carving knife.

"Tell me about that massy vault, the one that's bigger on the inside than on the outside."

"You have the book right in front of you."

"I can't read in this light. What does the vault look like?"

Dart grimaced at the amount of mud still clinging to the knife. "What does it look like on the outside? I'll have to give you the whole sentence so you get the atmosphere. *'With many a fearsome and ferocious glance, many a painful jab about the ribs, many an adjustment of her enormous hat, Madame Lyno-Wyno Ware led Pippin through the corridors of her spider-haunted mansion to a portal bearing the words* MOST PRIVATE, *thence into a chamber of gloomy aspect and to another such door marked* MOST MOST PRIVATE, *into a far gloomier chamber and a door marked* MOST MOST MOST PRIVATELY PRIVATE, *which creaked open upon the gloomiest of all the chambers, and therein extended her gaudy arm to signify, concealed beneath a tattered sofa, a homely leaden strongbox no more than a foot high.'* That's all, 'homely leaden strongbox no more than a foot high.' From there on, it's about Pippin's disappointment, that little thing can't be the famous massy vault, but the boy bites the bullet and forges ahead, says the right words, and it all turns out all right, kind of."

He rinsed the carving knife, brought it near his eyes for inspection, and rubbed the soapy cloth into the crevices around the hilt.

"The golden key brings him to Madame Lyno-Wyno Ware?"

"Lie? No. Why, nowhere." Dart picked up his glass with a dripping hand and finished the vodka. "The truth is all-important, can't lie to Mrs. Lyno-Wyno Ware, nope." Twitching with impatience, he watched her stuff paper into the bag. "That'll do. Scamper into the kitchen and get me a refill."

When she returned, Dart took a mouthful, set down the glass, and meticulously dried the knives. A hard red flush darkened his cheekbones. "Clean the mess out of the tub. Work fast, I have a lot to do, must prepare for the arrival of sweet Marian."

Nora knelt in front of the bathtub. A few dimes and quarters glinted in the slow-moving brown liquid. The thunder of rainfall on the roof suddenly doubled. The window over the tub bulged inward for a second, and the entire cottage quivered.

Nora came out of the bathroom. Dart was staring at the ceiling. "Thought the whole thing was going to come down. Put the bag on the table and bring me the rope. Hardly need the tape, wouldn't you agree?"

She placed the bag on the table. "Coat." Dart removed his tie and draped it over a shoulder of the suit. Nora unsnapped the red slicker, put it on the hook, and, her heart beating in time to the drumfire on the roof, carried the rope toward him. "Slight possibility I may have overdone the vodka, but all is well." He concentrated on arranging his shirt on a hanger.

Aligned with Dart's usual care, the knives had been placed beneath the pillow on the left side of the bed. "Rope." She came close enough to hand him the coil of clothesline. He yanked off his boxer shorts. "Sit."

Dart drew the carving knife from beneath the pillow, cut off two four-foot lengths of rope, and stumbled around to the side of the bed. "Hands." Eventually he succeeded in lashing her hands and feet. "Little sleep. Party isn't over yet."

Nora worked herself up the bed and watched Dart fussing to align the knife under his pillow. He stretched out on the bed and closed his eyes. Then he rolled his head sideways on the pillow and seemed to consider some troubling point. The rope bit into her ankles and wrists. "What the fuck you care about the massy vault, anyhow?" Wind and rain thrashed against the kitchen windows.

"I like hearing you quote," Nora said.

"Right. Worry not, I'll wake up in time." He was asleep in seconds.

97

CANDLELIGHT FELL TO the floor in a shifting, liquid pool. On the other side of the table, paler light filtered through the bathroom door. All else was formless darkness. Dick Dart began sending up soft, fluffy snores barely audible under the drumming on the roof. Her hands were falling asleep. Drunk and hurried, Dart had made the knots tighter than before, and the rope was cutting off her circulation. She made fists, flexed her fingers, slid her wrists up and down. A dangerous tingling began in her feet. With her eyes on the pool of light wavering across the smooth floor, Nora explored the knot with her fingers.

Dart's failure to include what her dream-father called "the choke" meant that Nora could fight the rope without immobilizing her hands. If she could locate the end of the rope, slide it under the nearest strand, unwind it once around, and pass it beneath the next strand, the entire mechanism would collapse. But every time her fingers traced a strand, it disappeared back into the web. The first time she had escaped this knot, Dart had tied a single hand in front of her; with both hands tied behind her back, she would have to find the end of the rope with her fingers.

The shoulder beneath her ached, and her wrists were already complaining. Her feet continued their painful descent into oblivion. She rolled her eyes upward in concentration and found the darkness obliterated by the yellow afterimage of the candlelight. If she wanted to see anything at all, she would have to look away from the light.

Groaning, she swung up her knees and flipped onto her back. A flaring red circle blotted out the ceiling. Another shift of her body rolled her over to face Dart. His breath caught in his throat before erupting in a thunderous snore. Nora tried to force her wrists apart, and increased the pain. Again she closed her hands into fists, extended and stretched her fingers, slid her wrists from side to side. There was some give, after all. The tingling in her hands began to subside.

How much time did she have? Not even Maid Marian was desperate enough to run through a deluge to sleep with Norman Desmond, but Dart's vanity ignored storms. He expected eager Marian in something like twenty minutes. Even drunk, he was probably capable of waking up in time.

Nora folded her hands, rubbed the tips of her fingers over the web of rope, and felt only interlocking strands. She maneuvered herself back onto her other side and shifted toward the end of the bed. She swung her legs out and lowered her feet to the floor. They registered only a profound, painful tingling. Her fingers probed the knot without success. She had to increase the amount of rope she could reach, and the only way to do that was by sliding the whole structure closer to her hands.

If she could put it between her wrists and pull her hands up, the doorknob might work. She stamped her feet on the floor, and a red track burned all the way from her soles to her knees.

Time's running out, girl.

The first two fingers of her right hand plucked at a thread. The thread moved. Her heart surged, and her breathing accelerated. Something flapped above her head. She urged the thread up from the knot, and mingled terror and hope flared white hot in the center of her body. The thread jittered out of her fingers and slipped away. Another nonexistent being chattered from the kitchen counter. She fumbled for the thread and met only interlocking strands.

Move!

She planted her burning feet on the floor and stood up, biting her tongue against the pain. Her ankles dissolved, and she fell like a tower of blocks, in sections, her hips going one way, her knees another. A hip struck the floor, then a shoulder. Dart belched, coughed, resumed snoring. Nora adjusted to her new pains. A pair of happy red eyes gleamed at her from the bathroom door. *Screw you.* She considered sitting up and noticed that roughly three inches above and behind her, a brace ran from the bottom of the bed to its head. A brace was probably as good as a doorknob.

She curled her knees before her, grunted, and jerked herself up. Flattened under her legs, her feet continued to burn. She inched backwards until her forearms met the brace, twitched herself a few inches farther back, and settled the rope against the edge of the wood. Then she pushed down and groped for the loose thread. Nothing. Gasping, she pushed again. The knot slipped an eighth of an inch, and her fingers met the raised line of the thread. Sweat poured down her forehead. A soft, high-pitched sound seemed to leave her throat by itself. The thread crawled out and came free.

She closed her eyes and worked it around and under. The braided handcuffs went limp. She shook her wrists, and the knot fell away. Her feet slid from beneath her thighs. Panting, she bent over and sent her fingers prowling through the rope around her ankles. A push, a pull, an unthreading, and the rope tumbled to her feet.

She moved away from the bed on hands and knees, then got one foot beneath her. The foot didn't want to be there, but it was not in charge of this operation; it would do what it was told. She levered herself upright, took an experimental step forward, and managed not to fall. The storm, suspended since she had noticed the wooden brace, exploded back into life.

Where had Dart put the gun? She could not remember his putting it anywhere, so it was still in his jacket. She limped toward the closet. Feeling returned to her feet in stabs and surges, but her ankles held. She stretched out her hands, moved forward until she felt the fabric of Dart's suit, ran her fingers down to a pocket, and thrust in her hand to discover the keys. She took them out and reached into the empty pocket on the other side.

Gripping the keys in her left hand, she inched up alongside the bed. Dart had put the knives under his pillow; why not the gun, too? He smacked his lips. She extended a shaking hand, touched the edge of the pillowcase, and found a wooden handle. Beside it was another. Millimeter by millimeter her trembling hand slid them from beneath the pillow. Dart sighed and rolled away. She groped for the revolver and touched metal.

"What?" Dart said, and reached into the space where she

should have been. Too frightened to think, Nora snatched up the carving knife and jabbed it into his back. For an instant, his skin resisted, and then the blade broke through and traveled in. He jerked forward, carrying the knife with him. Nora scrabbled beneath the pillow, and her hand closed on a metal cylinder. Dart twisted around and lunged toward her. The revolver in her hand, she pulled away and ran to the other side of the room.

He was staggering past the end of the bed. She yelled, "Stop! I have the gun!" and tried to find the safety Dan Harwich had mentioned, but could hardly see the gun. "I'll shoot you right now!"

"You stabbed me!" he yelled.

Nora ducked behind the second bed and moved her thumb over the plate behind the cylinder. Wasn't that where the damned thing was supposed to be? The pistol Harwich had given her had no cylinder; did that make a difference?

Dart stopped moving when he reached the table. Astoundingly to Nora, he laughed, shook his head, then laughed again. Although she could be only a vague suggestion in the darkness, he found her eyes with his.

"I have to say this hurts."

He twisted his neck to look at the knife sagging from his back. "I thought we were past this kind of bullshit." He looked, sighed, and reached back. "I may require the services of a nurse." He closed his eyes as he pulled out the knife. "Don't think I can overlook this matter. Serious breach of conduct."

"Shut up and sit down," Nora said. "I'm going to tie you up. If you're still alive in the morning, I'll get you to a hospital. With a police escort."

"Sweet. But since you already tried to kill me once, twice if we count Springfield, I tend to think Nora-pie doesn't actually have the big bad gun. If you did, you'd shoot me now." He clamped a hand over his wound, tossed the knife into the darkness, and took a step past the table.

"Stop!" Nora shouted.

"Why don't I hear any noise?" He took another step.

Because she had not found the safety, Nora pulled the trigger in despair and panic, certain that nothing would happen. The explosion jerked her hand three feet off the bed and released a lick of flame and an enormous roar. Her ears closed.

Dart vanished into the darkness. She aimed where she thought he had gone and pulled the trigger again. The gun jumped, carrying her hand with it. She fired again, causing another explosion which yanked her hand toward the ceiling. Nora gripped the wrist of her right hand with her left and trained the revolver back and forth against the rear of the cottage. A vivid mental picture of Dick Dart crawling across the floor sent her backwards until her shoulder struck the wall.

With nowhere else to go, she crawled under the bed. An unimaginable distance away, candles she could not see burned on a table she could not see. She crawled forward and realized that she had left the keys on the floor. When she reached the other side of the bed, she slid out and sat up.

A huge shadow rose up in the middle distance and charged toward her. Nora clenched her teeth, clamped her left hand over her right wrist, and aimed without taking aim. She squeezed, not jerked, the trigger, this also being a lesson Dan Harwich had given her. Dirty-looking fire blew out of the barrel, and the gun jumped in her hands. The charging shadow disappeared. She felt but did not hear a body strike the floor.

Nora crawled back under the bed and waited for the floorboards to vibrate, a hand to snake toward her. Nothing happened. She moved forward, and her hand touched warm liquid. She slithered out and moved to the foot of the bed. A dark shape lay a few feet away.

With the gun straight out in front of her, Nora moved around the body in a wide circle. It did not move. She came closer. A ribbon of blood curled away from Dart's head and trailed glistening across the floor. She jabbed the barrel into his forehead and for what seemed a long time applied pressure to the trigger, released it, pressed it again. The idea of touching him made her stomach cramp.

She tottered to her feet, remembered to get the keys, and pulled on Marian Cullinan's coat, surprised to feel nothing but a dull acceptance. The demons had fled, and only numbness was left. The rest, whatever the rest was to be, would come later.

Her ears ringing, she rammed the revolver into the pocket of the red coat and thrust her feet into Tony's rubber boots. She unlocked the door. When she pushed it open, the storm wrenched it out of her hands and threw it back against the front of the cottage. All of Shorelands, maybe all of western

Massachusetts, was like the center of a waterfall. For a moment she thought of staying inside until the storm ended; then she imagined the candles burning down and the two of them, she and Dart, waiting for the night to end.

She slapped Marian's hat on her head and heard a wheezy cough. Her heart froze. A vague shape pushed itself up on its knees, collapsed, hauled itself an inch forward. She fumbled the gun out of the pocket. The shape gathered into itself and surged ahead like a grub. The gun in her hand released another flare of light. The explosion yanked her hand three feet into the air, and something smacked into the kitchen cabinets. The grub stopped moving.

Then she was on the porch and moving toward the waterfall with no memory of having gone through the door. She thrust the gun into her pocket and ran off the porch.

98

HER FEET SLITHERED away, and a fist of wind smacked her into the muck. Cold ooze embraced her legs and flowed into the coat. She scrambled to get up, but the ground slipped away beneath her hands, and for an eternity she crawled through gouting mud. At last grass which was half mud but still half grass met her hands. She struggled upright, and another endless wave of wind-driven rain sent her reeling.

Miraculously, in another few minutes she was no longer blind and deaf. The trunks of massive oaks framed her view. A few feet away the deluge continued to assault the sluggish river which had once been a path. The wind had thrown her into the woods, where the canopy of leaves and branches broke the rainfall. Her breath came in ragged gasps, and her heart banged. Behind her, the trees groaned. She turned toward Main House and took a step. Wasn't Main House off to her right, not her left? She took a step in what seemed the wrong direction as soon as she had taken it. An enormous branch cracked away above her and crashed to the ground ten feet in front of her. Deeper in the woods, another limb broke off and tumbled to earth. When she looked back she saw that she had managed to get only a little way beyond the cottage.

Dim light flickered in the doorway; a second later, the silhouette of a large male body filled the opening. Reflected yellow light glinted off a flat blade. She backed into a tree and yelped. The man jumped off the porch and vanished into the darkness. Nora plunged into the woods in what she hoped was the direction of Main House.

She stumbled over fallen branches and walked into invisible trees. Waist-high boulders jumped up at her; streaming deadfalls towered over her, branches smacked her forehead and thumped her ribs. She moved with her hands in front of her face; now and then, she set a foot on empty air and went skidding downhill until she could grasp a branch. She fell over rocks, over roots. The weapon in her pocket bruised her thigh, and the rocks and branches she struck in her falls bruised everything else. She had no idea how far she had gone, nor in what direction. The worst thing she knew was that Dick Dart, who should have been but was not dead, followed close behind, tracking her by sound.

She knew this because she could hear him, too. A minute or two after she had run from the sight of him leaping off the porch, she had heard him curse when a branch struck him. When she had taken a tumble over a boulder and landed in a thicket, she had heard the harsh bow-wow-wow of his laughter, faintly but distinctly, coming it seemed from all about her. He had not seen her, but out of the thousands of noises surrounding him, he had heard the sounds of her fall and struggle with the thicket and understood what they meant. He could probably hear her boots slogging through the mush. She ran with upraised arms, hearing behind her the phantom sound of Dart picking his way through the woods.

A few minutes later this ghostly sound still came to her through a renewal of the waterfall's booming; Nora pushed her way past nearly invisible obstacles and came to the reason for the noise. On the other side of a veil of trees, a curtain of water crashed down onto a black river. She had come to another path, which made it certain that she had run in the wrong direction:

paths led to cottages, and there were no cottages in a direct line from Pepper Pot to Main House. Dart's ghost steps advanced steadily toward her.

Nora came up to the trees bordering the path, bent her head, and moved out into the deluge. Fighting for balance, she trudged forward, the boots sticking, slipping. At length the tide began to solidify underneath her feet, and she peered ahead at another wall of trees. The barrage diminished to heavy rainfall.

Nora looked back and thought she saw a pale form flickering through the woods on the other side of the path. She dodged into a gathering of oaks and began to work down a slight grade. The ground softened, then dropped away, and her feet went into a sliding skid. Instinctively, she crouched forward to keep her center of gravity in place and slipped down past the oak trees, skimming around rocks, tilting from side to side to stay upright. She stayed on her feet until a low branch struck her right ankle and sent her tumbling into a tree trunk. Sparks flared in front of her eyes, and her body slipped into a slow downhill cruise. When she came to rest, Marian's hat was gone, her head was pounding, and the lower half of her right leg seemed to be underwater. Her leg came out of the water when she crawled to her knees.

She was on open ground, and the storm had begun to slacken. At some point during the trip downhill, the wind had lessened. Dizzy and exhausted, she raised her right leg to pour water out of the boot. Her muscles ached and her head throbbed. The sky had grown lighter. More quickly than it had come, the storm was ending.

Before her a five-foot sheet of water moved swiftly from right to left. Rain dimpled and pocked the surface of the water. A river? Nora wondered how far she had come. Then she realized that fattened with rainwater and overflowing its banks, this was the little stream running through the estate. Behind her, some enormous object creaked, sighed, and surrendered to gravity. Dart was gaining on her. She had to hide from him until she could get to Main House.

Why didn't he just bleed to death like normal people?

She strode forward into the quickly moving water, and slick stones met the soles of the boots. The rain dwindled to a pattering of drops. Wind ruffled the surface of the water and flattened the coat against her body. Overhead, a solid mass of great woolen clouds glided along. With a shock, she realized that it was now a little past nine on an August night. Above the storm, the sun had only recently gone down. She climbed over the opposite bank of the stream and waded through the overflow into the fresh woods to conceal herself.

She heard laughter in the pattering rain and the hissing leaves.

Through the massed trunks Nora saw what looked like gray fog. She moved forward, and the fog became an overgrown meadow where grasses bent before the cool wind. On the other side of the meadow, high-pitched voices swooped and skirled, climbing through chromatic intervals, introducing dissonances, ascending into resolution, shattering apart, uniting into harmony again, dividing and joining in an endless song without pauses or repeats.

Singing?

For a second larger without than within, like the massy vault, Nora dropped through time and awakened to unearthly music in a bedroom on Crooked Mile Road in Westerholm, Connecticut, scrambling for a long-vanished pistol. Then she realized where she was. Instead of going south, she had run almost directly west. The meadow in front of her was the Mist Field, and the voices came from Monty Chandler's Song Pillars. Unable to hide, she pulled the gun from her pocket and whirled around to look for Dart. She ranged in front of the woods, jerking the gun back and forth. Dart did not show himself. She moved right, then left, then right again, waiting for him.

Then she understood what he had done. Dick Dart had half-followed, half-chased her across the stream and toward the Mist Field. He wanted her to cower in a hidey-hole and wait for him to move past. In the meantime, he was on his way to Main House.

"Oh, my God," Nora said. She began to run along the edge of the meadow toward a point in the woods where she could wade back across the stream, cut past Honey House, and approach Main House from the west lawn. She stopped to pull off the clumsy boots. Bare-legged, the ground squashing beneath her feet, she started running again.

A pale figure emerged from the woods at the far corner of the Mist Field. Nora froze. The revolver wanted to slip out of her muddy hand. Maybe it was empty, maybe not. If not, maybe it

would fire, maybe not. The figure moved toward her. She raised
the gun, and the man before her called out her name and became
a drenched Jeffrey Deodato.

99

NORA LET HER arm fall. Jeffrey had lost his Eton cap. Covered
with muddy streaks and smears, his raincoat clung to him like a
wet rag. Other streaks adhered to his face. Because he was Jeffrey,
his bearing suggested that he had deliberately camouflaged himself. He got close enough for her to see the expression in his eyes.
Clearly she looked a good deal worse than he did.

"You came after all," she said.

"It seemed like a good idea." He looked down at the gun.
"Thanks for not shooting. Where's Dart?"

Apparently Jeffrey had learned a good deal since their telephone conversation. "I killed him," she said. "But it didn't work."
She lifted the revolver and looked at it. "I don't think there are any
bullets left in this thing, anyhow."

Jeffrey delicately took the gun from her. "So you got away from
him."

"It started out that way. But I think after a while he was chasing
me away. He wanted me out of his hair so he could enjoy himself
with the women at Main House. Then he could come back and
have all the fun of hunting me down. We can't stand around and
talk, Jeffrey, we have to get moving."

He snapped open the cylinder. "You have one bullet left, but
it's not in a very safe place, unless you want to shoot yourself in
the leg." He moved the cylinder, clicked it back into place, and
handed her the revolver, grip first. "Let's get out of here and find
a phone."

Frantic with impatience, Nora rammed the revolver back into
her pocket. "The phones don't work." She looked around wildly.
"We have to get to Main House." Jeffrey was still examining her.

The spectacle she presented obviously did not inspire much confidence in her ability to deal with Dick Dart. Nora glanced down at the ruined coat and her streaky legs. She looked like an urchin pulled from a swamp.

"Main House?" Jeffrey asked.

She grabbed the sleeve of his coat and pulled him back toward the woods. "If we don't, he'll murder everybody. Come on, if you're coming. Otherwise I'm going by myself."

She saw him decide to humor her. "We'll make better time if we stick to the edges of the path." She started to say something, but he cut her off. "I'll show you. All I need to know is where Main House is from here."

"There." She pointed into the woods.

Maddeningly, Jeffrey began jogging back in the direction from which he had come. She ran after him. "We're going the wrong way!"

"No, we're not," he said, unruffled.

"Jeffrey, you're lost."

"Not anymore, I'm not."

At the end of the meadow Jeffrey pointed to the strip of wet but solid ground directly in front of the trees. He was right. The path had turned into soup, but they could move along beside it without falling down. The faint light was fading, and Nora remembered what it was like to move through the woods in the dark. "Okay?"

"Go," she said.

So close to the trees that Nora could feel roots under her bare feet, they began to move at a steady trot. "Too fast for you?" Jeffrey asked.

"I can run as well as you," Nora said. "What did you do after we talked?"

Waiting out the storm in the gas station, Jeffrey had grown increasingly uneasy. Nora's explanation of how she had come to Shorelands and her reasons for sending him back to Northampton seemed flimsy, her attitude unnatural. He had managed to coax the MG over the drowned roads to Shorelands and seen the Duesenberg in the parking lot. Just getting into his truck, Tony had ordered him off. *Where is Mrs. Desmond?* Jeffrey had asked. Tony said, *If you're a friend of that asshole Desmond's, you can go to hell.* His roof leaked; he could make it to his sister's house in Lenox; he didn't care what happened to Jeffrey. Jeffrey had pleaded with him to call the police, and Tony said that he couldn't call the police even if he wanted to because the phones were out. *Where is Pepper Pot?* Tony had sworn at him and driven away. Jeffrey set off on foot through the storm. He passed Main House, moved up the path, found Pepper Pot empty, and entered the woods again. He realized that he had no idea where he was going. Then the storm relented, and he found himself at the edge of a field. Far off to his right he saw a muddy scarecrow, and the scarecrow pointed a gun at him.

"I guess Tony doesn't care much for Dick Dart," he said. "Tell me about what's going on in Main House."

Before them, the bridge in front of Honey House arched up out of a flat, moving sheet of water. Nora walked out from under the dripping trees and waded into the flooded stream while Jeffrey kept pace beside her, the bottom of his coat floating behind him.

"I wish I knew. There are four women in there. Marian Cullinan, who works for the trust, Margaret Nolan, who runs the place, and two guides who used to work here in the old days." On the opposite side of the streambed, they began trotting beneath the oaks again. "He wants to kill them, I know that much. A normal psychopath would sneak into their bedrooms and take them one by one, but Dart wants to have a party. He's been chortling all afternoon."

"A party?"

At the end of the avenue between the rows of oaks, Nora could make out the edge of the pond. "He loves to talk, and he loves an audience. He'll want to get them all together and give himself some entertainment. He'd love the idea of making them watch while he kills them one by one."

"I hate to say this, but wouldn't he want to get it over with as soon as possible so he can get away?"

"Dart feels *protected*. He assumes he'll be able to walk away, no matter how long he takes."

Jeffrey considered this while they moved toward the pond and open ground. "How much time has he had already?"

"My sense of time went south with my sense of direction." She tried to work out how long she had flown through the woods. "He really was chasing me at the start. He was in a rage. I stabbed him, and then I shot him."

"You shot him? Where?"

"He was lying on his front, so all I could see was blood coming out of his head. He sure looked dead to me, but I couldn't see the wound. I would have checked his life signs, but I couldn't stand the idea of touching him. I guess I just grazed him, damn it. Anyway, I ran out, and about a minute later, he somehow got up and came after me. Hold on, Jeffrey, I want to do something."

She trotted up to the lip of the pond, plunged her muddy hands into the water, and scrubbed them clean before running back to him. "I don't want that blasted gun to slip out of my hands."

He began gliding up the sodden lawn. "Could he have had half an hour?"

Nora stopped moving. She stared at her wet hands, realizing that Dart had given them more time than they thought.

"Not that long. He probably spent at least ten minutes coming after me before he changed his mind. He made sure I knew he was close behind me, and then he started toward the house. That might have been twenty minutes ago. It would take him ten or fifteen minutes to get to the house, but he wouldn't start right away."

Jeffrey scratched his forehead, leaving a muddy smear which increased the camouflage effect. "Why not?"

She held up the hands she had washed in the pond. "This guy is one of the most fastidious men on earth. The first thing he'd do when he got inside would be to clean himself up. There's a bathroom in a little office corridor downstairs. He may even have taken a *shower*. Everybody was upstairs, and he had plenty of time to clean himself up for his party."

"This isn't a joke?"

"Jeffrey, this is a guy who goes crazy if he has to go a day without brushing his teeth. If he isn't presentable, he won't have half the fun he wants."

Jeffrey clearly decided to believe her. "I hope he doesn't have another gun."

"No. But the last time I saw him, he was holding a cleaver, and the kitchen is full of knives."

They looked up over the lawn to Main House. Real night had arrived, and the curving stone steps rose indistinctly to the terrace. Beyond the terrace, the big windows of the lounge blazed with light. As Marian had predicted, the power had been restored with astonishing speed.

Nora looked upward. All the second-floor windows were

dark, but at the top left-hand corner of the house, the windows of Lily's and Marian's rooms showed light. "Dart likes knives," she said.

Jeffrey pointed at the windows of the lounge. "Is that where you think he'd take these women?"

"He's in a mood to strut his stuff. He wants to use the best room in the house, and that's it."

"If that's true, we'll be able to see what's going on." Jeffrey unbuttoned his raincoat, yanked his arms out of the sleeves, and dropped the coat onto the grass. He broke into a businesslike jog across the lawn. When they had gone half the distance, they began moving in a quiet crouch.

Together they glided up to the terrace stairs and squatted in front of the bottom step. They glanced at each other, came to a wordless agreement, and went up side by side, bent low to stay out of sight. Four steps from the top, they peered across the terrace floor to the bottom of the lounge window. Nora saw only the white fringe of a carpet, the wooden floor, and the polished cylindrical legs of a table. She put her head closer to Jeffrey's and saw only a little more of the carpet.

Jeffrey crept up another two steps and leaned out onto the terrace. He looked back at Nora and shook his head, telling her to wait for him, then flattened out and began crawling slantwise across the terrace. Nora came up behind him and watched the soles of his shoes work across the wet tiles. When they were about six feet away, she lowered the top of her body to the floor and crawled after him, grating her knees and toes on the stone. The coat's metal clasps made a high-pitched sound of complaint against the terrace floor, and she scrabbled ahead on forearms and knees. Jeffrey slithered on before her with surprising speed and reached the window at the far end. Rain dripped steadily from the gutters.

For the first time Nora became conscious of the deep silence encasing the sound of raindrops pattering against the ground, the delicious freshness of every odor carried by the air. Even the rough tiles beneath her face sent up a vibrant smell, sharp and alive.

Jeffrey lengthened himself beneath the window, and she flattened out with her face next to his head, raised her neck, and looked into the lounge.

In a blue nightgown, Lily Melville sat lashed into a chair near the middle of the room. Another length of rope stretched from her ankles to her wrists, which had been pulled behind the back of the chair. Her head was bent nearly to her chest, and her shoulders were trembling. Facing the window, Margaret Nolan, still in the dress she had worn to dinner and similarly bound, was speaking to her, but Lily did not seem to hear what she was saying.

Margaret glanced over her shoulder, and Nora slid away from Jeffrey to be able to see the opening into the front hallway. Just appearing in the entrance was a hysterical Marian Cullinan, propelled from behind by Dick Dart. She looked as if she were trying to do pull-ups on the arm clamped around her neck. Dart held a long knife against her side with his other hand, and his face was alight with joy.

100

MARIAN HAD PUT on a low-cut, black, sleeveless dress for her poetic encounter. Dart was naked and completely clean. Only slightly mussed, his freshly washed hair fell over a bloody strip of gauze taped to the side of his head. He dropped Marian into a chair facing Lily Melville, shifted to her side, and bent down. She bolted forward. Without even bothering to look at her, Dart thrust out his left hand, closed it around her throat, and pulled her to the floor. Marian's scream penetrated the window. Nora felt her body clench.

Dart put down the knife and reached for something out of sight. Marian shot forward and flailed at him, and Dart pulled her off the floor by the neck, as if she were a kitten.

"What are we going to do?" Nora whispered to Jeffrey.

"I'm thinking about it," he whispered back.

Shaking his head, Dart raised Marian until her feet were off the floor. Then he dropped her, caught her around the waist, and pinioned her arms. While she thrashed against him, he brought a hand holding a rope back into view. He carried Marian back to the chair and slammed her down.

She screeched again.

Margaret turned her head toward Dart and said something surprisingly measured. Ignoring her, he knelt behind Marian, passed the rope twice around her, and released his hold. She jumped up and tried to sprint away with the chair on her back. He pulled her back and passed the rope over her shoulder, down, under the seat of the chair, then duckwalked to the front of the chair. She kicked at him, and he snatched her ankles, looped the rope around them, and worked it back beneath the chair. He sliced through the rope and knotted it behind her back. Margaret spoke to him again. Whatever he said caused her face to quiver.

"Strong son of a bitch," Jeffrey whispered.

Marian bucked in her chair, bucked again, then sagged back.

Dart jerked her chair into place and moved frowning past the three women, rubbing his chin. On either side of Margaret and a few feet in front of her, Marian and Lily sat facing each other. Dart came to a halt in front of them and stepped backwards toward the terrace. Considering the women, he gently fingered the gauze pad he had succeeded in taping over the wound in his back. His body winced, and a blotch of red at the center of the pad darkened and grew.

Jeffrey tilted his head toward Nora. "Isn't there another woman?"

She pointed upward. "Sick in bed."

Dart wandered around the women, measuring the effect he had created. They watched him, Marian sullenly and Margaret in thoughtful concentration like Dart's own. Even the back of Lily's head expressed stunned terror. Marian flipped her hair and moved her lips in a sentence Nora could read: *You hurt me.* Dart went behind Lily, shifted her a little way toward the window, and patted her head. Margaret clamped her mouth shut as Dart tugged her chair a few inches backwards. Marian spoke again: *Norman, why are you doing this?*

Margaret uttered a brief sentence. Marian's body went rigid, and all emotion left her face.

Dart, whose real name had just been uttered, held out his arms and twisted from side to side, acknowledging imaginary applause.

"What are we waiting for?" Nora whispered.

"For him to tell us what to do."

Dart swayed up to Marian and kissed her cheek. Talking, he went behind her chair and shook her hand. He stroked her arms, her hair, drew a finger along the line of her chin. Margaret watched this procedure without any demonstration of emotion. Marian closed her eyes and trembled. The freckles blazed on her face. Still talking, Dart went around the chair and kissed her. She jerked her head back, and Dart slapped her hard enough for the sound to carry through the window, then kissed her again. When he pulled away, the red mark on Marian's cheek obliterated her freckles.

Raising his hands as if to say, *I'm a reasonable guy,* Dart backed away from Marian and addressed all three women. He smiled and pointed at Marian. He put a question to the two older women. Margaret gave him an impassive stare, and Lily shook her head. Dart put his hand on his heart, he looked hurt. He bounced up to Lily and lifted her chin. Nora saw his mouth utter the words *Lily, my darling, I love you.* Then he sauntered over to Margaret and spoke to her. Margaret clearly said, *No.* He staggered back in mock disbelief. He was having the time of his life. For a time he wandered back and forth, engaged in some hypothetically puzzled debate. He waggled his head sadly. He walked over to the knife on the floor, pretended to be surprised to see it, and in glad astonishment picked it up.

Nora looked at Jeffrey. Jeffrey shook his head.

Dart strolled toward them across the carpet. First his head, then all of his body above his knees, disappeared behind the table. Jeffrey touched her hand: *Don't move.* She jerked her head toward her side: *The gun?* Jeffrey barely moved his head, telling her, *Not now.* Dart's legs spun around, and his feet padded away. When the rest of his body came into view, he was no longer holding the knife. He snapped his fingers and disappeared. Margaret's eyes moved, and Marian twisted her neck to watch him go. The women's faces registered Dart's reappearance, and when he sauntered into view he held the cleaver. He displayed it to the women, chopped the air, and padded toward the table.

Jeffrey somehow managed to flatten himself nearly to the lip of the sill below the French doors. Nora folded her arms over her head and held her breath. When she risked peeking at the

window, Dart's hairy legs still bulged out below the table. He
was aligning his tools. One of his feet slid sideways as he turned
to look back at the women in the chairs. One of them must have
asked him a question. "The little woman?" he said, close
enough to the window to be heard through it. "When last seen,
my former companion was charging in full flight through the
forest primeval. At the moment, she cowers in a thicket waiting
for me to give up the hunt." He came up to the window. "*Norma! Nor-ma!* Come home, honey, the fun's just beginning! Can
you hear me, sweetie?" He turned to the women and lowered
his voice. "Maybe she's hiding right outside! Let's see!"

Nora's heart stopped, and her body went cold. She sensed
Jeffrey gathering himself to leap.

If Dart came through this window, his foot would land about
three inches from Nora's elbow. She lifted her chin, peered in,
and her heart started back into life with a massive thump. He
was moving away from the table toward the other windows.
In seconds, he passed out of view. Down the terrace a handle
rattled, and the French door opened. It was all part of the performance, a show for the ladies. In high good humor, Dart was
demonstrating their helplessness. He leaned out and bellowed
her name. "*Norma! Norma! Mrs. Desmond!*"

He must have looked back into the room. "Hear anything,
Marian?"

Softly, Marian said, "No."

He was still leaning out through the French door. "You know
who she is, don't you?"

"The woman you kidnapped," Marian said.

Margaret Nolan said, "Nora Chancel."

Dart sighed lightly, mockingly, as if lamenting Nora's
treachery.

"You made a serious mistake, Mr. Dart," Margaret said.
"You let her go. Please understand what I'm telling you. Mrs.
Chancel isn't cowering in the woods. She's on her way to find
help. You should get away now. You can go back to Pepper Pot,
put on your clothes, and take a car. If you waste a lot of time
with us, you will certainly be captured by the police. You see
that, don't you?"

"*Captured?*" Dart said. "Wonderful word. Suggestion of the
jungle beast."

"We aren't asking to be untied. But if you want to keep your freedom, you have to leave Shorelands now. Mrs. Chancel is probably already talking to Tony."

After a long moment of silence, an owl hooted from the other side of the pond. Drops pattered down onto the tiles. Dart snickered. She glanced sideways. He was smiling up at the sky.

"What a worry. If Nora-pie does talk to your charity case, he'll come up here to check out her story. I can take care of Tony. But do you know what's really going to happen? In a little while, Nora is going to sneak into this house. Written in stone. The girl knows my little ways. Won't be able to help herself. Never abandon you, not possible."

"That's stupid," Marian said. "Save yourself. Leave now. You don't even have time for clothes."

"Like me naked, don't you, Marian? I like me naked, too. Love standing here, the fresh air drifting around my body. Arouses me. I do especially enjoy being aroused, as you will discover. Do you have freckles on the soles of your feet, Marian?"

For several seconds, she said nothing. Dart waited her out.

"No."

"What a pity. Shall we see if Nora's already here? Promised her a treat, and I dearly wish to keep my promise." Dart shouted her name, cupped a hand to his ear, shouted it again. "No answer, girls. Must carry on by ourselves. Never fear, Nora's arrival won't spoil our fun." He pulled himself back in, and the French door grated shut.

Jeffrey jerked his head toward the front of the terrace and was instantly slithering over the tiles, making no sound at all. With a superhuman effort, Nora pushed herself up onto her hands and knees and followed him.

Jeffrey slipped around the edge of the pillar at the top of the steps and waited. When she reached him, he led her down the stairs to the grass, moved sideways to the wall beneath the terrace, leaned his head back against the stone, and stared out at the dark lawn.

"Is he always like that?"

"Pretty much," Nora said. "What are we going to do?"

"We have plenty of time. He's still winding himself up." He smiled. "You know, as long as you didn't care too much about who he killed, Dick Dart could have been a terrific combat soldier. He's incredibly strong and quick, he can absorb a tremendous amount of pain and keep going, he thinks ahead, and adverse situations bring out the best in him. So to speak."

"You're asking me to admire Dick Dart?"

"Not at all," Jeffrey said. "I'm describing him. If I don't take him into account, I don't have a prayer of defeating him. I don't suppose he was always like what we saw just now?"

"Being brought in for murder liberated him. He didn't have to hide what he was like anymore."

Jeffrey smiled again. "*Escaping* liberated him. After that, all the normal rules were suspended. He's a brand-new person in a brand-new world, stretching his wings, discovering himself."

This was so accurate that Nora set aside her impatience.

"He's not going to get around to doing any damage to those women for at least half an hour. He's having too much fun. In the meantime, he'll be waiting for you to show up. Is the front door locked or unlocked, do you know?"

"Unlocked," Nora said.

"Okay." Jeffrey looked up at nothing and wiped his face. "Does he know that *you* know it's unlocked?"

"Yes."

"That's where he expects you to come in." He walked out onto the lawn and looked up at the house. "Let's cook up a little surprise for Mr. Dart." He ran his eyes along the rear of the building. "The French doors weren't locked, either. Farther down from where we were, there was another set at the back of the room he went into to get the cleaver."

"The dining room."

"I bet every window in the building is unlocked. They rely on their isolation and Tony to keep them safe. They've probably never had a break-in. You say there's another woman in the house, some kind of invalid?"

"Agnes Brotherhood."

"What floor is she on?"

"The second."

"All right. When I was trying to find you, I saw a ladder next to the wall in the court. Some workmen must have left it behind. I'll go in through an upstairs window. Once I'm up there, I'll make some kind of noise, and Dart will think Agnes is about to join the party. He'll be delighted. You go back up there and stand at this end of the lounge. When you see him leave the room, go into the dining room and *stay* there."

"All right."

"We have to play this by ear, but hide in the dining room until you know you can take Dart by surprise. He won't expect you to come in that way. He won't be expecting me, either. If I can take care of him, I will. If I can't, he's going to bring me into the lounge, and that's when you come out."

"You should take the gun," she said.

"No, you keep it." Jeffrey raised one leg, untied his shoe, wiggled it off, and set it beside the wall. He did the same with the other shoe. "You have one bullet left. Don't waste it." He tapped the center of her forehead with his index finger. "Put it right here. This guy is made of iron."

"I know," Nora said, but Jeffrey was already slipping away through the dark.

101

MARIAN'S COAT FELT like a ridiculous encumbrance. Nora took the revolver from the pocket, ripped open the snaps, hitched her shoulders, and lowered her arms. The coat slid off and landed heavily on the grass. Except for the parts of her legs washed by the stream, the entire front of her body was dark with mud. She settled the revolver in her hand and moved up the stairs to the terrace. Quietly, she slipped across the tiles and flattened herself against the building beside the second set of French doors. She tilted her head and looked in to see three-fourths of the bright lounge. Marian Cullinan's back obscured half of Lily Melville. Margaret Nolan, fully visible, faced the all too visible Dick Dart. He was holding a champagne bottle in one hand, his half-erect penis in the other, and talking to Margaret, no doubt on the subject of the many delights he had given elderly women. She looked at him unblinkingly.

For the first time Nora began to doubt her assumptions about why Agnes was not with the others. Dart would not have left her in her room simply because she was too weak to get out of bed. Maybe he had tied her up and stashed her in a part of the room they could not see, saving her as a spider leaves extra meals in its web. If he had brought Agnes downstairs, he would know something was wrong the instant he heard a noise inside the house, and Jeffrey would be in even greater danger.

Dart swigged champagne and offered the bottle to Lily. When she did not respond, he moved in front of her. Nora thought he was putting the bottle to her lips. He made a sideways comment to Margaret. Of course. She was the one he hated most; he was performing for her benefit. He carried the bottle to Marian, tilted it like a waiter to display the label, and put the bottle to her mouth. Whatever Marian did or said evoked an expression of unhappy disbelief. Dart backed away, pouting, and walked across the room to pick the knife off the table. He explained what he would be forced to do if she did not join him in a drink and tried again. She must have allowed him to pour some of the liquid into her mouth, because he gave her a happy smile. He went to Margaret, who grimly opened up and let him tip in champagne.

Dart gulped from the bottle and turned to Marian. He tilted his hips, offering the cucumber. No? He put the bottle on the floor and said something which involved pointing to both the knife and the cucumber. Still talking, he tugged at himself, and the obedient cucumber plumped forward. Pleased, he displayed it to the other two women. Lily's eyes were closed, and Margaret barely glanced at his prize. Returning to Marian, Dart again indicated the knife and the cucumber. The back of Marian's head gave no clue to her response. Dart moved up beside her and rubbed the cucumber across her cheek. He glanced at Margaret, whose face settled into bleak immobility. Lily dared to take a peek at him and instantly squeezed her eyes shut again.

What was Jeffrey doing, admiring Georgina Weatherall's bedroom?

Dart backed away, raised the knife, and fingered the loops of rope binding Marian to her chair. After selecting one, he slipped the knife underneath it, severed the rope, and knotted it in a new place. Marian's right arm was freed to the elbow. It was an exchange of favors. Be nice to me, I'll be nice to you.

Stroking himself, Dart moved in front of Margaret. He waved himself at her and went through the same grinning pantomime he had with Marian. For Margaret's benefit, he manipulated himself into another inch of bloat. Pulling and stroking, a dreamy expression gathering in his eyes, he extended himself in front of her face, demanding admiration. He stroked her hair with his free hand. Then his head snapped sideways.

The muscles in Nora's arms and legs went tense. Dart said something to Marian. Marian shook her head. He whirled away from Margaret, bounded to the side of the entrance, and pressed his back to the wall. Marian turned her head, and Margaret quizzed her with a look. They had all heard something, and no one in the room thought it was the sound of Agnes Brotherhood wandering down to the main floor. Nora stared at the empty opening. Dart put a finger to his lips. A few seconds ticked by. The women strained in their chairs.

Dart licked his lips and stared at the entrance, ready to leap.

Nora's body decided for her. Before she had time to think, she moved across the window and pushed down the handle. Dart jerked his head sideways and stared at her in shock, surprise, and rage. He took a step forward, baring his teeth. Nora yanked open the French door, put a foot inside the lounge, and turned to stone as Jeffrey flew into the room. He somersaulted over, bounced to his feet behind Marian, and instantly began circling toward Dart, his body bent forward and his arms slightly extended.

Dart shifted his eyes to Nora, then back to Jeffrey. "Who are you supposed to be, Action Man?" He sidled away from the wall. "Ladies, say hello to Jeffrey, the manservant. You'd be dead already, Jeffrey, if the mudpie hadn't distracted me."

"Norma!" Marian shrieked. "Shoot him, shoot him!"

"Shut up," Nora said. She moved alongside Lily, who was gazing at her in pure terror.

"Shoot him, Norma!" Marian yelled.

"Baby, she's a lousy shot, and the gun's already empty," Dart said. Already wholly adjusted to this turn of events, he was once again in confident good humor. All he had to deal with was an unarmed man and Nora-pie, who was a lousy shot, especially when the gun was empty. He loved his odds. Jeffrey was still circling toward him. "Come on, manservant," Dart said.

Jeffrey had not glanced at Nora since he had rocketed into the room. So focused on Dart that he seemed not to have heard Marian's outbursts, he advanced with one slow, deliberate crab-step after another. Dart rolled his eyes in amusement. Jeffrey was not a serious threat. He threw out his arms and shrugged at Nora.

"Should tell you the bitter truth, sweetie. I lied to you. The tits aren't pretty. Too small and too flat." He glanced at Jeffrey, and his smile widened.

Nora said, "Do you ever wear women's clothes, Dick?"

He lost his smile, then began to move toward Jeffrey with the air of one having to conduct a necessary but tedious bit of business.

Lily looked up fearfully at Nora. "Is that you, Mrs. Desmond?"

"It's me, Lily." Nora touched her shoulder. The men drew closer. Nora was aiming the revolver at Dart, but she had no confidence in her ability to hit him. She said, "I can see your closet, Dick. There are two dresses inside it, and nobody's ever seen them but you."

Dart growled and sprang, and Jeffrey seemed to flow backwards. Dart sailed four feet through the air and thudded down onto his stomach. In a second he pulled himself upright and went into a crouch. "So we know you're fast," he said, and bunched himself to charge.

Jeffrey jumped right, then left, so quickly he seemed not to have done it at all. He moved directly behind Margaret, who, unlike Lily and Marian, was looking at Nora. Her eyes moved to something near the windows, then back to Nora. Nora looked behind her and understood. She ran to the table and picked up the cleaver. "Are you crazy?" Marian yelled. "You have a gun!"

Dart twitched right, Jeffrey twitched left, a mirror image.

Marian screamed at her to shoot.

Dart ripped his knife through the empty air where Jeffrey had been, then pivoted and charged forward. Instead of floating back, Jeffrey ducked sideways, gripped Dart's arm, rolled his body over his hip, and spun him wheeling to the carpet a few feet past Marian. Nora remembered that Jeffrey had once been, among a dozen other unlikely things, a karate instructor.

Wincing, Dart picked himself up nearly as quickly as he had the first time. "Cool," he said. "Faggy martial arts. Way you fight when you can't really fight." He jumped forward, jabbing, and Jeffrey faded back. Six feet from Dart, Jeffrey glanced at her over Marian's head and spoke with his eyes. Nora switched the cleaver into her right hand and chopped at the ropes running across the back of Margaret's chair.

"Now me!" Marian yelled.

Margaret pulled herself forward. The ropes fell away from

her chest, but her hands were still tethered. *"Me!"* Marian screamed. Nora put down the gun and knelt to saw the cleaver between Margaret's wrists. Lily cried out, and a body hit the floor. Dart was getting up on his knees, holding a bloody knife. Jeffrey dodged toward the hallway. An oozing, foot-long slash ran up the side of his chest, and his face looked as though he were listening to music. He filtered through the air, caught Dart's arm, and slammed him back down on the carpet. Instead of waiting for Dart to twitch himself upright and charge again, Jeffrey followed him over in one smooth, continuous movement. With the electric immediacy of a bolt of lightning, Dart twisted to one side and thrust the knife into Jeffrey's ribs.

During an endless few seconds in which Nora tried to convince herself that she was mistaken, that she had seen something else entirely, the two men hung locked into position. A red stain blossomed on Jeffrey's wet shirt, and then he sagged down onto Dart's body. Nora wavered to her feet.

Marian shrilled to be set free.

Dart released a sigh of triumph and pushed Jeffrey off his chest. Jeffrey pressed a hand over his wound and lay still.

Sitting up, Dart was sliding backwards to disentangle his legs from Jeffrey's. Nora took a step toward him. Jeffrey looked up at Dart and grunted, the first sound he had made since he had come hurtling into the room. The stillness of intense concentration had not left his face. Marian sent up insistent waves of sound. Frantic, Nora cocked the cleaver over her shoulder and walked toward the men.

Dart pulled himself easily to his feet and spun to face her. "Really, Nora."

Playful, taunting, the knife punched out at her. It was impossible, she could not do it, he was too fast for her. The knife jumped forward in another parody of a thrust, and Dart came smiling forward. Nora backed away, holding up the cleaver, knowing she could not hit him before he stabbed her. Superior, silvery amusement ran through him. "I expected a little more of you," he said, and then his eyes enlarged and his body dropped away in front of her with amazing, surreal speed.

She looked down. His arms around Dart's ankles, Dart's heels pressed against his chest, Jeffrey pulled him back another inch.

In the second of grace Jeffrey had given her, Nora sprinted

forward, raised the cleaver high over her shoulder, and slammed it down into one of the tufts of hair on Dart's back. The fat blade sank two or three inches into his skin, and blood welled up around it. She tugged at the handle, intent on smashing the cleaver into his head. Dart shook himself like a horse and twitched the handle away from her grasp. "Hey, I thought we were friends," he wheezed. He kicked himself free from Jeffrey's grip and dragged himself forward. He wheezed again, got his elbows under him, and pulled himself toward her. She stepped back. He looked up at her, eyes alight with ironic pleasure. "I don't understand this constant rejection."

Nora's heel came down on the barrel of the revolver.

Marian's screams floated to the ceiling. Nora wrapped her hands around the grip of the revolver and took two steps forward, her mind a white emptiness. She squatted on the soles of her feet and pressed the barrel against Dart's forehead.

"Cute," Dart said. "Pull the trigger, show our studio audience the show must go on."

Nora pulled the trigger. The hammer came down with a flat, metallic click. Dart gave out a breathy chuckle and clamped a hand around her wrist. "On we go." He pulled down her hand, and she squeezed her index finger again. The revolver rode upward on the force of the explosion, and the last bullet burned a hole through Dart's laughing eye, sped into his brain, and tore off the back of his skull. A red-gray mist flew up and out and spattered the wall far behind him. *A bullet in the brain is better than a bullet in the belly.* Even Dan Harwich was right sometimes. Dart's fingers trembled on her wrist. Faintly, as from a distant room, Nora heard Marian Cullinan screaming.

102

HALF AN HOUR later the larger world invaded Nora's life, at first in the form of the many policemen who supplied her with coffee, bombarded her with questions, and wrote down everything she said, thereafter as represented by the far more numerous and invasive press and television reporters who for a brief but intensely uncomfortable period pursued her wherever she went, publishing their various inventions as fact, broadcasting simplifications, distortions, and straightforward untruths, a process which led, as always, to more of the same. If she had agreed, Nora could have appeared on a dozen television programs of the talk-show or tabloid kind, sold the rights to her story to a television production company, and seen her photograph on the covers of the many magazines devoted to trivializing what is already trivial. She did none of these things, considering them no more seriously than she considered accepting any of the sixteen marriage proposals which came to her in the mail. When the public world embraced her, its exaggerations and reductions of her tale made her so unrecognizable to herself that even the photographs in the newspapers seemed to be of someone else. Jeffrey Deodato, who endured a lesser version of Nora's temporary celebrity, also declined to assist in the public falsification of his life.

Once Nora had satisfied her laborious obligations to the law enforcement officers of several cities, what she wanted was enough space and time to reorder her life. She also wanted to do three specific things, and these she did, each one.

But this long, instructive process did not begin until forty minutes after she put Dick Dart to death, when the world rushed in and snatched her up. In the interim, Nora freed the other two women and let Margaret Nolan comfort Lily Melville while she held Jeffrey's hand and tried to assess his injury. Clearly in pain but bleeding less severely than she had feared, Jeffrey said, "I'll live, unless I die of embarrassment." Marian Cullinan retreated to her room, but sensible Margaret volunteered to drive Jeffrey to the hospital and used the imposing force of her personality to dissuade Nora from coming along. She would try to call the Lenox police from the hospital; if the telephones did not work, she would go to the police station after leaving the hospital. She ran to the lot and returned with her car. Staggering, supported by Margaret and Nora, Jeffrey was capable of getting to the door and down the walk. While easing him into the car, Nora remembered to ask Margaret what had happened to Agnes Brotherhood.

"Oh, my Lord," Margaret said. "Agnes is locked in her room. She must be frantic." She told Nora where in her office to find the key and suggested that she might want to clean herself up and put on some clothes before the police came.

Nora had forgotten that she'd been naked ever since she had taken off Marian's coat beneath the terrace.

Margaret raced off toward Lenox, and Nora walked back toward Main House and Agnes, who had escaped the attentions of Dick Dart because he had been unable to get into her room.

She walked past the lounge without looking at Dart's body. The keys, each with a label, were in the top left-hand drawer of the desk, just as Margaret had said. Nora pulled on Margaret's big blue raincoat and went down the hall to Agnes's room.

The thin figure in the bed was sleeping, Nora thought, but as she took two steps into the room, Agnes said, "Marian, why did you take so long? I don't like being locked in, and I don't like you, either."

"It's not Marian," Nora said. "I'm the woman who saw you this afternoon. Do you remember? We talked about Katherine Mannheim."

A rustle of excited movement came from the bedclothes, and Nora could make out a dim figure pushing itself upright. "They let you come back! Or did you sneak in? Was that you who tried to get in before?"

Agnes had no idea of what had gone on downstairs. "No, that was someone else."

"Well, you're here now, and I know you're right. I want you to know. I want to tell you."

"Tell me," Nora said. She bumped into a chair and sat down.

"He raped her," Agnes said. "That terrible, ugly man raped her, and she died of a heart attack."

"Lincoln Chancel raped Katherine Mannheim." Nora did not say that she already understood at least that much.

"You don't believe me," Agnes said.

"I believe you absolutely." Nora closed her eyes and sagged against the back of the chair.

"He raped her and she died. He went to get the other one, the other horrible man. That was what I saw."

"Yes," Nora said. Her voice seemed to come from a great distance. "And then you told the mistress, and she went to Gingerbread and saw them with her body. But you didn't know what she did after that for a long time."

"I couldn't have stayed here if I knew. She only told me when she was sick and taking that medicine that didn't do anything but make her sicker."

"Did you ask her about it? You finally wanted to know the truth, didn't you?"

Agnes started to cry with muffled sniffs. "I did, I wanted to know. She *liked* telling me. She *still* hated Miss Mannheim."

"The mistress got money from Mr. Chancel. A lot of money."

"He gave her whatever she wanted. He had to. She could have sent them both to jail. She had proof."

Nora let her head roll back on her shoulders and breathed out the question she had to ask. "What kind of proof did she have, Agnes?"

"The note, the letter, whatever you call it. The one she made Mr. Driver write."

"Tell me about that."

"It was in Gingerbread. The mistress made Mr. Driver write down everything they did and what they were going to do. Mr. Chancel didn't want him to do it, but the mistress said that if he didn't, she would go back to the house and get the police on them. She knew he wouldn't kill her, even though he probably wanted to, because she put herself in with them. Mr. Chancel still wouldn't do it, but Mr. Driver did. One was as good as two, she said. She told them where to bury that poor girl, and she put that in the note herself, in her own writing. That was how she put herself in with them."

She managed to say what she knew. "And she put the note in her safe, the one under her bed, didn't she?"

"It's still there," Agnes said. "I used to want to look at it sometimes, but if I did I'd know where they buried her, and I didn't want to know that."

"You can open her safe?"

"I opened it a thousand times when I was taking care of her. She kept her jewelry in there. I got things out for her when she wanted to wear them. Do you want to see it?"

"Yes, I do," Nora said, opening her eyes and straightening up. "Can you walk that far, Agnes?"

"I can walk from here to the moon if you give me enough time." Agnes reached out and closed her hand around Nora's wrist. "Why is your skin so rough?"

"I'm pretty muddy," Nora said.

"Ought to clean yourself up, young thing like you."

Agnes levered herself out of the bed and shuffled toward the door, gripping Nora's wrist. When they moved into the light, she took in Nora's condition with shocked disapproval. "What happened to you? You look like a savage."

"I fell down," Nora said.

"Why are you wearing Margaret's raincoat?"

"It's a long story."

"Never saw the like," Agnes said, and shuffled out into the hallway.

In Georgina Weatherall's bedroom, the old woman switched on the lights and asked Nora to put a chair in front of the bed. She twirled the dial. "I'll remember this combination after I forget my own name." She opened the safe door, reached in, extracted a long, once creamy envelope yellow with age, and held it out to Nora. "Take that with you. Get it out of this house. I have to go to the bathroom now. Will you please help me?"

Nora waited outside the bathroom until Agnes had finished, then conducted her back to her room. As she helped her get back into bed, she told her that there had been some trouble downstairs. The police were going to come, but everything was all right. Marian and Lily and Margaret were all fine, and the police would want to talk to her, but all she had to do was tell them that she had been locked in her room, and they would go away. "I'd rather you didn't say anything about the letter you gave me," she said, "but of course that's up to you."

"I don't want to talk about that note," Agnes said. "Especially not to any policeman. You better wash yourself off and get into some real clothes, unless you want a lot of men staring at you. Not to mention tracking mud all over the house."

Nora showered as quickly as she could, dried herself off, and trotted, envelope in hand, to Margaret's room. A few minutes later, wearing a loose black garment which concealed a long envelope in one of its side pockets, she went downstairs. Seated at the dining room table, Marian jumped up when Nora came in. She had changed clothes and put on fresh lipstick. "I know I have to thank you," Marian said. "You and that man saved my life. What happened to everybody? What happened to *him*? Are the police on the way?"

"Leave me alone," Nora said. She went to a chair at the far end of the table and sat down, not looking at Marian. A current of emotion too complicated to be identified as relief, shock, anger, grief, or sorrow surged through her, and she began to cry.

"You shouldn't be crying," Marian said, "you were great."

"Marian," Nora said, "you don't know anything at all."

From the front of the building came the sounds of sirens and police cars swinging into the gravel court, bringing with them the loud attentions of the world outside.

ONE DAY AT THE END OF AUGUST

One day at the end of August, a formerly lost woman who asked the people she knew to call her Nora Curlew instead of Nora Chancel drove unannounced through the gates on Mount Avenue and continued up the curving drive to the front of the Poplars. After having been ordered out of the house by his father, Davey had been implored to come back, as Nora had known he would, and was living again in Jeffrey Deodato's former apartment above the garage. Alone in the house on Crooked Mile Road, Nora had spent the past week dealing with endless telephone calls and the frequent arrivals of cameras, sound trucks, and reporters wishing to speak to the woman who had killed Dick Dart. She had also contended with the inevitable upheavals in her private life. Even after she told him that she wanted a divorce, Davey had offered to move back in with her, but Nora had refused. She had also refused his invitation to share the apartment above the garage, where Davey had instantly felt comfortable. *You told the FBI where I was,* she had said, to which Davey replied, *I was trying to help you.* She had told him, *We're finished. I don't need your kind of help.* Not long after this conversation, she had called Jeffrey, who was out of the hospital and convalescing at his mother's house, to tell him that she would see him soon.

Alden Chancel, whose attitude toward Nora had undergone a great change, had tried to encourage a reconciliation by proposing to build a separate house, a mini-Poplars, on the grounds, and she had turned down this offer, too. She had already packed most of the surprisingly few things she wanted to keep, and she wished to go someplace where few people knew who she was or what she had done. Nora was already impatient with her public role; another explosion of reporters and cameramen would soon erupt, and she wanted to be far away when it did. In the meantime, she

515

had three errands to accomplish. Seeing Alden was the first of these.

Maria burst into a smile and said, "Miss Nora! Mr. Davey is in his apartment."

A few days after being suspended, Maria had been rehired. The lawsuit against Chancel House had been withdrawn, and Alden no longer feared revelations connected to Katherine Mannheim.

"I'm not here to see Davey, Maria, so please don't tell him I'm here. I want to talk to Mr. Chancel. Is he in?"

Maria nodded. "Come in. He'll like to see you. I will get him." She went to the staircase, and Nora walked into the living room and sat down on one of the long sofas.

In a few minutes, radiating pleasure, affability, and charm, Alden came striding in. He was wearing one of his Admiral of the Yacht Club ensembles: white trousers, a double-breasted blue blazer, a white shirt, and a snappy ascot. She stood up and smiled at him.

"Nora! I was delighted when Maria told me you were here. I trust this means that we can finally put our difficulties behind us and start pulling together. Davey and I need a woman around this place, and you're the only one who would possibly do." He kissed her cheek.

A week ago, announcing that she had finally had enough of his abuse, fraudulence, and adulteries, Daisy had left the Poplars to move into a suite at the Carlyle Hotel in New York, from which she refused to be budged. She would not see or speak to Alden. She had emerged from her breakdown and subsequent immersion in soap operas with the resolve to escape her imprisonment and revise her book. During one of his pleading telephone calls, Davey said that his mother wanted "to be alive again" and had told him that he had "set her free" by learning the truth about his birth. He was baffled by his mother's revolt, but Nora was not.

"That's nice of you, Alden," she said.

"Should we get Davey in on this talk? Or just hash things out by ourselves for a while? I think that would be useful, though any time you want to bring Davey in, just say the word."

Alden had been impressed by the commercial potential of what she had done at Shorelands, and Nora knew from comments passed along by Davey that he was willing to provide a substantial advance for a first-person account of her travels with Dick Dart, the actual writer to be supplied later. The notion of her "true crime nonfiction novel" made his heart go trip trap. trip trap, exactly as Daisy had described. But the most compelling motive for Alden's new congeniality was what Nora had learned during her night in Northampton. He did not want her to make public the circumstances of the births of either Hugo Driver's posthumous novels or his son.

"Why don't we keep this to ourselves for now?" she said.

"I love dealing with a good negotiator, love it. Believe me, Nora, we're going to come up with an arrangement you are going to find very satisfactory. You and I have had our difficulties, but that's all over. From now on, we know where we stand."

"I agree completely."

Alden brushed a hand down her arm. "I hope you know that I've always considered you a tremendously interesting woman. I'd like to get to know you better, and I want you to understand more about me. We have a lot in common. Would you care for a drink?"

"Not now."

"Let's go into the library and get down to the nitty-gritty. I have to tell you, Nora, I've been looking forward to this."

"Have you?"

He linked his arm into hers. "This is family, Nora, and we're all going to take care of each other." In the library, he gestured to the leather couch on which she and Davey had listened to his ultimatum. He leaned back in the chair he had used that night and folded his hands in his lap. "I like the way you've been handling the press so far. You're building up interest, but this is about when we should do a full-court press. You and I don't need to deal with agents, do we?"

"Of course not."

"I know some of the best architects in the New York area. We'll put together a place so gorgeous it'll make that house on Crooked Mile Road look like a shack. But that's a long-range project. We can have fun with it later. You've been thinking about the advance for the book, haven't you? Give me a number. I might surprise you."

"I'm not going to write a book, Alden, and I don't want a house."

He crossed his legs, put his hand to his chin, and tried to stay civil while he figured out how much money she wanted. "Davey and I both want this situation to work out satisfactorily for all three of us."

"Alden, I didn't come here to negotiate."

He smiled at her. "Why don't you tell me what you want, and let me take it from there?"

"All I want is one thing."

He spread his hands. "As long as it's within my powers, it's yours."

"I want to see the manuscript of *Night Journey*."

Alden stared at her for about three seconds too long. "Davey asked me about that, hell, ten years ago, and the thing's lost. I wish I did have it."

"You're lying to me," Nora said. "Your father never threw anything away. Just look at the attic of this house and the storeroom at the office. Even if he had, he would have kept that manuscript. It was the basis of his greatest success. All I want to do is take a look at it."

"I'm sorry you think I'm not telling you the truth. But if that's what you came here for, I suppose this conversation is over." He stood up.

"If you don't show it to me, I'm going to say things that you don't want people to hear."

He gave her an exasperated look and sat down again. "I don't understand what you think you can get out of this. Even if I did have it, it couldn't do you a bit of good. What's the point?"

"I want to know the truth."

"That's what you came here for? The truth about *Night Journey*? Hugo Driver wrote it. Everybody knows it, and everybody's right."

"That's part of the truth."

"Apparently your adventures have left you more unsettled than you realize. If you want to come back in the next couple of days to talk business, please do, but for the present, we have nothing more to talk about."

"Listen to me, Alden. I know you have that manuscript somewhere. Davey once came to you with an idea that would have made you even more money from the book, and you never even bothered to look for it. He did, but you didn't. You knew where it was, you just didn't want him to see it. Now I want to look at it. I won't open my mouth to a single human being. I just want to know I'm right."

"Right about what?"

"That Driver stole most of the story from Katherine Mannheim."

Alden stood up and looked at her in pity. Just when she could have turned things around and joined the team, Nora had turned out to be a flake after all, what a shame. "Let me say this to you, Nora. You think you know certain facts which could damage me. I would rather not have these facts come to light, that's true, but while they might stir up some publicity I could do without, I'll survive. Go on, do whatever you think you have to do."

Nora took a folded sheet of paper from her bag. "Look at this, Alden. It's a copy of a statement you probably won't want made public."

Alden sighed. He came across the room to take it from her. He was bored, Nora had thrown away her last chance to be reasonable, but he was a gentleman, so he'd indulge her in one final lunacy. He took his reading glasses from the pocket of the blazer, put them on, and snapped open the paper on his way back across the room. Nora watched this performance with immense pleasure. Alden read a sentence and stopped moving. He read the sentence again. He yanked off his glasses and turned to her.

"Read the whole thing," Nora said. Until this moment, she had wondered if he had already known. The shock and dismay surfacing through his performance made it clear that he had not. She could almost feel sorry for him.

Alden moved behind the leather chair, leaned over it, and read Hugo Driver's confession and Georgina Weatherall's postscript. He read it all the way through, then read it again. He looked up at her from behind the chair.

"Where did you get this?"

"Does it matter?"

"It's a fake."

"No, Alden, it's not. Even if it were, would you want that story to get out? Do you want people to start speculating about your father and Katherine Mannheim and Hugo Driver?"

Alden folded the letter into one pocket, his glasses into another. He was still hiding behind his chair. "Speaking hypothetically, suppose I do have the manuscript of *Night Journey*. Suppose I satisfy your curiosity. If that were to happen, what would you do?"

"I'd go away happy."

"Let's try another scenario. If I were to offer you two hundred thousand dollars for the original of this forgery, solely for the protection of my father's name, would you accept my offer?"

"No."

"Three hundred thousand?"

Nora laughed. "Can't you see that I don't want any money? Show me the manuscript and I'll go away and never see you again."

"You just want to see it."

"I want to see it."

Alden nodded. "Okay. You and I are both honorable people. I want you to know I never had any idea that . . . I never had any idea that Katherine Mannheim didn't just walk away from that place. You gave me a promise, and that's my promise to you." He recovered himself. "I still say that this is a forgery, of course. My father followed his own rules, but he wasn't a rapist."

"Alden, we both know he was, but I don't care. It's ancient history."

He came out from behind his barricade. "It's ancient history whether he was or wasn't." He moved along the bookcase and swung out a hinged section of a shelf at eye level to reveal a wall safe, another massy vault larger within than without. He dialed it open and with more reverence than she would have thought him capable of reached in and took out a green leather box.

Nora came toward him and saw what looked like the bottom of a picture frame on the top shelf of the safe. "What's that?"

"Some drawing my father squirreled away."

Alden pulled the drawing out and showed it to her before sliding it back into the vault. "Don't ask me what it is or why it's there. All I know is that when Daisy and I moved into the Poplars, he showed it to me and told me to keep it in the vault and forget about it. I think it must be stolen. Somebody probably gave it to him to pay off a debt."

"Looks like a Redon," Nora said.

"I wouldn't know. Is that good?"

"Good enough."

She took the box to the couch and looked inside. A small notebook with marbled covers sat on top of a lot of typed pages. She picked up the notebook. Katherine Mannheim's signature was on the inside cover. She had written *"Night Journey, novel?"* on the facing page. Nora turned page after page filled with notes about Pippin Little; this was the embryo of Driver's book, stolen from

Katherine Mannheim's bag. *He who steals my trash steals trash.*
She put the notebook beside her and took the manuscript from the
box. It seemed such a small thing to have affected so many lives.
She opened it at random and saw that someone had drawn a line in
the margin and written in a violent, aggressive hand, *p. 32,
Mannheim notebook.* She turned to another page and saw in the
same handwriting, *pp. 40–43, Mannheim.* Lincoln Chancel had
demanded the stolen notebook, kept the manuscript, and marked
in it everything Driver had stolen from Katherine Mannheim. If
Driver ever ruined him, he would ruin Driver.

"Do you see?" Alden said. "Driver wrote the book. These
Mannheim people don't have a leg to stand on. He borrowed a few
ideas, that's all. Writers do it all the time."

Nora returned the manuscript and notebook to the box. "I'm
grateful to you, Alden."

"I still don't see why it was so important."

"I just wanted to see it all the way through," she said. "In a day
or two, I'm going to be moving to Massachusetts for a little while.
I don't know where I'll be after that, but you won't have to worry
about me."

Alden told her he would say good-bye to Davey for her.

"I already did that," Nora said.

The second of Nora's errands took her to the post office, where
she withdrew from an unsealed envelope addressed to *The
New York Times* a letter describing Hugo Driver's debt to the
forgotten poet Katherine Mannheim and an account of the poet's
death and her burial a few feet north of the area known as
Monty's Glen in the Shorelands woods. To the letter she
added, in her hasty hand, this note: *"Katherine Mannheim's
original notebook and Hugo Driver's manuscript, with Lincoln
Chancel's marginal notes referring to specific passages taken
from the notebook, are in a wall safe located in the library of
Alden Chancel's house in Westerholm, Connecticut."* Having
kept her promise never to speak of these matters, she refolded
the letter, wrapped it around another copy of Hugo Driver's confession, put them back into the envelope, sealed it, and sent it by
registered mail to New York.

Nora's third errand brought her to Redcoat Road. Natalie Weil's
house was still in need of a fresh paint job, but the crime scene

tapes had been removed. She pulled up in front of the garage door,
walked up the path to Natalie's front door, and pressed the bell. A
friendly female voice called out, and footsteps ran down the stairs
to the door. As soon as Natalie saw her, she immediately tried to
slam the door, but Nora thrust herself inside and backed Natalie
toward the stairs. "I want to talk to you," she said.

"I suppose you do," Natalie said. She seemed aggrieved and
reluctant, which did not displease Nora. "I know how you feel, but
all of a sudden three new listings showed up, and I have to show
my boss I can still do my job, besides which there's a little
problem with the police, some crap about drugs, but that won't
stick, so what the hell, right? Come upstairs and have a beer."

"You're calmer than I expected," Nora said.

"You win some, you lose some. I'll have a beer, even if you're
not going to."

Nora went up the stairs and waited for Natalie. Despite her
Westerholm weekend uniform of a faded denim shirt and khaki
shorts, she looked wary and defensive, and though not as ancient
as she had appeared on Barbara Widdoes's couch, older than Nora
remembered her. She pulled her refrigerator open, took out a
bottle of Corona, and popped the cap. "Come on in, sit down,
we've known each other a long time, what's a little husband
fucking between old friends? I can't blame you for being mad at
me, but it was hardly a big deal, if you want to know the truth."

"Yes," Nora said. "I do." She came into the kitchen and sat
opposite Natalie at her kitchen table. "That's exactly what I want
to know."

"Join the crowd." Natalie drank from the beer bottle and gently
put it down. Her eyes looked bruised. "Hey, at least for the time
being, I'm still in the real estate business. You know what that
means? We sell dreams. Truth is what you say it is. Right?"

"A lot of people think so," Nora said. The handcuff photographs had been taken off the corkboard, and the refrigerator magnets had been thrown away.

Natalie took another swallow of Corona. "How do you like
being famous? Is it neat? I wouldn't mind being famous."

"It isn't neat."

"But you killed Dick Dart. You wasted the bastard." The beer
in front of Natalie was not her first.

"So they say," Nora answered.

Natalie toasted her with the Corona bottle. "You and Davey all right?"

"He moved back in with his father and I'm leaving town. So, yeah, we're probably all right."

"God, he's going back to Alden." Natalie twisted her mouth into a half smile. "I heard Daisy took off. About time. That guy is bad news, and he always was. I mean, you make mistakes, but Alden was about the worst mistake I ever made. Well, let's drop that subject."

"Let's not," Nora said. "After all, you and Alden caused me a lot of trouble. I was about to be arrested when the wonderful Dick Dart abducted me."

"Nobody's perfect. For what it's worth, Nora, I'm sorry." Natalie was having trouble looking at her. "Sometimes you do things for the wrong reasons. It's a lousy deal, you know? You get strapped, you agree to stuff you'd never do otherwise. I never wanted to get you into trouble—shit, I *like* you. I always liked you. The whole thing was Alden's idea in the first place. It was just business."

"Bid'ness is bid'ness," Nora said.

Natalie made a wry face. "Know how many houses sold here last year? Exactly nineteen. And not precisely at my end of the market, no siree, I get the top of the bottom end, like your place, no offense, but the office doesn't give me the two-million-dollar properties." She swallowed more beer and put down the bottle. "Alden's a jerk, but he's willing to put cash on the table, I'll say that for him. And I got you off the hook, didn't I?"

"Yes," Nora said. "But you almost got me arrested for kidnapping."

Natalie took another swallow of Corona. "It was never supposed to get that far, Nora. He just wanted to jerk Davey around, that's all. He was pissed off. We didn't know that whole thing with Dick Dart was going to happen, who could know that?"

"Tell me about the blood in your bedroom."

Natalie smiled at her like a conspirator. "One of Alden's brilliant ideas. He wanted to get everybody worked up, tie my thing into the murders. Stir the pot, you know? He got this pig blood from a butcher and wrecked my bedroom. But you're okay now, aren't you? I went through my act, it's all over, what's the difference?"

"If you don't know, I'll never be able to explain it to you," Nora said.

Natalie turned her head away.

"Natalie," Nora said, and Natalie looked at her again. "You disgust me. Alden *bought* you, and you ruined my life."

"You didn't like your life anyhow. How could you, married to that baby?"

"How much did he pay you?" Nora asked.

"Not nearly enough," Natalie said. "Considering what's probably going to happen to me. I'd like you to leave my house, if you don't mind. I think we're done. If you ask me, I did you a favor. You came out of this deal a lot better than I did."

"I didn't volunteer," Nora said. "I was drafted."

An unfamiliar car was nosed in toward Nora's garage door, and thinking it belonged to yet another reporter or to one of the unknown men who had proposed to her, she nearly drove on to the end of Crooked Mile Road until she saw Holly Fenn get out of the car and walk toward her front door. Nora turned into her driveway, and Fenn waved at her and started moving slowly back to the garage. She pulled in beside his car, got out, and walked toward him. He needed a haircut, he was wearing the ugliest necktie she had ever seen, and there were weary bags under his eyes. He looked great.

"So there you are," he said. "I called a couple of times, but all I got was your machine."

"I'm not answering my phone all that much."

"I bet. Anyhow, I wanted to see you, so I thought I'd take a chance and come by." He tucked in his chin, stuffed his hands in his pockets, and looked at her from under his eyebrows. A spark of feeling jumped between them. "I have something to tell you, but mainly I just wanted to see how you were."

"How am I?"

"Holding up pretty good, I'd say. I like your new hair. Cute."

"Thanks, but you're lying. You liked it better the old way. I did, too. I'm going to let it grow out."

Fenn nodded slowly, as if agreeing with her on a matter of great importance. "Good. You getting your life back together okay?"

"I'm taking it apart pretty well, so I guess I am, yes. It isn't the same life, that's all. Holly, would you like a cup of coffee or something?"

"Wish I could. I have to be somewhere in five minutes. But I thought you ought to know something I learned about that old nursery school on the South Post Road. It occurred to me that I didn't know who held the lease on that building, so I checked. The lease is made out to a guy in New York named Gerald Ambrose. I called him up, and he told me that a citizen here in Westerholm rented it from him for the rest of the summer."

"Ah," Nora said. "You're a good cop, Holly."

"Yeah, maybe, but I turn out to be a little on the slow side. If I'd checked this out before, I could have saved you a lot of trouble."

She smiled at him. "I don't blame you, Holly. Who rented the building?"

He smiled back. "Do I get the feeling you already know, or am I making that up?"

"I have an idea, but tell me."

"The citizen who rented the building is a big-time publisher who told Ambrose he needed temporary storage for some over-stock. Are you on good terms with your father-in-law?"

"My soon-to-be-ex-father-in-law and I have a long history of mutual loathing." She remembered Alden Chancel stroking her arm and saying *I'd like to get to know you better.* "Holly, if you stop in on Natalie Weil, she'll probably tell you an interesting story. I just saw her, and she's sort of killing time until her world caves in."

Fenn wiped his hand over his sturdy mustache and nodded, taking in both the remark and Nora. "Your friend put on a pretty good show."

"She even fooled Slim and Slam."

Fenn's eyes crinkled. "I gather some money changed hands."

"Not enough, according to Natalie."

Fenn grinned at the driveway, marveling at the ingenuity of the human capacity for committing serious error. "And you called me a good cop."

"I think you're pretty good all the way around," Nora said. "You stuck by me."

"Yeah, well, I tried." He gave her a rueful glance which managed to encompass compassion for what she had endured and anger at having been unable to spare her from it. "Anyhow," he said, "I better get going."

"If you must." She walked him to his car.

"Look, maybe this is none of my business, but did you say that you were leaving your husband?"

"I already left."

Fenn looked away. "Are you going to stay in town?"

"I think I'll go to Northampton for a while. I can work with a woman who runs a catering business for a couple of weeks. I want to get away from the telephone and clear my head. After that, who knows?"

Fenn nodded his big, shaggy head, taking this in. "After I'm through with Mrs. Weil and your soon-to-be-ex-father-in-law, do you suppose I could come back here and take you out for coffee or something?"

"Holly, are you asking me for a date?"

"I'm too old for dates," he said.

"Me, too. So come back later and we won't have a date, we'll just knock around together. I want to hear about your encounter with Alden. You can tell me all your favorite war stories."

Fenn smiled at her with every part of his face. "And I promise not to ask to hear yours."

"Or tell me any lies."

"I wouldn't know how to lie to you."

"Then it's a deal," Nora said.

"Well, okay." He lowered himself into his car, winked at her through the windshield, and backed away from the garage. A few seconds later, he was gone.

And don't miss

Peter Straub's

In the
Night Room

a Random House hardcover
available wherever books are sold

1

About 10:30 on a Wednesday morning early in a rain-drenched September, a novelist named Timothy Underhill gave up, in more distress than he cared to acknowledge, on his ruined breakfast and the *New York Times* crossword puzzle and returned, far behind schedule, to his third-floor loft at 55 Grand Street. Closing his door behind him did nothing to calm his troubled heart. He clanked his streaming umbrella into an upright metal stand, transported a fresh cup of decaffeinated coffee to his desk, parked himself in a flexible mesh chair bristling with controls, double-clicked on Outlook Express's arrow-swathed envelope, and, with the sense of finally putting most of his problem behind him, called to the surface of his screen the day's first catch of e-mails, ten in all. Two of them were completely inexplicable. Because the messages seemed to come from strangers (with names unattached to specific domains, he would notice later), bore empty SUBJECT lines, and consisted of no more than a couple of disconnected words each, he promptly deleted them.

As soon as he had done so, he remembered dumping a couple of similar e-mails two days earlier. For a moment, what he had seen from the sidewalk outside the Fireside Diner flared again before him, wrapped in every bit of its old urgency and dread.

2

In a sudden shaft of brightness that fell some twenty miles west of Grand Street, a woman named Willy Bryce Patrick (soon-to-be Faber) was turning her slightly dinged little Mercedes away from the Pathmark store on the north side of Hendersonia, having succumbed to the compulsion, not that she had much choice, to drive two and two-tenths miles along Union Street's increasingly vacant blocks instead of proceeding directly home. When she reached her destination, a vast parking lot with two sedans trickling through its exit, she checked her rearview mirror and looked around before driving in. Irregular slicks of water gleamed on the black surface of the lot. The men waiting to drive out of the lot took in the young woman entering their field of vision at the wheel of a sleek, snub-nosed car; one of them thought he was looking at a teenage boy.

In the lot, Willy drifted along past the penitentiary-like building that dominated the far end of the parking lot. Her shoulders rode high and tight, and her upper arms seemed taut as cords. Like all serious compulsions, hers seemed both a necessary part of her character and to have been wished upon her by some indifferent deity. Willy pulled into an empty space and, now at the heart of her problem, regarded what was before her: a long, shabby-looking brick structure, three stories high, with wide metal doors and ranks of filthy windows concealed behind cobwebs of mesh. Around the back, she knew, the dock that led into the loading bays protruded outward, like a pier over the surface of a lake. A row of grimy letters over the topmost row of windows spelled out MICHIGAN PRODUCE.

Somehow, that had been the start of her difficulties: MICHIGAN PRODUCE, the words, not the building, which appeared to be a wholesale fruit and vegetable warehouse. Two days earlier, driving along inattentively, in fact in one of her "dazes," her "trances"—Mitchell Faber's words—Willy had found herself here, on this desolate section of Union Street, and the two words atop the big grimy structure had all but peeled themselves off the warehouse, set themselves on fire, and floated aflame toward her through the slate-colored air.

Now, she asked herself, *was that an accident?*

Willy had the feeling that she had been led here, that her "trance" had been charged with purpose, and that she had been all along *meant* to come across this building.

She wondered if this kind of thing ever happened to someone else. Almost instantly, Willy dismissed the strange little vision that blazed abruptly in her mind, of a beautiful, dark-haired teenage boy, skateboard in one hand, standing dumbstruck on a sunlit street before an empty, ordinary-looking building. Her imagination had always been far too willing to leap into service, whether or not at the time imagination was actually useful. That sometimes it had been supremely useful to Willy did not diminish her awareness that her imaginative faculty could also turn on her, savagely. Oh, yes. You never knew which was the case, either, until the dread began to crawl up your arms.

The image of a teenage boy and an empty house added to the sum of disorder at large in the universe, and she sent it back to the mysterious realm from which it had emerged. Because: hey, what might *be* in that empty house?

3

The memory of the messages he had seen on Monday awakened Tim Underhill's curiosity, and before going on to answer the few of the day's e-mails that required responses, he clicked on DELETED ITEMS, of which he seemed now to have accumulated in excess of two thousand, and looked for the ones that matched those he had just received. There they were, together in the order in which he had deleted them, *Huffy* and *presten,* with the blank subject lines that indicated a kind of indifference to protocol he wished he did not find mildly annoying. He clicked on the first message.

From: Huffy
To: tunderhill@nyc.rr.com
Sent: Monday, June 16, 2003 8:52 AM
Subject:

re member

That was the opposite of dis member, Tim supposed, and dis member was the guy standing next to dat member. He tried the second one.

From: presten
To: tunderhill@nyc.rr.com
Sent: Monday, June 16, 2003 9:01 AM
Subject:

no helo

Useless, meaningless, a nuisance. Huffman and presten were kids who had figured out how to hide their e-mail addresses. Presumably they had learned his from the website listed on the jacket of his latest book, *Lost: This Boy, This Girl*. He looked again at the two e-mails he had just dumped.

From: rudderless
To: tunderhill@nyc.rr.com
Sent: Wednesday, June 18, 2003 6:32 AM
Subject:

no time

and

From: loumay
To: tunderhill@nyc.rr.com
Sent: Wednesday, June 18, 2003 6:41 AM
Subject:

there wuz

There wuz, wuz there? All of these enigmatic messages sounded as though their perpetrators were half-asleep, or as though their hands had been snatched off the keyboard—maybe by the next customer at some internet cafe, since the second messages came only minutes after the first ones. Wait, wait . . . what were the odds that four people savvy enough to delete the second half of their e-mail addresses would decide, more or less simultaneously, to send early-morning gibberish to the same person? And how much steeper were the odds against one of them writing "no helo," whatever that meant, and another deciding, with no prior agreement, upon the echo-phrase "no time"? Although he thought such a coincidence was impossible, he still felt mildly uneasy as he rejected it.

Because that left only two options, and both raised the ante of Tim Underhill's comfort level. Either the four people who sent the e-mails to him were acting together in conspiracy, or the e-mails had all been sent by the same person using four names.

The names, *Huffy, presten, rudderless, loumay,* suggested no pattern. They were not familiar. A moment later, Tim remembered that back in his hometown, Millhaven, Illinois, a boy named Paul Resten had been his teammate on the Holy Sepulchre football team. Paulie Resten had been a chaotic little fireplug with greasy hair, a shoplifting problem, and a tendency toward violence. It seemed profoundly unlikely that after a silence of forty-odd years Paulie would send him a two-word e-mail.

Tim read the messages over again, thought for a second, then rearranged them:

re member
there wuz
no helo
no time

which could just as easily have been

re member
there wuz
no time
no helo

or

there wuz
no time
no helo
re member

which wasn't much of an advance, was it? Another possibility came to mind, that "helo" could be a typo for "help." *No time/no help* made more sense than *no time/no helo.* "Remember, there was no time, no help."